# VODKA

By the same author

*Messiah*
*Storm*

# VODKA

## BORIS STARLING

HarperCollins*Publishers*

This novel is entirely a work of fiction. The names, characters
and incidents portrayed in it are the work of the author's imagination.
Any resemblance to actual persons, living or dead, events or
localities is entirely coincidental.

HarperCollinsPublishers
77–85 Fulham Palace Road, London W6 8JB
www.harpercollins.co.uk

Published by HarperCollins 2004
1 3 5 7 9 10 8 6 4 2

A catalogue record for this book
is available from the British Library

ISBN 0 00 711945 3

Set in Meridien by
Palimpsest Book Production Ltd
Polmont, Stirlingshire

Printed in Great Britain by
Clays Ltd, St Ives plc

*For Mills*

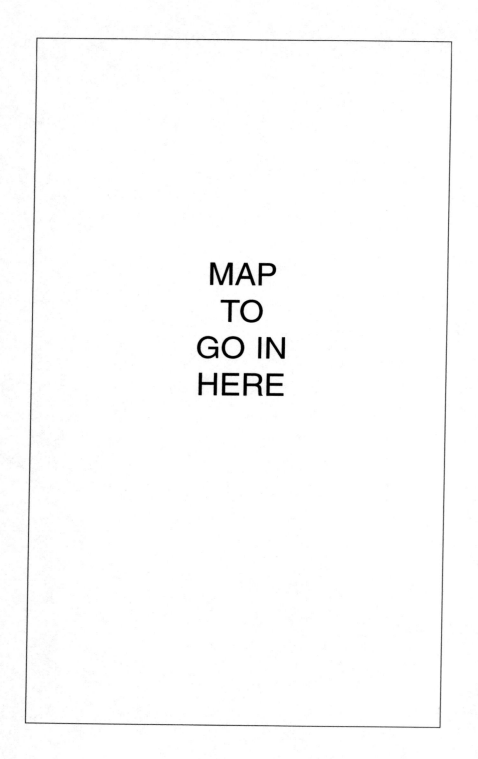

*Vodka* was a very personal labour of love, and yet I couldn't have written it without being helped by scores of people, all of whom have my gratitude and affection.

My publishers and agents were endlessly patient as deadline after deadline vanished into the ether, and infinitely wise in their judgement on the drafts that did finally appear; my thanks to Julia Wisdom, Nick Sayers, Anne O'Brien, Brian Tart, Caradoc King and Nick Harris, and to Kelly Edgson-Wright for marketing services beyond the call of duty.

My family – David and Judy Starling, and Mike and Belinda Trim – were, as ever, my most trenchant critics, most ardent supporters, and finest chefs. Richard Fenning first fired my interest in Russia; Samantha de Bendern, Guy Dunn and David Lewis fanned the flames. Mark Burnell, Godwin Busuttil, Charles Cumming, Juliette Dominguez, Fiona Kirkpatrick, Fiona McDougall, Rory Unsworth and Iain Wakefield all spent more time than they could spare to read a gargantuan first draft and give me their thoughts. Ben Aris took me under his wing in Moscow; the Apple workshop in Granada performed miracles with a sick iMac; and the Fell-Clark family rented me their tower by the sea, the most magical place to write.

I read more books than I care to remember during research, many of them by authors who clearly share my passion for Russia. It is for me the most fascinating and inspiring country on earth, and I hope that in *Vodka* I've done some small measure of justice to an extraordinary nation and a unique people.

Boris Starling

# RUSSIAN NAMES

All Russians have three names: their given name (what Westerners would call their Christian or first name), their patronymic (a derivative of their father's name), and their family name (surname). To show respect, formality or distance, Russians use both the given name and the patronymic. Friends and family use only the given name or a nickname derived from it (e.g. Kolya for Nikolai).

# PROLOGUE

*Wednesday, 21 August 1991*

Moscow at dusk, the great city hanging suspended in all its contradictions: halfway between day and night, past and future, east and
west, sanity and madness, picturesque and squalid, good and evil.

The coup was over. For the first time since it had begun, the night
was dry and moonlit. The troops had that afternoon started to withdraw from around the White House, the Russian parliament building. They were retreating from Moscow as Napoleon and Hitler had
done before them, but they were doing so with pleasure, relieved
that they'd not had to massacre their countrymen, and pursued by
the grateful cheers of demonstrators who threw sweets, cakes and
coins in through the hatches of their armoured vehicles. Four tanks
were left empty in the grounds of the White House, garlanded with
flowers and Russian tricolours; the rest snaked away in long columns
of belching gasoline and churned asphalt, and the parliamentary
defenders had never smelt anything sweeter.

They'd been there since the very start, three days and a lifetime
before, flimsy lines facing down the Soviet army and the world's
press, and this was their moment. Everyone shared a common look
of astonishment, as if each person had individually ventured to drop
their lifelong mask and show their true face. Middle-aged teachers,
muscled truckers, suited office workers and feckless students
wandered with expressions of recognition, as in 'I know you'. They
picked their way through rocks and crushed machinery, sidestepped
the armfuls of flowers laid on the street to cover dried bloodstains,
and grinned in joyful disbelief that the building – that Russia itself –
was safe.

And among all these Russians, there was not a bottle of vodka
in sight; not one.

Inside the White House, Lev – parliamentary deputy, distillery

1

director, criminal godfather, champion weightlifter, his shoulders as wide as two men's, the crown of his head seven feet above the floor – walked the corridors and surfed waves of intelligence and rumour. Gorbachev was on his way back from the Crimea. The coup leadership had disbanded and flown out of Moscow. The three ugly sisters – the Party, the KGB and the Ministry of Defence – were in disarray. Between them, they hadn't even managed to produce a decent coup.

Lev felt a hand on his elbow. It was Nikolai Arkin, the brightest of the young reformers and, if parliamentary gossip had any credence, hot favourite to be the new Prime Minister. He grinned at Lev with teeth white enough to suggest German dentistry, and steered him towards the nearest balcony. Out on the Moscow River, bobbing tugboats let off flares and called themselves the Russian navy. The crowd were singing now. "We've won! Victory is ours!"

Arkin waved a papal arm over the throng. "Is there a greater nation in the world?" he said. "They've been repeatedly beaten to their knees, but they've never forgotten how to stand up. The people who walked in darkness have seen a great light." A breeze caught his dark forelock and lifted it from his brow. "You know what that is?" Arkin asked, the euphoria making him ever more melodramatic. "It's the wind of change."

Lev looked at Arkin with the weary indulgence a parent grants an excitable child. "Change?" he growled. "*Change*? Aren't things bad enough as they are?"

# 1

*Monday, 23 December 1991*

Television newsreaders, metro workers, shop assistants and *babushki* in the market all said the same thing: "the Soviet Union is no more." Eleven of the fifteen constituent republics had met in Alma-Ata over the weekend and agreed to dissolve the union, nine days short of its seventieth birthday. "The Soviet Union is no more", indeed, but no two people said it exactly the same; the phrase came loaded with hope, fear, relief, apprehension, joy, anger, excitement and nostalgia, and each person's mixture was different.

"No matter how much we hated the old system" – Lev never used the words 'Soviet Union' – "it provided a kind of order. It was predictable. But now the authority is gone, the police are weak and afraid to deal with the black-asses from the south – especially the Chechens. They've been allowed to establish a presence here in Moscow, and it looks like it's up to us to send them back home, back to their blood feuds and their tribal armies. We haven't survived communism just to let a bunch of niggers fuck us in the ass."

There were three men at the table, Lev, Testarossa and Banzai, all of them vory – thieves-in-law who had abandoned their given names in favour of noms de guerre and relinquished their right to a home or family in favour of the brotherhood of criminals. Between them, they ran Moscow's three largest Slav gangs. Lev was in charge of the 21st Century Association, Testarossa the Solntsevskaya and Banzai the Podolskaya. They had come to this dacha north-west of Moscow for a summit meeting. Each man had an ashtray in front of him. There was vodka on the table and smoked fish on the sideboard. Outside, the snow was falling again, whirling against a wan sky. Cigarette ends glowed like fireflies through the windows; three gang leaders meant scores of bodyguards.

Lev ran his hands over his head. In accordance with tradition, as the man with the most jail time (and the only one to have been officially designated an enemy of the state), Lev had seniority over the other two.

"As it stands," Lev continued, his voice croaking, "we're not organising ourselves in the most productive manner. We compete with each other for control, be it of Moscow districts or business sectors. Testarossa, you want some of my pie in Kitai-gorod; Banzai, I want your counterfeit vodka interests. In normal times, this is perfectly healthy; honourable vory come to a mutually acceptable arrangement, and if they can't do so, then the strongest man wins. But these aren't normal times, my brothers. If we keep fighting among ourselves, the Chechens will take over. They're the enemy now. So I propose a truce; we suspend operations against each other and join forces against the Chechens."

"Until when?" Banzai said.

"Until we've beaten them."

"And then?"

"And then we take their interests and divide them up between us, equally."

Banzai's features – the narrow eyes and plate-broad cheekbones of Sakhalin, just across the water from Japan – arranged themselves into something the far side of scepticism.

Lev turned to Testarossa. "What do you think, brother? This can't go ahead without your agreement; it's your men and your firepower we'll be calling on the most."

The Solntsevskaya was the largest single gang in Russia, let alone Moscow. Testarossa could call on four thousand men and at least five hundred Kalashnikovs, one thousand machine pistols, fifty Uzi rifles and a handful of Mukha grenade launchers. The 21st Century Association had no more than half this capacity; Banzai's Podolskaya only half that again.

"Do you even need to ask, brother?" When Testarossa smiled, his eyes were liquid smoke beneath a blaze of red hair. His hairline sat low on his brow, virtually nudging his eyebrows. In the prison camp at Magadan, he'd tattooed his forehead: *Fucked by the Party*. The authorities had pulled down his scalp to cover it. "A vor should support another vor in any circumstance; isn't that our first rule? What have we become, if we don't define ourselves against the enemy? We'll band together against the narrow-films, and be proud of it."

"Spoken like a true vor. I thank you." Lev looked at Banzai.

4

"And you, little brother? You need this alliance more than either of us."

"*Little* brother. That's it, isn't it? I lend you my men and my weapons, and when it's over you two divide the spoils between you and I get fucked."

"When it's over." – Lev's voice was suddenly hard – "we'll negotiate freely and fairly. We're men of honour. I won't let petty money-grabbing undermine the criminal brotherhood which we're all sworn to defend. Remember, vory must always tell the truth to fellow members."

It took Banzai a moment to recognise the implicit threat behind Lev's words. "What are you saying?" he asked. "What truth?"

"There's nothing you haven't told us, little brother?"

"No, nothing."

"A trip to Kazan, perhaps?"

Banzai's head went back and up a fraction; back in surprise, up in defiance. The Tatar capital of Kazan was the processing centre for 3MF, trimethyl phentanyl, a dry white powder several times more potent than heroin and impossible to detect when mixed with water.

"The thieves' code specifically bans traffic in drugs," Lev said. "Whatever else we fight them for, the Chechens can have the narcotics, all of them. They're animals anyway, so let them lose their souls."

"The drug trade's worth millions of dollars, Lev. Better *we* control it than them."

"Banzai, have you forgotten what it means to be a vor? It's not just money."

"Don't talk to me of what a vor should or should not do, Lev." hissed Banzai. "A true vor should not co-operate with the authorities, right? But you're a parliamentary deputy. A vor must never accept a job at a state-owned institution, *right*? But you run the country's largest distillery. A vor must not fraternise with communist organisations, yet you have a KGB man, Tengiz Sabirzhan, as your trusted deputy."

Lev pushed his chair back and stood. Upright, his dimensions came into sharper focus. He rarely used his size deliberately to intimidate; he knew that it usually did so without his having to try. He placed his hands on the table; then, suddenly, reached out and slapped Banzai across the face, the traditional punishment for a vor who'd insulted another vor. When Lev spoke, his voice was Vesuvian.

"The *Russian* parliament, whose resistance helped destroy the Soviet Union. The distillery whose appropriation was approved by the vory at the Murmansk summit back in '87, because it benefited us and hurt the KGB, all at once. As for Sabirzhan, he's simply a tool to be used when it suits my purpose, nothing more."

He subsided back into his chair. "Everything's up for grabs – cars, weapons, haulage, prostitution, gambling, banking, vodka. *Everything.* Smuggling income's going to go through the roof; each successor republic will now exercise jurisdiction only within its own borders, so goods stolen in Russia can be legally traded anywhere outside. The central finance system's gone to shit, so there's millions to be had from currency speculation. We've a freedom of movement unthinkable even a year ago. The country's changing day by day. It's the revolution all over again. If we're to take our rightful place in the new Russia, *now* is the time to strike. But in order to seize this opportunity we too must change."

Lev fingered the home-made aluminium cross that dangled from his neck. The cross, like his habit of wearing his shirt outside his trousers with a waistcoat on top, was a deliberate homage to the vory who'd ruled the camps in the last years of Stalin's reign.

"No." When Banzai shook his head, his plaited dreadlocks jerked like a Turkish bead curtain. "You talk about the Chechens as though they're an organised army. They're nothing of the sort. They're ignorant, undisciplined psychopaths who'd as soon murder their own brothers as any of us. Their idea of refinement is to take their meat rare rather than raw. Thank you, but no. I prefer to take my chances alone."

"But you're outnumbered, little brother, and we can't have you outside the tent pissing in. By a margin of two to one, the decision is taken: we unite." Lev wagged his finger to emphasise the point. It was tattooed with a symbol: *In life, only count on yourself.*

"Over my dead body," said Banzai.

On the other side of Moscow, at the foot of the old hilltop royal estate of Kolomenskoe, three Chechen ganglords – Karkadann of the Tsentralnaya, Zhorzh of the Ostankinskaya and Ilmar of the Avtomobilnaya – were meeting in similar circumstances. They were not vory; Chechens never were. Instead, they styled themselves *avtoritety,* 'authorities', and they saw themselves as harder and more pragmatic than their adversaries.

The Tsentralnaya gang was the most powerful of the three, and so it was to Karkadann's house that Zhorzh and Ilmar had come; Zhorzh from his base at the Ostankino Hotel in the northern suburbs, and Ilmar from inspecting some of the South Port car showrooms for which his Avtomobilnaya group provided protection.

"Be free!" they said as they greeted each other.

Karkadann's face was rawhide, a tangle of crevasses and creases: cheekbones like raised daggers, shadowed holes for eyes, a bent nail of a nose. Here was a man who walked down the darkest avenues, wielding his face like a club. He took his visitors outside, despite the weather and his limp; his garden was vast, and he wanted to show it off. They talked while shuffling down pathways lit by undersized streetlights.

"I'm meeting with Lev tomorrow," Karkadann said. "He's seeing his vory now. I speak for us, he speaks for them; that's what we've arranged. He may offer us a deal, he may not. If he doesn't, it's war, plain and simple. If he does . . ." He grinned, as sharp and menacing as a sword unsheathed; "if he does, it's still war, even plainer and simpler."

"You don't know what he'll offer," Ilmar said.

Karkadann reached down into a bucket, pulled out a raw steak, and tossed it at the caged bear he kept to intimidate his debtors. "Whatever it is, it won't be enough."

"It won't be everything, you mean."

"Take it how you like." Karkadann jabbed at the air with a gloved hand. "Even if we did make an agreement, do you think those bastards would honour it? Not for a moment. Why would they? They've hated us for centuries. They hate us, the police hate us, every useless drone in this city hates us. As far as they're concerned, the only good Chechen is a dead Chechen. The *only* reason they tolerate us is because they're scared of us. And if we make a deal with the Slavs, we've lost even that. So there it is. All or nothing, a fight to the death. If you have any doubts, speak now."

He hobbled towards the walled garden. His right leg was ten centimetres shorter than his left, but no one was certain how this had happened; some said a mafiya attack, some a childhood deformation, some the revenge of a jealous husband. It was typical of Karkadann that no one knew for sure; equally typical that he chose not to enlighten anyone who asked.

Zhorzh shook his head. The white streak in his hair made him look like a cross between Trotsky and the devil in a medieval icon.

"The Slavs have got – what? I'm guessing five, six thousand men," Ilmar said. "We've half that at most."

"Ha! Then *they* should be quaking," Karkadann shouted. "One Chechen is worth ten Russians! Have you gone soft, Ilmar? What's happened to your mountain pride? What is agreement, if not surrender? And when did you last see a Chechen surrender, eh?"

Ilmar had softer features and lighter skin than his fellow *avtoritety*. He rubbed at his chin and said nothing.

The singing fountain, which in the summer emitted different notes depending on the height of the water, stood in winter stasis. As they walked, Karkadann checked that there were no gaps in the wire or the netting around the perimeter fence. His guards made the rounds every day, but there was nothing like checking for oneself.

"All right," Ilmar said eventually, but his unhappiness was plain to see.

"You're not serious," Lev said.

"Over my dead body," Banzai repeated, and it was clear that serious was exactly what he was being. He'd made his name in the camps for attacking guards; the other vory had taken bets on when, not if, the authorities would give Banzai the bullet. Now, Lev's slap had marked not just Banzai's face but also his reputation.

"I want no part of this. I want simply to be treated as a vor." Banzai was agitated, speaking fast. "But you refuse to listen to me – you slap me." He shrugged extravagantly. "What choice do I have? I'm walking out of here, and the only way to stop me is to kill me."

"Banzai, you're being ridiculous," Testarossa said.

"Kill me," Banzai repeated. "And Testarossa, it's you that'll have to do it." Lev could have snapped Banzai's neck like a breadstick, but vory tradition dictates that the senior man present can't dirty his hands. "So!" Banzai's voice was almost jaunty. "*Do* you dare, Testarossa? Do you dare kill a fellow vor, for nothing more than disagreeing with you? Hah! The system's been dead two days, and already you're acting like the KGB." He pushed his chair back and it fell with a crash.

The bodyguards were outside, facing away from the windows. What went on within the dacha was not their business.

"This is getting out of hand," Lev said, realising too late that he had miscalculated badly in expecting Banzai to understand that his proposals were motivated not by self-interest but the good of the vory. The thieves' code had much to commend it – indeed, they would never have survived the Soviet system without it – but a creed that dated back to the days of bandits and highwaymen was inadequate to the demands of these changing times. The very inflexibility that had been its greatest strength would doom the vory to

8

destruction if Lev failed in his bid to drag the brotherhood towards the 21st Century. Banzai was willing enough to ignore the ban on drug-trafficking, but any alliance with the state – even when the vory had the upper hand in the partnership – was anathema to him. Now he was prepared to challenge Lev and risk death over a mere slap, because the code demanded it. And if Lev's progressive leadership were to survive the challenge, he must deal with Banzai according to the code.

"You leave, Banzai, and you're compromising the very future of the brotherhood," Lev said.

Banzai started for the exit as if he hadn't heard. He walked at normal pace, allowing Testarossa to reach the door and cut him off two paces short. Testarossa was ten centimetres taller and ten kilos heavier than Banzai; it would hardly be a fair fight.

"You really want me to do this?" Testarossa asked, pushing himself back against the door.

"Do you dare?"

Lev was sitting at the head of the table. Testarossa looked to him for guidance, as if seeking the emperor's verdict on a gladiator.

"You have your knife with you?" Lev asked.

Testarossa tapped at his right hip. "Always."

Lev's head rose and fell: a simple movement, a death sentence.

Testarossa placed his hands on Banzai's shoulders and began to spin him round, slowly at first, as Banzai resisted, and then with increasing ease. A full circle took away the victim's soul and supposedly made it easier for him to accept death; it was the point of no return in the vory death ceremony. When he next faced Testarossa, Banzai's eyes were wide, as though he'd been playing a game and only now saw that his brinkmanship had backfired. Testarossa manoeuvred Banzai against the wall; he was firm, but took care not to be rough.

Lev watched from the table, five paces away and as remote as Vladivostok.

"Die like a vor," Testarossa said, only marginally more statement than question.

Banzai gripped his own collar with sweat-slimed palms, knuckles drained white, and ripped his shirt open. Neither he nor Testarossa were watching Lev; had they been, they'd have seen his face twitch in a momentary wince.

"Take my soul," Banzai said, and Testarossa drew the knife from his belt and plunged it into Banzai's throat, right up to the hilt, the way they'd used to kill people in the gulag.

\* \* \*

9

Ilmar stood by his limousine and indicated his watch. "I'll miss prayer if I don't hurry," he said.

"Good for you," replied Karkadann. "I don't know how you manage it. I can never fit in my three times a day."

They hugged sideways, Chechen-style. "It's five times a day, actually."

"Oh well . . ." Karkadann's voice was bright. "The more the merrier."

The television schedules had been cleared for Gorbachev to announce his resignation – with the union gone, there was nothing for him to be president of any more – but when the television crews were allowed into his Kremlin office, they were greeted by an empty chair.

"It's all come as a bit of a shock to him," one of the presidential staff explained. "He needs time to get used to it, that's all."

They showed the empty chair on TV until it was time for the next programme.

# 2

*Tuesday, 24 December 1991*

There is in central Moscow an island shaped like a walrus moustache, bound to the north by the river which shares its name with the city and to the south by the Vodootvodny drainage canal, originally dug to prevent the city centre flooding in spring when snowmelt swells the river. The island follows the river's extravagant sweep past the Kremlin and down to Moscow's oldest monastery, the Novospasskiy. It's so narrow that the bridges on the north and south sides almost run into each other.

The river was frozen, of course; had it not been, Karkadann would have come by speedboat rather than his Mercedes 600, for it was much safer to travel on an empty river than on Moscow's increasingly congested roads. There was less traffic on the river, less chance of being ambushed by attackers who would pluck a mafiya boss's car from its escort as easily as one would pick lint from a lapel.

Karkadann's Mercedes was book-ended front and rear by Land Cruisers with tinted windows, and it wallowed low under the weight of its armour-plating. Mercedes had been happy to carry out the modifications free of charge, recognising a growing market when it saw one; its 1992 forecast predicted more orders for 600-class limousines in Moscow and St Petersburg than across a region stretching from Dublin to Berlin.

Each door of Karkadann's Mercedes was painted with a wolf's head, the symbol of Chechnya. Chechens see the wolf as they see themselves: fierce, brave and untameable. No matter how long a wolf is kept penned up, it will always howl at the moon for its freedom.

When the convoy reached its destination, Karkadann's bodyguards piled out of the Land Cruisers, scanning rooftops, doorways, windows and traffic. They formed a human wall between the limousine and the restaurant's front door. The restaurant where Karkadann and Lev were meeting had no street sign, just a bell. When they rang, the owner, an elderly woman, opened the door herself.

"Good afternoon," she said, showing neither surprise nor trepidation; the mafiya used her premises for this purpose quite regularly.

Baltazar Sharmukhamedov, Karkadann's chief bodyguard, opened the door of the Mercedes, and Karkadann limped out. He was wearing shoes crafted of alligator skin, to emphasise that he didn't have to step in the filth of Moscow's streets.

The old lady led her visitors through a room lit only by candles. After the brightness of the winter sun, it took a few moments before their eyes adjusted. Patterned carpets from the southern republics and oil paintings from St Petersburg covered the walls. It was late afternoon, and the place was empty; the lunchtime crowd had gone, the evening diners were yet to arrive, and the guitarist who usually strummed Georgian folk songs had been given the day off. It was the kind of place where, when the waiter asks how many bottles of wine you want, he means each. Georgian restaurants are like that. Even the Russians admit – grudgingly, of course – that Georgians know how to drink.

The dining-room gave way to a corridor, and the corridor in turn to a wooden door. For a moment, Karkadann seemed to be scratching himself like a Barbary ape, so fast were his hands moving around his body. He handed his guns to Sharmukhamedov. Karkadann always carried three guns: one in his right trouser pocket, another under his left armpit, and the third in his left outside coat pocket. Only in places like these did he relinquish them.

"I feel naked without them," he said, and his guards dutifully laughed, because naked was exactly what he was going to be.

11

Karkadann pushed open the door and stepped into a small changing-room which smelt of lavender. Lev had already gone through; his clothes lay in a neat pile underneath a sports jacket with shoulders as wide as an albatross' wings.

Karkadann undressed without hurry, arranging his clothes with care. Off came the necklace, the rings and the bracelets; the metal would get too hot and the rings too constricting as the skin and capillaries swelled in the steam.

When he was ready, he hobbled into the banya. Russian steam baths often served as meeting places for rival gang leaders. For a start, it is all but impossible to conceal a weapon on a naked body. Moreover, the feeling of well-being which the banya produces is supposed in turn to promote accord and a willingness to work problems through. The choice of venue said much about the parties' intentions. Very public or very private places tend not to lead to violence. Everywhere else is suspect.

Both men had brought bodyguards; neither moved without them. Some ganglords come alone and unarmed, which is very brave or very foolish; it's also how reputations are made.

Karkadann could see nothing through the steam bar a muscular arm which looked as though it was sheathed in colourful Chinese silk.

"You're late," said Lev The in a voice which seemed to start somewhere deep beneath the river. Being late for a meet was against gangster etiquette; failure to show up at all automatically meant defeat.

"Traffic," Karkadann replied, knowing Lev would see the lie; mafiya limousines jumped lights and used forbidden lanes, and there was not a traffic cop in Moscow who dared stop them.

Karkadann hoisted himself on to a bench and rubbed his palms on to his thighs. Unlike a sauna, which slowly bakes the sweat out, the banya is so saturated by moist steam that perspiration blooms in an instant. When the vapours cleared, Karkadann realised that what he'd taken to be Chinese silk was actually a carpet of tattoos, not just on Lev's arm but rioting over his entire body. Vultures, bleeding wounds, spectres and snowscapes crawled over the ribcage. A map of the gulag stretched above Lev's waist, names distended and elongated by the rise and fall of his chest: Magadan, Tashkent, Vladimir, Kolyma, Vorkutia, Potma, Lefortovo – places where the empire's waste had been quarantined to prevent infection of the glorious Soviet nation. Just as the vory had refused to recognise the state – declining to carry a residence permit, pay taxes, take up arms on behalf of the state – so the state had returned the compliment. Since organised crime could not logically have existed in a socialist utopia, the vory had been awarded the ultimate accolade of invisibility. There'd been no crime in the Soviet Union, merely asocial behaviour, political dissidence, and mental illness.

The only blank space was on Lev's breastbone, where a white scar shone. The sheer incongruity drew Karkadann's eye to it; in an extravagance of activity, it was easiest to pick out the void, the paler space where a picture had been taken from the wall.

Lev pointed to it: "Lenin." He turned round to show another scar on his back. "Moustaches." Stalin. The twin heroes of the Soviet Union were common faces on the skin of those who'd rejected their every doctrine; it was thought that a Soviet execution squad would refuse to shoot at either image.

"The authorities removed them?" Despite himself, Karkadann was curious.

"No. I did. The day the devil's spawn came back from the Crimea, I took a soldering iron and burnt them off myself." The devil's spawn was Gorbachev, because of the mark on his forehead.

They sat sweating in silence for a few moments, feeling their bodies reacting to the banya. The heat produces an artificial fever, urging every organ of the body into action, furiously cleansing the body from inside out through the largest organ of all, the skin, and its excretion, sweat.

"Let's get straight to it." Karkadann was impatient.

"Very well. No one in Moscow wants you here. Go back to Grozny. We'll pay you more than fairly for your interests." Turf wars were destructive, co-operation was easier on everybody. It would, Lev reflected, be the perfect Marxist solution: from conflict to synthesis.

Karkadann snorted. "You must be crazy."

No, thought Lev, *you* must be crazy. He weighed twice as much as Karkadann and could easily have snapped him in two, but the Chechen seemed entirely unintimidated.

"You must be crazy," Karkadann repeated. "There's not enough money in Moscow to make me leave. Not enough just to leave Red October alone."

Lev had wondered whether Karkadann was going to mention that. Lev was director of the Red October distillery, a few streets down from where they were sitting. In truth, it was more than a distillery, it was the spiritual home of Russian vodka, the largest and most famous of its kind anywhere in the federation. He who controls vodka controls Russia, goes the old saying, and Lev had a hand in every stage of the vodka process. He provided protection for and shared in the profits of distilleries. He ran underground bottling plants for counterfeiting; for every bottle of vodka produced officially, another was produced on the side. He ran his own trucking firms to take care of distribution. He managed vast warehouses where the vodka was stored. He controlled the shops and kiosks where the vodka was sold. And he imported foreign vodka, which had social cachet and was seen as good value for money. Importing vodka into Russia may have seemed like taking samovars to Tula, but there was still great demand for it.

"You have a week, until New Year's Eve, to consider my offer," said Lev. "The price will be fair; I'm a man of honour."

"Spare me. The world has moved on." Karkadann's eyes were glittering black holes, and behind them was endless night. "No one gives a shit about the vory generation any more, Lev; the hell with you."

In the banya, silence but for the hissing of water on hot rocks.

It's tradition that, if the meeting results in reconciliation, the men will go upstairs and eat. They'll be offered bagels, cream cheese, borscht, and some of the specialities of the house: traditional baked bread stuffed with thin layers of cheese; fried strips of aubergine rolled around a walnut paste filling; or perhaps some tsatsivi, cold chicken and turkey in a soupy walnut sauce.

Neither man suggested going upstairs.

Since Lev had been the one to call this meeting, he stayed in the banya until Karkadann had showered, changed and left. It's embarrassing to be in a man's company once you've failed to find agreement with him.

# 3

*Wednesday, 25 December 1991*

A soft parcel wrapped in brown paper arrived at Red October just before lunchtime, brought by a courier because only a fool trusted the Russian postal system. The word 'Lev' was scrawled across the front of the package; there was no sender name or return address. Red October's security guards checked for protruding wires and grease stains where any explosives might have sweated; finding neither, they made doubly sure by passing the parcel through the rickety fluoroscope which had been liberated from KGB headquarters following the August coup. Only when four men had satisfied themselves that it wasn't a bomb – the Soviet Union hadn't encouraged individual initiative in its citizens – did they take it upstairs.

Lev unwrapped the package with efficiently minimal movements; his hands may have been bigger than any stevedore's, but they were also supple as a cellist's. When he pulled the item free from the wrapping, there was a short but dreadful hiatus while he grappled with the import of this gesture of Karkadann's. Then he gave a low whistle and a headshake, as if the Chechen's capacity to insult was simply beyond his comprehension, and looked up at his secretary Galina. Her eyes were pea-green and her hair was like a gypsy's, jet black and scarcely tamed.

"Galya, go and get Tengiz Lavrentiyich, will you?" he said.

Tengiz Sabirzhan was Lev's deputy at the distillery and head of security for the 21st Century Association. Where Lev had come from the gulag, Sabirzhan was KGB to his bootstraps; the Sixth Directorate, to be precise, which had been responsible for industrial security and economic counter-intelligence. That the Sixth Directorate had now been subsumed into a new body, the MSB, altered the nature neither of the organisation nor the man. Sabirzhan had been appointed political officer at Red October in Brezhnev's day – every enterprise had a political officer, to recruit informers among the workforce and ensure ideological hegemony – but, as stagnation had grown deeper under Andropov and Chernenko, so the KGB had been forced to collaborate with the enemies of the state. Only by striking deals with the organised crime gangs could they prevent internal trade from grinding to a halt. Keeping the vodka industry running had been top priority; the people would accept the shortage of many commodities, even staples such as potatoes and timber, but vodka? Never.

Sabirzhan came immediately, as he always did, waddling into Lev's office with shirt straining at his gut and eyes bright with sweaty intrigue behind his pince-nez. Lev gestured towards the package. "This sweater – this . . . *thing*," he said, putting a metre of clean air between himself and the word, "is made of goat's wool."

To a vor, goat's wool – homosexual overtones aside – was the mark of a traitor, one who collaborated with the authorities against his own.

Lev stretched his arms out in front of him; from the end of one sleeve appeared a tattooed crest, the double-headed imperial eagle commemorating the troops of the White Guard who'd fought the revolutionary Red Army. He shook his head again. "That black bastard's gone too far this time."

Sabirzhan kept his wet-lipped mouth shut. Even after four years as Lev's deputy, he knew little of the vory. This was not through lack of interest on his part but a complete lack of informers. Though they made use of his services, to the vory Sabirzhan would always be an outsider, someone to be kept at arm's length.

Lev clapped his hands, as he did to shed excess talcum powder before lifting his weights. "Enough musing, Tengiz – to practicalities. If you want to drive out a wedge, hit it with another."

"You want Karkadann killed?" Lev found Sabirzhan's excitement at the prospect almost indecent; but then what else did he expect? KGB members had been tutored extensively in the science of inflicting pain; it was hardly surprising that many took enjoyment as well as pride in their work.

"Killed? No." Not for an insult, however heinous. Besides, Banzai's murder was pricking at Lev's conscience. "But . . . *warned*, yes. Threatened."

"How many men?" said Sabirzhan, eyebrows clinging to his skin like slugs.

"Two." They'd need no more, if Sabirzhan chose the best. Lev preferred to avoid employing small-time mafiya thugs, men with the intelligence of bullfrogs and the morals of camp guards. Instead, he picked men who knew for themselves the value of physical training: wrestlers, weightlifters, martial arts experts, and those who, like Sabirzhan, had worked in the security services. Yes, vory tradition prohibited fraternisation with the KGB – Banzai's accusation still stung – but Lev had always been quicker than most vory to appreciate how the country was altering, and if something benefited him then he was happy to accommodate it, always with the caveat that it was on his terms. He didn't have to be friends with all his men, but he had to trust in their abilities. So the 21st Century's gangsters went to the gym every second day and to the shooting range every week; they all knew that their professional value was in direct ratio to their physical fitness. The imperceptible tremor of a trigger finger, the slightest wavering of an eye, or a split second's hesitancy at the crucial moment could spell the difference between success and failure.

"I know just the ones," Sabirzhan said.

"Who?"

"Ozers and Butuzov." Two whom Sabirzhan had recruited

personally from the Army Institute for Foreign Languages, the school for aspiring KGB members which taught its pupils the darker arts of the service's tradecraft. Had they been born a decade earlier, Vyacheslav Ozers and Gennady Butuzov would have been pursuing minor dissidents around godforsaken Baltic towns. But if you were smart enough for the institute, then you would also be smart enough to see which way the winds of change were blowing under Gorbachev.

Lev nodded in approval. "Excellent. *Excellent.*"

At 7 p.m. Gorbachev went on air to take his leave of the Soviet people; the first, and last, Soviet leader to have departed office voluntarily, if one could describe his evident reluctance to step down as in any way elective. In every public place with a television set people fell silent and watched, their eyes narrowed in stoic acceptance of this latest twist in their history.

"I am ceasing my work as president of the USSR," Gorbachev said, dignified in his sadness. "I am very much concerned as I leave this post, but I also have feelings of faith and hope in you, your wisdom and force of spirit. We are inheritors of a great civilisation, and it now depends on one and all as to whether this civilisation makes a comeback to a new and decent living today." Behind owlish glasses, the twinkle seemed to be dying in his grey-green eyes; and then he rallied, proud to the last, the forehead with the famous birthmark still unwrinkled by worry or stress. "I have never had any regrets; never had any regrets. I consider it vitally important to preserve the democratic achievements which have been attained in the past few years. We have paid with all our history and tragic experience for these achievements and they are not to be abandoned, whatever the circumstances. Otherwise all our hopes will be buried."

He closed the thin folder containing the text and dropped it on to the table in front of him. When he went to sign the order authorising the transfer of the nuclear arsenal, however, his pen ran out. And so it was that Gorbachev's last signature as Soviet leader was made with a Biro borrowed from the American producer overseeing the broadcast. It was Christmas Day in the West, but not in Russia; Gorbachev's PR had always been better abroad than at home.

"I wish everyone all the best," he said, and then he was gone.

Lev was one of the millions who watched, and he felt no pity either for Gorbachev or the hated union he'd taken with him. Almost the first thing that Gorbachev had done on becoming General Secretary was to introduce an anti-alcohol campaign, and by way of example Lev had been singled out as Moscow's premier vodka crook and thrown in the Lefortovo jail. In typically Russian fashion, this was both a compliment and an insult: a compliment to Lev's perceived standing, in that Lefortovo was usually reserved for those committing crimes against national security; and an insult in that it effectively categorised Lev as a political prisoner – something akin to pond life in the eyes of the vory. Being inside mattered little to Lev; he ran his empire just as easily from behind bars, even extended it, and besides, he was released after only a few months in order to strike his deal with Sabirzhan. But Lev had never forgotten Gorbachev's slight, nor forgiven him for it.

Less than half an hour after Gorbachev had finished speaking, the hammer and sickle was taken down from the Kremlin flagpole and the Russian tricolour hoisted in its place, to scattered applause and a few whistles from the handful of tourists in Red Square. A light snow was falling.

The twentieth century had ended, eight years before time.

# 4

*Thursday, 26 December 1991*

"Why do we have to wait around here? Why can't things just work properly?"

"I don't know what your problem is, Lewis, but I bet it's hard to pronounce." Alice Liddell put her hand over her husband's and stroked at the fine hairs on his wrist. "Getting hoopie ain't going to help. Cool your liver. *Enjoy.*"

"Enjoy? This is the VIP lounge, right?" The languor of Lewis' New Orleans cadence accentuated his incredulity; his wife spoke twice as quickly as he did. "Come on, Alice. Port Authority's classier than this place."

He had a point, Alice conceded silently. Seat cushions were struggling free of their upholstery; unshaven men wrapped in ankle-length coats puffed cigars and eyed up girls in skirts short enough to pass for belts. Sheremetyevo Airport clearly had a more elastic definition of VIP than she was used to, but wasn't that part of the fun?

Lewis looked around the room twice in mute defiance before turning back to Alice, by which time she'd started on the nearest copy of *Pravda*, testing the Russian she'd spent the last four months learning. Gorbachev's resignation speech had coincided to the minute with *Pravda*'s deadline, but the paper made no mention of it; the Soviet Union's most notorious mouthpiece hadn't held the front page for its own funeral.

The Liddells had been assigned a triumvirate of officials – a man from the finance ministry, another from the airport, and a third from the American Embassy – and now all three came back at once, dodging a splash of technicolour which Lewis recognised through the murk as a huddle of African state dignitaries in robes. The apparatchiks were almost running in their childlike eagerness to be first back to the new and exciting visitors, each brandishing sheaves of papers like wise men bearing gifts: passports, currency declaration forms, hotel reservations, tourist brochures – *as if*, thought Alice, there'll be time for *that*. Each seemed caught in confusion about who they should hand the papers to, because Lewis was a decade older than his wife, more conservatively dressed and, most importantly, male, all of which put him in charge until proven otherwise, but even by Russian standards Alice was so striking in her bootcut jeans and leather jacket that eventually, beholden to the masculine reflex of lustful gawping, they went to her instead.

When the embassy man escorted Alice and Lewis into the taxi and climbed into the front seat, he gave the other two a small involuntary smirk of triumph, and it was all they could do not to lean in through the window and ask the rich Westerners for a little baksheesh, a goodwill gesture in these times of glorious international co-operation.

Alice was surprised that the embassy man – Quarrie, he said his name was; Raymond Quarrie, from Trenton, New Jersey – had come personally. As an International Monetary Fund advisor she was technically employed by the UN rather than the US. But America was the only superpower left now, which meant that Washington called the shots when it came to international aid. US, UN – what was a consonant between friends? Even friends who'd spent the best part of half a century eyeballing each other across Checkpoint Charlie and the Straits of Florida.

Quarrie swivelled in his seat to face them. His face was pale and blotchy; he'd not be shy of a vodka or two, Alice reckoned. "Don't worry about your luggage," he said. "It'll be sent directly to your hotel. You're staying at the Metropol, yes?" The Metropol had reopened earlier in the month, refurbished by Scandinavian companies. For the average Muscovite, a room there cost five years' wages. The rouble was trading at ninety-six to the dollar; clerks and technicians earned four hundred roubles per month, pensions were half that.

"Until we find somewhere more permanent," said Alice. "Or the IMF runs out of money, whichever is the sooner."

Quarrie laughed much louder and much longer than the joke was worth.

Armed guards stamping their feet to keep warm slid from view as the taxi eased out of the airport. Quarrie peered through the rear windscreen and then sneaked a surreptitious look at Alice when he thought she wasn't looking. She hardly noticed, it happened so often, even with her auburn hair cropped short enough to bristle up the back of her neck. She loved it; from one angle it made her look bold, and from another vulnerable. Lewis hated it. He called the cut a duck's ass and said it made her look like a dyke.

"It's quite a ride into town, so please take your coats off if you want to," Quarrie said, playing the old Moscow stager. "Are you warm enough?"

"Fine," said Alice. The heating was on full blast.

"You'll be used to the weather, anyway. Moscow winters aren't much worse than Boston ones." He smiled. "Your accent gives you away."

"My husband's from New Orleans," she said, realising that Lewis hadn't exchanged a single word with Quarrie.

"New Orleans?" Quarrie laughed. "You guys don't even have winter there, right?"

They passed the anti-tank hedgehogs that marked the place where the Red Army had halted the Wehrmacht's advance half a century before. Alice stared rapt as Moscow flashed changes at the window, rolling out for her delectation every cliché about Soviet cities, and then some: massive buildings of uniform grey with crumbling façades, roads with potholes large enough to be bomb craters. There were pockets of beauty – a Byzantine church here, a pre-revolutionary house there – but they only served to accentuate the gloom.

The taxi swayed left and right as the driver glided between the hollows.

The ugliness and dereliction didn't bother Alice. For her, the first glimpse of a new country was always exciting, vista on a world pregnant with promises of adventure and challenge. She glanced across at Lewis, knowing that he didn't share her animation. Lewis was still ambivalent about coming to Moscow. He was looking at exactly the same city as Alice, but she knew that for him it spelt discomfort and difficulty, an experience to be endured rather than enjoyed. After two years living on different continents – the IMF job had started out as a temporary assignment in Warsaw which then led to another in Budapest and then another and another – Lewis, having failed to talk her out of accepting the Moscow posting, had decided to join her. As soon as her work was done there, they would head back to Boston to settle down and have kids while he was still young enough not to be taken for their grandfather.

Alice reached for Lewis' cheek and ran her hand down it, past the silvering hairs at his temples. He gave her a weak grin.

Quarrie leant towards Lewis. "You're taking up a post at the Sklifosovsky, I understand." Lewis nodded, a blip in Quarrie's monologue. "Finest emergency department in Moscow; they say it's far better than the Kremlinovka, or whatever they call it now – the Central Clinical Hospital, something like that. Even an old Russia hand like me finds it hard to keep up with all the name changes. No more Leningrad, no more Sverdlovsk; streets and metro stations switch from one day to the next. In Moscow, only the weather's still the same."

The driver cut across three lanes without indicating; Quarrie, unconcerned, pointed out of the window. In the gathering darkness, the most radiant objects in the skyline were the ruby-red stars shining above the Kremlin towers. "Five points, for the proletariats of five continents," he said. "Fat lot of good it did them."

The Kremlin itself, so familiar from photographs and television footage, looked slightly out of kilter. It took Alice a few moments to realise that it was because the hammer and sickle no longer rippled from the flagpole. In its place was the Russian tricolour, striped in white, blue and red; the same colours, Alice thought, as those of America, Britain and France, the countries tasked with helping revive the stricken Russia.

"They put it on upside down last night, can you believe?" said Quarrie. "Down comes the hammer and sickle, up goes the tricolour – and the red stripe's at the top! Stupid asses. Too much vodka, I wouldn't doubt. Then the artificial wind machine to make the flag flutter didn't work. They had to give it a good kick to get it going. Percussive maintenance, I think they call it. That's the way most Russian problems get solved. To cap it all, they launched an enormous hot-air balloon in the same three colours. It rose a few feet, then crashed back to earth. Not the most auspicious start."

"Nor much of an omen," said Lewis, perking up for the first time since their arrival.

The Metropol was entirely to Lewis' taste, which was to say it was sufficiently luxurious to kid him that he wasn't in Russia. He retired to the bathroom to soak away thoughts of the great unwashed outside, while Alice plucked four Smirnoff miniatures from the mini-bar and drained them with systematic relish as she stood at the window, looking down at the patches of neon signs flickering uncertainly, the dancing headlights of crazy drivers, the gargantuan buildings which loomed like supertankers from the darkness, and the people, the people, scurrying fifty metres below the remote and omnipotent goddess who'd come from the promised land to spread the gospel according to the almighty dollar.

# 5

*Friday, 27 December 1991*

The limousine pulled up round the back of the president's official residence, a neoclassical triangular building that used to serve as the senate. The driver, a thickset southerner named Ruslan with beetle brows and an ill-fitting suit, opened the door for Alice. The cold was dry and seemed almost industrial; it hurt her nostrils the moment she stepped out of the car.

"I'll be waiting here for you when you come out," Ruslan said.

"You'll be keeping yourself warm while I'm gone?"

He looked at her blankly, perhaps surprised at how good her Russian was. Alice opened the passenger door and pulled a bottle of vodka from the glove compartment. Ruslan sized her up fast and smiled. "Best heating known to man," he said.

She grinned back. "Save some for me."

The president's office was at the end of a long corridor carpeted in red. Alice passed through an anteroom bulging with stone-faced men in grey suits and into a small conference chamber, where she waited until a secretary arrived to escort her into the inner sanctum.

Anatoly Nikolayevich Borzov, president of the Russian Federation and now the Kremlin's inhabitant, kissed Alice's hand, took a step backwards the better to admire her, nodded approvingly and steered her by the elbow towards a white leather armchair. Gorbachev had been gone barely thirty-six hours, and already there was no trace of him. Rumour had it that Borzov had moved in even before Gorbachev had left, piling Gorbachev's possessions in the corridor as though he were holding a fire sale. Now the office was a shrine to Russia and Borzov in equal measures.

Huge paintings dominated the walls: Lentulov's *St Basil's Cathedral*, Surikov's *The Morning of the Execution of the Streltsy*, Polonev's *Moscow Courtyard*. Along the plasterboard, smaller frames jostled for space: prints of pre-revolutionary streets and czarist armies, icons of apostles, and scores of photographs, all without exception featuring Borzov himself, his drinker's luminous face glowing under the statesman's stiff helmet of white hair. Borzov in a bulldozer, Borzov outside McDonald's on Pushkin Square, Borzov laughing with colleagues.

"You'll take a hundred grams with the Chief?" he said.

It was ten in the morning. "Of course."

Borzov filled two glasses and handed one to Alice. The vodka in his glass lurched as he sat heavily into the chair opposite her, but the preservative balance innate to the hardened drinker ensured that not a drop was spilt. "Your good health," he said, and moved to drain the glass in one before remembering whose company he was in and smoothly altering the action to a sip.

There was a knock at the door, and in came Arkin.

"Kolya!" Borzov launched himself from his chair and kissed Arkin on both cheeks. "Kolya, meet Mrs Liddell. Mrs Liddell, meet Nikolai Valentinovich Arkin – the son the Chief never had."

Arkin looked to be in his mid-thirties, two or three years older than Alice. He shook her hand and speared her with his good looks; skin glowing under well-groomed black hair, as tall as Borzov but many times more handsome as he shrugged off his Italian cashmere overcoat, a Russian as the West likes to see them. Untainted by any past association with the communists, Arkin was a perfect poster-boy for the new generation. At his inauguration as Prime Minister the previous month, he'd taken a stiletto blade from his pocket and slashed at the air in front of him. This is to be my trademark, he'd said; this knife is the symbol of my desire to cut through red tape and get things done. "I've no time for the enemies of progress," he'd proclaimed. Whether he'd mimicked the famous Soviet slogan deliberately or unconsciously was moot; that he understood the free market was evident.

"You two!" Borzov said, looking at Arkin and Alice as though he were presiding at a wedding. "So young, and already ruling the roost! There's hardly room for an old codger like Anatoly Nikolayevich these days, is there?" He winked at Alice to let her know that he wasn't being serious, and she understood instantly why he was such a hero to Russians; they were seduced by his bonhomie, but they also recognised the steel beneath it, and that reassured them. He'd stood on a tank outside the White House in August, he'd faced down the grey bureaucrats until the coup had disintegrated. He belonged to the Russian people, he was *theirs*. It was no wonder that Muscovites had rallied to him in those dark days the previous summer.

Borzov motioned Arkin to a chair, chided him good-naturedly for refusing a glass of vodka – "Don't say it, Kolya; someone has to remain sober, no?" – and then went to sit behind his desk, one side of which was covered with banks of telephones, some white and others coloured but all without numbers. Under the Kremlin telephone system, each phone was connected to only one other person, which meant that the number of telephones was a direct indicator of seniority. No one had more phones than the president, of course. A modern exchange, though infinitely easier and more flexible, would have defeated the point: what matters in Russia is not just who has the power, but who's *seen* to have that power.

"It's very simple, Mrs Liddell," Borzov said. "Russia is reforming, God knows, we're reforming. Prices are being freed next Thursday, we're stabilising the money supply, creating a new tax system, protecting property rights and contracts, and so on. It sounds very simple put that way, no?" He nodded towards Arkin. "Kolya understands all this much better, which is why Anatoly Nikolayevich made him Prime Minister, to see this whole programme through. And he tells the Chief that the one thing we need to do before everything else, the one thing that's of paramount importance, is to privatise. The state owns everything, absolutely everything: diamond mines, food stores, oilfields, barbers' shops. Yes, Gorbachev's reforms have ushered in some new beasts – leased enterprises, joint-stock companies, economic associations, co-operatives – but these are little more than variations on a theme. If we're to be a proper market economy, the state must own *nothing*, yes? As little as possible, anyway. So we put out some feelers. 'Who knows about privatising command economies?' we asked. We asked everyone – international organisations, other governments, embassies – and one name came up time and again. Yours."

Alice wasn't surprised; quite the opposite, in fact. She'd have been insulted if she hadn't been chosen. In the mid-eighties, she'd been the first woman to work on Milken's infamous junk-bond trading floor in Beverly Hills. Headhunted from Wall Street at decade's end, she'd spent the last two years running privatisation programmes in Eastern Europe, suddenly liberated after the momentous autumn of 1989 when government after government toppled, the Berlin Wall was dismantled and the Ceaucescus were executed by their own people. If there was a single person who'd shuttled between Budapest, Prague and Warsaw more than Alice had in that time, she'd yet to meet them. But she'd always been conscious that, however important her work there had been, it was little more than a dress rehearsal for the big one —Mother Russia herself.

"Speed is the key here, Mrs Liddell," Arkin said, and it was the smugness of his tone that prompted Alice to answer back.

"Speed is *always* the key in situations like these, Nikolai Valentinovich, but we can only move fast if you pledge to stick behind me all the way. I planned rapid privatisation in Warsaw, and was undone by the bureaucrats. I was more cautious in Budapest, and was criticised for being too slow. Prague was the best I managed, largely because Havel backed me all the way. If this is to work, gentlemen, your support must be unwavering; I can't do it other-wise."

"This is Russia," said Arkin. "You can't apply the same strictures here as elsewhere."

"Why not? You're all post-communist societies, you're all facing similar transitions; you're all the same, more or less."

The silence was so deep and encompassing that it seemed to swallow Alice's remark and whirl it down into the black hole reserved for heresies. The muscles in Arkin's cheeks stood out like walnuts; Borzov struck his clay pipe against the table as though it were a drumstick. It seemed an age before the president spoke, in the quiet and measured voice of someone trying very hard to control their anger.

"Russia is unique," he said. "It is categorically and absolutely not like anywhere else."

Alice, her hands held up to pacify, gabbled to rectify her mistake. "I'm sorry, I didn't mean to offend, I was just . . ."

"We respect your knowledge and experience, Mrs Liddell." It was Arkin this time, playing the peacemaker. "And in return we hope that *you* will respect *our* country. By the time your work is done here, you may love it or hate it – maybe both – but you'll most assuredly see that it is indeed like nowhere else."

Alice had the sudden and uncomfortable feeling of being a teenager again, chastised by an elder, someone more worldly and sophisticated than she'd ever be. She drank the rest of her vodka and looked around, trying to hide her embarrassment. On the nearest wall was a picture of Borzov, mushroom-coloured, emerging from the Moscow River. He was clad only in a tiny pair of swimming trunks, obscured at the front by the pendulous overhang of his belly.

"They break the ice and have a competition to see who stays in there longest," said Arkin, following her gaze. He'd noticed her discomfort and was now moving to assuage it. Alice was grateful, and confused. "Anatoly Nikolayevich always wins."

"Only because they let him," said Borzov. "They think he doesn't notice, but he does. He's not stupid just because he's old, but you try telling his doctors that. Now he's nearly seventy, they say he shouldn't swim in there. Fools!" He grinned at Alice. "Your husband would know better. Anatoly Nikolayevich will remember to ask for him next time he's carted off to hospital." Borzov peered gloomily into his empty glass. "Another?"

"Please."

He hauled himself out of the chair, refilled their glasses and resumed his place, tamping tobacco in his pipe with excruciating slowness. He was larger than he appeared on television; the screen conveyed the breadth of his shoulders but not his height, nor his depth. Borzov seemed to go *back* a long way, Alice thought.

She looked out of the window. There was a demonstration on the far bank of the river; doctors protesting against their pay – less than ten dollars a month, when miners were still on four hundred – and holding up banners saying *Hippocrates, please forgive me.*

Borzov spoke to Arkin. "Now, Kolya, you were saying; speed is of the essence."

Arkin was turning a book over and over. It was only when he stopped in order to speak that Alice made out the title: *Wealth of Nations*, Adam Smith's masterpiece of free market doctrine.

"The West thinks every Russian is delirious with gratitude for the end of the Soviet Union. Not so. There are millions, tens of millions, who fear that reform will lead the country to ruin, and they're well represented in parliament. Forget the resistance you saw during the coup, Mrs Liddell; parliament is stuffed full of reactionaries who hope and believe we can't do what we say we will. If we don't prove them wrong, and fast, then our window of opportunity will be gone. That's why something, *anything*, is better than nothing. We don't need you to run an entire privatisation programme, Mrs Liddell, not yet."

"But that's what I –"

"There's no history of private property in Russia. Communism succeeded czarism; czarism had succeeded feudalism. Privatisation will be as seismic as introducing money into a barter economy – I don't exaggerate. This is why we tell you that Russia's different. We need to hurry, but we also need to be realistic about what we can do. To privatise everything overnight, that's impossible. But a single factory, successfully sold off, to show that it *can* be done . . . Make that work, and the rest will follow. The dinosaurs will see that privatisation is going to happen whether they like it or not. How long would that take you, to sell off an enterprise?"

"In Poland, I did one that . . ."

"No, by Western standards. To sell an enterprise, with due diligence and so on; how long?"

"A year, perhaps. Nine months, at the outside."

"Parliament meets in the second week of March. You've got nine weeks."

They told her what was needed. The enterprise chosen would be in Moscow, just about the only place in the nation where more firms were still functioning than going to the wall. The guinea-pig had to be well known, stable and commercially viable; bidding would be stronger for firms with good export potential and a strong retail base. Finally, it must already be corporatised as a joint-stock company; corporatisation was a cumbersome process, and performing it anew would take too long.

With all these factors taken into account, there were seven possibles – *Seven!* Alice thought. In a country that spans twelve time zones, only seven! There was the Vorobyovy chocolate factory; the Moskovksie Brewery; Koloss, which made spaghetti, snacks and tea; Moscow Food Processing; the food wholesaler Torgovy Dom Preobrazenski; and the Bolshevik Biscuit Factory. All these were suitable in financial terms, but not politically; the government couldn't hold up a spaghetti manufacturer as the harbinger of the Great Leap Forward, for instance. For the test case, the flagship, they needed something more . . . more *Russian*, something quintessentially national.

The seventh possible enterprise was the Red October distillery, and the decision had already been taken. What could have been more appropriate? Vodka is just about the only recession-proof industry; the worse the economy gets, the more vodka people drink. In many of Russia's cash-strapped regions, vodka was a stable currency, making it as profitable as diamonds or oil. Alice had read that teachers in Murmansk were receiving their salaries in vodka (having rejected funeral accessories and lavatory paper) because the local authorities couldn't pay them. The nation's consumption of vodka borders on the heroic, and the figures remain staggering no matter how many times you hear them: Russia accounts for four-fifths of the world's vodka; a million litres are downed in Moscow each day; the average Russian drinks a litre every two days (the *average* Russian, including women and children – consider that for a moment).

"Choosing Red October – it's not just an economic decision, you know." Borzov held his glass up to the light and squinted at it, as though the nation's secrets were held within. "The people will understand why, because vodka's our lifeblood, the defining symbol of Russian identity. It's our main entertainment, our main currency, our main scourge. Vodka affects every aspect of Russian life, good and bad: friendships, business, politics, crime, and the millions of Russians whose lives are lonely, embittered and tough. If there's one thing which unites the president with the frozen drunk found dead on a Moscow street, it's vodka. Vodka's always been the great equaliser, from here in the Kremlin down to the hovels. The good, the bad and the ugly, they all drink it. No matter what's going on up above – monarchy, communism, capitalism – there's always vodka, and all life goes through it. Our history and our future depend above all on one thing: vodka, and our relationship with it."

This was a sacred homily for Borzov, and Alice respected that. Borzov lowered his glass and stared at her. "What's vodka, Mrs Liddell, if not all things to all men? It can be a folk medicine, a hallucinogen revealing the mysteries of the soul, a lubricant more commonly applied to sophisticated machinery than any conventional liquid – and of course it can simply be vodka too. Every aspect of the human condition finds its reflection in vodka, and its exaggeration too. Russians drink from grief and from joy, because we're tired and to get tired, out of habit and by chance. It warms us in the cold, cools us in the heat, protects us from the damp, consoles us in grief and cheers us when times are good. Without vodka, there'd be no hospitality, no weddings, no baptisms, no burials, no farewells. Without vodka, friendship would no longer be friendship, happiness would no longer be happiness. It's the elixir sipped sociably, spreading gregariousness and love; it's also the anaesthetic without which life would be unendurable. Vodka's the only drug that enables the dispossessed to endure the monstrously cruel tricks life's played on them. It's the only solace for desperate men and women for whom there's no other release. So where better to begin the second revolution than at the spiritual home of Russia's vodka production, the drinker's Mecca?"

Borzov's cheeks lapped over the edges of his bulbous nose. He clenched a fist and grinned at Alice; she raised her glass to him and then followed his lead – down in one.

"You drink like a Russian," he said, and meant it as a compliment.

"Nine weeks," she told Lewis over dinner. "That's ridiculously short. A quarter of the time we need, at best. They must be mad."

"I bet they got your measure the moment you walked in." There was more than a trace of irritation in Lewis' laugh. "You *love* it. It's just another challenge to you; something else huge and complex and impossible for you to pull off. No, don't insult me by arguing, Alice. I'm right, and you know it."

He *was* right, and Alice did know it. The thrill rose in her gut like a salmon leaping from clear Siberian waters. This impossible schedule was the latest in the endless series of obstacles against which she could measure herself and discover in that measuring whether she was all she hoped she was – whether more, perhaps, or whether less?

"It's not *just* another challenge to me," she said.

He shrugged. "Right, whatever." His tone warned her off this line of conversation. There was only one thing in Alice's life that she was happy with as it was, and that was Lewis himself. She'd told him more times than either of them could remember that he earthed her, he saved her from herself; when she shook things up in giant snowstorms of endeavour, he was the constant.

# 6

*Saturday, 28 December 1991*
Come summer, the old royal estate of Kolomenskoe creaks at the edges, but at this time of year Ozers and Butuzov had only the crows for company. Both men were dressed in light colours, the better to blend in with the white snow, the grey sky, and the dirty cream tent-roofed Church of the Ascension against which they were

standing. The only splash of black was the binoculars against Butuzov's face, swinging in a long, slow sweep from left to right.

Kolomenskoe stands at the top of a hill, and Karkadann's property was at the bottom by the river, almost large and impressive enough to count as a rival estate. Away from the riverbank, a line of poplars traced the manor's perimeter. Butuzov guessed they'd been planted more for aesthetics than security, to hide the endless march of smokestacks and grimy tower blocks. The real security began behind the trees; a razor-wire fence topped with netting to catch hand-grenades, a concrete wall behind that. An outsider would see nothing at road level, but from this high up Butuzov could make out stables, a landscaped garden, more outbuildings – garages and guest cottages, he reckoned – and finally the main house itself, dark red like a bloodstain on the snow. It had come from Norway; Karkadann had seen it, liked it, bought it, and then had it shipped over and reassembled brick by brick.

Butuzov lowered the binoculars, handed them to Ozers, leant his head back against the church's wall and peered up at the gables which climbed like artichoke leaves towards the spire. He could almost have forgotten that they were in Moscow at all; Kolomenskoe was sufficiently far from the main road for traffic noise to be a distant grumble and for the air to be halfway clear. Butuzov closed his eyes and inhaled as though sniffing a fine vodka; even mafiyosi on stake-out are children of nature at heart.

"Looks almost impenetrable," Ozers said disgruntledly; irritability was his default setting. "There's no weak link in the fence that I can see, and the gatehouse is manned. We'll have to get closer and see if we've missed anything."

"Just what I was thinking."

Butuzov lifted the binoculars to his eyes again and studied Karkadann's house. A streak of colour flitted across the viewfinders, brief enough for him to start. He scanned the area quickly and found it again; a van heading down the drive, away from the house. Butuzov held the binoculars firm and tried to read the name on the vehicle's side. It was hard to make out – the stencilling was old and the van was moving – but he got it after a few seconds: Comstar.

Butuzov lowered the binoculars fast and grabbed Ozers' arm. "Quick! Let's go."

"What's the hurry?"

"I've got an idea." Butuzov was already running towards the car park.

He'd fired the engine of their deliberately nondescript Volga saloon and was already reversing in an extravagant circle before Ozers managed to close his door. The Volga, sufficiently dirty to make the colour of its paintwork a matter for conjecture rather than observation, shot down the Kolomenskoe access road far quicker than either its suspension or the road surface warranted. Broken nose and straggly beard arranged in violent concentration, Butuzov took two right turns and, after slowing briefly at a junction to get his bearings, a third on to a side street pocked with cheerless apartment blocks. He stopped with a lurch and reached under the dashboard for the lever to release the bonnet catch.

"What's wrong?" said Ozers.

"Pretend we've broken down."

"In this piece of shit? That won't be hard."

Butuzov walked round to the front of the car, propped the bonnet open and began to peer at the Volga's innards. He was not a moment too soon; the Comstar van was already coming round the corner. Butuzov straightened, turned and held out his hand. For a moment, he thought that the driver hadn't seen him or was simply ignoring him; then the van pulled into the side and stopped a few feet away. The driver leant out of the window.

"Thanks for stopping," said Butuzov. "You got some jump cables?"

"You got some vodka?"

"A bottle in the boot."

"Then I've got some jump cables."

"He'd have done it for free in the old days," muttered Ozers. Everybody wanted to be paid nowadays, and vodka was the universal currency.

The Comstar driver got out of his van. His trousers flapped an inch or so above his ankles; his socks were thin enough in places to be leaking skin, and his shoes were cheap Soviet plastic.

There were several bottles in the Volga's boot; few Russian motorists venture on to the roads without. Butuzov picked the cheapest and fished out three glasses from a cardboard box; it's the height of bad manners to swig straight from the bottle.

"Here we go," he said, handing them each a glass. "Keeps the cold out." He pulled the foil top off the bottle and poured them each one hundred grams. "I'm Kiril, he's Eduard."

"Maltsev, Yaroslav." The Comstar man shook their hands; his palm was slippery from patting the gel on his hair. "My friends call me Yarik."

"Well, Yarik, your good health." They clinked glasses. Maltsev downed his in one, Ozers and Butuzov sipped, for Lev banned any more than moderate drinking. "A drunken person has no secret," the vor liked to say, "and I've never met an alcoholic man of honour."

Butuzov indicated the Comstar logo on the side of the van. "Fixing phones?"

"Installing them." Maltsev jerked his head back towards Karkadann's estate. "Fancy house back there. Some coon with more money than sense. Top-of-the-range stuff, high-speed lines, nothing but the best. Black-ass could call the space station with that lot."

"It's Saturday; must have been a big job, to get you out at the weekend."

"That's the way it is now. Weekends, holidays – you need the money, you work whenever they say. If they pay you, who cares? Anyway, I've finished now."

"Let's get on with it, then," Ozers said.

Maltsev emptied his glass, went round to the back of his van and yanked open the rear doors. Butuzov turned to Ozers and whispered, "Pretend the car won't start. Make a big song and dance. Keep your foot on the throttle and flood the engine if you can – just enough to distract him for a minute or so."

Ozers nodded. The bags under his eyes were sufficiently pronounced to be knife scars.

Maltsev reappeared with jump leads dangling from his hand like grass snakes. He opened the van's bonnet, attached the clips to his battery, and repeated the process under the Volga's bonnet. When all the clips were attached, he started his engine and signalled to Ozers that he should follow suit.

Butuzov heard the Volga's engine cough asthmatically and die. He walked quietly round to the back of the Comstar van and looked inside. Everything he needed was within reach of the door, which was good; climbing inside would shift the van's weight and alert Maltsev. It would of course have been easier simply to shoot Maltsev and steal the van, but keeping civilians safe was one of Lev's most sacred tenets. Mafiyosi could harm fellow mafiyosi, Lev said, but never the man in the street.

"Try again," Butuzov heard Maltsev shout over the noise of his engine, followed by, "Don't keep pumping the gas, you'll flood the fucking thing."

Three abortive efforts at starting the Volga later, Butuzov re-appeared and gave Ozers a discreet nod. When Ozers next turned the key in the ignition, he twisted it fully rather than halfway as he had been doing before, and the engine started perfectly.

"Thanks for your help, Yarik." Butuzov handed Maltsev the vodka bottle. "Don't spill any, eh?" With the foil cap removed, there was no way of closing the bottle. Proper drinkers always finish an open bottle; when they go to the fridge, it's to get a new bottle rather than put the current one back for another day.

"I won't. You can count on that."

The flush in Maltsev's cheeks wasn't entirely due to the cold. Butuzov suspected that Maltsev would opt for the simplest way of avoiding spillage and relocate the vodka from bottle to stomach.

They watched the Comstar van leave. "If that bottle's more than glass and air by tonight, I'm a Chechen," Butuzov said.

"Would you mind telling me what all that was about?"

Maltsev's one working brake light flared dimly as he paused at the junction, and then he was gone from sight. Butuzov walked over to the nearest parked car and bent down to retrieve what he'd left behind the rear bumper; a set of Comstar engineer's overalls, and a toolbox.

# 7

*Sunday, 29 December 1991*

The guards at Karkadann's gatehouse – all Chechens, naturally, for Chechens trust only their own kind – frisked Butuzov and searched his van before letting him through. The precautions were standard, and there was no reason for the Chechens to be suspicious. They had no way of knowing that the Comstar logo had been painted on to the van only last night, or that the signwriter responsible had been paid five hundred dollars for his services and five hundred more to keep his mouth shut.

At the front door of the mansion itself, however, Sharmukh-amedov was more suspicious. His head was freshly shaved and his beard trimmed neater than usual; neither detracted from his air of menace. "What's going on?" he asked.

"There's a problem with your lines," Butuzov said.

"Not that we've reported."

"You wouldn't have. We picked it up at the central exchange about an hour ago."

"Who else is affected?"

"Hundreds of people. But our most valuable customers get priority."

Sharmukhamedov nodded, as if priority was no more than his

right. "What happened to the other guy? The one who was here yesterday?"

"Yarik? Sick. Stupid bastard drank some dodgy vodka."

Maybe it was the use of Maltsev's name, or the all too plausible intimation of vodka poisoning; either way, Sharmukhamedov's suspicions seemed to be allayed. He jerked his head back towards the interior of the house; in you come. A moment, a decision; a mistake.

Ozers had wanted to come too, of course, but Butuzov had disagreed and Lev had supported him. Two people for what was one man's job might arouse suspicion; unlikely, perhaps, but Karkadann was as paranoid as they came, so it wasn't worth taking the chance. If Butuzov was rumbled and things turned nasty, an extra person would make little difference in a house full of armed Chechens. So Butuzov had come alone, unarmed, and very scared.

"I'll need to see all the phones," said Butuzov, impressed at how steady his voice sounded.

"Sure. But I'm with you all the time, understand?"

Butuzov shrugged with a nonchalance he didn't feel. "Whatever."

The house was warm, huge, and unbelievably gaudy. To Butuzov the place seemed overblown and tasteless. Golden nymphs squatted on banister ends or pranced in crystal fountains. The paintings were hideous art nouveau, more often than not made even more vulgar by being set in relief. Karkadann's bedroom had spreads of scarlet satin and a mirrored ceiling; his bathroom boasted two jacuzzis.

There were thirty-two handsets in the house, but Butuzov knew the best place for him would be Karkadann's study. It was hard to see across the room; the overhead chandelier was the only light on, and each window was taped over with cardboard packing sheets. A layman might have assumed this had something to do with redecoration, but a mafiyoso knew better. The sheets were a precaution against snipers; denying a shooter visual into the room and diffusing the body heat of those inside, thus rendering infra-red rifle sights useless.

Lying on his back under the desk, Butuzov made a big show of unscrewing the wall socket and poking around among the wires in there; they'd taught him this at the KGB institute, of course, it was the kind of thing he could have done in his sleep. Even if Sharmukhamedov had been lying under the desk with him, he'd have seen nothing. Butuzov had the bug hidden between two fingers, and he simply pressed it among the wires as he fiddled,

pushing hard to compensate for the shaking in his hand. But crawling on the floor with a telephone repairman was several notches
below Sharmukhamedov's dignity; he stood and watched, missed and
failed.

Butuzov replaced the plastic covering on the socket and sat up
fast. He was too much of a professional to wince in anticipation of
his head hitting the underside of the table, even though he knew
it would have to hurt if it was to be convincing. He spluttered a
couple of expletives and rubbed his skull; a quick, almost imperceptible, movement of his right hand from scalp to the underside of
Karkadann's desk and the second bug was in place, stuck fast in the
middle of the table, far from the reach of straying hands. One device
on the phone line and one in the room; all bases covered.

Butuzov emerged from under the table with a wince – his head
really ached, there was nothing fake about that – and packed up
his toolbox. Sharmukhamedov didn't ask whether he was hurt.

"All done," said Butuzov, picking up the handset and making a
show of checking for the dialling tone.

# 8

*Monday, 30 December 1991*
Butuzov and Ozers took it in turns to man the listening post; four
hours on, four hours off, like naval watches. They both spoke decent
Chechen, enough to understand the gist of conversations, if not their
finer nuances. Much of the material was workaday and mundane –
Karkadann discussing dinner arrangements with his wife,
Karkadann arranging what sounded like a tryst with a mistress –
but two dialogues were sufficiently interesting for Butuzov and Ozers
to make transcripts in Russian and pass them on to Sabirzhan.

The first was a late-night disagreement – *another* disagreement,
by the sound of it – between Karkadann and Ilmar about the wisdom
of engaging the Slavic mafiya alliance in battle.

> K: *Are you working for those Slav fuckers or something? I don't under-*
> *stand you.*
> I: *And I don't understand you. This is business, not a pissing contest.*
> K: *This is war, and we're going to win.*
> I: *This is idiotic, and I tell you again: it's not too late to use common*
> *sense.*

The second, timed just before nine in the morning, was a brief exchange between Karkadann and Sharmukhamedov.

*S: Boss, I'm off now.*
*K: When's your flight?*
*S: Lunchtime; I can't remember exactly what time.*
*K: And you're back when?*
*S: Thursday.*
*K: New Year in Dubai, one man and his libido . . . I pity those poor Arab girls. Bring some of them back with you, yeah? I hear they're lush.*
*S: Why else do you think I'm going?*
*K: You don't like the girls I get you?*
*S: I'd like them better if you could get me sunshine and sand too.*

Sabirzhan handed the transcript back to Ozers and nodded to them both. "Well done, lads."

Sheremetyevo Airport is drab at the best of times, let alone on a sunless morning which spat uncertain flakes of snow as though the sky were trying to get rid of a bad taste. No wonder Sharmukhamedov was so looking forward to his holiday. Ozers and Butuzov prowled the airside beyond passport control and stepped smartly through drifts of arriving passengers. The foreigners penguin-walked with suitcases dangling from both hands and griped about the lack of trolleys. The Russians were almost invisible under mountains of boxes daubed with stylised drawings hinting at the contents within: cheeses and cognacs from Paris, children's bicycles from Abu Dhabi, Japanese stereos and video recorders from Frankfurt, discount computers from Prague. These cargo mules were ordinary workers who'd left Russia a few days earlier with all the savings they could muster, and were now returning in the hope that selling long-forbidden items from distant lands of plenty would recast them as wealthy merchants – as long as they could persuade bored customs officers that their goods were for personal use only, of course. Oratory usually failed; bribery usually succeeded.

There was only one flight to Dubai that day, and twenty dollars to the check-in girl had given Lev's men a look at the passenger manifest. There he was; Baltazar Sharmukhamedov, travelling first class. Ozers and Butuzov had then visited the customs and excise officer to whom Lev paid a handsome annual retainer in return for ensuring that vodka imported by the 21st Century Association received an uninterrupted passage, and impressed on him that the retainer also covered the loan of two customs uniforms, the requisite area passes, and a spare office.

All they had to do now was recognise Sharmukhamedov which, since he was twice the size of everyone else, shouldn't prove too taxing. Whether Sharmukhamedov would recognise Butuzov was a different matter. It was a risk, but Sharmukhamedov didn't seem the type to have paid much mind to a menial telephone repairman, let alone one he'd never have expected to see again. In any case, Ozers and Butuzov had been obliged to formulate their plan on the hoof and there wasn't time to change it now.

They found Sharmukhamedov striding towards the departure gate, taking two strides for everyone else's three. He noticed them when they were still several metres away, fanned out subtly but unmistakeably to prevent him going anywhere but backwards.

"Baltazar Sharmukhamedov?" Ozers was the one who spoke; he had the less threatening face. "Customs and excise. If you'd just come with us for a second?"

"What the fuck for?" Sharmukhamedov's eyes glowered sapphire beneath beetle brows.

"Nothing serious, of course. It's just that your boss has asked us to pass you an, er, an *item*, for your vacation, one he didn't want going through the security checks, and we'd prefer not to do it in public." Ozers looked almost apologetic, even overawed, as though dealing with gangsters was a huge but daunting thrill for a lowly customs officer.

"This item's so big that it needs two of you to tell me?"

"We're not performing this service for charity, you understand. My colleague will take the same commission I will; he doesn't trust me not to pocket it all."

Butuzov gave Sharmukhamedov a you-know-how-it-is smile, and saw no recognition whatever in the nod he received back. The Tsentralnaya had their tame officials at Sheremetyevo as much as any other gang; such co-operation was only to be expected. Sharmukhamedov would not have obeyed the orders of authority, but he *would* indulge them in a situation which showed the Tsentralnaya's dominance.

If Sharmukhamedov hadn't already been thinking of the beaches he was going to strut upon and the women he was going to fuck, perhaps he'd have been more suspicious; a man's reactions are always conditioned by the mood he's in. He gestured at Ozers to lead the way.

Ozers and Butuzov ushered Sharmukhamedov into their 'office'. The room was small and minimally furnished: a table and three chairs hemmed in by olive walls, solitary window gazing disconsolately on to a row of generators. There was nothing on the table, and no cupboards. Sharmukhamedov was just starting to ask where this precious item was when Butuzov unsheathed the truncheon from his belt and swung it in a wide arc, rising to the base of Sharmukhamedov's skull, just below the ridge where the back of his head swelled outwards. Ozers, standing in front of the Chechen, saw Sharmukhamedov's eyes widen in angry surprise before he pitched forward on to the table.

They draped his arms over their shoulders and carried him out, staggering under the weight. Sharmukhamedov's head lolled back, his mouth open to the ceiling as though hoping to catch flies. At that angle, no one could see the bruise which was already spreading across the back of his naked scalp. "The vodka," they explained to any passer-by who gave them more than a glance, "it was the vodka," and everyone nodded understandingly; it's never too early to be dead drunk in Russia.

Sharmukhamedov was pegged out on a metal table like an animal hide left in the sun to dry, a Gulliver roped down by Lilliputians. Thick steel bands secured his ankles, knees, waist, elbows and neck; any more than the slightest movement was impossible.

Sabirzhan walked all the way round the table. Sharmukhamedov's eyes, blazing with fury, swivelled in their sockets as they tracked Sabirzhan's progress.

Sabirzhan stopped, tapped his finger against his mouth and rocked back on his heels, the way people do in art galleries. "The problem we have," he said thoughtfully, "is this. Karkadann's home is too well-defended, and trying to pick him off in traffic is too risky." He gestured with one hand, inviting Sharmukhamedov to help him solve the puzzle; they could have been chess players, crossword fanatics. "So what we need is somewhere less secure, somewhere he's more vulnerable. Somewhere we can isolate him. The element of surprise is crucial, you understand that, Baltazar. This has to work first time, or not at all." He cocked an eyebrow over the pince-nez. "Any thoughts?"

Sharmukhamedov was silent. From the moment he'd regained consciousness and realised what had happened – more specifically, who'd seized him – he knew two things: firstly, that he'd have to resist for no longer than four days, because the moment he wasn't back from Dubai as planned Karkadann would get suspicious; and secondly, that no matter what he did or didn't tell them, they would kill him.

Sabirzhan's forehead prickled with sweat under his widow's peak. "No? Perhaps this will make you more talkative." Sabirzhan held a syringe up to the light and rubbed at Sharmukhamedov's arm. It was as hard as an oak banister; he must have been almost as strong as Lev, the two of them together could have formed a gang all on their own. Sabirzhan found a vein and jabbed the needle in with unnecessary force. Sharmukhamedov didn't flinch.

"Caffeine," Sabirzhan explained. "I've increased the dose to take account of your size. You'd have to drink ten, fifteen cups of coffee to get the same kick. You could recite *War and Peace* in the time it'll take to wear off."

Hours and hours of talking: Sharmukhamedov's fury at being suckered by such a simple trick; all the women he was going to have fucked this week; how not to cut yourself when you shaved your head every day; how he should have known that the fake phone engineer was a phoney; all the women he'd fucked in his life, especially the one whose cervix he'd split, now *that* was a tale; how the caffeine was making his heart flutter . . . An endless monologue about himself, telling Sabirzhan everything other than what he wanted to know.

Sabirzhan gave Sharmukhamedov a second injection, barbital sodium to depress his will.

"I want to wash my face," Sharmukhamedov said.

"You can wash it in your own blood by the time I've finished with you."

"Beat me all you want. I'll give it to you so that you'll be paying the medical bills for the rest of your life."

"Don't drag the cat by its tail. Come on, out with it; you'll save us both a lot of trouble."

"The entire collective's fucking your last girlfriend, you know." Sharmukhamedov laughed. "And your prick drips because a whore gave you a double-barrelled bouquet; the clap *and* syphilis. Ha!"

The barbital sodium proved as ineffective as the caffeine had. Sharmukhamedov stared at the ceiling and said nothing. At some point he closed his eyes; he may even have gone to sleep. At least he wasn't talking any more.

* * *

39

Lev sat at his desk, his chair pushed back to make room for his legs.

"Give him a steam bath," he said at length. It was prison slang for a no-holds-barred interrogation.

"Just what I'd have suggested," said Sabirzhan. He was hopping around like a pea on a hot griddle, flushed not only with elation at the prospect of inflicting untold pain on his prisoner, but also with eagerness for Lev's approval if he did it well.

Sharmukhamedov smiled when Sabirzhan showed him the stun gun. He'd used one many times himself, on those who wouldn't sign contracts or who quibbled about protection money.

Sabirzhan held the barrel against Sharmukhamedov's chest, glanced at his watch, and pulled the trigger. A terrible jerking against the restraints – one second – those sapphire eyes screwed tight shut, the first time the Chechen even looked to have felt pain – two seconds – how extraordinary, one hand was splayed open like a starfish, the other was clenched into a massive fist – three seconds and here they came, the unmistakeable sounds and smells of a body involuntarily emptying itself. A lake bloomed suddenly across Sharmukhamedov's crotch; sludge oozed from between his legs. Sabirzhan gagged on the cloying sweetness and held the stun gun aloft.

"Every time after this, Baltazar, I keep it on for a little bit longer. Three seconds, five, seven, ten. Irreparable paralysis begins to set in at ten seconds, you know?"

# 9

*Tuesday, 31 December 1991*

Alice arrived at the McDonald's on Pushkin Square ten minutes early. She'd chosen the venue deliberately; if privatising Red October was to be the real start of Russia's road to capitalism – capital couldn't function without private property, after all – where better to plot its course than in the bastion of consumer capitalism itself?

Harry and Bob were already there. Even though Alice had never met either of them before, she recognised them instantly, and would have done so even if she hadn't sent files on them beforehand. The locals were dressed in dull earthy colours, they were eating their hamburgers with the reverence one accords to an exotic delicacy, and hard living had lined their faces with trenches of strain. Healthy of countenance and with bright windcheaters draped over the backs of their chairs, Harry and Bob were tucking in without ceremony. Oh – and Bob was black, which in Moscow was enough to mark him out to a blind man.

Alice walked over to them. "Hey, guys. I'm Alice" – she adopted a jokingly girlish voice – "and I'm going to be your boss for the next few months." She stuck out her hand. "Welcome to the lions' den."

They were on their feet, laughing with her, glad to have another in their gang.

"Bob Craig, Houston, Texas –" thickset in a heavy sports jacket – "great to meet you."

"Harry Exley, Pittsburgh, PA –" like an excited freshman – "heard so much about you, Mrs Liddell. It's a real honour to be working with you, I was *so* thrilled to be asked . . ."

"Easy!" Alice chuckled to hide her embarrassment and take the sting from her reproach. "Harry, you're gonna have to kiss more ass than a toilet seat sees all year before this thing is out; don't waste your butt-licking on me. And the next time you call me Mrs Liddell, I'm going to knock you into the middle of next week, understood?"

"OK. *Alice.*" Harry pushed a paper bag towards her. "We were too hungry to wait lunch for you; sorry. And the queues were awful, so we bought you a hamburger meal to save you waiting. No cheese; is that OK?"

"Cheese, no cheese – they all taste the same anyway." Alice sat down on a plastic chair with too much yield in it to be truly comfortable and hoped she'd handled things all right. A vodka might have made her feel less awkward; sober, she was shy, and – especially when in authority – she tended to compensate by being abrasive. No matter, she thought. She'd know Bob and Harry soon enough, and then they'd forget their first impressions of her.

She began to sketch out the second revolution over hamburgers and fries.

When it comes to reforming command economies, there are two schools of thought. The first, shock therapy, holds that it's best to enact all reforms at once; the social and economic upheaval is so great that a short, sharp jolt is preferable to prolonging the torture with a piecemeal approach. The gradualists take the opposite view; for them, reforms should be staggered in order to avoid large drops in output and mass unemployment, which will in turn threaten political stability and therefore the reform process itself.

Borzov had decided to go with the former. They were going to raze the entire communist structure – clearly the institutions of the communist state were inimical to the spirit of enterprise – and in its stead erect a market economy. If this was implemented quickly and vigorously, the essentials of such an economy would begin to function almost immediately, and the economy would then gain the momentum it needed. The role of the state was simple: to establish the rules of the capitalist game and watch the new society unfold. This was where privatisation came in; more specifically, Red October.

"We're just going to do one auction to start with," Alice said. "The Red October distillery."

"Only one?" It was Harry; Alice bet he'd sat in the front row at varsity lectures.

"Yes, only one, to show it can be done. Parliament meets March ninth, and we need to have everything wrapped by then. So the auction will take place the Monday before that, the second."

"Two months?" Bob's bottom lip bumped against the straw of his Coke. "That's *absurd*." He gestured round the restaurant. "It took McDonald's fourteen *years* to open this place."

"You really think it's impossible, Bob, walk out now and I'll find someone else, no hard feelings. Yes, two months is very short – and even shorter because we can't go see Red October until next Monday because they're all on New Year vacation – but it's not absurd."

"We're gonna have to work twenty-four seven."

"You got a problem with that?"

"My wife might. She wasn't that keen on coming here in the first place."

"She should meet my husband. Harry?"

Harry shook his head. "Bring it on."

"No wife?" A redundant question. "Girlfriend? Boyfriend?"

"*Boyfriend*? Hardly. No, none of the above. Young, free and single." He looked round the room. "And keen-to-mingle. Bob, have you *seen* the chicks in here? I'm fouling my gutchies."

"Harry, you're depriving some village of an idiot," Alice said. "You're happy to give yourself to me for two months?"

"Is that an offer?"

Alice clicked her tongue. "It's a phase you're going through. You'll grow out of it."

"This afternoon, if there's a God," Bob said.

She saw herself suddenly as Harry must have seen her: smart and sassy and sexy, the girl everyone had wanted to befriend at school, the one who'd share a smoke and drink behind the bike stands, the first one to have a boyfriend, the one who never swotted but got good grades. He couldn't have guessed, this soon after meeting her, the depths below. No one ever could.

"OK." Alice's tone was serious. "Enough. We're gonna show these bastards a bit of good ol' American kickass. First up, division of labour. Working on the kind of model we used in Eastern Europe, I reckon the best way is to establish six working groups – we'll take charge of two each." She reached into a plastic folder and brought out four small dossiers. "I've tried to tailor these to your individual strengths and experience, so if you've got a problem with them, I want to hear it now rather than in a month's time."

She pushed the top two dossiers over to Bob. "Bob, you're a banker, and you've also done a bit of recruitment in your time, am I right? So I want you to head up procedures and staffing. Procedures involves devising a workable auction system in as much detail as possible: finding and preparing an auction centre here in Moscow, establishing communication links to the EBRD in London and the IMF in DC – and then pretending those links don't work whenever they say something we don't want to hear. Staffing means finding, hiring, training, paying . . . and firing when they're not up to it; and some of them won't be, you can count on that. Any questions?"

"Thousands."

"I'll hear them later." The other two dossiers went across the table to Harry. "Harry, your responsibility is all legal and company work. You have to study the relevant corporate documents to ensure that everything's above board, arrange for incomplete or illegal documents to be rewritten, and ensure that everyone understands what's legal and what's not. *And* you'll need to go through Red October's books with the finest toothcomb you can find. Accounts, figures, prospects, viability, strengths and weaknesses. Shove a microscope up their ass."

"How come *I* get the shitty jobs?"

"The shitty jobs?" Alice couldn't tell whether Harry was joking or not.

"Alice, no one here has the first clue what the law even *is* right now. How am I going to work out what's legal and what's not? And have you ever *seen* a set of Soviet accounts? My nephew's ten months old, and he makes more sense than they do."

"Your charm will overcome all obstacles, I've no doubt."

"And while we slave at the coalface, what are *you* going to be doing?"

"Oh, nothing much – just trying to stop the whole damn thing from sinking, that's all. And kicking your butts when you start bitching. I'll supervise the steering group, which will be in overall charge of the assignment, and will," – she made a show of checking her notes to get the phrasing correct – "'obtain rapid and effective decisions on all aspects of the case', or so it says here. I'll also look after PR; we have to promote and publicise this thing, and I'm prettier than either of you."

"Ain't that the truth," Bob said. The stubble round his goatee beard was like patches of blackened wheat. "I hate to sound negative, Alice, but – this could all go to shit, right?"

They were both looking at Alice intently, and she saw the depth of their apprehension.

"Yes," she said eventually. "Yes, it could. Even if we work our buns off, it could all go to shit. But it *definitely* will if we don't. Come on, guys. Be positive. It's an *adventure*."

When they left the restaurant – barely gone three, and already dark – a dozen or so vegetarian protesters had gathered outside, led by a young man wearing a fake silver beard and a padded coat. A placard round his neck read *Tolstoy says: "forget meat, stay with wheat"*.

"Tolstoy?" Alice said.

"I am the great Lev Tolstoy himself, reincarnated."

"What's your real name?"

"I told you, I am the . . ."

She skewered him with turquoise eyes until, shamefacedly, he muttered: "Vasily."

Above the beard, his skin was smooth. "How old are you, Vasily?" she asked.

"Sixteen." He offered her a veggie burger. "I'm a business student, you know."

The McDonald's crowd ebbed and flowed around them with haughty indifference. Most Russians find even the idea of vegetarianism absolutely bewildering; it's hard enough to find food as it is, let alone when you halve your options by refusing to eat meat. Vasily gestured disconsolately around him. "They don't understand," he said. "That's always the way it is in Russia. Any good idea you have here, it's ten years too early."

Sabirzhan had made Sharmukhamedov stand stock-still for hours, until the Chechen thought that the veins in his legs were going to burst. Then Sabirzhan had cuffed Sharmukhamedov's hands together, placed them between the Chechen's knees, attached the cuffs to a pulley, and hung him upside down. His belly was beach-ball round but hard as a quarried boulder; it didn't sag.

"The sparrow," Lev said, when he came to check on progress. "A gulag favourite."

"One of the KGB's premier techniques," Sabirzhan agreed. "I'm applying it according to recognised methods." 'Applied', as one would apply a soothing unguent.

Lev had twin lightning bolts tattooed on his right arm, a sign of never having confessed to anything. "What's he told you?"

"Nothing useful. But he will."

"We haven't got much longer."

"Forty-eight hours? He'll break long before then."

"And you can take a break too. We're leaving for the Vek in half an hour." The Serebryany Vek was a banya near the Bolshoi now converted into a restaurant where caviar was piled into mountains on the sideboards, chandeliers bowed deferentially from the ceilings, and liveried waiters whipped domed metal covers from dishes as though they were magicians performing tricks.

"Oh, go on without me."

"Tengiz, it's New Year."

"Yeah – and what's there to celebrate?" At midnight, the old regime would be officially extinct; joy enough for Lev, who'd refused even to recognise its existence, but calamity for Sabirzhan, KGB officer and sworn upholder of the Motherland.

Lev had asked out of courtesy and expediency, and was glad that Sabirzhan had refused. He'd no more have wanted to spend his New Year with Sabirzhan than with Josef Stalin, but Sabirzhan was powerful in Red October, and it never did to alienate one's allies unnecessarily.

"What are you going to do instead?" he asked.

Sabirzhan glanced towards Sharmukhamedov. The Chechen's bald head was visibly reddening as the blood flowed into it. "Spend some time with my new friend, probably."

Right next door to Red Square, the Rossiya Hotel is perhaps the quintessential example of Soviet architecture. An oblong hollowed out around two inner courtyards, it's almost a kilometre in circumference and covers ten acres. Even in a city with its fair share of ugly buildings, the Rossiya stands out, a greying monolith whose size is matched only by the numbing uniformity of its design. The Russians say that the best thing about staying there is that you can't see the Rossiya.

Lewis was unimpressed. "What a shithole. No decent city would allow that kind of eyesore."

The New Year clientele could have inspired Dante to rework the *Inferno*: stubble-scalped men with black turtlenecks and lumps under their blazers patrolled the lobby, while leggy Russian jezebels with dolphin-tight bodies strolled through the hotel stores, looking fetching in Chanel suits and impossibly high heels. Whores and pimps, small-time operators who'd bought concessions from the management to operate here, orbited around each other like planets, gravitating towards each potential client as though he were the firmament's brightest star. It was a *troika* of unholy fluidity, and one where every member could claim to be both exploiter and exploited.

Bob had swapped slacks and a sports jacket for a suit, though it clung uneasily to him and he knew it. His wife Christina peered at Alice from under her bob and proffered a damp hand. "Good to know you," she said, in a tone that suggested it was anything but. Christina was ten centimetres shorter than Alice and a similar amount wider through the hips; she knew where the men's attention would be, especially when Harry turned up with a stunning blonde called Vika.

"How much did you have to pay her?" Alice asked Harry once they were out of earshot.

He waved across the room at Vika and smiled proudly. "Not a dime." It was just about plausible; Russians found Westerners so exciting that they'd flock to anyone with English as a first language, no matter how unappealing their other attributes. For straight, single Western men, there was no better place to be, as Moscow was packed with more female beauty than practically any other place on earth. And not cold, haughty types either, but inviting, curious beauty, always looking as if they were just desperate to try something new, trade up, succumb to curiosity or pressure, fall into some wild adventure. There were vixens on every pavement, sly seductresses riding down the metro escalators, femme fatales pouring into the streets.

The beauty of Russian women is above all in their eyes, large and limpid and almost always accentuated by eyeliner.

"You must be from Texas," Lewis said to Bob.

"Never ask a man if he's from Texas. If he is, he'll tell you on his own. If he ain't, no need to embarrass him."

He was stretching his vowels so far that Alice feared they'd snap. She'd noticed that all their accents were noticeably, defiantly, regional: Harry dropping 'd's in the middle of words, just like a good Pittsburgher; Lewis stressing the start of almost every word, as though he'd forget if more than a syllable passed without emphasis. Asserting their roots so far from home. Alice wondered if she'd been doing likewise, playing up her Boston inflections.

The waiter brought vodka aperitifs and told them that dinner was a set menu: *blini* with black caviar, smoked salmon in marinated pumpkin sauce, sturgeon soup with dumplings stuffed with crab, breast of pheasant, fillet of beef in red wine, pears with chocolate mousse – all for a hundred dollars a head. A hundred bucks, Alice thought; Russians could work several months for that, perhaps close to a year. When Harry leant forward to light his cigar from the table candle, the waiter lunged forward with a Zippo; using candles as lighters is bad luck.

"Haven't seen a Russkie move so fast since they were kicked out of Afghanistan." Harry waved the glowing tube at the waiter's retreating back. "Anyone here been to New Orleans? Just like Moscow; everyone late for work and early home. You know what the Russkies think a workaholic is? An alcoholic in the office!" He tipped his head back and roared at his own joke.

"I'm from New Orleans," Lewis said.

"Then you'll know what I'm talking about!" Harry replied, missing the point by such a country mile that Alice actually laughed, half gurgle and half giggle, a saucy, choked chuckle that started high in her head, ended by her knees, and earned her a reproving stare from Lewis.

Alice sucked at her vodka and let herself melt into the evening. A couple more glasses and she was in the swing, holding court, the boss, taking their deference as her due, ignoring both her own mild unease at being the centre of attention and Christina's murderous stares as she kept the table enthralled with tales of restitution claims from aristocratic families whose land had been confiscated by the Bolsheviks – "there's one who wants half of Yekaterinburg back" – and some of the more eccentric privatisation applications. "A guy in Nizhny Novgorod rang me yesterday because he wants to build a distillery on the site of a former nuclear reactor, can you believe it? He's gonna distil the vodka in the reactor's water filters and call it 'Thermonuclear'. Get out of here, I told him, you can't be serious. And he told me straight, vodka cleans radioactive particles, and that's why they gave extra rations to crews of Soviet nuclear submarines."

They all laughed, even Vika. These crazy Russians, whatever would they think of next?

Five vodkas to the wind, she raised her tumbler. "We're going to perform the greatest transformation ever. We're going to make them be like us. To the end of history!"

Laughing, they all clinked glasses – all except Vika. "Your enthusiasm is infectious, but your expectations are too high," she said. Submarine vodka was one thing, but now a line had clearly been crossed. "If you ask me, anything less than complete chaos will be a success. Do you think you can control everything, bend everyone to your will? There are a hundred and fifty million people here, scattered over twelve time zones; you can't *make* them do anything." Harry was trying to nuzzle Vika's ear, but she pushed him away; she wanted to make her point. "Do what you can. Leave the rest to fate."

"But you've had political freedom," said Alice. "You've had perestroika and glasnost. Why is economic freedom so different?"

"Political freedom allowed us to reject our past; economic freedom forces us to confront our future." Vika paused. "We've always been good at the first."

There was a stage at one end of the room, and half an hour before midnight the restaurant manager appeared on it and called for silence. The chatter subsided like the ebbing of the tide, Harry the last one still talking – "and that's how it went on all semester, night after night, it was *wild*, man," – and the house lights were dimmed while a spotlight sought out the manager. He was holding a bottle of vodka; a single, perfectly ordinary half-litre of Stolichnaya. He tapped the microphone to make sure that it was working, and spoke into the bulbous head.

"Ladies, gentlemen, and anyone from Chechnya." The crowd laughed. "It's nearly midnight, the dawn of a new era, but we at the Rossiya thought we'd kick things off a little early, so we're going to have a little auction. The rules couldn't be simpler: one bottle of this excellent Stolichnaya, sold in Moscow's finer establishments for," – he puffed his cheeks while he thought – "Forty roubles, give or take. But tonight, it will go to the highest bidder. Let's start at the street price. Do I hear forty?" A forest of hands shot up. "Fifty? Seventy-five? A hundred?" Still the hands. "That's more like it."

"What's all this rouble rubbish?" Harry shouted. "Let's get on to dollars."

"Dollars?" The manager dipped a shoulder, as though the idea had never occurred to him. "Of course. Do I hear ten dollars? Fifteen?"

Harry raised his hand. Vika looked away, already disillusioned.

"Against the American gentleman with the cigar, twenty dollars." The price climbed faster than a pine auger runs up a tree. There

48

were four people left by the time it reached $50; three at $100; and when Harry pulled out at $120 – it was just a bottle of vodka, after all – the bidding leapt ahead as though suddenly freed from his weight.

"Expensive, terribly expensive," Vika cried, as though in pain.

Alice looked round for those still in the chase, and was surprised to find that they were both Russian. Westerners clearly no longer had a monopoly on wealth in Moscow. The bidders battered each other up to $300 until one shook his head; he'd made his point.

"Three hundred bucks for a bottle of Stoli!" Harry could barely make himself heard over the applause for the victor, who was shaking the manager's hand and holding the bottle up as though it were a boxing belt. "That's fucking *nuts*, man. Fucking *nuts*."

No, thought Alice; it was perfectly logical. The winner had bought the bottle just because he *could*, because there was no longer anyone to tell him not to: no central planner, no head of his factory party cell, no stern censor of morality in the workers' state. He'd bought it because after a lifetime of standing in line for milk and sausage, of greasing black-market palms to get a pair of blue jeans, of waiting ten years for a phone line and fifteen for a wheelbarrow with an engine marked 'Lada', after all this, money finally meant something. For a bottle of vodka, three hundred bucks was extortionate; for a middle finger to the Soviet Union, it was an absolute steal.

"Imagine how you'd feel if they'd stopped at a hundred and twenty dollars and left you with the bottle, Harry," said Bob. "What would you have done?"

"Given it to Alice, probably," muttered Christina.

# 10

*Wednesday, 1 January 1992*
"I gotta take a piss so-o-o-o-o bad. I need to pee like a Russian racehorse."

Alice needed three hands; one to push her off the bed, another to find the way to the bathroom because she couldn't open her eyes, and a third to clutch at her head and make the pain go away. Her hangover was a physical weight, pressing her down into a crouch that was more simian than human. She reached the bathroom by touch alone and flopped gratefully on to the first piece of porcelain she found, vaguely aware that the toilet seemed an odd shape and colder against her ass than she'd expected, but it was only when she was halfway through urinating that she realised why. Alice sighed, finished, stood on wobbly legs, and monkey-walked back into the bedroom.

"I just tinkled in the bidet," she said.

Lewis was getting dressed; his hospital shift began at ten, and his wide-awakeness sent a little thrill of shame through Alice. He looked at her and shook his head, too deadpan for her to know whether he was being serious. "You're a disgrace," he said.

"Why can't the Russians have one big porcelain throne in the bathroom, like Americans? What's with these people, Lewis? They refuse to shower regularly, but they want to have the cleanest asses in town." She moved over to him and closed her hand playfully around his groin. "Didn't we . . . ?"

"I'm surprised you can remember."

"*Course* I can remember. Christening a new city – how could I forget? It was *great*."

"That's what you always say when you were drunk." He adjusted his tie until the knot was just so. "I'll be back before seven."

It was past midday when Alice finally crawled out of bed for good. Coffee, a shower and ZZ Top on the Walkman couldn't cure her hangover; perhaps the winter air could. She wrapped herself in five layers and walked through deserted streets, realising that the entire city shared her hangover. Everyone was indoors, sleeping off the excesses of New Year's Eve and trying not to think about tomorrow, when – for the first time in Russian history – all prices were to be freed. For almost an entire century, Russia had been a giant laboratory, performing on itself giant innovations in social engineering. Now, for the second time, it was starting afresh, reshaping its state, society and economy all at once. One of history's most awesome experiments was ending, and an equally daunting one was beginning; only the experimenters had changed. It was a journey back from utopia, and towards – well, who knew?

Sabirzhan allowed himself only as much sleep as he thought suitable for Sharmukhamedov, which meant half an hour snatched here and there. Sharmukhamedov looked as unkempt as one would have expected from a man entering his third day of torture; Sabirzhan, on the other hand, felt fine, and then some. Administering pain seemed to energise him. In dark agonised corners of Lubyanka, his reputation still lurked; if a suspect needed to be worked on through the night, made to lap their own piss from the floor like a cat, Sabirzhan was your man.

The sparrow over, Sharmukhamedov was back on the table. Sabirzhan strapped a gas mask on to Sharmukhamedov's face, loosening the straps to fit better and lifting the back of the Chechen's enormous head from the table with something not far short of tenderness. He took a bottle of insecticide from the floor and gave the nozzle a few exploratory squirts. Even in such small doses, the chemical made him gag. He pressed the nozzle against the mask's mouthpiece.

"We call this the little elephant," he said, and noted with satisfaction that Sharmukhamedov's eyes were wide behind the perspex.

Sabirzhan pressed down hard on the nozzle and watched the mask fill with insecticide.

"Don't scream," he said softly, rubbing at the bridge of his pince-nez. "Don't scream, Baltazar; you'll only inhale it quicker."

Sharmukhamedov's arms jerked as he tried to tear at the mask, but his hands were pinioned to the table. He was mixing shrieks, sobs and coughs into the most inhuman clamour. Only when Sabirzhan saw the perspex splatter with vomit did he remove the mask. He didn't want Sharmukhamedov choking to death, not before he'd told Sabirzhan what he wanted to know. Besides, you couldn't have half as much fun with a corpse as with a sentient victim.

"Best New Year I've ever had," Sabirzhan said, and meant every word.

"I'm sorry if I was crabby this morning," Lewis said when he got back.

"You were annoyed that I got so smashed last night."

"I didn't want to go to work on New Year's, that was why."

"Really?"

"Really." And Alice chose to believe it as the truth, even as Lewis nodded towards the glass in her hand. "Is that vodka in there?"

"If it's not, I need to have a word with my taste buds."

"I'm surprised you can even take a sip without hurling."

"Hair of the dog, I guess."

"I've never seen you drinking on your own before."

"Lewis, I'm having a drink. I'm not drinking. Anyway –" Alice gestured towards the window and Moscow beyond – "when in Russia, do as the Russians do. Join me?"

The bottle was on the dressing table. To Alice, for an instant, it might as well have had a paper label tied round its neck with the words 'drink me' beautifully printed in 36-point type.

Lewis went over, poured himself a measure, filled Alice's glass up, and slumped into the nearest armchair. His collar and tie rode up around his neck. "I'm so tired, I could make dodo right now," he said. "Into bed, out like a light."

"How was work?" Alice asked.

"This place, this fucking place. It's New Year's, so gangsters get drunk, start arguing, pull out their guns – and guess who has to clean it all up? You got it."

"And they come to you because Sklifosovsky's the best emergency department in Moscow?"

"Gunshot wounds a speciality, and I haven't even had the pleasure of the weekly consignment of troops too stupid to work out the business end of a rifle. You should see what happens when a car with yellow number plates pulls in." Yellow number plates denoted a foreigner.

"Gravel burns as your money-hungry orderlies drag would-be patients from their cars?"

Lewis laughed, which pleased Alice; as a child seeks to impress a parent, so Alice liked to make Lewis laugh. "Something like that."

Alice picked up the vodka bottle with too much force; it was empty, lighter than she expected.

"We can't have finished it all," said Lewis. "I've only had a shot."

"I spilt some earlier," said Alice.

# 11

*Thursday, 2 January 1992*
Day zero dawned in deep blue and rich gold, a perfect Russian winter's morning. The temperature had risen as if in sympathy, hovering around freezing; monochrome Moscow shone in technicolour brightness. In a nation whose inhuman weather has shaped so much of its history, the elements were doing their bit to help the latest brave and foolhardy souls trying to drag Russia to the promised land.

Alice was out on the streets at nine o'clock sharp, fur hat down and collar up to keep the bare nape of her neck from getting cold. She walked round central Moscow all morning and watched the prices climb with the sun. Staff could hardly keep up with the changes; stock markets had crashed with less rapidity. For decades, bread had been thirteen kopecks; the price was so unchanging that it was baked into the loaves. By lunchtime, a loaf was two roubles. In a supermarket on Tverskaya, Alice heard a woman moan: "Bread is all I can afford to buy now." Polish sausage had doubled to sixty roubles per kilo; petrol had trebled to one rouble twenty per litre; the price of carrots had risen six-fold, from fifty kopecks to three roubles per kilo; a bottle of vodka was now ten days' wages. Everything cost what it cost, not what the state decreed it should.

The rising prices were a good sign, Alice thought. The billions of roubles hidden under mattresses throughout the country had created a vast monetary overhang, an ocean which had to be absorbed before the economy could start functioning properly. And yet, and yet . . . she could appreciate that economic sense dragged with it social trauma. The people hurrying from store to store looked like accident victims: shock and anxiety crowding their faces, eyes glazed and mouths hanging open, the usual reflexes of speech and action working at half-speed.

On Novy Arbat, a man in a hideous synthetic parka asked her where the market was.

"I'm sorry, I'm not from round here," said Alice.

"The market, the market. The one they've all been talking about, the one which starts today."

Alice laughed. "*That* market?" She waved her arm in an expansive arc. "It's all around you."

"No. They said a market which starts today." Parka Man was convinced that there'd be some physical infrastructure, a material manifestation of this great step forward. He looked about fifty; he must have spent all his life in pursuit of an ideal which, like Godot, had never come. Alice could hardly blame him for having lost his faith in intangibles.

Sharmukhamedov was in a terrible way. His body was a war zone floating with blood and unidentifiable parts, and he'd soiled himself so often and so fully that it was hard to tell where skin stopped and waste began. He lay absolutely still; perhaps he was unconscious, his mind kicking downwards from a surface which promised pain untold and delivered even more.

Sabirzhan came bustling in from out of the cold, rubbing his hands together like were a jovial uncle. He had only a few hours left to make Sharmukhamedov talk – the Chechen was due back from Dubai this evening, and Karkadann would be suspicious the moment he didn't return – but Sabirzhan felt curiously unworried. He could sense that Sharmukhamedov was close to breaking, and his judgement in these cases was rarely awry.

He took an ice pick and rolled it gently up and down his fingers. "Want your bones tickled, Baltazar?" A twitching of the stubbled head; Sabirzhan was getting through. High in the crowded field of Sabirzhan's favourite methods of torture, "tickling the bone" involved inserting an ice pick under the skin and scraping it along the bone. Most people wince just at the thought.

"You're going to kill me anyway." Sharmukhamedov's voice sounded too feeble to have come from such a great frame. Sabirzhan saw that his beard was matted with dried blood, patches of saliva and mucus; it looked like roadkill.

"Then tell me what I want to know, and I'll put the ice pick away and make sure it's quick. You're a loyal man, Baltazar. You and I, we're devoted to our bosses, no? That's our job, that's what we're paid for. But how can you owe fidelity to a man who thinks only of himself?"

"You know nothing."

"Who does Karkadann answer to? Himself, that's who. No one else."

"Fuck off."

"His wife? He'd fuck every girl in Moscow, given the chance. Ilmar and Zhorzh? Hardly. *You*? As long as you're useful to him, Baltazar. But that stopped the moment Slava sapped you at Sheremetyevo. Karkadann would give you up in a flash if he knew where you were."

Sharmukhamedov went away for a while. Sabirzhan watched, holding himself as motionless as the Chechen. This was the time, he could feel it, this was the time, and the most important thing was not to push. Pushing would only make Sharmukhamedov dig his heels in.

The steel restraints were slick with blood; a human reduced to animalism, whimpering its life away in the jaws of a trap.

Sharmukhamedov cleared his throat. When he opened his mouth, two lines of saliva stretched across the inside of his lips, a vampire's fangs. Sabirzhan leant forward. He wondered vaguely if Sharmukhamedov could summon up the energy to spit in his face.

"Florist's."

"What florist's?"

"Zamoskvareche district. Corner of Staromonetny and Ryzevsky."

"The one he owns?"

"Yes." Sabirzhan knew the place, a stone's throw south-west of the Tretyakov Gallery, and one of the best florist's in all Moscow. He found it hard to reconcile what he knew of Karkadann with the thought of him knee-deep in blossoms, arranging a bouquet here and a wreath there, always with tender dexterity. Karkadann's attachment to this improbable skill was genuine but profitable. Almost every week, it seemed, there was an expensive order for yet another funeral of yet another underworld colleague hastened to the next world. In terms of Karkadann's other revenues, the place was a mere bauble; but money was money, and a well-arranged display gave Karkadann quite as much pleasure as, say, an opportunity to kill.

"When?"

"Saturday."

"What *time*?"

"Evening."

"Why then?"

"Wedding anniversary."

"He takes his wife there?"

"Flowers."

"How romantic." Sabirzhan thought of the adultery on the transcript. "What about the bodyguards?"

"Outside. Privacy."

"They stay outside to give Karkadann and his wife some privacy?"

"Yes."

"What's her name?"

"Valentina."

"She's Russian?"

"Yes."

Russians didn't marry Chechens, not if they could help it. Whoever said that money couldn't buy love was clearly in the wrong income bracket.

"How many ways into the shop?"

"Bodyguards. All entrances."

"So how do we get in?" Sharmukhamedov shook his head. "You don't know?" Sabirzhan asked. "Or you won't tell me?"

Silence. Sabirzhan stared into Sharmukhamedov's right eye and then his left, as though willpower alone could suck the answer free. He rested the ice pick against the Chechen's elbow.

"You don't know, or you won't tell me?" he repeated.

"Jewellers," Sharmukhamedov said.

"Jewellers?"

"Diamonds. Bring diamonds."

"The bodyguards let the jewellers in?"

"Yes."

"And they stay outside while the jewellers are in there?"

"Yes."

"Who are the jewellers? Where do they work?"

Sharmukhamedov told him so fast that Sabirzhan didn't even have time to threaten him with the ice pick. Sabirzhan made him repeat the jewellers' name and address twice, just to make sure; then he went ahead and tickled the bone anyway, breaking the skin at Sharmukhamedov's right elbow and ripping down his forearm until finally, mercifully, coming out at the wrist.

Prices may have been attaining escape velocity, but in other respects little seemed to have changed. By sundown, many shelves were still empty, many queues still long. "It's clear that the liberalisation has been a failure," said one television reporter. "Prices continue to rise, but if there's no food it matters little; ten times nothing is still nothing." Behind him, customers fought with staff and each other.

In their room at the Metropol, Lewis scowled at the television. "Fucking savages. You know what this place is, Alice? A banana republic. Without the bananas."

Alice found it hard to take Lewis seriously when he was angry; his good looks were too conventional and placid to survive the contortions of indignation. "It's all part of the charm, isn't it?" she said. "Enjoy it while it lasts – things will soon settle down."

"I hope so. Because if this is how it's going to stay, we may as well leave now."

A crappy Volga with number plates illegible beneath dirt and mud, driving fast up the north side of Smolensky Square; Butuzov at the wheel, swerving suddenly across traffic as they approached the Belgrade Hotel, where the Tsentralnaya gang maintained their head-quarters; cold air rushing in as Ozers wound the passenger window down; Ozers slinging his arm like an outfielder; an object arcing through the air, a bowling ball it seemed, turning end over end in a graceful parabola; tyres and transmission whining in protest as Butuzov gunned the Volga's engine and darted back on to the right side of the road; the shock of the Chechen doorman, the scream of the hooker chatting to him, as Sharmukhamedov's severed head bounced twice and rolled gently to a stop at their feet.

# 12

*Friday, 3 January 1992*

Ilmar was staring at Karkadann, prey hypnotised by his unblinking serpent's gaze. Chechen gutturals gurgled in tense throats as they argued.

"Chop off the head and deliver it to the victim's crew?" Globs of spit flew from Karkadann's mouth. He was finding it hard to keep his anger in check. "It's the Avtomobilnaya signature, Ilmar; it's how your lot claim responsibility for a murder. *Everyone* knows that."

"If everyone knows that, how can you be sure it was us?" Ilmar dabbed nervously at his cheeks.

"Twice now, you've tried to persuade me to seek accord with the Slavs. I listen to you, but I don't agree with you, and it's my word that goes here. But that's not enough for you. Kidnap my bodyguard, *that's* the kind of thing I'll understand, isn't it? *Then* I'll listen to you."

Karkadann thrust his hand out, fast enough to make Ilmar flinch and then curse himself for showing weakness, for Karkadann hadn't been trying to hit him; he was showing him something, an oblong of black plastic in his palm. "You know what that is?" Karkadann said. "Of course you do. Stuck under my desk – put there, in other words, by someone who's been in this room. Who was here the day before Baltazar went to Dubai? Who was here, telling me not to fight the Slavs?"

"You really think I'd have ordered something like this?" Ilmar said.

Zhorzh was now staring at Ilmar, and his very silence oozed menace.

"We may disagree, Ilmar," Karkadann said, "but we're also Chechens. We *trust* each other. We *trusted*." He flashed an unexpected smile, a jovial grin of sunny brutality. The lines and planes of his craggy face shifted and rearranged, his eyes shone as they narrowed, his nose was pulled upwards and outwards, and his jaw seemed to push back towards his neck.

Ilmar knew what the smile meant. He'd seen it before, but had never expected to be on the receiving end.

"No," he said. "This isn't the way to do it, even if I *was* responsible."

Chechens have a tradition of blood vengeance for violent death, but the revenge killing is not frenzied or impetuous. Quite the opposite; the process is slow and scrupulously legalistic. The families of victim and aggressor meet and negotiate. Only if the talks are exhausted and the victim's family cannot forgive the aggressor is he declared an outlaw and killed.

"There's no time for all that. We're fighting a war, and we need to be unified – our enemy is, you can be sure of that. But you're not with us, Ilmar. And I can't afford for you to be spreading dissent and discord. Better for us that you're dead; better even for you."

"Better for me? Why?"

"With what you've done, you're no longer a true Chechen."

Ilmar knew the insult was calculated to force him into retaliation. For Chechens, such a slur is punishable by death. "A wound by the dagger can be cured by the doctor," the saying goes, "but a wound by words can be cured only by the dagger."

"I won't have this," Ilmar said. "I didn't kill Baltazar, and that's all there is to it. Either take my word for it, or I'm leaving." He turned and started for the door.

"Turn round," Karkadann said, and Ilmar froze despite himself. Honour demanded that a Chechen kill his enemy in face-to-face combat, not while they're walking away, But since Karkadann had denied him due process, what was to stop him ignoring this custom too? "Stop, and turn around. You've it coming, Ilmar; face it like a man."

Even if Ilmar made it to the door, even if he made it out of the house with all his bodyguards, this thing would not go away. There were Chechens all over Moscow, and most of them belonged to Karkadann or Zhorzh. So he could turn round slowly and let Karkadann shoot him, or he could take matters into his own hands, spinning fast while he pulled the pistol from his waistband, sighting for Karkadann first and then Zhorzh. But even as Ilmar brought his weapon up he knew he was too slow. Karkadann held a gun in each hand and they were both kicking, dull impacts in Ilmar's chest. Down he went, priceless Turkmen carpet warm and smooth against his cheek, and Karkadann's crazy-paving face of contours and angles swimming from view.

Valentina, her hair wet and slicked from the swimming pool, was holding a magazine in one hand and a cigarette in the other, both looking damper than was good for them.

"Guess who's coming to Moscow next month?" Her voice was high and wobbled from word to word; Karkadann found himself thinking of the birds chattering in the poplars. She answered her own question. "The headmaster of Eton. I had us registered today."

Every new Russian worth the name wanted to send his children to boarding school in England; it was cheaper than bodyguards, for a start, and the standard of education was thought to be second to none. Headmasters of English private schools could fill Moscow conference halls two or three times over; they pulled in more punters than symposia on banking and oil.

Karkadann took the magazine from her. It was the latest edition of *Domovoi*, the primer for the *nouveau riche* of Moscow and St Petersburg. *Domovoi* instructed its readers in etiquette, kept them abreast of the latest fashions, told them how to treat their maids and furnish their luxury dachas, and ran diary pieces from Milan, Geneva and New York. It had the fastest-growing circulation of any magazine in Russia.

Good, thought Karkadann. They'd educate their son at Eton, shop at Harrod's and live in Knightsbridge, where he had paid cash for a house last year. *Cash*, as in a briefcase neatly packed with fifty-pound notes which had seen the estate agent close for the day and send his assistant out for vodka and caviar; as in an excellent way to launder money. The cretin had come back with a bottle of Polish Dubrowka and some revolting ersatz black eggs that had never been within half a hemisphere of the Caspian. Karkadann had killed men for less.

The stables, the fountain, the pool, the house – such wealth had been literally unimaginable a few years back, when possessing more than ten thousand roubles had been enough to merit the death penalty. But every rouble he'd accumulated came with riders: a petrol bomb, a falling shell, the parcel packed with explosives, bursts of machine-gun fire and screaming wounded. Some day, this war might end, but until then he would spend his money as if there were no tomorrow.

# 13

*Saturday, 4 January 1992*
Karkadann's bodyguards wore wing-tip shoes and silk suits whose cut was spoiled by the holsters beneath. It was a look which they accentuated by straightening their spines and letting their arms swing backwards. They glanced at the jewellers' polyester suits and

saw how badly they fitted, too tight round the shoulders on the younger one, the older one's too long in the legs. The Chechens saw too where the polyester had worn thin at the elbows and knees; trousers shiny from overuse, shoes clumpy and squared off at the toes. Men like these blossomed on every street in Moscow; bewildered, dignified people whose salaries had gone to shit and who didn't know the rules of the new game. The jewellers each carried a small dark red box, a necklace in one and a bracelet in the other; both diamond, and worth between them north of half a million – dollars, of course, not roubles. It was more money than these two could ever dream of; Karkadann had spent it in a morning.

But the bodyguards hadn't seen the journey Butuzov and Ozers had taken to get here – stepping into the jeweller's shop on Varkava Street as they were shutting up for the day, the blinds already down so no one could see in from outside; Ozers faking a collapse to bring the jewellers round from behind the counter and away from their panic buttons; Lev's men with their guns out, forcing the jewellers to undress before binding and gagging them, not without regret, no hard feelings but you know how it is, we can't have you raising the alarm too soon; Butuzov and Ozers pulling on the jeweller's suits with the crest on the breast pocket, and taking the diamonds as they left.

The bodyguards hadn't seen Butuzov and Ozers exchange a kiss for luck; they hadn't heard Butuzov ask: "All set?" Hadn't heard Ozers reply: "Ready."

A dog padded carefully along the pavement, wary of burning its paws on the chemicals which the city authorities use to melt snow. One of the Chechens reached across and opened the door of the florist's, and in they went, Lev's men here at last, right in the heart of the enemy and beyond, an advance guard behind the lines.

Valentina was pointing to an array which stood like a circle of flame in the middle of the shop; polyantha roses and geraniums in pink, crimson and scarlet, burnished with orange zinnias and splashed with dahlias of the same yellow as the bleached streaks in her hair. Karkadann was limping among his blooms, and it was a few seconds before he saw the visitors.

"Right on time. Excellent. Here, tell me what you think." He gestured towards the plants. "I always use rhododendrons for bases and backgrounds. You can do so much with rich greens and long branches. You see, here," – he beckoned Butuzov and Ozers closer with a wave of his secateurs – "I'm using them to underpin a display of berberis. The berries are fuckers to deal with, all those thorns, and the branches at the base of the stem have to be split or crushed, but it'll be worth it for the sheer brilliance of the colours when it's done. Oranges, pinks and yellows; you've never seen anything like it."

"Very nice." Ozers adopted a tone of suitable awe. Butuzov nodded in agreement.

Karkadann had his jacket off, but the holster under his left armpit was full and another gun distended his right trouser pocket. It hadn't just been the language difficulties that had made the Savile Row tailor ask twice for confirmation that yes, his client *did* want his suits made to accommodate a small arsenal of holstered weapons.

Valentina was coming their way. "Can I open the boxes, darling, can I?"

Butuzov turned towards her; he would hand her his box and grab her in the same moment, while Ozers covered Karkadann.

In the moment before Karkadann's lupine smile split his face, Ozers saw in him the wearied irritation which signals the beginning of the end of love. For Karkadann, Valentina's appeal was already beginning to fade, and in a few years she'd lose the harmony in her looks: her face would sag, her forehead and eyes would be crinkled with lines, her complexion would coarsen and redden, and her hips would become saddlebags. Her beauty was ephemeral and fleeting, like that of so many women.

"In a minute," Karkadann said, teasing. Then, seriously; "I'll have those."

He took the boxes from Ozers and Butuzov, one at a time, never allowing both his hands to be occupied at the same time. He was good, Butuzov thought, all the paranoids were, they acted as though everyone was a threat, even though half the time they didn't even know they were doing it. "Thank you. That'll be all."

Karkadann put the boxes down on the counter, its surface strewn with weapons: a curved Uzbek dagger, the blade from a Red Army M-16, Chinese metal throwing sticks, bracelets that could break a man's wrist.

Ozers and Butuzov glanced at each other; fleeting, imperceptible, enough. Butuzov turned to Valentina to wish her a good evening – he'd seize her now, Ozers was already moving into position behind him – and he was already reaching for her hand when he saw a little face poking between two buckets of white carnations. He started; Valentina followed his gaze.

"Aslan!" She seemed delighted. "Come on out of there, my treasure!"

Aslan was five years old, maybe six; he ran round from behind the buckets and clasped hold of his mother's legs. What was *he* doing here? Sabirzhan had said that they'd only have to deal with Karkadann and Valentina; he'd made no mention of a child.

"Who's been hiding from Mummy, eh?" Valentina was ruffling Aslan's hair while he batted at her hands and squealed delightedly. "Who's been hiding in all Daddy's flowers?"

The kid's screwed it all up, Butuzov was thinking. Children were different, even Chechen kids – but there was no more time to think, Ozers was past him in a flash, reaching down and yanking Aslan clean off the floor, spinning round to face Karkadann with the child struggling in his arms and his gun pressed to Aslan's head, and almost before Butuzov knew it his own arm was wrapped round Valentina's neck and his gun was tracing cold circles against the base of her skull.

Karkadann was holding two guns out in front of him already, damn but this guy was quick, the holster hanging open. This was his family, though, and he held his fire.

Outside, the bodyguards glared down passers-by and didn't look back inside the shop.

"Get out of Moscow," Ozers said. "Give us your business. Take your filthy black ass back to Grozny, and don't come back."

Karkadann took sightings down his lines of fire, his head moving smoothly from side to side.

"Tonight, and don't come back." Ozers tensed his arm against Aslan's wriggling. "*Tonight.* Say it, or we'll kill them both."

"Ilmar," Karkadann said, almost to himself. "*Ilmar.*" His eyes shone, seeming to reflect starbursts of zinnias and dahlias. "You tricked me. You people . . . *dared* to trick me, into killing one of my own. And now," – his words came in surges, he was breathing hard – "and now you *dare* to trick your way into my shop, take hold of *my* wife and *my* child, and threaten me?"

"We'll kill them," said Butuzov. "We *will*."

"What do you need to be in power?" Karkadann asked, not addressing them but himself; no longer angry, it seemed, but philosophical. "You don't need guns or money or numbers; you just need the will to do what the other side won't."

A gunshot cracked, loud in the confined space; bodyguards piling through the door and Karkadann yelling at them to hold their fire even as he dived for the floor, Ozers and Butuzov caught by surprise and looking to see whether the other had been hit because they themselves were fine, disbelief rolling over their bewilderment when

Aslan sagged in Ozers' arms and Ozers realised after a blip in time that Karkadann had done it, he'd shot his own child.

Another shot, and then another. Ozers crumpled to the floor with the boy, the life ebbing from them both. Valentina clutched at her throat, where blood snickered and bloomed. Butuzov was waving his gun around but he couldn't see Karkadann to get a clean shot off and the Chechens were there, multiple barrels all trained on him, they'd kill him the moment he so much as went for the trigger.

"Drop it!" shouted Karkadann. "Drop it!"

Butuzov let his weapon fall to the floor and raised his shaking hands. Valentina rolled away from him and slid back against the wall, still just about on her feet.

Karkadann had rolled behind the far end of the counter. He got up and walked over to Valentina, dragging his bad leg behind him.

She gave him the strangest look; one of trust, perhaps, saturated with fear and humiliation.

He fired again, between her eyes, and stepped back to let her fall.

Karkadann was in Butuzov's face now. "My family are better dead than violated by you, filthy trash. What hold do you have over me now, eh? You think of us as beasts, but it's you, Russian infidel, who is the animal. We Chechens never pursue vendettas against women, *never* – at least, not until an enemy has gone after our women."

He brought his hands up either side of Butuzov's head, a gun at each temple. It would be quick, Butuzov thought; there was that, at least.

"Tell Lev this: for everything that he's visited on me, I will have my revenge. Not one for one, but manifold. He makes me kill my wife; I will kill all his women. He makes me kill my son; I will kill all his children. He makes me kill my friend; I will kill all his friends. Have you ever head of the abreky, you ignorant pig? No? Of course not; it's not the kind of history they teach in *Russian* schools. Let me educate you. The abreky were Chechen bandits. They'd throw over family, clan, home, everything, and give their lives to fighting the Russians. These were my ancestors, and this is their oath – remember it, scum, remember it word for word, because when you get back to Lev, you're going to repeat it to him, and he's going to see what he's unleashed here."

Karkadann took the guns from Butuzov's temples and began to declaim. "I, the son of Shamil Khambiyev, himself the son of an honourable and glorious horseman warrior, swear to the saints to show no mercy to my own blood or to the blood of anyone else, exterminating others as if they were beasts of prey. I swear to take from my enemies everything that is dear to their hearts, their conscience and their courage. I will tear their babies from their mothers' breasts, I will burn their homes, and wherever there is joy I will bring sorrow. If I do not fulfil my vow, if my heart fills with love or pity, let me never see the graves of my ancestors, let my native earth reject me, let water not quench my thirst, bread not feed me, and the blood of unclean animals be poured on my ashes, scattered at the crossroads."

# 14

*Sunday, 5 January 1992*
Sabirzhan's presence in the Kullams' room was like smog: oppressive, enveloping, noxious and, above all, unwelcome. Alla Kullam regarded him with a degree of suspicion that fell marginally short of outright hostility; her husband German twisted his hands and rolled his eyes, as if squirming alone would banish the intruder.

It was German whom Sabirzhan had come to see; German, whose arms poked from the shortened sleeves of his polyester shirt like elongated potatoes and who had a face like a canker sore. German had worked at Red October for more than twelve years, latterly on the rectifier, one of two columns which formed the still where vodka was distilled. For nine of those twelve years he'd also worked for the KGB, keeping Sabirzhan apprised of any dissent among the workforce and any deviation from strict Marxist-Leninist principles. Informing, in other words.

"I'm sorry for visiting you at home, on a Sunday," Sabirzhan said, in a tone which suggested that he was anything but sorry. "You'll appreciate, however, that this is a sensitive matter, one best discussed away from the distillery. You understand, German? Excellent."

Sabirzhan would have asked Alla to leave the room, but there were few places she could go. The Kullams lived in one of the thousands of communal apartments which Lenin's men had conceived as a way of eradicating class divisions, subdividing large czarist houses for the proletariat and housing a family in each room. In the Kullams' case, the room was little more than five metres by five – and they were among the luckier ones. A bed less double than one-and-a-bit was wedged into the far corner, and four chairs huddled around a plastic-topped table. In his cardigan and pince-nez, sipping at the cup of tea Alla had made – "Vodka? Thank you, no." – Sabirzhan looked every inch the favourite uncle.

"Red October is scheduled for privatisation, German, and quickly. We've been chosen as the test case for reform; I need hardly tell you how important it is that the process be completed as smoothly as possible. But nor do I need tell you how resistant our people can be to change. You're one of my better assets on the shop floor, German. You've served your country with skill and distinction for almost a decade now; the state is grateful to you, and has rewarded you accordingly. Now is not the time to relax and pat yourself on the back, however. Your services are required more than ever."

German pecked nervously at the tumbler of vodka in his hand; not his first of the day, by the look of things. "What do you want me to do?"

"Nothing you haven't done a hundred times before: talk, and listen. Spread the word among your colleagues; privatisation will be good for them. Whatever fears they have, everything will turn out right for those who trust the management. Far from spelling the end of the workers' collective, privatisation will enhance their status. A suggestion here, a hint there – you'll have no trouble steering conversations around to the topic, I'm sure. And while you talk, you listen, and then you report to me: who agrees with you, who's agitating against our chosen course, who's wavering and can be turned . . ."

German finished the rest of his glass and sloshed it full again. His hands were shaking.

"I don't think so, Tengiz Lavrentiyich," German said, spitting his words out in a gabble, speed and vodka courage overriding his instinct to do as he was told.

Sabirzhan was still, calculatedly and unnervingly so; he held the silence until German's hands began twisting like a crankshaft. "I didn't quite catch that, German."

"I said – I said that I don't think so."

"You don't think *what*?"

"I don't think that I'm going to do what you asked me to."

"What I *told* you to."

"I'm not going to do it."

"Would you mind telling me why not?"

"Because – because it's not right. You believed in the glory of the socialist ideal, Tengiz Lavrentiyich; you more than anyone. You told me only a few months back how that ideal was being violated by yids and Western rapists, deluded fools and capitalist lackeys. And now you come here telling me how *good* privatisation will be. What am I supposed to think?"

"You think what I tell you to think, German. We must move with the times."

In the corridor outside, two children cycled past at speed. A moment later, the wall shook violently; one of them must have crashed. German looked uncertainly from Alla to Sabirzhan, and down into his vodka glass.

"I don't have to be afraid of you any more, Tengiz Lavrentiyich. Your people are gone."

"My people will never be gone." Under a different name, perhaps, but never gone. "And the money we pay you, the monthly stipend . . ." Sabirzhan gestured round the room. "You look like you could use it."

German mimicked his gesture. "Fat lot of good it's done me so far."

"It's not my responsibility if you piss it away on the vodka."

"We *could* do with the extra, German," Alla said. "You know we could." Prices were still rising fast, as they were scheduled to do for another month or two. Items on the borderline between essentials and luxuries, such as toothpaste and toilet paper, were hard to find, as was fresh food; suppliers were withholding deliveries in order to exploit the rising prices.

"I'm not taking cash off him any more," German said.

Sabirzhan got to his feet and brushed at the seat of his trousers, as though to forestall the possibility of having picked up some ghastly disease from the chair. "I sincerely hope you'll reconsider before tomorrow morning, German; then I can ascribe your reprehensible attitude to the vodka and we can carry on as before. If not –" he blew his cheeks out – "if not, then I'm afraid I'll have little choice but to make you regret your decision." He turned to Alla; she was small and mousy, not unpretty, but quite what she saw in her husband was entirely beyond Sabirzhan. "A pleasure, Alla, as always."

The door opened, rocking flimsily on its hinges, and a boy with delicate features and cheeks red from the cold came in at a bustle: Vladimir Kullam, German and Alla's only son.

"Vova!" Sabirzhan opened his arms wide and bared his teeth by way of a smile. "How wonderful to see you! Come to your Uncle Tengiz and tell him what you've been up to."

Alla glanced nervously at Vladimir and inclined her head towards Sabirzhan. *Go on, Vova, do as the man says.* Vladimir stood his ground by the door; discomfort jagged from him as he ran his hands through thickets of black hair.

"On the cusp of your teenage years by now, aren't you?" Sabirzhan said, apparently unaware that he was still foolishly holding his arms up like aeroplane wings. "I see you're wearing the coat I gave you two Christmases back. Have you been up to mischief on the streets of Moscow?"

"You were supposed to be back hours ago," German said. "Where the hell have you been?"

"At the kiosk," Vladimir said, his voice tight with defiance.

"What kiosk?" Sabirzhan asked.

"One of those new booths down near Novokuznetskaya Metro," German said. "You know the type; it sells vodka, magazines, perfumes, all that. I've banned him from going there."

"Only in term-time," Vladimir said. "Not during the holidays."

"He was playing hooky from school," Alla said.

"I know," Sabirzhan replied. "I ensure that Svetlana Khruminscha keeps me well apprised of what's going on in that establishment."

"Then why didn't you stop him? A child needs education." German's pleading cocked a cold trigger of satisfaction in Sabirzhan's dark interior. "You know what he did when I first found out? He offered me some of his takings! Times might be hard, but I have my pride. Taking money from your own son – whoever heard of such a thing?"

"Like I just told you, German, change is not always for the better."

German turned angrily towards Vladimir. "Kiosks are dangerous, Vladimir." He chose not to use a diminutive, to impress upon his son the depth of his anger. "They're run by gangsters who'll off you without a care in the world. You're not to go there any more; I forbid it. If I catch you there again, I'll smack the crap out of you."

Vladimir reached into the breast pocket of his coat and pulled out a wad of money: dark-green dollars, not the multicoloured floss of roubles. "I earn more than the president, did you know that?" He peeled four notes carefully from the top and let them flutter to the floor. "There you go, Dad. That should keep you in vodka for a few days yet."

Alla clapped her hand over the perfect circle of her mouth. German took an unsteady step towards his son. "You little shit. Come here and say that."

"Fuck you, Dad."

"You really shouldn't talk to your father like that, Vova," Sabirzhan said.

"And fuck you too, *pervert*!" As German lunged forward, Vladimir swayed easily, tauntingly out of reach. "Fuck you! Fuck you! Fuck the lot of you!" – making a song of it as he skipped down the corridor and back out into the streets.

# 15

*Monday, 6 January 1992*

There was a certain irony in Red October's name. The Bolsheviks had all but banned vodka in the first two decades of their rule, and had only reintroduced it during the Great Patriotic War to provide soldiers with energy and courage. Stalin used to sit at his Kremlin desk in the small hours and look across the river at the distillery; content that the essence of the Russian soul was within view, seething that the hated British were right next door to it.

A dozen-strong line was waiting for them at the distillery gates. At the head of the line stood Lev.

Alice had spent the past week studying the files Arkin had provided and reading everything she could get her hands on about Red October. But nothing could have prepared her for her first encounter with its director. "Lev will be easy to type," she had told Harry and Bob in the car on the way there, but the man in front of her seemed to defy all categorisation. She found herself transfixed, not just by the sheer size of him – she had been expecting a great bear of a man – but by the aura of intelligence that seemed to exude from him. It had seemed logical to suppose that the real seat of power would be the KGB man, Sabirzhan, not some dumb-brute gangster figurehead. Alice hoped that Bob and Harry would be perceptive enough to adjust the strategy she'd outlined for today's meeting; something told her it would be dangerous to underestimate this man.

Lev's dark eyes flickered with amusement, as if he could read her thoughts. "Mrs Liddell." Both her hands disappeared in one of his. She saw the tattoo on the back of his right hand, laid delicately over the subcutaneous latticework of veins: a line portrait of birds flying over the horizon, and beneath it the inscription: *I was born free, and should be free.* "How good to see you, and my apologies that this meeting has been so long in coming, but we both know how hard it is for two busy people to find a mutual space in their schedules." She was impressed and gratified that he'd come to her first, as the delegation's head, even though she was a woman.

Alice introduced Harry and Bob, and stifled a laugh when she saw Harry wince at the strength of Lev's handshake. Lev gestured them inside without introducing the others; they were clearly only for show. Perhaps they were from an agency, Alice thought: weddings, bar mitzvahs, factory visits. There were bodyguards there too, men built like linebackers and with eyes that were never still, though none of them was as big as Lev himself.

"Where are the toilets?" Harry asked.

"The executive washrooms are on the upper floor," replied Lev.

"I'd like to see the staff toilets."

"The staff toilets are not suitable for a man in your position."

"That's why I want to see them." To Alice, Harry whispered: "It's a little trick of mine. See what the john's like and you've got a picture of the whole enterprise, almost without fail." He nodded with assumed sagacity, as though he'd uncovered a great truth.

"If you insist." Lev pointed down a side corridor. "They're just there, round the corner. I'll send one of my men with you."

Harry was already on his way. "I prefer to go alone," he called over his shoulder.

He rounded the corner, out of the others' sight, and found the toilets easily enough; but the doors were not marked, not even in Cyrillic, let alone with any variation of the international stick-man/woman icon. With no idea which was the gents' and which the ladies', Harry opened the nearest door and stepped purposefully inside.

Two vast women were standing at the washbasins, and a third was emerging from one of the stalls, ensuring that all clothing layers were returned to the right order as she did so. There was a brief hiatus while Harry's presence was registered and analysed; then all three women began approaching him at considerable speed. He stepped smartly back out of the door and took several paces down the corridor, looking back to make sure that they weren't following. He was still looking back when he walked straight into the wall.

Several things became apparent to him in strict sequence. He'd walked into the wall because the corridor had turned a corner, and he'd kept going where the passageway hadn't. This corner was the same one he'd passed on the way down, which meant that everyone – Alice, Lev and Bob – everyone who was waiting for him could now see him again. This in turn meant that he had no plausible excuse for turning tail and going back to the gents, which after all had been the original purpose of the visit.

Harry straightened his suit and strode back to the group, nodding at Lev in apparent acknowledgement that everything had been to his satisfaction. Alice was staring fixedly into the middle distance and making small trumpeting noises into the back of her hand.

"Shit," said Harry, reaching down for his fly. "Kennywood's open."

They walked through an entrance hall and into the main body of the distillery, which stretched and soared to a ceiling five storeys above. Vast vats of stainless steel and wood marched in rows across two walls and back on themselves. Technicians bustled at their bases and hurried between steaming structures of glinting metal. Bottles wobbled on conveyor belts, abruptly passing from one state to another like the ages of man: now empty, now full, now sealed, now with a metal cap, now clinking out of sight into a cardboard box. The wash of running liquid murmured softly beneath the machinery growl and the sounds of humans: footsteps, chatter, the odd laugh or cough. The sheer size of the operation alone impressed Alice; Americans and Russians share a passion for scale, an appreciation of gigantomania.

"What base do you use?" she asked. "For your vodka."

"Wheat."

"Rye? Potatoes?"

Lev snorted. "Rye's what the Poles use. Potatoes are good for bathtub vodka only."

A sharp hiss away to their right made Alice jump. Two men were firing steam guns up the inside of ten-metre vertical pipes. The vapour left the nozzles in angry tight lines; by the time it spilled over the tops of the stacks, it was amiable and diffuse, like drunks stumbling out of the tavern at closing time. "They're cleaning the purification columns," Lev explained. "We filter the vodka through hot charcoal to remove contaminants. The more the vodka's filtered, the better it is."

"And the more expensive," Alice said.

Lev smiled in recognition; more expensive, yes, that too.

An indefinable shift in the atmosphere ran ahead of their progression across the factory floor. Wherever Lev went, everyone either stopped what they were doing or conspicuously and determinedly busied themselves with some task of great urgency. He seemed to have time for all the workers, clasping hands with the vat mixers and smiling benevolently at the bottlers; an enquiry about a sick child, a joke, a hand on the shoulder. When one of the cappers asked Lev a question, Alice saw that he answered instantly and decisively. Russians believe that the boss should know everything; to admit that any problem is not easily soluble is a sign of weakness and incompetence.

"This is my place," he said to her. "Not in my office, but down here with my people."

She took it as it was intended; a statement, yes, but also a warning. Red October was not simply a place of work for its employees; it was the very centre of their existence, even – *especially* – in a world changing as fast as theirs was.

Lev opened a cabinet displaying the distillery's commemorative paraphernalia. He passed the contents along to Alice one by one, cradling them with exaggerated care as though they were family heirlooms. Bottles made in various shapes: triangles, circles, squares; one in the form of a rocket – a special issue for Yuri Gagarin; another for Gagarin's patron Nikita Khrushchev, with a blade of wheat from his native Ukraine; a bottle of Gzelkha, modelled in the blue and white porcelain of the same name and in the form of a double-headed eagle; and Alice's favourite, a bottle cut in half to reveal the court jester's two faces, a smile reflecting the joy of drinking and a grimace for the hangover's misery.

"You must be especially careful with this one," Lev said, handing Alice a bust.

"Who is it?"

"Who is it? The reason we're here in the first place, Mrs Liddell. That's Isidor, the inventor of vodka. He was a cleric, Thessalian Greek, who was imprisoned by Vasily the Third and rationed to water and grain. Isidor distilled the two together to make an alcoholic spirit which he offered to the guards. When they were comatose, he escaped! Only a Russian would have cunning like that."

"You just said he was a Thessalian Greek."

"In his state of mind, he was a Russian. And that, Mrs Liddell, is how vodka was invented." He took the bust back from Alice and kissed Isidor tenderly on the forehead. "Never believe anyone who tells you otherwise, especially a Pole. Poles always lie, and never more so than when they tell you that *they* invented vodka. Pffff!"

Lev took the Westerners upstairs. They passed through three doors on the way, and he was careful to open each one for Alice, which again she took as it was intended; not as patronising but as typical Russian male courtesy, a cultural trait designed to show respect. Women's lib had yet to reach Russia. Russian men still wanted to pay for dates, uncork the wine, light cigarettes, carry shopping, do the driving – and, Alice thought, be waited on hand and foot.

Galina, Lev's secretary, was waiting for them in the antechamber to his office. She shook the Westerners' hands and smiled at them through bee-stung lips. Harry looked at her as a father looks at his teenage daughter's friends.

Lev's office had two panoramic views – one facing inside over the distillery floor, the other outside to the river and the Kremlin – and looked as though it had last been redecorated under Brezhnev. The tables and chairs were brown, the floor and walls grey, the two stock colours of the Soviet interior designer. Narrow gashes in the upholstery spewed out fragments of cushioning, and threads poked shyly through the carpet by the door and around Lev's desk. Alice sensed slow but inexorable decay; the place was tatty around the edges, and everything needed a good clean. Bob moved to close the door behind him.

"Leave it, please," Lev said. "My door's always open. Any of my workers who want to come and see me can do so, any time, even during a meeting like this." He didn't ask if they minded, and didn't look as thought he'd have cared much if they did.

Lev filled four glasses with dark brown liquid and handed them round. "Let's have a drink."

"Okhotnichaya," Alice said, even before she'd tasted it, and Lev nodded approvingly. Okhotnichaya was drunk by hunters returning from the kill. She sniffed at it and smelt aniseed; swirled it in the glass and sniffed again, finding ginger and pepper. When she drank it, she tasted the other ingredients – port, cloves, juniper, coffee, orange, lemon, tormentil, angelica.

"The flavours are well-balanced," she said. "You've played the dry and sweet ones off each other very skilfully."

"Thank you," Lev said. He seemed genuinely pleased at the compliment. "Vodka-making is not a science, Mrs Liddell, it's an art. Since this is the best distillery in Russia, in the *world*, and I'm the head of it, that makes me the greatest craftsman of the lot. I'm Repin, I'm Kiprensky, I'm Surikov, all rolled into one." He smacked his lips in approval of his own genius. "It's always nice to be appreciated, especially – I hope you'll take this in the right way, it's not meant to offend – by a woman, and an American one at that. Your countrymen aren't renowned for their prizing of good vodka."

That much at least was true, Alice knew. Vodka owes its popularity in America largely to its suitability as a cocktail base, which in turn stems from what Americans perceive as its lack of aroma or taste. For Russians, drinking vodka with mixers is an even greater crime than pissing on Lenin's tomb.

They chatted about this and that – their families, plays and ballets they'd seen recently – anything and everything, so long as it was unconnected with the business at hand. Russians like to get to know someone before doing business with them; it's a far cry from the American way, where warmth is turned on and off like a tap.

"I've read many of your literature's classics, of course," Lev said. "Henry James" – he pronounced it 'Khenry' – "Steinbeck, Scott Fitzgerald, Mark Twain; and of course Hemingway. I've read all his books, start to finish." He turned to Harry. "Tell me, Mr Exley; of all Hemingway's books, which is your favourite?"

Harry looked startled and guilty, an unprepared child undone by a teacher's questioning. "Er . . . *To Have and Have Not*, I guess."

"*To Have and Have Not*? The one that Hemingway himself called his worst book? Come, Mr Exley. That can't be your favourite."

"It is, actually."

"Then you can't have read any others."

"You're right; I haven't."

"Uncultured," Lev muttered to himself.

"I've seen *Doctor Zhivago*, though," Harry said.

"Tchah! Zhivago played by an Egyptian. Western pap. Desecration of a great book."

"There was a book?"

Sabirzhan came in, all smiles and unction. He kissed Alice on the hand and left an imprint of clammy wetness there; she wiped it surreptitiously against her jacket while he greeted Harry and Bob.

"So good to meet you all at last," he said. "So good."

The wall clock showed they'd been there two hours, and only now – a bottle of Okhotnichaya to the wind, and most of *that* consumed by Alice and Lev, because Bob and Harry had stuck at two glasses each – did they get down to business.

"This is the only way it can be," Alice said. "In the past, staff have come to work and they've been paid, irrespective of what they have or haven't done. Now, things are different. State subsidies are on the way out; in their place will come a share-holders' society, where people will have to provide for themselves. They'll come to work, they'll realise production, they'll get money. Workers should see the link between their own work and the income they receive. Make them shareholders too, and they'll work harder, because their livelihood is determined by profits."

"Their livelihood depends on me, Mrs Liddell, and it's a responsibility I take seriously."

"And that's going to change. Red October has apartments, a school, kindergarten, a day-care centre, supplementary benefits, yes? You can't maintain these on thin air, you'll need to start making profits. In a market economy, competition is cruel; it takes decisions independent of your will, as director here, or of what the shareholders want, even of the government's desires. The market economy allows only those organisations which have arranged their resources properly to remain afloat."

"It's merciless."

"It's fair."

"This is Russia, Mrs Liddell, and what you're asking of me is something profoundly un-Russian; to be the guinea pig. If I do this, what happens when the communists get back to power?" He'd said when, not if, Alice noticed. "They could confiscate my factory, prosecute me; jail me, even."

"Oh, come *on*. The communists aren't going to get back in."

"And you know that for a fact? No. You think that because you're American, Mrs Liddell. Americans believe in a brighter future, because that's all you've known in the past two generations. In Russia, it's always our past that's golden, never our future. There are no good times here, just bad times and worse times. That's why we're pessimists. You equate shareholders with opportunities; I equate them with trouble. Outsiders don't know the difficulties we face, and won't have any interest in them. They'll just sell their holdings the moment things get tough and leave us even deeper in the shit."

"What we want here is co-operation. It's not a matter of me thinking that my way's better than yours, or me trying to exploit you. We both want to help Red October operate to its full potential, and the best way of doing this is through combining our expertise and your experience."

Lev squinted at her, attempting to gauge whether she was being sarcastic.

"Let me explain to you how business works in Russia today, Mrs Liddell," he said. "Boris and Gleb meet. Boris wants to buy a cartload of, I don't know . . .'"

"Vodka." Alice smiled.

"A cartload of vodka, why not? Gleb says yes, fine, he'll sell him one. They agree a price. Then Gleb tries to find that cartload, and Boris tries to find the money."

"So?"

"So everything. That's the way we do business. You talk of market institutions, market culture, market memory – we've nothing of that."

When they'd finished the Okhotnichaya, Lev opened a bottle of Ultraa. It was distilled using the pure oxygen-rich waters of Lake Ladoga, he told them, and its recipe was based on one that had been used in the czar's imperial palaces. Alice's senses were not yet so numbed that she couldn't smell the delicate, lightly sweet aroma, nor miss the touches of needle in a smooth taste, nor fail to feel the very slight oiliness of texture.

"One of yours?" she asked.

He shook his head. "But I appreciate any vodka that's good, as long as it's Russian, of course. Not from anywhere else. Especially not Poland."

"Why do you like vodka?" Harry asked Lev. Alice buried her head in her hands.

"Why do I like vodka?" Lev snorted. "That's like asking why it snows in Russia. Only a foreigner could ask such a ridiculous question. It's like asking for a definition of the Russian soul."

Whatever the rights and wrongs of Alice's case, it gradually became clear that, on some basic level, she and Lev were still miles apart. The Westerners had come equipped with graphs, statistics, market research, forecasts and projections, Bob and Harry giving the kind of slick presentation they'd done hundreds of times before in airport hotels the world over. They emphasised contents and slighted context, guarded emotions and shared facts. Lev did exactly the opposite, trying to read between their lines while apologising that he wasn't much of a details man – he left that sort of thing to Tengiz, they should sort things out with him later. Lev refused to be drawn on any issue, particularly the twin prospects of redundancies and a reduction in his own personal position.

"My ears are swollen," he told them eventually. "I'm tired of listening."

"You're an uncompromising bastard," Alice said.

"That's the nicest thing you've said to me all day." He was genuinely pleased.

Alice goaded and goaded Lev; even she'd had enough of going nowhere. Lev's face began to flush red; Alice almost looked under

75

the table to see if he was pawing the ground. Bob tried to interject, then Sabirzhan, and finally Harry, but they were all brushed aside.

"You think I'm going to be shunted out of the way just like that?" Lev snapped. "You think I'm *so* stupid that I can't see what you're trying to do?"

"What am I trying to do?"

"Wreck the Russian economy, that's what; maintain Russia in some kind of semi-colonial tutelage to the West. You can keep your expertise and your theories. The only thing capitalists are creating is misery. People begging on the streets, folks dying faster than they can make the coffins, no potatoes in the stores, babies born with only half a face, people who can't take a piss because they've got the clap, pensions worth shit. You lot knock us to the ground and then want to buy the wreckage. That's not just shit, it's *insulting*."

Alice held her hand up to try and interrupt the flow, but she might as well have tried to hold off a tsunami.

"You were pushing each other out of the way to get on the plane when that fool Gorbachev rode off into the sunset. 'Shock therapy,' you tell us. 'A few months of pain and it'll all be over.' Yes, well, we're getting the shock all right, but I don't see much therapy. And what's the West doing? You sweep in here as if you're emissaries of light, bringing salvation to the natives living in the dark forest. You think you're heroes because people give you free drinks and ask your advice. You think that what works for you will automatically work for everyone else. Your teeth are whiter than ours and your clothes better, so suddenly you're the arbiters of public morality. You assume America's the ultimate model, and so you judge every-thing simply by how close it comes to your own ideal. You think you've *carte blanche* to remake Russia in your own image. You don't, and you won't – not here."

She was drunk, now, very drunk, riled and losing it. "You are backward, lazy, devoid of initiative and living in the past," she yelled.

"And you, Mrs Liddell, are blinkered, imperialist, patronising and rapacious. I don't like being treated as an aboriginal in my own country, and I don't like the prospect of your privatising this factory merely to make money. You're trying to rape us, pure and simple."

And with that, Lev pushed his chair back and stormed out of the room. If the door had been shut, his fury would surely have propelled him straight through it.

Lewis was shaking Alice awake with enough force to make her slap his hand away in irritation. "What time is it?" she slurred.

"Half past ten. Where have you been, to get this drunk?"

Alice felt synthetic fabric against her cheek; the sofa in their room at the Metropol. When she lifted her head, a line of saliva stretched from the corner of her mouth to the upholstery.

"Where have you *been*?" he asked again.

"Red October."

"That was this morning."

"Lasted all day . . . Lev . . . Fucking asshole."

"Why's he an asshole?"

"Fucking fuckstick."

"You got hammered with this guy?"

"Trying to get him to agree to privatisation." Lewis' face swam in her vision. The skin under his chin was beginning to pouch, she saw; he was going to get jowly if he wasn't careful.

"You could have done that without getting drunk."

"I'm a Westerner. I'm a woman. Why make things harder than they already are?"

"Did Harry and Bob get drunk?"

"Course not."

"So why did you?"

"Had to drink their share for them." She giggled.

"Alice, getting drunk at work is not the way normal people behave."

She forced herself to focus on him. He was being patronising; she wanted to slap him again, harder. "Lewis, it's a *distillery*. That's what they do in distilleries: they make vodka, then they drink it." Alice giggled again, a hand to her mouth like a naughty teenager. "And if you had to deal with someone like Lev, you'd be drunk too." She wagged a finger. "I'm gonna get him, Lewis. I'm gonna get Lev, I'm gonna teach that fuckstick not to mess with me. Next time will be different."

# 16

*Tuesday, 7 January 1992*

The temperature had dropped again, down to minus twelve. Piled high on the pavements, the snow had earlier shone lemon in the midday sun; now, with dusk approaching, orange was seeping like an aftertaste into its honey colour. Everywhere, like a mantra, could be heard the phrase *golod y kholod*: famine and freezing.

It was Orthodox Christmas, the first in almost three-quarters of a century reclaimed from the godless embrace of communism. The first, then, when worshippers needn't fear a visit from the ubiquitous KGB. Lev and his phalanx of bodyguards – he always took twenty men wherever he went; no gang leader in Moscow ever took his safety for granted – went to the Kazan Cathedral at the northeast corner of Red Square. 'Cathedral' is something of a misnomer; the Kazan is little bigger than a church and painted as brightly pink as a child's birthday cake. Stalin had destroyed the original and replaced it with a public toilet; only the quick thinking of the architect Pyotr Baranovksy, who had made plans of the cathedral even as Moustaches was tearing it down, had enabled Gorbachev to rebuild it as original, right down to the ornate window frames, ogee-shaped gables and domes in green and gold.

Lev bowed three times before the icon of Jesus above the door, and between each bow stood and crossed himself, from head to stomach and right shoulder to left, using three fingers rather than two in the approved Orthodox fashion. Inside the cathedral, it was almost dark; the only light came from candles and weak wall-brackets. The air was close and quiet, heavy with incense and short on oxygen. Candles burned and sputtered in pools of pearly wax; candle stands glowed like softly burning trees. Lenin had described religion as a hypnotic flame for a reason. From the walls, icons looked dolefully and impassively down, unsteady in the flickering haze.

As in all Orthodox churches, there were no pews; the congregation stood. Feet shuffled, clothes rustled; no one spoke. In the murk, Lev's bodyguards forced worshippers into the corners, meeting resistance only from an old woman dressed in black and holding a brass contribution plate covered in red felt. A can of oil to keep the flames alight was at her feet; in her free hand was a box of candles in various sizes. The prices for each size had been crossed out and marked over several times. When she tutted at the wrestler who'd tried to move her, Lev came over and placed five hundred dollars on the contribution plate.

"We pray for Russia's future," he said, "and for its soul."

Lev had studied the Orthodox scriptures in the gulag. That was how he knew that the conquest of death remains eternal and that human souls, as fragments of the godhead, will share in it if they escape damnation. Hell is the only alternative to salvation; the orthodox can no more imagine purgatory than they can envisage different kinds of truth, different shades of meaning, or bargaining along the path which leads to spiritual revelation. Their liturgy is beautiful, but it is calculatedly mysterious, inaccessible, designed to be accepted without question. Death in this scheme is not the end of life; it is a transition.

Alice heard the key click-clack in the lock, and Lewis came in trailing cold.

"Raw out there, huh?" she said.

"And the traffic was awful," he replied. He took off his coat and rubbed his shoulders. "I'd give anything to be back in New Orleans again. How long does winter last here?"

"Till May, sometimes."

"May? No chance. This goes on till May, I'm out of here. Oh." He felt in his jacket pocket. "I brought you this."

He handed her a banknote in fuchsia pink. It was a five-hundred-rouble bill, officially issued yesterday, the first she'd seen; the previous highest denomination had been two hundred. The banknote was folded and creased from being in his pocket; she had to put down her vodka glass to straighten it out and examine it properly.

"What are you watching?" he asked.

"News." The reporter was saying that those coping best were country people who, having chickens and gardens, could feed themselves. It was not hard to detect a note of schadenfreude in the reporter's voice; Moscow has always been resented by the rest of Russia.

Alice switched channels. Now Borzov was touring the upmarket Arbat Gastronom. Its red-and-white awnings were cheerful and clean. The shelves and floors had been swept free of litter. Clerks in spotless aprons stood in front of rows of tinned food, imported vegetables and jars of pickled spices, all neatly sorted by category and size. Cellophane-wrapped packages of meat and poultry were piled invitingly in a large, modern freezer. A kilo of chicken was forty-eight roubles, a kilo of smoked fish forty; eggs were selling at twelve roubles for ten. The place radiated enterprise and profit. It was the kind of blatant propaganda that would have made any Soviet commissar proud.

"I don't care how much food they've got," Lewis said. "This place is Third World until I can find a muffuletta." If there was one thing above all others that Lewis missed about New Orleans it was the cuisine, and the muffuletta sandwich – a round seeded loaf split and filled with ham, Genoa salami, mortadella, Provolone cheese and marinated olive salad – was a particular favourite. "So they got vegetables?" The word had four syllables – vedgeatibbles. "Bully for them."

79

Back in the Kremlin, tricolour at his shoulder, Borzov addressed the nation. "The hardest time is from now until the summer. After that, there will be stabilisation and improvement. Next winter will be easier than this one. Today we must all make a choice: well-fed slavery or hungry freedom? To make this decision requires the will and wisdom of the people, the courage of politicians, the knowledge of experts . . ."

He looked sincere and pained; Alice fancied that he was addressing her personally.

"Your president has made this choice. He has never looked for easy roads, but the next months will be the most difficult. If he has your support and trust, he is ready to travel this road to the end with you."

Borzov took a sip from the glass on his desk – Alice hoped and doubted that it was water. He narrowed his eyes. "For too long, our economy has been run on lines which can only be described as anti-human. As a result, we have inherited a devastated Russia. But we mustn't despair. We have the chance to climb out of this pit and to stop our constant preparation for war with the whole world. This will be a special year. We will create the foundations of a new life. We are abandoning mirages and illusions, but we are not going to lose hope. Hope we do have."

Vladimir Kullam was hurrying home. Brezhnev had once boasted that Moscow was the only capital city in the world where a person could walk the streets at any hour without fear of attack; no more. Vladimir had made good money on the kiosk today, more than he wanted to carry alone for too long. When he thought of the Chechens who'd threatened him yesterday, he upped his pace a little more and checked to make sure they weren't following him. The streets were badly lit; if anyone was there, he might not see them until it was too late. His youthful imagination ran merry riot in his head; he'd heard tell of what the black-asses did to people who'd crossed them.

An exclamation – "Vova!" – cut through Vladimir's thoughts. He was off before he knew it, three strides into a sprint, when the voice said "Vova!" again, and he realised who it was. He stopped running. "You want to be careful, coming up on people like that – you almost gave me a heart attack!"

The streetlight caught the dull glint of a vodka bottle. "You want to take a hundred grams with me?"

Vladimir shook his head. "I haven't the head for that stuff."

"Good lad –" And then Vladimir felt a sharp pain at the base of his skull, saw an explosion of light entirely at odds with the smoggy blackness of a Moscow winter, and heard his own sharp cry of surprise give way to a yawning silence.

# 17

*Wednesday, 8 January 1992*
Lev had boasted that his door was always open to his workers and, just before the start of his shift and in a state of some agitation, German Kullam was the latest to prove the truth of this.

"Vladimir's gone missing," he blurted.

Lev poured German a hundred grams, sat him down and made him recount what had happened.

German and Vladimir had argued on Sunday afternoon about Vladimir's working at the kiosk, something German had repeatedly told him not to do. (German omitted to mention Sabirzhan's presence; it would have raised all sorts of questions he'd rather Lev didn't ask.) Vladimir had stormed out. That was the last his parents had seen of him.

"Your son disappears on Sunday afternoon and you wait till *now* to tell me?"

"We thought he was being a hothead." German listened to himself and realised that he'd smeared the truth somewhat. "*I* thought he was being a hothead. Alla was worried right from the start. But this happens all the time: we fight, he leaves and doesn't come back for a night. Sometimes even two."

"And where does he go?"

"To friends."

"These friends – did you ring to see if Vladimir was with them?"

"With what phone calls cost nowadays?" The price of local calls had been almost negligible under communism, but telecommunications were no more exempt from rampant inflation than anything else. "Besides, it was up to him, wasn't it? To call, to come back, I mean. *He* was in the wrong, not me. He should obey his father."

"He's your *son*, German."

German looked at his hands. "I went down to the kiosk. They haven't seen him since yesterday."

"Have you been to the police?"

"What's the point? Those guys couldn't find their own assholes with a mirror."

"Too true. OK, German. You tell me everywhere you can think of where Vladimir might be, every place you've ever known him go, and I'll have my men check them out for you."

Endless pairs of men, wrestlers and weightlifters in dark overcoats who clutched smudgy photocopies of Vladimir's photograph, fanned out across the city like blips on a radar sweep. They went to every one of Moscow's eight mainline train stations, ticking them off as though they were destinations on a journey – Belarus, Riga, Kiev, Yaroslav, Leningrad, Kazan, Kursk, Pavelets – striding through air heavy with fried food and urine, ignoring the beggars who swarmed out of the pistachio gloom and tugged at the brightly coloured plastic bags that families were carting home across the federation's expanse. The searchers stood at ticket barriers in metro stations and thrust Vladimir's picture in the faces of commuters and station workers. They went to Red Square and questioned the hustlers who tried to sell tourists fur hats for ten times their value. They went to the vast GUM department store and prowled beneath advertisements for the Canary Islands promising eleven months' sunshine a year. They went to the Bolshoi theatre, the Tretyakov Gallery, the Lenin and Dynamo stadia, and to Gorky Park, where families skated and wrapped their faces in sticky pink candyfloss.

In every place the same result: no sign of Vladimir, no sign at all.

# 18

*Thursday, 9 January 1992*
It was just past eight in the morning. A British Embassy staffer was walking along Sofiyskaya, the road which ran along the north side of the drainage island, directly across the Moscow River from the Kremlin. The wind tore her copy of *Izvestiya* from her hands and sent it whirling towards the river; when she looked over the parapet to see whether the paper was retrievable, she saw a dark shape below the ice, hidden briefly and then visible again as the sheets of newsprint skittered across the top of it.

Juku Irk, once of the Estonian capital Tallinn and now senior investigator with the Moscow prosecutor's office, wanted to go home and start the day again. Russia really is the home of winter, he thought bitterly; the sun hauls itself wearily over the horizon after breakfast and is back in bed by teatime. The ground was grey with ice, the snow grey with dirt, the buildings grey with exposure; it was as though the bleak winter had robbed the world of its colour. Beneath Irk's feet, the mud was as hard as concrete, and the puddles might have been made of marble.

He'd had to show his card to gain access to the site. He didn't look like an investigator. An academic, yes. His features were small and clustered together beneath a slick of back-brushed grey hair; they made a face too soft and genteel for his job.

The police had set up some sort of small crane to lift the corpse out. The job needed two policemen, three at most; there were at least a dozen, arguing, shouting, smoking and getting in each other's way. Irk knew that scolding them would just make things worse; there was little love lost between police and prosecutors. Police caught criminals, answered to the Interior Minister, were uneducated and badly paid; prosecutors questioned criminals, answered to the prosecutor-general, usually had degrees and were better paid, though in Moscow salary and income tend to be different beasts altogether.

They were right by the spot where Red October's effluent pipes spewed into the river waste that was warm enough to keep the immediate vicinity from freezing over too heavily. Moscow city ordinances explicitly prohibited such discharge; Moscow city industries explicitly ignored such ordinances.

Shit day, shit job. Irk had travelled here by metro, for heaven's sake – all the squad cars were on calls or had broken down. It wasn't the inconvenience that bothered him, still less the implied loss of status, but the fact that on foot he couldn't help but see things he could ignore from a car. Homeless children jostled for space on metro air vents as they tried to keep warm. Queues formed outside state shops hours before opening, to get the lower prices at the start of the day.

Irk heard a low groaning, whether mechanical or human he couldn't tell, and the child came free from the water at last, a grappling hook in the back of his coat and his extremities streaming water as they hung limp and pathetic as though reaching for the sanctuary of his icy tomb.

Sabirzhan stood in the mortuary with his hands clasped behind his back and waited, perfectly still, for the attendant to bring out the body. Identification was often the worst part of any death; it was the final extinction of hope, and on such occasions there was nothing Irk could do other than hover impotently while someone nodded numbly and confirmed with quivering lips and red-rimmed eyes that yes, this was their loved one and yes, they were dead.

Irk was grateful to Sabirzhan for sparing Vladimir's parents this ordeal. Sabirzhan was a KGB officer; dead bodies wouldn't cause him the slightest discomfort.

There was no sheet over Vladimir's body. Preserving the dead's modesty is a Western affectation. Sabirzhan looked up and down the corpse without blinking.

"That's Vladimir," he said.

Was it Irk's imagination, or did he see Sabirzhan lick his lips as he turned away?

There was only one place which the squeamish found worse than a murder scene, Irk thought, and that was the autopsy room. A dead body was repellent enough when first found, whether curled under a forest tree with animals chewing at its face, leaking blood on to the cheap linoleum floor of a dingy apartment, or hauled bleached and bloated out of the river as this one had been. It seemed twice as loathsome when laid out on the examination table. Clinical and chemical, pathology was supposed to sterilise and sanitise death; in Irk's experience, the effect was exactly the opposite.

And there were no autopsies more disturbing than those like today's, when the body in question was that of a child. The examination table was large enough to take someone of Sharmukhamedov's size, or even Lev's; it dwarfed this small, hairless corpse.

"You understand, Syoma; this may not be mine at all," he said.

'Mine', of course, referred to operational responsibility rather than paternity. If Semyon Sidorouk, pathologist, decided that Vladimir Kullam, deceased, had drowned, then Irk would not investigate the case. Drownings were either suicides, who usually weighted their pockets with stones, or accidents – children overestimating their ability to swim, adults drinking too much vodka. There were plenty of easier ways to murder someone.

"My knowledge of Soviet procedure is still good, Juku." Soviet procedure, more often than not, had involved deciding the result in advance and shepherding the analysis in that direction. "Though in these trying times, you understand I have to charge for such a service, may Lenin forgive me." The dark skin of Sidorouk's shaven head gleamed under the lights; he was a Chechen, one of the very few working in Moscow law enforcement. He stubbed out a cigarette in a knee-high ashtray embraced by lead nymphs.

"That's not what I meant, Syoma." Sidorouk had assumed that Irk wanted to bribe him to falsify results. "I need your honest appraisal. It's just that" – Irk waved helplessly at the body – "would *you* want to investigate that?"

Sidorouk shrugged. Irk understood that the gesture was one of indifference rather than indecision. Sidorouk dealt with cadavers the way mechanics treat cars, midway between affection and exasperation, with a pitying condescension aimed at those who did not understand. To Sidorouk, corpses were objects to be examined and dissected, stepping stones on the path to truth. It made no difference to him whether they were young or old, thin or fat, beautiful or ugly; he showed no interest in the kind of person they might have been. In a pathologist, it was an excellent quality; in an investigator, thought Irk, it would have been disastrous.

Irk wondered how much of Sidorouk's attitude stemmed from the way other people treated him. It wasn't that they saw the Chechen first and the person second; they simply saw the Chechen, and that was enough to discourage further interest. As an Estonian, Irk was an outsider too, but he knew there was a difference between white outsiders and black outsiders.

"It's the season for deaths, Juku."

"It's *always* the season for deaths." Numbers were worse in times of upheaval, but upheaval was constant. In the thirties there had been collectivisation, in the forties war; liberalisation in the fifties, retrenchment in the sixties; the seventies had brought stagnation, the eighties perestroika; and now this, freedom or anarchy, depending on whether your vodka glass was half-full or half-empty.

"Have you ever investigated a drowning before?" Sidorouk asked. Irk shook his head. "Right, first things first: let's find out how long it's been there." Irk sighed inwardly. The moment Sidorouk had an audience, he treated every autopsy as an opportunity to lecture. Irk had long ago realised that it was easier simply to play along; trying to rush Sidorouk only doubled the journey.

"The body's temperature matches that of the river. Bodies in water cool at about three degrees centigrade per hour, twice as fast as they do in air. If the water's warm, they reach the water temperature within five or six hours; if it's cold, as it is now, twice that. So let's say the cadaver's been there twelve hours, minimum; that's too long an immersion to run diagnostic tests for blood gravity or plasma chloride levels, even if I could get my damn machines to work."

"That doesn't help me, Syoma. Vladimir was definitely alive on

Sunday afternoon, he was definitely dead on Wednesday evening – that's three days unaccounted for, I need something more specific. What about that?" Irk gestured to the boy's neck and chest, patched in greening bronze. "Does that tell you anything?"

"Post-aquatic putrefaction. That's happened since it was pulled out of the river. Changes happen very fast once a corpse is exposed to the air. Nothing to do with how long it had been in the water."

'It', 'the body', 'the cadaver'; Irk envied Sidorouk his facility with the dead, his ability to dehumanise them. Irk came to the mortuary as seldom as he could manage, and when he did he spent as little time there as possible; he didn't chat to the assistants or poke round the freezer cabinets. Hundreds of people worked here, in the Ministry of Health's criminal biological department, but Sidorouk was the only one whom Irk knew either by sight or name. It was a world which Irk found alien and frightening. There was talk at Petrovka, the central police headquarters, that one of the mortuary assistants, dealing with the body of a catwalk model, had found her charms unblighted by death. Irk knew there was no correlation between how comfortable a detective felt in the autopsy room and his ability to solve a crime – some of the biggest idiots in homicide seemed practically to live in the morgue – but still; this was an aspect of the job he felt he should be handling with more aplomb.

He shook his head as a dog would when emerging from a lake; he needed to concentrate.

"So." Sidorouk clapped his hands. "Now for the main course. Let's see if this is going to be one of yours or not, eh? This isn't as easy as it sounds; it can be very difficult to tell whether a body drowned or not. Immersion artefacts occur in any corpse which has been submerged in water, irrespective of cause of death. There are no autopsy findings exclusively pathonomic of drowning, so we have to prove that the victim was alive on entering the water, *and* exclude the presence of natural, traumatic and toxicological causes of death. Only then can we be sure that the victim drowned."

"In plain Russian, then, it's a process of elimination."

"Exactly. If it *is* one of yours, you'll know before you'll know that it's not, if you see what I mean." Sidorouk chuckled and bent over the body; Irk saw veins tracing paths across his crown like those of the Volga River as its delta splays into the Caspian. "Let's see what the injuries tell us. You see how the body is largely exsanguinated?" Irk nodded; the boy was less discoloured than whitewashed. "That's not surprising. Immersion leaches blood from ante- and post-mortem wounds alike. It'll be virtually impossible even to tell the difference this long afterwards."

Sidorouk examined the sparse blotches of dusky cyan on the boy's head and neck. "Cuts and bruises. Again, that's exactly what I'd expect. Corpses in water always lie face down, with the head hanging lower than the rest of the body, so it's these parts which take the brunt of the battering." He moved slowly down the body. "Three parallel chops, here on the left forearm – propeller cuts, perhaps."

"Propeller cuts? How many boats have you seen on the river lately?"

"Good point. Two straight cuts on the sternum, arranged perpendicular to each other. You see them? The ones that look like an angled 'T'?"

"Too neat to be accidental, wouldn't you say?"

"Yes." Sidorouk pressed at them. "But they're quite shallow. Not halfway fatal."

Irk nodded thoughtfully. "Abusive father? Juvenile gangs? Self-mutilation?"

"You're the detective, Juku, you tell me. Tell me this, too: what kind of equipment did they use when they fished it out?"

"Grappling irons, hooks – oh, and ropes as well. He was wedged up against a buttress."

"Well, they're clumsy oafs. Tell them to be more careful next time." Sidorouk pointed to grazing down by the waist and a gash across the left thigh. "These look like recovery injuries."

Sidorouk examined Vladimir all the way down to the toes, his face so close to the body that Irk thought of a sniffer dog, and then straightened with a shake of the head. "Nothing conclusive either way, I'm afraid. And the waters are further muddied – if you'll excuse my phrasing – by the fact that cold water's involved. Have you ever heard of vagal inhibition?" He didn't give Irk the chance to respond. "A sudden and dramatic change in temperature can prompt cardiac arrest or laryngeal shock: instant loss of consciousness, followed by death. It's still drowning, but atypically so. Pathologically, instant unconsciousness is hard to discern from a prior state of the same; the symptoms can be confusing." Sidorouk's goatee beard stretched around his grin. "You may want to go outside for a cigarette now, Juku."

Irk stepped into the corridor and lit up under a no-smoking sign. The first drag made him feel even more light-headed than before, and the sounds from behind the screen doors didn't help: the petulant whine of an electric saw as it battered against bone, a satisfied squelch as it cut through tissue. Sidorouk's disembodied head appeared round the corner.

"You've gone even whiter than before." He was amused, not concerned. "Pack your ear plugs next time. Ready when you are."

It was bad enough that Sidorouk was so obviously enjoying Irk's discomfort; what was worse was that Irk couldn't think of a single thing he could do to return the favour. He walked back into the autopsy room and almost turned straight round again; the boy had been sliced open, three cuts forming a perfect 'Y' from shoulders to sternum and sternum to waist.

Sidorouk was cradling a lung as though it were a lapdog. Patterned in marbles of grey and crimson, it shifted over the inside of his forearms as he moved; it looked like a water balloon, a saturated bladder, voluminous and bulky. Irk peered from lung to cadaver and back again. He couldn't see how one had fitted into the other. Sidorouk placed the lung on the table.

"You see the lighter zones, here and here?" He indicated patches of pink and mustard yellow. "Those are the areas of more aerated tissue. You want to feel it? No? It's doughy, and pits on pressure. Look —" Sidorouk's finger seemed to disappear as he poked at it. "It's not an unpleasant sensation, you know. Pass me that knife there, would you?" Irk's hand hovered uncertainly over a stainless-steel tray. "Not that one, the one two along. Yes, *that* one. It's just like being in the kitchen, isn't it? Do you cook, Juku?"

Sidorouk sliced into the lung. Dirty water spurted from the gash and flowed over the edge of the table. If Irk had been a moment later in stepping back, his shoes and trousers would have been soaked. He thought he was going to be sick.

"As I thought." Sidorouk seemed pleased. "No fluid."

Irk pointed at the spreading pool on the floor. "Then what the hell's that?"

"Oh, that's *water*." He sniffed. "The river's finest, by the smell of it. No, I was looking for *fluid*, the sort you get when air and water have been actively inspired. Passive flooding of lungs with water looks quite different. Not that this proves anything, mind you. The fluid's not always there, and when it is, it's indistinguishable from that caused by a pulmonary oedema."

"The sort you get in head injuries?"

"Lenin be praised, they teach you something in cop school after all. Head injuries, yes; also heart failures and drug overdoses. Anyway, there's no sign."

"What does that mean?"

"It means – no, it *suggests* – that you might be getting this case whether you like it or not."

"You're enjoying this, aren't you?"

"A man should take pride in his work, Juku. The days seem so long otherwise."

Sidorouk tripped happily over to a set of scales and lifted a small bag from the bowl.

"Stomach?" said Irk queasily.

"Juku! You'll be after my job next." Sidorouk looked closer at Irk's face. "Perhaps not. Yes, the stomach – and it's as good as empty. Drowning victims tend to swallow all kinds of material: water, of course, but also sand, silt, weeds, and other foreign matter. When it comes to the Moscow, you could probably make a nuclear bomb with all the shit that's floating around in there; it's moot as to whether you'd drown or be poisoned first. Where was I?"

"Empty stomach."

"Oh, yes. Talking of which, have you had lunch?" Irk clamped his teeth together and shook his head. "Probably for the best. Anyway – when the victim's dead before it enters the water, very little matter gets as far as the stomach. What you find is usually confined to the pharynx, trachea and larger airways." He held the stomach out towards Irk. "Hold this, will you?"

"Fuck off."

Sidorouk laughed. "You should see yourself."

"Just get on with it."

Sidorouk put the stomach back in its bowl, returned to the corpse, and lifted its right hand. "What do you see?"

The hand was clean and flat. "Nothing."

"Precisely. Victims struggling in water tend to clutch at whatever objects they can, objects that can be very hard to dislodge from fists in cadaveric spasm. But there are none here. There's nothing under the fingernails either. I even checked for bruises to the scaleni and pectoral muscles from thrashing around. No sign."

Irk pointed at a russet patch which ran over the boy's left collarbone. "Then what's that?"

"Haemoglobin inhibition, I would imagine. Uneven putrefaction can cause such areas to develop in the muscle. It's easy to confuse this with haemorrhaging."

Irk sighed. "There's not much doubt, is there?"

Sidorouk gestured extravagantly towards the corpse, a waiter showing off the chef's special. "Investigator Irk, I present to you your latest case. And don't bother asking me to look for fingerprints or hair strands or bodily fluids either. They'll all have been sluiced off long ago."

Petrovka – technically, number 38 Petrovka Street, the headquarters of the Moscow police – hulked a dirty beige, shabby and in need of a good clean. The grime was almost comforting on Petrovka's hideous main block; on the winged porticos which faced north and south down the street, however, it seemed an affront.

You could distil vodka in the time it took for the lift to arrive. Irk climbed the stairs to the fifth floor, and reflected ruefully on the panting evidence that he was getting no younger. He was still catching his breath when he saw that there was someone in his office – someone sitting in his chair, in fact. Sabirzhan.

"A rare pleasure," Irk said as he entered. "All the Lubyanka men I know see us as second-class citizens. They'd rather stick pins in their eyes than slum it in Petrovka. So to what do I owe the honour?"

"There's no need for you to get involved in the Vladimir Kullam case, Investigator."

"Oh?"

"I'm personally conducting Red October's internal investigation into this tragedy, and I need hardly remind you of my qualifications in this matter. Vladimir Kullam's father works at Red October. The distillery is being privatised. That makes it a political case." The public prosecutor's office investigated all crimes except political ones and those involving foreigners – those went to the MSB, the KGB's successor organisation. "A very sensitive political case, at that. You can imagine how twitchy the government will be about anything which threatens to derail the reform programme. You're also no doubt aware of . . . of an incident on Saturday evening? At a florist's in Zamoskvareche?"

The Chechens, Irk thought, always the Chechens, first to be blamed for everything. "Karkadann's shop?"

Sabirzhan nodded. "A triple homicide. Which I believe Yerofeyev is handling."

"Or not, as the case may be." Yerofeyev was Irk's counterpart in the organised crime division. Homicide, Irk's section, handled only non-mafiya killings, even though murder and the mafiya were hardly strangers.

"I spoke to him just now. Active work for the solution of the case is not being done at the present time." The doublespeak was pure Soviet; Sabirzhan's voice carried no mimicry.

"Shelved within twenty-four hours, if I remember rightly. Something of a record, even by Yerofeyev's standards. It was one of yours, along with Karkadann's wife and child, is that right?" Sabirzhan nodded. "Yerofeyev would have beaten Pontius Pilate to the basin on that one. But what's that got to do with Vladimir Kullam?"

"Karkadann wants control of Red October, that's no secret."

"And?"

"How better to pressure Lev than by killing Vladimir Kullam?"

Irk laughed. "You're joking."

"Not at all."

"Even by KGB standards, that link's extremely tenuous." Even as he said it, Irk knew that people had been sent to salt mines on flimsier evidence.

Sabirzhan raised his eyebrows, picked up Irk's phone, dialled, muttered something unintelligible, and held the receiver out to Irk.

"Hello?" Irk said.

"This is Lev. I'll tell you what happened in the florist's, if you keep it off the record."

"All right." It was no loss. Irk could have recorded the statement and had Lev sign it in triplicate and it would make no difference. Yerofeyev could lose a smoking gun on the way from one hand to the other. He was reputed to be the richest cop in Petrovka.

"Karkadann killed them all: my man, his own wife, his own son. He left one of my men alive to pass on this message: 'He makes me kill my wife; I will kill all his women. He makes me kill my son; I will kill all his children. He makes me kill my friend; I will kill all his friends.'"

"Forgive me, but I still don't see what this has to do with Vladimir Kullam."

"I'm a vor. We don't have families." Lev didn't tell Irk that the oath Karkadann had taken was uncomfortably close to that of the vory, whose own ancestry could also be traced back to bandits who, before setting out on raids, had sometimes killed their wives and own children to stop them falling into enemy hands. "Vladimir was the child of one of my employees. He also attended the school run by Red October. I regard all those children as my own, Investigator. Don't scoff, please. I'm absolutely serious when I say that. These people are my responsibility. Karkadann knows that. It has started."

Irk took Sabirzhan up one floor, to the prosecutor-general's office.

Denis Denisovich Denisov had the best office in Petrovka: floor-to-ceiling windows looking south through one of the porticos. Were it not for the snarled traffic and the thick Moscow sky outside, the room would have provided the perfect backdrop for pre-revolution

91

aristocracy. Not that Denisov would have appreciated this; he was the kind of man who seemed unaware that the Soviet Union no longer existed. On the wall behind him, posters of socialist advancement curled back on to themselves.

Sabirzhan reiterated what he'd told Irk: that the case was political or criminal, possibly both, but certainly not a matter for homicide. Denisov shook his head.

"You think you can come in here and push us around like that? You can't pull that state security crap on us any more – those days are gone. This case is ours, Juku's – unless and until he finds evidence to the contrary." Denisov turned to Irk. "You find me a concrete link between the murder and either the privatisation process or organised crime, then you can pass it on. Only then."

Denisov had three perfectly symmetrical lines of skin under each eye; they could have been remnants of a melted candle, perhaps, or tribal markings. The rest of his face was perfectly ordinary, standard homo sovieticus. Photograph Denisov and superimpose a black strip across his eyes, like they did in pictures of Spetsnazy special forces soldiers, and he'd be unrecognisable.

Kovalenko was the press liaison officer, and he worked out of a windowless bunker in the bowels of Petrovka. An apt reflection, Irk thought, of his status in an organisation committed to telling the public as little as possible about what they were (or, more usually, weren't) doing. Kovalenko's salary was even more risible than his colleagues'; he was more or less officially expected to make up the difference with payments from reporters grateful for tip-offs.

Irk set down a bottle on Kovalenko's desk. "Eesti Viin," he said. "Rich and creamy, bottled in Tallinn – not the muck the kiosks here sell."

Kovalenko was too well-mannered to grab at the bottle, but only just. "And in return?"

"In return, I want you to tell any hack who asks that the body fished from the river by Red October this morning was a drunk." Drunks were hauled from the Moscow – in it or on top of it, depending on the season – with monotonous regularity, usually with their flies open because they'd overbalanced when taking a leak. It was news when a day passed *without* such an episode.

"What was it really?"

"If you don't know, you can't tell anyone, can you?"

* * *

92

"All right," Sabirzhan said, "maybe this will convince you: Vladimir worked in a kiosk at the Novokuznetskaya metro station. I hear they had a visit from Chechens the other day."

"I'll go down there later."

"Why not now?"

"Because I have to do house-to-house down by the river."

"You? You're a senior investigator."

Irk shrugged. Of course a senior detective shouldn't have been performing such basic tasks; he should have sent his uniformed subordinates instead. But when it came to house-to-house, the uniforms invariably seemed to find other matters worthier of their attention; even the most resourceful policeman found it difficult to extract bribes on such assignments. Irk had given up trying to fight the system; it was easier to just get on and do it himself.

It wasn't as if it was going to do any good. Up and down piss-soaked stairs because the lifts were out of order, back and forth across death-race roads, only to discover what he'd suspected all along – that if anybody *had* seen anything, they certainly weren't going to tell the police. Even in Moscow, many people were slow to appreciate that a visit from the police was no longer an inevitable prelude to ten years in Siberia.

On the way to Novokuznetskaya, Irk thought how much Moscow was a city of lines. Pensioners crocodiled outside metro stations, holding summer dresses and sunhats against their chests, in the middle of a Moscow freeze; shop assistants stood in front of their own stores and offered goods cheaper than you could get them inside; kiosks were strung out on pavements and underpasses, jostling each other in glass and metal. If you couldn't find what you wanted at one kiosk, the next one would certainly have it, or the one after that. Japanese electronics and Danish hams here, French cheese and Korean condoms there. Ninja Turtles and Barbie dolls? Three units that way. Snickers, Mars and Bounty bars? Next one along, sir, but I'd check the expiry dates if I were you. Hey, while you're here, perhaps you'd like some bootleg tapes? We've got Elton John, Sting, Genesis, and all the Rod Stewart you could ever want.

It was typically contrary, then, that the kiosk Vladimir Kullam had helped run stood in proud isolation. Irk came out of the metro station and there it was, a stone's throw from the Tretyakov Gallery. The kiosk door was divided in two like those found in stables; when he was inside, the operator kept the bottom half closed and served

93

people through the top. The operator in this case was a sullen youth with red hair and freckles.

"Is this where Vladimir Kullam" – Irk checked his tenses – "works?"

The redhead regarded him suspiciously. "Yeah," he conceded eventually.

"And you are?"

"You can call me Timofei." He was framed by hundreds of vodka bottles. Irk held his investigator badge out like a talisman.

"Well, Timofei, did you know Vladimir?"

"Yeah."

"We fished him out of the river this morning."

Timofei shrugged.

"That doesn't bother you?" Irk asked.

"It happens." Timofei fished under the counter and brought out a couple of magazines. "You want some porn, Investigator?"

"Do I look like I do?"

"Every man looks like he does. Here, I've got *Penthouse* – fifteen roubles a peek, four hundred to buy. Or you can have *Andrei* for half that." *Andrei* was a home-grown and blurred version of *Penthouse*; the women were prettier, the production values inevitably much worse. All in all, thought Irk, it evened itself out. "Or there's *Rabotnitsa* for the wife." *Rabotnitsa* – literally, "Woman Worker" – owed its circulation of ten million to an anodyne selection of knitting patterns, recipe cards and porridge diets; there was nothing on career women, nothing on sex.

"I don't have a wife. Who runs this place?"

"I do."

"No, bonehead. Who *really* runs it? Who do you pay your protection to?" Irk's expression warned Timofei off repeating his claims to grandeur.

"The 21st Century."

That made sense. Kiosks were not only lucrative; as a cash business, they were also good for laundering dirty money. However, while the world was no poorer for one more dead mafiyoso, Vladimir Kullam's loss meant something. Even in Moscow, children were different.

"Not the Chechens?"

"Do the 21st Century look like Chechens? I don't think so."

"Ever had trouble from any Chechens?"

"No." Too quick. Irk cocked his head.

"Timofei, no one'll know what you tell me."

"What I'm telling you is this; the Chechens have never given me any trouble."

It was extraordinary, Irk thought; Timofei was protected by one of the most powerful gangs in the city, but still the Chechens had struck such terror into him that he'd lie about them.

"And what *I'm* telling *you* is this: tell me the truth, or I'll haul you down to Petrovka."

"On what grounds?"

"I don't need grounds, you know that as well as I do." Irk was bullying; he hated himself for it, but he needed to find out what had happened.

Timofei glanced left and right to make sure no one was looking, and beckoned Irk closer. He believed Irk's threats, and that depressed Irk even more. Like most people, Timofei clearly assumed that all officials were corrupt.

"They came round on Monday."

"Was Vladimir with you then?"

"Yes."

"What did the Chechens want?"

"The action – what else?"

"Had they ever been round before?"

"Once."

"When?"

"Last week."

"What did they do?"

"The first time, nothing. The second time, they reached in here, grabbed us by the collar, yanked us clean out of the kiosk and told us to go with them rather than the 21st Century."

"What did you say?"

"That they should sort it out with the 21st Century themselves. That's how these things work."

Timofei didn't tell Irk how he'd yelped as his shins had scraped the sill, and again when the Chechens had dropped him on to the pavement. He didn't say how he'd pleaded when the leader had pulled a switchblade from his pocket: "Don't stab me, please don't stab me, not with the gut-straightener," he, Timofei, gabbling in panicked soprano, a frightened child the moment he was out of his protective box. He didn't say how his eyes had brimmed with fear as the Chechen had flicked the blade, placed the knife against his shirt and sliced two triangles out of the fabric; why, he didn't know. He didn't say how, though they were on a main road, no drivers had slowed to offer help and no pedestrians had checked their stride as they walked past. He didn't say how the man's silence had been more frightening than any amount of threats.

He didn't tell Irk any of this, nor did he need to. Irk knew, the gist if not the details. He'd seen too many gangsters put the frighteners on too many of Moscow's little people.

The Chechens could have killed Vladimir as a warning, Irk thought. It was possible, no more.

"Would you recognise them again?" he asked. "The Chechens?" Timofei shook his head. "Not even one of them? Come on, Timofei, you can do better than that."

"There was one, yes. The leader, the guy who pulled me from the kiosk."

"Describe him."

"White streak in his hair."

"You didn't hear a name?"

"We weren't on a date, Investigator. Besides, he never said a word."

"No matter." Every official in Moscow knew what Zhorzh looked like. Irk changed tack. "How does it work? You and the 21st Century?"

"They take a bit, I take a bit."

"How much of each?"

"Seventy-five, twenty-five." The tone of Timofei's voice told Irk that he wasn't the one ending up with the lion's share. "But they sort out any crap for me. And I still earn in three days what my parents do in a month."

"What about *school*?"

"What *about* school? What's the point? There are special schools for chess, maths, languages, sporting prodigies, but none for people like me at the other end of the class. I got punished the whole time, ignored if I was lucky. Normal life is lousy, Investigator. I can get richer here than anywhere else."

Irk gestured to the vodka bottles. "You drink this stuff?"

"These particular bottles? They let me have one a week."

"You ever take any more? On the sly?"

"They'd kill me if I did."

"Literally?"

"Literally."

Irk felt his ears prick. "They told you that, or you've seen them do it to other people?"

"Not with my own eyes, no. But you hear things."

"And Vladimir – would he have tried to rip them off?"

Timofei shrugged again. "Maybe. Vova was a bright boy, and you get people who think they're too smart to get caught. If he was selling some under the counter without telling them and they got wind of it, then yeah, they'd have killed him. But it wouldn't have been because he'd taken it for himself. Vladimir never drank vodka."

"Why not?"

"He thought it would stunt his growth."

Men from all three Slav gangs – the 21st Century Association, the Solntsevskaya, and the Podolskaya – crammed into the ballroom of the Rossiya Hotel; hundreds upon hundreds of them, reeking of aftershave and anticipation. The chairs were arranged in strict order of rank, ranging from the lowest orders at the back to the higher echelons in the front rows. On the podium was a table at which sat the vory troika: Lev in the middle, flanked by Testarossa and Gibbous, the Podolskaya's new leader.

Their years in the gulags had taught the vory to appreciate the value of organisation. Their command structures were as vertical and rigid as those of an army or political party, and this was just as much a gathering of the faithful as any party conference had been, though these men dressed better and exercised more than any communist delegates ever had. Waiters traversed the rows with hundred-gram glasses and bottles of vodka. The gangs rarely came together like this for there was danger as well as safety in numbers: a single bomb would have wiped out an entire generation of vory.

When Lev stood and called for silence, he looked like a bear balancing on its hind legs. They watched him as raptly as any ideologue had ever been transfixed by Lenin or Trotsky.

"Brothers, we stand on the threshold of a vast conflict. We're up against an evil man, a man who will not listen to reason; a man who has chosen to launch his campaign with the most despicable and cowardly act imaginable: the murder of an innocent child."

This was the rub. Karkadann was a new creature for Lev, and one that he wasn't entirely sure how to handle. It wasn't just that the man was clearly psychotic; it was that there seemed such a simplicity to him. Most gang leaders play a tactical game, weighing the odds, waiting for the right moment to make their move. For Karkadann, it appeared, the only moment was now; everything was either good or bad, right or wrong, black or white, and the odds could go to hell.

"We outlasted Soviet power. The communists failed to destroy us because no matter what they did to us we remained true, we kept our structure, our ideology, we survived. Now we face a different enemy, but we'll triumph just the same. We're superior to the Chechens in culture and morality. We pay the hospital bills of our wounded, we provide for the families of jailed men. We're better trained, better disciplined, and better armed than they are. We *will* annihilate them, I promise you that."

They applauded when Lev paused; they stopped when he held up his hand for silence. Lev motioned that they should stand. It was time for the toast.

"We must remember that what's more important than anything else to us is not money, but brotherhood. That's what gives us our strength."

Glasses brimmed in sweating hands; there wasn't a man there who wouldn't have killed for Lev, and that was one of his greatest strengths.

"So let's drink to our cause, which is always to support one another, to remain united. If a person is alone, he counts for nothing. But if we are united and support each other, then we are strong and everyone will fear us. Let's drink, Brothers! To unity!"

"To unity, Father!"

# 19

*Friday, 10 January 1992*

What Timofei had said wasn't enough to get Irk off the case, not nearly. He went to see German Kullam, a visit which he knew should have been his primary concern right from the outset. The man of the family is always the prime suspect in Russian homicide cases. This is a matter not of cynicism but of fact. Gangland killings aside, Russian murders usually fall into two categories: firstly, drunken rage directed at family or friends; secondly, as a corollary to robbery, either premeditated and intentional or accidental and impulsive. The usual victim of the Russian murderer is the woman with whom he sleeps or the child he's fathered. Only a handful of homicides ever transcend the level of childlike stupidity. Again, these are mostly gangland killings. The gangsters always have to be different.

The Kullams lived next to a convent founded by a grand duchess who had been thrown down a mineshaft by the Bolsheviks. The relics of the revolution were everywhere, Irk thought, watching impotently as Alla sobbed into her husband's shoulder. German cradled his wife awkwardly and half-shrugged, half-smiled over her head at Irk. He seemed embarrassed at his wife's display of grief.

Alla eventually disentangled herself from German and looked at Irk through wide, red-rimmed eyes. "Would you like some soup?" she asked. "I made it myself."

He nodded numbly, more to avoid causing offence than because he was hungry, and avoided German's gaze as Alla busied herself in the kitchen. She came back with a bowl on a tray depicting the battle of Borodino. It was cold summer soup: beetroot, cucumber, sour cream and egg, the yolk floating in a sea of lilac. A soup for lazy days in the woods with friends and vodka; not a soup for the man who came to your house after your child was dead.

Irk made all the right noises about how sorry he was, this was a real tragedy, but he had to ask some questions and he hoped they understood. Yes, Investigator, yes, of course, anything he needed. So he asked and Alla answered: what they did for a living, when they'd last seen Vladimir and in what circumstances, when they'd first become worried about his safety. He didn't ask them why they hadn't gone to the police sooner; they all knew the answer to that one.

They'd gone over the same ground with Sabirzhan yesterday, Alla said. Irk was annoyed and surprised in equal measure; annoyed that Sabirzhan seemed to be everywhere before him, surprised that the KGB man should have bothered questioning the Kullams when his own suspicions so clearly lay elsewhere. Perhaps he was covering his bases.

Alla was both bright and pretty enough not to be cleaning offices. Maybe she'd been offered other jobs, secretarial posts, in return for sleeping with the boss, and she'd refused. Good for her, Irk thought. German was easier to read: life savings going in the transition to capitalism, vodka, a job which paid little, vodka, emasculated because his wife was forced to work to make ends meet, vodka, insulted because his son was offering him money, vodka, going stir crazy in these long winter nights, vodka, arguments with a wilful son who was not quite a teenager, vodka . . .

German Kullam had the look of a drinker. His nose was an archipelago of broken blood vessels, his eyes swivelled in viscous pools. Irk was unsurprised. Most murderers were drunks first and killers second, more so now than ever before. Many had assumed, at least implicitly, that people would drink less following the demise of the Soviet Union. A democratic society would surely provide more means of escapism than alcohol, and all of them constructive – books, a free press, foreign travel, consumer goods. Fine, when you could afford such things, but for now there was still only one escape when times were hard: half a litre of temporary paradise. There was talk of a magic water source in the Vologda region that could cure drunkenness. The headspring was at a disused well which had not been blocked properly; wives were taking their husbands there by the trailerload. If they could somehow organise a shift system to and from Moscow, Irk thought, he could put his feet up for good.

"If you'd prefer," Irk said to German, "we could do this down at Petrovka."

"Whatever for?"

It was the first time Irk had heard him speak, he realised. German's voice was high and reedy; no wonder he'd let his wife do the talking. Irk wanted to shake him and say, Come on, you know how it is, you know the score, this is the way things are done around here, and we have to play along whether we like it or not.

German looked as though he would burst into tears at any moment. Irk could forgive him that, whether he was innocent or guilty. For obvious reasons if innocent, and if guilty because the Russian prison system could have given Satan nightmares.

Irk filled in German's details on a badly photocopied arrest form. He could recite the categories in his sleep: family name, given name, patronymic, address, date of birth, place of birth, age, sex, nationality, profession, marital status. Irk was on autopilot to the point where he was halfway into his first question about the night Vladimir had disappeared before he realised what German had said.

"Divorced?" German nodded. "Alla's your second wife?" Irk glanced at the date of birth again: 12 April 1961, the day Gagarin had become a starman. That made German thirty. If Vladimir was born twelve years ago; German must have married young and divorced early.

German shook his head. "My first. Only Alla."

Irk shouldn't have been surprised. Unable to afford to move, couples often had no choice but to live together long after their divorce, sometimes continuing to share the same room and even the same bed. If either German or Alla resented their circumstances, they hadn't shown it, at least not in front of Irk.

"You get used to it, Investigator," German said. "Just make do with what you've got. I don't give anyone any problems. You want to see troublemakers, go and talk to the three alkies who steal food from the kitchen and invite bums up there for all-night vodka parties. When that happens, the rest of us can't sleep."

The government were talking about building cheap one-bedroom flats to replace these beehives of communal living, but with more than a quarter of a million families to be rehoused the programme would take years to complete.

"The walls are so thin that you can hear what people are saying, even when they're talking quietly," German continued. "It's so depressing. No one can do anything without everyone else discussing it. We're meant to live as a big family, but it doesn't work like that, even when we try. Last Christmas we tried to put aside our differences and pulled pieces of furniture into the corridor to make a long banqueting table, but the ceiling was leaking too badly. We all ended up sitting in our rooms and sulking."

Twenty-five people in one house, with one kitchen and one bathroom between them. The Bolshevik planners had seen this as an innovation that would forge bonds between residents, an exciting experiment in socialist living. Innovation, experiment – words for scientists, Irk thought, not for human beings.

Sabirzhan was in Irk's office again.

"Perhaps I should give you all my work and go home for the day," Irk said.

"Are you making progress with German Kullam?"

"Didn't you hear what Denis Denisovich said?"

Sabirzhan held up his hands. "We got off on the wrong footing, you and I, and for that I apologise. The truth is this: I think German Kullam is guilty."

"He doesn't look like a Chechen to me. Nor some kind of political kingmaker."

"I know, I know. But I spoke to him yesterday . . ."

"They told me."

". . . and he wasn't convincing, let's put it that way. So I got to thinking; what if it is as simple as that? Take out the Chechens and the politics. Take out our national desire to complicate everything. What if German *did* kill his son, and all the rest is coincidence?"

Irk considered this for a moment. "A domestic incident, could have happened anywhere . . . Less embarrassing for Red October, that's for sure."

Sabirzhan smiled and clapped his hands. "I knew you'd see, Juku."

"What about Lev?"

"I thought it would be better presented to him as a fait accompli."

101

"He doesn't know you're here?"

"He has enough things to worry about."

"I'm not going to stitch German up, I want you to know that. If we charge him, it will be because he's guilty, not because you want him to be guilty."

Sabirzhan looked offended. "Investigator, please. We're not in the dark ages now."

Irk asked German about Vladimir until he ran out of questions. What happened the night he had disappeared, who his friends were, who his teachers were, where his stamping grounds were – everything he could think of. Some of the questions he'd already asked back at the apartment, others he repeated three or four times here.

German's diatribe on communal living was, in retrospect, proving something of a soliloquy. His answers had the consistency and creativity of a metronome: yes, no, don't know. At one point Irk even asked if Vladimir had really been his son, more to shock German into a reaction than anything else. German had said yes without surprise or offence, the same way he'd say yes to someone who asked him whether he'd like bread with his soup.

"Why don't you just drop it all on the table?" Irk said. He needed to sound angrier, more exasperated. If he couldn't convince himself, there was no way German would fall for it. "Go through your memory like your mother searched your head for lice. You'll feel a lot better. Come on, German. You're like a virgin after seven abortions. All this posing the innocent doesn't wash with me. I know details can get hazy in the emotion of the moment. I'll remind you of what happened, and you let me know when you remember, yes? After all, I'm only telling you things you already know."

Sabirzhan and Denisov were chatting away like old friends when Irk walked in. Yesterday's animosity was gone. It was amazing, Irk thought sardonically, what communality of purpose could do for human relations. He sat down without looking at either of them.

"He didn't do it," Irk said. "German Kullam didn't kill his son."

"Just because he didn't confess?" Denisov snorted. "Of course he did it. You only have to look at him to know that."

Sabirzhan was nodding slowly, as though Irk would soon see the truth so evident to other, wiser men. They're in this together, Irk realised. Before Sabirzhan had visited Irk, he must have been to see Denisov and impressed on him their mutual interest in convicting

German. This was how it was in Russia; for Irk, truth and justice were too often mutually exclusive commodities.

"He didn't do it." Irk realised he was beginning to sound like German himself: didn't do it, didn't do it. "The boy was dead when he went in the water. German doesn't live too far from the river, but he hasn't got a car."

"So?"

"So how could he get Vladimir's body down to the Moscow without anyone seeing?"

"Maybe they went for a walk on the bank and he bopped him on the head there. We hold Kullam until he stops playing silly buggers. I want him here, isolated and shitting himself." Denisov peered at him. "You didn't offer him a lawyer, did you?"

"No. But he's entitled to one."

"What, because the devil's spawn said so? Don't make me laugh." The previous year Gorbachev had extended a defendant's right to a lawyer to the moment he was arrested rather than from the moment he was charged. Denisov had flatly refused to recognise this; as far as he was concerned, anything which had come from Gorbachev was an edict of Beelzebub, and should therefore be disobeyed as a moral imperative. Denisov ran the prosecutor's office on strictly Soviet lines: suspects could be held without charge for three days, and for another week after that if the prosecutor believed they had enough evidence to prepare a case. When these ten days were up, they had either to charge the suspect or release him.

"That's what the law says."

"The law doesn't know what it says from one day to the next."

"Besides, it's not as if these draconian conditions help. Our clear-up rate is still woeful, Denis Denisovich, or hadn't you noticed?"

"Just imagine how much worse it would be without them."

Denisov took over the questioning himself. He drew the line at inviting Sabirzhan to help.

"We've spoken to your wife, German. She says you've been drinking more and more lately, and when you get drunk you get angry, and when you get angry you take it out on her too. But I suppose you think that's the lot of a Moscow wife – cook up, shut up, get beaten up. Don't you?"

Irk wondered how much Denisov was speaking from personal experience.

"You want to see what real violence is, German?" Denisov continued. "Have you ever got a good kicking from the police? They're scientists at it, my friend, they're *artists*. They know where to hit you, and they don't leave traces. They'll take your arms and legs and swing you high up in the air before dropping you on the floor, flat on your ass, again and again and again. You know what happens after that? The next day, you'll be spitting blood. Two days after that, it'll feel like a monster has set up an amusement park in your urethra. Two days after *that*, your kidneys will pack up and you'll die. Still want to try and prove that you're not a camel?"

German's eyes seemed to fill half his face. Irk couldn't remember the last time he'd seen someone look so scared.

"Denis Denisovich," Irk said, "can I have a word? Outside?"

In the corridor – he thought briefly of his cigarette break while Sidorouk chopped up Vladimir Kullam inside the autopsy room – Irk said, "It's not him, I'm certain of it. And any beating we give him is nothing compared to what they'd do to him in jail, you know that."

"Yes, but *he* doesn't know that. He's going to spill the beans any moment, Juku. Get in there and take his confession. That's an order. If you won't, I'll find someone who will. Don't play the hero; there's no room for Sakharovs here, *comrade*."

"I hate being called 'comrade'."

"I know."

Three springs ago, Irk had been a link in the million-strong human chain which had stretched all way through the Baltics, from Tallinn to Vilnius via Riga. Irk had fought against the Soviet Union while it was still there. Denisov was fighting for it now it was gone.

"We can't keep German inside for a crime he didn't commit," Irk said.

"Why ever not?"

It was a genuine question, Irk realised with surprise. Why ever not indeed? Stalin had killed millions for crimes they hadn't committed.

# 20

*Saturday, 11 January 1992*
They had put German in a cell overnight and left him there; no food, no water, no company. When Irk returned at dawn, German was sitting up on the flat bench which doubled as a bed. His eyes were dull with fatigue and his hands shaking with apprehension.

Self-loathing grabbed at Irk; he knew that German wouldn't have slept much, if at all.

"I've bad news for you, German. If you don't confess, Denis Denisovich wants to charge Alla as an accomplice to murder. He's within his rights to do so. Neither you nor your wife notified the police that Vladimir was missing."

When a man was falling, crumbling, collapsing, it didn't matter how hard the final kick was, but how carefully it was placed. What was left of German's resistance flew from him like a startled pigeon. "Where do you want me to start?" he asked.

A confession is the only evidence which counts in Russia; it's the end to which every Russian policeman works. They may bungle the forensics, they may lack trained officers, but when a judge hears the magic words "I confess", he can destroy a life without a second's soul-searching. All of which suits investigators, as it's not unknown for those who bring cases that end in acquittals to lose their jobs.

Confession is seen as the cry of the guilty soul, overwhelmed by the urge to unburden itself. Many Russians believe that a defendant who doesn't confess cannot be punished. Why else did Stalin insist that the victims of his purges must undergo show trials, where they acknowledged conspiracies which never existed? If an admission contradicts the facts, then the facts are wrong; if the facts are wrong, they should be changed.

It only works on amateurs and innocents, of course. Professional gangsters would no more confess than suddenly burst into Latin.

Irk felt contaminated, polluted. German's confession was signed and sealed; he'd agreed enthusiastically with everything Irk had reminded him that he'd done and, as the hours had rolled on and he'd gradually become more confident, he'd even started to add some embellishments of his own.

"Excellent," said Denisov. "The case is orderly again. Disorderliness makes me feel ill."

The only ailments Denisov was in danger of suffering, thought Irk, were a brown nose and a numb ass. 'Disorderly', the all-purpose Soviet negative, was Denisov's favourite word. A driving violation was disorderly, a factory failing to meet its quotas was disorderly, prostitutes were disorderly, a dead child plucked from filthy waters was disorderly. Denisov hated disorder. Even his name, Denis Denisovich Denisov, made no concessions to disarray.

"A first-class display of law enforcement," said Sabirzhan. "We at the Lubyanka could have done it no better, and that's the highest praise. I thank you both as sincerely as I know how. Lev will be very pleased when I tell him." He gestured at Denisov's phone. "May I?"

Irk felt a childish pang of resentment: Sabirzhan hadn't asked before using *his* phone.

As far as Lev was concerned, Saturday was just another business day, so he didn't find it unusual or rude that Gusman Kabish, director of the Kazan distillery in the city of that name, should be calling him. Not rude, that was, until he heard what Kabish had to say.

"I'm afraid we're cancelling our agreement with you, effective immediately. We're getting our water from Baikal instead."

Red October and Kazan had for three years enjoyed a mutually beneficial deal. The quality of top-line vodkas was dependent, among other things, on the wheat and water used in their manufacture. Wheat in Tatarstan, the semi-autonomous republic five hundred miles east of Moscow of which Kazan was the capital, was the best and most cost-effective in all Russia. Kabish had more than he could use, so he sent the surplus to Red October. In return, Lev sent Kabish water from the reservoirs Red October maintained up near the Mytishchi springs; the water here was soft and free from calcium, which was perfect for vodka. This was the way all industry had worked in the Soviet Union. Central planning's inefficiency meant that every factory suffered shortages, and the easiest way round this was not to fight the planners but to find another factory which had what you needed. You would then pay, barter or trade with them in secret.

In business terms at least, Kabish's decision made no sense. Baikal was much further from Kazan than Moscow was, and the water there wasn't as good as that from Mytishchi.

Look below the surface, Lev told himself. In Russia, that's where the truth is to be found.

Tatarstan is nominally Muslim, as is Chechnya. Though the two republics are thousands of miles apart, Chechens and Tatars see themselves as brothers, united by the prejudice of the Russian infidel. It was an open secret that the Chechen mafiya were expanding into Kazan.

"Karkadann's got to you, hasn't he?" Lev said, and slammed the receiver down without waiting for an answer. The phone rang again instantly; Lev snatched the receiver back from the cradle and yelled into it. "Yes?"

"It's Tengiz. I'm down at Petrovka, and I'm very pleased to tell you that German Kullam has just confessed to Vova's murder."

* * *

106

Lev's size and fury seemed to fill Denisov's office.

"What the fuck do you think you're doing? That confession's a load of shit, and you know it. I will *not* have one of my employees fitted up because you lot are too bone idle or chickenshit scared to look for the real culprit. You release German right now and put his file in the incinerator."

"German confessed of his own free will," Sabirzhan said, "and –"

"Don't give me that shit, Tengiz. And please, don't insult my intelligence. What are *you* doing down here in the first place, when you know who the real culprits are? Are you afraid of the Chechens? If you are, just say so, and I'll get a real man to do the job."

"I'm not afraid of anyone. I came here to –"

"Then stop bullying someone like German, who can't answer back." Lev turned to Irk. "When we spoke on the phone a couple of days ago, Investigator, we talked like adults, didn't we? You seemed a decent enough man, and I'm not usually wrong about people – you can't afford to be, not in my line of work. Perhaps you've been forced into this against your will . . ."

"I must take my share of the blame," said Denisov. Irk started; he'd never known Denisov to admit to any share of any fault, *ever*. "I suspected that German was innocent – he simply didn't seem the type, and when you've been a copper for as long as I have, you get a sense of these things – but Juku had no doubt, and I let his zeal persuade me. I should have trusted my instincts."

There was not a trace in Denisov's face to suggest that he was being anything other than deadly serious. Irk actually felt his jaw drop open. Even Stalin might have blanched at such a blatant rewriting of history. Might have.

"Me too," said Sabirzhan. "As you know, Lev, I tried to persuade the investigator to drop the case, on the grounds that it was not his jurisdiction. But he wouldn't listen."

Irk looked at Denisov and Sabirzhan, and neither man flinched. Go on, their stares seemed to say, go on, we *dare* you to tell Lev what really happened. And of course Irk wouldn't tell, because it would be his word against theirs, one of them his superior and the other Lev's deputy. Why on earth would Lev believe him?

"You all know the system," Lev said. "Either you do as I ask, or I'll take the matter higher, and you know how high I can go. I'm sure you don't want to cave in, Denis Denisovich, but it's that or a transfer to Zigansk. I'm sure you'll make the right choice."

German Kullam was released from custody half an hour later.

# 21

*Sunday, 12 January 1992*

The school which Vladimir Kullam had attended was on the same
site as an orphanage. Red October ran the school and the 21st
Century Association the orphanage, though in practice both institutions reported to Lev himself. Raisa Rustanova hadn't been seen
at the orphanage for four days. It was lunchtime when her body
was pulled from the Moscow River at more or less the same spot
where Vladimir Kullam had been found.

The skin on Raisa's corpse was swollen and wrinkled, especially on
the palms. Irk was put in mind of a washerwoman, and perhaps in
time this little girl would have grown up to be exactly that, a plump
babushka with grandchildren darting between her knees. Instead,
she was lying naked and dead on the bank of the Moscow, a few
hundred metres upstream of the giant al fresco swimming pool
which was open year round and where in winter countless heads
bobbed like white balls above a cloud of mist. Irk thought of the
lido as a giant baptismal font to wash away Moscow's sins. At one
time it had been the biggest pool in the world; he felt it was no
longer large enough to cleanse the city's evil.

Sidorouk was wearing a pink-and-yellow bandana. All he needed
was a large gold hoop in his ear, Irk thought, and he could have
passed for a pirate. "How's life?" Irk asked.

"How's death, more like. I prefer it when they bring in gangsters.
There's nothing on children that's worth stealing."

"The cops would have beaten you to it anyway. They smear vodka
on corpses' gums to loosen gold teeth, did you know that?"

"Know it? I *pioneered* it. And you? How's life with you?"

"Nothing new. Tell me what you've found, Syoma."

"Same as before. Minimum twelve hours in the water, can't
tell a maximum – but that's your responsibility anyway, you find
out when she was last seen alive." German Kullam could have
killed her before Irk had taken him into custody, Irk thought
wildly. If that's how the evidence fell, he didn't relish telling Lev.
"But look –" Sidorouk led Irk over to the examination table and
turned Raisa's head so that the right side of her neck was more
visible. Even through crumpled and distended skin, Irk could

clearly see what Sidorouk was indicating – a long knife slash.

"That's what killed her?"

"Almost certainly. It's the only injury which could have been fatal, and she didn't drown."

"So he cut her throat and then dumped her in the river?"

"In essence, yes. But it's not as simple as that."

"Why not?"

"Look at the cut. It's long, but precise. It slices through the jugular but doesn't sever the trachea. If you're going to cut someone's throat to kill them, the simplest way is to pull their head back and carve all the way across – take out their windpipe, stop them breathing. That's not what happened here. Even after her neck was cut, Raisa could still breathe, at least for a while. She died of blood loss."

"But you said last time that water makes post-mortem wounds bleed as much as ante-mortem ones; that you can't tell the difference between the two, in fact."

"Yes. But she didn't drown, so she must have been dead when she went under. The only way that wound could have killed her is by sustained haemorrhage."

"How long would that have taken?"

"Several minutes."

"And *then* he dumped her in the river. So he must have been with her while she bled to death. But if he wanted to kill her quickly . . . ?"

"He'd have done it another way."

"Which means he chose this way deliberately." A clumsy bashing on the head from some half-wit with hands shaped like a prick, Irk could understand. Even a ragged starfish gunshot to the head. But to hold a child down and cut her throat . . . *that* was unusual.

"And this could have happened to Vladimir Kullam too, yes?" Irk said.

"There's no reason why not."

"Anything else?"

Sidorouk picked up a pile of Polaroids and handed them to Irk. They were all of Raisa's corpse, leached even whiter by the flashbulb, before Sidorouk had cut her open to get at her internal organs. The photographer – one of the faceless assistants Irk had never bothered to meet, presumably – had snapped Raisa from what seemed like every conceivable angle. Whichever way you looked at it, Irk thought bitterly, she was still dead.

"There –" Sidorouk was pointing to a shot of Raisa's chest.

"Where?"

"*There.*" A mark, an incision, so bloodlessly faint against the skin that Irk wouldn't have seen it without Sidorouk's guidance. The cut was curved, a crescent; it looked like the swoosh logo on those counterfeit Nike sports shoes that were so popular in the open-air markets. It was also in roughly the same place as the T-shaped slits they'd found on Vladimir's body – the slits that were too neat to have been accidental. These marks must mean something, but Irk didn't have the first idea what.

He looked round the room. Sidorouk couldn't be faulted for his assiduous assimilation of top-flight equipment. His spectographs were German and his haemotypers Swedish, all gleaming as though they had just been pulled from their boxes.

"I want the works on this one," Irk said. "Every test you can run." He mimicked Denisov's voice. "There's no budget on justice."

"And there's no justice in my budget, Juku. In case you hadn't noticed, both commodities are in rather short supply."

Irk gestured at the electronic showcase. "What about all this?"

"Gifts from foreign police forces, the patronising shits. The machines are useless without their component parts, and guess what? I've got no funds, so I get no parts. They've been sitting like that since the day I got them."

No wonder they looked so new; they had never been used. Poor Sidorouk. Imagine being given a Mercedes 600 and not being able to afford the petrol, or a Bang and Olufsen without any recordings to play on it. "Haven't you asked Denisov?" Irk said.

"Hah! That miser wouldn't give you a snowball in winter. Says it's not his department."

Irk felt for Sidorouk, but his moans about equipment hardly made him a special case in law enforcement. Irk didn't have the capacity to run number plate checks or look up suspects on a computer database; Sidorouk couldn't do DNA testing or genetic fingerprinting. Same boat, different compartments.

"If you get anything," said Sidorouk, "it'll be in spite of my apparatus, not because of it."

"In that case, let me pick your brain. I presume *that* still works." Irk paused, trying to pick his words correctly. "This one here, and the one the other day – is there anything about them which might suggest the, er, the involvement of your people?"

"My people? You mean Chechens?" Irk nodded. Sidorouk sighed. "You that stumped for ideas already, Juku? Or perhaps I should be grateful that you held off asking until the second body, no?"

"It's not like that."

"It's always like that."

"No." Irk weighed up how much he could reasonably tell Sidorouk. "There could be a Chechen connection here – just trust me on that, Syoma. Could be, that's all. Mafiyosi."

"Don't look at *me*. I've nothing to do with those guys."

"You know people."

"Not mafiyosi."

"But you know people who know them?"

"And?"

"Just ask around. See what you can find."

"It won't do you any good."

Irk gestured at Raisa's body. "Nor will finding another like this."

Lev himself met Irk at the gates of the orphanage. After what had happened with German Kullam, Irk expected to be met with hostility, or at best indifference, but Lev shook his hand warmly.

"I can guess what happened at Petrovka," he said. "Don't worry, Investigator, I'm under no illusions about the kind of men Sabirzhan and Denisov are. I asked around about you, too. People think highly of you. You'll have no obstruction here, not from any of my people."

"Not even Sabirzhan?"

"Especially not Sabirzhan."

"And the internal investigation?"

"Is no longer his responsibility."

"I can't imagine he's too happy about that."

"That's not your problem."

They walked along freshly scraped paths which sliced between swathes of garden waist-deep in snow. In the summer, Lev said, there would be milky banks of cow parsley, greenhouses bulging with tropical palms and rare orchids, but at this time of year there were only trees buckling under the weight of snow balanced in rhomboids on their branches. One of the limes, a gnarled white patriarch with a lopsided trunk, was the oldest tree in the city, one of the few to have survived the fires of 1812. Beyond the walls, eight lanes of traffic thundered up and down Prospekt Mira.

The orphanage was an old Gothic building in dark red. Lev took Irk round the side and ushered him through a heavy wooden door. Irk found himself in a gymnasium where two teams of children were playing soccer with more enthusiasm than technique. They rushed around the room in swarms, kicking and pushing at each other, and occasionally the ball would shoot across the faded markings of the floor as though fleeing the mêlée, and off they all set in pursuit again.

"Children are our future, everyone knows that," Lev said. "Yet many are abandoned and left to fend for themselves. Self-reliance is an excellent trait, but it's dangerous when foisted on those too young to accept the responsibility. A few orphans rise above this and make something of themselves, but most of them, tragically, succumb to a life of fear and parasitism. Hence this orphanage. I burden the strong with taking care of the weak."

The ball found its way into the far goal, more by luck than judgement. Irk heard happy cheers and squealed recriminations. Sprawled on the floor beneath wall bars and ropes, the goalkeeper was making a point of blaming every one of his team-mates in turn. He'd go far, Irk thought.

"Our country's being overrun with drug addicts," Lev said. "Sport is the only means of saving the nation. We've taken the most robust of the neglected ones, and we'll build them up to be the nation's future superstars. That's why I'm setting up places like this and encouraging the love of sports – to divert young people away from drugs and perverts who'll pay them for sex. Those children who come here find it hard but rewarding: three hours' exercise a day, six days a week. I promise occupation and discipline, in contrast to the shameful neglect meted out by the state orphanages. As is so often the case, Investigator, private enterprise is doing the government's job."

A whistle cut through the hubbub: full time. Irk looked around to see who'd blown it; as far as he'd been able to make out, the only adults there were himself and Lev. When the whistle sounded again, Irk saw the referee and realised instantly how he'd missed him before. He had a man's face, thin dark hair giving on to long sideburns, and shoulders packed with muscle, but he was no bigger than his charges because, from the thighs down, he simply didn't exist.

"That's Rodion," Lev said. "That's who I want you to meet."

"Well done, everyone," Rodion shouted. "Good game. Tea's in fifteen minutes. I want you all showered and changed by then." He ruffled the hair of the nearest child. "Great goal, Kesha. Go on now, quick, quick – first ones to the washrooms get the hot water."

The children left at a rush. Rodion gathered up some books in a wide piece of cloth and hung it like a sling around his neck, then made his way over to Irk and Lev, moving fluently on his hands as he swivelled his torso from side to side. Irk thought of monkeys

112

swinging through the trees. Close up, Irk saw that Rodion was no beauty. Fleshy bags drooped beneath his small eyes and an elongated Adam's apple dangled like a pouch under his chin, suffusing his face with repulsion and sensuality.

"Rodion Khruminsch here runs the orphanage," Lev said. "Juku Irk, investigator with the prosecutor's office." Rodion extended a hand and gripped Irk's with more force than was strictly necessary. "You haven't told the kids about Raisa yet?"

Rodion shook his head. "Going to do it at tea; everyone will be there then."

"Good. That'll give you time to talk to the investigator. I'd like your mother there, too."

"His mother?" Irk said.

"Svetlana – she's headmistress of the school here. And Rodya's wife Galya is my secretary. Red October's a family, Investigator."

Lev excused himself; he had to get back to the distillery. Irk followed Rodion out of the gymnasium and into a matrix of corridors through which children ran shrieking until Rodion good-naturedly scolded them. He moved fast on his hands; Irk could barely keep up.

Svetlana was in the kitchen. She clasped Irk by his upper arms; her grip pulsed with fervour, as if she believed he could somehow deliver Raisa back to life. She wasn't exactly fat but somehow swollen, like a sack of grain. Her nose was large and looked distorted, and when she smiled she exposed teeth that looked too long for her mouth. She was fully made-up; her foundation looked as if it had been applied by a roadmarking gang, and her hair was shiny and black, like wet paint. It needed a sign, Irk thought, such as those advising people not to sit on freshly daubed benches.

When Irk looked closer, he saw she'd been crying.

"You'll have to excuse me," Svetlana said. "These kids are very precious, and this whole thing's rather hard. Rodya feels it too, but he's a man, he won't show it."

Irk sat down at the table and took off his coat and gloves. "I wanted to work organised crime, you know," he said. "I went to homicide because there was more chance of doing something good; everyone's too afraid of the gangsters. And look where I end up."

"Gangsters!" Svetlana snorted. "For you, maybe. For me, seeing what they do here, they're as honourable and decent as anyone else in this country. The real gangsters are the politicians and bureaucrats, the state criminals, who enrich themselves without helping children or the elderly."

Irk had been trying to make conversation and put them at their ease. Another partial success, he thought. "But have you ever thought about where the money for this place comes from? I could tell you things that would turn your stomach."

"Ach!" Svetlana hawked deep in her throat. "Who cares where the money comes from, as long as it's put to good use?"

"OK, OK." He held up a pacifying hand; this argument wasn't what he wanted at all. "Let's agree to disagree, and get on with it. What kind of procedures do you have here, to keep track of absenteeism?"

"It's not as easy as you think." Rodion's voice crackled with hostility. "Some of these kids are more or less wild; you can't just –"

"Rodya, he wasn't accusing you of anything." Svetlana put her hand over her son's, and her touch seemed to mellow him. Irk was grateful for her intervention. "Look, Investigator, there's no point keeping the kids here against their will; they come and go as they please. Those are Lev's direct instructions."

"He told me it was hard but rewarding. I'd have thought he'd take a much tougher line."

"Did you spend twenty years in the gulag, Investigator? No? Then don't talk to me about the rights and wrongs of locking people up. Like I said, there's no point keeping anyone here against their will. We take a roll-call every other day, as much for catering and administrative arrangements as anything else. Raisa wasn't at last night's register, or on Thursday; she *was* here on Tuesday. To be honest, we wouldn't have thought any more of it had it not been for Rodya."

"I overheard two of Raisa's friends talking in the corridor, wondering why she'd left," he explained. "She'd come and gone a couple of times over the past year or so, but she seemed happier these last few weeks than ever before. That's why they were surprised she'd gone, I guess." He made a moue; for the first time, his face softened. "Little did they know, poor things."

Irk looked at the clock on the wall behind Svetlana. Each time the minute hand moved forward, it first jerked slightly backwards, as if gathering itself for the leap. It was like Russia itself, Irk thought, where progress is never made without a retrograde step before and after. "What about security?" he asked.

"There are always a couple of guys from the 21st Century here," Rodion said. "But this is a big place; there's only so much they can do. Besides, which kid would have the courage to come in off the street or go back out there if the place was crawling with muscle?"

"Even after Vladimir was found, and Lev was worried about the Chechens?"

"That was Thursday, no? Raisa was already gone by then."

"And the Chechens?"

"Around here? None that I've seen. Mother?"

Svetlana shook her head, and then, almost as an afterthought: "Tell you what, Investigator, why don't you come over to our place for dinner tonight so we can talk about it some more?"

"*Our* place?"

"Of course – Rodya's, mine, and Galya's." Rodion lived with his mother. No wonder he looked so miserable. Irk began to protest, but Svetlana cut him off. "You're too thin, look at you. You need feeding up. You play the cuckoo, I bet." Playing the cuckoo means to live alone; the phrase comes from the cuckoo's habit of slipping her eggs into other birds' nests for hatching.

"Yes." Irk felt like a naughty schoolboy being reprimanded.

"And I bet there's no food in the house."

"Again, yes."

"I know your type too well – you're one of those men who think they can manage without women. Come, Svetlana will feed you up." She tilted her head as though to see him better; he was a good twenty centimetres taller than her. "Has anyone ever told you that you look like Keres?"

Paul Keres had been a chess grandmaster. Dead since 1975, but still just about the most famous Estonian in the former Soviet Union. Irk nodded. "Frequently."

"Good." She gave him the address. "Seven thirty do you? Don't be late. You stand me up and I'll come round and eat you."

The Khruminsches lived in an apartment on Preobrazenskaya, out in the eastern suburbs. Svetlana kissed Irk on both cheeks, took his elbow and steered him between walls covered in strips of adhesive brown plastic patterned with unconvincing wood-grain finish. Her forearms were massive, like a man's; in the stale light, the dark hairs on them crawled like centipedes.

Rodion and Galina were in the kitchen; Rodion sitting at the table, Galina jumping to her feet and greeting Irk with smiles and tinkling laughter. What was someone like her, so sultry and alluring, doing with someone as ugly as Rodion? thought Irk. And then he remembered the ease and warmth with which Rodion dealt with the orphans, and chided himself for his shallowness.

Svetlana guided Irk to a chair, shooing away the cat sitting there.

Irk saw a flash of blue as the moggy leapt to the floor and ran between them. *Blue?* A black cat running between two people was supposed to be bad luck, but . . .

"Blue, of course." Svetlana dismissed Irk's question as though it were the stupidest she'd ever heard. "No, it's not a genetic mutation. Lyonya's a pure-bred Archangel blue; very rare, very classy. The first recorded blue belonged to Peter the Great, did you know that? We moved here with them. A cat should always be the first creature to cross the threshold of a new home. All seven came in before us, so they should have given us seven times the luck. Hah! Tell that to poor Raisa. But they've all won prizes. Look –"

She pointed to rows of rosettes on the wall, bright colours splashed in serried ranks. Vladimir and Konstantin had won at Solkoniki Park; Nikita was the reigning Grand International Champion of Europe; Josef had triumphed in Kiev, Yuri in Saratov, Mikhail in Krasnoyarsk. Vladimir, Josef, Nikita, Leonid, Yuri, Konstantin and Mikhail, Irk thought; Lenin, Stalin, Khrushchev, Brezhnev, Andropov, Chernenko and Gorbachev. Svetlana was evidently one of the millions pining for the Soviet Union.

"They don't have to parade like dogs. They just have to sit still and look pretty." Svetlana beckoned Leonid back to her. "Look at their fur. If you brush it one way, it's blue; the other way, and it's silver." Leonid looked at Irk with big emerald eyes, his slender ears sticking up like chimney pots. Svetlana leant forward and tapped Irk's knee. "I'll let you in on a secret. You know what keeps them *so* blue? Vitamin pills and courgettes. And I wash them every other day in automatic laundry detergent. Some of them like it more than the others, of course; they've all got their quirks. Lyonya here, for example, needs vodka in his milk. Two months ago, he knocked a bottle of vodka off the kitchen table – whoops! – and licked the entire contents off the floor. Now he's become a raving alcoholic, and won't stop running around until I give him a couple of shots of vodka."

"Waste of good vodka, if you ask me," said Rodion. Irk had almost forgotten he was there.

"So," Irk said, "let's talk about Raisa."

Galina and Rodion had their heads close together, speaking in low voices as though their conversation was a litany of secrets. They looked at Irk and then at Svetlana. By some form of family decision, invisible to Irk's alien eye, it was Galina who was elected to speak for them.

"There *is* someone we think might be responsible," she said, "but it's difficult to say who."

"Difficult because you don't know?"

"Difficult because he's a powerful man, and he's well connected."

"Don't tell me it's Lev."

"*Lev*? Heavens, no – impossible!" they all chorused in union. "Do you have any idea what he's done for this family, Investigator?"

"Why don't you just tell me who you've got in mind?"

The Khruminsches looked at each other again. "This can't have come from us, right?" Galina said. "You understand that?"

"The prosecutor's office keeps its sources strictly confidential," Irk said, and caught himself. "Sorry; I sound like a pompous ass. Yes, I'll keep your names out of it. If need be, I'll fabricate evidence to justify further investigation."

"It wouldn't be the first time, I bet," Rodion said.

"You're right," Irk said equably. "It wouldn't be the first time."

"It's Tengiz Sabirzhan," Galina said, as though in the confessional.

Even among a people who pride themselves on their solicitousness towards children, Sabirzhan showed what some – the Khruminsches included, though they said they were by no means the only ones – felt to be an excessive interest in the school and orphanage. He was often round at the Prospekt Mira site, they said, though he'd no real reason to be – he didn't have a child at the school, and he wasn't officially involved with the orphanage. Of course, none of the staff there dared take issue with him. Rumours of Sabirzhan's cruelty and passion for torture preceded him like outriders. If nothing else, Sabirzhan was KGB, and the legacy of fear which those initials engendered was dying hard.

What had really convinced the Khruminsches to come forward, though, was the fact that Sabirzhan had a handful of favourites, and he was brazen in showering gifts and attention on them. Vladimir Kullam and Raisa Rustanova had both been among the "lucky ones". The tone of Galina's voice made it clear that she regarded such status as a mixed blessing.

"Sabirzhan was round at Vladimir's house this time last week," Rodion said.

"How do you know?" Irk replied.

"German told me."

"I interr— I questioned him. For hours. He didn't mention it."

Rodion shrugged. "And then Sabirzhan was round at the orphanage on Wednesday."

"The day before Raisa failed to turn up to roll-call."

"Exactly."

"We really shouldn't speculate as to what happened," Svetlana said, before spending ten minutes doing exactly that. Maybe Sabirzhan had tried to seduce the children and they'd resisted. Perhaps, not knowing the violence he was capable of, they'd threatened to expose him to Lev or someone even higher. Whatever the truth, there was something not right with the man, that was for sure.

Irk chewed on his lower lip. Sabirzhan had been keen to get Irk reassigned right from the get-go. His reasons had seemed plausible enough at the time, but his actions made even more sense if he was the guilty man. As far as Irk was aware, serial killers tended to confine themselves to one gender. Admittedly, his knowledge was scant; officially, there had been no serial killers in the Soviet Union, and therefore investigators had no need to study their motives and methods. Another triumph for totalitarian law enforcement.

They ate – chicken legs from the US, known as Bush's legs because imports had begun under the current Washington administration – and drank. As the evening progressed and the level in the vodka bottle diminished, so the conversation moved away from the case and everyone seemed to relax. Svetlana bustled around and flirted with Irk in a matronly way. Galina spoke enthusiastically of all the Western pop bands she and her friends were listening to, though of course there'd never, *ever*, be any group half as good as the Beatles. Even Rodion began to lighten up, rattling off a succession of jokes filthy enough to have made a tart blush.

They discussed how the city was being knocked off its bearings, forcing its citizens to fend for themselves, and agreed that their defencelessness was not only material, it was inner, psychological, a feeling of desolation. Moscow has always been a city of kitchens; great kitchens, to be sure, kitchens with the world's best conversing, drinking, schmoozing, seducing, plotting and (most importantly for any Russian) philosophising. With vodka, food, cigarettes and a handy guitar, Russians will settle down to swap stories, teach each other a few songs, and indulge in heart-to-hearts as only they can. Muscovites have always relied on this kitchen unity as a spiritual lodestar which guides them in difficult times.

Irk was enjoying himself. Even a man as content with his own company as Irk was could only be solitary for so long, and when he looked at his watch, he was astonished to see that it was gone one in the morning, too late for the last metro back. He could have gone into the street and flagged down a car – people were so desperate to make money that virtually every driver on the road offered himself as an impromptu taxi – but the Khruminsches were having none of it. There was a sofa-bed here in the living-room; he could take that, and they'd all go into work together tomorrow. Irk glanced at Svetlana to see whether this was her roundabout method of seduction, but all she gave him was a demure kiss on the cheek before disappearing into her room.

Irk liked to read before going to bed so he took the first book he saw from the shelf. It was Pushkin, of course; every Russian house has Pushkin, it's almost a constitutional requirement.

"What have you found?" asked Rodya.

Irk opened it at random and began to read. "The horses once again are riding: Jingle-jingle go the bells . . . I see: the ghosts are gathering amidst the whitening plains."

Rodya snatched the book from Irk's hands, slammed it shut and tossed it on the floor. "Ghosts!" he said. "Ghosts, from Afghanistan. How can I listen, when in my head the horse is an armoured transport vehicle, the bells are the clanking of its treads, and the white plains are yellow sand? I don't even have Pushkin any more, fuck it!"

# 22

*Monday, 13 January 1992*

Irk and the Khruminsches left the apartment on Preobrazenskaya just after seven in the morning. When they descended the stairs – the elevator was out of order, *again*, Svetlana said – Irk could barely keep pace; Rodion had the balance of a cat. Once in the street, Galina handed Rodion a small wooden trolley and a thick pair of gloves. He sat on the trolley, pulled on the gloves, and propelled himself along the pavement with strong, confident pushes.

"I've had enough practice," Rodion said, and Irk heard the bitterness in his voice.

Svetlana stopped to chat briefly with two janitors wrapped in padded jackets and orange hats against the grim freeze. Every winter, armed with snow shovels, twig brooms and ice-hammers, they and thousands like them battled to clear half a billion cubic metres of snow from the streets. Their struggle was a very Russian one: unceasing, mighty, and with the maintenance of normality its only aim – normality, in this instance, being open roads, passable pavements and roofs free from deadly icicles. Only in the summer, when their duties turned to planting tulips, tending lawns, sweeping litter and generally brightening up the neighbourhood, could anything as radical as improvement be considered.

Galina kept walking; Rodion kept pushing, weaving between cracks in the pavement and angled paving stones. Irk hesitated, unsure whether to go on with the youngsters or stay with Svetlana. He ended up walking by himself. Svetlana caught him up, puffing from the effort, and gestured angrily at her son and daughter-in-law.

"An exchange of pleasantries, that's all it is. Yet they have to make their point, don't they?"

Every Soviet leader since Stalin had used janitors as informers. Sly old women denounced their neighbours to the secret police or pointed out the flats which housed enemies of the people. Galina and Rodion were of a generation which knew change; they saw no reason to fraternise or ingratiate themselves with such people.

Two men in hooded coats were standing in front of Galina and Rodion, forcing them to stop. For a moment Irk thought that it was accidental, the kind of thing that leads to an absurd dance as both parties go for the same space two or three times before finally getting it right with laughing apologies. But when he saw the deliberateness of the men's stance, and the darkness of their skin beneath their hoods, he knew they were Chechens and this was trouble.

"Pretty girl." It was the taller of the Chechens who spoke to Galina. "You should think about doing some work for us." He used *ty*, the form of address usually reserved for intimates – unless the intention is to patronise or insult, as it was here.

Irk and Svetlana reached Rodion and Galina, and stopped. Passers-by swirled around the contretemps, shying involuntarily as they clocked the presence of the Chechens before pretending that they simply weren't there. Chechens engender fear wherever they go, and they know it; it's their bubbleskin, their forcefield. But Galina seemed not in the least afraid. She tossed her head as if in revulsion at a bad smell.

"I know my friends, and I'm sure I don't know you, so if you want an answer, it's *vy* not *ty*."

"It won't be much," the Chechen said. "Passing on some of the information that comes across your desk, that's all."

"Leave us alone, will you?" Rodion said.

Both Chechens looked down at Rodion as though he were an impertinent child. The derision in their stares flushed Irk with anger – worse, he thought, with shame and a vicarious pity.

120

"Did the cripple say something?" the smaller Chechen said.

"I didn't hear," replied his colleague.

"I'm a war veteran, not a cripple," Rodion snapped. "And I can still remember how to fight, so why don't you just let us past before this gets ugly?"

"You want to see ugly, my friend, look in a mirror."

"I'm an investigator with the prosecutor's office," said Irk, stepping between them, badge in hand. "I suggest that you scarper, unless you want a trip to Petrovka."

The Chechens glanced at each other. They were small fry, Irk saw; their boss wouldn't have sent anybody valuable to intimidate a secretary on a Moscow street. "Go on," Irk said. "Fuck off out of here."

"Think about it," the smaller Chechen said to Galina. "We'll contact you again." They melted into the crowd and were gone.

"My boys!' Svetlana clapped her hands and hugged Irk and Rodion close to her. "My brave soldiers, protecting their women!"

Galina's emerald eyes were shot through with rage. "How *dare* they?" she said. "On the street, in full view of everyone, with all of you here? Who the hell do they think they *are*?"

Rodion was silent. The Chechens' jibes had stung him, and he bristled with all the hostility Irk had seen last night. Irk realised now that Rodion's belligerence had not been aimed at him, the interloper, but at the world in general.

As for Irk's own part in the incident, well, it had all happened so quickly, but he couldn't help thinking that he, an officer of the law, should have spoken up a lot sooner.

They took the metro in from Elektrozavodskaya. Irk watched subtly and not without admiration as Rodion negotiated stairs, escalators and crowded carriages; not a ramp in sight to make his progress easier.

"Wouldn't prosthetic limbs be easier?" Irk said.

"Forget it. They're produced like every other Soviet product – to fulfil a quota, not to meet the needs of those who use them. All the ones I tried left me with dreadful sores or lesions."

Galina was going all the way to the distillery. Svetlana and Rodion changed trains at Kurskaya to take the Circle Line up to Prospekt Mira. Irk decided to stay with Galina. "I've got plenty of reasons to see Lev," he said. "Your name won't come into this."

She looked hard at him. Penned in by commuters on all sides and by the fur hat on her head, she seemed to Irk extraordinarily

121

alluring, a spirit of the steppe jammed into a cage that could hardly hold her.

Red October was in turmoil when they arrived. Normally, the workers ambled, walked or bustled around the distillery, depending how near the end of the month it was and how far behind their schedules they were. Today, however, a crowd several hundred strong had gathered beyond the filtration columns. They were shouting and gesturing at Sabirzhan, who was standing on a staircase and making calming motions with his hands.

"I tell you, the situation is in hand." Sabirzhan was having to shout to make himself heard over the hubbub. "I am personally investigating these regrettable incidents, and the perpetrator will be brought to book in the near future."

Once a KGB agent, Irk thought, always a KGB agent.

"What if there's another one, Tengiz Lavrentiyich?" someone shouted. "And one after that?"

"These are difficult times, I know. But," – Sabirzhan puffed as he searched for the right words – "but your patience is a great help."

"What kind of person are you looking for?" It was German Kullam speaking, up on tiptoes and looking twice the size of the wreck Irk remembered from Petrovka. "Someone like you yourself, perhaps, Tengiz Lavrentiyich?"

Sabirzhan recoiled as if he'd been pushed. Irk understood that the gasp which ran through the crowd was not one of disbelief at German's accusation, but of recognition that he'd dared say the unthinkable. Emboldened by their approval, German hurried on. "A man who enjoys torturing and killing – doesn't that sound like you? How do we *know* it wasn't you, eh? You should be on trial anyway, Tengiz Lavrentiyich, you and your friends at the Lubyanka."

A mass reckoning for the KGB was something many people – Irk included – favoured, but Irk knew it would never happen, if only on the grounds of practicality. Millions of people would be involved. Perhaps this was Red October's substitute.

"That's enough!" Sabirzhan was hopping around in agitation. "Back to your workstations, all of you!"

"We want an answer, Tengiz Lavrentiyich!" The crowd scented blood; they followed where German had dared to tread. "Come on, defend yourself against these accusations!"

"That *is* enough." Lev's voice rumbled like cannon fire. As he descended the staircase, the sheer force of his presence impelled

Sabirzhan to step aside. "The murders of Vladimir Kullam and Raisa Rustanova have struck a blow at the heart of the Red October family. I share your anger, German, and I feel the loss of those two children as keenly as if they were my own son and daughter. I give you my word that I will hunt down their murderer as if I were their father. I will move heaven and earth to find him, no matter where he is hiding, and I will make him pay. I know how difficult this is, especially for those of you whose children attend the school, but I ask you to put your faith in me. I have just this minute returned from Prospekt Mira, and the children are well guarded. Whatever fiend is committing these crimes, the discord I see here will only serve his purpose better. If you want to talk to me in private, my door is always open; otherwise I ask you respectfully to get on with your work. Thank you."

The crowd began to drift away. Sabirzhan sneered at their retreating heads. His salmon face was clammy with sweat, and he was breathing hard. "You see that?" he said. "The sooner you have me back on the case, the better."

Lev turned to him. "A word of advice for the next time you're tempted act the peacemaker, Tengiz: don't."

Irk sat in the canteen with German Kullam; a cup of strong tea each, and a severe dose of nerves for German. The canteen was three-quarters empty, but those that were there were only feigning nonchalance. Word had got around that Irk was an investigator. German looked about him as though working out which way to bolt.

"This isn't very comfortable for me," he said.

"I can see that, German."

"Couldn't we do this somewhere more private?"

"Why didn't you tell me about Sabirzhan?"

"What about him?"

"You tell me."

"How do you know there's anything to tell?"

"That's not what I asked. Vladimir was one of Sabirzhan's favourites, wasn't he?"

"You're not going to get me on this, Investigator."

"*Wasn't he?*"

German cast more panicked glances towards the four corners of the room. "Vova didn't ask to be. We didn't ask for him to be. Sabirzhan just . . . he just *decided*. He took a liking to Vova, and that was that. It's not like we could have stopped it."

"Are you afraid of Sabirzhan?" Irk smiled; soften, flatter. "It didn't seem so back there."

"No, I'm not afraid of him. Not . . . not when there's lots of people around, or even when it's just me and him, face-to-face, sometimes. But if I'd told *you* . . ." German looked down at his tea. "What would have happened then? You'd have ignored me, or told me not to try and pin the blame on other people. He's one of yours, Investigator."

"He's *not* one of mine. He's KGB. I'm from the prosecutor's office."

"Different names, same thing. Doesn't matter what you call yourselves, it all ends up the same."

"If you'd told me, I'd have questioned him – which is exactly what I'm going to do now."

"OK, Investigator, so you question him – then what? He's got friends in high places, hasn't he? He'll know I talked to you – there's probably someone reporting back to him right now – and then he'll really make my life a misery."

"You signed a confession rather than land him in the shit? I can't believe this."

"Then you can't understand how things work round here. Nothing personal, Investigator, but I wish I'd never met you."

"What more evidence do you need?" Lev asked. He ticked off the points on his fingers. "I tell you what Karkadann said. Vladimir was working at a kiosk run by the 21st Century. A couple of those black bastards threatened my secretary this morning on her way to work – and *still* you don't seem to take me seriously, Investigator."

"If I could find a Chechen connection, I would. If only so I could hand this case over to Yerofeyev and be shot of it. I want to get rid of it as much as you want to get rid of Karkadann. But all that's circumstantial at best. It's certainly not enough for me to start poking round the Chechen gangs. All that's going to do is piss them off and piss Yerofeyev off, and being pissed off is the only thing that makes Yerofeyev even more objectionable than he is normally."

"Then I'll have to deal with the Chechens myself."

"You will anyway." Irk saw Lev shrug slightly, conceding the truth. "The main reason I'm not convinced it's the Chechens is that another suspect has come to light; someone much closer to home."

"'Someone' as in German Kullam?"

"No. Someone as in Tengiz Sabirzhan."

Rule five of the vory code was that members of the Communist Party were to be despised – and never, Lev thought, had this been more true than with Sabirzhan. Oh, Sabirzhan seemed utterly innocuous at first glance, even given the ancestral suspicions of the brotherhood. His grey cardigan, pince-nez and big head reminded Lev of an owl, and his outward manner could be gently and abstractly benign – the amiable professor. Sabirzhan could speak better Russian than anybody else Lev knew, even though he was a Georgian. When he wanted to, he could wind his phrases through subsections, qualifications and subtleties, all hinting at the coldly precise brain behind.

But as Lev had got to know him, he realised that Sabirzhan was a man with no friends, only informers. Not for nothing had his fellow KGB agents christened him Dripping Poison. He heard everything, even the murmurs of love from a couple in bed and the leisurely conversations of his neighbours as they sat round their table. As for the shrieks of agony, he was so inured to them that he probably would have been awakened only by their ceasing, as a miller would awake when the millstone stops its creaking.

They had an accommodation, of course. It dated back five years, to the vory summit at Murmansk where it had been decided that Lev could take over Red October. The 21st Century had had the distribution and transport networks necessary to keep the distillery running; KGB involvement was the government's price for handing over control – essential if they were to keep tabs on their investment. At the time, Lev and Sabirzhan had found use for each other. Since then, however, power had shifted Lev's way. His empire was expanding; Sabirzhan's influence was on the wane. The one thing they still had in common was Red October and their interest in its successful privatisation. Because Sabirzhan's natural instinct was to reject the free market, Lev had offered him a generous stake in the auction. Lev knew that every man had his price, and that in the final analysis greed would always beat ideology. He also remembered the words of Don Corleone: keep your friends close, and your enemies closer.

But there was a limit. There was always a limit.

Lev thought of Sharmukhamedov strapped to the table and hung upside down by his hands. He thought of the glee with which Sabirzhan had gone about the torture. He thought of how Sabirzhan had chosen to spend New Year – the most historic New Year of their lives – inflicting pain on another man. He thought of all the times he'd gone over to Prospekt Mira and found Sabirzhan there. Lev thought of all this, and remembered something Sabirzhan had once said: Suspicions can only be proved, never disproved, because a suspicious person will not be satisfied with anything but affirmation.

* * *

Irk arrived at Sabirzhan's office to find it empty. He resisted the temptation to sit in Sabirzhan's chair and act as though he owned the place; instead, he stood by the window and let the gentle cadence of the distillery floor far below soothe him. There was little urgency in people's movements, and Irk thought he understood why. The Russian worker wants a place where he can talk about fishing, his wife, the hash the government's making of things, whatever – above all, a place where he'll be *understood*. He wants not only his colleagues but also his boss to accept him in this way. He wants work to feel like home; he needs time on the job to chat, time off the job for special occasions. The atmosphere he seeks is one of serenity.

Sabirzhan returned a few minutes later, shaking water from his hands. "First I come to you, now you repay the compliment," he said. "This could be the start of a beautiful friendship."

"I'd like to ask you some questions."

"About what?" Sabirzhan's tone was lightly curious; Irk could detect no defensiveness.

"About Vladimir Kullam and Raisa Rustanova."

Sabirzhan waved an expansive hand. "Anything. Anything I can do to help."

"I'd rather do it at Petrovka."

Sabirzhan was suddenly very quiet. His eyes simply weren't those of a human being, Irk thought; they seemed to be made of some yellowish resin.

"Do you mean what I think you mean?" he asked eventually.

"It's just a few questions."

"You have absolutely no idea, do you?"

"No, Tengiz," Irk said. "*You* have absolutely no idea."

"Lev will have your balls for cufflinks when he finds out."

Irk shrugged, and Sabirzhan knew: Lev was letting this happen.

No one has faith in the Russian justice system, least of all someone who knows its workings from the inside. Sabirzhan should have shouted and screamed. That was what Irk would have expected an innocent man to do. That was what he would have expected a *Russian* to do. Sabirzhan's anger, ice-cold rather than red-hot, was dangerously alien.

A squad car came to pick them up. Irk sat in the back with Sabirzhan and started counting the pimples on the back of the driver's neck. He gave up when he reached fifty.

"I've heard of you," Sabirzhan said. "Irk the incorruptible. Just my luck. Ninety-nine per cent of cops are on the take . . ."

"I'm an *investigator*, not a policeman," said Irk.

". . . and I get the one who isn't."

Irk bit down on his anger. In return for risking their lives the police were paid a pittance. Nowadays they didn't even qualify for special housing, even though many officers were from beyond the city limits and desperate to get their hands on a Moscow residence permit. So was it any wonder ninety-nine per cent were on the take? Only those with no alternative would take on such a thankless job with such low prestige, and the low quality of recruits in turn perpetuated the poor reputation of the force. Even the name by which they were known belied a reluctance to take the job seriously: in the Soviet Union the police had been the *militsia*, as if they were just a group of civilians working together. Only bourgeois societies had police, because only bourgeois societies had crime.

Irk could afford to be principled – he was a senior investigator in the prosecutor's service, paid just about enough to live comfortably – and having integrity was healthy for his conscience. Maybe it was the Estonian in him, he conceded, the civilised half-Westerner feeling morally superior to the primal Russian; but, if so, if he walked the straight and narrow purely to feel pleased with himself, did that vanity negate all the good?

An hour in Sabirzhan's company had left Irk feeling clammy. He put him in a cell and went back to his office, where he found a message from Sidorouk. The pathologist had asked around, and found nothing. Irk wondered how hard Sidorouk had really tried.

There was a large map of Moscow on the wall opposite the window. Irk looked at it, and saw something he'd never noticed before. As the river meandered through the city, it seemed to trace the profile of Mother Russia herself, the great lady in repose. The locks of her hair flow from the statue of Yuri Gagarin up to the site proposed for a monument to Peter the Great; the crown of her head abutted the Kremlin; her nose swelled beneath the Novospasskiy; her mouth pressed up against the Simonov; her bosom stretched beyond Andropovka Prospekt and down to Kolomenskoe; while her legs reached languidly out towards the east.

Irk wondered when Mother Russia would next cough up one of her children.

# 23

The meeting was scheduled to start at ten. Alice had hammered down the arrow on that, confirming it with Galina on three separate occasions. As it was, Alice arrived to find that Lev had been delayed.

"Annoying, huh?" Galina said.

"Not all men are annoying," Alice replied. "Some are dead."

Lev called her into his office just after eleven. She was alone, which not only surprised him but, he was loath to note, pleased him too. He made her wait for another hour while he went through his correspondence line by line. She'd known that he made every major decision at Red October; she hadn't expected him to make every minor one too. He refused to let even the most trivial of letters, payments, invoices or contracts be issued without both his signature and the imprint of the company stamp, of which – surprise, surprise – he possessed the only model.

Alice didn't let it get to her. She stood by the external window and looked across the river towards the eruption of onion domes which marked St Basil's, Russia's most famous symbol. Ivan the Terrible had built the cathedral with money taken from Kazan in 1552, and St Basil's eight domes symbolise the eight assaults Ivan's troops had been forced to make before Kazan had finally yielded. Even by Russian standards, Ivan's troops had been bloodthirsty, and yet from the carnage of their conquest had come this impossibly exquisite building, its cupolas rich in texture and shade. Alice saw the scales of a golden fish and a serpent's enamelled skin; the changeful hues of a lizard, and the glossy rose and azure of the pigeon's neck. It was no wonder that, when the cathedral was complete, Ivan had blinded the architect to prevent him from building anything so beautiful ever again.

"Where's Sabirzhan?" she asked, when he finally turned his attention to her.

"Sorting out some figures."

"That's more important than meeting with the privatisers?"

"I don't see your colleagues here either, Mrs Liddell."

She smiled: touché. "Harry and Bob are up to their eyes in background work. Besides, it's not as if any of them got the chance to say much last time."

He took it as it was meant, a peace offering, and shook her hand. "We start from a clean slate today, yes?" he said. "Let bygones be bygones."

"Well, if we argue again, you might find that I bite."

He laughed. "I'll take your word for it. Let's get things off on the right footing, then."

He sat her down and gave her two vodkas to taste. Russkaya had been filtered through birch-tree charcoal and quartz sand, and tasted of cinnamon. Alice preferred the Altai Siberian. It was sweet, rich and oily, smoothed with glycerine and lingering long on her palate, without a background burn worth mentioning.

Her skin was Elizabethan pale, almost translucent; he could see the veins beneath the surface, the blood pulsing through them, as though there was nothing to mar her beauty within or without.

He showed her how not to get drunk. "Smell the vodka first, take a sip and hold it in your mouth for a couple of moments. Then you swallow, and right after that you eat something. After every toast, a chaser; it's the beauty without which the beast is incomplete. Getting drunk is all well and good, but it's not the entirety of what vodka's about. If you equate vodka purely with inebriation, it's like saying love's the same as venereal disease."

Alice was unaccountably happy that Charming Lev had turned up, as opposed to Angry Lev. It wasn't just that she wanted things to run smoothly. Accustomed to dealing with adversaries she could manipulate, she had been caught off-guard by Lev. She had allowed him to goad her into losing control. If this privatisation were to happen in nine weeks she needed to maintain control. And since browbeating clearly wasn't going to work, charm seemed her best ploy.

For insurance, she'd brought a pin with her, which she held in her left hand. If she felt herself getting angry, she would jab it into her palm as a reminder to calm down. Not that she needed it to start with. Gently, gradually, as though she were massaging a lover, Alice worked on convincing Lev that privatisation was in his best interests.

As the subject of the inaugural auction, she said, Red October would secure better terms than those enterprises which came into the process later. Lev's foresight would also free him from the influence of apparatchiks, and give him access to Western capital, which in turn would help attract a strategic foreign investor. Society was changing, she reiterated; better to move with it and help shape it than stand, Canute-like, on the shore and be swept away.

"I despise the rationality and harshness of the new market economy," he said.

"Why? Russia's a harsh country."

"Yes, but it's not rational."

They went at it all morning, Alice and Lev, Beauty and the Beast; Alice's prettiness as Russian as her attitudes were alien, Lev a towering presence which she found unnervingly unreadable. He'd spent decades in the gulag, and now he was one of the most powerful men in Russia. She'd never felt so aware of and intrigued by someone. How long would she have to spend with him, she wondered, before she could fathom what made him tick?

"What I propose is that Red October has minority insider ownership," Alice said. When Lev tried to interrupt, she held up her hand, determined to assert herself. "Hear me out, please. Twenty-five per cent of shares go free to employees and managers. Another ten per cent will be sold at discount. Then there's a final five per cent which top managers can buy if they want. The remaining two-thirds are sold to the public at auction."

"That's totally unacceptable. It doesn't give the workers enough rights – not even close."

"What you mean," said Alice, getting angry despite herself, "is that it doesn't ensure that you retain control of this place." She jabbed the pin into her palm and imagined the ire draining out around it, as though her rage was a boil which could be lanced.

Lev shot Alice a look which took her a second to read. It was not that she was wrong in her assessment of his reasoning; rather, he was disappointed in her vulgarity at enunciating a truth which was tacitly and best left unspoken. She felt gauche, teenage.

"I'll make you a counter-offer," he said. "Insider control – management and workers combined – is set at seventy-five per cent. The remaining twenty-five per cent is offered for sale to the public, with a cap on how much any one individual or institution can own. Oh – and no foreign involvement." He tried to make it sound like an afterthought, but Alice knew better.

"*What*?" He hadn't demurred when she'd talked about Western capital earlier. To Alice, it was a no-brainer; American and European firms would bring expertise, cash, technology and access to world supply chains, and would make bidding more open and pricing more important.

"You heard me perfectly well, Mrs Liddell. Bidding must be restricted to Russians only."

"Why? Foreigners are already involved in the process."

"As advisers, yes; not as participants. In Poland, you planned national investment funds to manage and have equities in privatised enterprises, didn't you? And who was to manage these funds? Foreign firms. Foreign firms who'd gain control of Polish assets, who'd strip such assets for short-term profits, who'd sell off Polish firms at bargain basement prices or shut them down altogether. You must be a fool if you think I'm going to allow you to repeat that here."

It was ironic, Alice thought; it had been that very privatisation programme in Poland which had first introduced her to this kind of xenophobic paranoia. British Sugar and Peat Marwick had been accused of trying to destroy local rivals. The Polish accountants and lawyers who had helped Alice had been denounced as traitors; some had even received death threats.

"That's total flam," said Alice. "No one intends to take your country over or wreck your economy. Quite the opposite – Western business could be a great help to you, if you'd only let it."

"If I wanted help, Mrs Liddell, don't you think I'd have asked for it?"

Alice couldn't think of an answer. Trying to buy time and defluster her thoughts, she looked round Lev's office, and saw that it was full of presents: an engraved paperweight here, a picture with an inscription there. That was how people had expressed their appreciation in Soviet Russia.

"I don't see what's wrong with my original scheme, to be honest," she said at last, and cursed herself for how uninspired it sounded. "The free and discounted stock offered to management and workers is effectively giving you the option of a leveraged buyout through a no-interest, long-run state loan. With inflation going through the roof, this is a giveaway."

"For a democrat, Mrs Liddell, you seem very keen on trying to impose your will on mine."

"A democrat shouldn't compromise on the essence of democracy; a free-marketeer shouldn't compromise on the fundamentals of such an economy. These are extraordinary times. They'll only become ordinary after we've laid the foundations of democracy and the free market."

Irk had been in Sabirzhan's office since breakfast, blinds down and door locked. He'd waded through reams of correspondence, all written or annotated in Sabirzhan's neat handwriting, and found nothing. If he never saw that copperplate again, Irk thought, it would still be too soon.

Stretching his arms and blinking his eyes, he walked along the corridor to Lev's office. Galina leapt up from her desk the moment she saw him. "You can't go in there, Juku."

→ "Why not?"

"He's with the American woman who's come to do the privatising."

Irk understood perfectly. Negotiations were doubtless at a delicate stage, and of all the reasons to keep the murders secret, this was one of the most important.

Profit and loss, shareholder rebels, corporate raiders, bankruptcy – these were all alien concepts for Lev, and they made him afraid. The prospect of an annual shareholders' meeting whose remit included the election of directors, the appointment of the auditing committee and the company's reorganisation or liquidation was particularly unnerving. One man, one vote, he said. Alice tried to reassure him: the meeting needed to be attended by half of all shares; directors would be elected by a simple majority for a two-year term, at the end of which they could seek re-election as long as they were still alive; reorganisation or liquidation needed seventy-five per cent approval. It was one *share* one vote, she explained. One man one vote, he argued; one man one vote, even when she explained that under that system he'd have no more power than the humblest of his workers.

In the old days, Lev hadn't needed to know – and consequently wasn't interested in – anything other than what would help Red October meet centrally imposed schedules. Everything else had already been settled at levels high above him, in the upper echelons of central programming. Gosplan set the plan, Gostsen the prices, Gossnab distributed supplies, Gostrud decided labour and wage policy, Gostekhnika directed research and technology. The disillusioned referred bitterly to Gostsirk, the state circus which specialised in bureaucracy gone crazy.

This was why Lev knew nothing about marketing, finances, product quality, customer service or investor management – because such notions had never applied to him. A director's status and power were measured by how many employees he had under his direction. He didn't have to please legions of shareholders or consumers, to look nervously over his shoulder at the competition, or keep up

on current market trends and product innovations. He'd never had
to learn the language of the market.

They broke for lunch. Alice picked at the food Lev had laid out,
discovering with unexpected pleasure the way vodka brought out
certain flavours in sausage, dill cucumbers or pickled mushrooms;
flavours that she'd never known they possessed.

"Vodka's a wonderful drink," Lev said. "It's good with food, before
food or after food. Whatever anyone tells you, Mrs Liddell, remember this: there's no such thing as Russian cuisine, just things that
happen to go well with vodka."

Alice rang Arkin from a spare office and relayed the gist of the morning's debate.

"He won't budge," Arkin said when she'd finished. "You'll have
to go with what he wants. Most of it, at any rate."

"No way. Majority insider control, no foreign ownership – what's
that going to achieve, Kolya, except to swap one makeshift system
for another?"

"It'll get property out of state hands."

"And into the hands of Lev and a thousand others like him.
Where's the difference?"

"The difference is political. A new class of investor, a new kind
of stakeholder. That's what we need most of all right now. If this is
the price we have to pay, then it's worth it, it's a necessary evil."

Alice thought of the men in Washington, in New York, in Paris
and Brussels and Geneva and London and Frankfurt, all wanting a
piece of the pie. They had made their help contingent on Russia
treading an approved path. She felt the pin press into her palm
again.

"Just for now, just to get it through. We haven't got the time
otherwise," Arkin said. "You know how fast things change; it'll all
be different in six months' time. Don't sweat the foreign exclusion
on this one. There are still plenty of ways into the market: joint
ventures, trade agreements, consultancies, all that. Remember, the
last time property rights were transferred wholesale in Russia was
after 1917, and the Bolsheviks enforced that at gunpoint. We've
neither the means nor the will to do that. It's this or nothing, Alice;
and if it's nothing, then your work here's done, you can get the
next plane out."

And that was the bottom line, thought Alice. For all that Lev
teased and parried with her, it was Arkin, her ally, who'd found her

weak spot as surely as if he'd taken the stiletto knife of which he was so proud and plunged it straight through her ribs.

Sabirzhan's apartment was south of Kropotkinskaya, near the river in a district studded with foreign embassies fluttering bright flags from Africa and Asia. Irk checked the front door for KGB tradecraft: the strand of hair across the lintel, an item on the other side of the door which would be pushed out of position by someone coming in. It was a moment before he remembered that it didn't matter; of course he'd be searching a suspect's apartment, that was to be expected.

The place was almost preternaturally tidy, scored through with the yawning absences which mark a man living alone. Sketching the apartment's layout on his notepad – he'd have brought a Polaroid camera, if Petrovka's allocation hadn't all been sold on the black market by enterprising young detectives – Irk set to work.

A filing cabinet in the study yielded up the names of Sabirzhan's informers at Red October, and then some. There were almost two hundred of them, and each was awarded a dossier; some held only a couple of sheets of paper, others bulged with material. It was classic KGB stuff: records of payments made; transcripts of telephone calls; copies of informers' reports complete with grammar and spelling mistakes, all corrected by Sabirzhan as though he were a schoolmaster; and sexual peccadilloes desiccated by official prose. "Attempted intimacy with female employee Natasha R—, at our request, and was rebuffed." *Our*, Irk thought; *us*, the KGB, the power. There was a file for German Kullam, of course. Irk didn't recognise any of the other names, but he noted them down anyway. Should he tell Lev? Only if it proved germane to the murder inquiry, he thought, and chided himself for the ingenuity with which he achieved irresolution.

The workers; it always came back to the workers. "For thirty, forty years, we had a factory sanatorium by the Black Sea," Lev said. "We sent thousands of workers and their families there every year for their summer holidays. Now, even if they could afford it, they couldn't go there. It's Ukrainian territory, it belongs to someone else. Some of my staff go to their allotments, but that's a matter of survival, not fun. This distillery is my life, Mrs Liddell."

"You're a vor. You're a parliamentary deputy."

"I'd give the latter up before this, any day of the week. I know every inch of this place. There are five thousand workers here, and I know most of them by name. I don't like employing outsiders; I want *my* people to work here, I want to keep the factory a family business. Administrative procedures are nowhere near as effective in controlling people as peer pressure from their family and friends. That's why I only take people by recommendation. I don't have any problems filling vacancies; they're snapped up in no time. I *reward* my people, Mrs Liddell. I try to keep them fed. Red October owns two farms outside Moscow, and we sell the fruits and vegetables at subsidised prices. I'm proud of the apartments, the school, the orphanage, the sports complex, the cultural palace. How can I let outsiders take a stake in my company? How can anyone know better than me how to run operations here? Who knows the suppliers, the customers, the officials as well as I do? I make all the decisions. If I have to sack people, Mrs Liddell, I'll become a caricature of the evil capitalists they warned us about in school."

"You must at least consider the possibility of redundancies. There are ways you can hoard labour while reducing wages – pay freezes, direct cuts, delays in payments, reduced working hours, temporary layoffs with minimum pay, unpaid leaves of absence. In economic terms . . ."

"That's all you Westerners think about, isn't it? Economic terms." He'd snapped again; Alice was getting better at testing the boundaries, but she still couldn't tell when to pull back – or perhaps she should simply accept that she couldn't cross difficult turf without sparkling him off. "Well, this is Russia, and economics aren't enough. Have you been listening to me? I can't dismiss a man in his fifties or a woman with two children. I don't throw people out in the cold when they become old or tired. The workers wouldn't stand for redundancies, and I've neither the authority nor the power to implement such changes against their will."

"Oh, come on. You said it yourself: nothing gets done in this place without your say-so."

"Only as long as my say-so doesn't contradict the wishes of the majority. The manager is expected to be authoritarian, assertive, even inspirational – but he's also expected to understand and work with grass-roots feeling. An enterprise is a democratic institution. Everyone's entitled to have his or her voice heard, and even the humblest employees feel free to speak to the boss. If the manager stands up for his workers' interests, and if he exercises his authority with firmness and frankness, then he can count on the loyalty of his workforce."

"The more democratic he is, the more dictatorial they let him be?"

He smiled. "I couldn't have put it better myself."

She saw that this was his own benevolent dictatorship, strong but fair, a place that worked despite itself. Red October was a microcosm of Russia, in every way; and it would change just as the country was changing, Alice was sure of that. She wondered how much he was telling her about himself when he talked about Russia.

Alice left Lev with a final offer that he said he'd consider. Insider control – management and workers combined – would be set at fifty-one per cent, at a multiple of the defined enterprise value; twenty-nine per cent would be offered to outside investors; and the remaining twenty per cent would remain with the state.

At first glance, it looked as though they'd reached more or less a midpoint between their two positions, but Alice knew better. She'd conceded foreign exclusion *and* inside ownership. It was Lev who'd won this round, even before he'd agreed to anything. She felt drained, bitter and resentful – at Arkin, for making her negotiate with her hands tied, and at herself, for being weak enough to submit to that. When she gathered her notes up, she saw that they were speckled with blood, though she hardly remembered using the pin.

Lev shook her hand warmly when she left. She shied instinctively from his smile, wanting to believe that it was strictly crocodile, but when she looked again it seemed perfectly genuine.

There were books on Sabirzhan's shelves and rugs on the walls, but little sign of personal taste; it could have been a museum, a library, a hotel room. Only in the living-room did Irk find anything which smacked remotely of humanity: a photograph album, and even that was crammed on top of a bookcase as though best forgotten. Irk took it down and leafed through it.

There were pictures in black and white, Sabirzhan's parents perhaps, their clothes and the lack of spontaneity in their poses dating them as accurately as tree rings. There were some of Sabirzhan graduating from KGB academy, even then half a pace away from his colleagues. After that came Sabirzhan shaking hands with Brezhnev, Andropov, Chernenko, looking in the last two instances as though it was only his touch that was preventing the doddering geriatrics from falling over altogether.

The children were near the end. They covered nine pages in all, four or five pictures to a page, and each child probably appearing twice. Twenty different children, give or take; a lot of favourites for one man to have. Some had been taken at the orphanage or the

136

school – Irk recognised the backgrounds – others at Moscow landmarks such as Victory Park, where Vladimir Kullam squinted into
a pale sun, or the Chaliapin House. What struck Irk most, however,
was the uniformity of the expressions. None of the children were
smiling; most looked like they'd rather be somewhere else.

The last photograph in the album showed Sabirzhan himself,
sitting upright with a girl of about eleven or twelve on his lap. He
was smiling for the camera; she was in profile, staring away from
the lens. In the context of the album, it was an unremarkable snap-
shot, and Irk had to look twice before he saw two things. Firstly,
the girl was Raisa Rustanova. Secondly, she was pushing down with
both arms as she tried to wriggle off Sabirzhan, whose forearm was
tensed round her waist with the effort of restraining her.

Children know, Irk thought; children always know.

Alice walked the streets to clear her head, and saw that the economic
outlook was not universally gloomy, at least not on the main shopping drag of Tverskaya. There were three kinds of sausage in the
shops: kilogram sticks of the rubbery boiled flesh-coloured kind,
smoked salami, and pale link ones. There were eggs, frozen chickens, butter, cottage cheese, smoked and tinned fish, red caviar, soft
rose meringues in boxes and long beige strips of pastila sweetmeat.
No one was asking for ration coupons. Bookshops unable to cram
their wares on to shelves spilt them on to the pavement, spreading
the books across rugs. Alice rifled excitedly through the editions,
finding Agatha Christie and James Bond, computer manuals and
analyses of the USSR's collapse, translations of Smith, Keynes, Hayek
and Galbraith, Bibles, books on yoga and meditation, Sakharov's
autobiography – everything, in fact, apart from Marx and Lenin.

She took a wide arc through the back streets until she found
herself outside the old KGB headquarters: Lubyanka. What she saw
there stopped her dead. A line of people stretched for half a mile
or more, starting outside the Children's World toyshop, continuing
over the traffic mound where Feliks Dzerzhinsky's statue had been
so unceremoniously toppled in August (the decision to build the
toyshop here in the first place had apparently been in tribute to Iron
Feliks himself, who in true Russian style had combined the found-
ing of the secret police with chairing a commission on children's
welfare), and snaking all the way down the hill, past the Bolshoi
and into Red Square.

Even by Soviet standards, it was too long to be a queue of
shoppers. Alice went closer, and saw they were traders, sellers. They

were offering pens, brassieres, coats, shoes, kettles, perfume, vodka, food. They cradled their wares to their chests, or laid them out on filthy newspapers and upside-down wooden crates. Like protective body armour or some superstitious religious talisman, each novice trader had carefully clipped out from the newspaper the presidential decree on free retail trade and pinned it on to their heavy winter coats. A fortnight ago, they could have been thrown in prison for this.

It looked like some kind of firesale, but Alice knew better. She was witnessing the beginning of capitalism in Russia. Was she being melodramatic? She didn't think so. Perhaps it took a rare, imaginative gift to see the shivering huddled masses as harbingers of the entrepreneurial spirit. No, it wasn't aesthetic; nor was it seemly or civilised. But newborn infants aren't beauties when they first appear; only the parents can see what a gorgeous person will, in time, grow of that crumpled red creature. It was shabby and messy and amateur, but it was *there*.

Russia's nascent merchants came in all shapes and sizes: a young woman with glasses rubbed shoulders with an old man in a Red Army greatcoat; two *babushki* wearing headscarves chatted in low voices. Alice made for the nearest person, a middle-aged man holding a pair of pink women's shoes.

"How much do you want for the shoes?" she asked.

"Whatever you'll give me. I'm a teacher, I'm not used to this sort of thing."

"You'll never make any money that way," she said. "It's up to you to set a price. Decide what you think is fair and add a bit more. A buyer will start lower than what he thinks is fair. You haggle back and forth for a while and meet in the middle."

The teacher looked down at her feet. "Anyway, they're not your size."

Alice smiled at him and walked away, ecstatic. She knew that market economies always start from trade. When supply is limited and demand great, entrepreneurs concentrate on selling goods with high mark-ups – clothes, perfumes, electronics, liquor – and they do so in big, rich cities. Only when the market is reasonably saturated do they move upstream, from small-scale consumer production to heavier industrial manufacturing. That the traders were here at all confirmed Alice's view that men and women are natural, instinctive capitalists, and that – regardless of what Lev had said back at the distillery – Russians are no different from anybody else. The planned economy may have held back their inherent entrepreneurial ability, but it hadn't managed to quench their innate human desire and drive to take risks, accumulate capital and better themselves. These people would be the driving force for change in Russia, she'd have bet her house on it – until she remembered that she lived in a hotel.

# 24

*Wednesday, 15 January 1992*
Irk's car was still being repaired, and available squad vehicles were becoming rarer than teetotallers, so he took the metro again. Moscow had become a city of posters, he realised as he walked to the station; posters plastered everywhere, *everywhere*, on lamp-posts, trees, telephone boxes, walls, shop windows, even the metro itself, which the Party had boasted would never carry a single piece of capitalist advertising – but here they were, placards of a city trying to pull itself up by its bootstraps, shrieking about crash courses in economics and banking and computers and foreign languages, or selling flats and dachas and cars, no timewasters and no roubles, serious dollar buyers only.

There were two staircases leading to the platform. Like everyone else going down, Irk ignored the 'no entry' sign and headed for the staircase reserved for passengers ascending from the platform. This should by rights have caused a bottleneck, with the downward flow colliding with people coming the other way – but of course all the passengers coming up were using the staircase reserved for those coming down, again simply because it was marked 'no entry'. It was exquisitely Russian, he thought; superbly communal, breaking regulations purely because they were there, and flipping the system on its head while still making it work. A million minor contradictions somehow produced overall order. The biggest contradiction of all was when there was no contradiction, surely?

Irk hadn't seen Sabirzhan since he'd brought him into Petrovka more than thirty-six hours ago. This was deliberate. Sabirzhan was a professional interrogator; he'd probably forgotten more about extracting information than Irk would ever know, which meant that he'd know every resistance technique around. Irk had therefore figured that his best strategy was to be counter-intuitive. Even Sabirzhan might be put on edge by a day and a half cooling his heels, wondering what evidence the prosecutor's office were digging up. Now was the time for Irk to see if he could exploit such uncertainty.

He'd prepared a bare room for the interview, stripped of anything that might take Sabirzhan's focus away from him. Tables and chairs had been removed; there were no bookcases, filing cabinets or windows, no posters, maps or calendars. The walls had been repainted white, so there were no irregularities or damp patterns from which Sabirzhan could make shapes and faces. There would be one light: an ordinary desk lamp in the corner which would be barely bright enough for them to see each other.

Irk went to Sabirzhan's cell himself rather than send a policeman. It would be just the two of them, right from the start; that was the only way it could work. His reservoir of patience was inexhaustible. He would search for Sabirzhan's weakness, and if it was there he would find it.

Irk talked about himself to start with, to put Sabirzhan at ease. He spoke of his childhood on the small island of Saaremaa – a part of Estonia largely untouched by Soviet industry and immigration – and the fantastic medieval castle at Kuressaare where he'd played with his friends. He spoke of the wrench he'd felt when moving to the capital Tallinn, and how he'd clung to the fairytales of his youth by wandering the cobbled back streets of the beautiful Old Town on misty Sunday afternoons. He spoke of Moscow and the way in which it simultaneously energised and depleted him. He spoke and spoke, lacing his words with affability and self-deprecation, and watched for the moment when the habitual suspicion in Sabirzhan's eyes began to fade.

"I think we'll grow to like each other, Tengiz Lavrentiyich," Irk said. "I sincerely hope so."

Interrogation is usually a duel which ends in one of two ways: confession or acquittal. Irk was unusual in that he looked for something beyond either of those eventualities; he sought the truth. He wanted to find out *why*. It was not enough for him to say that this was Russia and these things happened. He wanted Sabirzhan to hand him his soul.

Irk told Sabirzhan that he'd found the pictures of the children in his apartment. He'd recognised Vladimir Kullam and Raisa Rustanova; the staff at Prospekt Mira had identified the others, and were keeping a close eye on them.

"I sympathise," he said, quietly to make Sabirzhan strain and concentrate to hear him. "It must be terrible to have a disease which society can't understand – won't understand, perhaps?" Even in the low light, Irk saw a bubbling of sweat at Sabirzhan's temple. "Let's face it, Tengiz, we don't live in the most enlightened country, do we? The law still classifies homosexuality as a mental illness; it's hardly going to push the boat out for child molesters, is it?"

He paused to let Sabirzhan answer, and went on himself when he received silence. "Are you queer, Tengiz? The person who's doing this, it wouldn't be surprising if they were queer. Society teaches homosexuals to loathe themselves, and self-loathing leads to destructive behaviour. If you *are* queer, Tengiz, you'd better tell me, and soon. You'll be classified as mad, not bad. You'll go to hospital, not jail; you'll be treated, not left to rot. You'll get life, not death. You must have seen the inside of prisons here, Tengiz. Imagine what they'd do to you in one of those, when they found out you were inside for slicing children open. They'd tear you limb from limb."

"You can talk all you want, Investigator," Sabirzhan said, "but I didn't do it."

He was still at the dead point of absolute denial. Irk had to get him away from that; he'd be in business only when he did. All he needed was the first yes, and the rest would come. It was like murder itself. Once a man has murdered, he has two choices: stick or twist. It's a strong man who can stick and still live with himself. Crimes mean secrets, secrets mean isolation, isolation means an urge to confess. Twisting is in many ways easier; the first time's the easiest. Once that barrier has been breached, the natural compulsion is to keep going, to kill again and again.

"Do what you want, Investigator, but you'll never get me to admit it, because it's not true."

Not true? Irk felt fury rise in him. The KGB had arrested tailors for making suits which didn't fit; they'd arrested musicians for playing badly at a concert and spoiling the evening for a Party grandee; they'd arrested teachers for giving low grades to investigators' daughters. They'd put these people in cells fifty centimetres square and watched them go insane – and Sabirzhan had the gall to talk about what was and wasn't *true*?

Irk only spoke when he'd let his anger ebb from him. "Do what I want? What does that mean, Tengiz? Do you mean torture? Of all the people I've ever interrogated, Tengiz, I've never hurt one. Electrodes on their genitals? Never. Pulling out their fingernails? Not me. Pentathol truth drugs? I wouldn't know where to start."

Two man, a bare room, a prizefight with their minds and wills the only weapons; that was where Irk felt most in the mix. He was a predator hunting prey, and when he was here he cared little for his reputation. The praise which came with success left him indifferent; he shrugged off the criticism which followed failure. He felt that Kipling would have been proud of him.

"What time is it?" Sabirzhan said.

They'd been there hours, though without any light from outside it was impossible to tell exactly how long or whether darkness had fallen.

"I've no idea."

"Look at your watch, then."

Irk pushed back his sleeve. "I took it off." He gestured to himself and then to Sabirzhan. "I'm wearing no more than you are, Tengiz. I'm sitting on the same hard floor you are, I haven't eaten or drunk any more than you, I'm hungry and thirsty like you. We're in this together."

"What a load of shit."

A knock on the door signalled food. Irk opened the door just wide enough to collect the tray. Two meat-filled pastries known as 'gastritis', for obvious reasons; two cups of tea; three hunks of bread.

"The Petrovka canteen is renowned throughout the federation for its haute cuisine," Irk said, but not the faintest trace of a smile disturbed Sabirzhan's fat cheeks.

They ate in silence. Irk left the third piece of bread for Sabirzhan. It sat on the floor between them for more than an hour – that was Irk's estimate, anyway – before Sabirzhan picked it up. He crammed it into his mouth with the frenzy of a man sliding down a slope.

Sabirzhan lay on the floor and closed his eyes. Irk couldn't tell whether he was sleeping or merely pretending; either way, he chose not to disturb him. The KGB manual would have counselled sleep deprivation for subjects as a matter of course. Irk would therefore do the opposite. The KGB had thrived on inhumanity; how better to subvert it than through humanity?

Sabirzhan began talking when he opened his eyes.

"Thou shalt not kill is a sanctimonious commandment, Investigator."

"Why so?" There was curiosity in Irk's voice; no excitement, no sense of triumph.

142

"The proletariat should approach this rule in strictly utilitarian fashion, from the point of view of class utility. Murder of the most incorrigible enemy of the revolution, murder committed in an organised manner by a class collective on the order of class rulers in the name of salvation of the proletarian revolution is lawful, ethical murder. The metaphysical values of human life do not exist for the proletariat, for whom there exist only the interests of the proletarian revolution."

"Zalkind," Irk said. *"Revolution and Youth."*

Sabirzhan smiled, thrilling and unnerving in the gloaming. "An educated man!"

"Are we talking about Vladimir Kullam and Raisa Rustanova here?"

"What do you think, Investigator?"

"What about the informers you keep?" Irk asked.

"What about them?"

"How do you select them?"

"Select them?" Sabirzhan snorted. "People queue up to volunteer, Investigator."

"For what reasons?"

"They want to serve their country. They want the money. They're angling for promotion."

"Do you promise you'll help them out?"

"All the time."

"And do you keep your word?"

"Things don't always work out, Investigator. People insist that you promise them the moon, and then wonder why you can't make good on those promises."

"But by that time they're working for you anyway."

"Exactly."

"They all sign the statements?"

"Of course." Sabirzhan began to recite the text; Irk had seen enough such statements to know how they ran. "'I, Ivanov, Ivan Ivanovich, voluntarily declare my wish to co-operate with the organs of state security. I have been warned of the penalties for divulging the fact of co-operation. I will sign the material I submit with the pseudonym 'x', followed by the date and signature. It's very necessary, Investigator. There are enemies of the people in all branches of industry."

"The system's finished, Tengiz."

"The system will *never* be finished, Investigator. You know why?

Because we're all involved. People bleat about how awful and unfair it is, but it couldn't have happened without them. Only men like Sakharov and Solzhenitsyn are exempt; they held out, and suffered the consequences. Everyone else is to blame. You let Sakharov and Solzhenitsyn suffer; you let it happen."

They talked like old friends; trading stories, arguing, putting the world to rights. Irk had split his mind in two, one half chatting away and keeping the conversation going, the other filtering everything Sabirzhan said for something he could work on, and finding nothing.

"It's a funny thing, Investigator. A year ago, I'd never have been here, being interrogated by you. The KGB was the power, everybody was terrified of us."

"And now they're not."

"Not as much; and they resent us because they despise *themselves* for having submitted. It's a hard shift to accept, Investigator."

He still maintained his innocence, though he admitted a sneaking admiration for the perpetrator. Not for the killings, of course – they were reprehensible – but for covering his tracks in a manner worthy of the KGB.

# 25

*Thursday, 16 January 1992*

Irk spent the night with Sabirzhan. They slept with their backs against the walls and their legs on the floor, like drunks passed out. They had neither blankets nor pillows, and when the bulb popped in their solitary lamp they had no light either. They took it in turns to fumble for the bucket which Irk had agreed to accept for calls of nature; and still, in their windowless prison, Sabirzhan did not confess, even when Irk said: "I'm your friend, Tengiz. Friends don't lie to each other."

Denisov himself came to the interrogation chamber and asked Irk to come to his office. Irk left the room on wobbly legs, screwing his eyes up against even the corridor's dim glow. Streetlights dropped amber pools through windows. "What time is it?" he asked, as he followed Denisov up the stairs.

"Half past seven."

"Morning or evening?" It would be dark in either case. Denisov stopped and looked round.

"Are you serious?"

"Perfectly."

"Morning." Denisov shook his head. "No wonder you look like shit."

In his office, Denisov sat down behind his desk without offering Irk a chair. Irk looked at a Soviet propaganda poster which showed Andropov opening a new school, and read the caption below: *Children are our only privileged class.*

"How are you doing with him?" Denisov asked.

Irk puffed his cheeks. "Slowly, slowly."

"Slowly's no good. Go get yourself tidied up, Juku, then either charge Sabirzhan or release him."

"You can't be serious."

"Do I look like I'm joking?"

Irk shook his head; Denisov and jokes were mutually exclusive concepts. "I'll have him in another week, no problem. Three days, then another seven, that's how we work, isn't it?"

"Not in this case."

"Why not?"

"Why do you think, Juku? Sabirzhan's KGB; he still has friends in high places."

"You let me take him in to start with."

"Yes, but now we cut him some slack."

"I thought I had ten days. I'd have done things differently if I'd known otherwise."

"Too bad. You know how it is." Denisov shrugged.

Irk did indeed. Power in Russia is a complex and mutable entity; Sabirzhan didn't have enough influence to save him from arrest, not when Lev had given his approval, but he had enough to ensure that he was released as quickly as the law provided. "Three days expires this afternoon, Denis Denisovich. I won't get him to confess in that time."

"Then you'll have to let him go."

Much as Irk wanted to will Sabirzhan into confessing, he could find no way in which to do it. His strategy had been predicated on time; time to lower Sabirzhan's guard, time to establish trust, time to wheedle away until he broke. Hurrying things up now, after a visit from the prosecutor-general, would only have alerted Sabirzhan to Irk's desperation and therefore to his own imminent release, and he'd have clammed up with the speed and finality of a Venus flytrap. Since he had to let Sabirzhan go, Irk decided that his best course would be to act as if he'd given up on him; send Sabirzhan on his way with the impression that Irk's interest in him was over, then see what he could dig up on the sly.

Sabirzhan went straight back to Red October. Lev poured him a glass of Russkaya.

"I'm not going to apologise for what I did, Tengiz," Lev said. "I had no other option. This thing needs to be solved, and I'll do anything to make that happen."

"You suspected me?"

"The prosecutor's office suspected you. I'm glad they let you go."

Sabirzhan shrugged. "It's no big deal. No hard feelings." His hand disappeared inside Lev's, a gesture of conciliation. "Really, none. The investigator and I had a good talk. He understands, you know."

"Understands what?"

"How difficult it is for a man like me to make sense of what's going on in Russia right now."

"For us all, Tengiz. It's happening, whether we like it or not. We must adapt or die."

"You had a good meeting with the American woman?"

"Very much so. I made her give up more than I conceded, much more."

"I'd have expected nothing less."

Lev searched Sabirzhan's face for insincerity or mockery, and found none. Sabirzhan seemed serious enough, though Lev would reserve final judgement for now. Lev had been used to thinking of Sabirzhan as a creature who swam in murky waters; now Sabirzhan seemed . . . well, *cleansed*, for lack of a better word. It was not what Lev had intended when he'd allowed Irk to take Sabirzhan away three days before; then again, it was not a result of which he disapproved.

The salt taste of disappointment grazed at the back of Irk's throat. First Denisov had made him extract a confession from a man quite obviously innocent; now he'd insisted on the opposite. Irk's job was hard enough as it was, harder still if his boss kept pulling the rug from under him. He should go up to Denisov's office and have it out with him, but what good would it do? Denisov wouldn't relieve him of the case; he was on it until he found proof that this was related either to privatisation or to the mafiya. Besides, every other investigator Irk could think of was incompetent, corrupt or both. All he could do was keep plugging away and hope for a break.

146

Irk's phone rang. He picked up the receiver. "Prosecutor's office."

"It's Galina Khruminscha here." Her voice was high, and she was talking fast. "I'm at the apartment. You must come, Juku, quick as you can. Something awful's happened."

The rain was falling hard, which made Moscow driving even more hazardous than usual, as did the fact that Irk had left his windscreen wipers at home. Wiper blades were in short supply – what wasn't? – and a vehicle left unattended with blades attached didn't remain that way very long. Intent on the traffic as if engaged in combat, hearing only the tearing of water under his wheels and the squeaking of his own horn under an insistent palm, Irk peered at the gondola flow of running lights and the melting of shop windows. In many ways, he reflected, driving without wipers was easier on the nerves; what he couldn't see couldn't hurt him.

The Khruminsches' front door had splintered at the hinges, and their living-room was covered in blood. Irk's first thought was that one of the family must have been injured – or worse – but they were all there waiting for him, and all unhurt.

That was as far as the good news went. Galina had her hands clasped to her temples, as though to keep her head from bursting; Svetlana was sobbing in heaving wet gulps; and Rodion's jaw was set into a snarl of masculine impotence at whoever had done this.

The cats were dead, islands of blue and silver in an archipelago of red. Lying on their sides, they could have been asleep, except for the slashes across their throats. Seven Russian blues, fed on vitamin pills and courgettes and washed every other day in laundry detergent; all with the life now drained from them. The prize rosettes on the wall swam as wreathes in Irk's vision.

"Fucking Chechens," Rodion said. "Fucking, *fucking* black bastards."

"They said they'd be back, didn't they?" Galina berated herself. "And I ignored them, I thought they wouldn't dare, and look what they did . . . Mama, they were your pride and joy, I'm so sorry."

Svetlana turned to her daughter-in-law. "It's not your fault, my sweet."

"She's right, Galya. You mustn't blame yourself," Irk said. He moved as though to hug her, but the gesture felt awkward and he turned it into a stretch of his arms. Galina sank to her haunches and hugged Rodion, kissing his forehead; Svetlana rested her head against Irk's shoulder.

147

"Let's clean this place up, anyway, and give them a proper burial," Rodion said.

"What about the police?" Galina said. "This is a crime scene, isn't it?"

Rodion belched a snort of derisive laughter. "You think the police would be bothered by something like *this*? They wouldn't give this the time of day, would they, Juku?"

Irk shook his head and flushed; he felt the failings of the force as his own. "I'm afraid Rodya's right. Let's clean this place up, and I'll find someone to fix the door."

The men shooed Svetlana and Galina out of the living-room and set about clearing the cats away. The first corpse flopped over Irk's hands as he lifted it from the floor into a plastic bucket; he took to grasping the others by the back of the neck, as if he were scragging them. Feline cadavers were no more appealing than human ones, and Irk tried not to look at them. The dull squelch as he dropped each one into the bucket was sufficient test for his squeamishness.

Rodion skidded on his stumps from blood lake to blood lake, soaking up the gore with cloths which he wrung dripping into the bucket before scrubbing angrily at the remaining stains. He worked with such a frenzy that Irk felt it best to keep silent; not that he felt much like chatting.

Even though none of them were hungry, Svetlana cooked dinner and pressed it on them. She bustled from table to kitchen counter and back again with salted salmon, telling them as she did so how it was best cooked: remove the small bones from the fillet, sprinkle with coarseground salt, let it stay at room temperature for three days and then serve.

Galina and Rodion were silent; Irk's appreciative noises at the food were drowned in Svetlana's incessant chattering. "I reuse everything rather than discard it," she said. "Stale bread goes to the guy along the corridor who keeps chickens at his dacha, milk that's gone bad is boiled and used for cooking, old jars are kept to store food." She even filed papers in colanders and sieves rather than drawers or folders, she said. Irk didn't try to shut her up or encourage the others to talk. He'd seen the shock that followed trauma many times. Everyone handled tragedy in their own way, and there was nothing he could do except be there for them when they needed him.

# 26

*Friday, 17 January 1992*

Alice was up to her eyeballs with work, Lewis was pulling long night shifts at the Sklifosovsky; breakfast was about the only time they managed to see each other. She'd got up an hour earlier than usual this morning and demanded that he not go to bed just yet – there was a fantastic apartment for rent in Patriarch's Ponds, one of central Moscow's more upmarket districts, and if they didn't move fast it would be gone.

"What do we need with an apartment?" he said.

"You like living in a hotel?"

"It's comfortable, it's clean, everything's done for us. Yes, I like it."

"It's not *ours*. I want somewhere that's ours."

"We've got somewhere that's ours."

"Back in Boston. Not here." She kissed his cheek. "Think about it – our own kitchen. You can make cush-cush till you explode." Cush-cush – browned cornmeal served hot with sugar and milk for breakfast – was another of those New Orleans dishes Lewis pined for when away from home. "At least come and look at it with me."

"All right, all right." There came a point in every argument when Lewis took the path of least resistance and backed down; anything for a quiet life.

The apartment was in a large, pale blue block on the east side of the square where the patriarch's pond, now singular, was located. There was little point in paying the premium for south-facing residences when half the year was winter. The realtor looked barely old enough to have started shaving; his suit was sharp and his shoes even sharper.

"Western *remont*," he said. "All fittings and furniture; Western materials, Western labour." Western *remont* was the best you could get in Russia. The next level down was 'semi-western' – Western materials with Russian workmanship – which was fine if you were prepared to risk the hugely expensive Smeg gas cooker squirting water everywhere because it had been connected to the wrong mains. Below that was simply 'Russian': poor build quality and shoddy workmanship with gaudy aesthetics to boot.

The apartment had everything they needed: two bedrooms, each with an en-suite bathroom; a kitchen, a living-room, a dining-room and a small annexe which could be used as a study.

"A lot of people are interested in this place," said the realtor. "It'll be gone by the weekend, that's for sure."

Alice went to the window and looked out across the square. This was where Satan had first materialised in *The Master and Margarita*, Bulgakov's classic tale of how the devil had caused havoc in the capital. Alice fancied that, if she looked hard enough, she could see Bulgakov's ghost, floating like marsh gas over the pond where the patriarch used to keep his fish.

Lewis came over to join her. "It's OK," he said. "Nothing special."

"It's perfect."

"If you're really determined to leave the Metropol, at least look at other properties first."

And stall, that was his thinking, she saw it as clearly as if he'd told her straight out. Alice loved this apartment because it was a home, something permanent. Lewis was happy to stay at the Metropol indefinitely, because hotels are transient, no matter how comfortable or how long the stay. An apartment excited Alice for the same reason it dismayed Lewis; she was beginning to belong.

"Lewis, this is fine. If I have to spend another week cooped up in that place, I'm going to go nuts." She turned to the realtor. "We'll take it."

Lewis put his hand on her arm. "That's not what we –"

"I knew you'd understand, Lewis. God love ya."


Timofei had just opened up his kiosk at Novokuznetskaya when the Chechens came back; Zhorzh in the lead, his bodyguards fanning out around. Zhorzh raised his eyebrows questioningly at Timofei: Have you decided whether or not to switch allegiance? Unnerved as before by Zhorzh's silence, Timofei's hesitation was answer enough.

Zhorzh leaned inside the kiosk, took two vodka bottles from the shelf nearest Timofei, snapped the tops off, and produced from his pocket two pieces of cloth. Timofei recognised them as the triangles Zhorzh had cut from his shirt the first time the Chechens had come, and he knew with sudden and complete horror what was going to happen. The fear seemed to be nailing his feet to the spot.

Zhorzh splashed some vodka on to the rags, shoved them into the bottles' necks, pulled a lighter from his pocket, set the rags alight and placed the makeshift Molotov cocktails back in the kiosk, nestling them as deeply among the other bottles as possible. Timofei, the power of movement at last restored, tried to push past him, but two of Zhorzh's bodyguards were pressing strong hands against his chest. They shoved him back into the kiosk and shut the door on him, locking it from the outside with the keys still hanging there; Timofei hadn't even had time to remove them.

The flames rippled, licked and caught at the neighbouring bottles, hesitantly at first and then boldly. The bottles were shattering now, little tinkling explosions until the whole kiosk was on fire, a flaming pillar on a Moscow sidewalk. Timofei kicked twice against the glass before going down, and the humane would have hoped that the smoke got him before the flames did.

Irk smelt of smoke and anger; smoke from the burning kiosk, anger because Timofei had been inside. He knew the Chechens were responsible, but the issue for Irk was whether the attack was tied in with what had been going on at Prospekt Mira.

He'd barely had time to consider his next move when a squad car pulled up and disgorged Yerofeyev's smugly corpulent form. Yerofeyev seemed more bloated every time Irk saw him, as though he sat on a bicycle pump when he went home.

"There's nothing here for you, Juku." Yerofeyev could have given a bull mastiff a lesson in territoriality. "You can go back to Petrovka."

Irk quickly explained his interest in the incident, racing to duck under the edge of Yerofeyev's notoriously short attention span. Yerofeyev clicked his tongue dismissively. "This isn't the only kiosk to have been torched today, Juku. We've had reports coming in from all round Moscow: four on Novy Arbat, two on Pokrovka, another three on Valovaya." Yerofeyev recited the names as though the burning kiosks were tourist landmarks. "So it's an organised crime case. On you go." He swatted a pudgy hand in the air before running it through hair slick with lotion. "Leave it to the big boys."

Moscow seemed to be crawling with policemen as Irk drove back to Petrovka. They reminded him of the Soviets in Tallinn under communism; an alien, occupying force, equally resented and feared by the local populace. No wonder the whole city drank. Every time Irk turned a corner he saw someone with a bottle to their mouth, a population of suckling babies. Before work and after work, at construction sites and on shop floors, in apartments and office blocks; liquid energy was everywhere, *everywhere*.

Irk parked between a Cadillac and a BMW – there were always a few foreign cars in the car park at Petrovka, on loan to the cops who offered their protection to Western auto dealerships. In his office, breathing from the walk upstairs, he ran a finger over his small Estonian desk flag. It was striped horizontally blue, black and white, to represent the sea, the land and the sky. He found the combination of colours soothing, which was more than could be said for the thoughts which chased round his brain.

The phone trilled. For Irk, its very ring carried the threat of bad news. "Prosecutor's office."

"It's Rodya. Another one's gone missing."

"From the orphanage?"

"Yes."

"One of Sabirzhan's?"

"She wasn't in the photo album. Her name's Emma Kurvyakova."

"How long's she been missing?"

"She wasn't at register yesterday morning, or today."

"And you only tell me now?"

"I told you, Juku: they come and go. The other night, when I told the kids about Raisa, I said that we'd be checking every day, and we'd start looking for them after twenty-four hours."

"Why not sooner?"

"Because then we'd spend every day trawling the streets, that's why."

"OK, OK." Irk didn't want to waste energy arguing. "Have you . . . ?"

"Yes, we've looked in the river, we're not stupid. No sign. There's more, Juku. I saw some Chechens hanging round here earlier."

"Where?"

"Just outside the main gates. Three guys, watching the place from across the road."

"Would you recognise them again?"

"I was a long way away." The underlying implication was clear: blacks all look the same. "You have to help us, Juku. You can imagine what this is doing to the orphanage. Some of the kids are terrified, crying and jumpy. Mama's beside herself, of course. Help us for her sake, eh? She trusts you, Juku; don't let her down."

It never rains but it pours, isn't that how the saying goes? Irk's life felt like a monsoon.

He went down to Kolomenskoe, thinking little and caring less about what Yerofeyev would say if he found out. Traffic was surprisingly light, and the journey took less than half an hour; too short, perversely. He was putting his head in the lion's mouth, and he'd expected more time in which to prepare himself.

Irk needn't have worried. Karkadann's house was like the *Marie Celeste*: a deserted, ghostly place, its emptiness mocking its splendour. The gates were tight shut and the perimeter fence unbroken, but there wasn't a soul in sight; no guards, no chauffeurs chatting by Mercedes limousines, no swarthy gangsters cutting deals. The lawns were buried under swathes of virgin snow, and the windows were dark behind their cardboard fillings. When Irk walked round the side, he saw Karkadann's bear lying on the floor of its cage, though he couldn't tell whether it was asleep or dead.

What use did a man have for all this luxury, when he'd killed his own wife and son?

Irk hurried back to his car and span it through a three-point turn with a haste that surprised him. The sense of loss and decay pursued him all the way back to the Belgrade Hotel.

There was the usual mix of types milling around outside the Belgrade – businessmen, gangsters, ordinary citizens – but they were divided sharply into two groups: those with the ability to open sesame, and those without. Russia was two societies divided by currency. Rouble Russia squatted in the ruins of the Soviet Union, immense, impoverished and angry. Above it was another world, elite, sleek and smart: Ru$$ia – dollar Russia, peopled by those with access to hard currency. Security guards kept the two sides apart; and, as at all the best parties, those not invited far outnumbered those who were. Hotels were like embassies now, accessible only to the rich and the alien; the doormen were there not to usher the elite in but to keep ordinary Russians out. The only natives to gain admittance were the most threatening ones, the kind who were accustomed to breezing straight through security.

The doorman at the Belgrade saw Irk, took half a pace forward and stopped, confused. Irk fell midway between all categories, and the doorman didn't know what to make of him. He wasn't a Russian, clearly – he was an Estonian, dammit, and proud of it – but equally, he wasn't a prosperous Westerner for whom passage was a divine right.

Irk flipped his badge, and the doorman retreated with a grateful smile; confusion spared.

The Chechens kept Irk waiting an hour while they discussed his proposal. Phone calls gave way to huddled conversations broken by suspicious glances in Irk's direction. Irk had brought a copy of *Moskovskie Novosti*, and read it from cover to cover while waiting for them to make up their minds. Shootings, muggings, nails in the coffin of hope; the newspaper was like his life.

Finally, two Chechens approached him, both bearded and both with AK-47s hanging casually from their shoulders. "Come with us," they said.

They took Irk down to the basement car park and shepherded him into a Land Cruiser. He sat in the middle of the back seat; the two Chechens took up position either side of him, unslinging their guns as they climbed in.

"You'll have to wear this," one of them said, handing him a blind-fold.

They let Irk tie it himself, but the vehicle only began to move when both his guards had tugged at the material to check that he really could see nothing. Irk tried to work out where they were going – up a ramp, left, right and then immediately left again – but it was more for the mental exercise than a serious attempt at remem-bering the journey, and it wasn't long before he gave up. The man to his right smelt of okra, and he could feel the barrel of the other's gun digging into his ribs whenever they went over a bump – about five times a minute, given the state of Moscow's roads.

"I hope the safety catch is on," he said airily, and received a resounding silence in reply.

They were on the road for half an hour, and barely stopped once. Irk wondered how many red lights they'd jumped. Only when he heard the engine die did he know that they'd reached their desti-nation. He waited for the guards to get out and shuffled along the seat, feeling for the exit with his legs. They took his arms and pulled him on to the pavement, not without care.

Inside; a corridor, to judge from the darkness behind the blind-fold and the echoing footsteps. Then a brighter haze, warmth, and a chair beneath him as his shoulders were pushed down.

"Take the blindfold off," Karkadann said.

The room was small and damp. Wallpaper was peeling off in fillets; there was a plastic table, metal chairs, a samovar. They could have been anywhere in Moscow, which Irk guessed was precisely the point. Karkadann was sitting opposite Irk, his chair turned round so he could rest his arms on the backrest. Zhorzh hovered like a vampire at Karkadann's shoulder.

"If Yerofeyev wants to talk to me, he can come here himself," Karkadann said.

"Then tell me something that lets me pass my case on to him."

"I've absolutely no idea what you're talking about."

"Vladimir Kullam. Raisa Rustanova."

Karkadann's face was unreadable. "Never heard of them."

"Vladimir worked at a kiosk on Novokuznetskaya." Irk looked at Zhorzh; Zhorzh looked steadily back. "One of those you firebombed today, in case you forgot. Vladimir attended the Red October school on Prospekt Mira. Raisa Rustanova was at the orphanage on the same site."

"'Attended'? 'Was'? You use the past tense, Investigator. These young people are dead?"

"And now another one's missing. You had nothing to do with this?"

"You think I do?"

"You want the Red October distillery."

"There are many ways pressure can be applied. We're bandits, Investigator. A bandit never pays out, only collects. Businessmen owe bandits, not vice versa. No one collects from me, *no one*."

"I know what happened in the florist's, too."

Karkadann turned his head slightly, acknowledging Irk's line of thought. If a man could shoot his own child in cold blood, what was to stop him killing others? Whether by accident or design, the light caught the trenches in Karkadann's face and painted them in deep shadows. He looked suddenly haggard, spectral; a man struggling to keep his dignity as he lost his humanity.

Irk understood. No more Valentina and no more Aslan, because Karkadann had murdered them himself; no more mansion in Kolomenskoe, because killing Ozers and the oath he'd taken had meant war on the Slavs, so he couldn't afford to stay in the same place all the time, no matter how well defended it was. He was a guerrilla leader now, hiding out and always on the move; all he needed was military fatigues, and the look would have been complete. Karkadann had brought all this on himself, but he still thought life had screwed him. He was a shell.

Irk felt a sudden urge to place his hand on Karkadann's shoulder and say that he knew; that bad things had happened to him too, things that had made him feel less a man than a husk, and there was no manual for learning to live with it. "I'm sorry about your family," he said.

"People will think it's us anyway, regardless of the truth." Karkadann's voice was shot through with bitterness. "Bloodshed's in our blood, isn't it? It's our nature; like vampires, *isn't it?* The wicked Chechens – that's what you Russians think."

"I'm no more Russian than you are."

"A fair chance, is that too much to ask? Clearly so, because it's something we've never had. My parents were born in Kazakstan." Irk knew instantly what he meant. Stalin had deported the Chechens to Kazakstan en masse in 1944; they'd only been allowed to return after his death nine years later, and every Chechen carried the shame and anger of that exile like a dagger. "For those denied a Soviet legacy – no money, no power, no connections – violence is the only way to make money. Do you know why so many Chechen towns are named Martan? It's the Chechen word for battlefield. Urus-Martan, Achoj-Martan – they're all scenes of great Chechen battles against the Russians. Let me tell you this, Investigator: it won't be long before my people start referring to this place as Moscow-Martan. This is our battlefield. This is where we will win."

# 27

*Saturday, 18 January 1992*
No matter how cold it was outside – up above, rather – it was warm down here in the sewers, and Irk's skin had turned into a giant sprinkler; sweat gushed from every pore, slickening the inside of his rubber suit and stinging eyes already squinting in the dim light. The policemen alongside him walked with exaggerated caution, arms held away from their bodies and legs spread wide; this was a strange new world, one in which they were cosmonauts. Irk himself could have been at a market or on a picnic for all that the conditions seemed to bother him; he'd been a veteran of the sewers ever since a metro driver who owed him a few favours had taken him for a ride in the cabin of his train. The gang of orange-suited women nearby were sombre and quiet, for sure, but that wasn't because of the damp or the fetid air; it was on account of the body they'd found earlier, the body over which Irk now stood as though he were a mother bear protecting her cub.

The body of Emma Kurvyakova, in fact.

At first glance, Emma had the pose of someone sleeping off a vodka hangover; flat on her back, right leg drawn up to her chest and left hand clasping the opposite shoulder, the kind of contortion that only the seriously drunk can maintain without discomfort. She even wore the grin of the stupefied, though the smile was plastered on her neck rather than her mouth – a slash across the jugular. The accretion of gas had made her eyes bulge but hadn't yet appreciably distended the abdomen, and her skin was unblistered.

The sewer water lapped at his ankles and sighed in eddies round Emma's head. Irk choked on his own rancour. He should have thought about investigating the sewers before. He'd spent enough time down here, after all; but with everything else that had been going on it hadn't occurred to him until now, too late for Emma Kurvyakova. He felt nauseous. A man hoped he was hardened to death, and in the blood-cloyed heat of a rancid sewer he knew that he was not.

Emma's body had been caught against a mesh screen gate at the point where the main sewer, which runs perpendicular to the Moscow River, meets the intercepting sewer, travelling parallel with the river. The sewage workers had found her on a trip to clean away the debris backed up against the filter: paper, rags, corks, sticks, leaves, vodka bottles, disposable nappies (which only the wealthy could afford), and laddered tights, all washed down drains or flushed down toilets – all, that was, apart from a girl's body.

There's an old Russian superstition that a murderer's image remains on the eyes of his victim. Irk aimed the beam of his torch at Emma's face, and instantly cursed his own stupidity. He was an Estonian, the most Western of all former Soviet peoples; he should have known better than to entertain that sort of peasant mumbo-jumbo.

"You went to see Karkadann?" Denisov said. "Then this case should go to Yerofeyev."

"No."

"What do you mean, no? I thought that's what you wanted."

"I do." Well, he had done, until it had become clear that the Khruminsches, and particularly Svetlana, were relying on him to solve the case. He didn't mention this. A personal motivation? Denisov would no more understand that of Irk than he'd understand nuclear physics. "But what can you do? Three deaths, and already we've had three separate suspects. German Kullam was innocent, that's for sure. Sabirzhan was still in custody when Emma Kurvyakova went missing. And Karkadann wouldn't give me a straight answer."

"So give it to Yerofeyev, let him deal with it."

"Deal with it? Forget about it, more like. Look at the facts, Denis Denisovich. Vladimir Kullam and Raisa Rustanova were two of Sabirzhan's favourites. How likely is it that the Chechens would choose them? One's coincidence; two is deliberate."

"Maybe they wanted to frame him."

"They'd need to know an awful lot about his habits to do that. Perhaps they have someone on the inside; but if so, why would they have bothered threatening the Khruminsches the other day? Everything about the Chechens is circumstantial. So I've been thinking. If we let the facts lead us to a theory" – *as proper police departments do*, ran the unspoken subtext – "what do we have? A repeat offender – a serial killer."

"Highly disorderly," Denisov said. He was, as usual, wearing hideous grey plastic Soviet shoes. Irk was almost tempted to buy the man a pair of decent shoes out of his own pocket, until he remembered all the kickbacks Denisov must be getting.

He told Denisov what he'd managed to ascertain. The filter screen, three-millimetre mesh, had been erected on Wednesday to stop solids clogging the duplicate inverted siphons which ran under the river. The body had been discovered during a routine check – miraculously performed on time – to ensure that the gate had been properly installed and the mesh was intact. Maintenance of the Moscow sewers is a perpetual job: debris must be jetted, flushed, blowboarded or rodded away, and there's a running battle with the highway authorities about excessive road grit dropping into the sewers.

It seemed that the killer had disposed of the previous bodies by bringing them into the sewers and letting the flow take them out into the river. The water was moving under the ice, of course. It had just been the killer's dumb luck that he'd jettisoned the corpses near the outflow from Red October: warm water brought things to the surface. If the killer had continued right up to the sewer junction he would have seen the new screen. That he appeared not to have known of its existence implied he'd been leaving the bodies further up the tunnels, where access was easier, and letting the stream of sewer water do the rest.

Either way, he must at some stage have been in the sewers with the bodies. Every sewage worker in the capital was therefore a suspect. Getting beyond that was the hard part. Sidorouk couldn't establish a specific time of death for any of the victims, so there was no mileage in checking work schedules and duty rosters; and even if there was, what good would it do, when people were marked down as turning up for work when they hadn't and vice versa?

Public works departments were just about the worst offenders in the culture of slack second-ratedness that the reformers were trying to beat out of Russia, and berating them about their ways was futile; you might as well tell them they couldn't drink vodka. Most of the sewer workers would be doing two or three jobs just to survive, like everyone else Irk knew. It was a wonder that anyone had time to eat or drink, let alone go round murdering children.

Except gangsters, of course. Gangsters always seemed to have time.

So Irk would check out the sewer workers. He would also need to go back over the lists the police had made of the hundreds who had access to Prospekt Mira: parents, suppliers, staff. An insider would have known who Sabirzhan's favourites were. But Vladimir Kullam hadn't been at school when he'd been killed; both Raisa Rustanova and Emma Kurvyakova could have left the orphanage before being taken. Sabirzhan had been in custody when Emma had disappeared, but not when she'd been found. He was still a suspect, that was for sure. Or maybe it was something totally unconnected, and the connection with Vladimir Kullam and Raisa Rustanova *was* just coincidental. The moment Irk thought of a solution, his mind sprouted a hydra of objections.

Irk had bribed the press officer Kovalenko to keep Vladimir's death quiet. Now there were more bodies, he wondered whether he'd been too hasty.

"Perhaps we should welcome publicity, Denis Denisovich, not hide from it."

"Absolutely not," Denisov said. "You know my views on this."

"People can't help if they don't know there's something wrong. If we release the news, maybe it'll jog someone's memory. They'll remember their neighbour behaving weirdly, or something."

"Everybody's neighbour behaves weirdly, Juku. No. I forbid it. The disadvantages of going public far outweigh the advantages."

That was reasonable, Irk conceded; what wasn't reasonable was that Denisov was still stuck in the Soviet mindset, which refused to acknowledge that such crimes could occur in the workers' paradise. There'd been no serial killers in the Soviet Union, not officially; serial killers were an abomination found only in the West, as were racists, gangs, whores and the unemployed. Criminals were a priori déclassé elements – Marxist for life's flotsam. These déclassé elements even had their own categories: Easy Morals, Drifters, Adolescents, Retards.

And yet, and yet . . . down in Rostov, Andrei Chikatilo was due to go on trial in the spring, and if anybody could shatter the myth that communist Russia had been quiet, predictable and law-abiding, it was surely Chikatilo. He was charged with fifty-two murders – fifty-two! – beginning in Brezhnev's day, and a greyer, more apparently normal man would have been hard to find. Chikatilo had children, grandchildren. He was a teacher, the quintessence of the man next door, and children had gone with him to the woods around Rostov again and again because in Soviet society children had been taught to obey adults without question. None of the adolescents Chikatilo had picked had been sufficiently independent to challenge or doubt him. Why should they? He was a kindly old uncle, wasn't he?

Chikatilo called himself a 'mistake of nature', but Irk didn't buy this. Like every Russian, Chikatilo's past dipped into darkness, and some of those shadows were now being illuminated. His brother had supposedly been eaten by starving peasants during the Ukrainian famine of the thirties, his father had been captured by the Nazis during the war and imprisoned as a traitor when he returned home, making Chikatilo the son of an enemy of the people – a terrible cross for a child to bear in Soviet Russia. Chikatilo wasn't nature's mistake, Irk thought; he had motivations, threads which patchworked together, just as the killer whom Irk sought would have, and Irk would need to unpick these strands before he could understand the man who left dead children in the sewers, and he'd need to understand the man before he could catch him. Chikatilo had eaten parts of his victims, but he was not an exception; he was an exemplar. As far as Irk could see, every Russian crime was cannibalistic to some extent; no people feed on and off each other more than the Russians.

Irk had too many questions and not enough information to answer them. Even if he did have the knowledge to hand, would he have the aptitude to use it? He was nothing if not conscious of his own limitations. The West, the decadent capitalist West, knew how to breed serial killers. Through necessity, they had also learned how to catch them. Moscow detectives had not.

"It might be worth considering bringing in outside help on this one," he said.

Denisov's eyes narrowed in a parody of suspicion. "What do you mean, 'outside help'?"

"The FBI? Scotland Yard, perhaps."

"You must be joking."

"They've repeatedly said they're happy to help if we need them."

"And I've repeatedly told them they can go piss up a rope."

"I'm digging up the ground with my dick on this one, Denis Denisovich. I need more than I'm being given if I'm to skim off the cream."

"You and Sidorouk, you're just the same – always blaming your tools, the pair of you. Everyone else manages, Juku, so why can't you? But no, you have to be different. Why do you assume the Westerners will be better than us?"

"They have more experience than we do. Much more."

"So would you if you had the crime they do."

"We *do* have the crime they do. Very nearly, at any rate."

"I'll tell you what they'd say – *nothing*, that's what. When they could be bothered to peel the whores off their cocks and crawl smirking out of their three-hundred-dollar beds at the National, they'd fob us off with revelations of the bleeding obvious: the killer's a man, history of mental illness and drug use, he's a loner, he's paranoid, he's probably fucked his mother, fuck your mother! He eats, he sleeps, he breathes, he drinks vodka. I could find out more from the damn horoscopes."

A vast map of Moscow covered the wall behind Denisov's desk. It was an old Soviet chart, and half the street names were out of date, changed since the August coup. Nevertheless, Denisov would still have this map in a decade's time, Irk thought, he was the kind of guy who'd always refer to Tverskaya as Gorky Street, Yekaterinburg as Sverdlovsk, St Petersburg as Leningrad.

"The FBI and Scotland Yard have an excellent record in solving –"

"I see where you're coming from, Juku, don't get me wrong. The only reason you even speak Russian is that you were part of the Soviet Union. Your alphabet is Roman not Cyrillic, you're Catholic rather than Orthodox. Deep down, you Estonians have always been Western, no matter how much we've tried to educate you. If you want to adopt Western ways, you've only to reach deep inside and recover a part of yourself, whereas I would have to go far outside myself, give up part of myself. You might be prepared to do that; I'm not. I went to Estonia on holiday last year, did you know that? To Parnu, by the sea. Lovely place – until the waiter threw the food in my lap, just because I was Russian. Estonians are chickenshit, all of you. What did they say during the Baltic uprisings? Estonians would die for their freedom – to the last Lithuanian. It's true, isn't it? Thirteen dead fighting the Soviets in Vilnius, five killed in Riga – and in Tallinn, a big fat zero. So I've had enough of all your griping about how Russia's shit and Estonia's so much better, how the kroon's pegged to the deutschmark and the rouble to thin air. I know all that. But I know this, too: Estonians live better and complain more than anyone else in the Soviet Union." Irk thought better of correcting Denisov's geopolitics.

161

"You're all whiners. If your precious Estonia is so wonderful, why the fuck did you leave?"

"You really want to know?"

"Unlike you, Juku, I don't ask questions for the sake of it."

"I left because my wife and best friend were killed. They were in a car crash, hit by a lorry on the road to Tartu. Imagine that, Denis Denisovich; imagine having to go and identify the bodies of the two people who meant more to you than anyone else in the world. Imagine then discovering that they'd been fucking each other behind your back for six months. What could a place hold for you after that?"

Denisov was silent; for once, Irk seemed to have got through to him. He went on. "So I asked for a transfer out of Tallinn. Where do you want to go? they asked. Anywhere in the union, I said. I'd had the Russian language forced down my damn throat since I could walk; I figured I might as well use it. They came back with three options: Magadan, Minsk or Moscow." Irk snorted. "That's the kind of choice they used to give you in the labour camps, isn't it? Do you want a bullet through the temple or in the mouth? So *that's* why I moan; because I had my country taken from me twice, first by you fuckers, the Russians, the people I hated, and then by Elvira and Mart, the people I loved. And when I left, where did I go? To Moscow, right to the heart of the enemy. Tell me that's not a *Russian* thing to have done."

Irk stood up and strode, almost ran, towards the door.

"Where the hell are you going?" Denisov's voice was agitated; a detective walking out on him would certainly count as disorderly.

"To the mountain to steal tomatoes, to the village to catch butter-flies. None of your business."

Irk stalked angrily from headquarters and down the avenue, past the statue of Vladimir Vysotsky, guitar slung across his back and his arms flung wide. Irk had seen Vysotsky play Hamlet in Tallinn in the late seventies, not long before his death; he'd been *electric*, his black-jeaned prince a lone voice not in the court of Elsinore but in the asphyxiating closeness of the Soviet Union. Hamlet was the archetypal Russian tragedy, Irk thought, because everyone died: Hamlet died, Ophelia died, Polonius and Laertes died, the King and Queen died. Hamlet's father *started* the play dead. Shakespeare should really have set it in Moscow. Irk wondered what Vysotsky, Russia's own bard, would make of this freedom he'd fought so hard for.

There were two people looking at the statue, a father and son.

The father was small with greasy hair; his glasses were cracked, and his cheap suit hung off him like sackcloth. The son was a replica in miniature. If anything, his clothes fitted even worse: the jacket was two sizes too big, and the collar of his shirt flopped from his neck. They looked like they were going out for the evening; it was probably the only time in the year they could afford to do so. Perhaps it was the son's birthday. Where were their coats? It was freezing. Irk wondered where the mother, the wife was. The possibilities – divorced, dead, separated – reminded him of what had happened back in Tallinn.

As they stood looking at the statue, the son turned to his father and wrapped his arms round his waist, clasping him so tightly that he knocked his glasses half off his nose. Irk watched them for a second, son with father, father with son. It was a moment of warmth to melt this cold, cold city, and Irk felt his eyes prick even as he remembered that Moscow did not believe in tears.

# 28

*Sunday, 19 January 1992*
Lev's penthouse was in the Kotelniki building, twenty-four storeys above the junction of the Moscow and Yauza rivers. The Kotelniki is one of the so-called Seven Sisters, Stalin's gothic skyscrapers which dominate the Moscow skyline like vast, layered wedding-cakes pock-marked with windows and girded with crenellations, their vertiginous spires topped by glowing ruby stars as they reach for the clouds. The Kotelniki aside, there's an apartment block at Kudrinskaya Square near the American Embassy; two ministries, Transport and Foreign Affairs; two hotels, the Ukrainia and the Leningradskaya; and the Moscow State University in the Lenin Hills.

Lev was brooding, and it was Karkadann who loomed spectral in his thoughts; Karkadann, the man who was surely behind the deaths of three children already; Karkadann, now in hiding and nowhere to be found.

There would be less to brood about, Lev thought, if he could comprehend more. As someone who had spent much of his adult life in prison, how could he hope to understand a hoodlum barely out of school who was already earning millions? It was like appointing a member of the Communist Youth to the Politburo. A man needed to grow, to accumulate experience; he shouldn't expect things to be his by right. Lev had worked hard to be where he was, he'd done his time – that was what being a vor meant.

Decades on, he still recalled with pride the words of the three vory who had sponsored his entry into the brotherhood (three sponsors, when you only needed two for the Party): "His behaviour and aspirations are totally in accordance with the vory worldview," they'd said. "He staunchly defies camp discipline and is practically never out of the punishment cell. His soul is pure, so let him in."

Let him in they had, rechristening him Lev, the lion. The name was initially for his flowing mane, but it wasn't long before it also stood for his natural leadership. He'd never used his birth-name again – there was no one left who remembered him by that name; he had no family but the vory now. After the initiation ceremony came the admittance tattoos – a dagger-pierced heart and a suit of aces inside the cross – the first of the hundreds which now swarmed his skin. News of his admission had spread through the gulags, from the harsh northern route of Vologda, Kotlas, Vorkuta, Salekhard, Norilsk, Kolyma and Magadan; down to Komsomolsk and Sovetskaya Gavan near the Mongolian border, to Bratsk and Taishet in western Siberia and the Kazakh hellholes of Karaganda, Ekibastuz and Dzhezkazgan.

Camp life was different once you were a vor. Lev was now entitled to a corner of the cell to himself, away from the door and the communal toilet where the small fry and homosexuals were forced to cluster. When Lev wanted to watch television, his underlings were made to pedal exercise bikes to ensure a steady flow of electricity; if he wanted them to take a fall for him, that was their duty. But he had responsibilities too: he couldn't lose his senses when drinking vodka, he had to honour his debts and, most importantly, he was charged with making and enforcing regulations, gathering information, organising prison life and taking necessary and sometimes unpleasant decisions. Without these, effective leadership was impossible.

Lev was jerked out of his reverie by the arrival of Juku Irk. It was the first time the investigator had been to the apartment, and he seemed suitably impressed. The ceilings were high, the finishings marble, steel and hardwood. The bar was topped with leather, and the carpet on which he walked – having first exchanged his shoes for the slippers provided for guests – was thick and white. On the far wall of the living-room, an icon sat atop a prayer: *O Mother Russia,*

164

*your role is sacrifice. No land like ours has been called upon by history. No land like ours has the deep will to respond.*

Lev gave Irk a handshake, a vodka and an armchair; Irk began to give Lev a précis of the investigation's process, but only got as far as his visit to the Belgrade when Lev interrupted.

"You went to see Karkadann?" Lev exclaimed. "Where is he?"

"They blindfolded me. I couldn't find it again if I tried."

"How was he? What did he look like?"

"What did he look like?" Irk considered the question for a moment. "Hollow."

"Did he admit responsibility?"

"He didn't give me a straight answer."

"For heaven's sake – it's so *obvious*."

"I'm keeping an open mind."

"You're keeping an empty mind, Investigator. I expected more of you."

"All right." There was only so much bullying a man could take. "Let's assume you're right. Let's assume that Karkadann *is* behind all this. Why not negotiate with him?"

Lev steepled his fingers. "You're an educated man. You know what Kutuzov told Napoleon."

"That was different."

"Not in the slightest." Lev quoted the great general: "'I should be cursed by posterity were I regarded as the first to take any steps towards a settlement of any sort. Such is the spirit of my nation.' And so it remains, Investigator. Even if I *could* get Karkadann to talk with me, what would be the point? In Russia, it's victory or defeat, nothing else will do. Feuding's bad for everyone, but the only way to peace is hegemony, and the only way to hegemony is by eliminating the opposition."

Irk had heard it all before. Russians may enchant with their arts and inspire with their courage, but horror, tragedy and drunkenness spiral through their genes. He finished his vodka and got to his feet.

"How can I help you, Lev, if you won't help me?"

# 29

*Monday, 20 January 1992*
Everyone in Russia knows there are only two certainties, death and taxes; but since no one pays their taxes, death is doubly sure.

Alice returned to Red October with a legion of short, matronly and ineffably formidable women: the representatives of every branch of the tax inspectorate – customs, bankruptcy, monopoly, pricing, and several more whose names and functions she hadn't caught – all supplied for her on Arkin's express order. Each inspector was accompanied by two armed tax policemen. Collecting taxes was a high-risk profession; most businessmen felt that evasion was their right, given that they were having to pay separately for protection services the state should have provided. Inspectors were frequently shot, beaten up, blackmailed, kidnapped, or found their offices and homes torched.

Red October's security force took one look at the raiding party and stepped aside, deterred more by the women than the men. Even Lev wouldn't take on a detachment straight from the Kremlin. The tax posse marched across the factory floor, where the workers seemed to be more industrious than on Alice's last visit, and into Lev's office – his door was always open, after all – brandishing demands for every tariff Alice had thought of and several she hadn't: VAT, income, profit, property, salary, municipal transport, export, import, garbage collection, ecological . . . Alice stood with her arms folded in the corner by the door. It was truly Marxist, she thought; as in Groucho, Chico and Harpo, rather than Karl.

Lev pushed his chair back from the desk and retreated across the room on its castors so fast that Alice thought he might plough straight through the plate glass of the internal window and down on to the distillery floor. He stopped just in time and held his hands up. "Enough! Enough! What's all this about? What about the energy giants? They owe *billions*, trillions even; far more than I do. Why don't you go after them first?" He pushed himself to his feet. "The tax I pay one month is gone, raised, lowered or superseded the next. Even if I *wanted* to pay taxes, I couldn't get anyone to tell me what I owe."

That at least was true, Alice conceded. She looked out of the external window, down at the traffic crawling along Sofiyskaya. As she watched, a pedestrian on the sidewalk raised his arm, and two vehicles dived for the kerb, one of them a police car. The drivers got out and began to argue as to who'd take the fare. From up here, the cars with their opened doors looked like insects, legs splayed either side of their bodies.

When she looked back into the room, Lev was smiling appreciatively at her. This time she'd dominated him rather than vice versa.

It was as if she'd flipped him on to his back and sat astride him.

"I'll do it," he said. "I'll let you privatise this place."

Lev escorted Alice to the sideboard by the internal window; it was just the two of them now, the tax dragons had all gone, mollified by promises of this and that. He offered her some Pertsovka vodka, nut-brown with red tinges. It contained infusions of cubeb berries and pepper pods, red and black. Touches of aniseed and vanilla played on Alice's nose when she sniffed it; it was surprisingly sweet on her lips, and as she sipped she saw Lev chuckling. Before she could ask him what was so funny, she found out as the aftershock from the pepper suddenly ignited on her gums and tongue.

"You could have told me," she spluttered.

"Here." His fingers brushed hers as he passed her a bowl of rice. "It'll dampen the fire. Besides, Pertsovka highlights the seasoning and nuttiness of rice. Vodka does that, you know, brings out the flavours in food. If you have herring and soured cream, the vodka melts the cream's richness and slices through the herring's oiliness. Or take caviar. Vodka promotes beluga's creamy, nutty relish, together with a hint of sweetness which recalls almonds and marzipan. The lightly fishy, brie-and-roquefort taste of oscietra becomes even smoother with vodka. And vodka softens the sea-salt flavour of sevruga, which can be a little harsh."

Alice felt absurdly enthusiastic in the face of his knowledge, as though she were a schoolgirl with a crush on Teacher. Watching him over the rim of the glass – a gaze which they both held a beat too long – she wondered whether his kiss would taste as explosively violent as the Pertsovka.

"I suppose there's no point in asking you to make beer too?" she said at last.

"Beer? *Beer*? Over my dead body. Beer's not alcohol, for heaven's sake. Have you ever drunk beer and felt like you knew the secrets of the world, felt like you understood love and art and music? Of course you haven't. Beer's a hangover cure, no more and no less." In Russia at least, this is true; supermarkets stack beer in the same section as they do mineral water and cola.

Alice's face was as red as Lev's, but in her case it was from laughing. "I was joking. I wouldn't want you to offend the Great God of Vodka."

When she looked back towards St Basil's, she saw the domes as vodka bottles. Vodka, not religion, was the true opium of the masses. She shook her head to clear the image, and when she looked again she saw the onion domes – Russia's other perfect symbol. Onions have multiple layers, and the more you peel away, the more you weep.

Lev was happy simply to shake hands on the deal, but Alice wanted something in writing. Not that an agreement was worth the paper it was printed on. Russians don't view contracts the same way Westerners do. With constant shifts in power a fact of life, Russians need to be free to renegotiate, modify, ignore, abrogate or apply conditions selectively – whatever the new circumstances dictate.

Worse, contracts mean legal agreements, and after seven decades of living under cruel, arbitrary and punitive legislation the Russian people have learned to consent in public and seek loopholes in private. Fundamentally, there are only two laws which have ever been recognised in Russia: one for the rich, the other for the poor.

Lewis was on the phone when Alice returned, jabbing angry fingers into the air as he talked. "Fat lot of good that'll do." He looked up at Alice. "Bob, gotta go. Alice has just come in. Yeah, talk to you soon." He put the phone down, but didn't get up.

"What's wrong?" she asked, slurring the elision slightly.

"Damn car's been stolen." A Mercedes mid-range sedan, unexceptional by American standards, bought two weeks before from a showroom on Novy Arbat. "From out of the hospital parking lot, you believe that? And not insured, of course, because we couldn't get insurance, because nothing in this country fucking works." The last two words came at a yell, and Alice took half a pace back; Lewis shouted about once a year. "Damn reds'll pinch anything that's not nailed down."

"Lewis, it could have happened anywhere."

"Anywhere? I haven't had a car stolen in twenty years back home. But the moment I come to Moscow, look what happens. Jesus. Might as well hand the keys to the nearest guy and invite him to help himself. *Jesus.*"

Alice went over and knelt beside him. He kissed her on the cheek, distracted and perfunctory, which annoyed her. "Lewis, please. It's just a car. We'll get it back."

"You think so? Who's going to get it back for us? You think the Russian police are gonna give two hoots for our stolen Mercedes?"

"The police, no. But I know a man who will."

"Who's that?"

"Lev."

"Oh, *Lev.* Lev will find the car for us, of course he will. Tell me;

168

has he agreed to privatise yet, or is he still jerking you around?"

"We agreed today." His expression didn't change. "Aren't you going to congratulate me?"

"Not when you smell like that."

"Like what?"

"Like you're drunk. Every time you go to that distillery, you come back drunk."

"Lewis, this is Moscow. *Everyone* drinks a lot. *Everyone*." She spun the word out, sing-song.

"I can't remember the last time I saw you turn down a drink."

"That's the way it is here. You go to a meeting, you go to a reception, they virtually hold you down and pour it in."

"Not where I work."

"Lewis, you work in the Skil. . . the Slik. . . – that hospital. It's not a business culture there. If I took all the drinks I was offered, I wouldn't be able to get up. I'm drunk, yes. Beautiful. So what? I'm your wife. I'm not an infant, I'm not a pet. I'm a functioning adult, and I can make my own decisions. Let me live my own life."

"And me? And *my* own life? Am *I* enjoying myself here? What do you think? I'm too old for this, Alice. I want a comfortable life in a civilised country with my lovely wife and my adorable kids. I don't want to be in a city where I'd be out of a job if people were sober. I don't."

# 30

*Tuesday, 21 January 1992*

Arkin bestowed his movie-star smile on Alice. "It's rather fitting, isn't it, that we're here to celebrate privatisation on the anniversary of Lenin's death?" he said.

Alice had already had three vodkas before arriving at Lev's penthouse. Tonight was a big occasion and she wanted to rise to it; there was no quicker or surer method than vodka, the cold rushing river which swept her away from the dangerous rapids of trouble and stress and into the calmer pools of happiness and contentment. A quick dab of the elixir, and gone was the gauche and tense Alice who always seemed to appear when she was least wanted. That no one else seemed to notice this awkwardness – Alice felt herself as adept an actor as she was a drinker – didn't make it any less real. With vodka came the Alice that everybody would love and want to know: confident Alice, funny Alice, mature Alice, sophisticated Alice, cynical Alice, a smooth operator who could thrive and survive in the asylum that was Moscow. The real Alice, she liked to think; *in vodka veritas*. Vodka was a liquid makeover from the inside out.

The party had brought together an eclectic mix of people, but then Alice would have expected no less of Lev. Arkin was with some men from the finance ministry, grey of suit and even greyer of face. Sabirzhan kissed her hand again, this time leaving behind a thin trail of saliva. Galina bubbled with excitement as she introduced Alice to Rodion and Svetlana, who pinched Alice's cheeks and told her she should forget that stupid American obsession with diet and eat properly. Lewis was more handsome than all the other men in the room put together. Harry had come with a date, not Vika from New Year's Eve but another Moscow vixen cast from the same impossibly blonde mould. Bob and Christina had brought their son Josh because there was, in Christina's spitting words, "no one in this damn city to baby-sit for us".

"No one you'll trust to do the job, you mean," Alice said uncharitably, though Christina's disgusted tutting revealed that Alice had been all too accurate. Alice sank to her haunches and looked Josh in the eye. "How old are you, Josh?"

"Six and a bit."

"When are you seven?"

"Soon." Against the white carpet his coffee-coloured skin looked darker than it was. "Do you want to hear a joke?" he said.

"Sure."

"What noise annoys an oyster most?"

"I don't know."

"You have to repeat the question."

"Oh. OK. I don't know; what noise annoys an oyster most?"

"A noisy noise annoys an oyster most." Josh burst out laughing; his smile was a split galosh.

Alice reached under his armpits and tickled him, which made him laugh even more. "That's a *terrible* joke," she said. "You deserve to be tickled all evening for that."

He squirmed in her arms and tried to tickle her in return, but she held him away so he couldn't reach her. He thrashed his arms in giggling impotence.

They were interrupted by the shrill tinkling of metal against glass: Lev, calling for silence.

"For a drinking-party like this," he said, "one shouldn't hesitate to slice the last cucumber. It's my house, my party, so I'm the toast-master. I'll start with an old favourite."

Lev waited while his bodyguards went round filling glasses. "Two-thirds full only," he reminded them. "Only Philistines fill to the top, because they don't mind spilling vodka down their shirtfronts. And this is good vodka – Kubanskaya, made by Cossacks in the Kuban lowlands, a little bitter. Everyone ready? Good."

Alice was aware that she was staring at Lev, and she forced herself to look away before Lewis noticed. Then she remembered: Lewis wasn't the jealous kind. Lev cleared his throat. "There are two types of vodka; good and very good." The audience roared their approval. "There can't be not enough snacks; there can only be not enough vodka." More laughter. "There can be no silly jokes; there can only be not enough vodka. There can be no ugly women; there can only be not enough vodka." Rodion and Harry catcalled; Galina and Svetlana gasped in mock outrage. Lev was working the audience, call and response, including them all in the process. "There can't be too much vodka; there can only be not enough vodka. The first glass is drunk to everyone's health; the second for pleasure; the third for insolence; and the last for madness. So – to your health."

Alice clicked glasses with as many people as she could reach, bent her elbow, assumed the expression of a Tolstoy character ponder-ing life and death, inhaled deeply, and drank her glass down in one gulp. Without question, she thought, the cold simplicity of vodka is an invitation to toss a glassful down the throat and wait, eyes water-ing, for the lovely blast in the stomach as the liquor explodes. Vodka lacks the subtlety of whisky and the bourgeois splendour of brandy, but in its craggy purity it stands on a peak of its own.

An oblong of tables in the middle of the room made an island of food. There was green sorrel soup with rye bread; silver-grey salted herring, its meat bright, succulent and soft; beet juice flowing through the diagonal cuts of onion bulbs sculpted as flowers; open cakes of cottage cheese and jam; and rose-shaped petals in cheese, cinnamon and poppyseed. Alice picked one of each, determined not to miss out on anything. Lev laughed.

"I *knew* you were a connoisseur," he said. "When it comes to mixing vodka with food, you can take the high road – caviar, smoked murlofish, veal Apraksin – or you can take the low road: herring as bony as you can find, and Ukrainian fatback, pink as a baby's butt. Both paths are equally worthy of respect. Whichever one you

171

choose, you'll find tomatoes, mushrooms, peppers, cabbage and sauerkraut. All are honest, upstanding chasers, as beautiful as any Grecian urn and as virtuous as a pre-Nabokovian teenager. You know why vodka goes so well with food, Mrs Liddell?"

"I've no idea." She cocked her head playfully. "Enlighten me."

"Because so many foods are suitable base materials for vodka, that's why. You can use anything with a starch content that can be converted to sugar: barley, rye, maize, wheat, beetroot, onion, carrot, apple, pumpkin, bread . . . even chocolate."

"Chocolate vodka. Imagine that." Alice whistled. "Two addictions in one." She looked around for Lewis, saw that he was deep in conversation with Bob, and beckoned Lev closer. "Can I have a word? In private?"

She found it impossible to tell what, if anything, was hidden behind his nod. He led her out of the living-room – a *troika* of body-guards started to move with him, but he waved them away – and into his study. Alice felt impossibly daring.

There was an old bureau against one wall and a green leather sofa opposite, darkened and shiny with age. The study led not only back to the living-room but also through to Lev's bedroom. Through the half-open door, Alice could see his bed. It was enormous, of course. Alice wondered who shared it with him. He wasn't married – Arkin had told her that wives were banned under the vory code – but there was bound to be someone. Or many someones; most Russian bosses expect their female employees to sleep with them as a matter of course.

She imagined him in that bed with his lovers, and jealousy jagged briefly through her.

"My car's been stolen," she said. "*Our* car. My husband's and mine." She felt it both absurd and necessary to emphasise Lewis' involvement, even though the evidence of her marriage was here on her finger and in the next room. Lev took a pad and pen from the bureau.

"Give me the details. Make, colour, registration number, where it was stolen from." As she gave him the information, he wrote in quick, jerky strokes. "No problem," he said. "Leave it to me."

"You're sure?"

"Of course. You'll have it back within the week."

"I'm very grateful."

He smiled, but his eyes gave nothing away. "I'm sure you are."

Suddenly and unusually, Alice could think of nothing to say; or rather, she could think of many things to say, but none of them seemed at all appropriate. Lev lit a cigarette, holding it along the length of all four fingers, the way workmen do.

"It's a great party," Alice said, cursing herself for sounding so prosaic.

"It's a proper Russian party, that's why. American cocktail parties are barbaric. There's nowhere to sit, nothing to eat, and they stop after one or two drinks. That's worse than torture. Parties are like sex – why start if you're not prepared to go all the way?"

"Why indeed?" Alice said, but she felt it sounded pompous rather than flirty.

There was another pause, even more awkward than the first.

"Your husband's out there," he said, gesturing that she should go ahead. She set her face into deliberate neutrality as she walked back to the living-room.

"Everything all right?" Christina said.

"Yeah. Fine."

"You were gone a long time."

"Who are you, Christina, the KGB? We had a few details to sort out, that's all."

"Details?"

"Yes, details." A childish defensiveness stopped her from telling Christina about the car; it was none of Christina's business what Alice was doing. "Shop talk, boring stuff about the distillery, stuff best done quickly and without interruption." Alice knew she was gabbling. Don't give so much information, she thought, it makes you sound guilty. "That's all," she concluded lamely.

Lev was nowhere to be seen. Alice understood and appreciated his delicacy; it might have raised questions had they emerged together, and such questions were . . . well, out of the question.

Josh was clinging to Christina's legs. "My ear hurts," he said. "*Still.*"

"I know, darling," Christina said. "Mom's trying to find something to make it better."

Alice felt angry sympathy for Josh. Few of the expats who came to Moscow brought their children. They thought the city was too rough and harsh for their offspring, which was ridiculous; Russians dote on children more than virtually any other people in the world. How many kids of his own age would Josh get to know here in Moscow?

"He's had earache for more than a week, poor lamb," Christina said. "You can't get any proper medicine in this place."

"Let me have a look at him," Lewis said. "I'm sure I've got some stuff at home."

"Medicine? For an earache?" Lev chortled. Alice hadn't even heard him approach. "You don't need *medicine* for an earache." He nodded towards one of his bodyguards, who went into the bathroom and came back with a wad of cotton wool. Sitting on the floor, but still towering over Josh, Lev soaked the wad in vodka and held it up in front of Josh's face. "This won't hurt, I promise. You trust me?"

Josh nodded, lips tight with determination. Alice wanted to hug him.

"Vodka?" Lewis' voice was thick with condescension. "What good's vodka going to do?"

"Which ear is it?" Lev said.

"This one." Josh pointed to his right ear. Lev pressed the cotton wool against it. He could have held Josh's entire head in one enormous hand. "Best cure in the world," Lev said, as Josh grinned up at him with the fearlessness that only small boys have for their new friends, no matter how outsize.

"That's ridiculous," Lewis said.

Lev bestowed a smile of beatific equanimity on him. "You don't need medicine in Moscow, Dr Liddell. Vodka's the cure for all known ills. Stomach ache? A glass of salted vodka. Flu? Peppered vodka and a hot bath. Fever? Rub vodka all over your body." He looked at Josh again. "You hold that in place for an hour, young man, and you'll feel right as rain. But whatever you do" – he lowered his voice conspiratorially – "don't drink it."

Alice called for silence. The guests applauded her; Harry whooped as though cheering a home run in the ninth. Alice turned to him. "I like you, Harry. You remind me of when I was young and stupid." She quelled the laughter with a smile and an upraised palm. "It makes me very proud that America, my country, is helping a great nation back to its feet," she said. The Russians clapped even louder than before, not least for the quality of her Russian. "So, on behalf of all my colleagues at the IMF, I'd like to propose a toast: to Lev's generosity in hosting this magnificent party, and to his guests' gratitude that he's doing so."

It was a good toast, eloquent and heartfelt, and they applauded her for a third time. When everyone had inhaled, drunk, exhaled, reached for some orange juice and chewed some herring, Lev raised his own glass. "To Mrs Liddell's beauty," he said simply.

Lewis looked proud. Alice glanced quickly, daringly, at Lev, and then away again, smiling as the guests cheered. But it was not the admiration of the crowd which intoxicated her; rather, it was the rapture of one. It was Lev who kindled the flame in her eyes, Lev who curved her lips into their bow of pleasure. She tried to restrain these giveaway signs, but they appeared on her face of their own accord. The blow had fallen. The room was crowded, but Alice felt as though she was alone with Lev. And if there was something terrible and cruel in his charm, so too was there in hers, and the uncontrollable radiance of her eyes and her smile burnt him as he drank. Every moment bound them closer, every moment suffused Alice with joy and fear as it pushed her nearer the gate of the unknown.

There were more toasts and still more, all of them accompanied by cries of *"pey dadna!"* – "Drink to the bottom!" One called for world peace; another for eternal friendship; a third for exuberance, enthusiasm, eloquence and grandiloquence. Alice was first to finish every toast and first to refill.

"The way that lady drinks," Alice heard Svetlana say, "her guts must be on fire."

"If they weren't before," Rodion replied, "they will be now."

Lewis touched Alice on the arm. "I'm going home," he said.

"Are you in a bad mood?"

"Not at all. Just tired. And sober."

Harry staggered up. "You should stay here and defend your wife's virtue." He gestured towards Lev. "I think he's got his eye on her."

"That brute?" Lewis snorted. "I hardly think he's your type, is he, darling?"

He was gone before she could answer, which was just as well. What would she have done – laughingly agree with him, betraying the bond she and Lev already had, or tell Lewis the truth: yes, Lev was her type, and it angered her that Lewis was too stupid to see that. No, not stupid – *complacent*, that was it, that was what tore at her. All Lewis wanted was an easy life, which was his choice. But what was life if it was easy? She felt sure Lev could tell her a thing or two about what it meant to really live.

Harry and Bob were singing, so out of tune that it took Alice a few moments to work out what the song was: "Sweet Home Alabama". Americans are loud, boisterous drunks. Russians are more serious, drinking until they fall with dignity, like trees. Alice realised she was the exception that proved the rule. She sat in a corner, cocooned in a fluffy vodka haze. Josh was asleep in her lap. She clasped her arms under his neck and felt his breath slide over her skin. Lev sat heavily down beside them.

"Are you drunk?" he asked.

"Just tipsy."

"Tipsy? The amount you've drunk, you should be paralytic."

"Hard head."

"A Russian's like a sponge, you see. You don't know his true shape until he's soaked." Lev pressed Alice in the hollow of her throat, taking what seemed like elaborate care to avoid touching her breasts. "Do you know why I agreed to privatise Red October, Mrs Liddell?"

"Because I brought the tax police in."

"No."

"Yes."

"Perhaps. Up to a point. But you have to look deeper, you have to *understand* – and I think you do, or at least you have the capacity to. You remember the first time you came into my office? You brought graphs, statistics, market research, forecasts, projections, this and that. None of it meant a thing to me. Russians don't trust figures or facts; to us, they've always meant lies. We respond to feelings, Mrs Liddell, *feelings*. We don't think like you do, therefore, we don't act like you do. There's so much about our psyche you must consider: our attitudes to money, our fears about being drawn into another ghastly social experiment, our anxieties about your motives."

"I can assure you, my motives are entirely honourable," Alice said, and was glad that they were talking for now of professional rather than personal terms.

"What does America's western frontier mean? Freedom and opportunity. But when we Russians look to *our* west, we think of invasion and terror. We remember Napoleon, we remember Hitler. Our suspicion of the West is . . . *ancestral*. You simply cannot over-estimate it. We're afraid that even the most innocuous statement can set terrible events in motion. You remember Gromyko?"

"Of course." Andrei Gromyko was the veteran Soviet foreign minister whose dourness had earned him the nickname 'Grim Grom'.

"Well, a Western diplomat once asked Gromyko whether he'd enjoyed his breakfast. Gromyko considered the question for hours, turning it over in his mind, examining it from every angle for hidden meanings, innuendos, dastardly capitalist plots . . . and eventually replied with a single word. You know what that was?" Alice shook her head. "'Perhaps.'"

Alice laughed. Not a polite tinkling laugh, but a throaty cackle which had Christina swivelling in remonstration. Lev looked from

Christina to Alice in amusement. "She doesn't approve of you," he said.

"She's got a banana up her butt."

"Such a charming son, too. She's one of those who looks down on the natives?"

"You got it."

"It's a common failing among your compatriots, Mrs Liddell. Always thinking you're best, and lying when you're not."

"*Lying*?"

"Armstrong. The moon."

"What *are* you talking about?" Alice couldn't tell whether he was being serious.

"Who put the first satellite in space? The first dog? First man? First woman? Who made the first unmanned lunar landing? We did, the Russians." Russians, not Soviets, Alice noted. "Sputnik, Laika, Gagarin, Tereshkova, Luna Nine . . ." Lev rattled the names off as though taking roll-call. "And yet we're supposed to believe that suddenly, on the hardest mission of all, the Americans turn it round? Tchah! You faked the moon landing, just as you faked all your so-called scientific discoveries. Who invented the light bulb?"

"Thomas Edison."

"Wrong! Alexander Lodygin. Who flew the first aircraft?"

"The Wright brothers."

"Wrong again! Alexander Mozhaisky, a full decade before. What about the radio?"

"Marconi."

"Alexander Popov – everyone knows that. Why else does the sun rise in the east and set in the west, if not as evidence that the Russians are superior?"

Alice circled her finger at her temple. "You've gone nuts," she laughed. She'd decided to assume he was joking whether he was or not.

"Do you respect me?" he asked.

"Of course I do."

"You're sure?"

"Sure I'm sure." Alice knew that the American imprimatur of recognition and respect is precious to all Russians, no matter how much they deny it. Russian serfs and American slaves were freed in the same decade, the 1860s, a time when the number of million-aires in Moscow and New York was about equal. It's the progress that both nations have made since then which makes the Russians so twitchy. The more threatened Russians feel, the more prickly they become. They show the same kind of backhanded respect to the Germans, the mortal enemy with whom they fought toe to toe on the eastern front. The Russians reserve indifference only for the little nations, the Frances and Britains.

"Good, because . . . because the Russian lyre has three strings: sadness, scepticism and irony. The sad fate of our country is to show the rest of the world how not to live."

"Huh? You were just telling me how great Russia is."

"Embrace chaos," Lev said. "Reconcile yourself to the loss of a few details. Hope that in the end it will all even out." He pushed himself to his feet and walked away before Alice could ask whether he was talking about the party, privatisation, or something else entirely.

# 31

*Wednesday, 22 January 1992*

Another day, another anonymous apartment, this time in an equally faceless high-rise in the northern district of Ostankino, a few blocks from the national television tower. Karkadann had arrived just before dawn, sneaking in under cover of darkness. His men stood guard discreetly but purposefully at all the block's vulnerable points: at the main entrance, on the fire escapes, and of course within the apartment itself. Karkadann sipped green tea and wished he was back at Kolomenskoe. This was no way for a man of honour to live, but the only alternative was to return to Grozny, and that he would not do, not while there were still battles to be fought here.

He carried Lev's image in his head. With every day and every fresh indignity, skulking from safe house to safe house like a fugitive, he wished more pain and destruction on his enemy. When it was all over, and he had brought Lev to his knees, then he would kill him – not before. Karkadann would take the agonies he was suffering and visit them on Lev, with interest.

There were shouts from outside. Karkadann saw alarm bloom on Zhorzh's face – was this it, had the Slavs somehow found where they were? – but the bodyguards were well trained, and none were running in to hustle them away. Zhorzh went to the edge of the window and peered out.

"Some kind of demonstration," he said.

In the street below, placards waved above crowded heads.

Karkadann joined him at the window and saw a poster of Borzov clutching a bottle of vodka in one hand and a naked girl in the other, with the caption *Happy New Year, life is getting better*. Fifty metres away, on the other side of the road, he could make out Borzov himself, and Arkin too. But it looked as though their gentle walk-about was turning into a near-riot.

As the crowd surged and jostled, the bodyguards recoiled and pushed back, movements like seawater finding channels on a beach. Some people lost their footing on the icy pavement. In the bitter air – it was seven degrees below – tempers were beginning to fray. A woman with dark roots and thick foundation appeared in front of the presidential group. "What are we supposed to eat?" she yelled.

"You can slice the president up," said Borzov, "but that won't last you long."

It was the kind of throwaway line he had been applauded for back when he'd been helping shoulder the Soviet Union to the cliff's edge. Now, it seemed callous and facetious. Arkin, who had been walking half a pace behind, moved forward, all but shouldering Borzov out of the way before he could say anything else inflammatory.

The president was accustomed to being received rapturously wherever he went, hailed as the heroic defender of a nation. Now, for the first time, Borzov was moving out of kilter with the Russian people. The reaction to liberalisation, Arkin thought, was proceeding faster than the process itself: from shock to trouble, via hope, in three weeks flat.

"You've misinformed the president, Kolya," Borzov hissed at Arkin. "You assured him that liberalisation was proceeding well and that the people were making the best of it."

Arkin had told Borzov no such thing, though saying so would be pointless. When Borzov was in a mood like this, there was no reasoning with him.

The bodyguards ushered them through the crowds and into the nearest store. Ostankino was dirty and down-at-heel, yet the shop would not have looked out of place on the Arbat. Its stone floors were scrubbed spotless, its paintwork was new and gleaming. The place had clearly been tarted up for their visit.

The store's owner, almost overwhelmed by the great honour being paid to his establishment, introduced himself as Artur Kapitonov, took Arkin's hand in both of his, and practically prostrated himself in front of Borzov. It was, he said, a compliment to have such eminent men in his humble store; they could take anything they wanted, on the house, it would be his pleasure.

Borzov was in no mood to be soft-soaped. He peered at the price labels on the shelves – six roubles for a loaf, sixty for a bottle of vodka – and snapped, "Is this really what you charge people?"

Kapitonov blinked furiously, as though he hadn't understood the question. The lines at the edges of his eyes, footmarks of an entire flock of crows, furrowed and deepened.

"*Is it?*"

"It's what the market dictates, Anatoly Nikolayevich," Kapitonov stammered.

"It's ripping people off, that's what it is. You will halve all these prices, *now*."

"Anatoly Nikolayevich, my suppliers already charge –"

"Then you're fired." Borzov turned to his bodyguards. "Empty the store, give the goods to the people." He cut short Kapitonov's protests. "You did say we could take anything we wanted."

Kapitonov could do nothing but watch as the presidential bodyguards cleared his shelves. Bread, biscuits, onions, cabbages, potatoes, eggs, poultry and vodka all went. Borzov led the guards from the store and beamed as he watched them wade into the crowd, where the merchandise was snatched from them before they could even start handing it out.

When the bodyguards, sweating despite the cold, had extricated themselves from the throng, Borzov asked how much cash they had on them. The president never carried money himself, of course. "Come on, come on," Borzov said, clapping his hands, "hand it over." He then plunged into the crowd himself, handing out sheaves of roubles to the startled protesters: a hundred roubles here, two hundred there, five hundred roubles to another. Those people whose hands weren't full from the previous giveaway could hardly grab the cash fast enough. It was all the bodyguards could do to pull Borzov back from the grasping hands when the last roubles had gone.

"Anatoly Nikolayevich, you can't go round doing that," Arkin remonstrated. "It runs counter to all prevailing economic policies. We can't conjure up cash from thin air."

"Anatoly Nikolayevich can do what he likes," Borzov said. "*Shef darit*." The Chief gives.

They piled back into the presidential limousine and were gone.

\* \* \*

Watching from his window, Karkadann shook his head. "How hard can it be to win the war, when that buffoon is Lev's biggest protector?"

Back in the Kremlin, Borzov slurped at his vodka. "This isn't a country; it's a mass of bruises," he wailed. "Ach, this whole thing is going to be a disaster. Is it too late to stop it?"

"Yes, it is. And you mustn't think like that, Anatoly Nikolayevich."

"But, Kolya, there's no precedent for this. No country has ever shed an empire, reformed its economy and developed a democracy all at once. And now it falls to Anatoly Nikolayevich to accomplish it all. The Russian people are in a different country than the one they knew, and they don't like it. And who are they blaming? Anatoly Nikolayevich, that's who. It's Anatoly Nikolayevich who has to mount the scaffold, Anatoly Nikolayevich who has to put his head under the fucking guillotine. It's all going to turn out for the worst, Kolya."

"You know what I'm thinking about?"

Borzov regarded him sullenly, a petulant child. "What?"

"Your plane crash last year. You remember the pain, Anatoly Nikolayevich?"

"How could the Chief forget it?" Borzov had been taken to hospital in Barcelona with a displaced disc. "It was horrible, impossible."

"Exactly. You couldn't move your legs. The doctors operated immediately, there was no time even to return to Moscow. The next day, they told you to get up and walk."

"And Anatoly Nikolayevich laughed in their faces."

"Exactly. If this had been Russia, you said, you'd have been in bed for six months. But they insisted: Get up and walk." Arkin lit a cigarette. "You looked round for crutches, and found none. Get up and walk. So you did. One step, another, the sweat pouring off you. You made it to the wall and back, and again, and again." Arkin exhaled a stream of smoke. "If you could do it, why can't Russia? We've hooked up market electrodes to the frail body of the Russian economy. We're rousing our paralysed system and making its vital centres work. We're dragging the patient off the bed and forcing him to walk."

# 32

*Thursday, 23 January 1992*

Lev was full of surprises, not all of them pleasant. If Alice had thought that the privatisation agreement – not to mention their behaviour at the party two nights ago – would suddenly turn him into a model of co-operation, it took him three hours to change her mind. The three hours, in fact, between the time they were supposed to meet and the moment he deigned to turn up.

"I know you're a busy man, but we're really pushed for time." Alice was careful to make her tone reasonable; she'd already run the full gamut of reactions to his lateness, from irritation to resignation via anger and exasperation. "Punctuality is . . ."

". . . a trait foreign to most Russians, Mrs Liddell." *Mrs Liddell*, still; it threw Alice. Hadn't they crossed some sort of bridge at the party? If so, why was he being as formal as ever? If not . . . Well, if not, she must have just been reading too much into something that wasn't there. She pulled herself back to his words. "You never lived under the old system, Mrs Liddell, when people had to wait five years for a new car and ten for a private telephone line."

"I see your point, but I still think you're full of shit." She smiled to take the sting from the words. "I've got another meeting back at the ministry starting in half an hour. Now I have to cancel it. I thought we'd be through by now – long before now, in fact."

"If you want to see two people in the same day, schedule one for early morning and the other for late afternoon." Lev was unfazed, even amused. "Find the most liberal estimate of time needed to do something, and double it. The fast stream never reaches the sea, Mrs Liddell."

Wasting time is a very Russian trait; it's how Russians remind themselves that life is more than just a series of goals and results spiced with numbers.

Lev tapped a bottle. "Here. Take some vodka with me."

"You can't soft soap me with that 'take some vodka with me' shit any more," Alice snapped, angry above all that he could rouse her to ire so easily.

Lev smiled. Alice wondered whether it was recognition of the effect he was having on her. "Ah, but this vodka is *very* special," he rumbled. "I'm trying out a new process, and I'd like your input. You've already proved yourself a connoisseur."

She twisted her wedding ring against her finger, pulling at the skin. "We don't have . . ."

"It's a new process of triple rectification. The first distillation takes the purity up to eighty per cent, the second and third to the high nineties. Try some." He poured her a glass. After a moment of resistance, Alice took it, sniffed, drank, and wrinkled her nose in disappointment.

"Tastes bad?" he asked.

"No, not bad. Not anything. Bland. Boring."

"Exactly!" He slapped his hands together. "It emphasises purity at the expense of character, that's *just* what I feared. Peter the Great loved triple-distilled vodka, you know. Maybe we need to dilute it with some anis, perhaps some other congeners too, because as it is, it tastes like Absolut. Typical Swedes – take the danger out of driving and the character out of vodka."

"Enough! I need you to give me the company books," she said.

"Why's that?"

"So Harry – my colleague, Mr Exley – can evaluate the strengths and weaknesses of Red October's commercial position."

"Why does he want to do that?" Lev looked genuinely puzzled.

"So we can show the public what kind of company they'll be buying into."

"*I* can tell them that."

"With all respect, you're hardly unbiased in this matter."

"You don't trust me?"

"Don't make this personal. It's not a question of trust."

"That's how it seems to me."

"What I'm asking is standard procedure. No one in the West would think twice about it," and then, catching herself, she forestalled his reply. "I know, I know – we're not in the West now."

The sewage system is divided into sectors, and individual workers tend to operate only in one, two at most; the legacy of Soviet bureaucracy and its mania for compartmentalisation was everywhere. Irk hadn't managed to find anyone with a working knowledge of the entire labyrinth, nor had he located a map of the sewers, or at any rate not a complete one covering the Moscow metropolitan area. The public works department had told him to try the mayoralty, the mayoralty had told him to try the water agency, the water agency had told him to try the public works department. Everyone he'd spoken to had been sure that there was a map somewhere, or at least there *had* been once upon a time, *But you know how it is, Investigator* . . . Thousands upon thousands of documents had been lost in a transition so chaotic that people would have mislaid their heads if they hadn't been screwed on. Even the offer of a half-litre of Eesti Viin had no effect. The map really was nowhere to be found.

Not that it mattered. Irk reckoned that he knew the sewers as well as anybody. He'd spent countless hours down there, hooked from the moment he'd first seen the metro tunnels from the train cabin. That was how it had started: by memorising the configurations and conjunctions of all the different lines, he'd come to know every dip and dogleg in the track, learning the lie of the city from the bowels up. He'd gone beneath the metro platforms and got into the machinery that drives those massive escalators. Then he'd followed the municipal service tunnels and the ventilator shafts, just to see where they led. Stuck in a sprawling grey city without friends, where else was there to go but down? It was his version of rebellion, a private obsession which didn't count because it took place in the reverse world. He'd never mentioned it to any of his colleagues.

Irk splashed through the subterranean labyrinth. He walked down a trunk sewer where two or more channels came together, the pipes stretching high and wide around him, freeways of waste, before veering off down a side duct so low and narrow that he had to lie on his stomach and crawl through, his nose and mouth inches from illegally dumped chemical refuse, petroleum spirit and calcium carbide. He flicked a butane lighter and checked the flame, looking for a slight orange tinge which might indicate trace levels of natural gas. The pipelines climbed and dipped, twisted and went straight, now following the contours of the ground above, now swerving round cellars and mains lines, now kinking to make room for a drain outlet.

And always there was water, dripping through cracks in the brickwork, racing itself through the conduits, making sodden sounds and soggy noises. Ancient underground rivers burrowed through the city, blind and unseen currents with lost directions. Sometimes half the basements in Moscow cried. Beyond the constant chords of water, Irk could hear a low chattering: human voices. People made homes for themselves here, complete with chairs and sofas, bare bulbs, stoves, vodka bottles. They set up camp by hot-water pipes, for the warmth; and sometimes those pipes burst and boiled alive anyone who happened to be nearby.

Irk was ostensibly looking for clues, but he'd have been down here even if not for Emma Kurvyakova. He wasn't sure what he was looking for, only that he was looking. Through the alkalic twilight came more sounds: the movements of sex. There were plenty of places down here where people could screw without fear of disturbance, certainly more than there were up above. Young Muscovites had few ways of testing their feelings. There was nowhere to meet for romance, to flirt and learn about making out; apartments were small and offered little privacy, restaurants and hotels were too expensive, few people could afford to own cars, and bars and discos were only for the rich. No wonder people came down here to fuck.

The tunnels were shaped like eggs. Irk had to walk with one foot on each slope, as though he was hoofing along a ditch, and his ankles ached. A white fungus slicked across the walls, and shafts of watery light trickled down from the streets high above. There were manholes every two hundred metres or so, as well as at each change of gradient and all points where two sewers intersected. The underbelly of Moscow is six levels deep on average, and in some places as many as twelve or fifteen, going down almost a kilometre. You start with gas and electric and telephone lines, then the sewer systems and the subways, both mapped and clandestine – Stalin was rumoured to have built a second ring of metro lines on the city outskirts, probably to shuttle bombs around the capital. Then you find where the Soviets burrowed deeper: secret tunnels, KGB listening posts, fallout shelters for the elite.

The city's jumbled secrets, Irk thought, pressing on each other like tectonic plates.

He ended up by the screen where Emma Kurvyakova's body had been found, and surfaced at the nearest manhole. Orienting himself, he felt his memory jolted by the red, green and white blocks of the flag which drooped above the Madagascan Embassy. He'd seen the flag recently, but where? From the window of Sabirzhan's apartment, *that* was where. And sure enough, there it was – right next door to the embassy. Why hadn't he made the connection when they'd first found Emma, then? Because they'd come from a different direction, he remembered, via Ostozhenka rather than the embankment.

He remembered something else too: he had never been convinced of Sabirzhan's innocence.

# 33

The first thing Alice saw when she arrived at Red October was her Mercedes, sitting inside the main gates and looking as good as new. It had even been cleaned, a genuine rarity in Moscow. She went to Lev's office and thanked him profusely and genuinely, momentarily tempted to kiss him in gratitude. "How did you find it?"

"With my eyes shut, it was so easy. The dealership you bought the car from is run by the Solntsevskaya group. I had a word with Testarossa, my fellow vor, and presto! Your car."

"The *dealership*?" Alice looked puzzled. "What's the dealer got to do with my car being stolen?"

"Who else do you think took it, Mrs Liddell? Koskei the Undying? You're not that naïve, surely? They kept a spare set of keys, noted your address, and took it back as soon as they could without arousing suspicion."

"Then what? They'd resell it?"

"Of course. Change the number plates, forge the papers and repeat the process. If you do that twenty or thirty times . . ."

"You make a million dollars."

"On each car, yes. If there's an easier way of making money, do let me know."

"This place," Alice shook her head. "This place. Just when I thought I was getting to grips with it. Anyway –" she shrugged – "I've got the car back, and that's what matters, so thank you."

"My pleasure, Mrs Liddell. And the Solntsevskaya know not to do it to you again."

It was no idle boast. Alice saw the return of the car for what it was: a kind gesture, yes, but also a glimpse of the awesome power Lev could wield. "I bet they do."

He looked at his watch. "Will you excuse me? I have to be on the factory floor."

"I'll come with you."

"No. I won't be long, and I'm sure you've got plenty to do here." Alice felt like an errant child, duly chastised. "Sabirzhan will give Harry the books either today or Monday," Lev added. "You have my word."

He touched her hand and was gone.

Privatisation was agreed, Harry would have the books; they were really starting to make progress, Alice thought, and not before time.

It was almost a month since she'd first met Borzov and Arkin – where had all the days gone?

Alice wandered through to the antechamber, where Galina was bashing away at an old typewriter. "You might be able to help me, Galya," she said, and Galina looked up, flushed with excited enthusiasm. "I need a hundred and fifty people – keen, intelligent, honest people – to help out on the day of the auction, but I haven't got the time or resources to advertise and interview thousands of applicants."

"I'll handle it," Galina said instantly. "Let me handle it." The doubt on Alice's face made her hurry on. "I've got friends, friends of friends, people I was at university with – they'd chop off their right arms to be involved with something like this, they really would."

Perhaps it was a conflict of interest, perhaps not. Alice had neither the time nor the inclination to care, as long as Galina delivered. "That would be great. Thanks, Galya; I owe you."

"My pleasure."

Alice walked back into Lev's office, crossed over to the internal window, and looked down at the factory floor. Today was payday, the penultimate Friday of the month, and a long line – a typically Soviet queue, Alice thought – of employees stretched away from the cashier's window through copses of columns and stills.

She watched as the cashier checked a worker's name off on a list – hard copy, of course, Red October had yet to dip more than a toenail into the scary waters of information technology – counted out his pay from shrink-wrapped piles of roubles, and pushed the money through in a metal tray beneath the glass partition. The employee – this was where Alice's attention was pricked – then walked over to Sabirzhan, who was standing a few paces away, counted out some notes from his pay packet, and handed that portion to Sabirzhan before walking off.

That was strange, Alice thought, though there was probably a perfectly innocent explanation. Perhaps Sabirzhan had lent the man some money and was claiming it back; perhaps it was payment for some rare item that Sabirzhan, with his contacts, had managed to procure.

She saw the next man in line do exactly the same thing, then the next one, and the one after that, and the one after that.

Lev came into view and walked across the distillery floor towards Sabirzhan who, collecting money with the impassiveness of a Roman tribune, barely seemed to acknowledge him. Lev said something to

Sabirzhan; Sabirzhan said something back, his attention still on the supplicants.

Alice was about to go down to the distillery floor herself when she saw a third man join the huddle. He looked gentle enough, but his arrival had clearly prompted tension. Lev shook hands willingly enough, but for Sabirzhan the gesture seemed to require a monumental effort.

Lev took the man a few paces away, towards the edge of the floor. Sabirzhan turned his back on them and continued to collect the money. A small queue had formed in the hiatus.

Alice went downstairs at a brisk trot.

The door which led from the staircase on to the distillery floor had a small porthole inset at eye level. Alice noted vaguely that this window seemed to have been blacked out, and she was reaching for the handle when she heard voices from the other side. She realised that the blackout was Lev's back, obscuring the entire aperture as he leant against the door.

It was the tone of the men's voices that first held Alice frozen as she stood. They were arguing. She warmed to the daringly clandestine thrill of eavesdropping even as she battered away another image, that of the banisters on the landing of her childhood home in Boston, where she'd watched and listened as her parents – her father sober, her mother steaming drunk – had squabbled.

"Let's not lose sight of the most important thing." It was the other man speaking; Lev's voice was too distinctive to be mistaken. "The quicker these murders stop the better, for both of us."

It was another hour before Lev returned to his office. Throughout that time Alice's curiosity nagged at her like scabies. She had so many questions that she hardly knew where to begin, and she couldn't imagine that the answers to any of them were going to be what she wanted to hear.

"What the hell was all that about?" she said, when he finally came back.

"What was all what about?"

She gestured down to the factory floor. "Sabirzhan, taking people's cash off them."

"Oh, that." He flapped a hand in the air. "That's standard procedure."

"Not anywhere I've seen, it's not." Alice wanted to say that it was bullying, but there is no such word in Russian. The notion that it's unfair for a powerful person to threaten someone weaker is very much a Western one; in Russia, everything gets done by bullying.

"I don't have time to explain it to you now, but it's all perfectly normal. Anything else?"

If Lev had been forthcoming about Sabirzhan, Alice might have left it at that, but there was little she disliked more than being kept in the dark, and her anger skidded her forward.

"What murders?" she asked.

Lev bluffed and stalled and denied, but Alice wasn't about to let this one go. It took him a quarter of an hour to relent and tell her about events at Prospekt Mira, as quickly and succinctly as he could, as much to minimise the evident horror on her face as anything else. He took her to the window and pointed out German Kullam. He hadn't wanted her to know, he said, for several reasons. What they were trying to do with Red October was complex and unprecedented. He knew the West was keen to see it succeed, but he knew too how squeamish Westerners could be, and he hadn't wanted to complicate the situation any further.

"*Complicate?*" Alice didn't even try to hide her sarcasm. "Children are being murdered, probably by a Chechen warlord hoping to put pressure on you, and you think that's a *complication*?" She looked away, feeling as deceived as if he were a cheating lover; there was the same indignity of being the last to know, the same dulled anticipation that there might still be more left undiscovered. "Didn't you think I *should* know?"

Lev shrugged. "In Russia, Mrs Liddell, what you should or shouldn't know is of no consequence; the only thing that matters is what you *do* know." He moved as if to take her hand; she pulled back. "Please, Mrs Liddell. These are my children. Not biologically, of course. But it's my sworn duty to keep these young people safe, and I'm failing. Don't you see? I didn't tell you because I'm *ashamed.*"

She looked at him; *into* him. "I'm ashamed," he repeated, more softly, and she knew he was telling the truth. A man who would not let himself love a woman or have children, had taken on others' children by proxy and loved them in his own faltering, uncertain way as if they were his own.

Alice knew that a line had just been crossed. She was still determined that nothing would happen between them. And equally certain that if it did, she'd be powerless to resist.

"Vodka?" he asked, his voice wavering as he turned away from her and busied himself at the cabinet, selecting a bottle. She nodded mutely. "Here – a bottle of the finest Tolstoy. You think he'd have seen the funny side? A teetotaller – worse, an abstentionist propagander – and he's immortalised in vodka! You might as well name a synagogue after Adolf Hitler." He handed the bottle to her. "You pour."

Alice's hands were shaking so violently that she had to touch the bottle's neck to the glasses in order to stop the vodka from spilling. She was vaguely aware of Lev crossing the room. When she looked up, he was on his way back towards her, and she saw that he'd closed the door – the door, she remembered, which was always open, *always*.

He moved his lips to hers, and she was destroyed.

He looked as though he'd been painted, top to bottom. His toes were ochre claws, his feet sapphire and sage. Tongues of primrose licked up his calves to rows of crimson stars across each kneecap, each point on the stars representing a year inside. He saw Alice's stare.

"No one's ever made me kneel," he said.

How long did it take to cover such an enormous man? How long, and how painful? Prison tattooists didn't come with coloured ink, disposable needles and sterilisation kits; they mixed charred shoe leather and molten rubber with water, sugar and piss, sharpened sewing needles on the concrete floors of the cells, and – if you were lucky – waved them through a flame before setting to work.

She was dissolving with desire, arcing into him as his fingertips traced fire the length of her silken spine. She felt his need, his *compulsion* to be steeped in her. When he entered her his eyes opened, not just the lids but the pupils themselves, as if the room had suddenly become dark.

Lev was lying across her, but Alice was not conscious of his weight. She felt blurred and primitive, satiated and insatiable. It was as if she had shed her skin, making her feel everything with immeasurably greater intensity, at once incredibly fragile and incredibly strong.

He stirred and she pulled him closer, holding him like a child after a nightmare. Around him ebbed her discomfort, her pain, her tension; her life as she'd known it, in fact.

"I've been waiting for you," she said, and she knew the truth of this only at the moment she spoke it, as though thought and speech had also become one. "For a very long time, I think."

"When I first saw you," he replied, "I knew I'd met you before. I'd heard your voice, I'd smelt your fragrance. I'd already tasted you before I kissed you. I didn't need to touch you to know how you felt. You're inside me, too."

190

"Perhaps you could start calling me Alice, then," she said, and they laughed.

Alice left her car at the distillery. She wanted to get some air. More, she chided herself, she wanted an excuse to return to Red October tomorrow. Besides, the half-bottle of Tolstoy they'd shared afterwards had surely made her too drunk to drive, though she must have been the only person in Moscow who cared about that.

She walked round the west side of the Kremlin, where the snow was thick on slopes which fell steeply away from the imposing crimson walls. Under the benevolent and indulgent eyes of their parents, a few children were sledging on trays, flattened bin liners or simply their own asses. Alice passed two women perched on a bench with their bottoms on the rim of the backrest and their feet on the seat where snow was compacted between the slats.

"Children are the flowers of life," one said, watching the sledgers.

"Yeah – on their parents' graves," the other replied.

In the darkness, it seemed to Alice that the streetlamps glowed with the brilliance of searchlights, illuminating everything in crystal clarity.

An old woman glided smoothly along, only her head and torso visible above snowdrifts piled high on grass verges. When her whole body became visible, Alice saw that her feet were trotting along nineteen to the dozen, a furious motion entirely at odds with the serene progress of her upper half. Alice thought of a swimming duck, fluid on top but paddling like fury underneath; she thought of herself.

She reached the Tomb of the Unknown Soldier. It was five to seven, and they changed the guard every hour. It would be good to see the ceremony, Alice thought, hoping it would slow the pace of her chattering heart. She stood by the barriers and read the plaque which told her that the soldier – *your name is unknown, your deeds immortal* – had died at kilometre 41 on the airport road, the point at which the Red Army had halted the German advance on Moscow.

The tomb and eternal flame were guarded by two sentries in small glass shelters. They held bayonets in their right hands and their feet were aligned at ten to two. Their replacements came goose-stepping in perfect synchronicity. A score of people had joined Alice now, most of them materialising in the last couple of minutes as though from the ether. She smelt vodka on breaths, heard giggling and the fizz of soft-drink cans being opened. An old woman was crying; perhaps she'd lost her husband to the Nazis. Her companion tutted at the disrespectful young.

191

It was not until the guard had been changed that Alice realised the reason for the laughter: the eternal flame had gone out.

Alice took a tube of mints from her coat pocket and popped a couple into her mouth. She didn't want Lewis to smell vodka, or worse, on her.

The door was on the latch; he was home. She took a deep breath and stepped inside. "Hi," she called, and her voice didn't waver. She listened to it as though it had come from outside her skull, and almost nodded in approval: she'd caught just the right tone.

"Hi," he called back. "I'm in the bedroom."

His unsuspecting voice brought home to Alice the enormity of what she'd done. Lewis trusted her implicitly, and she'd betrayed him. What cut her most was the blithe ignorance in his words; he had no idea what had just happened. Even if he had, would he have believed it? For all his intellect and medical aptitude, Lewis was in many ways a simple soul. If he wasn't capable of something, he didn't see how anyone else could be. Depravity and immorality were alien to him. Lewis would no more have considered being unfaithful than he'd have stuck needles in his eyes.

Alice felt a keening of dereliction. She'd failed Lewis, failed their marriage; failed *herself*.

She went into the bedroom and kissed Lewis lightly on the lips, once. Not too passionate, not too distant. Again, spot on.

"Is there something you're not telling me?" he said.

For Alice, the room seemed to hold in still life for a moment; only her pulse hammered. She forced herself to take a long deep breath, an attempt to lasso her heart rate which she disguised as a show of exasperation. "Such as?"

"If you're not telling me, Alice, then I wouldn't know. Would I?"

She switched from misunderstood vexation to wounded indignation. "Lewis, what are you trying to insinuate? I was late because I was working."

"That wasn't what I meant. I don't suspect you of having an *affair*, darling. At least, not beyond the one you're already having."

"You've lost me." She almost believed it herself. "What affair?"

"The one with this –" Lewis reached into the wardrobe and pulled out a bottle of vodka. The rush of relief was so strong that it made Alice want to vomit, which in turn made her laugh. She could drink vodka till the cows came home, but the sight of it almost made her puke.

"Oh, *that*." She flicked an airy wrist. "I bought it the other day, the same time as I got that blouse and those jeans on Neglinnaya. I must have just put it in with them when I was unpacking and forgot all about it." She felt shame at the lie, pride at the ease with which it came. Lewis scratched at a thin strip of sideburn; he was unconvinced. "Come on," Alice pressed. "It's not even open, is it?"

"It was *hidden* among your clothes."

"It was not hidden."

"It was jammed underneath a pile of sweaters."

"You were looking through my drawers?"

"You'd deliberately concealed it."

"I said, were you looking . . . ?"

"Alice!" The unexpected sharpness of his voice made her jump.

They sighed in almost perfect stereo. "All right, all right," said Alice. "I *did* hide it."

"Thank you. *Why* did you hide it?"

"Because you think I drink too much."

"You *do* drink too much."

"I hid it because I didn't want to annoy you. I realised we already had some, and I didn't know what to do with it, so I just buried it there and forgot all about it. I shouldn't have bought it, if that's what you want to hear. I shouldn't have bought it."

"So why *did* you?"

"I told you, I thought we needed some. And besides, I'd had a shitty couple of days at work. It's all over now. Things are going ahead, the pressure's off for a while."

"I don't know why you need to drink so much."

"I don't know why you don't loosen up about it."

"There's nothing wrong with me." He folded his arms across his chest. "Just because I don't like to get drunk doesn't mean I'm uptight. I'm just not mad about losing control."

Oh, I am, thought Alice, I am.

# 34

*Saturday, 25 January 1992*

There had been a mafiya shoot-out at the Intourist Hotel on Tverskaya, and traffic was snarled even worse than usual around Red Square. In a classic case of bolting every stable door long after even the slowest nag would have left, the police had closed all roads within a half-kilometre radius, but only after two hours of letting people walk in and out of the hotel unhindered. Now, the police were engaged in a futile hunt for clues, cavorting around Lenin's mausoleum as if they'd found him resurrected.

Alice was angry, not merely at the delay but at Lev. He hadn't been at Red October when she'd gone to pick up the Mercedes. Not that she'd have known what to say to him in the cold, sober light of a winter morning, but she'd have liked to have had the option of making a tongue-tied, quasi-teenage fool of herself, that was all. Either way, she was in no mood to sit in traffic for hours.

The jam was even worse than a Boston gawkerblocker, when drivers slowed to a crawl to check out an accident on the other side of the road. Alice pulled out of the queue, turned hard left and headed through a no-entry sign on to a side street. The road was empty and she'd almost made it to the other end when a traffic policeman stepped smartly out from between two parked cars and twirled his baton at her like a drum majorette. "Stop!"

Her first reaction was to pretend she hadn't seen him, but if her vision was that bad then she shouldn't have been anywhere near the wheel of a car in the first place. Besides, the cop would simply radio through to the next guy down the line, who'd give her twice as much hell. She pulled over, and the policeman smirked when he saw her yellow number plates; foreigners are easy shakedowns because they can usually spare more money than time. Harry reckoned on being stopped about once a fortnight, Bob once a week – it was a black thing, he averred. At least her plates were clean, Alice thought. The slightest splash of mud sends dollar signs whirring behind policemen's eyes.

Alice pulled the vehicle documents from the sun visor and her personal ones from her purse, checking instinctively that she had them all: the *tekhpasport*, which gave her name and vehicle regis-tration number; the *tekhosmotr*, which confirmed that the car was roadworthy (making it the nation's biggest-selling work of fiction); her international driver's licence, open at the Cyrillic page; and her Russian visa and work permit. The cops always ask to see them all, and if any are absent or expired, then it's the long walk home and a car abandoned to the tender mercies of Muscovites. "Without docu-ments," the Russians like to say, "you're shit."

She got out of the Mercedes and walked over to the policeman. Sometimes it's better to play the dumb foreigner and hope they get bored of trying to elicit a bribe from you, but usually it's easier just to pay whatever they ask and go on your way. You can stand and fight, but then they confiscate your licence and you have to pay the fine anyway to get it back. It simply isn't worth the hassle – which is almost certainly why the system evolved that way to start with.

The policeman's nose was curved like a cucumber and large enough to cleave his face in two. His features were too adjusted to meanness to be anything but ignoble. Alice looked at the name badge on his lapel: Uvarov, Grigori Eduardovich.

"This is a one-way street," Uvarov said.

"And how many ways did you see me going?"

The joke did not register. He squatted down by the bumper. "Your headlights are faulty."

"My headlights are fine."

"Driver's licence." Uvarov put out his hand and she gave him her licence. His eyes travelled slowly down the page. "What is your nationality?"

"I'm a drunkard."

"What?"

"It's from *Casablanca*. Major Strasser asks Rick Blaine . . ."

"Ah, *Casablanca, Casablanca*." He switched to bad English, more amused now. "'Here's looking at you, kid.'"

"Exactly."

"A hundred bucks." He was speaking Russian again; playtime was over.

"Shall we go and sit in your car?" It's illegal for policemen to accept money in public. He shrugged; there was no one around to see them, why not do it here? Alice handed over five twenties; Uvarov licked his finger and counted them.

"You want some caviar?" he asked. "I have some in the car. Good price."

"No, thank you."

"Very good price. Very good caviar – Caspian. Not the shit from the far east."

Alice shook her head. Uvarov shrugged again. "Very well. A hundred dollars, for violation of traffic direction and faulty head-lamps."

"I told you, my lights are fine."

He whirled sharply and drove his baton into the offside lamp. Serrated splinters of glass plopped on to his shoe. "You don't buy my caviar, your headlights are definitely faulty." He handed her a card. "This is my brother's number. He runs a repair garage on Dolgorukovskaya. He'll fix it cheaply for you. Don't take it to those crooks at the big places, they'll rip you off."

Alice took the card and turned it over. On the back, she wrote down Uvarov's name and badge number. "Grisha" – she used the diminutive deliberately and patronisingly – "I work for the IMF, and I report directly to Nikolai Valentinovich Arkin. I'm going to mention this little incident to him, and I imagine the only way I'll ever see you again is if I happen to find myself looking for a parking space in Tomsk."

Uvarov looked horrified. Alice walked back to the car and got in.

"My brother will do it for free," he said. He'd gone white. Alice backed the car up a touch, mimicked his shrug – little more than a twitch of the shoulders – and pulled out from the kerb in an arc wide enough to avoid both Uvarov and the puddle of glass for which he was responsible.

Alice knew that the police didn't get paid a salary worth the name and depended on petty extortion for a living. She didn't begrudge Uvarov the cash – she *had* been breaking the highway code, after all – but smashing the headlight when she wouldn't buy his caviar had overstepped the mark. That was why Alice had taken his name. And she *was* going to tell Arkin, of course she was. She'd been in Russia long enough to know you should never make a threat you're not prepared to carry out. More important, you should never up the ante unless you were sure who you were dealing with. It was Uvarov's fault if he'd forgotten *that*.

# 35

*Sunday, 26 January 1992*

Sabirzhan was on the move just after breakfast. For Irk, who'd pulled up across the road barely ten minutes before, it seemed like serendipity. He put his car in gear and followed Sabirzhan through the light Sunday traffic, taking care to keep at least one vehicle between them; Sabirzhan was KGB, trained in counter-surveillance techniques, and it wouldn't do for him to recognise Irk in his rear-view mirror. Irk had no idea where Sabirzhan was going or even whether this would yield anything useful, but he felt he was doing something positive, and that was the main thing.

Irk tracked Sabirzhan's silver BMW as far as Khlebny Avenue, where Sabirzhan entered an apartment building just down the road from the Egyptian Embassy. Irk half-got out of the car and then thought better of it. There would be at least fifty apartments in that building, and there was no way he could find out which one

Sabirzhan was visiting without risking exposure. So he sat and waited, a hunter in repose. The shops nearby had plastered their doors with dollar-only signs. Gorbachev should have won the Nobel Prize for chemistry, Irk thought: he'd turned the rouble to shit.

Sabirzhan came out forty minutes later. Irk looked for a jaunty step or the jerkiness of anger, and saw neither. Sabirzhan gave nothing away, even when he thought he was alone. He got back into his car and the trail began again: out west to Kudrinskaya Square, north round the Garden Ring, left on to Krasina and then left again towards the zoo. Another apartment building, another visit; another wait in the car for Irk with nothing to do except note the address and speculate whom Sabirzhan might be visiting. Family members, whores, friends – Irk couldn't tell.

*Friends?* Did a man like Sabirzhan have *friends*?

Irk thought about ringing Petrovka for more people to help tail Sabirzhan, in case Irk was spotted, or someone to find out who lived in the apartment buildings. He felt in his pockets for two-kopeck pieces and found none. With inflation what it was, public phones were the only thing kopecks were used for now. Enterprising babushki sold stacks of them outside the central post office; ten two-kopek coins for thirty roubles, 150 times their face value!

Even if he'd had the change, there was little point making the call. Petrovka barely had the manpower to investigate a loaf of bread. Irk knew of detectives who were reduced to tailing suspects by bus, using phone booths rather than radios, and even charging foreign journalists to accompany them on patrol. Under current re-equipment schedules, it would take the police twenty-five years to get equipment parity with any half-decent gangster. Twenty-five years! Twenty-five years from now would mark the centenary of the revolution.

The problem, Irk thought, was fundamental: Russians didn't understand crime. Lambasting criminals as 'socially dangerous', the Soviets had equated crime with politics. As socialism was perfected, the theory went, so the social base for crime – and therefore crime itself, of course – would gradually disappear. Consequently they had seen no point in spending money on modernising the police, training prosecutors or improving the courts. It was wholesale institutional blindness, and it was men like Irk who were suffering. How could he do his job when all he could find was a small piece here, another piece there? It was like trying to do a jigsaw by touch alone.

Irk was so lost in thought bordering on self-pity that he almost missed Sabirzhan when he came out of the apartment building on

Zoologicheskaya. Gears ground and tyres squealed as he strove to keep his quarry in sight. The chase, such as it was, went on all morning and through lunch, a slowly unwinding procession of street names and building numbers: Petrovsky, Zvonarsky, Kolokolnikov, Ipatevsky. It was at the seventh destination, just as Irk was about to give this up as a waste of time – though what else would he have done with the day? – that he had some modicum of success. Sabirzhan drove down Bolshaya Ordynka, past the Convent of Martha and Mary, and was just pulling into the kerb when Irk recalled that he had been here before. This was where German Kullam lived.

Sabirzhan got out of his car and went up the steps to the Kullams' building. Irk slowed just enough to be sure that he'd got the right place, and then turned tail and headed for home.

The guy who ran the bookstall on Irk's street was packing up when Irk arrived.

"All over for another day, Nikulsha?" Irk asked.

"All over, full stop. I'm closing."

"Closing? Russians love to read."

"Books are expensive, Investigator, and food even more so. Can you eat a book?"

"What will you do?"

"I'll survive."

Irk wished him good luck and went inside his apartment block, happy as ever to be home. He always felt uplifted the moment he walked through the front door. Perhaps he was becoming more Russian than he liked to concede; a Russian's apartment is more than a physical living space, it's a sanctuary from life outside, even when it's as nondescript as Irk's. He had few items that were new, and even fewer that were valuable. His sofa doubled as a bed, his phone was the old rotary-dial model and his books were old and tattered. According to tradition, a host is bound to hand over any item that a visitor praises, though there was little enough danger of that happening here. Irk's possessions were junk, and he never had anyone round.

The police file on Sabirzhan was in the drawer of Irk's desk. It should have been at Petrovka, of course, but it was safer here. If Sabirzhan had enough connections to get himself released from questioning early, he had enough connections to make files disappear.

Irk flicked through the file – his own reports, photographs of

Sabirzhan's apartment and office, sundry correspondence – until he found the list of informers he'd copied from Sabirzhan's records. He ran his finger down the address column – it was in alphabetical order, of course; neither Sabirzhan nor Irk would have stood for anything else – and the street names popped up for him like targets on a shooting range:

> Bolshaya Ordynka, 328/34 – Sissikin, Albert G.
> Zvonarsky, 96/8 – Durakov, Filipp V.
> Zoologicheskaya, 263/52 – Ossipov, Innokenty S.
> Ipatevsky, 14/25 – Myshkin, Alexei D.
> Kolokolnikov, 58/2 – Tupikov, Mark S.
> Petrovsky, 82/11 – Zaitsev, Otar K.
> Khlebny, 47/9 – Serdzekorol, Vasily M.

Not relatives, whores or friends. Sabirzhan had been visiting his informers. Irk felt the spearing thrill of connection, and hot on its heels the gentle anticlimax of deflation. Sabirzhan had been visiting his informers; so what? In some ways, it would have been strange if he hadn't been. Did it make any difference to Irk's hunt for whoever had killed those three kids? Not that he could see. Perhaps Lev would like to know what Irk had worked out. But if Lev was worried about it, Irk thought, he could tail Sabirzhan himself.

Irk made chicken soup with boat-shaped pastries and turned on the television, flicking through the channels in an attempt find something that wasn't a commercial. Soviet television had shown reports of beggars scavenging for food in New York trash cans or miners in Yorkshire battling with the police; modern Russian stations carried advertisements for cash machines and dishwashers. Few viewers had fully believed the news reports; everyone wanted the commercials to be true.

# 36

*Monday, 27 January 1992*
"Good morning, Mrs Liddell. I believe I owe you an explanation."

Lev's tone was civil, no more and no less, and it was shot through with an indifference that cut Alice deep. Civil is what you are with clients and acquaintances, she thought, not with someone with whom you'd lain naked in this very office. He'd used the word 'explanation', and her mind shied away from the implications even as her gut tugged them in one by one. As far as Alice was concerned, 'explanation' usually meant 'excuse'.

"I thought we'd agreed that you would call me Alice." Her voice trembled with the effort of staunching; apprehension, anger and tears were all queuing up.

"You asked what was going on with the workers." He was gone from her, as impassively remote as an Easter Island statue. "It's very simple. The money they were handing over to Sabirzhan came from several sources." He ticked them off on his fingers. Alice wished she had the strength to reach across the table and snap them one by one. "Bonuses they've earned, free allowances from the trade union, rewards for efficiency proposals, fictitious wages paid for fictitious work."

"So why the hell do they give it to *you*?"

"Because it's not really theirs to start with, and because it's not for my personal enrichment."

"And the rest."

"You doubt me? You doubt my integrity, *Alice*?" He spat her name, and she felt sick. "That money provides bribes and gifts for suppliers and contractors; that money, therefore, is needed for the future of this factory. No bribes equals no permits, no raw materials, no retail space. No bribes equals no jobs. They get their wages, but their wages aren't paid in full unless the plan is met, and the plan will not be met without subterfuge."

The plan – that was the way all industry had worked in the Soviet Union. Every last aspect had been planned, no detail too picayune: what should be produced, at what cost, from what materials, for what price, for which customers, on what time schedule, with how many workers and at what wages. The plan. For the atheists of central communism, it had been the Godhead; to the high priests of capitalism, it was devilry.

"That's exactly the kind of shit privatisation will stamp out."

"Maybe so, but until then, things go on just the same as they always have. If I didn't do this, my workers would starve."

"You run a criminal gang. You could afford to pay the lot of them from your own pocket."

"They make more from me than I take from them."

"That's *bullshit*."

"You'd like to think that, wouldn't you? Have you ever heard the saying *ne pesh, ne mash* – if you don't drink, you're not one of us? In this case, it's slightly different. *Ne beresh, ne mash*: if you don't take bribes, you're not one of us. Either we subordinate ourselves to the laws of corruption governing the trade system, or we find ourselves ejected from that system."

"That system is history."

"That system is alive and kicking, and the sooner you realise it, the better."

Lev had offered Alice, Bob and Harry one of the distillery's better offices, and Alice spent ten minutes in the ladies' toilet composing herself before going back there. 'Better' was in this case strictly a relative term. The fluorescent swathes on the ceiling washed the room in a milky radiance which highlighted the room's shortcomings. It was barely a few strides from one side to the other, and the walls were patched with grey paint. Even the smell of cabbage seemed stronger than usual.

Western executives are used to vast corner offices, tinted glass and brushed steel; this place would have disgraced a student magazine, but Alice loved it. It was suitably humble for the great transformation she would help wreak. The French Revolution had been hatched on a tennis court; the Nazis had met in a Munich beer cellar; the Bolsheviks themselves had plotted on the Tottenham Court Road in London. Great changes need unassuming beginnings, she felt.

Bob was nowhere to be found. Harry was rootling around on all fours beneath a desk all but invisible beneath towers of documents. "The fuck are you doing, Harry?" Alice said.

"Looking for my pen."

"Harry, there's only one part of you that's visible, and I have to say, it seems a somewhat unlikely orifice for you to be speaking through."

Harry backed out and up, brushing dust off the pen. "Are you OK?" he asked.

"Fine. Why?"

He studied her face. "You look . . . preoccupied, I guess."

*I should tell him,* Alice thought. Harry and Bob had a right to know that children were being killed because of what they were doing. She should tell him – and she didn't, because she knew what his reaction would be. Lev had said how squeamish Westerners were, and he was right. If Harry or Bob wanted out – and at least one of them surely would – Alice would be back where she started, and she couldn't afford that, not with so little time left.

She changed the subject. "How you doing with the books?"

"I can understand about one word in ten, and all of those are probably lies."

"Find a recording of Brezhnev's speeches, and you'll get used to it fast enough."

Harry shrugged. Any information he could glean from the books would probably be insufficient, misleading, irrelevant, or all three. The law required that valuation be based on the book values for fixed assets, current assets, current liabilities, net current assets, net assets and capital, but all these were badly distorted. Book values were traditionally overstated to make it appear as though production targets had been reached and quotas filled; these particular ones had been set on New Year's Day, and therefore took no account of subsequent inflation.

Decoding Russian balance sheets was more of an art than a science. Russian accounting was still based on the Soviet model, designed to detect misuse of state funds rather than provide information about company performance. A popular Soviet joke had the director of an enterprise interviewing candidates for the post of chief accountant. He asked each candidate the same question: "How much is one plus one?" The man who got the job was the one who answered: "How much do you need, Comrade Director?"

In Western business, intangibles are usually minor and easily dealt with. Here, the situation was reversed. How could Harry evaluate cash flow when the majority of every enterprise's dealings involved promissory notes, barter and unpaid receivables? How could he put a value on the underground economy? How could growth figures be taken seriously when everyone had an incentive to exaggerate?

Always assuming, of course, that Harry had been given the genuine books in the first place.

Practically every Russian company keeps two sets of books: the official ones which are sent to the authorities and on which taxes are paid (or, more usually, aren't); and the unofficial ones which record the unreported cash transactions as well. The Russians call it 'accounting out of the safe'. A businessman chooses how much of his activity to conduct above ground and how much below, and what the ratios of cash and barter will be in the latter.

For an accountant, the distortion of figures is a nightmare. What looked bad on paper could look much better with all the information to hand. It could also look much, much worse.

"You know accountants," he said. "If we can't count it, it don't exist."

"Greenlight everything, unless it's totally and irrevocably ludicrous."

"That's ridiculous, Alice."

"That's also how it is," she said, teaching him lessons she was still learning herself. "You got the payroll there?"

Harry extracted a file from the middle of one of the document stacks, steadying the top of the pile with one hand while he pulled the file out with the other. "Here you go. Watch out for the gum band holding it together; it's frayed."

"*Gum band*?" she teased, picking at the rubber band he'd indicated. "It's called a 'lastic."

"Not in Pittsburgh, it's not."

"And we're nearer Boston now." She nodded down towards the distillery floor. "I'm off to the jungle. Look after Vladimir for me."

"Vladimir?"

Alice nodded towards a bust of Lenin which had been turned to face the wall. "Vladimir."

The distillery floor was busier than Alice had witnessed before, though it was only when she saw a large digital clock with the time and date displayed in fading red LEDs that she realised why. It was nearly month's end, and Russian industry divided each month into three ten-day work periods – decades, they called them. The first decade was *spyachka*, sleepy time, when the previous month's quota had been met and the pressure was off; then came *goryachka*, the hot time; and finally *likhoradka*, fever: a headlong rush to complete by any means necessary.

Alice went to the bottling department first, because it was the nearest. The payroll listed more than two hundred employees in this section. By the law of averages, even Russian averages, at least one of that two hundred would surely be co-operative. Alice stood for a moment, watching the bottles tottering down the conveyor belts like an army of penguins, and then marched up to a woman in a white coat. She had rounded cheeks and her nose was pointed: a snowman's face; a snowman's body too, square and thick. A kerchief covered her greying hair, and her stumpy legs were sheathed in rubber boots. "What's your name?" Alice asked.

The woman regarded her with a mixture of suspicion and curiosity. "What's yours?"

"You were paid on Friday, right?"

The woman looked around and up – for Lev, Alice realised, as though he were Big Brother, omniscient and ubiquitous. "Right," the woman said at length, as though expelling a stone.

"The money you got – did you keep it all?"

"All that I was entitled to."

"What does that mean?"

"It means what it means."

"That's not very helpful."

The woman gestured to the nearest wall, where a metal rack held squares of printed cardboard – timecards. "I clock in, do my work, go home. It's not my job to be helpful."

The rack was ten rows across and seven down, with two compartments blank: sixty-eight timecards. Alice turned back to the woman. "Those timecards . . ."

"What about them?"

"They're just for those people here today, right?"

"You work in this department, your card's there."

"Even if you're not in today?"

"You think people take their cards home and frame them?"

"OK. Thank you."

Alice turned back to the payroll and counted again. The list of bottling department employees ran to six and a half pages; at thirty-three lines a page, that made more than two hundred, she'd been right the first time. She looked at the title page: the document was dated this month, it was current.

The far side of two hundred bottlers on the payroll, but only sixty-eight of them had timecards. What had happened to the other two-thirds?

# 37

*Tuesday, 28 January 1992*

Alice had discovered the same pattern all the way across the distillery. For every employee she'd physically found – and even then Red October was overstaffed, Alice had reminded herself, like all inefficient Soviet industries – there'd been another, perhaps two, who appeared on the payroll. Of the 25 filtration column washers listed, she'd unearthed only 12; of the 399 recorded as working on the storage vats, just 187. By the time she'd reached the fourth department, the question was not whether the official and actual tallies would be different but by how much. She didn't tell anyone what she'd found, because she didn't want news getting back to Lev. Instead, she asked every department head for the names and numbers of those employees under their supervision, and told each one that everything was just as she'd expected.

Alice left the site at Prospekt Mira until last, not merely because it was off the main premises, but also because of the murders; she needed time to steel herself before going. She felt an irrational resentment towards Lev for not telling her earlier. They were lovers now, why should they have secrets from each other? Then she thought of Lewis, and the gulag.

It was late in the afternoon when she arrived. Two of Lev's men were at the main gate. They checked her credentials and let her through, pointing her towards the entrance of the school. Term had resumed last week after the Orthodox Christmas holiday, and Alice walked through corridors which streamed with children in sombre uniforms and high spirits. She was surprised, and a little disturbed, to see that no one, pupils or teachers, gave her a second glance, even with everything that had been going on here. Whatever the bogeyman looked like, it clearly wasn't Alice.

Svetlana's door, unlike Lev's, was not always open. Alice knocked, waited a moment, and entered. Svetlana was talking to a man whom Alice recognised instantly as the one who'd come to the distillery on Friday; the one, indeed, who'd inadvertently apprised her of the child killings in the first place.

Svetlana broke off her conversation and came quickly across the room. "Mrs Liddell!" She clasped Alice's forearm with both hands. "We met at the party last week, you remember?"

"Yes, of course."

"But you haven't been taking my advice, have you? You should eat more. Look at your face: skin and bones. Well, you Westerners don't know best, not in this case. Come, Sveta will feed you up. I've some speckled hen in the kitchen. Have you ever had speckled hen? Chicken strips, cucumber slices, minced prunes, mayonnaise, walnuts, eggs – sound good? Juku, you will have some too. Have you two met? No? How rude of me not to introduce you earlier. Mrs Liddell, this is Juku Irk, the finest investigator in the Moscow prosecutor service and a close friend of mine. Juku, this is Alice Liddell, who's come to privatise the factory and tell us how we should be living. I'll go get the speckled hen – won't be a minute."

Svetlana bustled from the room. Irk gestured that Alice should sit down.

"Investigator." Alice said. "Of course. What else?"

What else, indeed? Irk had thought of nothing else for days. A psychiatrist would doubtless have told him that he was suffering attack psychosis: he awaited the next murder with such keen anticipation and imagination that it seemed almost as though he was either experiencing such an attack for real or trying to conjure it into existence through sheer force of will. Either would have done, as the only thing unacceptable was silence. He needed either to find the murderer or new murders with fresh clues, and since there was no sign of the former, it had to be the latter. The enemies Irk knew – politicians, bureaucrats, mafiyosi – were finite in their power to threaten, frighten or dismay, no matter how potent their influence. Not so the enemy he was unsure about.

"I know you must have a great interest in this case," Irk said, sounding as pompous as he usually did when he wasn't sure how to go about things. "I assure you I'm doing all I can to solve it. I want to see reforms go ahead too, you know."

"That's why you're making such efforts?"

"No. I'm making such efforts because I don't want to see any more dead children."

"Who do you think is responsible?"

"I'm keeping an open –"

"For God's sake, Investigator, if this gets out, it could jeopardise the entire process. I don't want the party line – I want you to tell me what you honestly think. Is it the Chechens?"

"I don't know."

"Do you *want* it to be the Chechens?"

"I want to find the truth," he said, simply and without flourish, and Alice realised with a flash of shame that she'd underestimated him. She'd been prejudiced enough to take him for homo sovieticus, mendacious and venal, concerned only with his career, his reputation and his bank balance, in no particular order. There was much more to him, she saw now. He was like her, a seeker, a searcher, one of those unquiet souls who keep digging even when they know they shouldn't, because when you dig you can't stop halfway down, you have to go on and on till you get to the end, and you can't ever hide what you've uncovered – not from yourself, at any rate.

"I'm sorry," Alice said. "I got you all wrong. I thought you were . . . well, you know . . ."

Irk nodded; he knew, all too well. "Did you come here to see me?"

"No. I'm checking personnel details. Boring admin stuff."

"But someone's got to do it, right?"

She laughed. "Right. Just like someone's got to deal with all the dead people in Moscow."

"Just wait till spring, when all the snow flowers bloom."

"'Snow flowers'?"

"The bodies we find when the snow melts. It's one of our busiest times." Irk looked wistful. "Lucrative, too, if you're ruthless enough."

"There's always someone who makes money out of death."

"You can say that again. I've investigated cases of ambulancemen coming to people's houses and saying that this or that relative has been involved in an accident, just so they can get into the family's home and steal their things while everyone's crying and carrying on with grief. Or ambulancemen tipping off body-snatchers: fifty bucks, corpse removed the same day. Actually that's not such a bad bargain, when it can take the state a week to arrive, if they make it at all."

Irk's tone was curious, Alice thought. It was as though he were trying to impress, or depress, her with the city's squalor. He went on: "I've had to examine bodies which have been thrown out of windows. You get to them by following the footprints of those who've already been there to strip the corpse of anything valuable. The other day, *Pravda* had to sack the guy who compiles the death notices because he wouldn't guarantee a space in the paper unless the relatives gave him a bribe. People are starving and freezing to death every day; he was making a small fortune."

Something stirred in Alice's brain. Horror, yes, the inklings of black humour too, but also a connection. "*Pravda* publish death notices?" she asked.

"Every day. You die in Moscow and someone remembers you, in goes your name."

# 38

*Wednesday, 29 January 1992*

The entire front page of *Pravda* was taken up by the headline: PLEASE DON'T BUY THIS NEWSPAPER. An article inside explained that *Pravda* had calculated its prices for 1992 the previous autumn, when newsprint had cost four thousand roubles per tonne. Newsprint now cost twenty thousand and rising, but if the cover price increased then no one would be able to afford it. So *Pravda* was losing money on every copy produced, and the more readers it had, the more it lost. Alice thought the whole thing must be a practical joke or a deliberate lie – *pravda* is Russian for truth, but the old joke was that there was no truth in *Pravda* – yet the staff in the *Pravda* office seemed serious enough. A newspaper that didn't want people to buy it. Only in Moscow.

The newspaper archivist, a pale young man who looked as though he hadn't seen the sun since Brezhnev's death and possibly before, couldn't have looked less interested in Alice's request had he tried. Back copies of the newspaper were kept over there, he said, jerking his head vaguely towards the far wall. Alice should look in the large dark red files, each containing exactly a month's worth of issues. She didn't even have time to reply before the archivist turned away from her and continued sorting through a mountain of card indexes. He'd probably calculated his rate of progress, Alice thought, to finish the sorting at exactly the moment his working day ended.

He was also just about the only Russian man she'd met who'd shown absolutely no recognition of her beauty. She didn't know whether to be relieved or insulted.

Alice went over to the files, pulled out the ones for the previous November and December, and set them down on the nearest spare desk. There were fifteen or twenty death notices a day, more on Thursdays and Fridays when the Monday deaths had been incorporated – half of all Russian men die on a Monday, usually after a weekend of solid vodka drinking.

There were two versions of the Red October payroll: one organised by department, the other alphabetical. Using the latter, Alice started to work backwards through *Pravda*, cross-referencing two lists. It was a job best done on a computer, and she feared that the mind-numbing tedium of checking down reams of names would cause her to lose concentration and miss something, but she struck gold almost immediately: Salnikov, Roman R., died 12 November in Basmanny, now listed as working in the accounts department of Red October. A few days earlier, there was another one: Breus, Mikifor G., died 3 November in Meshchanosky, now listed as a forklift operator.

Far from being tedious, the methodical task was proving therapeutic, balm for her weary soul. The names totted up. Goikhmann, Piotr D., died 28 September in Donskoy, now a tasting technician. Polivoda, Stassis K., died 19 July in Sloboda Kutuzova, resurrected as a security guard. Ratsimova, Marina R., died 1 June in Zyuzino, a spectral presence in the cleaning department.

Alice wondered what these people had been like when they were alive. Had they worked at Red October, or had Lev just picked their names from the death columns? She wondered too what their relatives would think if they knew their loved ones were being used this way. If there was money in it for them, she thought bitterly, they'd probably approve.

She stopped counting when she reached the start of 1991, by which point she had thirty-two matches, and even then she'd probably missed some. Conclusive proof, either way.

When she walked past the archivist's desk, she saw that his pile of card indexes had hardly diminished at all. Perhaps he was working towards finishing by the end of the week rather than the day. He looked up. "Good day?" he asked, suddenly friendly.

Alice nodded towards the indexes. "Better than yours."

Lev was waiting for her when she arrived back at Red October. "Where have you been?" he asked. "Your men have been asking after you all day."

*Her men.* She wondered if he'd chosen the phrase deliberately. "I'd things to do. What's it to you, anyway?"

He took her into his office and shut the door. Despite herself, Alice remembered what had happened the last time he'd done that.

"I'm very busy," she said.

He picked up a thick hundred-gram glass and handed it to her, his fingers brushing hers. "Handwashed in spring water – no scented detergent, please, not for our purposes. You see, the glass is stemless, and fits neatly into your palm? This warms the liquid, which is good; room temperature is best for testing. Long-stemmed glasses are better for pleasure, when the vodka is freezing and the afterburn icy, but this isn't pleasure. Master craftsmen must be particular about their equipment."

There were three small glass bottles on the sideboard. Lev removed the stopper from the first and filled Alice's glass. "I'm making it harder for you, I confess," he said. "The easy way to detect faults is to cut one measure of room-temperature vodka with two measures of pure, bottled spring water in a wineglass, swirl it to release the vapours, and then inhale. Most faults will then become so apparent that they virtually scream at you. But you don't strike me as a woman who needs to start at the beginner's level."

He held her gaze a beat too long for comfort, and then gestured at her to try the vodka. She dipped her nose to the rim of the glass and inhaled. The vodka was off, she could tell that without even having to taste it. She shook her head. "It smells bad."

"Be more specific."

"It smells of toffee." She sniffed again. "A faint layering of caramel, too."

"They both mean the same thing: diacetyl, burnt sugars from incomplete fermentation. You're right, that batch is no good. We'll have to throw it away. Perfumes are a dead giveaway. Amyl alcohol smells of nail-polish remover, DMTs of boiled cabbage or drains. Acrolein is sharp, acrid and pungent. The scent of green apples means acetal. Methyl thiazole, you can't mistake that one, it smells like cats. What else? Oh yes, ionone; that's heavy and sweet. *All* are bad news. Now, how about this?" He took another glass and filled it from the second bottle. This one she *did* need to taste; from the smell alone, she couldn't tell whether anything was wrong.

"Too heavy," she said. "Too greasy."

Lev clapped his hands together. "I'll be offering you a job at this rate. You're exactly right. We've overdone the fusel oil."

"The what?"

"It's a combination of butyl and iso-amyl alcohol. We use it in tiny quantities to make the vodka smoother. Not tiny enough here, clearly – not enough to be sold commercially, though I could fill a few bottles and peddle them to the bums outside without too much trouble. Last one." Another glass, another bottle, another sample. It was vodka infused with horseradish. Alice sniffed, swilled and swallowed.

"Excellent." She savoured the burn, extra strong with the infusion.

"Flawless – flawless."

"I'm tempted to have another sample, just to make sure."

"That would be greedy. I never need to make sure. I know first time when I've got it right."

He gestured, and Alice understood. The last sentence, perhaps the entire demonstration, hadn't just been about vodka, but about the two of them. Lev took a deep breath.

"Yesterday, I owed you an explanation," he said. "Today, I owe you an apology. I've behaved badly these past days, since . . . since what happened last Friday, and I'm sorry, I shouldn't have, but it's just that . . ." – she waited him out, giving him nothing – "this is difficult for me, because of the situation, the factory, and also because . . . because I'm used to Russian women, and you're different, you're like them in many ways but you're not in many others, and so if I'm behaving like a teenager, then that's why."

The blurting confession sounded strange coming from a man so mountainous, and it melted the hardness Alice had set in herself as surely as if it had been a blowtorch.

"I've been meaning to talk to you too, about what happened the other day, and . . . it was lovely, it really was, but you see, I'm married, I love my husband, and anyway; you must have the pick of all the women you want, all younger and prettier than me."

"You're beautiful," he said simply. It wasn't an empty compliment, she knew that. "It's you I want, Alice," he said, "you I *need*. A man considers himself frozen, stagnant, halfway lifeless; then the right flame draws him as though he were a moth, and when he gets close, it melts him."

With one hot hand she held his, while with the other she pushed him away. "Don't say such things," she pleaded. "We're supposed to be negotiating an auction, we can't . . . whatever you want, I'm not the one who can give it to you."

Those were her words, but her eyes said something very different.

"Is that what you really think?" he asked, and he knew the answer as well as she.

"No." Her voice was so soft as to be almost inaudible. "Of course not." She got up from her chair and came round the desk, never letting go of his hand.

"Is it true you had to fuck Arkin to get this job?" he asked through a laugh.

"No." She paused. "I blew him."

Alice hitched her skirt up and sat lightly on Lev's thighs. "Kiss me." There was nothing flip in her voice any more; she was deadly serious.

Lev cradled her face with his hands, making Alice feel small and adored and alluring, all at the same time. He took her lower lip between his and chewed gently on it, as though to eat her up one tiny, exquisite portion at a time. When he used his teeth, the impression was so soft and tender that Alice hardly felt it, but she knew instantly what it was and what it meant: a drop bite, his incisors leaving the tiniest of marks inside her mouth, a secret sign.

Alice and Galina walked past kiosks selling delicacies: smoked sausage, salami, even oysters. Business was good. Since all food was expensive, consumers had decided that they might as well buy the upmarket stuff before it disappeared. Everyone was tired of staples like canned sprats in tomato sauce – nicknamed 'unmarked graves' because they were such abominable blobs of bones and boiled eyes. The horror of empty shelves and lines was too recent and shallow to be confined to memory; people wanted the capitalist plenty they'd heard so much about, even if they couldn't really afford it.

They went to a bar on Tverskaya. The front of the bar top, where customers could rest their elbows, was stainless steel; the rest was solid ice, a channel lined with freezing coils which Firsov, the barman, called his hockey rink. Originally, the entire bar had been done in ice, but so many people had ripped their skin off when getting up that the design had been rethought. Firsov handed Alice a bowl brimming with pungent stalks of pickled wild garlic – an excellent accompaniment to vodka for those strong enough. Alice took one and chewed happily on it. Galina asked for coffee.

"I've only got the fake stuff," said Firsov. His eyes were shaped like teardrops. "That's how you can tell a real bar, you know: real bars can only afford ersatz coffee. The only places with real coffee are the fake bars, tourist traps." He shrugged; such contradiction was commonplace.

Tonight, Alice felt, she'd *earned* her vodka, and there was nothing quite like the first proper vodka of the day – tasting sessions like this afternoon's didn't count, not really. The first proper vodka was a ritual, and Alice approached it with due reverence. She opened the bottle with a quick, sharp turn of the wrist, then splashed the liquid into the glass, watching it rise high around the sides before settling to a level surface. She savoured the smell as the glass came up and the burn as the vodka went down.

It was passion, it was sensual pleasure, it was a paramour. It deadened the conflicting feelings inside her: a longing for intimacy but a terror of it, a wish to merge with others without being consumed. She was a gregarious introvert, she decided, that was her problem. She didn't like being alone, but equally she was very shy. At work, she could hide behind her professional persona: the proven privatiser, the market messiah. No matter how many questions she was asked, she had all the answers and one more.

It had been Galina who'd suggested the drink, and Alice recognised her courage in doing so. Galina was a secretary; to her, it must have seemed as though Alice had come from another galaxy, and Alice wasn't so self-absorbed that she couldn't see how intimidating she was capable of being. Galina had said that she wanted to improve her English, which had been culled almost exclusively from Sherlock Holmes stories and Beatles songs. "Your English is fine," Alice said, but she herself kept lapsing into Russian to prevent the conversation from stagnating while Galina stumbled over her words.

They spoke about this and that – what parliament would think of the privatisation plan, how Moscow compared to other cities Alice had visited, the merits of American and Russian hockey – but somewhere along the line Alice was conscious of talking too much. She was hardly taciturn at the best of times, but tonight she seemed overly chatty, too determined to cover all the natural pauses in discourse. Her cadence, her pacing were wrong. She knew Galina had picked up on it, for Russians are accustomed to people using words as a smokescreen rather than a window.

Galina cocked her head to one side. "What is it you're not telling me?" she said.

"Nothing. Why?"

"There *is* something, I know it."

"How can you know it, Galya? We barely know each other."

"That doesn't matter. You've got a secret, I can tell."

Alice smiled through a sigh. "Is it that obvious?" she said, knowing that it was. It was as if an excess of vitality so filled her being that it betrayed itself against her will; now in her smile, now in the light of her eyes. Glee and guilt pressed at each other within her. She was on to her fourth vodka, and she was desperate to tell *someone*. This was one secret she couldn't share with her usual confidant, Lewis, and Galina was the closest thing she had to a friend in Moscow.

The alcohol was working its way through Alice, carving out paths for itself, straightening her kinks, coaxing her tongue loose, tempting her to indiscretions she knew she should eschew. She put her finger to her lips. "*Tsss*! Shhh!"

"I won't tell anyone."

Alice glanced left and right, parody of a paranoiac. "It's Lev."

Galina knew instantly what she meant. Her mouth formed a perfect circle. "No!"

"Afraid so."

"You're insane." Galina mistook the amusement on Alice's face for offence. "Oh, I don't mean – I mean, you've done so much in your life, Alice, you know so much more about the world than me, so forgive me if I'm talking out of line or missing something, but . . . is this a good thing for you to be doing? I mean, you wouldn't have told me unless you wanted my opinion, would you?"

"Why don't you think this is a good idea?"

"For a start, you're married."

"And I've never done anything like this before."

"That's no excuse to start now, is it?"

"Have you ever cheated on Rodya?"

"He's the only man I've ever slept with."

"Oh." Alice thought briefly of the various lovers she'd had in college and on Wall Street: students, tutors, colleagues, clients – all received in the hope that they could help her find what she wanted. She wondered how anyone could know that they had found Mr Right without working their way through a few Mr Wrongs, and was startled when Galina mistook the source of her puzzlement.

"You're wondering how we do it, right?" By the time Alice realised what Galina was talking about, Galina was half a sentence on, taking Alice's silence for assent. "The same way as everyone else, that's how. Rodya didn't lose any of *those*, you know. But people see he's got no legs and think he must have lost the rest too." The words poured out of Galina in torrents; she'd damned them up for so long, Alice saw, taking every slight against Rodion as her own. "Everyone who sees us thinks two things, whether they say so or not." She ticked them off on her thumb and index finger. "One, how do they do it? And two, what the hell's she doing with him? He's no beauty, let's face it. Even back when we were kids, he was nothing special to look at. And you know something, Alice? I couldn't care less. He's got the best, kindest spirit in the world. You see him with the kids at the orphanage, and then you think of all he's seen and done in Afghanistan, all the things that have broken so many of those guys you see begging on the streets, and you realise that his warmth and generosity are even more amazing. He's my husband, and yet there's something so childlike about him that he's like my son too, so until we have a real child, I get two for the price of one!"

"I knew all Russians were capitalists at heart," Alice said, and they both laughed until Galina, embarrassed at the vehemence of her outburst, remembered where the conversation had been heading. "You're married, you're trying to privatise the distillery, and you sleep with the director?" she said. "Imagine what'll happen if this gets out."

"It won't get out."

"How can you be so sure?"

"You're the only person I've told."

"Then keep it that way. What about Lev?"

"I doubt *he'll* be shouting it from the rooftops."

Galina shook her head, unfathomably disappointed. "Why are you doing this? You're not a Russian, Alice. You're used to holding your destiny in your own hands. This isn't a game. All you're going to do is cause a whole heap of trouble for yourself. You want my advice? Get out while you can."

# 39

Rodion came into the factory with Galina first thing rather than
going straight to the orphanage; he wanted to see Lev personally.
A ceiling fan moved lazily, and Rodion felt something flickering
through his memory, something wasn't quite there – then it came
to him, of course, that the movement of the blades should be accompanied by their flat blatting sounds and the staccato roar of a helicopter's engines.

He hopped on to one of Lev's chairs, refused the offered
hundred grams with a shudder, and got straight to the point.
"There've been more Chechens hanging around outside the gates,"
he said.

"The same ones as before?"

"I'm not sure. But . . ."

"What?"

"I don't know, I might be wrong, I don't want to be responsible
if . . ."

"Rodya, you tell me what you think, and I'll decide what to do
about it."

"OK. I don't think this lot were watching our site."

"You said they were hanging around outside the gates."

"But they weren't facing in our direction, and they didn't seem
to care if we saw them."

"So?"

"Well, this is something I remember from my army training –
surveillance and positioning and all that. Perhaps their attention was
somewhere else nearby."

Lev steepled his fingers. "You know what 'somewhere else nearby'
might be, Rodya?"

"Yes. I've helped out there before."

"Good. Thanks for telling me this. We'd be better off if everyone
was as observant as you." Lev had been tipped off about Chechen
activity in the area a week ago, but Rodion would have been crushed
to learn that his precious nugget of information was worthless.

The compliment seemed to swell Rodion. "I can help guard the
place, if you need more men."

"Men are the one thing I'm not short of, Rodya."

\* \* \*

The night sky was darkened smog, hazy and moonless. Any watchers would have found it hard to make out the score of men moving silently into the underground car park beneath Prospekt Mira; they were swathed in black and kept to the shadows, far from the security lights and their weak pools of amber which illuminated the signs warning of dogs and patrols. Neither were to be seen, of course. It was too cold for anything other than a polar bear to be outside for long, and any guards would have been inside, huddling round gas fires and passing the time with vodka and cards, laughing at the man with the losing hand at the end of each round.

The car park went down five levels. At the deepest, covering the entire expanse of one wall, was a corrugated iron door that could be rolled back to allow deliveries to the subterranean vodka depository beyond. It was by this door that the Chechens congregated. Two of them attached plastic explosives to nine points on the door – the four corners, the midpoints of each side and slap in the middle, making three neat rows of three. The men worked fast to keep the others from freezing; several minutes standing around in that kind of cold felt an eternity, and men flexed their toes and fingers to keep the circulation going.

When the explosives were set and primed, the Chechens retreated to the other side of the car park and ducked behind parked vehicles as the fuses were detonated. The shock waves bounced around the walls, and the noise could have woken the dead, but this was Moscow – no one in their right mind would investigate an explosion in the middle of the night. There was smoke and tangled metal, a rich smell of burning, and the Chechens were through what had a few seconds before been a door. They fanned out in a line, squinting through the smoke for the slightest movement, but when the air cleared they saw nothing but crates of vodka stacked floor to ceiling: the booty they'd come for in the first place.

They brought three vans right up to the entrance and arranged themselves into teams: two in each van to stack, three to carry the crates to them. The containers were heavy, and the men were soon sweating despite the cold. Four Chechens stood guard outside; the others slung their carbines across their backs or put them down on the floor to make the crate-carrying easier.

The vans were half-full when Lev's men emerged from behind what was left of the screen of vodka crates. They came silently and in a rush. They didn't call for surrender or line the intruders up against the wall before tying them up; they simply shot them where they stood. Nothing clinical, no double-taps to the head and simple takedowns. This was carnage, machine-gun rounds like stitching, the Chechens torn apart by hollowed-out bullets tipped with wax and filled with mercury explosive. Holes the size of dinner-plates blossomed in chests; arms spun from bodies as if sliced off. Men seemed to burst under the weight of blood, scalps were rolled back from skulls, chunks flew from faces as though torn by the teeth of wild dogs. The screams stopped long before the gunshots.

When it was all over, Butuzov stepped out into an eerie ringing silence and began to stalk the aisles of the dead, checking that no one was left breathing. Lev had given him charge of this operation, as revenge for what Karkadann had done to Ozers in the florist's. Butuzov had been waiting here for a week now, night after night, rubbing his own bullets in garlic to promote gangrene in the wounds of anybody not immediately killed, but the precaution now seemed unnecessary – there wasn't so much as a twitch. Where two men lay tangled with each other, he kicked them apart to make sure neither was playing dead. He wasn't worried that any survivors would go to the police. The police would do what they always did: nothing. Besides, Karkadann's men prided themselves on their code of silence, they wouldn't tell. Butuzov was simply following Lev's orders: no survivors.

# 40

*Friday, 31 January 1992*
The underground repository yawned mockingly behind the fluttering tape. It had been cordoned off by the 21st Century rather than the police. Irk was the first law enforcement officer on the scene, and then only because the Petrovka switchboard operator had mistakenly put the call through to him rather than Yerofeyev. He remembered how Yerofeyev had behaved at the kiosk on Novokuznetskaya, and wondered how long he had before Yerofeyev arrived here and started throwing his weight around again.

Irk's most immediate problem, however, was a thick-necked man in a black bomber jacket standing four-square in front of him and saying: "You can't come in here." A mafiyoso telling a cop to stay out of a crime scene – only in Moscow.

Irk reached in his pocket and flipped his badge open. "Juku Irk," he said. "Chief investigator, prosecutor's office."

The bullneck peered at the badge. "Has anyone ever told you that you look like Keres?"

"Every day," said Irk.

The man shrugged and stepped aside. "It's not pretty in there."

"It never is."

Warehouse, slaughterhouse; Irk saw slicks of blood on the floor and bodies piled against a wall like discarded mannequins. He shuddered, partly from cold, more from squeamishness.

Sabirzhan was bending over one of the corpses, his salmon face clammy with sweat. Irk wondered whether seeing so much death up close was arousing him.

"There's nothing here for you, Investigator," Sabirzhan said without looking up. Irk felt momentarily wounded, as though the time they'd spent in Petrovka together meant nothing. Then he remembered trailing Sabirzhan round Moscow the previous weekend, and felt that Sabirzhan had a right to his hostility, even if he didn't know it.

"How much vodka's kept in here?" Irk asked.

Sabirzhan straightened, adjusted his pince-nez, and decided to answer. "A wagon and a side cart." A large amount.

"How much, exactly?"

They looked an odd couple: Sabirzhan with yellow eyes behind his pince-nez, Irk's softened features neatly clustered together, too cerebral and gentle for all this. Sabirzhan relented, as though humouring an old friend. "If we hadn't stopped them, they'd have got away with more than a million bottles."

Irk's left eyebrow was naturally arched; he raised his right to join it. Muscovites drink a million bottles of vodka every day. It's a hell of a number, whichever way you look at it.

"And there's, what, twenty men dead in here?"

"Twenty *trespassers* – that makes it their own fault. You're not the one being fucked, Juku, so don't make the motions."

Irk knew Sabirzhan was right, up to a point. The mafiya's quarrels were with each other rather than with the man in the street. So long as they didn't affect members of the public, why not let them batter each other to death? In any case, the argument was academic. Once the Pooh-Bah that was Yerofeyev got hold of this case, he'd administer a coat of whitewash sufficiently comprehensive and swift to make any builder proud.

Irk walked gloomily round the warehouse, more to show that he wasn't going to be pushed around than in any real hope of uncovering anything useful. Chechen cadavers lay tangled together in contortions that wouldn't have been out of place at an orgy. If there was ever any dignity in death, Irk thought, it hadn't found its way here.

He caught a glimpse of something, an image subliminal enough to be a memory. He blinked and looked again, knowing for sure what he'd seen and unsure whether he hoped he was wrong. *There*, beneath two dead Chechens who looked to have fallen on top of him, lay a young boy.

Irk leant down and rolled the first Chechen away. The body was brittle hard under his fingers – rigor mortis was setting in quickly. The second Chechen seemed to be clinging to the boy. Taking a deep breath, Irk yanked the man's arm from round the child's torso. Irk's stomach heaved, and he bit back the bile as his mouth filled with saliva; it wouldn't do to be sick here, in front of half the 21st Century. The Chechen went spinning on to his mate and the boy was left exposed, alone, bloodied and naked.

There they were: the same marks as on the other bodies. They were clearer this time, much clearer, perhaps because the victim was slightly less decomposed than the others had been, or perhaps because the killer had been more adept at inflicting them. Irk didn't care which. He cared only that he knew now what they were.

Not a crescent, or an angled letter 'T', but both, laid across one another. Together they made the most famous Soviet symbol of them all – the hammer and sickle.

Rodion and Svetlana arrived at the repository a few minutes later; the school and orphanage were just across the road, after all. Irk met them at the edge of the scene and took them aside.

"I don't know if you've ever seen a dead body before," he began, "but . . ."

"I was in Afghanistan," Rodion said indignantly.

"I meant Sveta."

"Never." Svetlana shook her head and swallowed nervously.

"Then I should warn you, it's pretty horrific in there. Think what you will of the Chechens, but there's a boy in there who's one of yours . . ." They looked more resigned than horrified, and why wouldn't they, when this was the fourth? "Someone you knew and cared for, perhaps more than the other kids, perhaps less, but . . . I'm sorry I have to do this, I'm so sorry, but I need to know what his name was, and at least one of you will have known him."

Irk clasped Svetlana's shaking hands between his. "OK?" She nodded.

As he led them back through the slaughter, Irk was grateful that the 21st Century men stood aside and didn't crowd them. They knew that there were those for whom death was part of life, as it were, and those for whom it wasn't. Irk took Svetlana and Rodion up to the boy's body and stepped away. Svetlana gasped and crossed herself. Irk thought he saw her swaying, but when he reached out to steady her she batted his hand away; she was fine. Rodion, closer to the corpse than either of then, shut his eyes and shook his head.

"No," he said, and Irk thought he heard anguish in his voice.

"I need his name, Rodya."

Rodion opened his eyes again and looked up at Irk. "I meant, no, I've never seen him before."

"Me neither," Svetlana said.

His miniature Estonian flag apart, Irk's desk was empty. Its blank cleanliness stood like a reproachful tract of Siberia in the crowded hubbub of ancient typewriters and crime reports piled into tottering turrets. A man who'd taken five weeks' vacation would have left his desk like this, not a man working on a case of serial murder.

Missing Persons were still checking their files to see if they had any record of a boy answering to the victim's description. That he wasn't one of Prospekt Mira's had come as a shock, there was no denying that, but the more Irk thought about it, the more it made sense.

For a start, he could no longer deny that the Chechens were responsible. The child had been with the men who had attacked the repository. Sidorouk reckoned he'd been dead longer than twelve hours, which meant they must already have killed him before going to the repository. They must have intended to leave him there as a signal, a warning. The only alternative was that he'd been killed earlier by Lev's men, there in the repository, and whichever way Irk looked at that, it made no sense.

As for the kid not being from Prospekt Mira, perhaps the Chechens had decided it would be more effective to spread the net wider. Until now, Lev had been obliged to explain himself only to the thousands of people who worked at Red October, but if news of the latest murder was made public he would have to answer to millions of Muscovites, all fearful that their own child would be next. It was, Irk acknowledged ruefully, smart thinking from Karkadann.

As for the hammer and sickle – well, Irk had to look no further than what Karkadann had said to him about the Chechen diaspora and the national exile to Kazakstan. The carvings were a defiant display of hatred against a regime now gone. That Lev had despised the Soviet Union just as much as the Chechens seemed to have escaped Karkadann's notice, or perhaps not. In

Irk's experience, men's hate is greatest when they see themselves reflected.

When he went down to the squad room, the uniforms were packing up. Irk called over to them.

"Gents, have you got a moment? I need some manpower."

"Nothing doing, Investigator," one of them answered. "We're due at Mytninskiy in half an hour." Mytninskiy was Moscow's largest audio, video and computer market, way up in the northern suburbs. It was open daily until six. Irk checked the duty roster. The men's shifts for today were over; they were going to the market not as policemen, but to act as muscle for one of the gangs who controlled the place. It was known as 'extra-departmental guard duty', just one more form of semi-institutionalised corruption.

"Hell, we've got to get some greens somehow," said a second man. He turned to his mate. "Yarik, you got my pager?"

"What do you need pagers for?" Irk asked.

"So we know when the exchange rate rises. We pass the news on to the traders, and they put their prices up. Sorry, Investigator. Another time, and all that."

They left the room at a jog. Irk looked at the calendar on the wall: the last day of January. Was it only a month ago it had seemed that, having got rid of the communists at last, everything would fall into place? The boil had indeed been lanced, but the doctors, instead of caring for the patient, were busy going through his pockets.

The door was still swinging behind the uniforms when Denisov came in. He hadn't been down here in so long, Irk wondered how he'd found the way without help.

Denisov had his hands behind his back, his traditional marker of bad news. "You know what I'm going to say," he said.

"And you know what *I'm* going to say."

"That he'll fuck it up completely?"

"Of course. You take the case from me, Denis Denisovich, and it's as good as unsolved. You know that as well as I do."

"I can't help that, Juku. The kid was found at a gang shoot-out. Give the case to Yerofeyev – you have no choice."

Irk shook his head. Denisov opened his mouth, and then closed it again.

"What?" Irk said.

"Nothing." Denisov shook his head twice and left the room without a backward glance.

It had been an apology, Irk saw, the words that had died on

Denisov's lips. It had been an apology, only Denisov didn't know the word for "sorry".

Irk rang Lev to tell him that he would be dealing with Yerofeyev from now on. Lev clicked his tongue. "If you'd listened to me, Investigator, perhaps we wouldn't be in this state now."

Hadn't Lev given Irk his full confidence? How many more people would let Irk down over this? He snapped back an answer before he could stop himself: "In that case, how many more children have to die before you change your mind about talking to Karkadann?"

"I'm not the one killing them, Investigator."

Irk slammed the phone down. It rang again instantly.

"Prosecutor's office."

"Is that Investigator Juku Irk?"

"Who's this?"

"I'm phoning from *Pravda*. I'd like to talk to you about the child you found this morning."

# 41

*Saturday, 1 February 1992*

It had turned even colder than before, a frigid morning under brumal skies to remind Muscovites that progress towards a brighter future, whether political or meteorological, was never smooth.

If it was chilly outside, the atmosphere in Borzov's office was positively glacial. Borzov himself stared gloomily at his hands and said nothing, wheezing through a blocked nose. Arkin did most of the speaking, from between teeth clenched so tightly that Alice feared he would grind them down. His message could hardly have been clearer had it been carved in ice. "Does everyone understand me? There is nothing – *nothing* – more important to the reform programme than this auction, and I will not have it jeopardised under any circumstances. I need assurances from each of you that you remain fully committed to the auction."

"I won't negotiate with that barbarian under any circumstances." Lev said.

"We're talking about children's lives here," said Alice. "Surely the priority has to be putting an end to these murders."

"Mrs Liddell, if the reform programme collapses in ruins, *millions* of children's lives will be at stake, not to mention their futures. Of course the murders are horrific, but for the international community to withdraw its support would be to give in to the killers. More than that, it would send a message that their tactics have succeeded. Is that what you want? No, the auction must go ahead. Those responsible for the murders deserve punishment, not victory."

"And you have Petrovka's word that we'll leave no stone unturned," Denisov said. "The case has been passed to organised crime" – he indicated Yerofeyev, who dipped his head with a modesty that hardly became him – "and our best men are working on it."

"Investigator Irk?" Arkin asked.

"This is no longer simply a homicide case," Denisov said. "Departmental rules –"

"Departmental rules be fucked. Everyone I've spoken to says Irk's the best man in Petrovka." Yerofeyev's incompetence remained implicit. "He's been on the case from the start, hasn't he? Then put him back there, *now*."

"With all respect, Prime Minister –"

"That's a direct order. This could make or break the country's good future, Denis Denisovich. Your handling of the case will determine whether it makes or breaks your career."

News of his reinstatement pleased Irk for all of several seconds. His anger was consuming. It wasn't just that *Pravda* had got the story – how, he didn't know, but he'd move mountains to find out – they had also found the boy's name, Modestas Butautas, while the police were still trawling missing persons files. Once more, Irk felt the police's failings as his own.

*Pravda* had devoted the front page and the next four to the story, and they'd got most of it right: the victims' names, the fact that the latest was a street kid originally from the Latvian capital Riga, the circumstances in which they'd been found, and the power struggle for control of Red October. All in all, Irk acknowledged, a pretty good job – perhaps he should ring the reporters up and offer them jobs at Petrovka. They seemed a damn site better at unearthing facts than most of the detectives he worked with.

He thought about going down to the basement to have it out with Kovalenko, once the Petrovka press department's Cerberus and now its lapdog, but what good would that do? He'd given Kovalenko a bottle of Eesti Viin; *Pravda* had obviously offered a crate. A man's loyalty nowadays was not to whoever paid his salary, but to whoever paid his bribes. The only surprise was that the story had taken so long to get out.

It was the main feature on all TV news bulletins by mid-morning, replete with grainy video footage – the Chechens had delivered a tape to one of the news agencies of Karkadann ranting at the camera: "For decades, Russians have been guilty of the most barbarous cruelty towards Chechens. Now, perhaps, you will start to understand our suffering." Channel One, the government station, was circumspect in its reporting, offering commentators with expressions of suitable gravity; Channel Two, with no official remit, thrust microphones into the faces of people on sidewalks and found answers to satisfy any demagogue: the mafiya should sort themselves out, privatisation should be stopped, the country was going to the dogs.

It was the kind of story – perhaps the *only* kind of story – capable of shocking Muscovites out of their habitual mixture of smug complacency and cynical resignation.

The lights in Irk's apartment flickered, rallied, and went off for good. Irk sighed. It was the third blackout in as many days, all caused by the same thing: residents using heaters so inefficient that they overloaded the antiquated electricity grids and blew fuses throughout entire buildings. He decided to pay the Khruminsches a visit; their apartment would be warm and light, a veritable Hilton compared to this place.

Irk's car started second time. Traffic on a Saturday was lighter than during the week, and he made good time. On Bolshaya Yakimanka, he passed a series of flyover struts, built and willing but as yet without a flyover to support. The stems of steel and concrete stretched forlornly skywards like flowers searching a sun, emblematic of a city on the rise, disposed to take any direction as it long as it led upwards.

This headlong, lemming-like quest for a better tomorrow had always been the root of Russia's problems, Irk thought. First the never-never utopia of socialist brotherhood, and now the rush towards capitalism in which business was equated with crime. Greed is a natural human attribute, but whereas Western countries had regulations to check the worst excesses of businessmen intent on accumulating money and connections, Russia did not. The successful Russian businessmen's strategy was therefore twofold: to build his own power base, and to demolish the competition through malicious rumours, brute force or subterfuge. How could you run an economy and a country on these lines without ruining them too? It was impossible. Organised crime all too easily perpetuates the conditions in which it can flourish. Left unchecked, it would soon become an indivisible part of the body politic.

Outside Okhotny Ryad metro station, women clutching goods for sale formed a line along the pavement. Each stared straight ahead, like suspects in an identity parade. As Irk drove past, he saw the line suddenly fragment and dissolve. When three police officers appeared a moment later, they found nothing other than a crowded street of people going about their business. The moment the cops had turned the corner, the line reformed as easily as it had evaporated. The women weren't breaking the law, just avoiding having to pay bribes.

Everyone was at it, that was the problem. Everyone was at it because that was the only way to survive. Irk wasn't simplistic. He knew that Russia's problems ran way deeper than the mafiya. The country could not hope to change its crime without changing its police, its politics, its morals, its values. Like Moses, the Russians needed to spend forty years in the desert so that the old generation could die off and a new, liberated one emerge. In the meantime, a man did what he could.

Rodion answered the apartment door, propelling himself smartly backwards when Irk extended a hand in greeting. "It's bad luck to shake hands over the threshold of a doorway," he said. "If you do, you'll have an argument." He tutted at the scepticism on Irk's face. "You Estonians, you're all the same: you think superstition's for peasants and bumpkins."

"Isn't it?"

"Of course not. Just because you can't explain something doesn't make it any less true. Come on in."

"What happened to your chest?" Irk said as he followed Rodion into the sitting-room.

"My chest?"

The top button of Rodion's shirt was undone and the next one was missing. Irk indicated three diagonal scars on the skin left visible in the plunge.

"Afghan medals," Rodion said. When Irk narrowed his eyes in confusion, Rodion explained: "Gorbachev himself decorated us, in Red Square on Victory Day. I pulled my collar open and pinned the medals into my bare flesh, so that they'd draw blood – because into those little pieces of metal we had poured the blood of our friends, the blood of those who died and those who went as children and returned as old men. Those medals held the pain of our hearts."

\* \* \*

These dinners with the Khruminsches had become the high points – the only points, come to think of it – of Irk's social life. Tonight, they talked about the case – what else?

"Lev should start negotiating with the Chechens," Svetlana said.

"That's what I told him," Irk said.

"That would be giving in to blackmail and threats," Rodion said. "You can never go down that path."

"Rodya, these are *our* children they're killing," Svetlana said.

"And so the only way is to wipe the Chechens out."

"Spoken like a true Russian," Irk said.

"And *that* was spoken like a true, patronising Estonian."

"Stop it, you two," Svetlana said. "What's more important? Who runs the factory, or the lives of children?"

"It's not that simple, Ma."

"It *is* that simple, Rodya. Galya, you're closer to Lev than all of us; can't *you* persuade him?"

Galina shrugged. "If Lev's made up his mind, he's made up his mind."

"Couldn't you at least talk to him? I can't believe you approve of this."

"Of course not. But I can't see what difference I can make either."

"You could say you tried."

"Ma, leave her alone," Rodion said. "Galya's right. We're the little people, all of us – even you, Juku. Every big decision gets taken without consulting us or thinking how it'll affect us. That's the way it's always been, and it's not going to change now."

# 42

*Sunday, 2 February 1992*

The lobby at Petrovka was full of children, most of them half-drowned by filthy clothes several sizes too big and looking around with defiant apprehension. Irk skirted round the edge of the throng and buttonholed one of the duty sergeants behind the main desk. "What the hell's going on here?"

"Street kids, all brought up from the sewers this morning."

"On what grounds?"

"Denisov told us to."

"For their own protection?"

"It was a nightmare, Investigator. We had to work in shifts."

"So the police have got manpower problems – tell me something I don't know."

"No, there were enough men, but we didn't have enough protective uniforms. Plus the maps were rubbish and the radios didn't work, so we all got lost."

One of the sergeant's colleagues was talking to a group of children while filling in forms – arrest forms, Irk noted with disbelief. "You're *booking* them?" he said. "On what grounds?"

"There are always grounds, Investigator."

Irk went straight up to Denisov's office and marched in without knocking. "Why are the police hassling these children instead of protecting them?" he shouted. "It's all for show, isn't it, for statistics which'll be falsified anyway? Those kids will be back underground the moment they're released. The whole thing is unutterably pointless, Denis Denisovich."

"Once again, Juku, you've failed to see the bigger picture. The prime minister has –"

"The prime minister has bleated about curfews for children, that's what he's done. He's blamed aid agencies for encouraging the homeless to come to Moscow because they reckon life's better here. Who does he think he's kidding, Denis Denisovich? Moscow controls four-fifths of Russia's revenues – is it any wonder people think the streets are paved with gold?"

Posters started to go up around Moscow later that day. They were written as a message from Lev, with pictures of the four victims and – in bigger type than everything else – a reward for anyone who provided information leading to the perpetrator's capture. The 21st Century had slapped the placards on to every surface they could find, overlaying bulletins advertising sports events, or the circus, or dance schools and theatres. To the cynical, the hunt for the killer seemed another form of mass entertainment for a city which craved diversion.

"We need to talk," Lewis said.

Alice was midway through pouring herself a vodka. She filled her glass, put the cap back on the bottle, and walked back to her chair. "OK. You go first."

"I think we should leave here."

"Because of the murders?"

"Yes, because of the murders. Don't sound so dismissive, Alice. I've seen people who've lost kids – I've *operated* on some of those kids – and when they're gone, there's nothing worse. Maybe you think those lives are casualties of war, a price worth paying. I don't."

Lewis spoke so slowly that, as always, Alice was itching to get her reply in way before he'd finished talking. "I think giving in would be worse than going on."

"For God's sake, Alice, you're not the government, you don't have to impress me with how tough you are. These people are killing kids because they want the distillery. Do you really think they won't come after *you*, if it suits them? Or me, to get to you? What are we to them? I'll tell you: we're prey. This thing'll go ahead with or without you. It's not worth getting killed over."

"This thing won't go ahead without me. There's not enough time."

"Oh, you're indispensable now? Alice, come on. This is the Wild East, this is the mafiya."

His tone was so condescending that Alice had a sudden urge to tell him everything about Lev, just to spite him. Lewis had no idea how deeply she was in with the mafiya, and they with her. Not for the first time, she thought how hard it was to take him seriously when he was angry. Where passion suited Lev, it sat uneasily on Lewis, like someone else's clothes. Every battle Lev had fought was etched on his face; Lewis was unlined, untouched, a sculpture in smoothed marble.

But it wasn't Lev about whom Lewis was worried, it was Moscow. Already, Alice loved Moscow with the infatuation of a new romance. She knew it wouldn't always be this way, and that her love would eventually be that for a difficult child or a temperamental lover: deep and resilient, but shot through with lines of hatred, resentment and anger, layers in rock.

Love it she did, however. Moscow set her senses jangling, it put her on full throttle every day. It was a city charged with history, even more than Berlin or Paris, and Alice could feel the overlaying of present with past wherever she went. There it was, lurking at the street corner; there again, oozing round her feet as she hurried along the pavements. The perpetual fight for life, the combat, the uncertainty, the excitement, the sheer unreality – Moscow energised her. She'd heard that Russia changed people. You went in as one person and came out as another. Tension stalked you with a shadow's impassive remorselessness. You woke with it, worked with it, ate with it, loved with it, slept with it. Some people couldn't take it and fled. Some grinned and bore it for as long as they had to. Some took refuge in eccentricity, some went insane. And some, like Alice, embraced the Russian bear and danced with it.

"Let's go home," Lewis repeated. "We can always come back in a few years' time, once this place has sorted itself out. If we still want to."

If we're still together, she thought.

# 43

*Monday, 3 February 1992*

February is always a gruesome month in Moscow. The early charms of winter snow have worn off, the consolation of the New Year holiday is long past, and there's still months of grimy slush to slog through before spring brings relief. Slimy sleet inside boots and grey wind in souls, darkness when work starts and darkness again when it finishes, the sun barely making it through the combination of noonday dimness, hangovers and the unknowable fear of the future.

It was the coldest day of the year, twenty-five below and falling. The cold was a presence, an organism; in the few steps between the front door of her apartment block and Arkin's limousine, Alice wondered briefly whether hell was freezing rather than roasting. Her earrings seemed to be burning into her flesh. She unfastened the flaps of her fur hat and pulled them down over her ears. Inside the car, Arkin greeted her with a bottle of vodka. "Rub this on your face," he said. "It'll help."

En route, Arkin pointed out the sights as though he personally had built the Kremlin, cobbled Red Square and erected the dome on St Basil's. "This is the greatest city in the world. The third Rome," he said, holding up three fingers on one hand and four on the other. "Built on seven hills, just like Rome was." Alice recalled Rome's history: a flea market of stolen goods and vanquished peoples, a city of hell and heaven, slaves in one and gods in the other; humans fed on dog flesh and vice versa, iniquity twisted like intestines on a butcher's block. What was new?

They bumped off the road and on to the pedestrianised section of Manezh Square. To their left, the Moscow Hotel was a monument to strained pomposity. "See the towers on either side of the central block?" Arkin said. "They're different from each other. Schusev, the architect, prepared two treatments for the façade, illustrating both on one drawing. He gave the sketch to Stalin, who approved and signed it as shown, not realising that Schusev wanted him to choose between the two. Schusev was too scared to point it out. So that was how the hotel was built: two wings, two designs."

Ahead of them the police were trying to clear demonstrators out from under Resurrection Gate so that the prime ministerial limousine could pass into Red Square. Alice saw that some of the placards targeted her personally: one portrayed her as a vampire, sucking the blood from the Russian economy; another as the devil in a dress; a third showed her as the Pied Piper, playing merrily while Borzov and Arkin led the line following her towards a river marked 'Doom'; in a fourth, she was a female Rasputin, bewitching and befuddling hapless politicians. She was foreign, and therefore cavalier with Russian money and sensitivities alike; her looks brought jealousy on the coat-tails of admiration. An easier target would have been hard to find.

Alice found herself shaking. This was the first time public opprobrium had been turned against her personally, and she felt violated by the depth of hatred. It was all right for Borzov and Arkin, they were used to it, in fact they *courted* it. For the people's elected representatives, it went with the territory. But she was nothing more than a paid official, why should she have to put up with it?

Her shaking, she conceded, might also have something to do with the amount she'd drunk last night. Well, that was Lewis' fault for pissing her off so much. When she'd finally crawled out of bed and gone to open the curtains, she'd had to brace herself against their weight; good Russian curtains are always heavy, to keep out draughts in winter and daylight in summer.

"Murderers!" someone shouted. "Stinking murderers, the blood of innocent children!" Another demonstrator half-broke through the police line. He brandished a sheaf of roubles at the limousine, and yelled: "You know what I'm using these for? Papering my walls, and wiping my ass. That's all they're good for!" The last words trailed away as the police finally managed to wrestle him to the ground.

Alice knew he had a point. Inflation becomes hyper when it rises fifty per cent month on month; the rate was past that now, and getting worse every day. Hyperinflation is self-feeding, increasing exponentially rather than linearly. If Russia were a Western company, Alice thought, the receivers would have been called in, the assets sold off, and the employees made redundant. Of course, it was insane to consider privatisation in such conditions. Of course, this was Russia, and they would continue.

The press was out in force for the official announcement of both the Red October auction, to be held exactly four weeks time, and voucher system under which all privatisation would take place. Every one of Russia's 150 million citizens was entitled to a free voucher, nominal value ten thousand roubles, which they could either invest directly in a privatised enterprise, put in a voucher investment fund, or sell for cash.

The voucher didn't look much: the paper was flimsy, and the design – grandiose banners proclaiming "Russian Federation" and "Privatisation" across the top and bottom respectively, between them an embroidered oval containing a stylised drawing of the White House from across the river, and a serial number in the lower right-hand corner – made it look less like a banknote than a lottery ticket. Which in a way, Alice thought, it was.

Arkin had initially been loath to give the vouchers away – the state needed money, and even the lowest of prices was worth something when multiplied by 150 million – but Alice had quoted his own words back at him: what mattered more than anything else was getting enterprises into private hands. They needed millions of owners with a handful each, not a handful of owners with millions each. It didn't matter who got it or whether they were ready or what they could do with it, so long as the state no longer owned it.

Besides, price liberalisation had wiped out everyone's savings, so the only people who could lay their hands on vast amounts of cash were foreigners and mafiyosi – and even Arkin couldn't think of a way to sell either possibility to the Russian people. In theory, cash privatisation was beautiful. In practice, it would be dangerous, untenable, cataclysmic. It would allow, even encourage, a small group to buy the whole economy, which in turn would spark resentment and upheaval.

Finally Alice's arguments had won the day and Arkin had agreed to give the vouchers away rather than sell them. She felt extraordinarily proud of herself. Could this be the same woman who'd shouted across Wall Street trading floors, "I got ten million IBM eight-and-a-halves to go at 101, and I want those fuckers moved out of the door *now*!"; the woman who'd herded clients into corners and sat on them until they'd puked gold coins; the woman whose first reaction to the Chernobyl disaster was to buy up as much crude oil as possible (nuclear stocks would take a hammering, less nuclear power meant an increased reliance on oil) and more potatoes than Idaho could produce in a year (fallout would contaminate vast swathes of European crops, putting a premium on clean American substitutes).

Arkin was taking questions, and they were coming thick and fast, the first from *Pravda*, even though the paper's reporters were supposed to have been banned from the room as punishment for last weekend's exposé. "How can you justify this process when children are being murdered in its name?"

Arkin arranged his features into an expression of suitably regretful solemnity. "We're in a time of transition, and transition always encourages transgression. Like all right-minded citizens, I abhor what the Chechens are doing. What we have here is terrorism, groups trying to coerce us into doing what they want. Yes, these things are happening at the distillery, and yes, they're horrendous; but far more horrendous would be to let them intimidate us into submission. Just because we're now a democracy doesn't mean we've gone soft. Those are my last words on the subject; I'll take no more questions about that."

Several hands which had been up went down. A woman got to her feet and peered over her reading glasses. "Why isn't Anatoly Nikolayevich here?"

"He's been under the weather, so he's recuperating at Sochi." Sochi is on the Black Sea; Borzov couldn't use the traditional presidential dacha at Foros in the Crimea, where Gorbachev had been detained the previous August, as the Crimea was now Ukrainian territory. "But he has sent us a message of support, and is fully behind the great progress we're making."

Translation, Alice thought, pleased with her perceptiveness and irritated that she hadn't seen it before: the president is distancing himself. If it all went to shit, Borzov would step away as smartly as a matador dodges a charging bull.

Arkin clapped his hands together. "No more questions. I want to show you our television commercials."

Half-slumped in her chair, Alice sat up fast. This was the first she'd heard of television commercials. She tried to catch Arkin's eye, but he was too busy supervising the technicians setting everything up. When the lights went down, Lyonya Golubkov appeared on the back wall of the conference room.

Lyonya was the archetypal Soviet buffoon, the modern-day version of Ivan the Fool. The idiot savant hero of countless Russian fairy tales, Ivan the Fool's default mode is to sit on the stove and do bugger all, occasionally rousing himself to catch a magic fish which will grant him three wishes, find a magic horse which will bring him riches and love and fame, or catch the firebird who's been stealing golden apples from the czar's garden and claim the imperial reward – half the kingdom in the czar's lifetime, the other half after his death.

The advertisements were divided into two sections: before and after. In the first, Lyonya, wearing a thick canvas jacket and shabby hat with ear-flaps piled on top, was a backhoe driver – though he could just as easily have been a plumber, a loader, or any kind of unskilled labourer. He was carrying his very last roubles to pay the administration fee for his voucher. "I'll buy my wife some boots!" he said, grinning at the camera. "Well done, Lyonya," said the narrator. In the Sberbank branch, Lyonya met other characters in the same boat as himself: Marina Sergeyevna, a single woman who didn't trust anybody but had faith in the vouchers; a couple of dirt-poor newly-wed students; and a pensioner whose glasses were held together with string. All of them had clearly been passed over or ruined by economic reforms – but, the message ran, these very reforms would now give them their lucky break. All they had to do was go to the nearest branch of Sberbank and pick up their voucher.

The contrast between before and after was as subtle as a sledge-hammer. Lyonya and his wife were now seen in a newly furnished apartment: ski boots in the hall, expensive fur coats hanging in the closet, a shiny new Mercedes outside. Marina Sergeyevna had abandoned her threadbare clothes and was admiring herself in the mirror of a luxurious boudoir. The students had also moved into a new apartment, all their own, no in-laws or friends or strangers hunkering down with them. And the pensioner was packing fruit and toys to send to his grandchildren in Barnaul.

The screen went blank as the tape ran to the end. The lights came on.

Alice's hangover suddenly reared again, and her mouth began to fill with saliva, a frothing, choking sensation which only ever heralded one thing. She pushed her chair back and walked quickly but unhurriedly from the room. It was only when she was in the corridor that she started sprinting. The gents' toilets were nearer, and it was those that she made for – any port in a storm. She threw open the door and slid the last few feet into the cubicle like a batter stealing bases.

She was still singing psychedelic praises to the depths of the china bowl when Arkin came in.

"Are you OK?" He looked concerned.

"Fine."

"You looked ill. I thought I'd better check on you."

"Something I ate, probably." She spoke through panting breaths. "I had herring and salmon last night, perhaps one of them was off."

"You can't waver, Alice."

"I'm not wavering."

"You're strong – that's why we picked you. Nothing great is ever achieved without sacrifice."

"I said, I'm not wavering."

Arkin made a moue of acceptance. "What do you think of the commercials? Pretty good, eh?"

"Honestly?"

"Honestly."

"I hate them."

"I know the production values aren't great, but it wasn't bad for a rush job, was it?"

Alice felt that she took eons to find her voice. "Those are blatant lies, Kolya. Wishful thinking, at the very least. You can't put that kind of stuff out on air. It's not going to happen like that, and you know it."

"Well, either we sell them that, or we watch the whole thing fall down around our ears."

"I won't be a party to this."

"You *are* a party to this. You're here to privatise the distillery. The more people who pick up and use their vouchers, the better for you."

"I don't want you to submit those commercials."

"Too late. They're going out tonight."

"Tonight? Then you must pull them from the schedules."

"It's too late. I can't do that."

"You're the prime minister, you can do whatever you want. Pull them."

"*No.*"

Alice saw that there was no doubt in Arkin's mind that he was in the right. He reminded her of a line from Dostoyevsky: if you gave him a map of the stars overnight, he'd return it the next morning covered with corrections.

Arkin turned on his heel and stalked from the room. Alice went over to the basins and splashed her face. It couldn't have been the amount she'd drunk, that was for sure; she'd drunk much more than that before without any ill-effects. All those television lights had made her hot, the protesters had made her nervous . . . Stress and seafood, that's all. And she'd got up and gone to work and done her job regardless. She wasn't collapsed in a gutter or in bed bemoaning her life. She'd done fine.

# 44

Alice's office phone trilled: the double ring which indicated an external line, so it wouldn't be Lev. She felt a gnawing sense of disappointment as she picked up.

"It's me," said Lewis. "Just to let you know I'll be late home."

"Trouble at the top?"

"A whole Schwegmann's bag full. More people to sack." His tone was neutral; Alice couldn't tell whether this was a prospect which excited or appalled him, or neither.

"Poor bastards," she said.

"Most of them, yes. Apart from one guy who's been stealing blood from the hospital stores."

"To sell on the black market?"

"Presumably. He's the first to go, and good riddance to him."

There was a knock on the door. "*Kto?*" Alice said. "Who is it?"

"*Kto, kto, ded Pikhto.*" It was a nonsense rhyme: "Grandpa Pikhto, that's who." Lev came in, doffing an imaginary hat as he blocked the doorway. His thick hair was swept back from his forehead and tucked behind his ears; tendrils curled up on themselves at the base of his neck. Alice held up a finger: one minute.

"Good riddance to him indeed," she said into the receiver, her voice unhurried. "Take your time, I might be late too."

Lewis hung up. Other men tell their wives they love them at the end of phone calls, and sometimes it irked Alice that Lewis was not like that. Today, however, she was relieved – he'd spared her the embarrassment of reciprocation in front of Lev.

They drank Sibirskaya, distilled from winter wheat and repeatedly filtered through birch-tree charcoal. The wafts of aniseed on the nose were repeated on the palate, this time with liquorice tones attached; a delicate and light aroma giving way to a large, fragrant taste, quite sweet and almost creamily smooth until the extra alcohol began to bite through a long finish.

"I saw you on television yesterday," he said.

"And?"

"You looked prettier than Arkin."

She laughed. "I didn't feel it."

"It's a lousy idea, the vouchers."

"It worked in Eastern Europe – I know, I know, Russia's

different. Why is it a bad idea? People can do with them what they want."

"They should be made to invest them in the enterprises where they work."

"I'm sure most of them will. But if they don't, you can't stop them." Lev was silent; Alice detected the lightest brush-stroke of amusement on his face. "Not even here," she said.

"What makes you so sure?"

"What are you going to do? Force them to sell you their vouchers?"

"Yes."

"You can't."

"I can, and I am. I've had their contracts amended to that effect."

"That's illegal."

"Not at all. I'll pay them face value, so they'll all make money from the deal. There are special provisions for the workers as it is. I'm just making sure all the vouchers go to the right place. What kind of signal would it send out if Red October's employees didn't want to invest in their own company?"

"Every worker?"

"Every worker."

Something jogged in her brain. "Every person on the payroll?"

"That's what I said."

Feeling vaguely nauseous, Alice made her way down to the distillery floor. She didn't like what Lev was doing, didn't like it at all, not least because she couldn't square it with the man she so desired. Until she was sure of what was going on, however, she would not confront him.

The first person she saw was German Kullam, staring into space. It was the start of the month, with production targets again weeks rather than days or even hours away, and the sense of urgency was all but invisible.

"What are you going to do with your privatisation voucher?" she asked. He looked first at her and then up towards Lev's office high above the distillery floor; the same motion as the woman in the bottling department, she remembered. "And you're happy about that?" she said.

"Lev knows best."

"German, this is a factory, not a damn cult. Are you happy about selling him your voucher?"

"You want to know what makes me *un*happy? Being invaded by Westerners on hardship packages. You get luxury flats, the best tickets for ballet and the theatre, restaurant allowances, six-figure dollar salaries – and on top of all that, *allowances* for 'deprivation'. That's not hardship, you shits on sticks. Come and live where I live, come and work where I work, come and earn what I earn – then you'll see what fucking hardship is." He tapped his chest, a warrior feeling for his medals. "We're the people without tears. Straighter than you, more proud. You see me – how old do you think I am?"

His face was scored with lines, anxiety and vodka in equal quantities; his hands bore the creases of a million experiences. "Forty-five?"

German snorted in derision. "Thirty-one. What about her?" He pointed at a woman working at a technician's bench.

"Fifty-two," Alice said.

"Forty," German said, his voice not without triumph, as if he'd just confirmed a great truth about pampered Westerners.

"You don't seem very busy," she said.

"Waiting for supplies."

"Isn't there someone else you could be helping?"

German looked blankly at her. It was not that he didn't like the question, Alice saw; rather that he didn't understand it. A Russian worker felt responsible only for his allocated task. If one worker had finished and another still had much to do, the first would never help the second, no matter how easy the work, and the second would never ask for help. Under Soviet law, every citizen of able mind and body had been obliged to hold a job or face prosecution. This meant that enough work had to be found for everyone, which in turn meant that each worker did his own and only his own specific share. "We pretend to work, and they pretend to pay us," the people had lamented under a system which gave little reward for hard work and didn't punish sloth. Suddenly they were expected to behave as though they were salesmen working on commission; it simply wasn't going to happen.

Alice went back upstairs to find Harry suggesting performance initiatives and bonuses.

"You understand nothing, do you?" Lev snapped. "*Nothing*. What you're suggesting would destroy this place. The moment you start paying people differently, you create envy, dislike, factionalism. This place runs on equality, Mr Exley, equal pay across a group. There's no room for individual ambition."

Harry tried again. "In that case, you need to raise prices. Sell your vodkas at greater margins."

"Who's going to buy them then, eh? How many ordinary Ivans have you seen ambling down the street counting their millions? Our prices are high as they are, to distinguish us from the third-rate poison that inferior distilleries and private piss-artists put out. If we go any higher, people will either switch to our competitors or they'll start making their own. Either way, we'll go from some margin to no margin. There's an old conundrum which goes like this: 'If they raised the price of vodka to the price of a suit, which would you buy?' 'Why, vodka, of course. What would I need with such an expensive suit?'"

Irk had been trying for three days to get an audience at the Belgrade Hotel; the phone call came through now, giving him half an hour to get there or miss his chance. Jump, the Chechen mafiya said. How high? asked the senior investigator.

They went through the same rigmarole as before with the blindfold, except this time the Chechens also searched him for tracking devices. Their paranoia was clearly on the up. The journey lasted longer than before, and Irk knew even before the vehicle stopped that they were somewhere in the countryside; the sounds and smells of Moscow's streets had long since evaporated, and the ride had been sufficiently bumpy to smack his head twice against the roof.

When they bundled him out of the jeep, they were rougher than before. Irk removed the blindfold and squinted against the snow glare. They were in a field, bounded on two sides by lines of poplars and on the other two by dirt tracks. It could have been anywhere.

"Where's Karkadann?" he said.

There were four men, all with their guns trained on him. None of them answered. He nodded towards the weapons. "Where the hell do you think I'm going to run to?"

They waited ten minutes in silence before another jeep appeared, listing drunkenly over the dirt track, and disgorged Zhorzh. He rummaged in his pocket as he approached Irk and brought out a wad of dollars, from which he peeled off a large chunk – the size, Irk thought, was as much a reflection of a gloved hand's lack of dexterity as it was of Zhorzh's generosity. Zhorzh placed the money carefully in the breast pocket of Irk's overcoat. With equal care, Irk took it out again and handed it back. Zhorzh scowled.

"You shouldn't insult us by refusing our generosity," said the gunman standing nearest Irk.

"And *you* shouldn't insult *me* by assuming my dishonesty."

"Leave this case alone."

"I couldn't, even if I wanted to. The prime minister himself has appointed me."

Zhorzh pursed his lips, thought for a second, and nodded at the gunmen. The one who'd spoken kicked suddenly at the back of Irk's knees, toppling him forward on to the ground. When he tried to push himself upright, snow clinging to his cheek, he felt a metallic ring pressed against the back of his head: the end of a pistol barrel, very, very cold.

Irk held his breath and waited, waited, as though seeing how long he could stay underwater. He'd never been one of those thrill seekers for whom life was incomplete without facing death. It seemed unfair that death should come looking for him when so many others went looking for it. Unfair, that was all. Unfair, such a prosaic word. If there was a great epiphany to be had at the last, Irk was surely missing it, and he felt disappointed at the mundanity of his thoughts. He didn't even feel particularly afraid. If you didn't have much of a life, how could you fear its loss?

Long beats of silence, ragged breathing which was his own, footsteps which clearly weren't.

Irk heard engines revving and the crunch of snow under tyres. It was only then that he realised there was no longer a gun pressed against his head, but he kept still until silence had floated back over him like a blanket. When he looked up, the Chechens were gone.

It took Irk an hour to find the main road. A ten-dollar bill clamped between shaking fingers ensured that a car stopped for him within the minute, and was good for a journey all the way to Petrovka.

Denisov offered him round-the-clock protection, which Irk turned down. A couple of prognathous youths in a clapped-out squad car wouldn't be able to save him from anything more dangerous than the common cold. Lev, too, offered him round-the-clock protection, and again Irk turned it down, not because he doubted its effectiveness but because he knew it would spell the end of his own neutrality.

Svetlana fussed over him and told him he had to be careful, there was a shortage of good men in Moscow as it was.

"When your time comes, your time comes," he told her, and wondered if he really believed it.

# 45

*Wednesday, 5 February 1992*
The rate of provisional voucher take-up – the vouchers themselves weren't to be released until a week before the auction, ostensibly

for security reasons but in reality because they were being printed on presses which were old and temperamental – had soared since Arkin's advertisements were aired. Western audiences would never have fallen for the idea that a voucher could transform lives, but for Russians it was seductive. People who no longer believed in politics or nationhood were ready to trust a commercial that promised to make them rich overnight. So frenzied was their quest to enter this looking-glass world that they forgot to ask themselves the most crucial question of all: would there be milk there? And if there was, would it be good for them to drink?

Sabirzhan came in carrying an armload of files, which he put on Alice's desk with an exaggerated flourish and a theatrical wipe of his brow. She smiled her thanks and started on the nearest file even before he had left the room. They were behind schedule, there was far too much for Harry to cover by himself, and Alice had proved during her time on Wall Street that she could read a company's finances as well as anybody.

The files were routine stuff, boring but essential: real estate contracts with the Moscow city government, agreements with suppliers, budgets for research and development. Alice soon got into a rhythm of speed-reading, deliberately slowing her breathing so as to keep herself from going too fast and missing something. It took her all morning and most of the afternoon. Towards the end, her eyes were beginning to blur from looking at too many faded and badly copied documents. By the time she got to the last file, she was ready to call it a day; but she'd made it this far, she thought, and another half-hour of concentration wouldn't hurt her.

The file was labelled 'Suyumbika', and Alice saw instantly that the contents were dynamite.

There was no way Sabirzhan could have meant for her to see this, she thought. Yes, Red October was obliged to give her full co-operation and disclosure, but Alice was becoming more realistic about how much work they had to do and how little time they had in which to do it. There must have been an entirely plausible alternative file that Sabirzhan should have given to her instead, and she'd never have known the difference.

It was clear what Alice should do: take all the files back to Sabirzhan, thank him for them, and hand them over. The auction was less than a month away, why rock the boat now?

Why indeed. Because that was the kind of person she was: a prober, an inquirer, restless and ambitious, and you could no more show a file like Suyumbika to her and expect her not to act on it than you could dangle a bottle of vodka in front of an alcoholic and expect them not to drink it.

In the toilets, Alice saw that she wasn't the only person removing items surreptitiously from the premises. Two women were decanting vodka into hot-water bottles which they then strapped to their chests. They didn't miss a beat when they saw Alice, which annoyed her.

"What are your names?" she said. "I'm going to report you."

"For what?" said one. "If everything belongs to everybody, nothing belongs to anybody."

"That's not the case any more, and you know it."

"That's always the case. We take what we can get: *that* hasn't changed."

"Report us all you want," said the other. "The guards won't care. Everyone knows the limits."

Wasn't that the truth? Alice thought. Theft was fine, so long as it was at an acceptable level.

Outside Pushkinskaya metro station, Alice had to fight her way through a queue which seemed to stretch halfway round the block. She followed it all the way to its source at a post office. Post offices had insufficient funds to pay pensions, so the staff waited until someone came in to mail something and then paid the next person in line with the money just received. If you went away and came back the next day, you'd find that your pension was worth much less than it had been the day before, so no one dared leave, and the queues got longer and longer.

A police car shot past, leaching blue neon into the smoggy darkness. Alice caught a glimpse of two Chechens in the back seat, each cuffed to a grabhandle, each staring out of the window with the sullen disillusion of aliens wondering what kind of world they'd landed on.

"We've got enough for a couple of soccer teams, and none of them are saying a damn thing." Denisov hawked deep in his throat and spat into the trash can. "I don't tell him how to run the country, so what gives him the right to tell me how to do my job?" Because he's the prime minister, Irk thought, but didn't say it. "Oh, I forgot – you're his new favourite, aren't you?"

Irk understood Denisov's anger perfectly well. Arkin had demanded that the police not only do something, but be *seen* to be doing it. So the order had gone out: round up low-level Chechen gangsters. The exercise was excruciatingly pointless. Any Chechen mafiyoso insufficiently well-protected to escape the trawl was by definition too junior to have any useful information about Karkadann's whereabouts. So nothing had been achieved, and everybody was pissed off: a bunch of Chechens in leather jackets who had better things to do with their time; Denisov, who'd lost face by being forced to authorise the farce; Yerofeyev, who'd now have to explain this whole farrago to those higher up the Chechen food chain who paid his bribes; and Irk, who seemed to be collecting enemies as though they were football stickers.

# 46

*Thursday, 6 February 1992*
Alice read until the small hours, undisturbed because Lewis was on night shift. By the time she'd finished, she'd confirmed her worst fears, and then some. Red October was selling vodka at artificially low prices to a shell company, Suyumbika, which was then exporting the vodka at much higher (and tax-free) international prices, and pocketing the difference. In the past year alone, Suyumbika had cleared more than twelve million dollars. The file included hundreds of bills of lading, detailing each shipment's nature, size, source and destination.

There was hardly a country in the developed world to which Suyumbika hadn't made a sale – nor, it seemed, a country in the former Soviet Union. The fourteen republics which along with Russia had made up the USSR were now foreign countries, and vodka sold to them was therefore export rather than domestic trade. Alice found bills of ladling to Yerevan, Tashkent, Riga, Tallinn, Tbilisi, Kiev and Minsk. Clearly, the union's disintegration was proving lucrative for Suyumbika.

In contrast, the official figures for Red October over the same period listed less than four million dollars' worth of exports. The profits from these sales went into the distillery accounts and were therefore included in the privatisation assessment, whereas the profits from Suyumbika presumably went straight to the pockets of Lev and whoever else was in on the scam. To Alice, they were technically untouchable.

This was the way things worked here, wasn't it? That was the easy way out. Alice could make excuses for Lev all she wanted. This was the man with whom she was sleeping, this the man for whom her feelings were already dangerously strong and deep; this was the man who was ripping off his own company.

Sabirzhan was waiting for her when she arrived at Red October.

"I was just wondering whether you'd finished with the files I gave you," he said.

"Oh, sure." She gestured towards the pile on her desk. "Be my guest."

Sabirzhan picked them up, flicking through the covers like a croupier. "There's one missing."

"There is?"

"The one marked 'Suyumbika'."

"I haven't seen it."

"You haven't read that file?"

"No. Not that I can think of." She laughed. "Read them all in one go, it's hard to tell which is which." She looked down at the ground. "Oh, there it is." Crouching quickly down, the desk shielding her from Sabirzhan's line of vision, Alice let the Suyumbika file slide from her bag into her hand. Surfacing, she gave it back to Sabirzhan. "Must have fallen on the floor."

"Must have." She couldn't tell whether he was being sarcastic.

"Shouldn't I read it?" she asked, feeling mischievous.

"There's no point. It's just a duplicate of this one." He tapped the uppermost file and left.

You can lie as smoothly as I can, Alice thought. Of course he could: he was KGB.

"Have you come across something called Suyumbika, Harry?" Alice asked.

"Suyumbika? What's that?"

"Just a name I thought I recognised."

He shook his head. "Not that I member. Too much vodka, making you imagine things."

"Probably." Alice wasn't ready to share her discoveries with Harry and Bob. She should have done, she knew, but she felt that this was between her and Lev. She hadn't told her colleagues that she'd known about the child murders before *Pravda* had made the story public; as far as they were concerned, they knew everything she did, and vice versa. They were a team, right?

"The books don't balance," he said. "Not even close. As far as I can make out, we're dealing with debts of hundreds of millions of roubles here, even at the old values."

He showed her the workings: the amount owed to suppliers was well into nine figures, the amounts owed to banks and the state were eight each. It wasn't surprising. Enterprises ran up such huge debts because they could. The creditors with the capability to enforce payment – government agencies – didn't do so because the administration were afraid the resulting bankruptcies and plant closures would provoke social instability. As for the banks and suppliers – well, if they didn't have the muscle to enforce payment, who cared what they thought?

"It's taken me ten days, I've worn out four ink pens, and to be honest, I could go round and round till the end of time without knowing whether I was any closer to the truth," Harry said. "It's like standing in a jungle and looking into the trees. There's something in there, and though the camouflage means you can't tell whether it's a tiger or a snake, you know it's not nice. If this was a potential M&A in the States, I wouldn't touch it with rubber gloves and a bargepole."

"Well, it's not. Nor is it helpful to apply those standards here. What you got?"

"I've calculated Red October's statutory capital at 45,214,000 roubles. Divided by a nominal value of 1,000 roubles, this gives 45,214 shares. Ordinary shares held by management and workers make up 51% of the total, that's 23,059 shares. We offer 29% per cent – 13,112 – at auction; and the remaining 9,043, the last 20%, are held back by the state. That's it."

Figures made it official, Alice thought; figures meant it was really going to happen. She wanted the auction to go forward, it was what she had set her heart on, the pinnacle of her career to date. Yet at the same time she wanted to uncover whatever darkness there was at the heart of this place, whatever the harm to her cause. These twin contradictory thirsts for achievement and knowledge tugged at Alice, just as she was torn between love and guilt, loyalty and betrayal, desire and ambition, friendship and lust. The time was coming when, caught in the conflicting currents, she must hold her nose and take the plunge.

# 47

*Friday, 7 February 1992*

In addition to Lev's penthouse, the Kotelniki building also housed the Illusion cinema, in Soviet times the only one in Moscow which had shown undubbed foreign films. Now, a painting advertised *The Silence of the Lambs*; the artist had improbably but spectacularly contrived to make Anthony Hopkins resemble Ivan Lendl, and Jodie Foster Pinocchio.

Lev had invited Alice for dinner. She was going to be strong, she told herself as she stepped into the elevator, strong and professional. She would tell him that she'd discovered his scams, that the West would see them as unacceptable, and that he'd better have a good explanation. She wouldn't let him pour her any vodka, and she wouldn't let him undress her.

She ran her hand over his belly, marvelling at its hardness.

"If it wasn't like that, I'd break my back every time I lifted weights," he said.

He kissed her round the back of the neck, just below the hairline; he kissed her on her eyelids, licking from their centres to their edges; he kissed her in her ears, blowing gently in one and nuzzling the other; he kissed her on her hands, looking up at her as his tongue traced lazy circles across her palms; and he kissed her where her wrists pulsed, the lightest of touches.

He was a heart too hot to hold, a flame that burnt her soul.

In Gozo, years back, Alice had swum through the Azure Window – a cave that led from the sea into a small lagoon. As she'd scissored through the water, she'd felt bubbles rising from the depths beneath her. When she'd looked down, she'd seen nothing but ever-deepening shades of blue, extending to infinite darkness. She had known then that if she were to stop swimming and let herself sink, she would never reach the bottom – the monster breathing those bubbles would have eaten her first.

She was experiencing a similar sensation now, held in suspension over the abyss to a strange and hazardous world.

Lev's right foot was covered in tattoos of cats, signifying his life as a thief. Several cats together across the top showed that he was part

245

of a gang, while the tom's head on his instep represented good luck and warned that the bearer was not to be messed with.

"Tell me about him," he said.

"Tell you about who?"

"Lewis."

Alice thought of the wedding photograph in her sitting-room: the two of them laughing as they ducked a shower of confetti. Lewis was beautiful – handsome to the point of ugliness, like he'd just stepped off the pages of a glossy magazine, the kind of guy who appeared in adverts. When it came to handsomeness, he was streets ahead of every Russian man she knew. But now Alice found his looks flat and antiseptic. Lev's face was much rougher than Lewis'; Alice felt she could lose herself in Lev's features for ever.

She was reluctant to answer. "Why do you want to know?"

"Why not?" Within Lev's parameters, the question was entirely normal.

"OK. *What* do you want to know?"

"What's he like?"

"Everything I'm not. Quiet when I'm loud, dependable when I'm all over the shop, sober as a piece of glass when I'm oinking like a pig, part of the furniture when I'm the garish centrepiece."

"He doesn't know about me?" She shook her head. "Does he suspect?"

"No." Alice had convinced herself that she could partition her life into small, separate compartments. Lev's existence, her drinking – it was easier not to explain things to Lewis. The best way to keep the harmony was to maintain his ignorance. "It's enough that he thinks he's losing me to Moscow."

"He's right."

She shrugged. "You know when I first wanted to come here? I was working up in Lake Placid at the Winter Olympics, twelve years ago. I was a student, it was a volunteer job, crap pay, endless fun. I was one of the stewards that day at the ice hockey, when we beat you . . ."

"That team played under the hammer and sickle. It was *not* mine."

". . . and when the hooter went, I was looking not at the Americans but at the Soviets. I'd never seen a team look more upset – they were devastated."

"What did you expect them to be?"

"Automatons. That was what we'd been fed, remember: that these unsmiling people would come here, win the gold medal without a flicker of emotion, and go back home to their grey cities. Only it turned out they weren't robots, they were human beings. Ever since then I've wanted to come here. Last year, when I was offered the privatisation job, Lewis begged me to turn it down. He didn't want us to come here, even when the Sklifosovsky approached him. I persuaded him that this was the land of opportunity. We were stagnating at home. I wanted that buzz again, the one I'd had in Eastern Europe: that sensation of being at the cutting edge, where history's made."

"And so you should. Foreigners who are drawn or sent to Russia become part of our history, in all its restlessness and unpredictability, no matter how much we like to pretend they don't."

"But how many of them realise it? Most of the chowderheads here see this as just another foreign posting. They might find it *exciting*, but does it grab their soul the way it does mine?"

"Then that's their loss, and there's nothing you can do about it. If a man's a fool, he'll stay that way for good. Being part of history is easy. Shaping it, less so – that privilege is given only to the chosen. Have you ever read Alexander Blok?" Alice shook her head; Lev quoted from memory: "Dear overseas guests, go to sleep. May your dreams be blissful; forget that darkness falls on the cage we struggle in."

"Isn't it my struggle too? We – *I* – came here with the best of intentions; to make a difference, to transform this society. The West had won the Cold War, it was up to us to show a winner's magnanimity, be helpful in the hour of our triumph."

"Alice, Russians don't like it when foreigners talk like that."

"But it's *true*, Lev – I can't help that. It's just that living in Moscow has done different things to us. The more my horizons expand, the more Lewis' seem to contract. I'm twice an outsider, an American woman in a world dominated by Russian males; but I feel more at home here than I've ever done in Boston, in D.C., even in New York – and if there are two places on earth you could confuse with each other if you don't look too hard, it's Moscow and New York. Look at their . . . look at the dirty vibrancy they share, look at the people's fuck-you attitude, look at all the Mercs and Beemers and limos on the streets. I love Moscow, Lev, I *love* it. I should hate it. I should hate its fumbling drunks and its racism and its unmade roads and its callous authorities and its violence – and I *do*, I do hate all that – but I still love the place."

"Of course you do. What's life, if you live it on a flat line? No great downs, true, but no great ups either. You might as well be dead. Ups and downs are proof that you're alive. Flatlines are what happen to patients in hospital when their bodies give out on them."

"Tell that to Lewis: he spends his days watching for vital signs."

"Why don't you leave him?"

"Do you want me to?"

"That's not what I asked."

She took a deep breath. "All right. If I left him, I'd be admitting failure. I've never failed at anything in my life, and I don't want to start now. I still want him to love this place as much as I do. He's already talking about going back to America. If he does that, either I leave him or I leave here."

"And if you leave here, then you leave me."

"And that I can't do."

Alice drained her glass and shook it at him. "Fill her up."

He paused a moment, looked at her, and poured. "You're tucking that away behind the tie."

"Taking it to my breast, and it feels good." She drank half the hundred grams down in one.

"When did you start drinking?" he said.

As far as Alice could recall, Lev was the first person ever to have asked her that. Most people just accepted her drinking as a part of her, as innate and integral as her spleen.

"As a teenager, I guess. It used to be a big thing, going out and getting drunk – you know, rites of passage, experimentation, all that. Boys thought it was really cool to know a girl who could out drink them. Once they'd got over the blow to their machismo, they treated me like some kind of party piece. They loved me for that, and it made me feel popular and wanted – and sexual too, of course. It lowered my inhibitions, made me feel randier, and most teenage boys couldn't find their own assholes with a mirror, they're so fumbling and clumsy, so it was just easier to be drunk." She paused, as thought she'd just articulated the thought for the first time. "That's it, I guess: it was *easier* to be drunk than not to be. It's more ingrained and complex now, but that's where it started. There was always liquor round the house, it was too easy."

"Your parents drank?"

"My mother, especially." Alice reached for her glass. It was empty, and for a moment she felt disconcerted, she couldn't remember having finished the last measure. "She was . . . she was an alcoholic. I know, I know, alcoholism can be genetic and hereditary, transmission's more often maternal than paternal – I know all that. I'm lucky to have escaped it, I reckon."

"Do you remember her drinking, when you were a child?"

"Oh yeah. And I know all the psychobabble, I had all that shit rammed down me about the way children behave in those situations. Whether they try to act the hero and achieve things in school or sports or drama or whatever to get love and appreciation; or whether they go for the caretaker-come-lost-child approach, taking responsibility for the family and looking after it by blending gently into the background and keeping the peace when they can."

"I'd never heard of those."

"You're not American. In America, you can hardly walk out of your front door without being mugged by shrinks. It's all bullshit. Therapy schmerapy. Let's leave all that crap in America, where it belongs, and talk about something else, shall we?"

Sensing the hurt behind her cavalier dismissal of the subject, Lev acquiesced, even though he would have liked to know more. On the surface, Alice was the typical brash, hard-as-nails American bitch – or so she would have everyone believe. But there were chinks in that armour-plated surface that offered tantalising glimpses of the woman within. A woman who was anything but typical.

Perhaps it was something common to every only child, this need to belong and yet to be alone. Alice could count on the fingers of one hand the number of friends she had; proper, true and valued friends, that was. There were many others, of course, who dropped into her life and then left again, like Bob and Harry, coming and going. Alice had tried in the past to join groupings of people, but it hadn't worked. She was too singular. Her beauty and vulnerability were those of a woman; her haircut and clothes were masculine. Without siblings, an only child puts up boundaries and cordons. Alice was born lonely and had grown up lonelier.

There was a complete absence of guilt in Alice. It was the only thing that made her feel guilty. What she and Lev had was beyond regulation. It couldn't be negotiated like treaties, rationed like food parcels or ignored like background noise.

"I only wish to save myself," she told him, "but I don't know how."

His eyes were grey. Skin scooped under his cheekbones and ridged around his mouth. He had no answers, no questions, only a statement.

"I love you," he said.

It was the response Alice's soul desired and her reason dreaded.


"Where've you been?" Lewis asked. His voice was distant; he was in the bedroom.

"Working late." *With my lover.*

The apartment was stuffy and hot. Alice turned on the humidifier and opened the window. She went through into the bedroom, and as usual the guilt came flooding back the moment she saw Lewis' beautiful, trusting, bland face. But now his features were not those she remembered, he looked somehow different. Alice looked again, and realised that it was she, not he, who'd changed. She noticed things about him that she'd previously taken for granted. The lobes of his ears kinked sharply upwards just before they fused with his jaw – how had she missed that? Look how lightly the puffs of skin beneath his eyebrows rested on his eyelids. Lewis was one of the central staples of her accepted life, but now everything seemed fractionally off-centre: a twin who wasn't quite identical, a room which had been searched and left infinitesimally out of kilter, a voice heard on tape rather than from inside the owner's head.

This was their home, their life, hers and Lewis', where everything had its own poetry, sincerity and warmth. Alice wanted very much for it to be safe and whole again.

Lewis flipped through a medical journal as he talked. "You'll be glad when it's over, huh?"

"It's not for very much longer, and . . ."

And then, numbed by the recollection of her treachery, she ceased hearing a word of what she was saying. She felt her nerves being stretched like strings drawn tighter and tighter round pegs. Her toes fidgeted inside her shoes. It was her passion for Lev which had caused this, a flood of white light in which her former world, illuminated without mercy or respite, looked like a dead landscape on an extinct planet. She saw Lewis bend the magazine back on itself and settle down to read an article, and she wanted to scream at him that it didn't matter, none of it mattered. He couldn't be aware of her happiness, and she pitied him from the bottom of her heart.

His light was out by the time she came back from the bathroom. All the forms and sounds in the swaying semi-darkness struck her with unusual vividness. Her thoughts swarmed and whirled, seeming to move in skeins which constantly tangled and untangled themselves. For a long time she lay perfectly still, thinking of Lev, her eyes wide open and so bright that she fancied she could see in the darkness.

# 48

*Saturday, 8 February 1992*
"I want out," Alice said.

Arkin was nothing if not a professional politician. He showed no surprise, still less alarm. He merely cocked his head and said "I'm sorry?" as if they were talking on a bad phone line.

"I want out," she repeated. "The privatisation programme – I've had enough."

Arkin's look said it all; this was the woman who'd sat on a podium with him earlier in the week and swelled with pride when they told the world's media how the programme was going ahead come what may, and the nay-sayers be damned. She'd given him her word that she wasn't wavering – and here she was, swaying like a larch in a hurricane. "May I ask why?"

"Because the process has moved too far from what we started with." *Because I'm falling in love with Lev.* "Because two mafiya gangs are fighting over the distillery." *Because I'm falling in love with Lev.* "Because children are being killed there." *Because I'm falling in love with Lev.* "Because we haven't enough time to do this properly." *Because I'm falling in love with Lev.*

Sitting at his desk, his mouth pursed, Arkin considered what Alice had said for several moments before replying. "Alice, the auction of Red October takes place in three weeks. Even if you were to leave now, your achievement would be considered heroic. But if you leave now, who could possibly take over? No one, that's who. You're invaluable, and you know it as well as I do."

The dim lighting pouched his eyes in shadow. "I hear what you're saying, and I understand your reservations, but I ask you to reconsider. This isn't just about you, or me. What we're doing is for the Russian people, so they can live in a normal country, not one run on lies and sophistry. We used to laugh at the six paradoxes of socialism. You know what they were?"

Alice shook her head. Arkin began recite: "There's no unemployment, but nobody works; nobody works, but productivity increases; productivity increases, but the shops are empty; the shops are empty, but fridges are full; fridges are full, but nobody's satisfied; nobody's satisfied, but everyone votes unanimously. You want Russia to go back to that? Would you live with yourself, if you walked away now?"

"It's not that."

"Then what is it?"

She couldn't tell him. He had demolished every objection she'd put up, of course he had, because what she'd told him wasn't the truth, and she couldn't tell him the truth, so she couldn't in all conscience step down. Arkin had her over a barrel.

"I'll stay," Alice said. "I'll stay until it's over."

# 49

*Sunday, 9 February 1992*

Lev was asleep when the phone in his bedroom rang. He knew before answering that it must be important; very few people had his private number, and none of them were without influence. When he picked up, his first reaction was surprise that the voice was Karkadann's. His second, more pressing, was alarm that the voice was Karkadann's.

"The reservoirs. Potassium cyanide," Karkadann said, and rang off.

The reservoirs in question were the ones Red October maintained up near the Mytishchi Springs, whose soft, calcium-free water the Kazan distillery had stopped taking the previous month. It took Lev minutes to assemble a twelve-vehicle convoy, five men to a car. At that time on a Sunday morning, traffic was light, though it would have made little difference had it been rush hour on a Friday: the convoy jumped red lights, ignored one-way signs and trebled the speed limit on occasion, and not a traffic cop in Moscow would have dared stop them.

The Mytishchi reservoirs were protected by two concentric rings of razor wire and permanent patrols of armed men in uniform and dogs. Lev himself strode up to the security officer in charge: V. Golovin, according to the laminated nameplate on his chest. In his hurry to stand to attention, Golovin practically snapped himself in half.

"Have you had any break-ins?"

"No."

"No alarms, strange incidents?"

"None."

"No Chechens in the area?"

"They're the first thing we look for."

"All your men accounted for?"

"Yes."

"Go and check the perimeter fence, every centimetre. Draw off samples of water from each reservoir and have them sent to Petrovka for analysis; the boffins there do it, for a fee."

The phone was ringing in the guard hut at the main entrance to the reservoir complex. Golovin gestured diffidently in its direction. "May I?"

"Of course."

Golovin hurried into the shed and snatched up the receiver. Lev saw Golovin's body stiffen, his face urgent as he snapped words soundless behind the heavy bullet-proof glass. In an instant, Lev was in the hut, taking the phone from Golovin and filling the tiny space with his anger. It was Sabirzhan calling: a 21st Century convoy bringing grain from Krasnodar had been attacked on the Garden Ring, and it was carnage.

Blue and red emergency lights rotated lazily in the pale light of a winter morning. The ambush had taken place at Serpukhovskaya Square, where the main road from the south meets the Garden Ring. It was a logical enough place to have mounted an ambush: any traffic coming from Krasnodar to Moscow would have had to pass through here.

There must have been thirty vehicles at the scene: ambulances and police, with civilian cars being filtered round them. There were no trucks; the Chechens must have stolen the lot. Lev strode angrily through the police cordon. A young officer moved to stop him, but then thought better of it and backed away.

Bodies littered the ground. Lev recognised the drivers and their guards, sprawled and stretched across the road in pools of darkening blood. It looked like a mock-up, the kind of tableau used to teach rescue workers about safety procedures. Young men, Lev thought, young men who in other times would have had twice as much life ahead of them as had already passed, but who as mafiyosi could expect three decades if they were lucky. Their bravery in facing death was no more than he would have expected. Those who joined the warrior elite traded rich rewards for a life of tension and an inevitably violent end. They had been happy to live fast and die young. Russians are all too used to death; when twenty million died defending the Motherland against the Nazis, Stalin simply sent in twenty million more.

The warning about poisoning the reservoirs had been a decoy. Karkadann had made Lev concentrate on a threat which didn't exist, and in doing so had left the door open for the Chechens to hit the Slav alliance elsewhere.

Lev's men had been primed for the attack on the repository the previous week, but this one seemed to have caught them unawares. Though every man in the convoy had been armed, Lev could see no dead Chechens. How was *that* possible in a mass gunfight?

Two paramedics were loading a man on to a stretcher by the kerb. By the care with which they handled the patient, Lev knew he was still alive – they'd have slung corpses in like sacks of garbage. When he got closer, he saw that it was Butuzov, his grey face beaded with sweat and blood.

"What the fuck happened?" Lev said.

"Police."

*"Police?"*

Butuzov shook his head, and winced at the movement. "Not real ones. Blacks. Dressed as police." It wasn't as ridiculous as it sounded; the police took recruits where it could find them, even from those whom they most routinely victimised. "Appeared from nowhere, pulled us over, ordered us out, disarmed the guards."

"Then what?"

"Shot us."

"Everyone else is dead?"

"I think so. Someone fell on top of me, that's why I'm still here."

"And the trucks?"

"Took them."

A bubbling eruption of blood spurted from Butuzov's mouth, and the paramedics were on to him in a flash. Lev turned away. He'd seen enough men die to know that Butuzov wouldn't make it. He remembered how Butuzov had installed the bug in Karkadann's office and helped snatch Sharmukhamedov from Sheremetyevo; remembered too how Karkadann had sent Butuzov back to Lev with the Chechen bandit oath ringing in his ears. Butuzov had been there almost from the inception of this conflict – it didn't seem right that he wouldn't live to see its end.

Lev looked back to the stretcher. Lying on his back, his blood wetting skin he could no longer feel, Butuzov stared sightlessly at the sky.

# 50

*Monday, 10 February 1992*

It was still dark, but the area round the Vera Mukhina sculpture was lit up like a television studio. Irk saw discarded McDonald's wrappers, three half-litre bottles of vodka – empty, naturally – and a young girl, whitened first by blood loss and then by the merciless glare of the arc lights.

The girl was lying on her back. Irk stepped forward and looked into her eyes. Once again, there was no reflection of the murderer; all he saw was himself, embittered, angry, bewildered and so very, very tired. Every option he took turned out to be useless against an enemy who was both ubiquitous and invisible. Damn Arkin, he thought, damn Arkin for putting him back on the case.

Vera Mukhina's stainless-steel rendition of the worker and farm girl is one of the most famous sculptures in all Russia. The worker clasps a hammer and the farm girl a sickle; they hold their hands high in solidarity as they stride boldly towards the glorious Soviet future, his apron and her skirt rippling out behind them in horizontal pleats. Stalin used to come at night and stare at the sculpture for hours. It was rumoured that Trotsky's profile could be seen in the drapery's folds.

The policemen on the scene hopped from foot to foot, wafting vodka with every exhalation. If the bottles by the sculpture hadn't been empty before, it was no mystery that they were now.

Irk looked away from the girl towards the VDNKh, the Exhibition of Economic Achievements Park. Marx himself would have been proud of the pavilions' names: Atomic Energy, Coal Industry, Biology, Education, Physics, Trade Unions, Electrotechnology, Agriculture and Grain. But their grandiose architecture now mocked the denuded halls where imported cars and televisions had ousted local products, and where merchants touted their wares as if they were in the souk.

Death of a child, death of a nation. Irk wondered whether he could still tell the difference.

Unsure whether to be reassured or disturbed that he still had an appetite, Irk stopped at the Petrovka canteen. His hunger lasted for as long as it took him to search without joy for solids in the watery ghoulash. Where the girl's corpse had failed, Petrovka cuisine had succeeded. His hunger evaporated.

He went up to see Denisov, who was so engrossed in the television that it was several moments before he noticed Irk. US Air Force carriers were arriving at Domodevo Airport with the first aid consignments of Operation Provide Hope. Transport aircraft landed with wobbling wings before disgorging the contents of their fat bellies on to the grimy snow. The pallets were unloaded by immaculately uniformed USAF officers, square of jaw and straight of back. Next to them, the assisting Russian conscripts looked like toy soldiers, pale-faced and shivering as they passed bottles of vodka round to ward off the cold.

"What are they delivering?" Irk asked.

"Food. Pre-packaged army meals left over from the Gulf War, which they're getting rid of because they're nearing their sell-by date. If we don't take them, they'll throw them away. It's an insult. Leftovers are what you give animals, not human beings." Denisov hawked again, but this time didn't follow through; his phlegm was clearly not rising as fast as his bile. "We're a great people, Juku. We'll settle things ourselves, with our state and our government. There's a world of difference between help and handouts. The West gives us this today – who knows what they'll ask in return tomorrow? This is free cheese in the mousetrap. For all I know, the meat there's been poisoned. I wouldn't feed it to my dog."

"I didn't know you had a dog, Denis Denisovich."

"I don't."

Rodion was waiting for Irk down in the lobby of Petrovka, ignoring the stares of the able-bodied. "I heard it on the news," he said. "Thought you'd like some moral support."

"I'd like a drink, that's what I'd like."

Rodion laughed. "We'll make a Russian out of you yet, Juku."

"Don't take this the wrong way, Rodya, but the longer this goes on, the happier I am to be Estonian. Yes, I'd love a drink, but I have to go back to the VDNKh."

"I'll come with you."

"It's a crime scene, Rodya."

"And I'm a . . . material witness – is that what you call it?"

"You've been watching too many cop shows."

"I'm part of the investigation, at any rate."

Irk thought for a moment. Two heads were better than one and, as always, he could do with the company. "All right."

The worker and farm girl is one of two statues outside the VDNKh; the other is the space obelisk, a shining rocket which trails a diverging jetstream and is faced in sheets of titanium which seem to ignite even in the palest sun. On one side of the plinth, engineers and scientists strive to put a cosmonaut in his rocket; on the other, Lenin leads the masses into space while a woman offers her baby to the sun.

As Irk and Rodion passed, a man was standing by the obelisk, endlessly declaiming to himself: "I was a cosmonaut. I knew Gagarin, I flew on *Voshkod 1*. I went all the way to outer space, and came all the way back. I saw the entire globe – the deserts, the seas, all the places I'd heard of but never laid eyes on. And of all the places on earth I could have landed, I had the bad luck to land right back in the Soviet Union."

The man saw Rodion and shuddered. Rodion stared straight ahead with the excessive determination of one who is hurt but determined not to show it. When it comes to the disabled, the Russians employ neither linguistic euphemisms or uneasy piety. If you're handicapped, you're in with the lunatics, the imbeciles and the idiots – unsuitable participants in the Soviet experiment, imperfect materials in a perfect society. It's an approach whose only merit is its complete lack of hypocrisy.

"Are you sure you want to do this?" said Irk, offering him the opportunity to leave without losing face.

"What, you think I'm bothered by jerks like him? I've had years to get used to it. I've long since given up on expecting people to understand. How could they? Afghanistan's the forgotten war, the buried war, the hidden-under-the-carpet war. Survivors of the Great Patriotic War – they're proper veterans, but not the *afgantsy*. They got medals for being at Stalingrad, Leningrad, Berlin; we got nailed to the cross to expiate a nation's sins. If they see me going to the window for war veterans, people say, 'Hey you, boy – you're in the wrong queue!' Me with no legs, fuck your mother! 'I defended the Motherland,' they go, 'what's *he* done?' It's a waste of time trying to talk to them about trauma and stress disorder, they just sneer and say it never bothered *them*, like they're made of sterner stuff or something. I've got no time for ignorant shits like that."

The crime scene was still cordoned off, though the sole policeman on duty seemed more interested in chatting up passing women than securing the area. He straightened when he saw Irk and tried to look officious, but it was too late. In a place where no civilian should have been allowed entry, Irk had seen a child at the base of the sculpture.

"What the hell are you doing?" Irk said. "This is a crime scene, not a pop concert."

"The area's secure, sir. It's just me here."

"Then what's that child doing?"

"What child?"

"That child," Irk said, pointing to the sculpture. The constable turned to follow his finger.

"There's no one there, sir."

And he was right, there wasn't.

Irk hurried over to the statue. The child was gone, but *where*? There was nothing but open space for a hundred metres in every direction. The kid would've had to be an Olympic champion to get away that fast.

Irk shook his head and slapped at his face. He was seeing spectres, hallucinating. He'd been working too hard, everyone at Petrovka told him so.

Rodion was by Irk's side – he moved fast for a man with no legs – and pointing upwards.

"What, Rodya – you think he flew?"

"No. *Look* –" Rodion was indicating the folds of the farm girl's skirts. After a moment Irk saw it too: the outline of an opening. "Service hatch," Rodion said, pulling himself up on to the cornice. He began to climb the girl's left leg. The metal was smooth, but there were plenty of handholds on the statue's contours. Rodion clung to them with the casual assurance of an orang-utan. The sinews in his forearms stood out like piano wires. He reached for the hatch's handle and pulled it open. "Come on up," he called down to Irk.

Irk had never been much of a climber, but if a legless man could get up there, so could he. He hopped on to the plinth, stood on a stack of *Yest Vykhod* magazines – the homeless sold them on Moscow streets – to get some height, and then launched himself up the same route Rodion had taken. Sweating, breathless and with his shins smarting from being bashed against the girl's substantial calf, he flopped through the service opening and inside the statue.

It was surprisingly spacious. Most of the interior had been hollowed out. By the light of three paraffin lamps on the floor, Irk saw half a dozen children, maybe more, curved against the swells of the girl's stomach. They regarded Irk silently. It was a moment before he spotted Rodion in the shadows. He was the same height as the children, of course, and next to them his face looked absurdly old, as though he was the victim of some dreadful ageing disease.

258

Rodion was sitting – did he sit, *could* one sit on stumps? – next to a boy who couldn't have been more than twelve. The boy's eyes were lavishly soulful, reined in by cool, appraising lids.

"This is who you saw," Rodion said.

"What's his name?"

"No names," the boy said. He reached inside his torn shirt and scratched at his armpit – fleas.

"How do you know him?" Irk asked Rodion.

"Been in and out of the orphanage." Rodion gestured around him. "Like most of them."

"What's *his* name?" The boy nodded towards Irk. "Looks like a cop to me. Rodya, what the hell are you doing?" He spoke fast through full, girlish lips. "You know I'm hiding from the cops. That's why I came here, to turn into a dot."

"His name's Juku," Rodion said. "He's a friend of mine."

"He's a cop."

"Investigator," Irk said.

"He doesn't care what you've done," Rodion said. "He wants to know about the girl."

"What about her?"

"She's dead," Irk said. The boy wiped a strand of hair from in front of his eyes and shrugged. Irk was incredulous. "That doesn't bother you?"

"You're here, you're gone. The dead are happier dead. They don't miss much, poor devils."

"What was her name?"

"Nelli."

"Nelli what?"

The boy shrugged: no idea.

"You seen any Chechens round here?" Irk asked.

The others stirred, muttered. Their voices were unbroken, and their sleeves extended six inches beyond their fingertips. The Chechens; always the Chechens.

"You come to take over their turf, Copper? That it? It doesn't matter, does it? Doesn't matter who runs things, as long as some-one's fucking the little people, yes?"

"The Chechens – would you recognise any of them?"

"Those coons? They all look the same."

Twelve years old and already a racist; the boy would make a fine Russian man, Irk thought, if he made it that far. "Did Nelli stay here often?"

"Sometimes. We move around. You see someone when you see

them." He rubbed at his eyes. "That's enough, Investigator. You can leave us alone now."

Rodion hugged the boy, and kissed a couple of the other children on both cheeks, Russian-style, as he headed back towards Irk. They all responded enthusiastically. Irk was struck by how well the children reacted to Rodion. Perhaps it was because he was so small, or because they were less quick than adults to judge on appearances.

Rodion and Irk climbed down the girl's leg on to the plinth, and from there to the ground. On the far side of Prospekt Mira, fairy lights glittered round the Kosmos Hotel's horseshoe outline.

"They like you," Irk said.

"As much as they like anyone. They're asphalt flowers, those kids. They know the world doesn't really care about them, Juku. If they don't grab something from life themselves, no one's going to do it for them. Most of them aren't even afraid of your lot. They know they can't be punished until they're fourteen."

"That boy was afraid. He didn't want me there."

"He's sixteen, that's why."

"Impossible. He looks about twelve."

Rodion shrugged. "No one looks their age in Russia."

A motorbike roared past them, its exhaust unmuffled and reverberating. Irk winced and put his hands to his ears, too late to miss Rodion's yelp. When Irk looked across, he saw that Rodion was panting, quick, sweaty, heaving breaths.

"What's wrong?" Irk said. "What's wrong, Rodya? Calm down, old man, it's only a motorbike."

Rodion rubbed his eyes; Irk heard his breathing begin to slow. "Sorry," Rodion said. "Sorry."

"What did you think it was?"

Rodion looked askance at him. When he answered, his voice was small. "A machine-gun."

"From Afghanistan?"

"You never really come home. War's not a film clip, you can't tear it from your memory."

Even the magnificence of the Komsomolskaya Station failed to lift Irk's mood. Some of Moscow's metro stations are more like ballrooms or museums than subway interchanges. Komsomolskaya is one of the finest, a sumptuous palace which exudes heroic triumphalism. The lower hall in particular is monumental, its vaulted ceiling held aloft by hundreds of columns. All the evening commuters wrapped up against the elements seemed unsuitably dressed; they should surely have been gliding through the marbled chamber to the strains of Rachmaninov, women swathed in rustling silk and men in tailcoats under the chandeliers. Irk was usually prone to such flights of romantic fancy, but today they flitted from his mind. All he registered were the negatives, the panels where Beria, Stalin and Khrushchev had once inspired the masses before they were airbrushed from history and the station alike.

Svetlana was in a strange mood: half glee, half sadness, sometimes both at once.

"Dad died today," Rodion said bitterly. "It's nothing to celebrate."

"Six years ago," Svetlana said, using her pestle to mash some ingredients to pulp in the base of a mortar. "Six years, this very day – a Monday, just as it is today. Stupid bastard went out drinking all weekend and didn't stop till he fell over. Better off without him, Juku, honestly I am."

"Don't say that," Rodion said.

"I did everything for him – made his breakfast, washed his dishes, cleaned his laundry, bought his groceries, packed Rodya off to school or day care, everything he thought wasn't a man's job. Just what *was* a man's job wasn't altogether clear – except in bed, of course, and that happened less and less as he got more and more drunk."

"You're bloody lucky he bothered at all, Ma."

"*You* should be grateful. You wouldn't be here otherwise." Sveta tipped the mortar's contents into a bowl. When she spilt some on the floor, she grabbed a broom from the corner and swept it up. "On his days off, he'd stay in bed till late. When he *did* deign to get up, he'd do nothing but read the paper and watch the television. Nothing but a waste of space. A true knight of the sofa. Don't get me wrong – he wasn't a violent drunk, he'd just pass out. And he wasn't a bad father to Rodya, once he'd grown up a bit. Men aren't interested in kids until they're about two, you know that? Before then, they're simply alien things, lumps of flesh. Men can't deal with that. My friends envied me, can you believe it? He didn't beat me up, didn't beat Rodya up, got paid more than even he could drink away. They told me I was lucky."

Praising someone by virtue of what they weren't rather than what they were; how Russian.

"None of this applies to you, of course. You're Estonian, a civilised chap. You must have all the Moscow matrons running after you!" She stroked Irk's cheek. "Here, look in the mirror. What a handsome man."

261

"Yes," Irk said, but what he saw was a dignified man aching with exhaustion, too tired to see an exit, too proud to take one.

# 51

*Tuesday, 11 February 1992*
Karkadann had sent a message to Lev: *Give in, and it stops.*

Lev understood both the message and what lay behind it. Karkadann had assumed that Ozers and Butuzov had been about to kill his family – they hadn't been, of course, but that's how Chechens saw Russians and vice versa – so he had killed them himself. It had been his choice: quicker that way, perhaps less painful. His choice, and it had destroyed him, shredding the last vestiges of his humanity.

Lev understood all this, but he couldn't tell Karkadann, because he didn't know where to find him. Invisible, Karkadann was behind everything: he was rumour, legend, curse, terror incarnate.

Channel Two was running vox pops between programmes, people too dissimilar to have been randomly selected telling the camera how much they disliked privatisation. Gosha, twenty-four, was first up. "If the state is giving it away," he said, "it can't be worth having."

Alice wanted to be with Lev, to help and support him while he tried to do the right thing over the child killings, but the auction was getting nearer by the day and she had too much to do as it was. Galina had asked her to come to the exhibition complex on Krasnaya Presnya, a few blocks along from the zoo in western Moscow, where Bob had hired one of the conference halls for the auction. Alice was needed to translate as much as supervise; Bob's thick Texan accent was proving something of a handful for the staff.

At first glance, Galina had been as good as her word. She'd found one hundred and fifty young people. When Alice looked closer, she saw combat trousers, stubbled chins, nose studs and earrings – hardly the average business crowd. Some of them were reminiscing about defending the White House during the August coup.

"Look at this shower," said Bob. "I've seen smarter people in precinct holding-rooms."

"They're Galya's friends, and I trust her. We haven't got time to give them handwriting tests and polygraphs, Bob. They'll be presentable enough on the day, that's the important thing."

"I'll beat a few of them like they were rented mules, that'll knock them into shape. Jesus, Alice, how did I let you talk me into this?" Bob cleared his throat and turned to face the room. "Listen up."

There was no reaction; everyone just carried on with what they were doing. Bob turned to Alice and gestured at his hands, his face; the colour of his skin. "Why don't we just hand out bananas so they can throw them at me? No, no, don't say it: because there's no fresh fruit in this shithole of a city, that's why." He turned back to face the room. "Hello? We're burning daylight here. Can we please get on with it?"

Slowly, reluctantly, the chatter subsided as the volunteers settled back in their chairs and waited for him to begin.

"Thank you." His voice dripped with exasperated sarcasm. "This is how we're going to divide y'all, so pay attention and work out which category you think you're best suited to. We need forty staff at the doors, to make bidders feel welcome and answer any questions they might have. Fifty tellers to take bids, verify they're legit, give bidders a receipt, and enter all the details on tally forms." He was writing the numbers on a whiteboard as he went along, as though the volunteers were kindergarten pupils. "Twenty-five controllers, to check the applications have been filled in correctly. Ten counters, who'll split the paperwork: applications go to the five sorters, tally forms to the two computer operators. Then we've got a first-aid person, a secretary, a translator, and fifteen floaters to fill in as and where you're needed."

Yarik, forty-five, said: "I buy vouchers off some people and resell them to others. Doing this, I make as much money in a day as I do at work in a month. I've a good brain, but I have to use it to survive – there's nothing left over for me to contribute to society. I could be working in a factory or an institute."

Bob took the volunteers through the principles of both types of bidding, passive and active. Passive bidders had to accept the strike price – the price reached at the end of the auction – but they were guaranteed at least one share. Active bidders would nominate a price at which they were prepared to buy a certain number of shares per voucher. Since active bidding would involve second-guessing an entirely unknown market, it was assumed that the majority of bids would be passive. Bob demonstrated several likely scenarios with a theoretical model of one thousand shares in various proportions of passive and active bids, the latter on a sliding scale from one share through five per voucher.

The strike price was to be calculated on the basis of three principles: at least one share for every passive bid; any remaining shares to be sold to active bidders bidding above the strike price; and no splitting of shares. As the number of remaining shares was gradually eaten away, the ratio of shares per voucher would decrease towards or all the way to its bottom limit – one. All this raised the possibility that a large investor would come in late on auction day and lower the strike price dramatically by gobbling up the remaining shares in one go. Not that it made much difference: vouchers were free and inflation rampant, so the shares would be virtually worthless whatever the strike price. It was going to be a giveaway.

"I'm too old to understand the whole business," said fifty-one-year-old Nellya. "I'd much rather the government had given me a new pair of shoes."

"Do you mind if I have a word with them, Bob?" Alice said.

"Be my guest."

Alice stood up and pointed to a man in the front row. "You, with the goatee beard. What are the three principles behind calculating the strike price?"

He looked blank. "Er . . . passive bidders get a . . . no, I mean active shares . . ." and tailed off. The others laughed; this was schoolroom stuff. Alice picked on the girl with the loudest laugh.

"OK, clever clogs, what's the bottom limit of the ratio of shares to vouchers?"

"There isn't one?"

"There *is* one, and it's one. Who in fuck do you people think you are? I looked round the room when Bob was explaining how the auction's gonna work, and I could count on one hand the number of you writing anything down. That's not on. If you don't want to do this, then fuck off and we'll find someone else – there are thousands of people out there who'd kill to be here, in your shoes. We'll pay you, and pay you well, depending on your performance. But in return, we expect you to turn up on time and work until you've finished your tasks for the day, whether that's at five in the afternoon or five in the morning. Whatever you've been used to before, understand this: I don't care. Problems are yours to sort out, not mine. I don't want to hear bleating about the boiler not working or your second cousin who's in hospital. From now on, these are the rules: one mistake, official warning; two mistakes, you're out."

They were cowed and silent. They hadn't expected a Western banker to use Bolshevik fear tactics. When Alice looked at Galina, Galina looked at the floor.

"It's just another way for the government to deceive people," said Stopya, sixty-three.

Irk had spent all day coming up against walls of mafiya silence and evasion, and was as drained of colour as the small victims of the monster he hunted. He felt he existed only in chiaroscuro.

When he saw Svetlana lying on her stove – "Best way to keep warm, Juku," she said – he had a sudden image of her as Baba Yaga, the hideous old witch with a huge distorted nose and long teeth. Rumoured to be the devil's own grandmother, she too would lie on stoves to keep warm. She was also said to live in a forest hut which stood on chicken legs, like the ones Svetlana had served last month; to eat those who failed to fulfil their part of an agreement, just as Svetlana had threatened Irk the very first time they'd met; and to travel in a giant mortar which she drove at high speed across the forest floor, steering with the pestle in her right hand and sweeping away all traces of her progress with a broom in her left, just as Svetlana had mashed up the ingredients and then swept them away yesterday.

Irk shook his head to clear the images. This was absurd. Sveta was his friend: a kindly, bustling, lonely woman for whom life had been hard. She was no more a fiend than he was. It must be his exhaustion, making him think like this. He wanted nothing more than to sleep.

# 52

*Wednesday, 12 February 1992*
Alice woke some hours after the vodka had knocked her out; long enough for it to drag her back to the surface for a few hours' restlessness before putting her under again before dawn. Perhaps she'd have found it endearing or exciting a month ago, when everything was new and exhilarating, but now it was simply tiresome, another hassle she didn't need. Everything suddenly seemed annoying and

difficult. The shine had come off, that was for sure. Alice could speak the language, but she couldn't yet understand how people lived. So far from home and so long gone, she felt she'd already lost a part of her identity without having replaced it with anything. Maybe she never would. What was Lev: the avenue to a new life, or the architect of her destruction?

Alice marked time until lunch, knowing what she had to do and dreading the moment when she had to do it. At twelve thirty, unable to stand the waiting any longer, she virtually yanked Galina from her chair and took her downstairs, out into air so cold they could hardly don enough layers, and along the road to a small café which took dollars only and served one dish a day, no menu. Today was an unspecified variation on beef. Alice took one look and ordered a vodka to go with.

They found half a table, next to a couple of builders who winked at them as they sat down. Galina lifted one leg above the table and pinched at the suede of her trousers. "You like?"

"Very much."

"Good, because they cost me a fortune. Much more than I can afford, but I saw these in the shop, they were just so *beautiful*, and . . ."

Alice understood, all too well. That's the way things are in Russia; spending money on luxuries rather than necessities is part of what keeps people human. Russians are the biggest dreamers in the world, and the maddest consumers, even though – or especially because – they can't afford to be. This month's edition of Russian *Vogue* carried a letter from a paediatrician in Omsk; with two children to support, she didn't have the money for a single item featured in the magazine – in fact, she had to save up even to buy *Vogue* – but for the four hours she spent reading it cover to cover, every word, masthead and disclaimers included, she was in heaven.

"I'm sorry about yesterday," Galina said. "I brought those people in, I told you they'd be good, and I just didn't think they'd . . . I mean, this is a new thing, right, and no one knows what to expect?" She looked so mortified that Alice wanted to reach over and hug her, but that would have undermined the reason she'd brought Galina here. "I talked to a few people afterwards, my friends, and told them to spread the word that everyone needs to buck up their ideas. What you said really shook them, I think. It won't happen again."

Alice nodded twice, curtly. "It had better not."

The food arrived, plonked unceremoniously in front of them by a girl with green hair.

"I've been invited to speak at a conference in London about the risks of doing business in Russia," Alice said. "I should tell the Guinness Book of Records."

"I'm sorry?"

"It could be the longest speech in history."

"Oh." Galina giggled, slightly sheepishly. "Who's the invite from?"

"A political risk organisation, I spoke at an event of theirs last year. They're offering me expenses, accommodation, thousands of dollars *and* the chance to bring a colleague. Want to come?"

Galina's eyes widened cartoon-style. "Are you serious?"

"Of course. We'll spend a day at the conference, another shopping, and a third going to your two favourite places in London." Galina looked blank; she'd never been to London, so how could she have a favourite place there? "Abbey Road," said Alice teasingly.

"Where I can walk across the zebra crossing barefoot!"

"And 221B Baker Street . . ."

Galina clapped her hands in delight. Sherlock Holmes and the Beatles – she'd cry tears of joy all the way back to Heathrow. "That sounds fantastic!" She made a moue. "If Lev lets me go."

"Why wouldn't he? It'd be with me."

The builders were leaving. Alice and Galina pushed their chairs back to let the men past, and realised too late that they should have got up. Alice got a faceful of paint-splattered crotch, Galina one of dusty ass. They were laughing before the men had even left the room.

The unloveliness of what she was doing circled in Alice's guts as though searching for the best place to strike. It was not too late for her to pull out, she could still leave this at what it was, part of her genuine warmth and friendship for Galina. But this is Russia, she reminded herself; here, friendships are *based* on who can do what for who.

"It'd be with me," Alice repeated.

"I guess so," Galina said, her uncertainty like blood in the water.

"You'd love London, you really would. Outside of Boston – and here, of course – it's my favourite city. Who knows – one day you could even go and work there. Or in America."

"Without Rodya? Or Sveta? No, Alice, no."

"They could come too."

"They'll never leave here."

"You want a child, Galya?"

"Who doesn't?"

"And when you have one, you think Lev'll keep your job open for you?"

"Of course he will."

"You're sure?"

"He's a loyal man."

Alice let her silence speak, and now Galina was confused. She knew about Alice and Lev, of course, but she also knew what Alice was driving at. In many Russian companies, taking maternity leave is equivalent to writing yourself out of a job. By the time you want to come back, the position's no longer available. Mothers are seen as unreliable employees: children are frequently sick, and people taking time off at short notice play havoc with work rosters. Several of Galina's friends had already had abortions rather than risk losing their jobs.

"Of course he will," Galina repeated, though with less certitude. "He's never foisted 'without complexes' on me, has he?"

'Without complexes' occurs frequently in job advertisements: applicants who aren't prepared to sleep with the boss need not apply.

"Galya, the West isn't perfect, but in terms of attitudes towards women it's light years ahead."

"It's easy for you. For Russians, bad things are there to be endured. We don't have the sense of power that you do. You Americans believe you can change the world."

"That's one of the reasons I'm doing what I'm doing, and" – Alice took a deep breath – "one of the reasons I need you to help me."

"Help you? How?"

This was Alice's last chance to turn back, and she stepped smoothly over the edge.

She outlined what she'd found at Red October. Galina looked surprised when she heard about the dead souls; she was impassive when Alice told her about the vouchers; she gasped at the extent of the Suyumbika scam. She'd known some of what Lev was up to, Alice realised, but not all – probably a mixture of Lev keeping her out of the loop and her own wilful blindness.

"We have to do this auction quickly, but we also have to do it properly," Alice said. "I need to know – and it's an awful thing to ask, we both have a stake in this place and in the man who runs it – but I need to know if there's anything else going on. If there is, I have to catch it *now*."

In the café, the chatter of the lunchtime crowd continued, banging plates overlaying chiming cutlery.

Alice had already wrestled with her conscience and won. Now it was Galina's turn to step on to the mat. Her loyalty to Lev, her ambitions, her nascent friendship with Alice, her desire for Russia to be a better place, guilt over what had happened with the auction staff yesterday, the promise of a trip to London and perhaps more – call it.

"I can't believe you're asking this of me," Galina said. When Alice was silent, Galina asked: "It really matters?" Then Alice knew she had her.

"I'll never tell where it came from."

Informing was in the Russian mindset, Alice thought, even for those who kicked against it.

Galina fished inside her handbag for a pen and wrote two numbers on a napkin. "Ring this number," she said, pushing the napkin across the table to Alice and pointing to the first set of digits. Alice saw that it was prefixed with an international code, though she couldn't recognise which one. "Ask them for transfer details on this account." That was the second number. "The password is 'Lefortovo'," she said, pushing her chair backwards, up and gone, her beef as cold and congealing as their friendship.

Sidorouk was cradling a dripping heart with reverence of an Aztec priest.

"Juku!" The pathologist was his usual jauntily lugubrious self. "How nice to see you." He put the heart into a stainless-steel tray and came across the room with his outstretched hand trailing blood. Irk recoiled with an urgency not far short of panic.

"Sorry!" Seeing the bloody hands that had so disturbed Irk, Sidorouk chuckled to himself, turned tail and headed for the washbasin. "My mistake. I used to work in an abattoir, you know. When winter came and it got really raw, twenty or thirty below, there was only one way to keep warm: by plunging my arms into the guts of a freshly slaughtered animal, right up to the shoulders."

The disembodied heart glowed like a pulsar in its tray. "How's life, Syoma?" Irk asked.

"They give you one rouble and charge you two." Sidorouk scrubbed his hands vigorously. "Things are pretty normal. People break in every week and steal whatever they can find." He finished washing his hands and reached for a towel.

"You've missed some bits." Irk pointed to reddish patches on Sidorouk's fingertips.

"Oh? That's not blood." Sidorouk laughed. "I take the same

light bulb from home to work and back again, every day – it'd get stolen otherwise. The marks are where I burn myself when I take it out of its socket. Now. You've come about the girl, I imagine?"

"Of course."

"She's over here." He led Irk across the room to the slab by the far wall, talking as he did so. "She's been sexually abused. That's a first in this case, isn't it?"

"The killer raped her?"

"Not necessarily the killer. The wounds around and inside her orifices are older than the ones on her neck and chest – the ones that killed her, in fact."

"How much older?"

"Enough to have halfway healed."

"So even if the killer held her for several days . . ."

"They'd still have appeared fresher than they did. I'd say they were inflicted some time in the past few weeks."

Irk recalled Nelli's friends – the "asphalt flowers", Rodion had called them – huddled under the skirts of the farm-girl statue. What was it that boy had said in response to his question about the Chechens? *Doesn't matter who runs things, as long as someone's fucking the little people.*

Alice went home; she couldn't risk being overheard or tapped within the distillery. A call to international enquiries – a service which hadn't existed in the USSR – revealed that the dialling code was for Nicosia, and Alice knew instantly what she was dealing with. In business terms, Nicosia is up there with Vaduz and Grand Cayman as a place where questions asked about money's origins decrease in direct proportion to the amount involved.

She rang the number, and her nerves jangled with the purity of anxiety which comes from knowing there's only one chance of getting it right.

A man's voice answered. "Bank Kormakitis-Plakoti." He spoke in English, heavily accented: a local.

"Good afternoon," Alice said. "I'm looking to check transfer details on this account." She gave the number.

"You have the password?"

"Lefortovo."

"Is that you, Galya? You sound different."

"Bit of a cold," Alice said, thankful that Galina's English was good enough for conversation and therefore impersonation.

"I'm not surprised, with the weather you have there. What do you need?"

"Incomings and outgoings."

He didn't ask why she wanted them; these kind of bankers never do. "For how long?"

"Past six months?"

"No problem. I'll fax them over."

"To work? No. The machine's broken. Use this one instead." Alice gave her home number and set the fax to receive.

"I'll send them over right away. Anything else?"

"No, that's all."

"Give Lev my regards."

"Will do."

She was shaking when she put down the phone, nervous reaction mixed with visceral triumph. Alice was developing quite a taste for detective work, also for the subterfuge and deceit which came with it. A well-crafted lie actually gave her pleasure: she admired the craftsmanship and elegant simplicity with which all the parts of a lie fitted together. There was a time she had hated lying, and falsehood had been alien to her nature, but now it was becoming so simple and natural it was as if some unseen power was helping her, clothing her in an impenetrable armour of lies. At the same time she knew it wasn't an impenetrable armour but a house of cards, and it would mount up and mount up – having started with little ones, she would build bigger and bigger ones on top – until one day the whole lot would come crashing down.

She waited and waited, anxiety gnawing at her. Had something gone wrong? Had she been rumbled? Had she made the man in Nicosia suspicious?

Time crawled. She had a couple of vodkas, to quell her nerves and keep her hands occupied.

It was forty-five minutes before the fax came through, a delay which, with the logicality of relief, Alice attributed to the precarious state of Moscow telecommunications rather than anything more sinister. There were seven sheets, and each one contained details of three or four transactions. They were spread, as far as Alice could see, fairly evenly throughout the period. The smallest was just below $3,000, the largest more than $750,000. Altogether, Lev had transferred more than $5,000,000 into the bank over the past six months.

Five million? It sounded a lot, but that was surely peanuts to a gang boss. The money could have come from anywhere, any of Lev's

271

myriad interests. But if it was nothing to do with Red October, why would Galina have told her? More to the point, how would Galina have known? She was responsible only for handling Lev's affairs at the distillery; there'd be others who took charge elsewhere, Alice reckoned, but only Lev himself would know the whole picture – a legacy of life in the gulag, where you trusted only yourself and compartmentalised your life.

Alice didn't dare ring Nicosia again. She'd got away with it once, she knew when to twist and when to stick. There was only one way to find out what those figures represented, and that was from Lev himself.

# 53

*Thursday, 13 February 1992*
Lev was in his office all day. There was no way Alice could get in there and look for the information that would allow her to determine what the Nicosia figures really meant. When she went in to see him, he told her he was busy and would come see her later. Normally, she'd have accepted this without question, but today it barked doubts and questions at her. He didn't care about her. Did he know what she was up to? Had Galina told him?

Galina herself would be no help, Alice had known that from the moment she'd seen her. Today Galina avoided eye contact and replied to Alice's questions strictly in monosyllables.

Harry was in the antechamber with an egg, which he handed to Galina. "I bought it off a guy outside," he said. "It's a fertility symbol." He winked clumsily.

"As far as you're concerned, Harry, it's a futility symbol," Alice said.

Ignoring her, Galina laughed and kissed Harry, entirely misreading his intentions. "Thank you. I'll draw a face on it, and it'll watch Rodion and me as we keep trying. It will be our icon."

When Galina had a baby, Alice wondered, would she still *want* to come back to work? Would Rodion want her to? A couple of kids down the line, and Alice could envisage a totally different Galina, the spark and soul gradually sucked from her by the relentless domestic demands of buying food, cooking, washing, cleaning, establishing order in her home and family. She'd have become tough, practical, sensible. The scatty, morally pure Galina whom Alice

272

wanted to enfold in love and protection would be gone. Oh, she'd still occasionally allow herself to be seduced by sentimental music or some impossibly expensive fashion item, but her excesses would be restrained by her duty to her family.

"Now she's what I call an executive sweet. Why won't she date me?" Harry asked Alice in mock exasperation.

"Because she's married. And she has taste."

Alice's attempts at reparation were too transparent. Galina was unmoved.

Alice spent the afternoon waiting for Lev to come and see her as he'd promised. Like a child counting the days before Christmas, the prospect underpinned and overhung everything else she was doing. She balanced Lev against her other lover. She wouldn't have a drink until he came. She'd have a drink because that would *make* him come. She needed to have a clear head to talk to him. She needed a couple of shots to steady her nerves.

Her phone rang at five. It was Yelena, the receptionist; a man was here to see her. When she went down to the lobby, she saw Lewis, leafing through a magazine, oblivious to the doe eyes Yelena was making at him. Yelena had a moon face, accentuated by the band which scraped her hair flat against her skull, and the violent red of her lipstick made her mouth resemble a bloodstain. She'd have been plain in the West; in Moscow, she was teetering on the verge of ugliness.

Alice gave an involuntary jerk of alarm, a movement which Lewis looked up a fraction too late to catch. "Darling," she said brightly. "What a surprise."

"We're going to dinner at the Craigs." He peered at her. "You can't have forgotten?"

"No, no." She *had* forgotten, totally. "I . . . I thought we were meeting at home, that's all."

"I told you this morning that I'd stop by here on the way."

"So you did. Busy day; must have slipped my mind."

"Is Harry ready? He's coming too, I think. Come on, let's not keep our friends waiting."

*Friends?* Alice didn't know whether they were *friends*. The thought of an evening spent in their company, listening to Christina whining about the hardships of an expat's life – secure in her palatial home, complete with jacuzzi and cinema – filled Alice with dread. But so far as Lewis was concerned they were strangers in a strange land, missionaries in a frontier town, and safety lay in cleaving to one's own kind. Seeing the eagerness in his eyes, she hadn't the heart to use any of the excuses that had been running through her mind. Feigning enthusiasm, she hurried back upstairs to collect her things. After all, an evening's penance was the least she could offer Lewis.

# 54

*Friday, 14 February 1992*
A woman in red stilettos and an electric blue skirt was picking her way across the road in front of Petrovka, listing as her heels skidded on the ice. Her hair was cut in a fringe like an army helmet, and she had put enough kohl round her eyes to pass for a panda. "Hey, copper," she shouted to Irk. "Wait up."

A tart. Irk sighed. It was a kopeck to a rouble that she wanted to ask him to pass a message to whichever member of the vice squad was taking his cut from letting her work the streets. In police forces overseas, undercover officers posed as whores; in Moscow, the more enterprising vice officers had recently begun reversing the process, registering whores as undercover agents. That way, the officer could justify regular contacts with the prostitutes, and the prostitutes could claim that they were not breaking the law but working to enforce it. It was genius, in its way. Irk wished he'd thought of it first.

One of the uniforms heading out of Petrovka puffed a cheek with his tongue as the tart passed him. "Darling, you want to take a wafer?" he said.

She didn't even break stride. "Not if your cock's as empty as your head."

Irk chuckled, and changed his mind about talking to her. If a tart wants to help, she can be a policeman's best friend. Working girls are streetwise. They look and listen; that's how they stay alive.

The officer who'd propositioned her called out to Irk. "Hey, boss, don't listen to Aldona. She's a drumstick."

"If I *have* got the clap," she shouted back, flipping the finger, "it must have been from you."

Irk noticed how thick Aldona's make-up was. Thick enough to cover bruises, let alone spots.

"You the one in charge of poor Nelli's case?"

Irk's pulse quickened. "You knew her?"

"She used to hang around with us sometimes."

"Did she work for the same pimp?"

"She didn't hang out with us *professionally*," Aldona said, indignant. "What do you take me for?" Irk raised a hand in apology. "As if there's not enough competition already," she added. Her mouth twisted, a smile in umber. "No. Nelli kept our company because it was better than anything else she had."

"You know where she lived?"

Aldona nodded. "Come with me, I'll show you."

The moment Irk stepped inside the internat on Akademika Koroleva, he stopped wondering why Nelli had chosen to spend time with Aldona and the other working girls.

The internat is a mixture of orphanage and asylum. On a scale of abomination, it comes in somewhere between the army barracks and the prison cell. Russians moan about their existence, Irk thought, but those who go through life without ever seeing the inside of internat, barracks or prison – and there are many – should count themselves lucky and shut up.

He walked the corridors as though treading nightmares. Two girls, naked from the waist down, scuttled shrieking past him. Irk saw a boy sitting chained to a wall, his knees drawn up so high that they seemed to have fused with his head. Open doors gave on to infernal vistas: children sprawled across filthy sheets, matchstick limbs splayed at impossible angles. Under shaven skulls, vacant eyes stared at him through clouds of flies. The rooms were dim, the beds pushed close together. At night, abuse would spread like a forest fire. The air was stacked with a pyramid of odours: breath, sweat, piss and shit; abandon, neglect and decay.

Nelli would have been one of the smaller children at the internat, prey, not predator. The evidence of sexual abuse Sidorouk had found didn't signal a change in signature or modus operandi as they had assumed. It was irrelevant, Irk thought, and almost choked on the guilt he felt at dismissing such trauma so lightly.

On a verandah, squatting children moaned and rocked in their own private perditions, heedless of the cold. Irk turned away when one of them waved at him and tried to say 'papa'. It would be so easy to persuade any of these children to go with him.

Aldona chatted in a low voice to a couple of staff members. When Irk looked surprised at this, she regarded him with no small measure of disdain. "The working girls help out here when we can," she said. "We outcasts must stick together, Investigator."

She led him into a kitchen with a table that was too large and a stove that was too small. A pot of dumplings bubbled away. Irk lifted the lid and rested his nostrils in the steam for a moment; it was the first thing he'd smelt in this place that hadn't made him want either to weep or vomit.

Dimenkova, Aldona said, that was Nelli's surname. "That was how she was registered, anyway. Like most kids here, she just blew in. They turn up and are taken in, and there's never enough room. It's like pissing against a hurricane."

"This place is funded by the state, isn't it?"

"Theoretically. If those pompous bastards have sent any money, do let me know."

Russia is no place to be a child without parents, Irk knew. The lucky few are sent to decent orphanages – decent in this instance meaning well-funded, and well-funded meaning privately financed, either by foreign organisations or local philanthropists such as Lev, and who cares where the money comes from? The rest are divided between the streets and the internats, their chance of a decent life gone either way. Everybody says that their plight's a disgrace. Everybody was saying the same thing twenty years ago; everybody will still be saying it in twenty years' time.

One of the older boys walked past the kitchen door, swigging from a bottle of vodka. Irk watched as he bent down to another child, a smaller one, asleep on the floor. "Come on, sleepy grouse. Let's go."

Sleepy Grouse opened one eye, saw the bottle of vodka and shook his head. Aldona leaned forward to follow Irk's gaze. "The younger ones don't drink," she said. "They think it stunts their growth. They want to be as big as they can."

Timofei had said the same thing about Vladimir Kullam. Good God, Irk thought; only the fear of not being able to look after themselves is keeping our children from the bottle. It wasn't much of a lookout for the future.

"When did you last see Nelli?" he asked.

"Last weekend."

"Is there anyone here who could have killed her?"

Aldona gave a short, barking laugh. "Is there anyone here who *couldn't* have?"

It was Valentine's night, and the only way Alice could deal with it was to be alone. Lewis had asked her what she was doing; she'd told him she was working late. Lev, apologetic for not making time yesterday, had also asked her what she was doing; she'd told him she couldn't make it. Both answers were true. Both concealed more than they revealed.

Logic said that Alice couldn't just go sneaking round the distillery after hours. What if she got caught? What would Lev say? What would he *do*? Would he harm her? She was his lover, sure, but she'd also be a spy, and he was a gang lord. The privatisation process was compromised enough as it was – what would the press say if they found out? Didn't Watergate start with an unauthorised break-in?

Logic also said that Alice should get Arkin to send in the cavalry and impound all Lev's files. But would he do so? She wasn't sure. With every extra person she involved, the chance of a snarl-up increased exponentially. Presenting this as a fait accompli was the only way to do it.

The distillery was closed for cleaning over the weekend. It would be empty tonight.

Red October at night, lights off and workers gone, seemed even more cavernous and intimidating than it did during the day. From where Alice stood at the window of Lev's office, the vast machines seemed to rise from the factory floor like darkened sentinels. Alice turned her back on them and set to work.

The office she'd been allocated had a storage annexe, and it was there that she had concealed herself until everyone had left for the weekend. She'd brought along a credit card to slip the lock of Lev's office if need be, but it was open; he clearly thought his own staff too respectful and the Westerners too scrupulous to sneak in behind his back. Odd, for one so paranoid, she thought; but even the most fearful sometimes grow complacent about their weakest points.

Alice went through desk drawers and filing cabinets one by one, grateful that Lev didn't use a computer. Alone and furtive, she kept the main lights off and shielded the beam of her torch with her hand; Red October was patrolled by the 21st Century's security guards, and they wouldn't be slow to come and investigate anything suspicious. If they found her, would any of them know that she was sleeping with their boss? Shit, this was more dangerous than letting a hungry weasel loose in a nudist farm hot-tub.

There was a bottle of Stolichnaya in the freezer. Alice took it out and filled a glass, watching the vodka as it separated and slid like oil over ice cubes: frigid lava.

Personal considerations intertwined with professional ones, guilt crawled over justice; she couldn't even see where to make the cut to separate them. Images of what she and Lev had done in this office, over this desk, against this window. She shut them all out and bent herself once more to the task.

Alice spent hours going through Lev's papers, looking for documents corroborating the bank transfer details. The trail was often patchy, incomplete or confusing – Lev didn't keep his records in any discernible order, either through accident or design – and it was well into the small hours before Alice had worked out for sure what he was doing. The realisation came to her gradually: a hint here, an inference there, allowing her to believe and disbelieve before gradually reconciling herself to the idea. It was better that it crept up on her rather than reveal itself all at once, because it was bigger than she'd ever expected. When she saw the whole picture, she was breathless at – and, despite herself, admiring of – his audacity.

Lev was systematically stripping Red October of its assets.

He'd established a new company called Suyumbika, also registered in Nicosia, to which he was transferring the distillery's buildings and equipment. The dates on the correspondence tallied with those of the bank transfers, and revealed a finely judged pace: not quick enough to arouse suspicion, not slow enough to risk being caught short before privatisation. At this rate, auction day would dawn with Red October – the guinea-pig for the entire reform programme, the company on which the future of Russia rested – little more than an empty shell.

Under communism, state factory directors who stole from the state were shot. Now, with the economy on its knees, those ruthless enough could obtain previously unimaginable wealth almost overnight. Russia, vast and laden with resources, was like a crashed bullion van, its contents scattered on the ground, and bystanders pushing each other away as they tried to grab the biggest bundle of cash – while the guards were trapped inside, crying uselessly for help.

Her eyes ached from straining to read by torchlight – she'd already had to replace one set of batteries – and in her excitement and fear she'd forgotten to eat the food she'd brought. She brought it out now: cheese, ham, salty biscuits and some stale bread.

No matter, she thought, there was a simple cure: bread soaked with vodka. She was in a distillery, after all, there was enough vodka here to last her a year . . . perhaps a month . . . well, a week . . . till dawn, at any rate.

# 55

*Saturday, 15 February 1992*

Dawn was when they started coming in, and they didn't look like cleaners. Lev and Sabirzhan were among the first to arrive. Sabirzhan wasn't the kind of person to bother himself with mundanities such as cleaning, and even Lev's insistence on controlling everything that went on in the distillery surely didn't extend this far. From beside the window in Lev's office, tucked out of sight, Alice tried to slow the churning in her chest. Her sense of guilt was no longer only about Lewis. Now it encompassed Lev too, as though the night she'd just spent was some sort of illicit affair behind *his* back, cheating on the man with whom she was cheating on her husband.

She watched Lev and Sabirzhan start up the production line, casual as could be. She heard sounds familiar enough to have become part of her subconscious: the steady sibilance of vodka washing through the machinery, the brittle clanking of bottles wobbling down conveyor belts. Above these noises came laughter and joking. In Soviet times, Black Saturday had occurred once a month, a compulsory workday. But there was nothing remotely downbeat about those here today. What else could this be other than a parallel production line, with neither output nor profits finding their way into the distillery ledgers, pure profit for those lucky enough to be in on it?

They were working faster than usual, Alice saw. Why wouldn't they, when their own money was at stake? Slow for the state, quickly for themselves. She couldn't even muster the energy to be surprised, let alone outraged.

No wonder Lev had initially been opposed to Red October's privatisation. It was amazing that he'd relented at all. Asset-stripping, voucher requisitioning, unregistered exports, and now this. He must have been making a fortune from this distillery, let alone all his other interests. Alice wondered how wealthy he really was – rich enough, surely, to keep accounts in Switzerland or the Caribbean, as well as the company in Cyprus. Perhaps even Lev didn't know his exact worth.

For Russia, one black market is considered two too few. There's the shadow economy of underground businesses, unrecorded, unreported and cash only. There's the virtual economy of Soviet-era manufacturing, which shelters from market pressures by retreating from them and existing instead by barter, credit notes and subsidies. And there's the offshore economy, where the serious money goes.

Three black markets, and Lev had fingers in all of them.

Alice's mind must have wandered. When she next looked down over the factory floor, Lev was nowhere to be seen. She was still searching for him when she heard the fire door at the end of the corridor open. It was Lev, she was sure; she could tell by the cadence of his stride, the long delay between each footfall as his endless legs ate up the ground, and he'd catch her in his office if she didn't move, *now*.

Lev's office gave on to the antechamber where Galya sat, and the antechamber had two doors – the main one out to the corridor along which Lev was walking, and a smaller side exit on to a gangway high above the distillery floor. Alice had little choice. She'd already filled a satchel with the most incriminating of Lev's papers. She slung it over her shoulder, hurried out of the office and across the antechamber, fancying that she heard the main door open even as she closed the side one behind her and stepped on to the gangway.

It was horribly exposed, that was for sure. The railing was only waist high, and the latticed metal treads looked a lot less secure than Alice hoped they actually were. When she looked down, she could see all the way through the grids to the floor; a couple of seconds' drop if she fell – or was pushed. How long would Lev be in his office? If it was only a few minutes, she should stay still, wait for him to leave, and sneak out that way. Any longer, and she should find somewhere more secure to hide.

Alice shifted the satchel against her hip and felt a hard bulge in its base. It took her a moment to remember what it was; she'd brought a camera with her in case she needed to photograph documents. Contenting herself with stealing them instead, she'd forgotten all about the camera. She had documents to back up everything else, but nothing to prove the existence of this illicit production. Pictures would be the icing on the cake, insurance even. Arkin might refuse to read documents, but even he couldn't ignore evidence on seven by fives.

The gangway was high enough to afford the perfect camera angle to capture faces – profiles, at least – rather than anonymous tops of heads. She wanted Lev in there too, but she could catch him when, *if*, he came back. Feeling like a private dick snapping a man with his mistress, she pulled out the camera, turned it on, adjusted the image in the viewfinder, and clicked.

The flash sparked, bright and impossible to miss even from twenty metres. It was automatic; Alice had forgotten to disable it. Even as her stomach twisted in self-reproach, the viewfinder picked out faces turning up towards her, fingers pointing, sudden, angry shouts where the laughter had been. There was no need for secrecy any more; safety was what she needed, and fast. Lev would be coming through the door behind her at any moment. The element of surprise she'd banked on had vanished. It was time simply to save her skin.

Alice ran.

The gangway swayed slightly under her feet, but she couldn't be scared of more than one thing at a time, and getting caught was more than enough to be going on with. She was most of the way across when she heard the door opening behind her and Lev yelling. Alice didn't even look round. The gangway forked in two and then in two again, branches across the roofs of vats which held more than a million litres each. If they caught her, would they throw her in one? What a way to go, she thought; she could open her mouth and literally drink herself to death. Talk about being pickled.

She zigzagged over the tops of oceans of vodka destined to fuel heated conversations, silly arguments, hysterical laughter, maudlin tears, pulverising hangovers, family scandals, acrimonious split-ups, violent rapes and agonising cirrhoses.

Alice scampered like a fox through landscapes of stainless steel. When the vats ended, she found herself in the treetops of the filtration columns, and even as she was looking behind to check whether Lev was following – he wasn't – her skin prickled as a column of scorching vapour spat and dispersed beside her. She looked down, and saw Sabirzhan, far below, holding one of the high-pressure steam jets they used to clean the filtration columns. A touch closer, and it would have taken some of her skin with it, even at this distance.

If she didn't know before, she knew now: these guys weren't playing around.

The more Alice ran, however, the less frightened she became. It must have been all the vodka inside her. She appreciated the danger she was in but felt somehow detached from it, as though this were happening to someone else.

A bolted steel ladder ran down the side of each filtration column. Alice chose the one nearest to the corner, the one most hidden from sight – if it was also the easiest to trap her on, then she'd take that chance – and clambered down it, using opposite arms and legs like a quadruped. In the wide-open spaces beyond, voices sounded loud and distorted as they chased her. At the bottom of the column – she'd come down almost fast enough to make her ears pop – Alice looked both ways, saw nothing, and then listened through the echoes to find out where her pursuers were.

Ten metres away, across an expanse of floor which looked about as inviting as a sniper's alley, Alice saw an alcove full of wooden forklift pallets stacked with vodka crates. She tucked her body low and ran to them. The pallets stopped a metre or so short of the alcove's ceiling, space enough for Alice to hide without being seen from above. The crates on the end pallet were piled at a slight angle, makeshift steps. She hauled herself up these and lay flat on top, pressing herself down as though by sheer force of will she could make herself invisible.

They ran past her, *under* her, ten seconds later, so close that she could have reached out and stroked the tops of their heads. Alice wanted to laugh at them, peek out and whistle before disappearing again; in her head, they were the Keystone Cops.

She was on the ground floor now. All she had to do was find an exit. Careful not to make a sound, Alice looked around her. It wasn't promising. The alcove enclosed her on three sides, and the main distillery floor lay beyond the filtration columns. She tried to remember the layout of the place. The main entrance was nearest, but she couldn't go out through there. With the threat of Chechen attack constant it would be too heavily guarded, even on a weekend. What about a side exit? None she could think of, not within reach.

Her fear had been subsumed while she was on the move. Now, with nothing to occupy her body, her mind began to twist again in quick turns of dread. Being alone was the worst of it. No one to look out for, sure, but no one to look after her either. She suddenly wanted someone else here, it didn't matter who – Lewis, Bob, even Harry.

*Harry.*

An image jumped into Alice's mind: Harry on his first day here, blundering into the women's toilets by mistake. The toilets were down a corridor which ran off the entrance hallway, and they'd have a window, even a small one for ventilation.

She squirmed very slowly across the top of the crates and looked out. The corridor was not far, perhaps double the distance between alcove and filtration columns. There were three men at the reception console, but if she kept close to the wall she'd be out of their line of sight. It was worth the risk; she couldn't lie here all day, they'd find her eventually if she did.

Alice gripped the edge of the pallet and levered her body over the side, taking the strain in her arms. It was three, four metres to the floor; at full stretch, she didn't have far to drop. A few surplus bottles had been lined up on the ground. Alice took two, for self-defence – a broken bottle was as good a weapon as any at close quarters, and no one in their right mind would come too close to a desperate woman jabbing at them with a smashed glass stump. If she got away cleanly, she'd drink them in celebration.

Movement would catch the eye of any watcher, but she had to take the chance. She walked quickly along the wall and turned sharply down the corridor. Not too hurried, not too furtive, nothing to suggest she didn't have a perfect right to be doing what she was. She stepped into the ladies' toilet, entered the nearest cubicle and locked it behind her. The door and lock were flimsy enough to be kicked off more or less instantly, but they were better than nothing.

The window was hinged at the top, and opened barely wide enough to accommodate Alice. Reluctantly, she set down the two bottles of vodka – there was no room for them in the satchel, and no other way of getting them out intact. Looping the satchel's strap round her wrist, she sent it through first, then, feeling ungainly and clumsy, squeezed after it, head first like a reluctant diver. The window was set too high for her to be able to reach the ground. She had to let herself fall, twisting as she did so to take the impact on her shoulder rather than her fingers, while her legs came over her head and hard on to the pavement beside her.

Moments later, brushing the snow off herself and rubbing at her bruises, she sauntered into the street and flagged down the nearest car: a dirty white Moskvich, the Ford Fiesta of Russia, so ubiquitous as to be all but invisible. An icon of the Virgin Mary and a topless glamour girl vied for space on the dashboard.

"Where to?" the driver asked, slapping the passenger window down with his hand.

"Patriarch's Ponds." Sweat on her brow, hearthammer beneath her shirt. She climbed in the back, sliding a violin case along the seat to make room. "Violin, or machinegun?" she asked.

He laughed. "Violin. One of my many talents." He reached in to his jacket pocket and brought out a stack of business cards, fanning them out between thumb and forefinger like a magician inviting her to pick a card, any card. Alice read the descriptions: Petropavlovsk, Sergei Mikhailovich, taxi driver, violinist, photographer, taxidermist, bookbinder, insurance salesman, counsellor, caterer, television post-production.

"I used to be a cabbie, but it cost too much. You have to bribe everyone at the depot – the depot manager, to get a decent car; the mechanic, to pass it fit for service; the garage manager, if you need repairs done; the controller, for giving you a favourable shift and cooking the time clock; and the guy at the exit gate, to let you leave. Once you've paid all that, fares and tips aren't enough, you need to find after-hours vodka, tours, whores."

He jinked left and right between two cars, and the Moskvich lurched like sloshing bathwater in protest. They passed signs on the pavement for pork chops, mashed potatoes, vanilla pudding – street canteens serving hot meals to the poor, the elderly, invalids, all those for whom winter bit particularly hard. Alice guessed that the food was from Operation Provide Hope, but she couldn't see whether the meals were being sold or given away.

She'd been into a lions' den and come out unscathed. She felt flushed with triumph, and it was all she could do not to yell at the top of her lungs. Instead, she gestured to the array of business cards. "Do you really do all these things?"

"Not all. But I know people who can. There are lots of us down on our luck, and nothing comes for free any more. The other day, I broke down in the middle of nowhere, coming back from Kiev. There used to be this unspoken rule that the first driver who passed a broken-down vehicle stopped and helped. How else can you run things, when you've got crap cars covering vast distances on bad roads? So the first driver stopped, as usual. But even before he'd looked for the teapot sign" – a window thus marked indicates that the driver is mechanically inept; Russians take a perverse pleasure in advertising this – "he asked me: 'D'you have money?' I wonder what this place is coming to." He swivelled round to look at her more closely. "You look like you need a drink."

"Damn straight, I do."

Petropavlovsk reached down into the passenger foot-well and picked up a bottle and a glass. Alice opened, poured and drank all in one movement.

"Ay, ay," Petropavlovsk said, wincing. "You drink like a Russian."

Back home, Alice was grateful to the apartment empty. She didn't feel up to talking to Lewis right now. She typed a report of what she'd found at Red October, ran the more incriminating papers through the fax to make copies, and added them as appendices.

Then she rang Arkin and said she had to see him, *now*. She didn't ask whether she was interrupting his weekend; Arkin would have made each day forty-eight hours long if it meant he could work harder.

In his office, she watched him read in a silence punctuated only by the dull tapping of a vodka glass against her teeth.

"Why are you doing this?" he asked when he'd finished.

What a question, she thought. "*I'm* not doing anything. If there was nothing to find, then I wouldn't have found it."

"You think this is going to help the process?"

"If this kind of stuff's going on, the process isn't worth it in the first place."

"What do you suggest, then?"

"This isn't incompetence or random pilfering. It's systematic fraud."

"You think I should fire him?"

"Do you have a choice?"

"What good will firing him do? You think we're ever going to get any of the money back? He'll have hidden it too well. More than that, Alice, we need Lev for privatisation to work. Sack him, and we can kiss goodbye to the whole process. Sack him, and you might as well give Karkadann the keys and invite him to help himself. You should have left this alone."

"And let the Russian people buy into a charade? No way."

"Alice, this is —"

"— Russia, I know, but that doesn't mean we can just brush everything under the carpet. Why do we need Lev for privatisation? The vouchers are distributed, the auction date set. This thing is bigger than one man. If he kicks up a fuss, we can destroy him publicly. Sacking him will prove once and for all that this really is a revolution, that people are called to account when they've done wrong. Coming clean now won't derail privatisation. Quite the opposite — it'll save it."

"That's not how things work here."

"You want me to take this to the president, Kolya?"

"Be my guest. You won't get a word of sense out of him."

"Oh?"

"He often leaves the Kremlin early, sometimes right after lunch, and makes for his dacha in Barivkha, giving orders that he's not to be disturbed. He's horrible to deal with when he's like this, and it's utterly impossible to get him to do anything. He'll only snap out of it when there's a crisis."

"What the hell's this, then, if not a crisis?"

"Not enough of one, that's what. He needs a full-on emergency – tanks at the White House, battle stations. Then you'll see him at his best: he swallows papers like a computer, the days are too short for him."

"Kolya, if you don't fire Lev, I'll go to the media and tell them myself."

There were four messages on Alice's answer phone when she returned home, all from Lev: the first bewildered, the second angry, the third frustrated, the fourth tinged with a desperation she'd never heard from him before. Lewis was in bed, asleep after a night at the Sklifosovsky. He wouldn't have heard the phone ring; it was in the living-room and, because it was a shoddy Soviet model, it rang quietly and sometimes not at all.

On the way into the kitchen to pour herself a vodka, Alice caught a glimpse of herself in the mirror and wasn't sure what she saw. A fearless crusader for truth and justice? Perhaps. Partly. But she wasn't yet so far gone that she couldn't see beneath that, down to the depths where she hated herself for cheating on a man who loved her, where she depended on a man she needed to get away from, where she was trying to make Lev hate her enough to finish their affair, to effect what she didn't have the courage to do herself.

# 56

*Sunday, 16 February 1992*

Alice went to watch Lewis play broomball at lunchtime. She needed to feel secure among her own kind, no matter how regularly she tried to disown them.

Broomball is ice hockey lite, and for Alice it was just about the perfect microcosm of expatriate life. It removes all hockey's danger: players use brooms tied with tape or string rather than sticks, rubber-soled shoes rather than skates, and pucks of plastic rather than vulcanised rubber. Despite this, it's still compulsory to wear helmets and face-guards, even though it's easier to get a tan in a Moscow winter than get badly hurt playing broomball.

Lewis slid round the ice with more enthusiasm than technique. Alice laughed with him when he fell over and cheered when he scrambled the puck into the goal, but she felt as though she were watching a son rather than a husband. She was keeping things from him, so her knowledge was greater than his, as an adult's is greater than a child's, and his resulting state of innocence was childlike too. Knowledge breeds power and power breeds pity – and pity, Alice thought, is the one thing you should never feel for a spouse. She still wanted to talk with Lewis and be his friend, go for walks and to the theatre, hug and protect him, everything that wasn't exciting, because what excited her were the very things she kept from him. What she didn't want, even though she could still admire his handsomeness, was to sleep with him.

Lewis' team was leading until the last minute, when he gave away a penalty and the opposition scored to level the match. Over on the touchline afterwards, as the players gathered their belongings, one of Lewis' team-mates, an attaché at the German Embassy, rounded on him.

"If you hadn't conceded that penalty, we would have won the match.'"

"If you guys hadn't invaded Russia," Alice said, "you'd have won the war."

It was a perfect winter's day, the cold matched only by the brilliance of the sun and the purity of a cloudless sky. Alice and Lewis went for a walk in a silence that he found companionable and she cagey. They passed like tourists through Resurrection Gate and into Red Square, a paved desert surely too vast to be contained in a city. Red Square looks as though it descended from the sky and simply erased an entire district. Its vacant tracts and towering walls make all those inside look insignificant. On the cobbles laid deliberately to recall the curvature of the earth, one can feel both at the world's centre and at its edge. This is no cosy, friendly courtyard; this is architecture as war.

Alice was struck by how the Kremlin draws all Moscow towards it, like a basin into which the city drains. In fact – another of Moscow's million absurdities – the Kremlin stands on a hill, like a huge Escher drawing in which a hill can be lower than the ground around it. The fortress is massive and impassive, and there's nothing subtle about it. It imposes, the towers stabbing the skyline, the golden domes swelling and glittering. It intimidates, a Mecca for those who believed, a Hades for those who opposed. More than any other place in Moscow, Russia, perhaps the world, the Kremlin says simply, "I am the power", and it itched at something atavistic in Alice.

\* \* \*

The men came for them when they were down by the river. There were two of them, and as they approached Alice watched with the curious detachment of the slightly drunk. They looked entirely normal, shapeless under heavy dark coats and fur hats, but there was something about the purpose and direction of their gait which pulsed warnings through the vodka fences in her head. As they came past, one knelt down to tie his shoelace while the other kept walking, and Alice was already shouting a warning to Lewis – she knew the impossibility of tying a shoelace when wearing thick gloves – when the first goon grabbed her from behind. He circled one arm round her neck and the other round her waist, pinning her fast. His mate, rising fast from the sidewalk, hit Lewis square in the face and knocked him to the ground before turning towards Alice.

A few cars puttering up and down the embankment, a family on the other side of the highway, a woman walking down towards the bridge – all as remote and unreachable as Mars.

A glint in the sunshine, a knife blooming in a gloved hand.

Alice felt less panicked than curious. For once, she was at the perfect state of intoxication: too drunk to be scared or feel much pain, not drunk enough for her co-ordination and reactions to have totally deserted her. She jerked her head sharply backwards and heard rather than felt the crack against the teeth of the man who was holding her. It was surprise as much as anything which made him loosen his grip, but surprise was all Alice needed. She felt for his balls through the thick fabric of his trousers and squeezed as hard as she could. When he took an instinctive pace backwards, she kicked flat-footed against his knee and heard him howl in pain above the crack of bone.

The knifeman slashed at Alice. She saw the blade disappear inside her coat, but didn't feel it go any further. She was moving, and he needed a clear shot to get through so many layers – she'd have been dead had it been summer. He pulled the knife out and raised it past his ear, intending an overhand shot. She grabbed at his wrist and brought her knee up into his groin, hard as she could, and with the fingers of her other hand she jabbed at his face, balls and eyes, balls and eyes, and now cars were slowing and people were looking, and he dropped the knife and ran.

Alice went after him, anger making her yell she didn't know what. When she passed a courting couple, their looks of astonishment made her realise what she must have looked like; a lunatic woman, loose on the city streets. At the same moment, she knew she wouldn't catch him, and she stopped as the adrenalin subsided.

Lewis was coming towards her. She was surprised at how distant he was, and therefore how far she must have run. His face was streaming blood, and he was shouting something at her. "Too dangerous," he bawled. "You see? You see now?"

The danger he'd meant was Moscow's, but it was also in Alice; a woman crazed with anger, who would have killed the man she'd been chasing if she'd reached him. The darkness in her was the darkness in the city, that was why Lewis hated this place so. She reached for him when he arrived. "What's doing?" she panted. "Are you OK?"

"Fine, fine." He brushed her hand away. "Nothing broken."

Alice saw the other man, the one she'd kicked, being bundled into a car. She was too far away to read the plate – not that it would have made any difference. The car was bound to be stolen, unregistered, or both. She turned back to Lewis.

"Thanks for asking how *I* am," she said bitterly.

# 57

*Monday, 17 February 1992*

Three adolescent beggars came towards Irk, swaying with the movement of the metro carriage as the train whistled through the tunnels. Street children had never been around under communism – correction, they'd never been *visible* under communism. Now they rode the carriages like pint-sized hobos, dodging the transport police and begging money off defiantly indifferent passengers. Street kids aroused as much fear as sympathy in adults. Homeless children were outsiders, the neglected ones. Most of them, Irk knew, had two options – begging or crime. When Irk opened his copy of *Argumenty y Fakty*, he saw Arkin reported as saying that "the number of homeless children and their criminalisation has reached threatening proportions. Urgent measures are required."

That last statement made Irk wince. Urgent measures meant one of two things, piss and wind or mindless brutality, neither of which would help the children. And this in a society which so prizes childhood. Irk thought of Lev's orphanage, one of the few places to be tackling the problem constructively – and look what was happening there.

The woman on the next seat nudged him. "What can we do?"

she asked. "What good can we do?" She waved the children away. Irk gave the nearest one a dollar and shook his head at the others. What good indeed? People felt they couldn't make any difference to social issues – they'd hardly been encouraged to do so before – and were reluctant to get involved in other people's problems. Keeping your own head above water was hard enough.

Alice had dressed down: no make-up, hair unbrushed and the most unflattering clothes she could find. She was punishing herself for being lovely, not knowing that this proud hostility to herself made her more attractive to Lev than ever.

Lev, unhurried as ever, took her by the elbow and guided her into his office. He must have checked his paperwork, he must have realised what she'd taken and what she'd seen. She wondered whether he would try to bribe or bludgeon or blackmail her into forgetting about it.

"I'm so glad to see you, Alice. We're developing a new vodka and it's a bit of a departure. I'd like you to taste it and tell me what you think."

"Lev, we don't have time for this. There are things . . ."

He slapped his tongue against the roof of his mouth in rebuke, as though she'd committed some dreadful rudeness. "Just when I let myself forget you're an American, you can't help but remind me again. Always in a rush, never time for the simple things in life. You *will* sit, Alice, and you *will* taste this with me."

She sat on the edge of a chair, a sulky schoolgirl, while he poured her a glass. "This is pear-drop vodka. The process is very simple, really; we spread a handful of pear-drop sweets across a sieve, place the sieve in the vat and let the alcohol pass over it. Esters impurities are sweet and fruity – we've kept a small amount in, to complement the pear drops. Some distillers prefer macera-tion, but I've always believed in circulation: six times a day for a week, and then the vodka's pumped into barrels to let the flavours fuse and settle for a couple of months. Of course, you get evapo-ration and a corresponding loss of strength – about ten per cent, which we adjust prior to bottling." He handed her the glass. "What do you think?"

Any aroma of pear drops was submerged under a slightly meaty smell, not unlike stock cubes. Alice knew this was due to the unspent yeasts burnt during the distillation. She was getting better. Lev, on the other hand, seemed to be losing his touch. Perhaps it was a sign of change.

She put the glass down and took a deep breath. "All right. *Enough.* Did you try to have me killed yesterday?"

"I'm sorry?"

"Two men, by the river. Whatever you think of what I did here on Friday –"

"Alice, I've no idea what you're talking about." His face was closed. He regarded her calmly, happy to prolong the standoff. "You were attacked?" he asked at length.

"Two men, a deliberate hit. They didn't want money, they wanted to kill me. Yours?"

"You believe that of me, you can leave here now and never come back."

She imagined, hoped, saw that it was the truth. "I'm sorry."

"Were you hurt?"

"Lewis was hit in the face. He's fine. I – I fought them off."

"I'd expect nothing less. I'm glad they didn't succeed."

"I suppose if they had been yours, they wouldn't have failed."

He checked her face to see if she was being serious. "I should sincerely hope not."

"I want you to read this –" Quickly, before the conversation ran away from her, she handed Lev a copy of what she'd given Arkin: her report, together with the appendices.

Lev read it through, his expression relentlessly placid even when he reached the photocopies of his own stolen papers. Alice waited for – what? Eruptive accusations of theft, indignant protestations of mistaken conclusions, savage denunciations of personal betrayal, but she got none, and it was the last that hurt her, because she *had* betrayed him, and she wanted him at least to recognise that. She wasn't sure which would be worse: if he really didn't see the extent of her treachery, or if he was simply determined not to give her the satisfaction of a reaction.

When Lev finished, he bounced the papers on their ends to straighten them and turned to Alice with a smile. "It's a shame the Cold War's over. The CIA could have done with your sort."

Like Arkin, he'd made no comment about her methods. Had this been America, every politician would have distanced themselves and every lawyer would have been daubing her in coats of inadmissible evidence and trespass. The Russians couldn't have given two shits. What she'd found was important; how she'd found it was irrelevant.

She handed him an envelope embossed with the prime ministerial seal. Lev opened it with the teasing deliberation of an

Oscar-night presenter. Inside was Arkin's order dismissing him from his post at Red October; dated yesterday, delivered to her house this morning. He read it with the same beatific equanimity as earlier.

"I must confess," he said, "I don't see exactly what I'm supposed to have done wrong."

"Are you being serious?"

"Perfectly."

God, she thought, there was so much she still had to learn about him. "You're stealing from the company – no, you're stealing the company. Without me, there'd have been nothing left of Red October by the time we got to auction day. The whole thing would have been a farce."

"Why's that?"

"What's nothing divided by forty-five thousand shares? Nothing, that's what."

"I'm not stealing the company."

"What are you doing, then?"

"Preserving it."

"*Preserving* it? Tell me how, exactly."

"This auction – who knows what'll happen?"

"It'll all be properly run."

"Afterwards, I mean. You start letting outsiders in, you open up a whole can of worms. But with everything that matters tucked away in Nicosia, under my control, I know it's safe."

"And?"

"And I can keep running the place as before, and none of my workers lose their jobs." He gestured at her report. "Sure, it's all true. But I'm only stealing from a government that'll otherwise steal from me."

"You're stealing from your workers – the same workers whose jobs you harp on about."

"*Stealing* from them? You've seen me with them, Alice. They respect me, no? They wouldn't respect me if I was ripping them off."

"They don't know you're ripping them off."

"They get their cut." Her surprise amused him. "You thought they didn't?"

"All of them?"

"Indirectly, yes."

"Your cronies, mostly."

"I distribute revenue among the workforce according to need as well as seniority. A married man with six children gets more than a single woman, that's only fair."

"But you get the most. You and your friends."

"Of course. The closer you are to product control, the more you take. That's obvious."

"It doesn't make you Robin Hood."

"Nor does it make me a shop-floor Ceaucescu. Tell me again: how am I *stealing* from them?"

"By forcing them to sell you their vouchers."

It had been so long since Lev had flipped, from affability to incandescence in an eye's blink, that he caught Alice quite off guard. "That? *That*? I'm doing them a *favour*. They get something useful – cash. I get a piece of paper which – like all the others the government issues – is worthless. Vouchers are worthless, roubles are worthless, and this –" he brandished Arkin's order at her – "is worthless."

"The order is served pending a criminal investigation."

"You can't prosecute me. I'm a deputy. I've got immunity."

"Not from an executive order." Lev shrugged. Alice continued: "There's two ways we can do this. You can leave now, or I call Arkin and he sends in the heavies and the television cameras, and all Moscow will see you being escorted from the building like a criminal."

Perhaps for the first time, Alice understood that either Lev would go or she would; they could not both stay. Only with him gone could she regain control of the auction and her life. She didn't ask what this meant for the two of them. This was the course she'd chosen, and she couldn't bear to consider the alternatives.

Lev nodded slowly. An oil slick of a smile spread across his face. He held up his hands. "Very well, Alice." His voice was as calm as it had, a minute before, been furious. "You win. You'll let me explain things to my workers before I leave?"

"Another time."

"At least permit me to say goodbye to them as I go."

Alice thought about this. They'd have questions, but once Lev was gone, she felt she could handle them. "Sure."

"Perhaps you'll walk with me through the factory."

"If you like."

"I like."

They took the elevator down to the distillery floor without speaking. Curiously, it wasn't an awkward silence, more the quiet of old friends who have come to the end of a long road mutually travelled. Alice was surprised by Lev's lack of animosity. He must be in shock, she thought. Logically, he may have taken on board the news that his time here was at an end; emotionally, she knew, it would take much longer to register. It would be the close of an era for the workers too, she realised. For the younger ones, Lev was the only boss they'd ever had. After five years, even some of the older ones would be hard pushed to remember what had come before him.

As they started out across the vast caverns of the distillery, she fell half a pace behind him. This was his moment, and she understood that she should allow him the dignity of taking it alone. She looked up and around her: at the gangways spanning the ceiling, the pallets stacked against the walls, all the places where she'd run and hidden from him, his cronies, her feelings.

Lev paused by German Kullam, leaned into him and whispered something in his ear. German was looking straight at Alice, and she saw the emotions flit like bats across his face: surprise, realisation, determination. He nodded once, decisive.

"What did you say to him?" Alice asked Lev.

Lev didn't answer. German was already walking away, to the person at the next station; another whisper, another nod, then they both moved down the line and passed the message on again, and so it spread.

The whispers came to Alice as though borne on the west wind. *Zabastovka*, the workers were saying, *zabastovka*.

Strike.

If Alice had been impressed at how quickly Lev had started up the machinery on Saturday morning, she was no less awed by the speed with which his employees were shutting the place down now. Conveyor belts creaked and juddered to a halt; bewildered bottles wobbled drunkenly as their endless passage was suddenly suspended, the gurgling and hissing from the stills subsided as though they were falling asleep. Alice heard only footsteps and lowered voices, tones of bereavement. Watching in amazement and not a little awe as Lev led the way through the main door – hadn't the poster under Resurrection Gate depicted her as the pied piper? – she stifled an urge to applaud.

Even Arkin couldn't find an entire workforce at such short notice. Alice suggested they bring in a skeleton staff from one of the more westernised eastern bloc countries, such as Estonia or Poland. Arkin said this would be useless. Lev's workers were valuable not because they were acquainted with the latest in distillery technology, but because they alone could operate the obsolete equipment which Red October had yet to replace.

"The auction's two weeks away," Arkin said. "We've no choice. We have to bring him back."

294

"With all that shit he's pulling? No way."

"That auction *has* to go ahead. I don't care what you've found, we can't do it without Lev. We tried, we failed, we've been outmanoeuvred – accept it. Rather that than this whole thing goes to shit."

"I –"

"You've brought this on yourself. Listen to me, Alice. Everything rests on this auction. If you mess this up, no international organisation will give you a job till the next millennium. Go to him, get what concessions you can, but get him back. At any price."

"You come with me."

"No. You've been working with him, you'll persuade him better. Use your charm."

It was not that Arkin suspected their affair, merely that he was distancing himself, just as Borzov had done by leaving Moscow. Arkin would blame Alice for anything that went wrong, saying he'd been mistaken to trust a perfidious foreigner. And it was precisely *because* she was a foreigner, because her life and career weren't here, that she was expendable. If it still went off OK, Arkin would claim the credit; if it didn't, dissociation was the only hope he would have of persuading parliament not to throw out the reformist administration. The reformers had no power base worth the name; they were a straggling handful trying to climb Everest, and their only clothes were tiny shreds of legislation liable to be ripped away at any moment.

Alice understood Arkin's logic, understood too that it was nothing personal against her. Personal and professional might be intertwined with Lev, but not with Arkin.

Lev seemed both pleased and unsurprised when she came to his penthouse, and Alice thought she knew why. In uncovering Lev's trickery and manoeuvring for his dismissal, Alice had shown power, steadfastness and ruthlessness; she'd used her alliances with powerful men; and she'd shown herself willing to adapt to local conditions. All of these were qualities Lev admired. Yes, they were lovers, but they were also adversaries.

"You want me to come back," Lev said. "You wouldn't have come here otherwise." Alice shrugged. "I can do this any time I like, you know. Bring my workers out on strike, I mean. I can make them run, jump, roll over, sit up and beg."

"I know." She'd realised that Lev had bought his employees heart, soul and conscience.

"So what are you offering?"

"It's not good for anybody, this way."

"What are you offering?"

"You have to wind down Suyumbika and restore Red October's assets. We can't run an auction with nothing, that's plain stupid."

"And in return?"

"Everything else. You can keep everything else the way it is." It was not a moral judgement, but a practical one. Alice thought how far her original ideals had been eroded. It had been a gradual diminution, a whittling away so subtle she'd hardly noticed it happening, because there'd been a good reason behind every compromise she'd made. "You can't keep running Red October this way for ever. In time, being majority shareholder in a well-run private company will earn you more money than you do now. Agree to that, and the dismissal order's rescinded."

He smiled at her. "Persuade me."

"We need you, but you love that factory. Fair's fair."

"No. *Really* persuade me."

She understood what he was driving at. "No."

"Why not?"

"It's not appropriate."

"Not *appropriate*?" He chuckled, and she felt herself swaying. He was quicksand, he was a whirlpool. "Not appropriate is hiding out in factories all night. Not appropriate is accusing your lover of trying to kill you. Come." He reached out a hand, a forcefield which dragged her closer. "You're very persuasive, when you put your mind to it. And I need a lot of persuading."

She nuzzled his neck. "This much?"

"More."

She kissed gently around the edge of his mouth. "This much?"

He shook his head with a look of mock disappointment, and she laughed as she unbuttoned his shirt and felt inside. "This much?"

"Ah. Finally, I'm beginning to see the merits of your proposal."

She worked at his belt. "This much?"

"Now, Alice, those are some *excellent* points you're making!" The rumbling of his laughter gladdened her heart.

# 58

*Tuesday, 18 February 1992*

Under communism, people had complained about the authorities; now they complained *to* the authorities. Every man and his dog seemed to be ringing Petrovka for a good old moan. It was Irk's misfortune to get saddled with a particularly vehement busybody.

"Why aren't you lot doing something about the niggers, that's what I want to know?" she shouted. "There are *hundreds* of them near me, riding round in their flash cars and causing heaven knows what kind of trouble."

"It's a free country, madam."

"More's the shame. Day and night they're here, putting good people in fear of their lives. It's a disgrace, that's what it is. I won't be letting my kids out of my sight, that's for sure – not now *he's* down here."

"He?"

"The gangster. The one who's on TV, ranting and raving. You know."

Irk's office was as overheated as every other room in Moscow, but now he shivered. "Where exactly do you live, madam?"

"Shubinsky Avenue."

"Where's that?"

"Off Smolensky Square, just round the back of the Belgrade Hotel. That's where they are."

Of course they were – that was their headquarters. "Let me get this straight," Irk said, hardly daring to believe it. "Karkadann's there?"

"Karkadann, yes, that's him."

"You saw him yourself?"

"With my own eyes, and there's nothing wrong with them. There I was in my kitchen, and from there I can see into the back court-yards of the Belgrade. I was looking out, minding my own busi-ness" – sure you were, Irk thought – "and there he was, getting out of one of those jeep-type things, a whole bunch of coons round him like he's the czar or something."

Irk was already halfway down the corridor.

Homicide didn't have enough men to spare. Organised crime did.

"An anonymous tip-off?" Yerofeyev said. "You must be mad."

"Let's say I'm not. She sounded genuine enough."

"Then this is a job for the OMON, even the Spetsnaz." OMON were the interior ministry's riot police; Spetsnaz were army special forces.

"And by the time we get permission to use either of those, Karkadann will be long gone. He's always on the move, you know that." Yerofeyev shrugged, not his problem, and Irk saw the reason for the apathy. "That's what you want, isn't it?" he snapped. "You've no reason to *want* Karkadann caught, not with the bribes he's paying you."

"You know what you should do, Juku? Ring Lev and get *him* to send *his* men over."

"And take sides in a mafiya war? Never."

"They'll do a better job than anyone we've got here."

"I need *your* men, and I need them now."

"No."

"Then I'll go to Arkin and tell him how co-operative you've been."

Four vans, six men in each, and two cars, four men apiece, all racing with blues and twos round the Garden Ring.

"I want roadblocks at each corner," Irk barked into his radio. "No traffic, in or out – is that understood?"

None of the men in the back of the van looked at him. There were half as many flak jackets as were needed; they'd had to draw lots for them. The ones who'd got jackets looked just as nervous than the ones who hadn't. "These vests might as well be made of newspaper, and *Pravda* at that, for all the truth about them being bulletproof," said one of Yerofeyev's men. "Ha! They couldn't stop a paper plane."

Why was Karkadann at the Belgrade? That was the last place he should have gone, and therefore, Irk thought with excitement and a dollop of grudging admiration, the most sensible place to have gone. One chance, one chance. Irk was momentarily surprised at how visceral his animosity towards Karkadann was, then he remembered that pretending to execute someone tended to breed enmity.

Smolensky Square loomed ahead, the Belgrade skulking in the shadow of one of Stalin's vampiric skyscrapers. Irk saw a half-assembled roadblock. "Clean shots," he said. "Watch your background; watch your background." Force markers, kicking in like adrenalin.

The police vans and cars slewing to a halt outside the wedding-cake ministry building; men piling from their vehicles; passers-by screaming and scattering. "Police – *move*," Irk shouted at the herd. "Stay down, stay still." Juku Irk, chess player reprieved from death, now in the mix and loving it as vengeful bile rose within him. Walking along the pavement, running, walking again. A bus and a lorry stopped in the square, perfect cover as he tried to see what was going on.

A furious volley; Chechens in the road, tipped off by the

roadblocks and waiting for the police; stars of flame bursting from the ends of their machine-guns, spent cartridges chattering in spurts to the ground. Dull slaps of falling men, dead before they landed: a Chechen, two cops. Weapons letting rip in concrete canyons; penetrations and ricochets, reverberation coming in patterns. Vehicles sinking and listing as bullets tore the air from their tyres. More men down, sprawling across each other like drunkards. Glass shattering on advertising hoardings of models in silhouette. A Western, a war film, come to Moscow's streets.

And there he was, right there, as though Irk had simply willed him into being: Karkadann himself, fascistic steel and glass towers behind him, this powerhouse of rampant self-interest with his legs apart for stability and hands spitting fire, a brace of guns spraying carnage as Zhorzh ran for cover behind one of the Chechens' jeeps. Irk saw in Karkadann the lust for havoc, the fever of blood madness to kill everything he could find, the darkness of the monstrous passions at the core of the human soul which lie ready to emerge when man's better instincts are suspended. Human civilisation itself was in abeyance; the laws Karkadann obeyed were jungle rules, and his dreams were the prehistoric reveries of cave dwellers. If his guns ran dry, he'd fight the cops with knives and iron girders. If those ran out, he'd fight with his bare hands. If he died, he'd take a score of men with him. But he wouldn't die, he was untouchable, as though he carried a forcefield around him. Behind Irk, a petrified policeman jabbered, barely coherent, of demons and dark forces. *This is our battlefield,* Karkadann had said. *This is where we'll win.*

It was Zhorzh's turn to give covering fire, even though he could hardly see through the blood running into his eyes. Only now did Karkadann move, speeding across the ground with his limp, even though he seemed only to be ambling. He crouched down and wiped the blood from Zhorzh's forehead. Three Chechens bundled them into the jeep and off they went towards the river, the only route the police hadn't yet managed to block.

Irk sagged against the nearest wall in deflated frustration. Yerofeyev's eyes were storm-whipped breakers of accusation, and Irk couldn't bring himself to meet them.

Nothing made Alice feel more like a Muscovite than riding the metro, and Revolution Square was one of her favourite stations. The bronze figures crouched under the arches gave her a comfortable feeling of companionship; there were sailors, soldiers, farmers and airmen, all with their weapons ready to protect the Motherland, to protect

Moscow, to protect Alice. The escalator hauled her and Galina up through heroic mosaics of Soviet endeavour. A man in a full gas mask passed them on the opposite stairway, heading for the city's bowels. Alice wondered whether he wore the mask because he was hideously disfigured, or because he knew something she didn't; was he a lunatic, or the last sane person in the asylum?

Outside the station, cars were parked all across the road, directly under signs proclaiming NO PARKING ZONE. Galina gestured to the signs. "No one pays any attention, as usual. But they should."

"What, to parking restrictions?"

"No. To the *zone*. The zone used to mean the gulags and the prisons, but these days we're all living under the zone's laws, we're all frightened. Look what's happened at Prospekt Mira. Look what happened today in Smolensky Square – twenty-two dead, they said, twice as many injured. Read the papers, watch the TV: bombings, murders, mafiya score-settlings . . ."

Not Lev, Alice wanted to say. She felt an obscure urge to defend him even when he wasn't the topic of conversation; she wanted to mention him whenever she could.

". . . robberies, assaults, maniacs on the loose. The rich kill each other with bodyguards and automatic weapons, the poor use vodka and kitchen knives, but they end up just the same, and the likes of me get caught in the middle." Galina reached into her handbag and pulled out a can of mace. "Every girl I know carries one of these. Some have electrical stunners too. There's a weirdo round every corner, Alice. Did I tell you what happened the other night? I found a man outside our building dressed in high heels – nothing else."

"Shit," Alice said. "I wish I had time for a social life."

They laughed as much as the small joke and their tentative rapprochement was worth.

For most Russians, the name 'Lubyanka' resounds like a gunshot at the end of a darkened corridor – the traditional method of killing prisoners in the KGB's notorious stronghold. Lubyanka, where every brick marked a grave. But for a lucky few, Lubyanka was Moscow's newest and trendiest nightclub. Alice had been sent an invitation for herself plus guest. Lewis, predictably, hadn't been keen to come – nightclubs were his idea of hell – so she'd asked Galina, hoping to make up with her.

They were whisked through an unmarked doorway and down a dark, shabby corridor dotted with piles of construction debris – subterfuge to deter undesirables who might be attracted to a new nightclub. Moreover, it's very Russian to hide one's light under a bushel, to ensure first impressions are wrong. In Russia, what you see is almost never what you get.

The corridor gave on to a hallway smelling of mould. It widened abruptly to a vast atrium wiped with neon and shaking with an impossibly loud bass-line. They'd come in at the mezzanine level, a gallery which ran round the walls high above the dancefloor. A vast head hung from the ceiling, its lifeless bronze eyes staring straight at Alice. It took several moments before she realised that she was looking at Feliks Dzerzhinsky – Iron Feliks, who'd founded the KGB – and that the noose which held it up was the same one which had pulled the statue from its plinth opposite the real Lubyanka following the August coup.

Alice shouted in Galina's ear. "It's a nuclear bunker. The defence ministry still owns it; the managers had to agree that they'd vacate the place within six hours if war's ever declared."

Galina shrugged. "The defence ministry's got to make money like everyone else, I guess."

The walls had been designed to mimic the Lubyanka's exterior: gunmetal cladding atop a smooth base of black stone; dour and sour shades reeking of military uniforms. It was a colour scheme, Alice thought, which hardly lent itself to jovial activity, but people seemed to be having a good time wherever she looked. Naked swimmers glided in a huge tank along one wall, pounding techno beats bounced off the glass ceilings and through the velvet-covered steel-tube furniture, while greying men with bulges in their jackets huffed and puffed with mini-skirted girls young enough to be their daughters. Location apart, it was a typical Russian nightclub: the music secondary to the idea, performance art and fashion wrapped in self-conscious mockery, and all somehow incomplete, the sum less than its parts.

Alice leant towards the man escorting them through the crowds and bawled in his ear: "It's very loud!"

"What do you mean? This is a quiet night."

"It is?"

"Sure it is. No one's been shot yet." His tie was patterned with bullet holes and blood. Alice had to look closer to see that they were part of the design.

He took them to a private room behind a mirrored wall on the main level. A vast buffet stretched the width of one wall. Sofas and armchairs lined the periphery, a dining table stood like an island in the middle, straining under platters of mushrooms baked in sour cream

301

and salted fish; smoked salmon and pickled cucumbers; herrings and meatballs; cold meats and cold fish; chilled soups with chopped pickles; and of course caviar, the black *zirnistaya* from the Caspian sturgeon and the red *keotvaya* from the roe of Siberian river salmon.

Sabirzhan was sitting at the table, smiling at them. Alice thought it must be a coincidence, and not an especially welcome one at that. She turned to Galina in surprise, but in return saw only shamed complicity.

"Well done, Galya," Sabirzhan said. "Sit, both of you. Please."

Alice slumped rather than lowered herself into the nearest chair, dropping as fast as her mood. She was annoyed at Galina, but held herself to blame; in Russia, everything comes around. Sabirzhan rubbed at her bare arm, his fingers tracing a snail's humid path that made her shudder. When he smiled at her, his lips looked like engorged maggots. She wanted to spit in his face.

"You like this place?" he asked.

Through the window, Alice could see a mock show trial being carried out on stage. "No."

"Shame. It'll do very well."

Alice looked at Galina. "What's all this about?"

Sabirzhan poured them each a vodka. Galina waited until Alice had finished her glass and called for a refill before she spoke. "You told me things would change," she said.

"I . . . *what?*"

"You told me things needed to change – in the factory, in Russia. I did something very bad, because I believed in what you said. And what happened? Nothing."

"The staff walked out. We can't get a new workforce."

"It's just the same as it was before. So what did I do it for? Why did you lie to me, Alice?"

"I . . ."

"It's not your fault? That's not good enough. So, *why?*"

There was no answer.

"Thank you, Galya." Sabirzhan flicked a smile at her. "I'll take it from here."

Alice watched as Galina left the private room and picked her way through the dancing couples. Alice had set this process in motion by encouraging Galina to betray Lev, so how could she complain now? She had known that the price of using Galya might be their friendship. The prospect jarred her, because Galina was the only Russian she felt halfway close to – Lev apart, of course. Yet Alice had never expected it to come to this.

It had pained her to see Galina's admiration for her slowly dissipating since the moment she had told her about Lev. What business was it of Galina's? Lev belonged to Alice and Alice alone. What they had together, the depth and intimacy of it, was the one part of her life which was truly secret. If she told Galina how she felt – even assuming she could find the words to describe it – wouldn't she be diluting its very preciousness? Besides, it sounded such a cliché. Every woman in love thinks her man is unique.

Sabirzhan was speaking. Alice wasn't really listening, until she heard him ask the waiter for another bottle of vodka – and an intravenous drip for the American lush.

"That's it," she said. "How many times do I have to flush before you go away?"

She got up to leave. He grabbed at her arm, and she sat again rather than let his slimy palm rest on her skin a minute longer than necessary.

"Stop the process," he told her. "Stop the auction, get it called off."

"Or what?"

"Or all of Russia will know you're screwing Lev."

"I haven't a clue what you're talking about."

"Your friend told me." Sabirzhan nodded towards the door through which Galina had left. "Seems you've disillusioned her somewhat."

"Why the fuck did she come to you?"

"She didn't."

"Then why did she tell you?"

"I speak to the Kormakitis-Plakoti Bank every week. They told me yesterday that Galya had requested printouts of all transfer details. I asked her why she needed them. She didn't have a good enough answer." He grimaced. "She soon found one. There's never treachery without co-operation, you know. I threatened to tell Lev. She'd have done anything after that."

He told her everything; Sabirzhan, the KGB man, eternally suspicious.

Sabirzhan, who'd found there weren't enough of his informers at Red October prepared to help him out. They used to be scared of the KGB, now they were scared of being seen with him.

Sabirzhan, who'd told Lev there were no hard feelings about what had happened at Petrovka, and then set about dismantling the privatisation behind his back. He'd given Lev his loyalty, and what had he got in return? Three days in a cell with Irk trying to pin child murders on him.

Sabirzhan, who'd given Alice the Suyumbika file accidentally on purpose.

Sabirzhan, who'd told *Pravda* about the murders at Prospekt Mira and beyond.

Sabirzhan, who'd been prepared to forsake the considerable fortune he stood to make from privatisation as long as it harmed Lev.

"How do I stop the process?" Alice asked.

"That's your problem. You've got twenty-four hours."

A Cossack dancer came on stage, so good that even Sabirzhan clapped in admiration. Legs kicking straight out and arms folded across his chest, the dancer's balance was impeccable. He could pick flowers in a minefield and not miss a bloom, Alice thought, and turned it on back on herself; what was her life but one long feat of equipoise, walking the thinnest of tightropes without so much as a balancing pole, let alone a safety net?

At midnight exactly, the music stopped and the Soviet national anthem came on. The clubbers cheered and whooped, revelling in the irony. They belted out the words with the zeal of victors mocking the fallen. "Indestructible Union of free republics, joined together for all time by great Russia! All hail the one, powerful Soviet Union, created by the will of the people! Glory to the free Fatherland. The friendship of peoples is our safe stronghold, the party of Lenin, the power of the people, will lead us to the triumph of communism!"

Sabirzhan was on his feet, singing lustily. This was still his doctrine. When the anthem was finished, he turned to Alice. "We sacrificed ourselves for the ideals of a better life under communism," he spat. "We planned and planned, then everything was lost. We were lied to. We lived for an idea. You Americans just live for money. Now it turns out you were right all along. How do you think that makes me feel?"

# 59

*Wednesday, 19 February 1992*

Alice went to look for Sabirzhan in his office, and then rang him at home, both without success. She fretted all morning. Finally, at lunchtime, she went to Lev, and had to wait for ten minutes while he bawled out Irk on the phone.

"Poor guy, I bet he's hubbing hell from everyone today," she said when Lev hung up.

"And so he should be. We'd have done the job for him, and he knows it. Now Karkadann's gone again –" he clicked his fingers – "just like that. Who knows when he'll surface again?"

"Are you calm enough to listen to me?"

His massive shoulders dropped as he exhaled. "Yes."

She gave him an abbreviated version of what had happened last night; abbreviated in that it omitted the nightclub and Galina, leaving just her and Sabirzhan as protagonists. The whole truth would surely have cost Galina her job, perhaps Rodion and Svetlana theirs too, and Alice didn't want that on her conscience.

"That fucking *prick*," growled Lev. "His face is just asking for a brick. How could I have been so stupid, not to have kept him on the tightest of leashes?. Short men have always caused trouble in Russia. Look at Napoleon, look at Hitler. The only people who cause more trouble than short men are Georgians. Sabirzhan's both, so was Stalin. That tells you all you need to know, my darling."

"What are we going to do?"

Lev steepled his fingers. "Ride it."

"How?"

"When you get home tonight, you tell Lewis about us."

"Are you mad?"

"Not at all. What's Sabirzhan banking on? That you'll do anything to prevent your husband from knowing. Take that away from him, and you leave him nothing."

"And then he publicises it anyway."

"So?"

"So the whole process looks compromised. You know how much opposition there is to this programme. It comes out about you and me – collusion at the highest level – the whole thing looks a farce. It might be the last straw. You get enough pressure on this government, who knows what'll happen? What if Borzov resigns? Arkin says he's unpredictable."

"The auction will go through."

"How can you be sure?"

"Because I am."

"I need more than that."

"The West won't back out. Public opinion in Russia's not strong enough to change a flat tyre. Parliament won't be able to do anything until it's too late. The auction will go through."

"No. Tell me why you're *sure*."

"Alice . . ."

"*Tell me.*"

He spoke through his sigh. "Because it's a done deal."

A done deal? She didn't understand.

"You know about presidential decrees, right?"

"Right." In the absence of a proper legislature, many laws were made by the president. Borzov would decide on something, commit it to paper, and voila! – it was law. That he could, and sometimes did, countermand or contradict it the next day was neither here nor there.

"Well, decree number 182 exempts the Sports Academy from all taxes and duties."

"The Sports Academy?"

"Runs training programmes, camps, and so on. Sport's the only way of saving the nation. We're for the public good, it's a worthwhile cause. Hence, we're exempt."

"So? No one pays taxes anyway."

"No, but this way we don't have to bribe tax and customs inspectors."

"I still don't understand what that's got to do with anything."

"The Sports Academy is the largest importer and exporter of vodka in the country."

"Vodka? Very sporty." Her sarcasm sloshed over him. "And the reason it's so big is that . . . you don't pay tariffs at either end."

"Correct."

"How much are we talking?"

"Ten million dollars, give or take."

"That's not so much."

"A month."

"Ah." Alice was beginning to see where this was going. "That's a hell of a concession." He waited her out, letting her reach the truth in her own time. "And for Borzov to have given you that," she mused, "you must have given something just as big in return."

"And what could Borzov want that's so big?"

She saw it now, and slapped her forehead in parody of sudden comprehension. "Light dawns over Marblehead! That's the price, isn't it? Borzov waives the taxes for the Academy, and you agree to privatise Red October. That's the price of your co-operation."

It was as cynical as used notes in brown envelopes. Lev smiled but said nothing. There was no shame, nor a facetious answer which would have patronised her. He was still waiting, she realised, waiting for her to find the last piece of the puzzle.

"So what the fuck have I been doing all along, if this was sewn up from the start?"

"Legitimising it." He spread his hands. "You make it above board, Alice. So long as you're involved, the West will be convinced everything's being done properly. Without you, every government from Dublin to Rome would think that a bunch of shady spivs had struck some dodgy backroom deal."

By Moscow standards, Machiavelli would have been – a cynic? Definitely not. A realist? Definitely. A liberal? Perhaps.

"And all this time . . . all this time we've been screwing, you never thought to tell me?"

"How could I?"

"You profess to have feelings for me. I'm nothing but a veneer of respectability."

"Listen, darling . . ."

"Don't you *dare* me call me darling. I was chosen for this job because I'm damn good. I fell into bed with you because you mean something to me. I feel this high –" She held her thumb and forefinger up, a couple of centimetres apart. "You can fuck off."

"You think I intended for this to happen between us? You're the last person I wanted to . . . And yet I did. It doesn't impinge on what I feel for you."

"Don't be absurd. It's all tied up together."

"And your behaviour's been above reproach, Alice? Sneaking round my office at night? Trying to have me sacked?" His eyes bored into her, spearing her with the memories of her own betrayals: Sabirzhan and the Suyumbika file, Galina and the bank details. "No, I haven't behaved well. Nor have you. So let's write it off and work out what to do."

"I can't . . . I can't just let it go that easily."

"You have to. Sabirzhan will ring you this evening. You have to know what to say to him."

"Does Sabirzhan know about this?" she asked. "About decree 182?"

"Sabirzhan knows everything."

Lev's alliance with Borzov went back seven years, to the start of Gorbachev's tenure. They'd seen in each other an ally in the task of dismantling the Soviet Union. Both men had defined themselves with regard to the communist system, one by his participation and the other by his opposition. Both had also appreciated the central irony of the situation; despite their implacable opposition, the party and the vory had been more similar than different. Both had been arranged round a paramilitary hierarchy, both had been hostile towards outsiders, both had rewarded their own, and both had regarded the law as an inconvenience.

Even as Lev had been doing his bit to destroy Gorbachev, he and the other vory had also been helping keep the system afloat. In the Soviet Union's final twelve months, the vory had controlled a black economy worth sixty billion dollars in spare parts, automobiles, timber, caviar, precious metals, gems, and of course vodka. The kind of deal struck between the KGB and the 21st Century in 1987 for control of Red October was repeated across the union, sometimes for tiny co-operatives, sometimes for massive industrial plants without which entire towns would have closed. By circulating goods and services around the union, the vory's smuggling had saved the state's industrial machine from choking on its own red tape – they'd been the closest thing the Soviet Union had to a service industry. The vory had been doing it for themselves, of course; any benefit to the regime had been entirely unintentional.

And now Lev and Borzov, having helped destroy the union, were helping to ensure its replacement. Not for free, of course; nothing ever comes for free in Russia. Criminals and politicians, politicians and businessmen, businessmen and criminals – the *troika* reinvented.

Alice cooked dinner and ate it without tasting a mouthful. Lewis was talkative, which suited her on two counts: it meant he didn't notice her distraction, and absolved her from the need to keep the conversation going by, say, confessing her infidelity. When the phone rang, she forced herself to stroll rather than sprint across the room.

"Hello?"

"Have you decided?"

Sabirzhan's voice was soft, and no less menacing for it. He was a creature of the twilight, Alice thought. Would he really fight his battles in public, as he was threatening? She couldn't stop privatisation, and she wouldn't tell her husband about Lev – why should she, until she absolutely had to? She should call his bluff; a bully couldn't coerce someone who wouldn't be intimidated. "I think you must have the wrong number," she said, and rang off.

# 60

*Thursday, 20 February 1992*

The revelation came to Alice with sudden and unexpected simplicity. She was watching Lewis gather his things for another night shift at the Sklifosovsky – he'd been working many of those lately – when she realised something at once intensely sad and deeply relieving: she was no longer in love with him. She'd always thought that whatever Lev gave her, whatever problems she and Lewis were having, Lewis was her husband and she loved him. But now, just as Lewis was buttoning his shirt, an unremarkable and pifflingly domestic moment, Alice saw in a flash that she didn't. It was like deteriorating vision; you get it so gradually that it's hardly noticeable, then one day you put on glasses and the world becomes once more as sharp and clear as it was always meant to be.

Alice had been lying to Lewis and concealing things from him ever since she'd met Lev, and maybe even before that. She recognised now that she'd also been hiding the truth from herself. It's an awful thing, not to love someone who loves you. The prospect of inflicting such a humiliating, annihilating blow on someone she cared about so deeply – and she could and did love Lewis without being in love with him – was enough to infuse Alice with terror. She *should* love him, of course, but wasn't there an absolute delight in loving the wrong man? Love is like a lump of coal, she thought: hot, it burns you; cold, it makes you dirty.

She knew every little thing about Lewis: that he liked to read biographies in bed; that he took ketchup but never mayonnaise with hamburgers, and mustard but never ketchup with hot dogs; that he often gave a quick three-pronged snuffle as he dropped off to sleep; that he walked with his weight slightly to one side, so that the heel of his right shoe wore away twice as fast as the heel of his left. She knew all these things, and many more, but it was no longer enough. There was no hope for her and Lewis any more. Lewis was wrong for Moscow, and Moscow was where she wanted to be. Ergo, Lewis was wrong for her.

With Lewis she could simply *be*, in a way she never could with Lev. Seeing Lev was always an event: she was always buzzing, always on top form, always superwoman. She and Lev had never spent an evening slumped in front of the television or reading in companionable silence. It was as though she was scared that the moment she stopped or even slowed, Lev would see her for a mistress of illusion. If he knew how unworthy she was, he'd surely stop loving her, and there was nothing she now feared more than the loss of his love.

The Hungry Duck was a Western bar on Pushechnaya which was working hard to maintain its reputation as one of Moscow's most degenerate nightspots. Tonight was ladies' night – women only and free drinks until nine o'clock. For Alice, it was the perfect place to blow off steam. There was no word from Sabirzhan, and she was going nuts sitting around waiting for the hammer to fall.

She found a quiet corner – well, quiet by Hungry Duck standards – and splashed vodka into her glass. The wall above her head was plastered with advertisements for other themed nights: Czar in the Bar, when a costumed actor roved the room ensuring that no glass remained empty for long, or Countdown, with a sliding scale of cut-price drinks, five for the price of one between eight and nine, four for one between nine and ten, and so on until normal service was resumed at midnight.

No one asked her to join them, which suited Alice just fine. She wanted to be alone; she wanted to be in a crowd.

At nine o'clock sharp, the doors opened on to – and, by the look of it, under the sheer weight of – a male tsunami. Scores of men brimming with vodka and testosterone came barrelling into the bar with the speed and relentlessness of a swollen mountain torrent, sniffing and yelping and licking at any women who were unfortunate enough not to get out of their way in time.

People didn't go to the Hungry Duck to talk, they went to unwind. It was the new, licentious Russia writ large. Every night, the place was packed to the rafters with thrill-seeking expats and Russians intent on drinking themselves blind, finding someone to fuck, and maybe getting into a fistfight or two – in short, everything they hadn't been allowed to do under communism.

Alice was at the bar when the first fight began. Two very drunk Russians were suddenly punching each other. She hadn't even seen it start, there was no preamble of raised voices, dire warnings, pushes in the chest and handbags at five paces. They just got stuck in.

Two more fights broke out, and then another two, like cells multiplying. Alice clambered on to the bar so as not to get knocked over. Her stomach lurched momentarily as she half lost her balance on a lager slick. One of the original combatants finally managed to knock the other to the floor and was kicking him in the head when security arrived, hauled him off and proceeded to beat the crap out of him – partly for their own pleasure and partly to encourage the others to pack it in. The crowd by the bar started shouting at Alice to dance.

"No way." She flipped them the finger.

"It might stop us seeing up your skirt," someone yelled.

"I'm not your type," she shot back. "I'm not inflatable."

There was nowhere for her to get down, so she started to shuffle from side to side, careful to keep her footing – she was drunk enough as it was, she wouldn't need much excuse to fall over – and they were clapping her rhythmically, wolf-whistling and cheering, so she started to do some sexy moves for them, gyrating her hips and running her hands down the sides of her thighs. Now she was loving this as much as they were – it felt good to have all these randy men egging her on, to know that she could have taken her pick, crooked her finger at them and watched them step on their cocks as they tried to get up there fast enough.

Someone propositioned her. She waved her hand in his face, showing him her wedding ring, and in that instant all her hypocrisies came pouring into her head, through the noise and heat and vodka, and she had to leave, she had to get out, *now*. She motioned to the crowd to clear a space for her, and they helped her down, hands groping her en route, but she just wanted out as quick as possible, she didn't even want to spend split seconds slapping the wandering paws away.

The stairs were as crowded as the bar had been. Alice barged her way down the flights and was almost at ground level when she saw what was going on. Girls were sliding down the banisters, all the way from the top, stark naked with their legs either side of the rail, and at the bottom men queued up with their tongues laid flat or their erections held down against the wood.

One girl lost her grip at the top and fell down the outside of the staircase, five metres or more to the ground, and when she landed it sounded like a small explosion. Even allowing for how drunk she was and therefore how limp and relaxed she'd have been when she hit the ground, she must have at the very least broken a limb, lying naked and spread-eagled with all her dignity gone. Not a single person moved to help her. The men were too busy yelling for another girl to come sliding down, and hurry the fuck up about it too.

"The wetter they are, the quicker they come down," Alice heard someone say.

She tried to fight her way through the mêlée to the injured girl, but there were too many people in the way, solid phalanxes of leering perverts. She heard American voices among them – dweebs raised in the suburbs, the kind of men who at home would have been afraid to jump subway turnstiles, now blind drunk, blowing chunks and thinking they were tough guys. There was a word for people like them, she thought bitterly: dorkadent.

Alice walked back through empty, frozen streets; but she was warmed from inside, a great molten core of vodka. Her thoughts seemed to flow down endless rivers of distilled spirit. Vodka was her friend. No one else really understood her, Alice felt, not even Lev. But vodka did, vodka made everything better. Everything better, she thought, everything better – until it made everything worse.

She was hiding, always hiding: behind the vodka at night, behind her professional persona by day. And sometimes, very occasionally, she peered into the gap between the two and spied what was left of her real self, trying to fight its way through, confused and frightened and lonely, pleading for help and trying desperately to be free.

When she was with Lewis, she felt guilty; when she was with Lev, she felt needy. The more this guilt distanced her from Lewis, the needier she became with Lev; the needier she became with Lev, the guiltier she felt about Lewis; the guiltier she felt about Lewis, the more she distanced herself from him, and so it went on. She drank to drown the confusion, drank to drown the shame and the slow erosion of integrity which accompanied duplicity. She felt dishonourable and evil, and her life was spiralling downwards, lubricated by vodka and made bearable by anaesthesia.

It didn't matter how fast or slowly Alice walked. Confusion stayed with her, a shadow that walked ahead in giant steps, shrank at the next lamp, then jumped out again. A telephone pole stretched longingly towards the stars, its wires joining with others – power lines, overhead bus cables – in a thick canopy above her, endless connections to all points urban which linked buildings divided by eclectic architectural patchworks and their own place in history.

Here were bulbous church domes and vast turn-of-the-century imperial government buildings coloured in pink and green or vast slabs of pale yellow and light blue; here were functional structures based on machines and a total absence of idle elements, granite and severe half-ruins from the cruel dreams and superwills of the century's most successful tyrants; here triumphant classicism reflecting post-war pride in cultural values and heritage; here softer and kinder socialist block apartments from the eras of Khrushchev and Brezhnev; and here the darkened glitter of new offices in chrome and glass.

Like the buildings around her, Alice felt she was now one thing and now suddenly another, a whole in spite of rather than because of the differing, clashing parts within. She'd lost her bearings. She didn't know anything about herself any more, not really. Sometimes she couldn't tell what she despised and what she admired. She felt as though everything was being doubled in her soul, just as objects appear twinned to weary eyes. Some schizophrenics are unable to recognise themselves in a mirror – would that happen to her? What would she see? Her own face, twisted and distorted? Two of her, identical twins? Someone else entirely? Or simply nothing?

# 61

*Friday, 21 February 1992*
Alice's hangovers came in degrees of awfulness, roughly divisible into three categories. First, the mild hangover, when her head throbbed like a fairground generator and her parched mouth felt as if someone had lit a small bonfire in it. These symptoms were amenable to, though not entirely cured by, a mixture of Paracetamol, water, cola and Vitamin C.

Then there was the moderate-to-severe hangover, in which general malaise was accompanied by paranoia (exactly what *had* she done last night?) and the feeling that Lilliputian secret policemen had spent the hours since her last drink pummelling her head and body – especially her kidneys – with small but lethally efficient rubber truncheons.

Finally, there was the humdinger hangover, when she'd wake with a ghastly start at five in the morning, overwhelmed by panic, dread, and the certain knowledge that the rest of the day, and possibly the following night too, was going to be lost to remorse, pain, self-pitying tears, chronic anxiety and insomnia. Unless she had another drink, of course – the only remedy that worked, at least temporarily, until the deferred hangover caught up with her all over again.

Alice's hangover this morning was at level two. She padded to the bathroom on legs which felt like suet and looked at herself in the mirror. Tiny blood vessels had burst along her nose and cheeks;

her hands trembled when she held them in front of her. She dry heaved over the basin, and saw her reflection in the curved metal of the taps. Her face was stretched and distorted; now long and flat, now bending round on itself, now back together with a snap.

The phone was ringing. It was early in the morning, no one called at this time without good reason. Alice hurried into the living-room, her head lurching in protest at the motion.

"Hello?" Her voice sounded as though she was swallowing a mouthful of treacle.

"It's me," Lev said, and her heart gave a quickstep of joy. Hearing his voice was always a thrill, as if he were not quite real, someone she could only love as much as she did if he were a figment of her imagination. "You can't have seen *Pravda* this morning?" he added.

"Why not?"

"Because otherwise you'd have rung me."

*Pravda* had it all, every last detail, or so it seemed: a copy of Presidential Decree 182, testaments from sources within distillery and government alike, details of the scams Alice had uncovered, the attempt to sack Lev and the subsequent walkout, and of course Lev's affair with Alice. The story ran across the first seven pages, and the reporters had done as thorough and efficient a job as they had on the child killings, to which this new story of course made reference.

Alice was summoned to the Kremlin. Borzov himself wanted to see her.

Lev and Arkin were there too. It was too early even for Borzov to have started drinking, though not too early to have stopped him working up a fury. "What the fuck is all this?" He flicked the back of his hand against a copy of *Pravda*. "What the hell are you two doing, sleeping with each other? Are you mad?"

No, Alice thought, just in love. But she didn't think it would be particularly helpful to say so.

"Fools, fools, fools, all around," Borzov said. "If Anatoly Nikolayevich had the choice, he'd sack the lot of you and start again from scratch. But it's too late, the auction's ten days away, we haven't got time. On the other hand, ten days isn't long, we can hold out till then. So here's what we have to do."

This was what Arkin had meant, Alice saw, when he'd talked about Borzov being on an upswing. This was a crisis, a real threat to his power; this was where he came alive. He pointed at Arkin. "Kolya, you're in charge of the government response. Deny everything. Say it's all nonsense cooked up by the enemies of reform. Tell

314

*Pravda* – and every other paper and TV station – that the next time they repeat such lies, we'll shut them down." Alice opened her mouth to protest, and shut it again almost immediately. She knew what they'd say, that this was Russia, this was how things were done here. "Flat denials. Act like it's an effort for you even to lower yourself to the level of answering such crap."

Borzov turned to Lev. "Red October: the president doesn't want a peep out of them, not a fucking peep. Tell them you're doing everything for their own good, blame it on zealous reformers. The president knows what kind of hold you have over your workers – use that now, keep them sweet.

"And you, Mrs Liddell . . . You must deal with the West. They hope the new Russia will be their grateful handmaiden. Right now it's a wild and wilful hooligan, but tell them it won't be like that forever and it shouldn't undermine their support for reform. What's important is that things get done, not how they're done – you can't make an omelette without breaking eggs, all that. Talk to Washington, London, Paris and all the number-crunchers in Frankfurt and Geneva. They're the ones you must answer to."

"You seem to have forgotten my husband," she said.

It was all Alice could do to put one foot in front of the other. The knots in her stomach seemed to be tying her limbs to the spot. It took five attempts before she finally succeeded in inserting her key into the lock, and she almost fell over herself as she stepped through the door. *The Marriage of Figaro* was playing on the stereo – an indication of Lewis' state of mind; he hated Mozart. Time to face the music, Alice thought, and tried to force a smile.

She went into the living-room. Lewis looked at her without speaking, and it his silence, so laden with accusation, hurt and betrayal, unnerved her more than any amount of shouting and screaming would have done. Alice burst into tears: great heaving sobs, the way a child cries.

Merciless in his stillness, Lewis didn't move a muscle. He waited for Alice to catch her breath and dry her eyes. He'd have waited there all day, it seemed to her.

"It's true, then," he said.

She jerked her head, approximation of a nod. "Yes. It's true."

"Do you love him?"

"Yes."

"And me?"

"Oh, Lewis." He waited her out again. She took a deep breath, knowing that no matter how much the truth might hurt, the lying hurt more.

"Do you love me?" he repeated.

"No. I don't." She looked away as she said this, not wanting to see his face. "I've tried to love you. But I can't deceive myself any more, Lewis. I love *him*."

It was, Alice thought, as though she'd been skating on the surface her whole life. Hairline cracks in the ice give you glimpses of what it's really like beneath, but afraid of the danger you steer away. Then suddenly one of those cracks opens up anyway and drags you down – and that's life, cold and dirty and exhilarating and a straight fight for survival. And the more you fight the more alive you feel.

Lewis was shaking his head, more in bewilderment than anything else. It had never occurred to him that he might love someone else, and therefore it had never occurred to him that Alice might; that was the way his mind worked. "No," he said, more to himself than her. "No. You must love me – look at you, you wouldn't be crying like that otherwise."

"Of course I'm crying, Lewis. I'm turning my life inside out."

"How long has this been going on?" Exactly four weeks, she thought, though it seemed like four years. "What are you doing, Alice? Looking for excitement? Glamour and glitz, is that what seduced you? Because you want to live dangerously?"

"It's not like that."

"Of course it is. I can see it all, Alice, I know you. I'm too dull for you, is that it? Too boring, too dependable? Just remember this: the problem with being swept off your feet is that you tend to land damn hard on your ass."

"Lewis, *you* couldn't sweep a damn floor. He makes me feel –"

"Don't blame *me* for this, Alice. Blame it on – oh, I don't know, those crazy hours you've been working, or my shifts at the hospital. We're displaced, Alice, both of us. We haven't given enough time to our marriage. We can change that, starting now. I'll take a few months off, we'll talk about it. We'll thrash things out, clear the air, start again, sort out your drinking. That's what has brought all this on – drinking and lying."

"What lying?"

"Screwing someone behind my back – that's not lying? It's the drink—"

"Don't say it!"

"Alice, you have a drinking problem. That's why you've taken up lying – that's what people with drinking problems do. They compartmentalise, and they lie. You've lied so much that you no longer know which way is up."

"Lewis, stop looking for excuses. It's too late. Yes, I feel guilty about lying and hurting you. Yes, I feel responsible. But I don't love you."

"And you love him?"

"Yes."

"*I'm* your husband, and *I* love you."

"Love!" she said. "You don't know what it is, Lewis. The love I have with Lev is something you'll never understand."

Bob, Christina and Harry would all side with Lewis. They were already on their way round to console him. Alice's friendship with Galina was dead. She went back to Lev. He was all she had.

# 62

*Saturday, 22 February 1992*

For Lewis, it wasn't the first few hours that were the worst; it was the morning after a sleepless, solo night, with the shock wearing off and reality beginning to bite. He went to the hospital, driving without consciously seeing the roads. He wasn't due on shift for another twenty-four hours, but if he couldn't help himself, the least he could do was help others.

Lev and Alice spent the day cooped up in the Kotelniki penthouse, trying to shut themselves off from the world. They were riding out the storm, what else could they do? They'd both done as Borzov had asked, as had Arkin. The government was denying everything, Red October's workers had been pacified, and the West had been reminded what realpolitik was all about.

"This place is bad for me," she said.

"This place is in your blood. You love the drama of it all."

"It's still bad for me. If it wasn't for you, I'd leave."

"Alice, you'd stay here even without me."

"Would I?"

She was lying on her stomach, naked. He took her right foot in his hands, cradling the heel in one palm while rubbing the other down the length of her sole, her soul, slowly pulling each toe towards him in turn, smiling as she shuddered at the touch. When he'd done the same with her other foot, he began to kiss all the way up the backs of her legs, around the orbs of her buttocks, lingering at their summits, then the downy hair at the base of her spine, feeling for it with the dryness at the very tip of his tongue.

Alice rolled on to her back and reached for him. Her head hung over the side of the bed, hair sprayed on the carpet, her pleasure magnified as the blood rushed to her head.

"Yes," Lev said, as they lay flushed and panting afterwards. "You would."

He offered her some Smirnoff Black, just about the best vodka in Russia. It's made from the highest quality neutral grain spirit, distilled in a copper-pot still to preserve the grain's natural mellowness and flavours before being filtered through Siberian silver-birch charcoal. Alice tasted tones of light rye overlaid with creamy charcoal and the slightest hint of acetone, tanginess ending with a brief sharp burn.

"You're my vodka," she told him.

"How so?"

"How many ways do you want? No matter how much I see of you, I always want more; too much is not enough. I count the time between when I last saw you and when I'm next going to see you. You drip-feed life back into me. It's the way you make me feel, up here –" she pointed to her head – "and in here –" she indicated her heart. "The way you make me glow, the way you make me forget my troubles . . ."

"Even though I'm the biggest trouble of all?"

"Even though you're the biggest trouble of all."

# 63

*Sunday, 23 February 1992*
It was Defenders of the Motherland Day, originally declared in memory of a Russian victory over German forces at St Petersburg on that date in 1918, now the second most important militarist holiday behind Victory Day itself. From his office in the Kremlin, Borzov looked down at the Red Square crowd through blue-tinted bullet-proof windows. The colour-staining, installed to protect the Kremlin treasures from sunlight, made the world outside look even colder and bleaker than it really was. The bulletproof glass bulged and refracted; seen through this lens the crowd seemed to repeat itself,

the distortion a mocking, physical manifestation of the ways in which the man up here was out of touch with those down there. Borzov wondered what he'd unleashed.

Red Square was packed. Above a sea of fur hats and flat caps swayed banners in the stark colours of protest: communist red, the nationalist blend of black, silver and gold. It was hard to tell who'd have been more stunned by this unlikely pairing of far left and far right, the Romanovs or the revolutionaries who'd murdered them.

The security forces had bickered about who was supposed to do what, so they'd been woefully unprepared when the protesters had arrived and the cordon erected to protect Red Square had been broken with embarrassing ease. Now the police, the OMON and the army troops could do little but form a sullen ring around the protesters and try to ignore the chanting and taunting. Their eyes darted nervously under ill-fitting helmets; when they banged their truncheons against cracked riot shields, it was more to lift their own spirits and keep warm than to intimidate the demonstrators.

Borzov's meaty, ruddy face creased with a sly smile. The combination made him look tipsy even when he was absolutely sober, scheming when he was at his most open, and menacing when he was at his friendliest – none of which applied at this precise moment.

"The president will address the people personally," he said. "It's time to show those ungrateful bastards who's boss."

There was a time when Borzov had worked crowds like a pro, chatting to everyone within range. Charm had flowed from him like liquid gold. Haughty and heroic in repose, his face had seemed transformed into that of a mischievous boy when he smiled. "Let's have a question-and-answer session," he used to say. "No holds barred." No Russian politician had ever done this, and Borzov's spontaneous openness had won him the admiration and affection of the people. Counsellor, confidant, faith healer – they had told him their problems, and he had listened. When they were desperate for truth and hope, Borzov had given them both; in return they'd given him adoration.

No more. Puffy-faced and enclosed within a phalanx of bodyguards and officials, Borzov seemed to have aged a decade. Cocooned from the world by a wall of muscle and deference, he no longer had that precious connection with the people. Now he stood atop Lenin's mausoleum and preached capitalism.

"When the distillery is privatised, and the reactionaries have seen the benefits and no longer rail against those who'd make this

319

country better, then Red October can produce a people's vodka. A high-quality vodka that the man in the street can afford." He puffed out his chest. "People of Russia, Anatoly Nikolayevich pledges this to you as your president: you will drink in comfort and safety. Anatoly Nikolayevich's name will be on the label, and above that his picture, so that the factory worker in Yekaterinburg, the salesman in Irkutsk, the football coach in Vladivostok, the soldier in Kazan – they'll all give thanks to their president every time they take a hundred grams."

The audience laughed and Borzov smiled, unwilling or unable to appreciate that the laughter was *at* him rather than *with* him. Protesters jeered and chanted. They held posters portraying Borzov as a vulture picking at a carcass, and his administration as Jews with yarmulkas, long beards, wide lips and hooked noses, all crammed inside a synagogue.

The deprivations Russia was suffering were serious, but hardly unprecedented. Now that Western levels of prosperity were seemingly round the corner, however, they *felt* more severe than before. De Tocqueville identified a similar phenomenon during the French Revolution: the most dangerous moment came not when the people were at their poorest, but when their expectations of significant improvement were raised only to be frustrated.

The protestors began to chant. "Borzov, go now!" With every repetition it spread and lifted until the entire multitude had taken it up. Behind the voices came a metallic banging, tuneless and yet somehow orchestral: it was the sound of thousands of empty pots and pans, symbolising the protesters' hunger, clanging in unison.

Around Red Square, the police flinched, the OMON snarled, the troops twitched.

More noise and yet more, as loud as it could go and louder. This was taking on a primal momentum of its own. Policeman and soldiers retreated behind their riot shields and backed up against their vehicles. Some of the men were scared, some sympathetic, others intolerant and itching for a scrap; a shot rang out as a panicky finger pulled a trigger – there was no way he'd have heard an order over this noise – and then it was all going off, the familiar rattling of gunfire, protesters recoiling and surging forward, old women trying to escape and skinheads rushing to the action, flurries of skirmishing limbs, tear-gas canisters tracing arcing clouds through the air, people choking and flailing and trampling. And somehow the television cameramen held themselves steady and trained unblinking lenses on the fighting.

The din carried to the Yauza River and through the thick windows of Lev's penthouse. Alice ran into the living-room and turned on the television. Channel One, the government channel, was showing an Uzbek film; Channel Two, more supportive of the protesters, was carrying live coverage. Sounds from outside mingled with the broadcast in eerie, staggered echoes.

"Jesus Christ, Lev, come quickly."

Alice had never seen so many abominably twisted faces, so much odium and animosity. They really hated what she stood for, what she was hoping to do for them. She rocked back on her haunches and stood up, still staring at the screen.

"We're trying to *help* you, for fuck's sake," she cried.

This wasn't just Defenders of the Motherland Day; it was also the forty-eighth anniversary of the Chechen deportations, when Russian troops had rounded up women and children, and those men who weren't away at the front, fighting the Nazis. According to folk belief, the day had been predicted by tribal elders who forecast that there would be snow at their backs – and indeed, though it was spring, a sudden snowfall had completed the fulfilment of the prophesy.

Villages had been sealed off and communications cut as lend-lease Studebaker lorries drew up to transport everyone to Grozny station, where hundreds of freight trains were lined up and waiting. The Russian soldiers had been drunk. They had given the Chechens twenty-five minutes to get ready before sending them off, thousands of miles across the desert wastes. The deportees were fed once a week, nowhere to wash, nowhere to piss, nowhere to shit, typhoid in the carriages, the harshness of the Kazak winters matched only by the coldness of the Kazaks themselves, who had been told that here were cannibals come to drink their blood.

Karkadann's grandfather had left the train at a stop to get some snowmelt to drink, and a Russian soldier shot him dead on the spot. Now, the Chechen warlord sat in an anonymous room in an anonymous part of town and seethed.

There was no one at Petrovka – every available policeman was down at Red Square. So Irk found himself alone, with time and space to think – though he'd have been better off with neither. What had happened in Smolensky Square would have cost him his job were it not for Arkin's continuing interest in the case. Yerofeyev was complaining to everyone in sight about the loss of so many men, as well he might. And still Irk waited in dread anticipation of another adolescent corpse.

With the auction getting closer, the Chechens should be upping the body count rather than throttling back. The delay seemed incomprehensible, and that worried Irk. He never liked what he couldn't understand.

"What's the point, Kolya?" Borzov stared gloomily into the dregs of his vodka glass. "What does the president rule, eh?" He gestured round the room. "Not Russia, not even Moscow, just this little fortress."

"Anatoly Nikolayevich, now's not the time for negative thoughts. Those idiots churning up Red Square aren't representative of the people."

"Anatoly Nikolayevich has never been the deputy, you know, always the boss. Not some apparatchik – the boss. In a thousand years, Anatoly Nikolayevich is the first politician to make it to the top because the people love him. That has to be worth something, surely?"

"It's worth everything, Anatoly Nikolayevich."

Borzov filled and drank, each drop dragging him further into the morass of depression. "Perhaps we're ahead of our time, Kolya. We can see what others can't. You play chess, Kolya?"

"Of course."

"In chess, you never play to the end. If you're going to lose, you resign, you don't go through the motions of a futile endgame and let your opponent humiliate you."

Borzov raised himself from his chair and went to look out of the window once more. "They used to love the president, Kolya. You remember? And now they expect miracles from him. They expect him to heal the sick, punish the corrupt, feed the poor. What else do they want? A human sacrifice? For Anatoly Nikolayevich to appear on the mausoleum and shoot himself?"

Arkin was at his side. "Anatoly Nikolayevich, if you give in now, I'll shoot you myself."

# 64

*Monday, 24 February 1992*
It was just after ten in the morning when four Chechens walked into the Sberbank branch on Ostozhenka. They ducked under a vast

banner advertising the privatisation and bypassed the Monday-morning queues, the manager himself ushering them quickly into his office – for who knew what Chechens would do if kept waiting? Producing warrant cards identifying them as representatives of the Ministry of Finance in Grozny, they informed the manager that they had come to pick up the privatisation vouchers which were due to be distributed today.

"Vouchers for where?" the manager asked. "Grozny?"

"The entire Chechen Republic."

The manager raised an eyebrow. "That's more than a million vouchers."

They gestured to a fleet of vehicles outside. "We've got plenty of room."

"There are no more elastic bands to wrap them with; is that a problem?" the manager asked. "The girls are using cut-up strips of condoms instead; they say it's no great loss, their husbands refuse to wear them anyway." He took a sheet of paper from a drawer. "I'll need you to sign the authorisation order. It allows you to take the vouchers away, and transfers responsibility for their safekeeping from us to you."

"No problem," they said, each man signing with an illegible flourish.

Another consignment of vouchers arrived at Red October, though this one numbered thousands rather than millions: one for each distillery worker, real or mythical. Lev took the packages into his office and locked them in the safe.

The intercom buzzed. He crossed over to the desk and flicked it on. "Yes?"

"Tengiz calling for you," Galina said.

"Tell him to go to hell."

"He'd really like to –"

"You heard me, Galya."

Galina clicked off the intercom and took Sabirzhan off hold. "He won't talk to you, Tengiz."

"Galya, I need to see him."

"Why?"

"This thing's gone far enough. Someone has to make the first move towards reconciliation, but since he won't let me in the distillery, what can I do?"

She sat up straighter. "You're all out of favours with me."

"Just tell me . . . is he going anywhere I could catch him?"

"Well . . ." She sucked air through her teeth. "You didn't hear this from me, but I've just made reservations for him at the Vek. Tomorrow night, eight o'clock. You could, I don't know, go there for dinner with a couple of people, accidentally on purpose, and act like it's a big surprise to see him."

"I'll do that. Not a word, eh? You're a star. Thanks, Galya."

"You can leave me alone now."

Sabirzhan walked across Red Square, where an army of municipal workers were still clearing up yesterday's debris. The display windows in the GUM department store gaped jagged where they'd been broken. Nearby, a man in a donkey jacket was scrubbing at a stain easily recognisable as blood, even against the dark red of the cobbles.

The riot had jolted the government, but no more. Borzov was still in power; Arkin had lambasted the rioters as hooligans and re-actionaries trying to derail the forces of progress; the West was still supporting the privatisation programme; and Lev was still in the distillery. Nothing had changed. The auction was in a week, that was all the time he had left.

Sabirzhan had one option remaining. It was a course of action he'd considered in the past but always rejected, save as a last resort. He got in his car and headed west – to Smolensky Square, where the Chechens were.

# 65

*Tuesday, 25 February 1992*

Same Sberbank branch and same manager as the previous day; four different Chechens, this time in the uniforms of the Grozny police. "There have been some irregularities in the voucher pick-up sched-ule," one of them said. "You still have the authorisation order?"

"Of course."

"Give it to me. We're taking it in for forensic testing."

The bank manager opened his drawer. "No," the Chechen said. "Don't touch it – we must do this properly." He opened a small bag and brought out a pair of rubber gloves, some tweezers and a clear plastic envelope. On went the gloves, the tweezers gripped at the paper, the authorisation order was dropped in the envelope.

"Shouldn't we report this?" the bank manager said, goggle-eyed at his bit part in such a drama. "To Petrovka – to the Kremlin, even?"

"Who do you think asked us to come here in the first place? Just let us handle it; there's a good fellow."

The Chechens were back at the Belgrade Hotel inside the hour. They had a million vouchers and the authorisation order. Sberbank had absolutely no record that they'd ever been there. When Karkadann heard the news, he corrugated his face into something which began as a grimace and ended as a smile – the first anyone had seen from him in a long time.

Officially, vouchers could be sold for cash, invested in an enterprise of the holder's choice, or put in a voucher-investment fund. Unofficially, and entirely predictably, a fourth market had sprung up overnight: vouchers could be traded for vodka, usually at the rate of one for three bottles. All over Moscow, kiosk owners put up signs saying: 'Vouchers bought here'. In the old central post office, now the city's raw materials and commodities exchange, a bust of Lenin watched inscrutably as dealers added vouchers to the list of goods bought and sold. On the pavement outside, Arkin could be found urging an old man not to sell his voucher, but rather to invest it wisely.

"Nikolai Valentinovich," the old man replied, "I'd sell it to you right now if I thought you were fool enough to buy it."

The maître d' at the Vek greeted Lev like a long-lost friend. It was the first time Lev had been there since New Year's Eve. Both Lev and Alice had dressed up for the occasion. Places like this thrived on exclusivity and patrons were expected to make the effort.

Even after everything that had happened over the previous few days, none of the other diners whispered or pointed fingers at Lev and Alice. She half-wanted someone to, just so she could give them a piece of her mind; her period wasn't far off, and a good rant would leach away some of her tension.

A table was presented, chairs pulled out, vodka and menus brought. The bodyguards sat at adjacent tables, close enough to see, too far away to hear. Lev chose an apple-filled goose, Alice a perch fish packed with mince and with olives for eyes. A jazz band played as softly and unceasingly as a river beneath the conversation. Outside, the dim sodium glow of the streetlights cast a suitably down-beat tinge on the perpetual stream of drones who trudged past. Home to work, work to home, nothing in between but survival.

Was it obscene, Alice thought, that they could come to a place like this and spend two hundred dollars a head? Of course. But then, many Muscovites were so poor that a trip to McDonald's seemed grotesquely extravagant.

They were halfway through their entrées when the attack came.

Three cars, BMWs by the look of them, passing at high speed, Chechens leaning out of the windows while their guns spat flames at the Vek's window. "Down!" Lev yelled. "Everybody down!" and they were plunging for the floor even as he shouted. In the half second separating chair from carpet, Lev saw everything with remarkable clarity: passers-by scattering and falling in terror on to the pavement outside; his own bodyguards waving their weapons around in frustrated impotence, unable to fire because the cars had gone and there were too many civilians in the way; Alice's face pressed against the ground, eyes scrunched shut in fear.

No, Lev thought, there's something wrong. He clambered upright with ursine determination, ignoring a warning from one of his guards that he should keep down. It was what he'd heard, or rather what he *hadn't* heard, like the dog that didn't bark. He hadn't heard all the things he'd expected to: he hadn't heard breaking glass, or grunts and screams from people taking bullets in their guts. Lev knew these sounds as well as he knew Pushkin, and there was only one explanation for their absence: the Chechens had been using blanks.

The others were slowly getting to their feet. They dusted themselves down and looked with bewilderment at the Vek's windows, entirely undamaged, and at the people outside, laughing nervously as they helped each other up. "They were using blanks!" someone shouted, and they could all see that, but Lev's mind was already one step on. Yes, they'd been using blanks – but why?

The answer came to Lev more by osmosis than conscious thought. He knew the reason before his brain had framed it into words, and it certainly wasn't conscious thought which had him toppling like a forest oak on to the floor again, a long way down for such a big man, dragging Alice with him as he yelled once more for everyone to get down, but they didn't understand. Surely, the danger was over. It was the simplest of double-taps and they couldn't see it, and his voice was lost in the twin impacts of his body against the floor and the first volley of real bullets through the window.

There were five cars in all, spaced at three-metre intervals, and this time they passed the Vek as though they were part of a funeral procession. Two gunmen were leaning out of each vehicle, and as they went past they laced the restaurant with methodical rounds, up and down, up and down. They made a double frieze, one at face height, the other at chest level, and from Lev's prostrate position he could tell what was happening only by the infernal noise of shattering glass and human howls.

The seconds stretched and stretched, and then the rearmost car accelerated away and time speeded up to normal again. Lev looked around. "Alice! Alice!"

She was lying on her side, covered in food. "Well, this was a total waste of make-up."

"You're fine," he said, and he knew she'd heard the anguish in his voice which showed that his love was for real. He peered cautiously up and around before daring to lift first his head and then his torso. The pavement was strewn as much with body parts as with entire people. The gunmen had been professionals, their slow and methodical stitching movement had torn heads from bodies and limbs from trunks.

The jazz band was still playing. They would not remember the tune afterwards, and their clothing was so saturated with nervous sweat that they needed to change even their shoes, but if they had stopped before their scheduled break, they would have been in breach of their agreement with the management. The Vek could then have withheld their fee – yes, even for a massacre right in front of them.

Inside the restaurant, people were whimpering and yelling, but it wasn't them Lev was worried about. He was looking for anyone who was silent, because the mute cases are always the most serious. No, everyone was alive. The person shouting loudest was one of the bodyguards.

"What happened to you?" Lev asked.

"Took a bullet in the shoulder."

"How bad is it?"

"Oh, not very. I'm more worried about my jacket." He picked at the leather so that Lev could see the bullet hole. "It was new, last week. Now it looks like it's come from my ass."

"Fuck your jacket." Lev glared through the gaping window at the destruction beyond, seeing that his cardinal rule of mafiya disputes had once more been well and truly broken: civilians had not only been involved, they'd been injured, killed. The Chechens' indiscrimination offended Lev. When he'd been behind the wire, his quarrel had been with the Soviet system rather than its people. His circumstances and opponents may have changed, but his principles had not.

Lev turned to the bodyguards. "Round up all the injured out there and take them to hospital, *now*. Don't wait for the ambulances, you'll be lucky if they get here before Christmas. And don't just drop them at those crappy municipal places, either. Take them all to the Sklifosovsky, and tell the staff there that I'll pay."

The restaurant was a mess, and there were no insurance policies in Russia worth the name. As his men hurried off, Lev yelled for the Vek's manager.

"I'll reimburse you for the damage," he told him. "Every last cent – you have my word."

# 66

*Wednesday, 26 February 1992*

The penthouse and Red October were the only places Lev felt safe. He sequestered Alice in his office at the distillery and stationed four guards with her. Another eight were in the antechamber where Galina sat. Lev called Sabirzhan and asked – demanded – that he come in.

"Only if you personally guarantee my safety," Sabirzhan said.

"I guarantee it."

There were no offers of vodka or chummy handshakes when Sabirzhan arrived; they got straight down to business. "Did you tell the Chechens where to find me?" Lev asked.

"How would I have known where to find you?" Sabirzhan was neither outraged nor defensive, there was no flicker in his eyes as he spoke. The doubt his impassiveness induced was enough to keep Alice quiet. She wouldn't condemn Galina without knowing for sure.

"That's not an answer."

"No. I didn't tell the Chechens."

This was why Lev had wanted to bring Sabirzhan in rather than just ask him on the phone: so he could see him face to face when he put the questions. But he found it as pointless as Irk had done back in Petrovka. You couldn't interrogate a man for whom interrogations were a forte; Sabirzhan knew tricks Lev hadn't even heard of. Lev could have asked Sabirzhan the same question, over and over until sundown, and still not known one way or the other.

It was luck of the purest kind that Sabirzhan should be leaving the distillery just as a man in a chauffeur's cap with Old Glory on the peak was approaching the reception desk.

"I've come to pick up Alice Liddell," Sabirzhan heard him say.

"And you are . . . ?" asked the receptionist.

"I'm from the American Embassy."

The limousine drove west towards the embassy, the Stars and Stripes fluttering proudly, provocatively, on its bonnet. Alice sat in the back, trying to work out what she'd say to the ambassador when he asked her about the assassination attempt and told her – not for the first time – how concerned Washington was about the way things were going. A solitary Range Rover rode shotgun, now alongside the limousine, now behind, never ahead. It was a simple run from Red October to the embassy; across the Kammeny Bridge, along Znamenka to Arbatskaya, down Novy Arbat and up Novinsky. They were making the last turn, the right from Novy Arbat to Novinsky, when the ambush came.

Have you ever seen orcas, killer whales, on the attack? They flash black and white as flukes and fins break the surface around a grey whale and her calf. The pod of orcas work together to tire their prey and separate mother from calf. They come again and again, sustained and violent, repeatedly ramming into the calf with extraordinary force as the mother tries to get between the killers and her baby, or to swim underneath it and push it out of their way. Eventually, battered to exhaustion, the calf begins to roll in red-stained water, its pectoral fins bleeding and studded with teeth marks where the orcas have been holding it under the water to try and drown it. The mother swims slowly shoreward. Her offspring is lost.

The Chechens came in four Land Cruisers. The first accelerated in front of the American convoy and braked sharply; the second and third tried to push in between the Range Rover and the limousine; the fourth took up position behind the battle, to block off following traffic.

The embassy limousine swerved round the first Land Cruiser with a lurch that threw Alice to the floor. She saw a Chechen face as she went down, and was torn between apprehension and admiration. Was there nothing these guys wouldn't try?

The first Land Cruiser darted hard to the right and smacked the limousine broadside. The next two took out the Range Rover, bumping it to and fro, never allowing it a path back to its calf, and finally sending it skidding across the carriageway and into the barriers. The fourth moved up behind the limousine. Double-up, separate and destroy; Admiral Nelson would have been proud.

All four orcas moved in on the calf.

Boxed in on every side, the limousine could do nothing but glide to a halt. Men out on to the road, guns levelled, urgent guttural cries which mean the same in every tongue in the world. The chauffeur turned to Alice. "Don't worry, ma'am," he said. "We'll get you out of this."

"If you think that, my friend, you must have drunk more than me."

The Chechens were motioning for Alice to come out or they'd shoot the lock and then her too. She'd no idea what they had in mind, but as long as it involved her being alive, it was better than sitting in the back of the limousine and waiting for a bullet through the temple.

She opened the door herself and stepped out. Her grace under pressure took the Chechens by surprise; a beat passed before the first man moved forward to grab her. It was strange, but she felt little fear, only curiosity. That was what a couple of vodkas first thing did for you.

Alice was thrown into the back of one of the Land Cruisers. As the vehicle pitched and yawed, she was blindfolded and trussed by Chechens reeking of petrol and cigarettes. She tried to remember which way they turned and how long they'd been driving, but soon gave up. There was nothing she could do now. She knew that at some level she must be in shock, and that the enormity of what had happened would eventually register, but for now she surrendered herself to bemused acceptance.

Hard on the brakes, a wide turn and hard on the brakes again. Doors open, men moving. Alice was dragged into the open and then back inside again, the cold a brief, burning brush against her skin. They hurried her through dank passages so fast that her feet touched the ground only intermittently, skating as a heron does when it lands on water. Into a room, down on to a chair. Even through the rag across her eyes, she could tell there was more light than before. She hoped for sunshine, but when they took off the blindfold, she saw that the glare was from a video camera held by a man with a white streak in his hair.

Still Alice felt a curious detachment. It was as if her brain was a building split into several separate apartments; each apartment with its own inhabitants, each inhabitant doing different things.

A man came in. His face was all angles and lines. Alice saw the way everyone else deferred to this man, and she knew who it was. Karkadann, her lover's arch-enemy. And now he had what Lev prized most.

Karkadann didn't greet Alice, or even look in her direction, but the intensity of his hauntedness singed her. She thought of Repin's famous painting of Ivan the Terrible, wide-eyed in desperate remorse as he cradles the son he's just killed; the painting which Repin himself said was inspired by the search for an exit from the unbearable tragism in history.

Karkadann motioned Zhorzh to focus on Alice, before personally checking the viewfinder to ensure he was happy with the shot. Then he stepped away and began to speak.

"This is a communiqué for Anatoly Nikolayevich Borzov, President of the Russian Federation. We have in our possession the American woman Alice Liddell, and we will release her on two conditions: that the privatisation auction scheduled for Monday is cancelled, and that all the holdings of the Red October distillery are transferred to the communal group which represents Chechen interests in Moscow and of which I am head. You have until midday tomorrow to accede to these demands, or Mrs Liddell will be killed."

That afternoon Borzov summoned the players to his office: Arkin, Lev and the American Ambassador, Walter Knight. Vodka for everyone, even Knight – two years in Moscow had eroded his resistance to drinking at all hours. He'd been here both for the August coup and the killings in Vilnius and Riga, but this was the first crisis to feature an American citizen centre stage, and his face was held rigid with tension.

"Our position is very simple," Borzov said. "Karkadann's demands are outrageous and non-negotiable. This is an act of terrorism. We cannot and will not accede to it."

"That's your public position?" Knight asked.

"As opposed to what?"

"As opposed to your private position." Borzov made a moue: go on. "Publicly, the US government and its major Western counterparts are in full agreement. But we must also consider the impact this will have on foreign investment in your country. If Mrs Liddell does not . . ." He swallowed, picking his words carefully. "If the worst occurs, the murder of an IMF advisor will hardly send out promising signals to institutions who are hoping to do business here."

"That's not our most pressing dilemma right now," Arkin said.

"It's one you should be keeping in mind, though. I need hardly tell you what Mrs Liddell's, er, husband" – he stared straight ahead, determined not to catch Lev's eye – "and friends think of all this." Knight had just come from the apartment at Patriarch's Ponds, where

Lewis had said little. "They want her out safely, whatever it takes. I wouldn't be surprised if they took the first flight back home after that."

"What else do you expect them to think? We can't take their feelings into account. Anyway, it won't come to that. We're already investigating other methods of resolving the situation."

"More hostages get killed in shoot-outs than at any other time," Knight said.

"But we'd be negligent not to plan for armed intervention. And in the meantime, we'll keep Karkadann talking, get him to extend the deadline while we negotiate. Don't forget, his hostage is his only bargaining chip. If he kills her, he's got nothing left."

Lev made a noise deep in his throat; more precisely, a noise was heard, and it was hard to tell whether it had been voluntary, or in what quantities it mixed assent and distress. "Anatoly Nikolayevich is right," he said. "Doing what Karkadann demands – that's out of the question. There's not a single worker at Red October who would want to be run by the Chechens. How could I give in to him without betraying all of them? How could I give in to him, full stop?"

"Exactly," Arkin said. "It's not like she's your wife, is it?"

Irk was called to the Kremlin and shown the videotape. Homicide, not kidnapping, was his speciality, but in Russia one all too often leads to the other. Besides, what was this if not a variation on the child killings? The protagonists were the same, as were their aims; they were upping the ante, that was all. One had to give the Chechens credit, Irk thought, for their persistence if nothing else.

"How did you get this?" he asked.

"Someone called the Kremlin switchboard and told them to look under a certain bench in Gorky Park," Arkin said. "We sent two of the presidential bodyguard. They found the cassette taped to the bench's underside."

"No way you can communicate with the kidnappers?"

"Not yet."

Irk watched the video all the way through, three times. He was looking and listening for anything which might give him an idea of where the recording had been made: a view through a window to a recognisable landmark, sounds from outside. Aeroplanes might mean they were near a flight path, traffic a main road, machinery an industrial plant. There were no signs, at least not to the naked eye and ear, and in Moscow a man's own senses were just about all any law enforcement official had. Sophisticated technical equipment could have isolated noises or enhanced images, but even with the Kremlin's full support Irk might as well have asked for a night with Miss World.

Borzov went on television, broadcasting from the presidential office with the full panoply of state power, the tricolour and double-headed eagle, arrayed behind him.

"The president will not be blackmailed into calling off a programme which is in the nation's best interests," he said. "How can we negotiate when we're in the right?"

The Chechens had stripped Alice naked and put her in a room not much larger than the average water closet. Underground, she thought, to judge from the damp and the absence of windows. They'd given her no food – no hardship, given that fear had clenched her stomach tight – and locked the door on her. She had felt round the walls to make sure that none of them were still in there with her.

Her mind was a thresher, trying to separate the wheat of hope from the chaff of doubt. In favour of survival: these were professional gangsters, so they wouldn't be panicked into anything rash. Against survival: she knew the odds against Borzov agreeing to their demands. What's more, her kidnappers had made no attempt to disguise themselves, and so they'd have no compunction in killing her if it suited. Best to think about *that* later.

They'd taken her clothes in order to humiliate her, make her afraid and defenceless. She could live with that, though. At least while they weren't there to cast sideways glances at her body. If they came for her, she'd try and foul herself to revolt them into stopping – if her imminent menstruation hadn't done that already, she thought wryly.

She felt guilt that she was putting everybody she loved through all this. She should have tried to escape at the beginning. The dignity she had shown stepping from the limousine was all very well, but look where it had got her. People depended on her and she'd let them all down. What about the auction? That was for the whole country, its present and future. Did anything matter more than that?

In the darkness, the vodka wore off. The gutturals of her captors beyond the door sounded to her like wolves tearing at a carcass. Alice dug her nails into her thighs to remind herself that she was alive, and tried not to think of the veneration with which Russians regard martyrs.

# 67

Karkadann himself came in with Alice's breakfast.

"I need the john," she said. "I've been holding it in all night."

He looked her up and down with carnal curiosity and shook his head. "After you've eaten."

"I can't wait that long."

"You'll have to."

Alice knew that antagonism would beget antagonism. So far she had done whatever they'd told her to, and had been neither too craven nor too defiant. They had every reason to hate her; she didn't want to give them any more. But she had her pride, too.

"If you're going to treat me like an animal," she said, "I'll behave like one."

Alice pushed herself into a squat. Karkadann stared at her, as if daring her to debase herself.

It should have been difficult, relaxing enough to urinate naked in front of a stranger, but Alice was so desperate that she had barely resigned herself to it when the stream came. Sweet relief, warm as it splashed off the floor and against her ankles. Karkadann said nothing until she'd finished, then he put his hand on her stomach and pushed her back into the puddle she'd made.

"Eat your breakfast," he said, offering her a grey pancake and some stringy broth which was several consistency grades short of soup. It was the first food she'd seen since being snatched yesterday, but the sight of it made her wish he hadn't bothered. "You got any vodka?" she asked.

Karkadann tipped his head slightly to look at her, as if he were examining some exotic creature in the zoo. "Are you being serious?"

"If you're going to kill me," she said, "I'd rather be drunk when it happens."

"Who says we're going to kill you?"

"You did, yesterday, on camera."

"We've extended the deadline."

"They're negotiating?"

"They're stalling. None of them want to give in to me, Lev least of all." Karkadann smirked when he saw the flutter of grief on Alice's face. "Let me ask you something. If you get out of here alive, will you stay in Moscow?"

"Of course."

"Why?"

"I love the city, that's why."

"Then you have no taste. Moscow is hideous. You should come to the Caucasus."

"Is that an invitation?" She felt goonish and awkward, trying to get him to like her.

"Snow on the mountaintops, year round. Sunlight which changes colour every hour. Air so pure you could drink it. Roses and pomegranates growing in the valleys, and you can't move for vineyards. We sit round and eat meat with flat bread and herbs and spices, and we wash it all down with brandy. You turn a corner, and there's a spring, there's a fountain, there's a courtyard. Ancient feuds settled with knives, horses which whisk you off into the night. It's *life*."

He left her with a copy of *Pravda*. Alice wondered what they'd have done for headlines over the past week without her. This was another multi-page splash. She read an interview with Lewis – "the cuckold", as the photo caption had him – in which he said he prayed for her safe release. And on an inside page was Lev, glowering at the camera from behind his praetorian guard. Alice looked at his face until the pixels blurred.

More hours alone. Alice tried to fill her mind and then to empty it; neither worked. In her head, round and round, Karkadann's words: "None of them want to give in to me, Lev least of all."

Alice knew that Lev loved her – she'd heard it in his voice at the Vek when he'd thought she'd been hurt – but she knew also of his pride in Red October and his hatred for Karkadann. If he sacrificed everything for her, he would surely resent *her* for being the cause. So he wouldn't give them up, he wouldn't surrender to Karkadann's demands. But if he wouldn't – the man who loved her – then who would? What if Karkadann was right? After all, she wasn't free yet, was she?

Doubt was corrosive, as was boredom. She was too used to rushing around, filling every last moment with activity. The auction was five days away. Arkin had told her she was indispensable. There were still a million and one things to do. How could she help when she was stuck here?

She tried exercising. Press-ups, sit-ups, squat thrusts, all wound down after a few minutes because she was drained of energy. She thought of Lev and began to fantasise, but even in an empty room she felt self-conscious about touching herself. There might be secret peepholes. There was no vodka.

After what felt like a few hours, they came and took her back to the room where she'd been filmed yesterday. Karkadann and Zhorzh were there again. Zhorzh was carrying a bed of needles and nails set in wax, which he placed on the floor behind Alice.

"This is called the silver chair," said Karkadann. "It's an old Red Army punishment. They used it on our people during the deportations. You have to squat over it until your thigh muscles give way. The lactic acid's bad enough, but the pain of the nails when you fall is many times worse."

The humanity Alice had seen in him earlier was gone, as though erased by a passing cloud. She inhaled sharply before she could stop herself, and he saw her fear. The wax bed was flecked with blood; she was clearly not its first victim.

"At least give me some clothes," she said.

"Feet flat on the floor, knees bent no more than ninety degrees." He nodded at her to begin.

"And if I refuse?" Alice said.

"It won't be worth your while to refuse."

"If assholes could fly," she said, "this place would be an airport."

Alice closed her eyes for a moment and then assumed the position. Karkadann knelt down to check that her legs didn't straighten a degree more than was permitted, and then stood again in apparent satisfaction. Behind its unblinking eye, the camera's red light was on. Her suffering wasn't just for here and now. In a few hours' time, she would relive it for four men in the Kremlin.

The pain started a few minutes later. Alice gritted her mind rather than her teeth against it; she didn't want her face betraying anything to Karkadann. The strain ran across the front of her legs and down the sides, stabbing and testing, retreating from one area before reappearing suddenly and violently in another.

Karkadann stood with his arms folded and smiled mirthlessly. She looked at him with all the contempt she could muster. The very force of her disdain seemed to knock her slightly backwards, and for a moment she thought she was going to fall, but she recovered her balance and redoubled her efforts to ignore the pain.

"Those points are awfully sharp," Karkadann said.

Alice didn't look down. She'd seen them already, and they were indeed sharp. Some were also jagged, others brown with rust or dried blood. She wondered what kind of infections lurked on those menacing tips.

The tape spooled.

When it came, the end was quick. Alice felt her legs going a fraction before they collapsed, and all the willpower in the world couldn't have kept her upright a moment longer.

The silver chair had made a hell of a mess. There were six or seven puncture wounds where Alice had landed, descending deep into the flesh. In addition there were tears and rips where she'd squirmed in agony, where she'd tried to push herself off and found that her numbed legs simply wouldn't respond, leaving her spread-eagled in front of them as though she were the cheapest kind of whore. The skin round these wounds glistened wetly, invitingly red, and when the camera lingered on them it felt to Alice like every kind of violation.

Another five o'clock meeting in the Kremlin; another round of vodkas; another tape, which they watched in silence, at first uncomfortable and then downright embarrassed when it came to the final shots of Alice's backside, the close-up almost voyeuristic in its intimacy. Lev got up and walked out, his throat twitching with the effort of keeping his temper under control. It was several minutes before he returned.

"Negotiations are continuing," Arkin said. "So far, Karkadann hasn't shifted his position at all."

"And if he hasn't by midday tomorrow?" Lev asked.

"He will. Either that, or he'll extend the deadline again. Like I said, she's all he's got."

"What about military options?" Knight said.

"A Spetsnaz team is on standby. They'll move into position the moment it's appropriate."

"What does that mean?"

"Precisely what it sounds like."

"Why aren't they in position now?"

"Was it not you who, only yesterday, cautioned against military intervention on the grounds that people get hurt in shootouts? Besides, it's not appropriate."

Denial and doublespeak, Knight thought. Once you knew your way through the thickets of disinformation, though, it was as easy to read as the truth. "You still don't know where they are, do you?"

"We're working on it."

"But you *don't* know."

"They're not making it easy, I have to say. Someone calls the

337

switchboard and tells us where to find the tapes. Yesterday it was Gorky Park, today Novy Arbat. Karkadann calls one of my private lines when he wants to talk, but he's never on long enough to get a trace. There's no way we can get in touch with them ourselves."

"Experts have examined the tapes and recordings of the calls for clues as to where they might be," said Irk. "But so far their findings have been inconclusive."

"A detachment of OMON troops raided the Belgrade Hotel this afternoon," said Arkin.

"They're not going to be *there*," Lev said.

"The OMON were looking for pointers as to where they might have gone."

"Did they find any?"

"It wasn't an entirely wasted trip."

"The answer's no, then."

"They did find *something*. Sackfuls of privatisation vouchers, to be precise. Vouchers stolen from the Ostozhenka branch of Sberbank on Monday."

Alone again and reduced to dependence on others for the very basics of food, water and shelter. They chose what they gave her. Whatever she asked for, she didn't get. That was why she had no tissues, even though her body was still counting the days. Her tears flowed with the blood; she wanted to continue leaking until there was nothing left of her.

# 68

*Friday, 28 February 1992*

The next tape must have been made overnight. The call to the Kremlin came before breakfast, giving a location near the Yermolov Theatre. Cars were sent for Arkin, Lev and Knight; they were all in the presidential office inside twenty minutes.

The footage began with a shot of Karkadann holding a rubber tube. Alice was tied to a chair. She squirmed against the ropes, seemingly more intent on easing the pressure on her ruined backside than trying to free herself. Karkadann walked over to Alice, flexed his free hand, clenched it into a fist and drove it into her stomach.

No one in Borzov's office dared glance at Lev.

As Alice gasped for air, Karkadann fed one end of the pipe into her mouth. Alice tried to bite down on it, but she needed the air too much to keep her mouth closed. The tube went further in, finding first the back of Alice's mouth and then her throat. Karkadann fed it slowly down, careful to get it into Alice's stomach and not her lungs. Alice's coughing gradually subsided to a low whistle. Like a conjuror producing rabbits, Karkadann pulled a plastic funnel out of his pocket and fitted it to the end of the tube.

Alice's eyes were as wide as her mouth. Knight rubbed at his face.

Karkadann reached down to the floor, disappearing momentarily from shot, and reappeared with a bottle of vodka. He opened it, held it above the funnel, and started to pour. Zhorzh's camera was not so tight on Alice's face that he couldn't get the bottle in as well, and he held firm, as though the steady glugging of an emptying vodka bottle had hypnotised him.

Alice was trying to say something, and she looked as though she was grimacing. Only Lev realised that she was in fact trying to smile, and heard the word she couldn't quite enunciate.

"More," she was saying, "more", with the abandon of someone with nothing left to lose.

It was the rubber snake as much as the vodka which made her stomach rebel, though there were few places for the vomit to go. Some made it out of her mouth, shooting from the sides and on to her cheeks and chin, but she swallowed just as much straight back again, and still the vodka kept coming, remorseless and relentless.

When the bottle was finished, Karkadann held it up to the camera and dropped it on the floor. Behind him, out of focus, Alice was thrashing around like a landed fish.

"This is your last chance," Karkadann said. "I've put back the deadline twice. You now have until eight o'clock tomorrow morning. After that, there'll be no more extensions. If my demands are not met by then, I will personally ensure that Mrs Liddell gets a traditional Tsentralnaya send-off."

The picture flickered and dissolved to static.

"What does he mean, a traditional Tsentralnaya send-off?" Knight said.

Lev looked at them with the pitilessness of a worldly man forced to shock cloistered people. "It's very simple. They strip you naked, wrap you in razor wire and put you in the trunk of a car, which they then set on fire. You either burn to death or shred yourself to bits trying to escape."

\* \* \*

Arkin had said there was no way they could get in touch with Karkadann off their own backs.

The man had murdered his own wife and son. He'd kill his enemy's lover in a heartbeat.

Lev went back to Red October and sat at his desk for an hour before dialling the Belgrade.

For a man accustomed to getting something at the snap of his fingers, the waiting seemed endless. Lev forced himself to think back to the gulag. He'd spent years there, every day like the last and also like the next. A few hours now was nothing in comparison.

Karkadann called late in the afternoon. Lev didn't know whether the message had taken that long to reach him, or whether he'd received it earlier and decided to make Lev sweat for a while before replying. He didn't much care either way. It was enough that Karkadann had rung.

"What do you want?" Karkadann said.

Lev thought of the way Karkadann had hit Alice. He thought of how traditional Chechen culture proscribed vendettas against women. He thought of what else the Chechens might have done to her when the camera wasn't on. He thought of the attempt to kill him at the Vek, and of the goat's-wool sweater. And then he banished all such thoughts to his innermost soul.

"I want to discuss settlement terms with you," he said, and his voice was perfectly neutral.

"No discussion. You have my terms – agree to them, or I hang up."

"They won't call off the auction, and they wouldn't allow me to transfer Red October to you even if I wanted; you must know that. I'll offer you the most you can reasonably expect to get."

"I can get what I asked for," said Karkadann, but his voice was already softening. Lev knew he was the first person in two days to have at least listened to the Chechen.

"Once the auction's gone ahead, it's too late for you, there'll be too much public dilution of the company. So, on Monday morning, I'll shift the auction's location at the last minute. My excuse will be the million vouchers you stole from Sberbank; I'll say the change of venue is a regrettable but necessary measure to protect Red October against Chechen corruption. The public won't know where to find the auction, so they won't get any shares. After that, on the quiet, I'll hand over Red October to you."

"That's insane. Borzov and Arkin will never forgive you."

"Borzov and Arkin are prepared to let Alice die. It's *me* who'll never forgive *them*."

"They'll declare war on us both."

"The auction in ruins, privatisation off, prices spiralling, parliament scenting blood – they won't even be in power."

The line hissed at Lev as Karkadann thought through his options. The rival ganglords against the Kremlin: it was an unlikely partnership, but then most alliances in Russia were.

"What do you want from me in return?" Karkadann asked.

"That you let Alice go. And that the child killings stop."

"How can I let her go, if this deal's secret?"

"You let her escape. Make it look as though she got out under her own steam."

Another pause. "OK."

"And the killings. You must call them off."

"Why are you doing this?"

"Like I said: because they won't. I sit with them, and they know full well it's my lover we're talking about. They see her naked, and they couldn't care less. She's *nothing* to them."

"I thought the vory didn't care for women."

Lev looked at the tattooed inscription on the inside of his left arm: *Fuck Soviet laws; the only rules I follow are my own*, it said.

"So did I," he said.

# 69

*Saturday, 29 February 1992*

Alice feigned sleep when she heard her door open sometime in the small hours. She could tell by the faint smell of rotting carrion that it was the one with the white streak in his hair. Beyond the flimsy barrier of her eyelids, she imagined him standing over her and licking his lips. He said nothing; he always said nothing.

She knew the deadline must be running close now, but she didn't consciously think of it. She could no more imagine the remainder of her life being counted in hours or minutes than she could conceive of life on another galaxy. To die here, alone and far from the one she loved – no, it was incomprehensible, her mind slammed doors on her, and the more she twisted to find the notion the more elusive it became, until she gave up altogether and thought of vile Chechens raping her because that was more direct, that was easier. Easier!

She heard Zhorzh's footsteps going back across the room. He opened the door, two steps through, and closed it behind him. She knew the sounds so well now: the strained squeaking as the hinges strained, the metallic rattle of door in frame, the rusty clunk as the lock engaged – except now there was no clunk.

Alice opened her eyes. No clunk, that was certain, and no sound outside the door either.

There were always sounds, the guards talking, moving back and forth.

It was a trick, surely. She'd open the door, and they'd be on her.

Why bother to trick her? They had her just where they wanted, didn't they?

She waited long minutes, her mind swinging like a pendulum from one extreme to the other. It was a trick, it was a mistake. These were her last minutes, this was her chance for freedom.

In Alice's breast, a strange sense of exhilaration. This was survival, this was escape, and all her education and achievements and beauty and success meant nothing.

What did she have to lose? That was where the pendulum ended: what did she have to lose?

She clasped the door handle, hard and then harder as the sweat on her palms slid against the metal. The handle turned beneath her grip and the door began to swing open through creaking which sounded like rifle fire. Alice held her breath, waiting for outraged shouts or worse. She only dared exhale when the door was open and she'd peeked into the empty corridor.

Time was telescoping; every step took an age. She'd barely moved in three days and eaten even less, not to mention the silver chair and the tube in the stomach. She wouldn't be able to fight an infant or even flee from one, let alone a posse of Chechens. Vodka would give her energy, vodka would give her courage.

Alice remembered something Lev had told her about the Siberian dilemma. At forty degrees below zero, a man who falls through ice into bitterly cold water has two choices: to stay in the water and freeze to death inside a minute, or to get out and freeze to death instantly. A true Siberian is supposed to pull himself out, even though this will kill him quicker. It's better to go and meet death head-on rather than simply wait around for it.

Alice went to meet whatever lay in store.

Along the corridor and up a flight of stairs, past a window which offered a glimpse of darkened streets and pulsing streetlights. Noise to her left, voices arguing in the room up ahead, one of them a woman, and Alice was momentarily stunned – if there was a woman here, why hadn't she seen her? – before she recognised the tinny cadences of a television set. She went low past the open door and didn't dare look in. At the edges of her vision she saw the backs of four heads, all focused on the programme.

A loud belch behind her and she froze, but it was just one of the TV watchers.

Alice was at the front door now. She opened it as softly as she could. A gust of cool moist air from the apartments' communal corridor outside and she was gone, forcing herself not to run, knowing that she couldn't have moved faster than a shuffle if she'd tried. Round a corner and up to the tenement block's main door, open and into the street past a coloured climbing-frame, the cold rasping like sandpaper at her bare skin and scraping ice crystals in her throat.

Freedom was a taste at the roof of her mouth, freedom was alien. How easy it was to get used to not making decisions. For a moment, Alice couldn't even settle on which way to go. It was the cold which jolted her into action. Naked in a Russian winter, her captors likely to discover her absence at any moment – it didn't matter which way she went, as long as she did. There was no point having come this far only to die of exposure.

She walked to keep warm and to get distance; she didn't care where she was. Street signs flashed changes at her – Dubininskaya, Zatsepskaya, Stremyanny – and still she walked, a mad woman naked on the streets as though in a dream, waving away the cars which were slowing for her until belatedly, through the fog in her mind, came the realisation that a car was exactly what she needed. When the next two glided towards the kerb, she chose the one driven by a woman.

"Kotelniki," she said, feeling a delicious blast of petrol-scented heat as she climbed into the back. "I've got no money."

The woman peered at her. "Aren't you . . . ?"

Alice nodded. "And I need my lover."

An American would surely have insisted on taking Alice to the police, doing things by the book. This Russian understood Alice all too well: what else would a woman want at a time like this, other than her lover? The driver laughed and pulled back into the road.

Lev took Alice in his massive arms and held her as though he'd never let her go again. She was smeared in grime and stank of filth and fear, and he clasped her as though willing her to transfer them

343

all on to him. He bathed her with tenderness and love, as one bathes a child, washing her clean of the ordeal she'd been through, gentle as he soaped the dirt from her wounds. He didn't ask what had happened, and she didn't tell; it was enough for her to know that his reticence came from respect for her privacy rather than lack of interest.

By the time he'd brought her breakfast, she was asleep in his bed, dead to the world. He worked the phones.

"Thank heavens for that," Borzov said through eddies of vodka relief.

"Good for her." Arkin's voice was edgier. "I knew that justice would win."

"I'm so glad she's safe," Knight said. "I'll pass the news on to her husband, if you like."

Arkin rang back. "We'll need to debrief her," he said. "Bring her to the Kremlin at once."

"She's been through hell," Lev said. "*You* can come *here*, when she wakes up."

Alice slept hard until lunch. When she woke, she wanted to bathe again; she still felt unclean.

"You should call your husband," Lev said as she lay in steaming water, putting a finger to her lips to forestall any argument. "No, you must. You know that."

Lewis held the phone away from his ear so that Alice's voice would seep into the apartment that was so devastatingly empty without her. He was glad she was safe, he said; that was the most important thing. He didn't ask her what it had been like, or if she was coming home. Nor did he tell her that he hadn't cried once, not during her captivity, not since she'd left him. Maybe he should have. Each to his own. They'd speak soon, he said.

Dressed and with coffee, Alice faced Arkin.

"You're OK for the auction on Monday?" he asked.

"For heaven's sake," Lev said. "Is that all you think about?"

The deadline had been less than three hours away. If Arkin suspected what Lev had done, he didn't mention it – and he *would* have mentioned it if he had suspected. But Arkin wouldn't have capitulated to Karkadann, and Lev would never forget that.

"I'm fine for the auction," Alice said.

"Darling, you've just suffered a . . ." Lev interjected.

"I said, I'm fine."

* * *

344

Alice told Irk what she could remember about the apartment where she'd been held. The street names she'd seen gave Irk a location, and she agreed to ride in an unmarked squad car to show him which building she'd escaped from.

"That's ridiculous," Lev said. "You can't take her back there."

"It's fine." Alice was adamant.

The area looked very different in daylight: safer, alien. Irk watched Alice for the shakes, but she'd had a couple of vodkas and her nerves were steady.

"That one, there –" She pointed.

"You're sure?"

"Positive." She remembered the climbing frame outside.

Irk wasn't going to take any chances with Petrovka's men, not after Smolensky Square. Nor was he going to use any men from the 21st Century, even though Lev was practically forcing them on him. An OMON squad raided the block an hour later. The apartment was empty.

# 70

*Sunday, 1 March 1992*

Alice had scheduled a full auction dress rehearsal at the Krasnaya Presnya exhibition complex and she was determined, against all advice that it could be left to Harry and Bob to run the show, that she would attend as if nothing had happened.

It started badly. She was barely out of her car when one of the volunteers came hurrying up.

"Mrs Liddell, I'd like to request a three-month leave of absence."

"Fedosia, after tomorrow you can do what you like."

"Tomorrow will be too late; I need to go *today*. I can offer my sister to you as a replacement."

"Without any training? Don't be absurd."

"She's very good, I promise."

"What's so urgent?"

"There's a job in Kazakstan that's just come up."

"Kazakstan? What the hell could you want in Kazakstan?"

"Satellite launching." Fedosia smiled shyly. "My background's in aeronautical engineering."

Alice almost laughed. Fedosia was a rocket scientist, quite literally, but here she was helping out at the auction, a job which Alice had thought that any young Muscovite would have regarded as the pinnacle of their fledgling career. Alice wondered how many of the hundred and fifty volunteers were doing this simply because they were down on their luck. The Russians call it dequalification, when you're forced to take jobs way below your station. In Moscow, it's commonplace. She could afford to lose one person, Alice thought. "All right," she said. "Go. Go to Kazakstan. Good luck."

There were a couple of protesters already in place, reserving their spots like shoppers in the winter sales. They waved a banner at Alice as she went past –*Yankee, go home!* – but she hardly noticed, because she could see trouble up ahead. Harry was arguing with a security guard. Alice quickened her step.

"What's the problem?" Alice asked, stepping between them.

"This guy won't let me through," Harry said. "I can't understand what he's saying, but he's giving me the shits." He looked past Alice's shoulder and said to the guard, in English: "Listen, buddy, this lady's in charge here, I'm with her, and so I go where I like. *Capisce?*"

He pushed through the doorway and immediately seemed to drop, as though he'd just fallen down a small step. The guard made a face: *I told you so.*

"What's happened?" Alice said.

Harry pulled first one foot and then the other clear of the sludge. They came out with extravagant three-syllable sucking sounds, like oxen tramping through mud. His trouser ankles and shoes were covered in mud, wet cement and paint. He had walked on to a building site, which the security guard had been trying to direct him away from.

Alice was heading through another door, the one which led to the main body of the exhibition hall. Studiously looking anywhere but at the security guard, Harry squelched after her. "I thought the guy was just being a typical Russian jag-off, trying to tell me what to do," he said.

"No, Harry." Alice was torn between being angry and trying not to laugh. "You were being a typical *American* asshole, not believing what he told you simply because he was Russian."

Harry was getting fatter by the week. Alice could see it in the way his jowls lapped at his collar, in the stretch of his shirt over his belt. She'd have thought that all that sex he was boasting about would be keeping him thin. His tan – *no one* had a tan in a Moscow winter – was suffused with orange, and seemed accentuated at the points on his temples where skin met hair. Definitely a sunbed job, thought Alice. Harry looked one notch up from a sex tourist in Thailand. She wondered how much he knew about her ordeal, about the video. Was the look on his face sympathetic or salacious? Either way, she didn't want to know. If she was going to get through today, and tomorrow, and the rest of her life, she was going to have to close the door on the whole sorry episode.

"How are you?" he asked. "After all the . . . I mean . . ."

"Do me a favour, Harry. You don't ask, and I won't tell."

Bob was waiting for them by the main desk. "How *are* you, Alice?"

"Ask Harry."

"Have you seen Lewis? He's been worried sick about you."

"We've got an auction to run here."

The auction was to take place in Pavilion II, Hall 3: three thousand square metres which was currently filled with tricolours, posters, tables and people. Alice ignored the hush that fell over the room when she entered. She stepped up to the podium, steadied herself against the lectern provided and began bombarding the staff with questions, to make sure they were on their toes.

Where did the applications go? To the sorters, who'd rank them according to the type of bid and then file them.

What about the tally forms? To the chief counters, for final checking before being sent to computer operators in the processing unit.

She was a passer-by without a voucher; how did they deal with that?

She filled out specimen forms but left them deliberately incomplete to see whether the tellers noticed; she missed out an address, an identity number, perhaps the number of vouchers bid or whether the bid was passive or active, even the applicant's name.

How many queues would there be outside? Two: one for individuals, the other for corporate entities, and on no account should the two be confused.

What identity did bidders need? Individuals required passports; corporate entities needed their charter, notarised copies of statutory documents, declarations of any state-owned interest in them, and of course the representative's authorisation to sign.

She shouted and screamed to check that security were alert.

Eighteen hours to go, and the staff were still getting things wrong. "If you're not sure," Alice yelled, "then do something very un-Russian: ask!"

\* \* \*

347

The rehearsal lasted until the evening. Alice felt as though she were revising for exams, and the point was approaching when she simply had to stop worrying and trust that everything would work out, if not perfectly, then more or less all right. She was going to cut a ribbon and open the auction at nine o'clock dead the next morning – Borzov and Arkin, still evidently hedging their bets, had both found pressing reasons why they couldn't do the honours – and after that, she didn't know whether to expect ten people or ten thousand.

She had no strength left. If she hadn't had the lectern to cling to for support she would have slumped into an exhausted heap. There was nothing she could do now but hope and pray – oh, and quell her nerves with the best part of a half-litre.

Lev was out on mafiya business and didn't get back till late.

"How was it?" he asked.

"Pretty average."

"Honestly?"

"Honestly, I'm shitting myself."

"It'll be all right," he said, kissing the crown of her head. "It'll be all right."

"You're more confident than I am."

He flicked through the channels on the TV and picked absently at some pickled herrings.

"You seem distracted," she said.

"Me? I'm fine."

"Tell me."

"Tell you what?"

"Tell me what you're not telling me."

He smiled playfully. "There are many things I don't tell you."

"Like what?"

"Like many things. I don't even know half of them myself. You're American, Alice; I'm Russian. You've one soul, I've two – a public one and a private one."

"You think that's exclusive to Russians? You should spend some time on Wall Street. On the trading floors, no one dares show sympathy, weakness, vulnerability, the slightest need for human kindness." Every day there had brought a test of one kind or another. She recalled how colleagues had left hardcore pornography on her desk to see how she'd react, and been chastened when she'd glanced at the pictures and told the nearest guy that his sister was looking well.

Lev's expression showed that he didn't think much of the comparison. He leant over and sang softly in Alice's ear:

> "What's your shell made out of, Mr Tortoise?
> I said, and looked him in the eye.
> Just from the lessons fear has taught us,
> Were the words of his reply.
> In Russia's land we find our way through
>     circles of deceit.
> The smiling mask cannot conceal your neigh-
>     bour's cloven feet."

The crevasses of his face were deep; scars and pits marking a latent thuggish belligerence born of necessity and laid down over the years, layer after layer, carapace against a hostile world. Whatever Lev chose to show her would be merely what he wanted to, the tip of the iceberg. From time to time the iceberg would rotate, bringing different parts to the surface, but it was too big for each part to receive its time in the sun. There'd always be concealed depths, areas forever clandestine.

# 71

*Monday, 2 March 1992*
Alice had hoped for good weather – sunshine would surely bring more people out – but she was disappointed from the moment she opened the curtains. It was one of those mornings when even starting the day requires an unusual, almost heroic effort. A mist of fine, drizzling rain enveloped the whole city, swallowing up every ray of light, every gleam of colour, and transforming everything into one smoky, leaden, indistinguishable mass. It was daylight, and yet it seemed as though it were still night.

On days like these, Moscow seemed not a city on the up but one mired in the depths of communist uniformity. People walked with their heads down, hurrying away from their past rather than towards their future. Although Alice was used to vast areas being little more than construction sites, it suddenly seemed that the builders were merely papering over cracks rather than laying proper foundations. When she looked across the skyline, she could hardly see a single crane. She couldn't believe that there was a capital city in the world, certainly in Europe and certainly of a large country, where less was actually being *built*.

She had arranged to meet Harry and Bob for breakfast in the Ukrainia Hotel, across the river from the exhibition hall. The lobby was packed and noisy when she arrived, with policemen shouting at gangsters, gangsters shouting at hotel staff, hotel staff shouting at policemen. Just about the only people who weren't shouting were Harry, who looked as if he was about to throw up, and four shell-suited men lying on the floor, dead. Alice hurried over to Harry.

"What happened?" she asked. "Are you all right?"

He looked at her vaguely before collecting himself and giving her a nonchalant, this-kind-of-thing-happens-to-me-every-day smile. "Shoot-out. I got here just as it was starting." Now he had an audience, he was warming quickly to his story. "Someone shouted, another guy pushed someone else, a fourth guy pulled out his gun and fired – and then everyone was diving for cover. It was like the Alamo. Wouldn't want to be the cleaners who have to redd this place up."

It was just past seven in the morning. The men, no doubt low-ranking mafiyosi, had almost certainly been drinking all night. Alice looked at the nearest corpse, slumped against the wall like a drunk. His face was fat and doughy, reeking of piggish stupidity even in death. Moscow was crawling with men like this, too brainless by half for any responsible authority to allow them within reach of a bottle of vodka, let alone a submachine gun.

Alice saw a knoll of humid ectoplasm sliding slowly down the wall behind the man's head, and felt a twinge of bashful guilt; she hadn't meant that he was *literally* brainless.

"You wanna go somewhere else for breakfast?" she asked.

"No, no. I'm fine." Harry glanced again at the wet flecks of grey. "I might go easy on the scrambled eggs, though."

Bob was coming through the main door. Alice hurried over, intercepted him before he saw too much of the carnage, and steered him firmly towards the dining-room. The maître d' wished them good morning and ushered them to a table. There was nothing in his manner to suggest that anything out of the ordinary had happened – he had the Russian ability to absorb the uncommon.

Harry went round the buffet tables as though he were participating in one of those supermarket sweep competitions where contestants are given a minute to cram a trolley with as many items as they could. If it was on display, it went on his tray: buckwheat porridge; egg fritters with cottage cheese; fried eggs; and of course a mountain of blinis. No wonder he was putting on weight.

Alice took a small plateful and picked at no more than half of it. She could hardly eat for worrying, and it wasn't even about whether the auction would be a success or not. Her mind was swimming with trivialities: personnel badges, generator back-up, food and drink – tea and coffee, that was, no vodka! – and spares, spares, spares.

"How're you feeling?" she asked Bob.

He swallowed nervously. "Like a long-tailed cat in a room full of rocking chairs."

Alice's first thought, confused but unworried, was that she'd walked into the wrong hall. The place was empty: no tables, no chairs, no dais for the supervisors. She clicked her tongue in irritation and was turning to leave when she saw two things more or less simultaneously: the sign on the door, which told her that she was indeed in Pavilion II, Hall 3; and a couple of privatisation posters left on the far wall as if to taunt her.

Suddenly very, very cold, Alice felt as though she were falling through space.

She was due to cut the ribbon in just under an hour's time, and the hall to which thousands of Muscovites would hopefully be flocking – there were at least a hundred outside already, she'd seen the queue on her way in – was as barren as the Siberian tundra. This place had been thrumming with activity only yesterday, when she'd conducted the dress rehearsal. Since then, sometime between about seven o'clock the previous evening, when she'd left, and now, everything had been – what? Stolen? Moved out? Burnt?

Bob was looking as though he'd seen Stalin's ghost.

"It's almost eight o'clock. Where *is* everyone?" said Harry, and Alice was about to round on him for asking such an irrelevant question – where was every*thing*, was surely the more pressing matter? – when she realised what he meant. The supervisors at least were supposed to have been here by now, and everyone else should be turning up in the next few minutes, but the three of them were the only people in the hall.

"Pinch me, Harry," Alice said, her voice wavering. "Hit me, bite me, do something to wake me up. This is all a bad dream, right?"

He shook his head. "Not unless I'm having exactly the same one."

\* \* \*

She found the security guard who'd tried to stop Harry tramping through the building site the day before. "My hall, it's empty," she snapped. "Where is everything? What the hell's going on?"

The security guard looked surprised. "The auction's been moved."

"*Moved?*"

"Of course." He nodded in Harry's direction. "He said you were in charge."

"Just tell me what happened," Alice said, spacing the words carefully as though cadence could make everything all right.

"A lot of blokes came along last night and took everything out."

"Didn't you ask them what they were doing? Where they were going?"

"They weren't the kind of people who appreciate questions, if you know what I mean."

"And you thought I had something to do with this?"

He shrugged. "Of course. I read the papers, you know. He's your boyfriend, isn't he?"

Alice rang the numbers she thought Lev might answer – penthouse and distillery – and several that he probably wouldn't, such as the Vek, on the grounds that she'd been there with him and it was the longest of longshots that he might be there now.

Wherever he was, he wasn't answering. She left Harry and Bob at Krasnaya Presnya, along with a growing number of bewildered journalists and camera crews, and, wiping panicked tears from her face, set off to track Lev down herself.

She'd barely turned the corner when she had to pull over and throw up into the gutter, dry retching long after her stomach had emptied itself. It wasn't just that this, the culmination of her work – right now, in fact, just about all she had to show for it – had disintegrated into fiasco; it was the fact that Lev was the one who'd pulled the rug from under her.

Lev, who'd said more times than she could remember how much he loved her.

Lev, who'd told her only last night that everything would be all right, when he'd just come back from putting a bomb under the auction.

Lev, who'd told her to go to breakfast with Harry and Bob because he had things to do, and that he'd see her in the exhibition hall.

Lev, who'd lied, lied, lied.

Alice went to Red October first, because it was closest. She ran past a couple of security guards and up the stairs, two at a time, to the executive floor. It was as empty as the *Marie Celeste*. When she went to the Kotelniki penthouse, there was no one there either.

Lev was the size of a small mountain, and he'd vanished into thin air.

There wasn't quite as much pandemonium outside the exhibition hall as there was in Alice's brain, but it was close. It was now half an hour since the auction had been scheduled to start, and Harry and Bob were trying to explain to journalists and would-be bidders alike what was happening. Alice slammed her car to a halt and ran up to them.

"What? What's going on?" she said.

"What does it look like?" said Harry. "The place is empty, and not a single member of staff has turned up."

Alice looked out at the agitated crowd: policemen trying not to laugh, punters who were telling each other how they'd always known this capitalism thing was too good to be true, and journalists almost visibly licking their lips at how juicy this story was.

"Look on the bright side," Harry added. "At least the day can't get any worse."

At ten o'clock, Alice made a public statement. She'd decided that the best way to play it was simply to be honest. Muscovites are so used to being fed lies that they laugh any 'we're-having-technical-problems' euphemisms all the way to Irkutsk. She confessed everything: that her staff, facilities and equipment were nowhere to be seen, and that, barring the kind of miracle unknown in a nation officially godless until last year, the auction of the Red October distillery was not going to take place today. She was jeered and whistled for this, and of course for being foreign, though pockets of the crowd also clapped her for her candour, which pleased her.

By midday, the waiting masses had begun to thin. About a third of the punters had wandered off in an all too-familiar legacy of dashed hopes. Some still clutched their vouchers, others had torn them up and thrown them in Alice's face. A proportion of the reporters had left too, convinced that the story had come and gone. Those who remained, in both camps, seemed to be there largely because they had nothing else to do.

At lunchtime, Alice drank vodka, three glasses more or less straight off, and started laughing – what else could she do? It was so bad that it was funny. Borzov and Arkin must have got wind of the fiasco; they hadn't been round, or even contacted her.

She rang Lev's numbers every thirty minutes, on the hour and at half past, and received no answer. She'd left raging messages at each number; she didn't have the energy for any more.

At six o'clock, the scheduled end of the auction, she, Bob and Harry reluctantly abandoned the exhibition hall and set off for the Ukrainia, where Alice fully intended to drink the bar dry.

At quarter past six, as they were crossing Kalininsky bridge, Lev rang.

Lev's sitting-room was vast, but Alice crossed it without seeming to touch the ground. She flew at him, talons outstretched. She wanted to rip Lev's skin from his bones and tear his eyes out. Until this moment, she'd never fully understood the old adage about there being a thin line between love and hate, but she got it now, she'd flipped the coin. He grabbed her wrists and pushed her against the wall so that she couldn't get enough leverage to kick him.

"How could you?" she shouted. "How could you?"

"What choice did I have?" he said simply. He held her close, both to restrain and comfort her. He was so much bigger than her that she had no real hope of hurting him.

"Let me go," she said.

He did so. "At least let me explain," he said.

"I'd like to see you try."

He told her what had happened, as quickly and simply as he could. There were copies of the staff list for the auction at Red October, of course. Last night, he'd sent two 21st Century men to every staffer's address – that was 300 mafiyosi, give or take. Each worker had been at home; anyone helping out at the auction would by definition not be earning enough money to go out on a Sunday night. Lev's men had given every helper one hundred dollars to stay at home the next day and ignore all phone calls. The money was the carrot; the stick came with the implicit threat of mafiya retribution if these instructions were not obeyed. Five people – a teller, a controller, a counter, a chief counter and a supervisor – had been given half as much money again and told to be at Tsvetnoy Bulvar metro station by seven thirty the next morning. From there, they'd been taken to the 21st Century's underground vodka warehouse beneath the Garden Ring, near the junction with Prospekt Mira, now cleaned of the bloodstains from the massacre of the Chechens.

This was where the auction had taken place. The warehouse had been open all day, in accordance with auction regulations, but since no one knew how to get there – or even what was going on – it

354

was unsurprising that there'd only been one bidder. This bidder had of course followed the procedure scrupulously, specifying that he was placing a type one, passive, bid. In doing so he had agreed to accept the final price reached, but had in return been guaranteed at least one share. At the end of the day's proceedings, with the total number of bids still standing at one, Lev had been presented with twenty-nine per cent of the shares in Red October for the grand total of ten thousand roubles – which, at prevailing exchange rates, was substantially less than one American cent.

Alice had sold a similar stake in a Polish soft-drinks factory to Pepsi for fifty million dollars.

"Why?" she spat. "*Why?*"

"For you."

"For me? You've ruined *everything*. How was that for me?"

"Karkadann would have killed you."

"You arranged this with *him*?"

Lev told her about their conversation, and how the Chechens had let her escape.

"You should have let me die," she said.

"Don't be ridiculous."

"I'm being perfectly serious."

"You value this auction over your life?"

"This auction *is* my life."

"You're drunk, you don't mean that."

"I'm not drunk."

"You are. I can smell it from here. I'm sorry about what's happened, I really am, but what else could I do? I live in my own system of co-ordinates, that's the pure truth. The new Russia is too fragile for Western morals and manners. It needs hard-hearted pragmatists, men like me, willing to dirty their hands and stain their souls, just to survive. My choice was a matter of life or death. I took the decision that your life was worth more than our auction. I'd take it again."

"You could have told me."

"And risk you go running to Arkin? No."

She was calming down, her thoughts were clearer. "When exactly did you arrange this?"

He looked her straight in the eye. "Friday."

"Three days ago."

"Yes."

"So all that time, when you were looking after me, you knew what you were going to do?" Her anger was rising again. It hadn't cooled very far, and it was coming back to the boil very fast. "When you were bathing me, and watching me sleep, and looking over me, you *knew*?"

"Of course."

"You *fuck*." It was a noun, not a verb. "I hope I never see you again."

"You're over-reacting."

"I think I'm being entirely reasonable."

"Coming in here half-cut and trying to scratch my eyes out is reasonable? You don't want to see me again, then fine."

"Fine? That's all you can say? *Fine*? For that, I should go to the Kremlin and tell them what you and Karkadann cooked up." He blanched; this was his weakness, and she could see that, the state she was in, he really thought that she might just do as she threatened.

"You do that, and I'll . . . I'll . . ."

"You'll do what? Kill me?"

"Don't push it."

"Or maybe I'll go to Sabirzhan instead. He'd love to hear it, wouldn't he? I know how much he hates you. He could put you on his slab and go to work on you."

"Alice, *don't*."

"Perhaps I'd let him fuck me too. You could watch."

"Enough! You need help."

"What for?"

"Listen to yourself. That's not you talking, all that sick shit, no matter how hurt you are. It's the vodka, frying your brain, making you volatile."

"Volatile? After what you've done, volatile is the very least I have a right to be."

"There you go again. Always finding excuses, always turning it away from yourself. This isn't about me, can't you see that? This is what you're doing to yourself. You don't want to see me again? Fine. Then take the time you'd have spent with me and use it to do something about your alcoholism."

"I'm not an alcoholic!"

"You're going to fuck everything up, Alice. And if you carry on like this, you can do it alone as far as I'm concerned."

"That's exactly what I'll do, then. Fuck off. Just fuck off."

Drunk and half-blinded by tears, Alice checked into the Budapest Hotel. It was the only hotel she could think of that didn't give her a view of either the Kremlin, the exhibition hall, the distillery, the Kotelniki or Patriarch's Ponds. The only one, in other words, which cut her off from her life.

She ordered a bottle of vodka and turned the television on. Flicking through the channels, she saw that every news programme was carrying footage of the auction fiasco. She hopped all the way through and all the way back before choosing Channel One, the government channel. As this had been a government initiative, its coverage should be the most sympathetic.

There she was, telling everyone what a fuck-up it had been. Interviews with disappointed punters, a reporter speculating about what had happened, and then a cut to Borzov, speaking from his office, playing the great statesman once more.

"What happened today was a farce, and for that Anatoly Nikolayevich apologises. In this instance, he has placed too much trust in the West, and in particular the blandishments of Mrs Liddell." Alice spilled some vodka as she started forward. Borzov distancing himself was one thing, but explicitly blaming Alice on national television was quite another. "The president was not the first man to be blinded by the promises of a beautiful woman, and he shan't be the last. Anatoly Nikolayevich admits freely: the devil confused him." Beneath the obscenities she was screaming at the screen, Alice caught the tone of Borzov's voice: there was more still to come. "Citizens of Russia, rest assured that your government has, as always, taken the most decisive steps available. Your president has dismissed Mrs Liddell from her post with immediate effect, and she will play no further part in the great reform effort, an enterprise to which she has contributed nothing but harm."

She'd always tried to defend Borzov. Now, when he'd been too cowardly, callous, discourteous and quintessentially Soviet to tell her in person that she was sacked, she finally saw what his critics meant. Russia hadn't elected as their first democratic president a man of great moral authority, as the Czechs had done with Vaclav Havel, and as the South Africans would surely do with Nelson Mandela. Russia had chosen a provincial communist party First Secretary. That was what they'd wanted, and that was what they'd got. Borzov was seventy this month, too old to do any more than partially re-educate himself. Sure, he'd learned much, but like everyone he had his limit, and when he came up against it he did the natural thing – fell back on his old communist thinking. That was the way he ruled. That was the way he'd treated Alice.

She poured herself another hundred grams and drank. The vodka slid down her throat, warm and seductively soothing. Her lover and her boss had both betrayed her; the bottle would never do so.

Alice's mind was clearing. It was almost a physical sensation, a scouring inside her skull. She'd pitied the millions of Russians who'd realised that everything they'd believed in and lived for was wrong. Well, what was she going through, if not exactly the same thing? Now, her job gone and her credo in tatters, she finally had the moment of revelation that comes to everyone who stays in Russia long enough, the moment when white middle-class Westerners finally understand what the rest of humanity has always known: that there are places in this world where the safety net they've spent so much of their lives erecting can suddenly be whipped away, where the right accent, education, health insurance and a foreign passport – all the familiar talismans which keep the bearer safe from harm – no longer apply, and where their well-being depends on the condescension of others.

The Russians brought down Napoleon and Hitler; they can bring down anyone.

Alice drank more and more. The real healing effects of vodka, the Russians say, begin only after the second bottle. Vodka in excess, brain in recess. It wasn't just that she wanted to blot out her self-pity and sense of failure, she was also looking to suffer.

She drank glass after glass of vodka, no water or orange juice between them, her aim twofold: to wake up tomorrow morning with the most agonising hangover, and to reach oblivion as quickly as possible tonight.

"Comfortably Numb" was playing in her head, and after a time Alice found out that Pink Floyd were right: there was no pain, and she was receding.

# 72

*Tuesday, 3 March 1992*
Moscow, centre stage in an endless drama, a great city for the shameless.

In public, Borzov denounced Lev for wrecking the reform effort.

In private, he stripped the Sports Academy of its tax-free status with a haste which reeked of spite.

Arkin was told that Lev had not in fact broken any law. The privatisation charter had given the company's director final say over where the auction was held, and not a single one of the lawyers who'd crawled over the document had seen fit to question it. The prime minister raged at anyone within earshot for more than an hour after he learned this.

His lover gone and the government on his back, Lev stayed in his penthouse and brooded like a dormant volcano.

Alice crept back to Patriarch's Ponds. She knew where everything was, she was comfortable there, and for the moment that was enough. She'd had enough excitement; what she wanted now was for Lewis to hold her, cradle her, make everything all right again. "I was wrong," she said. "I was wrong, I was seduced, I wanted to be something I'm not, and I'm so, so sorry."

"Do you have any idea how much damage you've caused?"

She nodded. "Some."

"And you really expect me just to take you back in?" He was holding out for his own pride, she saw. They both knew he'd take her back at the drop of a hat.

"I expect nothing from you. But I'm sorry from the bottom of my heart; you're my husband."

"And you don't love me."

"Lewis, we can still work it out."

"Not here we can't. We have to leave Moscow."

Moscow, her Moscow, the place Alice loved, the place which would swallow her absence without a ripple. So few people, particularly postcard-brained Westerners, appreciate Moscow's moody and elusive beauty. Uncovering it is like opening an end-less series of *matroshka* dolls: no one ever gets all the way to the end.

But that was what Alice was seeking, the answer, the truth, and by that she meant not simply the everyday *pravda* truth but the immortal *istina*, the inner light of truth. *Istina* is one of the few words in Russian that can't be rhymed. It has no verbal mate and no verbal associations; it stands alone and aloof. If *istina* existed, surely Alice would find it here.

# 73

*Wednesday, 4 March 1992*

Lev was working out. Wearing only a pair of shorts, he moved across the room with a powerful swagger, his massive arms keeping rhythm with the steady pump of his great thighs and his head swaying, gently but arrogantly, with each stride. Beneath his bare collarbones ran a slogan: 'He who has not been deprived of freedom does not know its value.' He radiated absolute peace and self-assurance. His face was composed in the benign, even saintly expression of an old-fashioned king certain of his divine right to reign. The scene might have benefited from some music, the "Hallelujah Chorus" perhaps, but it wasn't really necessary.

He'd had the floor strengthened in one of the rooms in his penthouse so he could use it as a weightlifting area. Unzipping a bag, he took out a white leather girdle and a package of talcum powder. He strapped the girdle beneath his belly, to diminish the immense strain on his stomach muscles when he hoisted the weights, and dusted his palms with talcum powder, slapping his hands together to get rid of the excess.

Then he went over to the weights themselves, great discs of iron stacked along one wall. He studied them for a moment, picked up two twenty-five-kilo discs as easily as if they were dinner plates, fitted one to each end of the bar, and lifted it three times with leisurely ease.

Lev added two more discs to the bar: ninety kilos in total. He spat into his palms, bent and gripped the bar. Gasping and grunting, he yanked it to shoulder level, paused, then raised it above his head, where he held it for a moment before letting it fall to the mats with an explosive crash. The savage clang of the falling weight was as unnerving as a grenade blast.

He rested for a moment, leaning silently on a padded gymnastic horse. He seemed to be concentrating very hard, as though slipping into some kind of trance necessary to perform superhuman feats. His chest and belly expanded with each inhalation, stretching the letters which spelt out the message that *Church is the house of God, prison the home of the thief.*

Some men find their escape in vodka; Lev's came when his vast muscles strained against vaster weights. This was where he found his grace, this was where he was exceptional. Three times they'd asked him to go to the Olympics: in Munich, in Montreal and then in Moscow. They'd come to the gulag and said he'd get temporary release for the duration of the Games. Three times they'd asked; three times he'd told them to get stuffed. What else could he have done? There was no way he could have worn the system's colours.

More discs on the bar. It was now up to something north of 150 kilos. This time, when he hoisted the bar above his head, he seemed about to burst; his belly strained against the leather girdle, the slabs of muscle in his biceps twisted and distorted the tattooed swastikas which signified the tough guy. Then Lev dropped the weight with the same hideous crash as before, squatted down, lifted it again, let it fall again. His chest was slick with perspiration. The sweat shone on the monasteries, cathedrals, castles and fortresses which crawled across his skin, the number of their spires and towers representing the number of years he'd been imprisoned.

The bar was up to 180 kilos now. With a bellow, Lev hoisted the weight to his shoulders, hesitated, gasped, and shouted with effort and exultation as he shoved it above his head. When the weight smashed to the mats this time, he threw out his chest, raised one arm and roared what sounded like a challenge to the heavens: "Victory or death!"

Lev and Karkadann had agreed to meet in the same banya as before. As before, Lev was first there; as before, he waited long minutes in the steam until Karkadann arrived. This time, however, he did not chide the Chechen for his tardiness.

"You're a man of your word," Lev said. "You let Alice go, and I thank you for that."

"What did you think I'd do? We're not animals, you know."

The silver chair? Force-feeding vodka? Lev choked back his bile. "And the children?"

"Have any more been killed?" Lev shrugged to concede the point. "There you are, then. Are *you* a man of *your* word?"

"I did what I said I'd do."

"And now? Red October's mine, yes? You've brought the paper-work?"

The flush on Karkadann's skin was not just from the heat, it was also the excitement of finally being able to touch what he wanted. In all human experience, there's little sweeter than victory.

"It's so good, to be in the banya after working out," Lev said. His arms, thick as tree trunks, were akimbo, the vast muscles at rest. "I never know when I'll train. Sometimes deep in the night, sometimes in the morning. I never repeat myself. Only I understand what's right for me. Yes, I've suffered sprains and ruptures, but I continued with my lifts regardless. The injuries didn't matter. They went away." He smiled. "Toss some water on the rocks, would you?"

Karkadann's initial reaction was to refuse, a childish antipathy to doing anything for anybody, but he hesitated only slightly before leaning forward and reaching for the water. He was nearer the rocks, after all, and he'd won; he could afford to show some magnanimity.

His eyes were off Lev for no more than a few seconds, but that was time enough. Lev curled his left arm round the front of Karkadann's neck, dragging him suddenly backwards. Karkadann instinctively reached not for the oak banister round his neck but for absent guns on a naked body, on his right thigh, under his left armpit. By the time Karkadann had realised his mistake, Lev had folded his right arm across the back of Karkadann's neck, left hand on right bicep and vice versa.

A man whose arms could lift almost two hundred kilos had no problem snapping another man's neck like kindling. Karkadann jerked twice and was still. Lev released his grip and laid Karkadann on a bench. He was quite, quite dead.

"Insults I could handle, even a direct attempt on my life," Lev said, "but to take a woman and threaten me through her, to strip her naked and humiliate her – no, no, that's not the act of a man." His black eyes shone from beneath the forest of his eyebrows, and he beamed a huge, beatific grin which made happy wreaths of his jowls.

He stepped out of the banya and into the ante-room, watching his skin prickle as the sudden coolness wicked heat from him. The two sets of bodyguards were waiting. Lev shook his head at them, to indicate there'd been a problem in finding agreement. Karkadann had called this meeting, so he'd be the one to stay in the banya until Lev had showered, changed and left, that was the etiquette. As before, when Karkadann had left first, it was embarrassing to be in a man's company once you'd failed to find common ground with him.

He showered quickly, but without visibly hurrying. Although the Chechens shouldn't go in to get Karkadann until Lev had left the building, Lev didn't want to take the chance. Within seven minutes he was dressed and moving through the restaurant with his protective phalanx, then out of the front door, on to the pavement and into the convoy. It was with a delicious leap of imagination that he fancied he heard the first outraged shouts from within as his car pulled away.

The television news played *The Godfather* theme as accompaniment to reports of Karkadann's death.

"It's an outrage!" Lev watched the footage through narrowed eyes. "He was an upstart punk, not a godfather. It's not an accolade you just put on like a coat – it has to be earned. That's the music they should play for *me* when *I* die."

# 74

*Thursday, 5 March 1992*

Near the tip of the Luzhniki district's marshy tongue lies the Novodevichiy Cemetery, and in all of Moscow only the Kremlin Wall is a more prestigious place to be buried. Nikita Khrushchev, the only Soviet leader not to be interred under the Kremlin, lies here under a bronze cannonball headlocked between jagged white and black monoliths, representations of the good and bad in his life. Nearer the main gate is Nikolai Gogol, the great writer with a pathological fear of death, mistakenly buried alive following a cataleptic fit. The inside of his coffin bears the claw marks of his desperate hands. Here too are Chekhov, Stanislavsky, Bulgakov, Shostakovich, Molotov, Eisenstein, Mayakovksy – and now Karkadann, his place secured by money, a reflection of an age as mercilessly accurate as Chekhov's plays or Eisenstein's films were of theirs.

Karkadann died as he'd lived, a Muslim in name only. Muslims should be buried among their own kind; Karkadann had chosen to lie amongst the Orthodox and the godless. Muslim graves should be built and marked in a simple way, for extravagance is false vanity; Karkadann's marble headstone was studded with diamonds and pictured him dangling the keys of his Mercedes from his right hand. Muslim corpses should be covered with plain white cotton sheets; Karkadann wore his best Savile Row suit. Muslims should be laid on their right side so they can face Mecca; Karkadann was on his back, as though taking a nap. Muslim traditions recommend a casket only if the soil is wet or loose; Karkadann's coffin was walled in layers of silver and bronze, its lid was thick plate glass, and the corpse lay on a couch of white satin and tufted cushions. The catafalque was enclosed in a chamber of black velvet trimmed with gold brocade and silver tassels, flanked by two pyramids of pink satin.

The scent of flowers wafted from Karkadann's grave like a chemical spill. A flowered heart the size of a man stood on an eiderdown of orchids, and around it was an extraordinary display: scabiouses in soft lilac, the greying blue of globe thistles and the firmer shades of hydrangeas and delphiniums; sorrels, spurges, hedge privets and hop flowers all in green; white splashes of gladioli, chalk plants, lilies, carnations and cornflowers; the pinks and reds of larkspurs, carnations, geraniums, snapdragons and roses; and crysanthemums in yellow, bronze, purple, apricot and champagne.

The florists must have worked all night, Irk thought. Even given that much of the preparation had been completed long before his death – gang leaders arranged their own funerals as a matter of course – it was still impressive. Only the seriously rich had the clout to get things done that fast. Moscow's morgues bulged with thousands of bodies unclaimed because there was no one to pay for their internment; even the most basic funerals, with vodka for the gravediggers, entertainment for the mourners and a simple coffin cost around three times the minimum monthly wage. If you were one of the have-nots in life, chances were you'd be one in death too.

Irk should have been celebrating with the rest of Petrovka. Karkadann had been behind the child killings. Karkadann was dead. The murders were therefore over. Yerofeyev, of course, had been quick to claim a share of the credit, though Irk had won the lion's share of the congratulations. As if he'd had anything to do with it, he thought bitterly. He felt only emptiness: the 21st Century had done what he, senior investigator with the Moscow procurator's office, had been unable to do. No, it was more; they'd done what he'd been *forbidden* from doing. Irk felt like a man sitting in a pile of shit with his hands and legs tied. He could see the shit, he could smell the shit, but he couldn't do a single damn thing about it.

Tradition dictates that gang leaders kiss the corpse of a fallen peer. Failure to do so is to admit responsibility for the death. The charade is followed even when the perpetrator's identity is known to all. So Irk watched the bosses come up one by one, kingpins of Russian gangland, all bending to kiss the corpse, some also leaving an envelope full of money to keep Karkadann comfortable into the afterlife. They came from all over the former empire: Testarossa from Moscow, St Petersburg's Ivan the Hand, Lenchik the Shaking Head from Vladivostok, Murmansk's Gibbous. Some were named for their appearance: Cyclops, who'd lost an eye in an attack; the Claw, who had an artificial hand; The Bearded, The Bald, The Kike, The Scar. Some had taken their noms de guerre from literature: The Possessed, The Idiot, Zhivago, Oblonsky, Raskolnikov. The only serious player missing was the Jap, who was rumoured to be in New York, attracting an unhealthy amount of interest from the FBI. The Jap was said to have spent so much time with the yakuza that he'd adopted their custom of inserting pearls between the outer skin of his cock and its inner core, one pearl for each year spent in jail. The amount of years *he'd* been inside, it must have looked like a studded club.

The last men up to the coffin were the ones who'd had most to gain from Karkadann's death. Zhorzh dipped his face silently and kissed the corpse: revenant, vampiric. Only Lev was left. He moved to the casket with the inexorable purpose of a zeppelin. The cemetery suddenly seemed very still, the living as silent and motionless as those whose sarcophagi they trod underfoot. No one seemed to blink or breathe as they watched Lev looking down at Karkadann's body.

Lev saw beyond the closed eyes of the dead man to the insolence and hubris that had consumed him. To kiss the corpse would be to signify respect and affection, when in Karkadann's case he had never felt either. "Most people have little confidence in tomorrow," he said, half to himself, "so they want it all today. They want to have everything and spend everything, all at the same time. They search and find and embrace their own excess, because they never know when someone might take it all away. It was like that in the gulag too, you know. We had no faith in tomorrow, so we measured our survival in half-days, the rise and fall of the sun. At sunrise, you'd hope to make it through to nightfall. At nightfall, you'd look towards dawn. It was a *system*." He looked down at Karkadann. "But you, you weren't of a system. You thought the world revolved around you. That's what got you killed."

Lev raised his head and walked away from the coffin.

A beat, maybe two, and the Chechens were raising their guns, but Lev's bodyguards were quicker, already swarming round their principal and hustling him away from the graveside. There the spurts of flame, there the harsh cracks as guns barked in Slav and Chechen hands alike; there the rips in shirts, there the blood billowing from chests, there the dull thud of men falling to the ground with the life flowing from them. Lev was out of the cemetery within seconds. When the firing stopped, the silence seemed absolute, redoubled. The cemetery was a wasteland.

\* \* \*

365

Irk went to the Khruminsches' apartment. They'd heard what had happened at Novodevichiy; they were glad Karkadann was dead, and they didn't understand the unfathomability of Irk's disappointment. "Life's not all neat ends and everything nicely tied," Sveta said. "What does it matter how Karkadann was killed, so long as he was?"

Irk said he'd take half an hour's nap before dinner. He slept straight through till dawn.

# 75

*Friday, 6 March 1992*
Alice had spent days in bed, clutching a succession of vodka bottles to her as a child hugs its favourite teddy bears. The shock of her kidnap had kicked in, delayed but no less real and visceral for that. She felt shy, unable to hold a conversation or leave the apartment; so weak that even a visit to the bathroom needing preparation and recovery; relieved, grinning like a loon at the oddest times; and afraid, the most innocuous sound making her jumpy. Most of all, she felt strange and detached, as though her skin and body weren't quite her own.

When Lewis tried to help, she turned away and stared at the wall, ashamed to have caused so much trouble and damage. When he told her to pull herself together and stop feeling sorry for herself, she yelled back at him to fuck off and leave her alone. He understood *nothing*, she shrieked, he knew *nothing*. It was as though she were willing him to throw her out again, and in doing so confirm her transformation from wife to witch. But he wouldn't; he was determined to make it work, even if she wasn't. When he was out and the phone rang, she let the answerphone pick it up, listening without enthusiasm and emotion to disembodied voices: Harry, Bob, Christina, Lewis himself from the hospital, sighing in frustration when she wouldn't answer.

Not Lev. Never Lev. Not that she cared about him anyway. She'd given strict orders to the whole of her body, down to the last hair, not to show him the smallest sign of love. She'd chained up her love in her heart under ten locks, and there it was suffocating. Her relationship with Lev was over, and she'd failed. The auction was over, and she'd failed there too. Raw, sucking wounds, the both of them, too fresh for scar tissue to have formed.

It wasn't the solitude that got to Alice first; it was the silence.

She padded into the living-room, eyes straight ahead so she wouldn't catch sight of herself in the mirror and see how ghastly she looked, and flicked through the mail she hadn't opened since leaving Lewis a fortnight before. He'd kept it all for her, stacked neatly – that was *so* Lewis, she thought.

One of the letters was from a district court in Moscow. Alice was already wondering what she'd done wrong when, reading further, she saw that it concerned the trial of one Uvarov, Grigori Eduardovich. Uvarov? Uvarov . . . She remembered now, Uvarov was the traffic cop who'd smashed her headlight a few weeks before. *Weeks,* she thought; weeks, as opposed to months or years, the usual timespan of a glacial system. They must have fast-tracked him, which in turn must have been because of her involvement. She was – had been – politically important.

Alice scanned the letter for a date. The hearing was today.

The court was running late. Uvarov's case should have started ten minutes before, but there was still a full hearing to come – not counting the one just coming to a close – before he would answer three separate charges: extortion (illegally demanding money from Alice); criminal damage (smashing her headlight); and the Soviet-sounding "activities incompatible with his status" (a back-up in case the prosecutor was too inept to make either of the first two stick).

There was hardly a room in the courthouse which wasn't in some way dilapidated. The ceilings wore polka dots of water stains, vast swathes of wallpaper were bidding for freedom. It was the kind of place held together by the plaster.

Alice lowered herself gingerly on to a hard wooden bench in the public gallery above the courtroom and tried to focus not on the pain but on the sorry procession passing below her: now a miscarriage of justice, now a miscreant. Judge Petrenko – juries had been eliminated by the Bolsheviks – confirmed to a kindly-looking old man that the government was banning the Salvation Army on the grounds that it had openly proclaimed itself an army, and was therefore a militarised organisation bent on the violent overthrow of the Russian government. The old man protested that the Salvation Army simply wanted to operate community centres providing food, shelter and clothing for the homeless and elderly poor.

There it was, Alice thought: Russian legislation in a nutshell. Most Russians think their laws are excessively harsh and nonsensical, the only saving grace being that they are rarely enforced. Decades of unjust and irrational rules had turned an entire people into a nation

367

of law-breakers. Could a system which had been slavishly devoted to the service of state and party now become a neutral arbiter of society, a defender of the constitution, a protector of civil liberties, contracts and private property rights?

When that system defined the Salvation Army as a terrorist organisation, the answer seemed clear. The judge shook his head at the old man's protests and rapped his gavel. "Next case!" Petrenko shouted. "Uvarov, Grigori Eduardovich."

Alice hurried down from the gallery into the courtroom and took her place in the witness stand. When Uvarov was led in, she almost recoiled in shock. Without his uniform, he seemed smaller, shrunken. He must have lost ten kilos since she'd last seen him, and he hadn't had many to spare in the first place. Set between hollowed cheeks, his cucumber nose looked even bigger than she remembered.

Uvarov didn't look at Alice until he was standing in the dock. She'd expected hostility, but what she saw, curiously, was sorrow. Petrenko read out the three charges and asked Uvarov how he pleaded to each.

"Guilty. Guilty. Guilty." Uvarov's voice was soft and reedy; the sound of a broken man.

"Good." Petrenko liked those who pleaded guilty. "Let's not waste any more time, then."

"Can I ask the defendant something?" Alice said.

"Do you have to?" Petrenko said.

"I'd like to."

"I suppose you've the right. Go on."

"Why did you do it?" Alice asked Uvarov, hearing as she did so the sigh from Petrenko which let her know what he thought: that it was just the kind of stupid question a foreigner *would* ask. For the money, dummy, why else?

Uvarov's first notion – Alice could see it in his eyes – was that she was being sarcastic, or having her own obscure fun at his expense. She nodded at him, to show she was being serious. "I really want to know," she added, thinking to herself, when did she ever *not* want to know?

Uvarov gripped the edge of the dock. "Because I hadn't been paid since December. Ten dollars a month – that was my salary. You'd think the police force could have found that amount, wouldn't you? Not for me, they didn't. Was that too much to ask – enough money to live? It's hard, when you've a wife and children. Do you know what it feels like, to wake up every morning wondering whether you can feed them that day? I saw you, I realised you were foreign,

368

and foreigners have money, everyone knows that. A hundred bucks to me was a lifeline. What was it to you? A night out." He looked like he was going to cry. "It was nothing *personal*."

Uvarov was right, Alice thought. What *was* a hundred bucks to her? To him it was almost a year's salary, even if he'd been paid it – even if he hadn't been sacked the moment she'd reported him. There was a reason why policemen were paid so little, of course: it was assumed that they'd make up the shortfall in bribes. They were practically on commission, for heaven's sake. What can encourage corruption more than assuming it?

Alice saw it all, as sudden and encompassing as a flashing light. It wasn't just that Uvarov was no longer a policeman; in his eyes, he was no longer a man. Without a job, he couldn't be the breadwinner, and providing for one's family is the *sine qua non* of Russian manhood. Wasn't Uvarov exactly the kind of man privatisation was supposed to be helping? The ordinary guy trying to make a living in difficult circumstances? Besides, it wasn't as though Alice had been blameless. She *had* been going the wrong way down the street; she *had* tried to joke her way out of trouble, twice. He'd been doing his job, more or less; she should just have paid up and gone on her way.

Uvarov was here because this was a political case. She had more power than him, she was higher up the food chain. Everyone kept telling her how weak the state was. True, it was weak when it came to taking on powerful organised interests, but, as if in compensation, when it came to the private citizen, it could be too strong.

If Alice was powerful enough to get Uvarov here, she thought, surely she was powerful enough to get him out, even now. She turned to Petrenko.

"Your honour, there's been an error. This isn't the policemen who stopped me."

Petrenko furrowed his brows. "What are you talking about?"

"I was mistaken. Grigori is an innocent man, that's clear." Alice looked from Petrenko to Uvarov and back again. It was hard to tell who was more shocked; easy to see who was angrier.

"Come to the altar," Petrenko hissed.

"The altar?"

"My bench. *Now*."

Alice stepped down from the witness box and walked over to the judge's bench. Petrenko leant forward, she stretched upwards; they could have been lovers at a window.

"Why are you doing this?" Petrenko whispered.

"I told you."

"The man is guilty. I'm not going to let him off."

"I'm the only witness, it's my word against his. What can you do?"

"Charge you with wasting police time."

"The police do a perfectly good job of wasting their time without my help."

"I can't let him off, Mrs Liddell."

"Why the hell not?"

"The judiciary has . . . standards."

"Standards?"

Petrenko lowered his voice still further. "Quotas."

"I see." Alice nodded; she understood. "And if you fill your quotas . . ."

Subtly, so no one could see, Petrenko rubbed his thumb against his middle finger. "We get paid. Payment you'd be depriving me of."

Alice sighed. "How much?"

"Two hundred."

"That's absurd." No, she thought, what was absurd was that she was haggling for Uvarov's freedom. "Grisha only asked me for one hundred; I'll give you that, to drop the case."

"Fine." It was more than Petrenko had expected, she saw, but it was too late to beat him down now. He sat back in his chair and rapped his gavel.

"The case against Uvarov, Grigori Eduardovich, is dismissed, with my personal recommendation that he be reinstated to his position in the GAI without further ado. The court will now break for lunch." He leant forward to Alice again. "That privatisation thing seems like a great idea, you know, even after what happened the other day. I don't suppose you've any spare vouchers lying around, have you?"

# 76

*Saturday, 7 March 1992*

Alice was killing time. She needed food, so she stopped by a gastronom, a large, box-shaped building with a battered metal door, a mud-covered floor, and walls in need of painting and washing. There were few things as time-consuming as shopping in a gastronom. First, Alice went round the store's seven counters noting the prices of the things she wanted; next, she waited in line at a cashier's window to buy receipts for each item; and finally she returned to the seven counters, queuing at each one in turn. When she reached the front of the queue, the shop assistant tore the receipt down the middle before handing over the food; Alice remembered her schoolteachers doing this on substandard pieces of work.

The whole process would have taken five minutes in an American supermarket; here, it took almost an hour. Alice was glad; she had nothing else to do. She wasn't living; she was existing.

Zhorzh came to the Kotelniki. He was unaccompanied, unarmed and seemingly unafraid for his personal safety, which made him either very brave or very foolhardy. Lev allowed himself a small smile less of triumph than of vindication before having the Chechen brought in to see him.

"I've come to seek accommodation," Zhorzh said. Karkadann was gone, Zhorzh was now head of the Chechen gangs; he'd found his voice at last.

"Why should I make a deal?" Lev asked.

"Because it'll save you a certain amount of trouble, and a fair few deaths too. We wouldn't go down without a fight. Why would you want to risk more damage to yourselves, when this way you can so easily avoid it? I'm the boss now. You'll find me more reasonable than my predecessor. What you did to Karkadann was entirely right. You can't deal with men like that, you can only get rid of them."

They hammered out the details with remarkable swiftness. The Slav alliance would pay the Chechens twenty-five million dollars for all their existing interests in Moscow. It was a fraction of what the Chechen portfolio was worth, but equally Lev could have taken the whole lot for nothing had he chosen to continue the fight. The money was his way of expressing appreciation for Zhorzh's sensibleness in coming to the table, and Zhorzh understood it as such. There was more than enough for him to take back to Grozny and invest there.

"You've got a week to leave Moscow," Lev said, "or the deal's off."

# 77

*Sunday, 8 March 1992*
Karkadann's death still gnawed at Irk. He wanted to be alone; away from Moscow, away from other people, and away, if he could have managed it, from himself.

The sewer streams were much deeper than usual. It was a few moments before he realised that this was peak time, when flows ran at three times the average and six times the night levels. Moreover, it had started to rain up above, which meant still faster streams as the surface water scuttled down the drains, burbling round Irk's knees as it hunted the outflows which would take it into the deeper foul sewers.

Irk could no longer see his breath, so he knew it was warmer down here than up above. But the chill seemed to have entered him from within, because he felt cold no matter how far he walked, and like a pilgrim he walked for hours. He came across a deserted laboratory whose floor was strewn with crystals; something about the skewed positioning of an ancient bakelite telephone and the haphazard piles of primitive respiration masks suggested that the room had been abandoned in a hurry, though whether it had been emptied five minutes or five decades ago, he couldn't tell. Later, in the distance, he heard echoes of Gregorian singing. Approaching cautiously, he saw a group dressed in monks' robes carrying torches around a stone altar. Suddenly he slipped on a patch of slime and fell heavily against the side of the tunnel. By the time he'd picked himself up, the worshippers had vanished.

Irk broke ground in Red Square, where endless currents of people seemed to materialise from the gloaming, swarming towards and around him. He felt as though he were still at the bottom of the sea, cut off from the surface, never to return. The square was criss-crossed with sons and mothers, husbands and wives – it was International Women's Day. In Soviet times, they'd shown televised vacuum cleaner races; now all the women were carrying flowers. The most impressive bouquets belonged to the wives or girlfriends of traffic cops, who'd spent the previous days in an orgy of imag-ined traffic violations in order to clock up the necessary fifty dollars for the best bunches on the block. Irk himself bought flowers for Sveta and Galya, who'd invited him over for dinner that night. Thirty bucks for two sorry-looking sprays – he had a good mind to bring the flower-seller in for extortion.

International Women's Day is the one time in the year when men are supposed to take on all the wives' chores. It rarely works that way. If there are children, they demand that the mother cooks them a proper breakfast; if not, the wife is so alarmed by the crashing and strange smells from the kitchen that she gets up to forestall a catas-trophe. Many men deliberately make a hash of everything in order to be exempted from such duties until the same time next year – not for nothing do Russian women refer to their men as 'the other child'.

Irk was aware of all this, but with the sterile knowledge of someone who's heard about it second-hand and never experienced it for himself. Perhaps that was a good thing, he thought.

# 78

*Monday, 9 March 1992*
Borzov knew that he'd need all his political savvy if he was to make it through the week unscathed. The Sixth Congress of People's Deputies, a five-day extraordinary session of parliament, was about to begin. Everything bad – rising prices, thousands more dropping below the poverty line – was being laid at Borzov's door. Everything good – the end of the child killings, peace between Slav and Chechen gangs, even the failure of a widely unpopular privatisation auction – was being credited to Lev.

Even if he'd felt like looking upbeat, it was impossible to maintain such an expression when squinting into howling winds and squalls of snow. It was one of those mornings when winter seemed determined to resume its sway with a last desperate onslaught. Halfway to a hurricane, devoid of either warmth or sunshine, the conditions seemed to reflect the reception Borzov was likely to get. Seven months before, he'd stood in front of the White House and hailed it as a bastion of freedom and democracy; now that same building was crammed with his most implacable foes.

Summer is the reformers' season; winter is the time for ruthless hardliners. On days when ice sits inches thick and light starts fading at lunchtime, the gloomy Cassandras have things all their own way: no scenario of chaos, degeneration and collapse seems too pessimistic to believe.

Over a thousand deputies from all corners of the federation had arrived for the congress. Many of the provincial representatives regarded these biannual assemblies as the highlight of their year: all expenses paid, grace-and-favour tickets to the Bolshoi, and a chance to spend some small part of the public revenue on luxury goods for the wife and – by way of balance for their spousal consideration – the finest girls Moscow had to offer. The deputies' new suits and shiny shoes betrayed their excitement. They stood in clusters, talking, laughing and shouting across the room at each other like children waiting for the teacher to call them to order.

Lev's was one of several vory among the deputies. For the most part, the vory got themselves elected not to debate the future of the nation, but because the position of deputy afforded the holder immunity from prosecution. Police investigators moaned that they could find more crime kingpins in the parliamentary chamber than in the cells at Butyurka.

At nine o'clock sharp, Arkin stepped confidently up to the rostrum. The harsh light picked out the features that cartoonists exaggerated and emphasised when they lampooned him: the full lips, the heavy-lidded eyes, the upturned nose, and most of all the unruly mop of black hair. He looked with barely concealed distaste at the representatives, knowing they'd give him a hard time, no matter what he said. He cleared his throat and began:

"In the most trying of circumstances, I'm delighted to say that the reform programme is still on course. If we're allowed to continue, I'm confident that inflation will start to decrease in the third quarter of the year. The austerity measures have been hard for everyone –"

The deputies howled him down. Arkin first tried to wait them out and then to outshout them, but neither tactic worked. He glanced at Borzov for support and saw only resigned dread, as if all the president's worst fears were being realised.

A forest of pink order papers shot up and one by one the deputies rose to lambast the government and harangue Arkin. Through it all, Arkin stuck to his guns, lambasting those who would stand in the way of progress.

Lunch was called at one o'clock precisely, and for ninety minutes the deputies' feeding frenzy became literal rather than metaphorical. Jeering the government was hungry work, and they piled into the cafeteria in search of mushroom juliennes, meat-stuffed pancakes, plum cakes and cream puffs. All these goodies, but no one there to apportion them because the cafeteria assistants were on their lunch break. So the deputies grabbed and scoffed and scooped and snaffled, trying to get their hands on the delicacies before they ran out.

After lunch Lev was first up, to wild applause. Many in the chamber saw him as a heroic standard-bearer, with the gnarled credibility of time in the gulag.

"I don't mourn the old system," Lev said. "We were treated like dogs, our only existence that of shadows, our only right that to die. In the gulags I served time with historians, mathematicians, astronomers, literary critics, geographers, experts on world painting, linguists with a knowledge of Sanskrit and ancient Celtic

dialects. I knew a man who was ten minutes late for work, twice –
and for this he was sentenced to five years in Vorkuta. And how
did these people spent their days? As manual labourers, or as trusties
in clerical jobs, or in the culture and education sections, or simply
wasting away, unable to find any practical application for their vast
knowledge – knowledge that would often have been of value not
only to Russia but to the whole world.

"That's why I supported our president and prime minister in their
efforts to help us build a new Russia. I thought, well, it won't be
perfect, and it may very well be unworkable, but it'll surely be better
than what came before. I believed they were good men trying to
do good things. No more."

They'd been prepared to let Alice die; he'd never, *never* forgive
them for that.

He looked at Arkin. "Kolya, you've forgotten your history. You
would do well to remember what happened to the False Dmitri, the
sixteenth-century czar who idolised all things Western – his subjects
murdered him and fired his remains from a cannon in Red Square,
as a reminder that Russia shouldn't go too far to the west. You know
what else you are, Kolya? You're a saltdick. You've got one foot in
Russia and the other in America, so your cock must be hanging
down into the Bering Sea."

The deputies stamped their feet in approval. Lev held his arm
up to milk the applause, before cutting it horizontally through
the air: enough, he wanted to get on. Dwarfing the lectern, he
turned to face Borzov. "As for you, Anatoly Nikolayevich, we
invested so much hope in you, so much hope. In electing you,
Russia saw not only a politician ready to demolish the state structure, but an individual who was trying to leave behind his old
habits and prejudices in favour of democratic values. You were
first secretary of the Sverdlovsk regional party committee, first
secretary of the Moscow city party committee, a candidate
member of the Politburo, a member of the central committee of
the CPSU – and then, at the age of sixty-five, *oplya!* You decided
you were a democrat, and the whole world believed you. If you
stick a wine label on to a bottle of vodka, it doesn't affect the
contents. The only way to bring about real change is to pour the
vodka out and pour the wine in. If democracy is to exist in Russia,
Anatoly Nikolayevich, it will exist not because of you but in spite
of you."

It was a bravura performance, and the deputies were enthralled.
Lev now turned to address them.

"I believe neither Anatoly Nikolayevich nor Nikolai Valentinovich is fit to hold his position. If I had my wish, they'd both be out on their ears. But the people have suffered enough uncertainty. They'd not thank us for plunging them into yet more by unseating their president. A prime minister, however, is a different matter. He can be replaced in this chamber, today, here and now. One vote is all that's needed. I propose that we take a vote of no confidence in Nikolai Valentinovich."

There'd been no preamble, no build-up, no rising percussion tide to herald this move, but Arkin felt the shock ripple through him almost before Lev had said the words. Borzov, his clay pipe dangling in limp surprise from the corner of his mouth, shot panicked glances between Arkin and Lev.

The chamber erupted. There were cheers from some quarters, but consternation and bewilderment in others.

Arkin knew how vulnerable he was. For all those who regarded him as Russia's great white hope, there were many more who hated everything he stood for. Knowing that parliament was a massive political spectacle, a great circus where only the most dramatic and breathtaking twists and turns can carry the day, he faced Lev.

"If such a vote is even taken," Arkin said, "no matter what the result, I'll walk out of this building and out of the government. Only a market economy can generate the wealth and dynamism that will renew Russia; only a market economy will enable this country to be a major world power. Vote me out today, and you'll harm Russia far more than you'll harm me."

Arkin had just about managed to have himself heard over the hubbub which had followed Lev's proposal; now, the noise in the auditorium was climbing somewhere towards that of a lift-off at the Baikonur cosmodrome. Borzov, as haughty as a popular tribune, glowered in the corner at this affront to his authority. As a rule, he kept himself aloof from such battles rather than risk destroying his popular mystique. But he knew this was no time to be timid. Whoever is shouting the loudest, gesticulating the most wildly, snarling the most ferociously will win the day. The only way to subdue Lev's fire was to counter-attack. He clambered to his feet.

"To sack a prime minister because you feel like it is mockery, not democracy. The chief will *not* be dictated to by a bunch of savages demanding human sacrifices."

The deputies were shouting at Borzov, and they weren't going to let up. He was right; they were savages, and the sacrifice they wanted was Arkin. No, said Borzov; they could control the appointment of certain ministers, the junior ones, but he wouldn't give them the prime minister. They howled and raged still more. He tried barter: offering to concede control of key portfolios, such as the security and finance ministries. A man on the run, doling out compromises and effectively dismissing his own officials to buy time. He was panicked, and they knew it.

At ten to six, the deputies voted to sack Arkin by a majority of 254.

# 79

*Tuesday, 10 March 1992*
When Borzov got up to speak on the second morning of the plenum, packs of deputies tried to howl him down. It was Lev who stayed them: he wanted to savour the president's humiliation. As the deputies quietened, Borzov nodded his thanks to Lev.

"Esteemed deputies," Borzov began, "the time has come for Anatoly Nikolayevich to apologise. Your president has not been vigorous enough in discharging his duties. He has compromised and vacillated. This isn't like him. It's time to return Anatoly Nikolayevich to Anatoly Nikolayevich. And this is where it starts." When he paused, there was silence; no one heckled. "The president refuses to accept the dismissal of Nikolai Valentinovich Arkin. In years to come, there'll be a statue to Kolya in every square in Russia. The chief won't have him removed before Russia has the chance to reap the rewards of his vision and courage. He will remain as prime minister until the Chief decides otherwise."

Currents ran round the chamber as though it were a power station. The heat which glowed from the floor, where Borzov and Lev once more faced each other, felt positively radioactive.

"The president has made many errors of judgement over the past few months," Lev said. "Now, in expressly disobeying parliament's wishes, he's gone too far, and is clearly no longer fit to hold office. Yesterday, we gave him the benefit of the doubt. By his own actions, he has shown himself unworthy. A vote to impeach him should therefore be held. More specifically, two votes: the first a ballot to decide whether an impeachment vote should take place at all, and, if this motion is carried, we will proceed with the impeachment vote."

Lev had read up on his rules, that was clear enough. Parliamentary officials consulted hurriedly amongst themselves and agreed: the impeachment procedure was as he'd outlined. They called the first ballot.

Of 1,012 deputies registered to vote, 338 were needed to carry the motion; Lev got 712. For the second vote, a two-thirds majority was required. If those same deputies voted against Borzov next time, the president would – technically, at least – be out of office.

"The motion will be carried if 675 deputies support it. All those in favour of the president being impeached, please raise their right hand."

There was a speaker, of course, but Lev seemed to have usurped the role. Borzov was looking at the deputies who had kept their arms down, because they were easier to count. If he had enough votes to survive, it wouldn't be by much. There was a long pause while the tellers counted, and then Lev spoke again.

"All those against the president being impeached, please raise your right hand."

Borzov's support showed in thickets, small copses of upraised hands dotted in the wilds of hostile seats. If anything, his position looked even more hopeless.

"All those abstaining," said Lev, in a tone which suggested very strongly that there'd better not be any; and indeed there weren't.

The tellers conferred briefly, nodding in satisfaction that their figures tallied. One of them approached the speaker's chair, his strides long and purposeful as the cameras tracked him; this was his few seconds of fame, and he knew it. He whispered the result in the speaker's ear, cupping his hand round it to conceal his lips as he spoke. The speaker cleared his throat.

"The results of the vote to impeach Anatoly Nikolayevich Borzov as president are as follows: abstentions, zero; votes against, 338 . . ." There was a murmuring among those sharp enough to do the maths in their head. The speaker moved smoothly on, putting the others out of their misery: "Votes in favour, 684." He raised his hand for quiet, but the deputies were too excited to pay him heed; they didn't need to hear the rest. "I therefore declare Anatoly Nikolayevich Borzov impeached and, by order of this parliament, removed from the office of president with immediate effect."

The applause was thunderous. Borzov looked at the hands blurring as they slapped together in appreciation, the mouths stretching as they yelled their approval, and recalled the words of the poet Tyatchev: "It's impossible to make sense of Russia, it's not amenable to reason. It's a place in which you simply have to believe."

Russians love the boss when he's new but inevitably fall out of love and into hatred as time goes by. Each time they hope that the new man will finally prove worthy of their adoration; and each time they grumble about being deceived. They loved the czars for the grandeur of their empires; they loved Lenin for destroying the hated czarist kingdom; they loved Stalin for restoring a national empire and purging the hated Leninists; they loved Khrushchev for ending the hated Stalinist yoke and mass terror; they loved Brezhnev for ending the hated Khrushchev follies and arbitrariness; they loved Gorbachev for ending the hated Brezhnev stagnation and for introducing freedom; they loved Borzov for ending the hated Gorbachev vacillations and launching reforms, and now they hated him for the humiliation, chaos and poverty with which his rule had left them.

"How about assassination?" said Arkin.

"Of Lev?" Borzov waved his vodka glass dismissively. "Don't be a fool, Kolya. The last thing we want is for Lev to be a martyr. No, he's done this constitutionally, and that's how we will respond."

"All right," Arkin said. "Let's take it to the people. A direct referendum, one question: who should be president?"

"No. Borzov's president, there's no question of that. The only way out of this is direct presidential rule: suspend parliament, call new elections, and govern by decree."

"And the West?"

"They want the president to stay in office at all costs, as you well know." He squinted at Arkin over his vodka glass. "You're testing Anatoly Nikolayevich, aren't you? You want to be sure that he's as steadfast as you."

Arkin smiled in admiring acknowledgment of the old man's perspicacity.

"The Chief knew he was right to stand by you," Borzov said, pouring himself another hundred grams.

# 80

*Wednesday, 11 March 1992*
Borzov's appearance on Channel One for the most momentous speech of his presidency was a study in nonchalance. The bigger the crisis, the more in his element he felt.

"Fellow citizens, your president," – he got that in early, to show them who was still boss – "is addressing you at a complex and critical moment. The Supreme Soviet is in a state of political decomposition. It has lost its ability to perform the main function of the representative body, that of concerting public interests, and has ceased to be an organ of rule by the people. It is pushing Russia towards the abyss. One can no longer tolerate this and do nothing.

"As president, Anatoly Nikolayevich's duty is to recognize that the current corps of deputies has lost the right to remain at the key levers of state power. As the guarantor of state security, Anatoly Nikolayevich – vested with authority acquired at the all-people elections in 1991 – has signed a presidential decree suspending the exercise of legislative, administrative and supervisory functions by the Congress of People's Deputies. The Congress shall no longer convene, and the powers of the people's deputies of the Russian Federation shall be terminated. In the interim, Anatoly Nikolayevich shall rule Russia directly, aided by Nikolai Valentinovich Arkin, who remains Prime Minister.

"Your president takes this decision to rule directly with a heavy heart, but he can see no other route out of the impasse. He is bypassing democracy in order to save it.

"Anatoly Nikolayevich appeals to the leaders of foreign powers to understand the complexity of the situation here. The measures he has had to take are the only way to protect democracy and freedom in Russia, to defend the process of reform and the still weak Russian market. He has no other aims.

"Most importantly, fellow citizens, your president appeals to you. The time has come when, by common effort, we can and must put an end to the profound crisis of the Russian state. Your president counts on your understanding, support, good sense and civic awareness. We have a chance to help Russia, and Anatoly Nikolayevich is sure we'll be able to use it for the sake of peace and tranquillity in our country. We are the heirs of a great civilisation, and its rebirth into a new, modern and dignified life now depends on us all. By common efforts, let us preserve Russia for ourselves, our children and grandchildren. Thank you."

The White House was surrounded by a line of men, in turn sullen, wary and defiant. They weren't in OMON livery or defence ministry regalia; they were from the parliamentary guard and the 21st Century. They were letting deputies, parliamentary staff and accredited journalists into the White House – no one else. They constructed makeshift barricades around the White House from whatever they could find: buses with their tyres slashed, trolley cars, garbage trucks, fences, concrete blocks, metal railings, park benches, armatures, scaffolding poles, even tree trunks. Parliament was under siege, for the second time in seven months.

At dusk, Borzov cut off the White House's electricity, heating and phone lines.

The assembly chamber, vast enough when normally lit, seemed even larger in the flickering light of hundreds of candles. The darkness which fled from the clutches of the glowing ellipses seemed to extend to infinity. Without a microphone, even Lev's basso profundo barely made it to the back of the hall.

"The government are scared," he shouted. "They know they can't win the argument, which is why they're resorting to bullying tactics, and so soon in the struggle too – that tells you all you need to know about how rattled we've got them. Fear not, my friends; with every moment that passes, we consolidate our grip on the situation. But I can't pretend that this is going to be easy. We could be here for days, even weeks. If you don't have the stomach for the fight, then it's better that you leave now. I need people who are with me fully or not at all. This is the last time I'll say this: go now, or stay with me till the end."

His thinking was spot on; better to have five hundred fanatics than a thousand waverers. If he kept the uncommitted in here against their will, he risked them spreading disillusion and dissent. Lev had spent half his life cooped up with others, and he knew that in such circumstances strains of thought spread and reinforce themselves, positive and negative alike; where willingness and zeal can strengthen the cowardly, disenchantment and grumbling can make doubters of the strongest. Nor was he under any illusions about the personal qualities of many of the little, grasping men who called themselves deputies. Given the choice, Lev wouldn't have shared a jail cell with half of them, let alone a parliamentary building.

Protesters started to gather in the streets around the White House after dark. They came in most of Russia's myriad shapes and sizes – children, old women, rough-featured labourers and young professionals shivering in thin raincoats – and the majority were supporting Lev. Several people carried posters which portrayed Borzov as Hitler, fringe and moustache drawn on, with a vodka glass in his hand, a pentagram between his eyes and the Number of the Beast on his forehead.

It was barely half a year since they – almost certainly even some of the same people – had come here to back the man they now lambasted. Russians like defenders, people who are protecting something, rather than aggressors. Last year, Borzov had protected the Russian people against the antisocial forces of an out-of-touch government; it was Lev's turn now.

# 81

*Thursday, 12 March 1992*
Patriarch Alexei took up the baton of conciliation, offering to chair negotiations between the two sides, and suggesting the Danilovsky Monastery as a suitably neutral location for talks. Portentous in his black robes and white headdress, Alexei's proposal demonstrated how fully the church had been rehabilitated since the atheist years of communism. That the church now felt itself a guarantor of national stability betrayed the feebleness of Russia's political institutions.

Both sides turned him down.

"We're denied basic essentials," Lev said. "Borzov has created a political concentration camp in the centre of Moscow."

"Parliament doesn't exist," Borzov stated. "So how can the president talk to it?"

Alexei asked that Borzov restore parliament's lighting, heating and water supplies.

Lev checked the stockpiles of arms dotted around the White House. Wherever you were in the building, the theory went, it should take you no more than a couple of minutes' brisk walk to reach the nearest weapon. The parliamentary guard had brought some of them. Lev's own 21st Century gang had supplied just as many. There were sixteen hundred automatic rifles, two thousand pistols, twenty machine guns and five grenade launchers in the White House alone, not counting the hundreds, perhaps thousands, hanging from the necks and shoulders of those outside.

Every time Lev looked out, the numbers flocking to his cause seemed to have grown: there were three battalions of Moscow reservists, one hundred crack troops who'd been serving in Moldova, police troops back from Riga, a detachment of Cossacks, and paramilitaries from the Workers of Russia Union.

Further out, hemming the building in on all four sides, were the police.

Alice stared at the television screen until her eyes began to fuzz, then she went to the window and looked out towards the west, as though if she stared long and hard enough, the intervening buildings would crumble and she'd be able to see the White House, ringed like Saturn with guards and police: arena, battleground, vortex, manifestation of this insane place that jabbed at her like a wire in her blood.

Once again she was watching history unfold. That was all it was. She wasn't thinking of Lev, leading the resistance; she didn't even care what happened to him. Wasn't, didn't. He could die in there for all she cared. Perhaps it would be better if he did. He wasn't in her life any more, so what did it matter either way?

Like all stand-offs, the siege was at once excruciatingly boring and unbearably tense. Minutes crawled, hours flew. The only thing that everyone knew was this: the moment the first shot was fired, the situation would take off like a rocket leaving Baikonur, and there'd be no holding it.

Alexei tried again to find common ground. Borzov refused to talk until Lev surrendered all the arms in the White House; Lev refused to talk until Borzov reversed parliament's dissolution.

Borzov summoned Sabirzhan to the Kremlin and, by presidential decree, placed him in charge of Red October. Sabirzhan's efforts at ruining the auction were history. He and Borzov were united in their hatred of Lev, and as ever, an enemy's enemy was a friend.

Lev's power at the distillery was absolute when he was there, but in his absence Red October was simply getting on with it – not without confusion or regret, perhaps, but those at the bottom in Russia keep going, no matter what happens up above. The workers didn't have time to worry about politics and infighting; their job was to work, to make vodka.

Lev had checked out the options for escape and evasion in case Borzov persuaded the army to storm the White House. He didn't let on to the deputies how flimsy their choices were. The building had a bomb bunker – it had been built when fears of an American nuclear strike had been very real – but the doors were hermetically sealed and no one knew how to open them. The metro passed directly underneath the building – it was on the orbital line, between

Kievskaya and Krasnopresnenskaya stations – but the tunnel from the White House basement to the line was rumoured to be mined. If Lev came out of the White House, therefore, it would have to be on to the street, and he'd only do that in victory, if Borzov had capitulated. If he left the building in defeat, he wouldn't be alive. He would die fighting, but he wouldn't surrender.

The White House's power and water came back on late in the afternoon. It was a concession to which Borzov had agreed reluctantly, and only when he'd been convinced that continuing deprivation was simply making Lev appear a martyr. He soured the pill by adding an ultimatum: "To the criminals still inside the White House – you have until midday tomorrow to leave the building. Anatoly Nikolayevich personally assures you safe passage if you comply. After that, he will not be responsible for your fate."

With lights suddenly blazing and radiators creaking into action, rumours and counter-rumours raced through the newly lit corridors like the west wind: Borzov had surrendered, Borzov was preparing for an attack, the American special forces were on the roof. Curiously, the restoration of the building's power and water seemed to be hindering rather than helping Lev's attempts to maintain spirits. By imbuing the defenders with a proper Russian sense of suffering, the cold and darkness had fostered a spirit of solidarity. Now, people were beginning to succumb to siege mentality in all its worst forms.

Lev called everyone into the chamber again, the better to show that his authority here was absolute. "We must remain sober!" he yelled. "Whether that imbecile Borzov tries to attack us may depend on how drunk he gets. Heaven preserve us if we lower ourselves to his level."

There was an argument away to Lev's left. It spun and escalated, sucking in more participants as it gathered momentum like a giant snowball, fragmenting, reabsorbing, reproducing. The deputies were middle-aged men two decades out of shape, and they fought that way, flailing ineffectually, pulling jackets and shirts over each other's heads, swaying this way and that, and probably managing to land less than half a dozen decent blows between them.

Lev waded into the mêlée, selected the two men nearest the middle, took a collar in each of his hands and cracked their heads together with such force that only his restraining grip kept them from bouncing halfway across the chamber. When he let them go, they dropped to the floor like sacks of grain. The others stopped fighting.

"That's enough!" he shouted.

He sat in the speaker's chair and led the deputies in a medley of old Russian folk songs: "Rustling Reeds", "Slender Roman-Tree", "Crimson Moon" and the "Song of Stenka Razin". His voice cracked when he smiled through the words; they were going to win this thing.

The police had been ordered not to fire. Everyone remembered what had happened on Defenders of the Motherland Day, when some-one had been panicked into pulling his trigger. The memory seemed to inflame rather than frighten the protesters. They began to push against the police, confident that they of all people wouldn't be up for a fight, and indeed they weren't. The policemen glanced at each other with wide and frightened eyes. This wasn't what they'd joined the force for, this wasn't something that responded to bribery or extortion, and they were massively outnumbered to boot, the thinnest of blue lines without any back-up from OMON black or army green. The retreat began almost imperceptibly, with the protesters disarming some policemen and beating others. As the pressure became greater, the line heaved and stretched and cracked, the policemen fleeing with their greatcoats flapping, half marching and half running, looking like frightened penguins. One of them tripped and fell. Rodya and Galina, who'd come to support Lev, jumped instantly on to the fallen cop – not to hurt him, but to prevent him from being trampled to death.

# 82

*Friday, 13 March 1992*

A faint unearthly pallor stole over the silent streets, dimming the watch-fires: the shadow of a terrible dawn grey-rising over Moscow. Superficially all was quiet, all the complex routine of humdrum life proceeded as usual. But beneath the surface, day broke on a city in the wildest excitement and confusion, a population heaving up in long hissing swells of storm. Ever-widening circles of unrest and excitement, another revolution, its difficult and fateful hour, the likelihood of its ultimate greatness.

Channel One had pulled all scheduled programmes and was showing *Swan Lake* – a bad omen if ever there was one; Tchaikovsky is the nation's harbinger of wars and coups d'état. At seven o'clock,

*Swan Lake* came off and Borzov came on to declare a state of emergency in Moscow, now divided into seven military districts: Borovistsky, Stretensky, Tverskoy, Vorobyory, Tryokhgorya, Taganka and Lefortovo.

The army had taken over the functions of the police, and Moscow was filling with troops by the hour. The first T-72 tanks were seen on the outskirts at dawn, and the pale sun was burning up the east by the time they came down Kutuzovsky Prospekt, slowly so as not to lose control on the slippery concrete, and pulled up on the Kalininsky Bridge opposite the White House. This was the same route the coup plotters had taken the previous year; the same route, indeed, along which Napoleon had entered Moscow in 1812.

The troops, most of them no more than boys with eyes streaming in the wind, came from all over: the Fourth Guards Kantemirovskaya Tank Division in Narofominsk, the 27th Motorised Infantry Division in Moscow, the 106th Guards Airborne at Tulskaya, and the Second Guards Tamanskaya Motorised Infantry Division in Golitsyno, widely seen as the toughest of them all. Their commanders had orders to fire if necessary.

The army had taken control of all the main bridges and arterial routes into Moscow, leaving snaking white tracks on the road as they patrolled the city. They assumed their positions round the White House, from where the police had been chased the previous evening. The building has nineteen storeys, and the tank barrels nodded slowly as they took sightings, as if wondering idly where to aim first. The message to the parliamentary guard who still circled the building was clear: the posturing would soon be over, it was time for action.

Midday, the deadline for the deputies' surrender, came and went. Borzov's resolve ebbed and flowed like the tide. He'd thrown down the ultimatum without a second thought. Now it had passed, he was suddenly more circumspect. There was so much that could go wrong, and he hadn't yet had the familiar flash of resolution which accompanied all his greatest decisions. Should he give the parliamentarians another ultimatum? Should he order still more troops into the area, to turn up the pressure? Or should he just go in with what he had, and perhaps catch them off guard by striking fast? The latter made his stomach jump; he was not naturally trigger-happy, and he knew that, irrespective of political persuasion, every Russian would thank him if he resolved the stand-off without resorting to violence.

He needed to clear his head, so he went to the Kremlin banya, by repute the most luxurious steam bath in all Russia, with benches upholstered in leather and thick pillows strewn across the floor. The heater was as wide as a truck and reached three metres to the ceiling; inside glowed a massive heap of round rocks, cannonballs in miniature. Borzov threw some vodka on the heated rocks, inhaled the vapours lovingly, and poured himself a hundred grams.

"Herald!" Borzov threw open the door. "*Herald!*" A herald was someone sent to buy liquor for his friends. One of the presidential guard came running. Borzov, his vodka face as round as a turnip, squinted at him and then began to shout again, even though the two men were no more than a metre apart. "Go fetch me another bottle, on the double. Go!"

Home alone, Irk watched the pictures from the White House with a sense of numb dislocation. It was happening again, he thought. Was this the way it would always be with Russians, their pretensions to civilised behaviour torn away every time an argument became intractable?

Denisov had ordered the police to support Borzov, and officially Irk was still bound by that. Not that he'd needed to be told, of course. If he, a progressive Estonian, wouldn't back the forces of reform, then surely no one would. But if there was to be an assault – and with all the troops involved there *would* be, maybe not today but certainly tonight, under cover of darkness – it would, Irk thought, simply expose Borzov as being no different from all his predecessors. If he was prepared to spill blood in pursuit of untrammelled power, if he was prepared to bomb his own people, he'd be no better than what he'd beheld.

Irk felt his way through thickets of unfamiliar feelings. Sure, Lev did bad things, but didn't everyone? He also did many good things. He stood by his own, he stuck rigidly to his code of honour, and he was a genuine philanthropist – look at the children's home, for instance. It was no hardship to respect and admire him. Technically, Lev was a criminal. So? The whole nation was becoming criminalised, just to survive. And at least Lev and his lot were competent, unlike Denisov and the halfwits at Petrovka. There was nothing Russia needed more than competence.

Irk had been unable to stop Karkadann, but perhaps he could make a difference now. There were few people more dangerous, he thought as he went to find his chemical protection suit, than idealists who've lost their heroes.

* * *

387

Outside the main entrance to the White House, Sveta scowled at the troops through her make-up and emptied on to the bonnet of the nearest tank the food from her shopping bag. She began feeding and scolding the soldiers simultaneously, as only a babushka can. "Who've you come to shoot at? Your mothers? Is that what we've brought you up for? Here, you – take this sausage. You look like you haven't eaten in months."

A colonel stepped forward to usher Sveta away, and she rounded on him. "You stay out of this, fatface," she snapped.

"Go home, Grandma," he said. "Your place is in the kitchen, making a borscht. Leave the politics to the men."

"We've been doing that since the time of Catherine the Great. A fat lot of good it's done us."

The colonel, knowing when he was beaten, stepped back.

His temporal efforts at negotiation having failed, Patriarch Alexei turned to peacemaking on an altogether higher plane. Trailed by priests whose black robes gave them the appearance of carrion crows, he went to the Yelokhovsky Cathedral and paraded the Vladimir Icon of the Mother of God. An image of the Virgin and the infant Christ, it is the capital's holiest icon. Many believe that it saved Moscow from Tamerlane. Now, clutching the precious figure tightly to him, Alexei prayed that Russia be preserved from catastrophe yet again.

It took Irk more than an hour to make the journey. He had to travel underground the whole way to be sure of avoiding the troops, who seemed to be on every street corner and at the entrance to every metro station. He was a senior investigator, of course, so it would have been damnably bad luck had they done more than check his ID and wave him on. But bad luck seemed to be Irk's speciality, and he decided not to take the risk.

The sewer flow seemed lower than before, as though Moscow itself was constipated while it waited to see who would triumph. Irk waded through cascades straight and spiralled, his progress measured by the baffles which appeared at intervals in the pipes. Hurrying through areas where the cast-iron pipes were badly corroded, he kicked up a splash around fish without either fins or eyes. And all this time, he saw no one. Only a cave-painting rainbow mural with red guitars dancing with musical notes betrayed that there was life down here.

He thought of Moscow's wobbly foundations: alluvial soils, the substrate pliable and sandy. On top of that, the water table's too high. There are underground lakes fed entirely by leaking plumbing and atrocious drainage. The bridge near Belorussky Station could tumble down at any minute, and it wasn't the only one. Every day, the city lurched closer to collapse. Well, Irk thought, he didn't need to be a speleologist to know *that*.

Perhaps he should give up being an investigator and run tours of the sewers: short ones, long ones, shallow ones, deep ones. How long would people want to stay down here? Less than an hour wouldn't really be worth his while. How about a whole night? He'd get them to pay twice: once at the start, and once to show them the right way out instead of abandoning them down here. He could do exhibitions too, in the city administration building or the Ostrovsky Museum. A cabaret under Red Square, or a safety-training centre for new initiates. He could go to the International Speleological Society in Alabama, get a new Land Rover, new suits, helmets from France – they were five hundred dollars each, but they were the best.

This was no hobby; it was a state of the soul. These places where he went were full of darkness and disease, collected there like a sponge. When he heard the water babbling in the sewers, it was as though he was listening to Moscow's ancestors. He heard their whispers bubbling up, and he was closer to them. People thought they were independent of these forces, but they weren't. They all depended on the underground. Like it or not, what had come before them, determined them.

It took Irk three wrong turns before he found what he was looking for: a door which led to the White House. He'd discovered it the previous year by chance, while looking for a way up to the Devyati Muchenikov church. The door was locked, naturally. Irk felt in his pocket for the skeleton key issued to all senior investigators and eased it gently into the lock. He felt the tremor as the tumblers clicked into place, and then he twisted the key anti-clockwise, hoping that the door hadn't rusted solid. The lock gave way. Irk gripped the door and pulled; it unpeeled itself reluctantly from the frame and gaped open before him.

The tunnel sloped upwards and was narrow, but higher than he'd expected. He had to do no more than duck his head and bend his knees slightly to walk through it, balancing on the balls of his feet to stop himself slipping backwards down the gradient. Navigating by the beam of his head torch, he went about twenty paces, turned right and then left again in a dogleg, went another twenty paces or so, and found himself at another door. This one gave way more easily; surprisingly so, he thought, realising that it hadn't even been locked. He stepped through it and found himself in a basement as dark, cold and damp as the access pipe had been, but this was unmistakeably terra firma. He was back once more from the reverse world.

Irk was just wondering whether or not to take off his chemical protection suit when there was a sudden flood of white light, and with it shouts and the sounds of safety catches being clicked – at least the catches had been on in the first place, he thought absurdly, as he tried simultaneously to cover his eyes and put his hands above his head. "Down!" rough voices yelled. "Down!"

Irk sank to his knees and then – less voluntarily, when someone kicked him hard in the back – to his stomach. He waited to be frisked, but none of them seemed particularly keen, perhaps, he realised belatedly, because his clothes were smeared with some of Moscow's choicest effluent.

"Who are you?" they barked. "What do you want?"

"My name is Juku Irk," he said, thinking that he sounded unbearably pompous. "I'm a . . ." he was going to say 'senior investigator with the procurator's service', but Denisov's public commitment to Borzov made him reconsider – "I've come to help Lev."

"He knows you?"

"Yes."

"What was your name again?"

"Irk. Juku Irk. But tell him I've come in a personal capacity. Be sure to tell him that."

He felt like Rudolf Hess, sneaking off to England without telling Hitler. Footsteps turned and faded, someone going to tell Lev what they'd found. When Irk raised his head to look around, a foot on the back of his skull dissuaded him. They were clearly taking no chances.

If Lev didn't want to see him, Irk thought, he'd be as dead as Lenin.

No one spoke. The silence stretched and stretched. Cities could have risen and fallen in the time it took for the footsteps to come back.

"Get up," said the same voice which had asked his name. "You're wearing clothes under that orange thing?"

"Yes."

"Then take it off."

Irk pushed himself to his feet and looked around. There were

390

four of them, all unshaven, pale and twitchy. Their eyes darted around the room like mosquitoes, never settling on one place for more than a moment. He was lucky that they hadn't shot him on sight.

When the chemical protection suit was on the floor, they took him to see Lev.

It was like walking through a military barracks. Every corner they turned and every staircase they climbed seemed to be guarded by two or three armed men, sometimes more; most of them affecting the sort of overly studied nonchalance which only the very nervous can attain. They were sure that an attack was coming, and that even the thousands of small arms they'd stockpiled would be no match for heavy tank and mortar fire. Their only hope was that Lev could somehow manage to change the army's mind before the first shots were fired. Failing that, the most they could wish for was to take some of the enemy with them as they died defending the White House.

Lev was in one of the conference rooms near the middle of the building. He was drumming his fingers on the tabletop and staring into space – gathering his energy or letting hope ebb away, it was impossible to tell.

"What do you want?" Lev said, in a voice devoid of either irritation or inquisitiveness.

"To help you," Irk replied.

"How?"

"By getting you out of here."

"I don't want to get out of here."

"Lev, Russia needs you, and it needs you alive, to help drag it back to its feet. You dying in the rubble here is no good to anyone."

"No. I've pledged that I'll leave here only in victory or death. These people are risking their lives for me, I can't leave them. And what do *you* care about us anyway, Investigator? You're Estonian, aren't you?"

*What do you care?* The question pricked at Irk. Why was he placing himself in the middle of the fight for a country that wasn't even his? Russia was under his skin, he guessed, and he hadn't even realised it until now. The more people who reminded him he wasn't Russian, the more compelled he felt to compensate.

"Why don't you believe in Borzov?" Lev added.

"I did."

"But . . . ?"

"And now I don't. The emperor's new clothes, I guess."

It existed in everyone, Irk thought, even in the most publicly infallible: those moments of weakness when the spring recoiled. Whether others saw these moments or not depended on little more than chance and timing. Irk saw the doubt in Lev's face, and he pounced. "Listen."

"To what?"

"What can you hear?"

People moving, pipes bubbling, floorboards moaning softly, an ambient hum; the cadence of a city, in other words. "Nothing."

"Exactly. It's too quiet."

The word leapt from person to person, wildfire through a building: "Attack is imminent. We're observing a blackout – extinguish all lights. Those with gas masks, prepare to put them on. Those without should tie wet cloths over their noses and mouths." In the sudden gloom, there was the stir of hundreds of people slipping on goggles, and tying scarves and handkerchiefs over their faces. After a moment, the lights were replaced with tiny red sparks which glowed and waned.

Lev stifled a laugh. Only the Russians, when prompted by the twin imperatives of staying invisible and minimising the effects of a gas attack, would consider cigarettes indispensable necessities rather than shortcuts to the next world.

There were four T-80 tanks on the Kalininsky Bridge, their turrets swivelling with the synchronicity of well-drilled chorus girls and unleashing 150mm cannon fire which scorched the White House black. The first shells hit the building with dull *crumps*, sounds which seemed too quiet and subdued to cause all the ensuing damage. Windows shattered and wept soot, walls and floors shuddered, and water pipes snapped and flooded hallways, extinguishing some of the fires which the shells had started.

The civilian protesters outside were the first to go. They'd seen off the police, but artillery was an entirely different matter. They ran for their lives, dispersing into the surrounding streets. The soldiers let them go, they had more pressing concerns. The parliamentary guard and other paramilitaries stayed at their posts until falling debris had killed several of them and injured many more; then they retreated into the White House. Most of the shells were hitting the building in its upper storeys, too high to seriously threaten its structural integrity. Perhaps the tanks were competing to see who could knock the clock tower off.

The army bombarded the White House until last light, by which time the commanders reckoned that both building and occupants were suitably softened up. As the last threads of day snapped, all television feeds were diverted away from the White House, to prevent any of Lev's men from seeing too much of what was going on outside. The troops cleared holes in the barricades through which Spetsnaz special forces made their way to the foot of the White House itself. They placed plastic explosive against the doors, each connected to the next by lengths of detonation cord.

The infantry assault began half an hour after sundown. One of the Spetsnaz boys lit the detonation cord, which burnt down at six kilometres per second. Even around a building with a diameter as large as the White House, it looked to the naked eye as though the explosions were actually rather than very nearly simultaneous. The soldiers came in hard and fast behind the explosions, throwing stun grenades into the suddenly gaping doorways and sweeping the corridors with gunfire as their barrel-mounted torches cut through the smoke. There was no one at the entrances, which was strange – they'd expected to be hurdling a few corpses fresh from the explosions. The defenders must have worked out what was coming and retreated further inside.

The troops raced down empty passageways, careful to cover each other at every corner and again before every doorway. Again, they found no one. There wasn't even any defensive fire for them to return. The first seven floors were all empty. There *were* people above that, but they were all dead, lacerated by flying glass or simply mangled by shells – the unlucky ones who'd taken the brunt of the bombardment. This was becoming decidedly strange. There had been more than a thousand people inside the White House, most of them armed, and they'd surely not go down without a fight; but they were nowhere to be seen.

It took the Spetsnaz and their less elite colleagues forty minutes to search the building from top to bottom and report, with ill-disguised incredulity, that the defenders had simply vanished.

At that very moment, when the army commanders on the Kalininsky Bridge were spluttering with incoherent rage at their troops' reports, Lev was emerging from a manhole on Gasheka Street, north of the zoo. Once he'd realised there was time for all the defenders to get out safely, he'd needed little persuading to follow

Irk's plan. He had known the troops would keep up the bombard-ment until nightfall; there was no military reason to send the infantry in during daylight, and only an eventuality such as killing hostages or some other political imperative would have seen them make the assault before last light.

Irk had led the defenders out through the sewage tunnel. The entire process had taken two hours, each man going through a couple of paces ahead of the next, moving fast but never rushing. All Irk had needed to do was get them clear of the military cordon around the White House; from there they could find their own way to the surface and continue the journey above ground, using the gathering darkness to dodge the army patrols where necessary. None of them had protective suits, of course, and they'd probably all fall ill in a day or two. For a safe escape, Irk reckoned, it was cheap at the price.

Borzov was furious. He ordered every law enforcement officer in Moscow to look for the escaped deputies – particularly Lev – and said that any policeman who returned empty-handed would be fired. Then he moved to consolidate his position by placing himself in charge of the National Security Council and introducing a whole raft of new measures against crime.

Police could conduct spot checks at will, detain suspects without charge for up to a month, search offices and dwellings without a court order, and examine the financial affairs of anyone suspected of involvement in organised crime. Residence permits were to be reintroduced in every city of more than a million people. Judges would be given improved protection. The tax police would be run by a special high-level enforcement body called the Temporary Extraordinary Commission, or VChK – a name deliberately designed to strike fear into tax cheats; the VChK was what the KGB had initially been called.

"I am power," Borzov proclaimed. "I'm not going to be pushed to one side. My task is to get everybody in hand and tell them all who's the boss. If they don't like it, they can send in their resignations."

The police – a round dozen of Yerofeyev's men, armed to the teeth – came to Patriarch's Ponds. "Have you seen Lev?" they asked.

"As if I'd have that dirty fucker here," she yelled. "As if! You can fuck off, the lot of you." They paid her no mind, sweeping her aside and turning the place upside down. "He's seven foot tall," Alice shrieked. "There's nowhere here big enough to hide him."

"It's nothing personal," Yerofeyev said.

"Don't be ridiculous. Of course it's personal."

"On the contrary. We're looking everywhere: at Red October, in the Kotelniki penthouse, at Testarossa's dacha, in every upmarket hotel and restaurant in the city." He didn't add the obvious rider: so far they'd come up with lint.

"What will you do to him if you find him?"

"*When* we find him."

"Whatever."

"Arrest him, of course."

"Not kill him?"

"Of course not."

"You were prepared to kill him a few hours ago – him and everybody else in the White House."

The police left mud on the carpets, dirty handprints on the walls, and ice between Alice and a gloweringly resentful Lewis. Having his apartment trashed and his privacy violated because of someone his wife loved was adding insult to injury.

# 83

*Saturday, 14 March 1992*

The Russian Orthodox Church buries its dead on Saturday. Thousands turned out to remember those lost the previous day, and to protest at Borzov's heavy-handedness, both in the way he'd handled the siege and the measures he'd announced after its resolution. In front of a still-smouldering White House the pavement was dotted with impromptu shrines of flowers, icons, fruits, bread, chocolate and cigarettes. The mourners came in dignity and silence, but their disapproval was clear. There was no euphoria now the stand-off was over; just shame, embarrassment and self-loathing. "How could we Russians so such things do each other?" they asked.

Some of the demonstrators carried banners with Lev's picture and the slogan *Fucked by the Party, Fucked by the Army*. Many of the deputies had been arrested or given themselves up, but Lev had gone to ground, and the image was all that anyone had of him. That, and a message he'd sent: "I ask forgiveness from the fallen men's families and friends; forgiveness that I was unable to protect them from the tragedy which befell them. As they rest in peace, I bow low before their will, their civic courage and the power of their spirit."

It wasn't the slightest bit strange that a gangster should be a popular hero. When Russians looked at gangsters, they saw the bold, the reckless, the forceful; they saw men who bent circumstances rather than let circumstances bend them. They idolised them even while they resented their success and methods.

It was enough to make Irk wish Karkadann was still alive. Four people in a filthy tenement apartment had been holding a drinking session, knocking back whatever they could get their hands on: vodka, eau de cologne, brake fluid, windscreen cleaner. The participants were a married couple, Valdemar and Astra Khrynin, and two brothers, Grigori and Pyotr Stonkus.

In one of Petrovka's shabbier interview rooms, Valdemar was doing all the talking. This was unsurprising, as he was the only one capable of coherent speech. Astra had attacked the arresting officers and was now restricting her testimony to a string of highly creative expletives; Pyotr Stonkus was under sedation; and Grigori Stonkus was in at least eight separate pieces.

According to Valdemar, the drinking session had proceeded apace until the brothers Stonkus passed out. "Drank themselves into their own asses," Valdemar said. "Astra and I, we kept going." After a few hours, possibly with a break for sex (he couldn't remember), the happy couple had become ravenous. "My innards were playing a march, I tell you. And what was there to eat in the house? Fuck all."

What else would one do in such a situation? They'd sized up the unconscious brothers, decided that Grigori was the fleshier (a marginal decision, Valdemar conceded), and set about him with an axe. Grigori's flesh had gone into the cooking pots, everything else into the heating furnace which the entire apartment block shared. By the time the meat was ready, Pyotr had come round. Where was Grisha? Gone home, they'd said. All the more for them, he'd said; he was as hungry as a horse. What were they cooking, anyway?

They'd told him it was dog.

Alerted by the stink from the furnace, the neighbours had called the police. The police had arrived, worked out that the Khrynins' haute cuisine was from a more elevated life form than the canine, displayed quite astonishing insensitivity in sharing this information with Pyotr, and then called homicide. "Why waste so much meat?" Valdemar asked. "It was very fresh."

Irk was still trying to think of a reply when the door opened and the duty sergeant beckoned him outside. "Can't it wait?" Irk said.

"Afraid not."

Irk sighed, got up, and followed the duty sergeant out into the corridor. "What is it?"

The sergeant swallowed, his Adam's apple like a ballcock. "Another one."

"Another what?"

"Another child. In the sewers. A girl. Dead."

It had started again. It *couldn't* have started again. The corpse would be an old one, killed before Karkadann's death and only found now. The corpse would be a new one; there was a copycat on the loose. Logic and emotion battered each other for primacy. As had happened too often recently for his liking, Irk found that emotion was winning.

Endless corridors, ceilings dripping, the uneven light of torches. Suddenly there were sea monsters flapping at Irk's face: tentacles curling out to sucker him, fins which could slice a limb clean off, serrated teeth sharp as a saw's blade, unblinking eyes boring into him. The shock made him want to scream, but as he looked closer at the monsters he saw that they were squids and sharks suspended motionless in formalin, and there were thick sheets of glass between him and them. A sign informed him that he was in the Academy of Oceanology warehouse. In all his years down here, he'd never even heard of it, but then again there were a million kilometres of sewer tunnels; Irk was amazed that anyone found anything here, ever.

The girl's body was lying near an interceptor chamber designed to catch oil, grease and chemicals before they did too much damage to the sewers. The worker who'd found her stood uncertainly nearby, shifting his weight as though he wanted to be elsewhere. His face, pouched in dim light and shy beneath a peaked cap, was almost invisible.

"When did you find her?" Irk asked.

"Couple of hours ago."

"What are you doing down here?"

"Stopping the pipes from collapsing. You name it, we're doing it: repointing mortar joints, replacing defective brickwork, pressure grouting, installing a plastic lining. You see, the pipes in this part of the system are made of fireclay –"

"I couldn't care less what the pipes –"

"– which absorbs water more readily than stoneware, and so isn't as strong. Fireclay needs glazing with salt, but you can't find salt for love or money now; a bit ironic, eh, for all those poor bastards sent to the mines?"

Elbowing the crime-scene photographer out of the way, Irk squatted on his haunches, careful to keep the seat of his trousers from dragging in the shallow stream of detritus. He shone his torch on the corpse, and the last vestiges of his hope fled with the light. The girl had only just begun to decompose. He reckoned she'd been killed twenty-four hours ago, forty-eight at the most. Karkadann had been dead ten days; he couldn't possibly have had anything to do with this one, who looked just like her predecessors, the hammer and sickle scored into a chest white with blood loss.

There was more: two blood-stained rings on the girl's stomach, both perfect circles, about ten centimetres in diameter. They looked as though they'd been caused by the impression of a cylindrical container, in the same way a coffee cup marks a desk.

Blood. Containers. Blood.

All the bodies had been partially exsanguinated, though that wasn't unusual for murder victims; even the smallest wound could leak a surprising amount of blood. But what if the exsanguination was deliberate? Blood was a valuable commodity in Moscow, Irk thought, and black-market prices were high, especially for uncontaminated plasma.

The photographer bumped against Irk, almost toppling him over. "Oi!" Irk said. "Watch it."

The man didn't answer; he was too busy snapping away. Irk thought that the photographer at his own wedding had taken fewer pictures than this.

"You need to put a ruler in there," he told the snapper. "There'll be no scale otherwise."

"Don't have one." The accent was a Minsk one – trust a Belarussian to be difficult.

"Then use your foot."

"I know how to do my job, OK?"

It's standard crime-scene procedure: every shot is taken twice, once with a scale to show the size of the object, once without in case the scale itself blocks a piece of evidence.

"What's your name?" Irk asked.

"Sluchek."

"Well, Sluchek, found any extraneous items?"

"Hundreds." The camera shifted slightly against Sluchek's face as he spoke.

"Remember to light all footprints from the side."

"There aren't any."

"The detail doesn't show up unless you do."

"I said, there aren't any."

"There must be. You think he levitates?"

Sluchek ignored Irk and kept on clicking. His photographic technique was as therapeutic as his character was abrasive; a gentle flex in his index finger as the lens blinked, the graceful crook of his thumb as the film wound on. Flex, click, crook. Flex, click, crook.

The tumblers fell in Irk's mind with the same mechanical simplicity. In long minutes of virtually continuous picture-taking, Sluchek hadn't stopped once to change the film.

Irk took two quick strides and tore the camera from Sluchek's face. The exposure meter boasted a big fat zero. Irk felt down the side for the release lever and sprung the camera open. The magazine gawped empty at him.

Irk shook the camera angrily. "You could roll a ball through it."

Sluchek shrugged. Irk prodded him in the chest, following as the man backed away, a slow dance round a child's corpse. "You sold the films on the black market, eh? And in a few hours' time, you'd have told me that someone had mixed the wrong chemicals in the darkroom and ruined the exposures. No wonder you fuckers want to be part of Russia again. You must fit right in here." He slammed the camera into Sluchek's hand. Its back lolled open, a dog's tongue.

"Are all Estonians patronising bastards, or is it just you?"

Irk swiped the air in front of Sluchek's face. "Fuck off out of here. Let me do my job."


Irk arrived at the Belgrade Hotel just in time. The week Lev had given Zhorzh to leave Moscow was almost up. Another ten minutes, and Zhorzh would have been on his way to Sheremetyevo; another couple of hours, and he'd have been in the air, bound for Grozny.

Breathlessly, Irk told Zhorzh what he'd found in the sewers. Zhorzh thought for a long time before answering – at least, it seemed to Irk like a long time, though in reality it was probably less than a minute. "It was never us," Zhorzh said simply.

"*What?*"

"Never. We'd no idea who was doing it, or why."

"But you claimed responsibility."

"Of course. It suited our purposes."

Irk shook his head, more to clear the fog than in disagreement with Zhorzh. "You wanted people to think that of you?"

"Like Karkadann told you, Investigator: we're Chechens. They think that of us anyway."

"OK. Tell me this: if it wasn't you, why did you try and scare me into surrendering the case?"

Zhorzh ran a hand through the white streak in his hair. "*Because* it wasn't us. Karkadann knew that if you dug around long enough, you'd realise all the evidence against us was circumstantial. Worse, you might find the real killer. The moment you did, all the pressure we were placing on Lev would have dissolved. It wasn't that we feared you proving we were responsible; we feared you finding out that it *wasn't* us."

Onwards, onwards; to stop, even to slow down, would have forced Irk to confront the humiliation of having got things so terribly wrong.

Investigators know surgeons, it's an occupational hazard of the job. Irk went from hospital to hospital, asking – in confidence, of course – what they knew of black-market blood. Some denied any knowledge outright; what they didn't say couldn't get them into trouble. Others hinted at the truth, leaving Irk to pick his way through shifting shapes of information and evasion. Yes, they'd heard it was a problem in other hospitals, but not here, heavens no, their own procedures were well tested and thorough.

Only one surgeon was totally frank with him, and if that was because he was American and therefore used to transparency, or if it was because Irk, having seen a photograph of the man's wife on his desk, had remarked that he'd had the pleasure of meeting her and that her beauty was matched only by her charm, well, so be it; a man got his breaks where he could. Lewis' accent made some words hard for Irk to understand, but that was offset by the slowness of his cadence.

"No offence to your country, Investigator . . ." he said.

"I'm Estonian. It's not my country."

"Even better. Black market? Yes, it's a problem. I had to sack someone the other day for raiding our supplies and selling them on. And of course you have to check all incoming blood too – you can't simply accept the supplier's word that it's safe. I've had to throw out stock that's contaminated, diseased, improperly refrigerated or otherwise substandard."

Children's blood was less likely to be substandard, Irk supposed; children had less time and opportunity to pollute themselves with vodka and heroin and AIDS.

"You deal with the suppliers directly?"

"You know how this place works better than I do, Investigator. Even the middlemen have middlemen. I keep well away from them."

Of course you do, Irk thought. You're American; your hands are cleaner than Pontius Pilate's.

"You saw the container marks on the body, I take it?" Sidorouk said.

"I've just been round hospitals asking about black-market blood."

Sidorouk paused. "I wouldn't dream of making suggestions, Juku, but . . ."

"You're going to anyway, aren't you?"

Sidorouk gestured at the cadaver. "Look at her neck." Irk did so. It was dotted with small tracts of dried blood. "Closer, down at the throat." Whorls of dark brown, smeared on the skin. "Now the left temple, next to the wound." A scab of desiccated saliva.

Saliva, whorls: licking, Irk thought, licking, tasting . . . The connection came in a rush. The killer wasn't taking the blood to sell on the black market; he was taking it to *drink*.

If a vampire was going to strike anywhere, Sidorouk said, Russia was as good a place as any. Looming large in Russian folklore is a bogeyman named Myertovjec, a brute with a purple face whose victims are the sons of werewolves or witches, or those who've cursed their own father or the church. Myertovjec responds to soft and hard treatment alike: if sprinkling poppy seeds along the road from the tomb to the deceased's house doesn't work, a stake through the chest to nail the beast to the coffin usually does the trick.

Vampires are supposed to command weaker wills; this at least was something to which Irk could relate. This vampire had drained Irk's energy even as he'd dominated his thoughts. Irk's lassitude had been debilitating. Some days, he'd climbed the stairs to his office only by grabbing the banister and pulling himself up arm over arm, as though hauling an anchor aboard a boat.

Why children? They were smaller than adults, of course, and easier to subdue. But why their *blood*? For rejuvenation? Reinvention? Was the vampire – the *killer*, vampires don't exist, he reminded himself – was the killer harking back to his own childhood, an idyll, real or imagined? Or perhaps he was revisiting the sins of a dreadful adolescence on these children?

*He?* Why shouldn't the killer be a woman? Sidorouk recounted the tale of the Transylvanian countess Erzsebet Bathory, who killed more than 650 young women and bathed in their blood, which she believed would keep her forever young. She'd been sentenced to life imprisonment in a windowless room, and had died there three years later.

401

The killer could easily be a woman, Irk thought. What about menstruation? Women lose blood every month, would a deranged female want to replace that somehow? The victims were children; did pregnancy have anything to do with it?

No, this was ridiculous. How would Irk know, one way or the other? He was a man, men know nothing about women, and the police force was a good generation away from being enlightened enough to employ women in anything higher than a clerical capacity.

So, assume that the killer's a man as opposed to a woman or a supernatural being. He would cast a shadow and have a reflection, and Irk would find him through detective work, steady and prosaic. The killer wasn't going to be a creature who could fly, or hypnotise a beautiful woman out of bed in the middle of a thunderstorm; he wouldn't be able to turn into mist and slither through keyholes, or command the elements, or survive on human blood alone. He wouldn't be as strong as twenty men, nor possessed of everlasting youth. He wouldn't be the master of bats, moths, wolves, rats, foxes and owls, and he wouldn't climb walls like insects.

Irk was sure of another thing: the killer wouldn't cease voluntarily. Only his own death or capture could contain the perverse fires within him that led him to kill. He was the ultimate consumer, unfettered by any kind of restraints apart from the need not to get caught, and he played off the weaknesses and moral contradictions which rent society from top to bottom. The vampire had chosen the darker path, and he was willing to go the distance.

Moscow at night is all shade and shadow, a city of sombre moods whose citizens drift in a void of moral weightlessness. Tverskaya was lined with an army of whores, five or six deep and wearing next to nothing, the cold making their bare legs blue under electric green miniskirts. In Pushkin Square, twelve-year-olds queued for hamburgers at McDonald's and sold them on at a profit. The queues stretched round the block; it was the slowest fast food in the world.

An old woman walked up and down the line, muttering to herself before grabbing Alice by the arm. "I wish my death would come sooner. I won't beg, I won't be pitied. You know why people pity beggars? Because, compared to beggars, they don't seem so pathetic themselves."

*I wish my death would come sooner.* Alice repeated the words to herself as she staggered down the pavement. She needed a permanent touch, like a radio which dissolved into static the moment you removed your hand from the aerial. She needed to be earthed.

*I wish my death would come sooner.* It would solve so many problems, and it would be so easy. All Alice would have to do was climb over the side of a bridge and step off, then down through the thinning ice, a couple of lungfuls of water, and she'd be gone.

You could skate across the surface when the river was frozen over, but in Moscow things moved in four dimensions, and time was taking her under and showing her the dark hearts of existence, as it did to everyone who wasn't just passing through. Maybe she could simply throw herself in front of a train the next time she was in a metro station. Thousands had been killed in the rush to complete the first line in the thirties, what difference would one more make? The metro was brutally efficient; she'd never have to wait more than three minutes.

No, no, it was stupid of her to think this way. However bad she felt, it would never be enough. Alice couldn't conceive of a despair on earth that was sufficiently powerful to extinguish her frenzied, perhaps even indecent, thirst for life.

# 84

*Sunday, 15 March 1992*
The cartoon in *Izvestiya* said it all. Three panels, from left to right: Lenin in ankle boots, because in his days Russia had only been inch-deep in shit; Stalin up to the knees in his trademark cavalry boots; and now Borzov, fishing waders flapping round his thighs as he looked thoughtfully at one of the full bodysuits worn by the sewer maintenance crews.

Borzov was drunk and maudlin. "You know your Shakespeare, Kolya? You know your *Macbeth*? What does a man need in old age? Honour, love, obedience, and a troop of friends. And what's the president got? None of them, that's what. Look outside, Kolya. Those oafs in parliament do untold damage to the nation, but when the president puts them in their place, the people turn against him. Newspapers, televisions, people in the streets with banners, they all say the same thing."

There was little Arkin could do but hear the old man out. He knew the problem perfectly well: the gap between reality and expectation had proved too much for people and president alike. Wounded by his own errors, by the implacable hatred and resistance of his enemies, and most of all by his inability to deliver miracles to this enormous, impoverished country, Borzov was proving too weak to manage the revolution and justify his people's trust.

The Kremlin doctors had suggested that Borzov was manic depressive. There had been depression, inactivity and despair; there had been energy, elation and activity. Nobody had thought out a plan more quickly, carried it out more slowly or abandoned it more easily.

As if deliberately confirming Arkin's fears, Borzov spoke again. "Anatoly Nikolayevich was too hasty in his reaction to the siege, Kolya. Perhaps we should quietly abandon some of these new policies before they become too entrenched."

"Anatoly Nikolayevich, that's absurd. This is what Gorbachev did, remember? Swing from one extreme to the other, make concession after concession. He tried to please everyone and ended up satisfying no one."

"Things are different now."

"Human nature's always the same."

"Why haven't those useless fools found Lev yet?" The discussion was over.

"He's got a network of supporters with no love for the cops. He'll be hard to track down."

"Find him, Kolya. We don't want him running around causing trouble."

The papers were full of the vampire, relaying every blood-engorged detail to their readers with lip-smacking relish and speculating wildly. One organised crime gang had lost a card game to another one, and the stake was fifty children's lives; Jews were sacrificing Christian children for their rituals; the murders were the work of a high-ranking government official who rode around in a black Volga sedan with a special licence plate beginning with the letters SSO – the Russian acronym for *Death to Soviet Children*.

Muscovites drank down every last detail and came back for more. The vampire, Irk thought, could be seen as a convenient form of retribution for the reformists' zeal. Muscovites, Russians, human beings want love, life and power, but in wanting these things they risk exactly the opposite: hate, death and exploitation. To understand this predicament was to understand the vampire, the true symbol of a society in decline and at war with itself.

* * *

Seven hours at Petrovka chasing up leads that went nowhere was enough for anyone. Irk went out west to Vagankovskoye Cemetery, where vampire-hunters armed with crucifixes, spades and stakes of sharpened aspen huddled round small fires and shared bottles of vodka. They were waiting for the creaking of a coffin lid or the sound of moving earth under the snow. The safest and surest way of cutting short a vampire's immortality was to trace it to its lair. They'd already been round the entire cemetery looking for empty coffins into which they could place crucifixes, which would prevent the vampire returning and send it crumbling to dust in the first rays of dawn. Inherent in Russian belief is the concept of the earth's purity and sanctity; the soil will not put up with dead sinners. "Trust the earth not to have you," the cemetery vigilantes muttered to their unseen enemy. "Trust the earth not to have you."

Across the rows of graves, Irk saw a familiar figure. Grateful for the relief, he hurried over like a swimmer striking out for land. "Rodya! What are you doing here?"

Rodion gestured at the nearest two graves. "Mates of mine; died in Afghanistan." There were a couple of women with him, wrapped like mummies against the cold. "These are their mothers, Ira and Lena," Rodion said. "This is Juku – he's an investigator with the prosecutor's office."

"Rodion's a friend of mine," Irk said.

"He's a good man," Ira said. "He always comes here, you know. Twice, three times a week. A lot of them don't bother."

"I wouldn't miss it for the world," Rodion said. "The mothers are always here, Juku. You see one hurrying from the bus in the evening after work, another already sitting by the graveside crying, a third painting the railing round her son's grave. That's how they get to know each other, that's how they got to know me."

Lena handed Irk a piece of paper, half-torn along the lines where it had been folded and unfolded on umpteen occasions. "This is what the government sent me," she said. He opened it and read: *Your son perished while fulfilling his international duty in Afghanistan.* "Not very comforting, is it?" Lena said.

"Tell us what it was like, Rodya," Ira said. "The truth, this time. You never tell us the truth, you lie to save our sensibilities."

"Mama, trust me. You wouldn't want to know the truth unless you'd been there, and if you'd been there you wouldn't have to ask for it."

"Why couldn't *he* have come back and *you* died?" Lena said suddenly, and there was silence, everyone shocked and no one knowing where to look. "I'm sorry, I'm sorry," she said.

"It's OK, Mama," Rodion said. "I understand. I'll see you next time. Come on, Juku."

Irk followed him through the cemetery. "Next time?" he said.

"There's always a next time, because there'll never be one for the poor sods we've come to remember. She'll be there with a bottle of vodka and a thousand apologies, embracing me as if I were her own son, saying over and over how she never meant it, grief does funny things to people, and we'll cry and hug. The mothers at least try to understand, Juku. No one else does, not really. 'We never sent you there,' they say. 'We didn't send you to Afghanistan.'"

Back at the Khruminsches' apartment, they settled down in front of a crime show called *Six Hundred Seconds*, each one counted down on a clock in the corner of the screen while the presenter – Alexander Nevzorov, a former movie stuntman and son of a KGB officer – narrated footage for which no detail seemed too gruesome. That was especially true tonight, when Nevzorov was dedicating every one of those six hundred seconds to the story of the Moscow vampire.

"When the need to kill arises," Nevzorov said, "the vampire can no more decide not to kill than a normal man can decide not to eat when he's hungry or not to drink when he's thirsty. The vampire can make and follow a plan to find a victim, even a subtle and convoluted plan. But until he obtains the release that killing offers, he'll be depressed and irritable, he might suffer from headaches or insomnia. Blood will no longer satiate him, it'll simply intensify the craving, a deadly snowball effect whereby the more he gets, the more he wants."

Like all the best programmes, *Six Hundred Seconds* was from St Petersburg. Moscow journalists couldn't make decent television if their lives depended on it. No matter how sprawlingly enormous it becomes, Moscow will always be a village at heart, retaining peasant superstitions. No wonder the vampire came here, Irk thought, because here people would believe in it. In contrast, Peter is a foreign, prodigal son, ashamed of its country-bumpkin mother. The vampire wouldn't have lasted a second in Peter.

Asleep on the sofa, too tired even to have got undressed, Irk fretted lonely in his nightmare.

He was walking through corridors lit in crimson, pathways to hell.

There were goths and rubber fetishists, men with tapestries of tattoos and women pierced like pincushions. Eyebrows had been shaved off and redrawn in eyeliner; lips were slashed crimson and traced black.

Irk was with a girl called Roza; her cheeks were snowy and her lips scarlet. People greeted Roza warmly, Irk more guardedly; in here, without make-up or ornaments, he was the freak. "You want to stay here," Roza whispered, pulling him into a side room, "we have to make you look normal." She pushed him down into a chair. "This won't take long." She rummaged in a wicker basket, and gave him a make-up job as basic as hers before holding up a mirror.

"You like?" Irk nodded. He thought he looked like a clown.

They went back out into the corridors, and from there into a cavernous hall where a band was playing on an elevated stage strewn with skulls and bones. Irk saw four musicians, stripped to the waist and soaked with sweat. In the pit below the stage, the crowd were loving it. When the singer yelled, Irk saw that his teeth were filed to gleaming points. In cages suspended above the stage, dancers flailed with whips and handcuffs, or writhed upside down, hanging like bats.

The band finished their set with triumphant howls and ran off the stage. In their place came an apparition in sweeping black, a woman with unnervingly real horns sprouting from her hairline.

"Plastic surgery," Roza said. "That's the Mistress, the head of the coven."

"She's young to be in charge, isn't she?"

Roza smiled. "She's eighty."

"Rubbish. She's half that, tops."

The Mistress' voice rang through the speakers. "Mortal life is short, but we are not of this world. We must liberate our souls from human flesh. We drink blood to reaffirm our membership of the religion of rulers. We are vampires, immortal masters of the earth. We drink for power, for surrender, for immortality. Those who fail are lost to the winds of time."

Irk saw objects being passed from person to person, metallic sheens glinting under the lights: scalpels and cups. Several were pressed into his hands; he was motioned to take one of each for himself and pass the rest on. Sleeves were rolled up, scalpels applied to skin. Three parallel incisions on the inside of the left forearm, the cups held beneath to catch the draining blood. Only Irk spoiled the symmetry.

Full, the cups were handed round in acts of communion. Irk waved away those offered to him and shuffled closer to Roza. Participants drank greedily and fast; those who sipped too leisurely would find the blood starting to coagulate. Irk felt the bile rise in his throat.

"I see a man who chooses only to observe," the Mistress shouted.

A moment dripped like blood on tiles. Irk realised that the Mistress was pointing at him.

"You wish to be lost to the winds of time, my friend?"

Her gaze squeezed at Irk's stomach. Dimly, slowly, he was aware they weren't playing games any more – if indeed they ever had been.

"The blood ritual can lead to a deeper understanding of oneself." The Mistress' voice was relentless. "If you won't become an active participant, then we'll use you as a passive one."

"What does she mean?" Irk hissed.

"If you won't drink our blood, we'll drink yours."

"No. No way."

"I thought you wanted to join us."

"Perhaps a sanctuary feed is in order," the Mistress said.

Roza looked away. Irk had to nudge her twice before she explained. "A sanctuary feed," Roza said slowly, "is when the entire herd converges on one donor."

Everyone was looking at Irk now, their faces heavy with anticipation. He felt their anger and fear. His investigator's badge was no use to him now; in here, he was the intruder, the outlaw.

Irk tensed himself to run.

"My friend is timid and reluctant," said Roza.

"And so his blood is tarnished," the Mistress replied. Was Irk imagining it, or was there a note of disappointment in her voice? "Very well. We'll find a *willing* volunteer for this most noble of services. Roza, would you escort your friend from the premises?"

Irk burst from sleep like a cork pops from a champagne bottle, and sucked in deep, gulping breaths as though Moscow air was the cleanest and purest of mountain breezes.

In his bag was a copy of *The Master and Margarita*, Bulgakov's classic tale of how the devil had created havoc in the capital. If Satan came back to Moscow now, Irk thought, he'd find his work already done.

# 85

*Monday, 16 March 1992*

Testarossa rang Lev early in the morning. "Borzov wants to offer you a deal," he said.

"How so?"

"He's embarrassed that they can't find you. It's making him look weak and stupid. Reading between the lines, he's also worried about how small his power base is. There's a lot of support for you out there. He'd rather have you where he can see you than always be wondering what you're cooking up against him."

"What's he offering?"

"An amnesty for what happened in parliament."

"And in return?"

"You agree not to stand as a deputy again. To stay out of politics altogether, in fact. And you give up all your interests in Red October."

Lev thought for long moments. "The first is acceptable. The second's definitely not."

"It's Red October that's caused all this trouble, as far as he's concerned. That's why he put Sabirzhan in charge."

"Don't talk to me about that scum. What else? From Borzov, I mean."

"That's it."

"*That's it?*"

"You can keep everything else. If you ask me, it's a hell of a deal. The old man's going soft."

"The old man is worrying about his popularity ratings."

Lev considered the offer for an hour. The longer he thought, the more he realised Testarossa was right: it *was* a hell of a deal. Borzov was old, his health was failing, he wasn't up to the job. In a couple of years tops he'd be out of office, and then all bets would be off.

President and vor were photographed together in the Kremlin at lunchtime, all smiles and handshakes. It was a new dawn in Russian politics, Borzov said: reconciliation between enemies. Russia was not yet so blessed with people capable of reconstructing the nation that it could afford to throw them in jail, he added. The flash of sincerity in his eyes might almost have convinced Lev that he meant it.

Petrovka was stuffy, smoky and overheated. Irk went for a walk to clear his head.

The snow was falling heavily again. When he looked behind him, he saw that the snow was already covering his footprints, erasing any trace of his progress. Story of my life, Irk thought, story of my –

And then he was running, footprints be damned, skidding like a penguin through the Petrovka gates, taking the steps two at a time past his astonished colleagues.

What had that asshole photographer from Minsk said the other day in the sewer? That there weren't any footprints. "There must be." Irk had replied. "You think he levitates?"

*There must be*, but there weren't, and none around the latest body either – at least none that hadn't been caused by heavy-footed cops tramping over evidence as though they were getting paid per item destroyed. Irk was annoyed – no, he was disgusted – that he hadn't registered the significance of this earlier. It was the kind of thing that only a chance observation would have uncovered. He could have stared at the case files for weeks on end without it coming to light. Reality lies in what's left out of the picture. Truth lies almost, but not quite, in looking away, in the detail nearly missed, the one that snags the imagination and makes it see.

Irk took the photographs of Nelli's body and went over them with a magnifying glass till his eyes ached. If something was going to show up, it would be here, on dry land by the VDNKh sculpture, where the endless running of the sewers hadn't washed away evidence.

*There* – tracks on the ground, faint and slightly knurled. Wheels, perhaps, with narrow tyres. A bicycle? Irk looked closer. The lines were parallel, as far as he could make out. If it was a bicycle, then the tracks would have to have come from two separate machines – unlikely – or the same machine repeating the same route. But no, the lines were symmetrical, perfectly so. Two wheels, separated by an axle. Not a bicycle. Too small to be a car, of course. A pram?

No, all the victims had been too old for prams.

What else had wheels?

A wheelchair, for a start.

That was stupid. None of the victims were disabled, and the vampire clearly couldn't be.

Why not?

The children were small and weak, they were no match for an adult, even a disabled one.

How would you get a wheelchair into the sewers?

You wouldn't, not without extreme difficulty.

Irk examined the photographs again, looking at each tyre mark in turn. The treads seemed even across their width. Wheelchair tyres would leave thicker marks on their outer edges than on their inner ones, since they were angled slightly towards the rider.

410

If not a wheelchair, then what?

Irk thought of Rodion and his trolley, and he knew. There were hundreds of those poor bastards on what were little more tea-trays. They haunted the metros and street corners, playing war ballads or simply holding out upturned hands beneath lowered heads.

How would he go about interviewing them all? Was there a list of Afghan veterans?

Irk's mind shied from the connection. A disabled veteran on a trolley; a man who knew at least the first three victims; a man whom Irk had seen win children's trust in a heartbeat; a man who'd offered to help with the investigation; a man who called himself Irk's friend.

None of the Khruminsches were home. Feeling like the most deceitful man alive, Irk used his skeleton key to open the door of their apartment. It was mid-afternoon, so he had a good couple of hours before any of them were likely to return home, but still he found himself holding his breath and creeping lightly on his feet.

What was he looking for? He didn't exactly know' a clue, a lead, something to clear Rodion's name or drag him deeper into the mire. Irk opened every drawer, ran his hands over every item of clothing, flicked through the pages of every book – and finally, in the margins of a memorandum about staffing at Prospekt Mira, Irk found something: *Studenetsky, Wed. 12th, 18.30.* A name, a date, a time – an appointment. Rodya's handwriting, Irk knew that much.

He checked back through his own diary. Wednesday had fallen on the twelfth last month, February; the next previous occasion had been back in June, and the memo was dated January this year, which ruled that out.

Not that any of this helped Irk much. Who or what was Studenetsky? Speculation was pointless; it could be anybody. Irk didn't even know whether the name was important, or if Rodya had kept the appointment. A telephone number would be priceless. A telephone number was exactly what Irk didn't have. Unless . . .

He recalled Sveta, chattering away after the Chechens had killed the cats – good God, Irk thought suddenly, blood lust was blood lust, animal or human. What if it was Rodya rather than the Chechens who'd sliced up the Archangel blues? – anyway, Sveta chattering away about how nothing ever went to waste, and *how she used colanders and sieves to file her papers.*

He went through into the kitchen.

The phone bills were in the third colander he tried, beneath a frying pan full of old newspaper crosswords, all blank, and above a skillet smeared with the pages of a letter. Phone bills had been itemised since the start of the year – it was one of Arkin's proudest boasts, that a modern city must have a decent telecommunications system. That wrong numbers were still ten a penny was of no concern to Irk now, so long as he found a Studenetsky at one of these numbers, he'd be happy.

He worked backwards, careful to check before each new number that he hadn't dialled it before. Three "you've got the wrong number"s, two failures to answer and one torrent of abuse later, he struck gold.

Studenetsky was a consultant at the Serbsky Psychiatric Institute.

Irk sat at Elektrozavodskaya metro station and moved his gaze slowly through a half-circle. He started with the curved ceiling where cupolas cradled electric lamps, passed through the rows of pylons crawling with marble reliefs, and finished at the black-and-grey paving slabs framed in pink-and-yellow Crimean marble. What counted more: his friendship with Rodya, or his job? He could no longer have both.

The Serbsky was a yellowing pile on Kropotkinskaya, halfway down the loop in the river by the Luzhniki Stadium. Yevgeni Studenetsky's white hair was brushed savagely back from his forehead. He looked more like a retired Red Army colonel than a psychiatrist, Irk thought, but then again, what did he know? People kept telling him that he looked more like a chess grandmaster than a homicide investigator.

"I'm not sure I like this whole affair," Studenetsky said. "The nature of the relationship I have with Rodion Khruminsch must surely remain between me and him? There is such a thing as patient confidentiality, Investigator – or are the thought police still with us?"

Such a gambit was usually a prelude to a bribe, but Studenetsky's voice didn't carry the knowing cynicism which Irk would have expected, and Irk saw in his face none of the almost imperceptible movements which represent the habitual financial come-ons of a Russian reluctant to part with information. Studenetsky wasn't holding out for money; he really was concerned about Rodion's right to privacy. The incorruptible man, Irk thought, was good at spotting the few who were like him; it was a secret society, almost.

"It's like this, Yevgeni Pavelevich," he said. "Rodya's a friend of mine, and I'd give anything not to be investigating him, but that's the way things go. I wouldn't have come here unless I thought it absolutely necessary. This is a serial killer we're talking about."

"I know that."

"If Rodya is innocent, nothing you tell me will make it beyond these walls, I promise you that. I won't even tell him I've been here. If he's guilty, his state of mind – whether he's insane or not – will be crucial in determining whether he's fit to stand trial. Either way, I'd rather do this in a civilised manner, gentleman to gentleman, than have to bring down a bunch of uniforms and impound your files."

"Are you threatening me?"

"I'm appealing to your good sense. My need for information is greater than Rodya's need for privacy; I'm trying to make you see that."

Studenetsky steepled his hands, and Irk knew he had him.

"What did Rodya come and see you about?" Irk asked.

Studenetsky gave a small laugh. "Where do you want me to start?"

"The basics."

"All right. Rodya suffers from a blood delusion." Good God, Irk thought, there goes the first nail in the lid of his coffin. Soviet courts had sentenced people to death on half this evidence. "It's been getting progressively worse, especially since Rodya came off his pills in mid-January."

"Pills?"

Studenetsky ticked them off on his fingers: "Desipramine, phenothiazines, benzodiazepines, lithium, Xanax, doxepin hydro-chloride, thorazine. Half a chemist's shop, and most of them past their sell-by date, dumped on us by the United States or coming from our own antiquated pharmaceutical plants before they were deemed environmental hazards and shut down. Some of them worked, some of them didn't. Rodya was down to only a few by the time he came off. Well, 'came off' is perhaps a misleading phrase. He didn't want to stop taking them – *I* didn't want him to stop taking them – but they simply cost too much. The clinic could no longer afford them, Rodya couldn't either, and the stuff on the black market is too expensive and cut with all kinds of rubbish – that stuff causes more harm than it cures. Say what you like about the old system, detective, but it kept Rodya in pills and his problems in check."

"And it never occurred to you to get in touch with Petrovka these past few days?"

"You know my position on that, Investigator, we've been over it."

Irk could have pushed the point, but decided he'd do better to

413

get as much as he could out of Studenetsky now. "Tell me about the blood delusion."

"Well, it stems from Afghanistan. More specifically, from when he had his legs blown off. The medics had run out of morphine, so they injected him with vodka instead. And from that moment onwards, he's feared that his blood – of which he now has less than other people, of course – is turning into vodka." Studenetsky saw the scepticism on Irk's face. "Believe me, Investigator, Rodion's mania is no joke. This obsession with his blood is so intense that we can't inject him with anything – he's too scared of needles. I once found him watching a televised angiogram and the sight of blood pumping through the veins had him utterly transfixed. I stood next to him for ten minutes before he even noticed me. It was as if he were in a trance."

Studenetsky left the room and came back five minutes later, clutching a video cassette.

"We tape sessions sometimes," he explained.

"With the patients' knowledge?"

Studenetsky made a face. "The clinic's policy is that the patients by definition are incapable of determining their own best interests."

Irk thought fleetingly of Studenetsky's jibe about the thought police. Studenetsky inserted the cassette into an old VCR machine and fiddled with controls on both recorder and television until a picture appeared. Rodion's face filled the screen, filmed in full zoom on a static camera, and Irk actually recoiled in his chair at the sight, it was so sudden and unexpected – so *real*.

"I try to hold it in," Rodion was saying, "but sometimes it's too hard. Dark thoughts, bad thoughts keep on and on, battering against the inside of my skull. It's chilly outside right now, but I don't feel too cold, and that sets me worrying, because it means that there's too much vodka in my blood again. My blood's turning to vodka, that's why it's not freezing, because vodka only freezes at very low temperatures. If I don't get some more blood soon, then that'll be it for me."

"When was this filmed?" Irk asked.

Studenetsky looked down. "February twelfth."

"And this didn't alert you that something might be wrong?"

"He often said stuff like that. You say you know Rodya, Investigator. Then you'll know how he can be . . ." Studenetsky searched for the right words: "So insistent, so . . . over the top." That was true enough, Irk thought. "He came in here once

414

claiming that someone had stolen his pulmonary artery. So when dealing with his delusion one must be careful to factor in his tendency to exaggerate."

Irk shook his head and turned his attention back to Rodion.

"When I was young," Rodion was saying, "I had such a head for vodka that my friends said I had hollow legs. Now my legs are gone, I've only half a body. There's more and more vodka, less and less blood. I can feel the blood thinning into vodka. If I look at my veins through the skin they're no longer dark with all the red blood flowing through them, but pale, like clear plastic tubes. I see all the vats and the machinery and the pipes in the distillery and I think, that's it, that's what my body looks like inside: a distillery. Without blood, my body's going to disintegrate, everything will shut down: blood stops flowing, heart stops beating, kidneys and liver stop working . . ."

Rodion kept talking, jumping from subject to subject; Irk watched and listened, rising to the thrill of finding his mark, falling at the way his friend had let him down.

"It was a perfect day to be alive. A hundred peaks, dazzling white in the sun; dragonflies buzzing around like miniature Mi24 helicopter gunships; the sound of a river rushing below us; clumps of the most amazing flowers – deep pink, purple, dark blue – blossoms everywhere you looked. And the air was full of birds: yellow wagtails with rich lemon-curd heads, hoopoes with their striped crests . . . But beyond the drone of the flies, the flutter of the birds, the shepherds watching our passing, you could see the rocket craters, the shrapnel scars, the twisted metal carcass of a downed helicopter napalmed so the Afghans couldn't get it, charred roof beams rising from burned buildings. That's why we hurried through this region.

"But hurrying meant taking chances, and chances in Afghanistan meant risks. A convoy had been down this road a couple of days before, and we didn't think there'd been time for the Afghans to re-mine it. I was hanging on to the outside of the trawler, ready to jump down and start sweeping the moment I got the order. To keep our minds off the prospect of being attacked, we were singing:

> Here in the mountains we have only one law,
> to stab and to slash the Afghan tramps;
> and if your chest doesn't catch a fragment of lead,
> it'll most likely catch a medal instead.

"We'd just got the words out when the vehicle suddenly jolted. I thought we'd hit a rock, and like a greenhorn I hadn't been holding on tight enough. My arms stretched out in front of me. But then I looked down at myself from up above and saw my body tearing itself off the trawler in pursuit of my hands. It must have been a huge rock, I thought; the trawler was in bits.

"Men were lying with their limbs hanging by threads, and the rocks were red and soft with intestines. I looked down and there was nothing below my waist, nothing but blood. I've lost my balls, I thought. Never mind my legs, I've lost my fucking nuts. I reached down and felt around. I found one, but not the other. Hitler only had one ball, that's what the veterans from Stalingrad had told us. But then I found the other, caught between my legs – caught between my stumps, rather. One, two, both my plums were still there.

"I called out to one of my buddies, the first guy I saw. 'Hey! Filya! I've lost my legs.'

"'No, you haven't,' he said. 'They're over there.'

"He should've been a comedian, Filya should. I looked where he was pointing, and saw he was right: there were my legs, with the identity tags glinting round my right ankle – except now it was somewhere near my left knee. We always wore two identity tags, one round our neck and the other round an ankle. That way, if you got blown in two, they still might be able to put your corpse together and send it home.

"The medics pulled my shirt open. My chest was all white, except for the pink patches left by the lice sores. They had to inject me with vodka, because they were all out of morphine. They said they'd get me drunk and knock me out, all in one go. It took four men to hold me down, I was struggling so much. They shoved a branch in my mouth for me to clench my teeth on; I'd have bitten someone's hand clean off if they hadn't. I remember the needle going in, feeling the vodka pump round my system and watching my blood draining on to the road – blood out and vodka in, blood out, vodka in, out, in, blood, vodka. The pain got louder and louder, until I was almost unconsciousness. And then all the thoughts wandering about my head seemed bright and new and sticky to the touch like fresh paint. It was a wonderful feeling.

"I knew I didn't have to worry any more about dying the worst way of all. I wouldn't need to keep a bullet or grenade in reserve in case the mujahidin got me. They did terrible things to the ones they caught, the mujahidin did. They'd kill a man with pitchforks. or peel off his skin and throw him on to hot sand, or slit open his stomach, bend him over and push his face into his own intestines . . .

"And who can blame them, when you know what we did to them in return? They used to interrogate men in threes, take them up in a helicopter, all blindfolded. The first guy got thrown out, no questions asked; all the others heard were his squeals. The second one sometimes talked, sometimes didn't – if not, out he went too. The third one always talked. And we'd cut the ears off the mujahidin we killed, so that later we could lay them on the tombstones of friends who never made it back. That was our way of telling our mates that they could rest in peace, that we'd avenged them.

"They gave me more vodka back at base. It took so much to knock me unconscious that my body temperature went right down, and my pulse and breathing were so shallow the medics thought I was dead. They put me in a zinc coffin and loaded me on to a black tulip – that's what we called the planes that carried the dead flowers of Soviet youth. Each coffin came with a slip, saying something like – I can't remember the exact words – 'nature of consignment: coffin with body of Ministry of Defence soldier. Weight: three hundred kilos. Declared value: zero roubles.' Worthless, in other words. Wasn't that the truth?

"Anyway, halfway through the flight I woke up. Coming round and realising that you've been buried alive . . . well, it's the worst fear imaginable. I banged on the coffin lid, but of course no one was back in the hold watching over the coffins, and the pilots couldn't hear me above the roar of the engines. I went nuts in there. Elbows, fingers, stumps – I beat them until they were scraped raw in my frenzy to get out. It was only when the flight landed at Tashkent and the engines were shut off that they finally heard me. And you know how I survived that long? Because the zinc coffin I was in was substandard. It wasn't airtight. In a normal, screwed-down box, I'd have been dead within the hour. If that had been a real corpse in my coffin, it'd have stunk the place out. Shitty Soviet workmanship saved my life."

Studenetsky fingered the cleft in his chin. "You may think we could have done more for him, Investigator, and in many ways I'd agree. This institute is one of only two psychiatric clinics which are qualified to treat Afghan veterans – the other's in St Petersburg. What use is that, if you live in Magadan, or Kazan, or Syktyvkar? But remember too how far we've come. Ten years ago, Rodya wouldn't have even had a chance of treatment. That we're having this conversation at all is a miracle."

* * *

The vampire hadn't just emerged from nothing. He'd been created by the old system and nurtured by the new, forged in the white heat of a revolution ushered through without the first thought for what it would do to people like him, the little ones, the forgotten ones. Rodion had been a product not of his own nature but of the insane society in which he lived.

The vampire wasn't to be found in Moscow, Irk thought bitterly; the vampire *was* Moscow.

Irk returned to the Khruminsches' apartment, past houses which sported dead cats and dogs on their thresholds in the belief that the vampire would have to stop and count every hair on the animals' cadavers, which would take it until dawn, when it would have to flee.

The vampire: Rodion.

Nelli had been killed a month ago. The tracks were visible beside her body. Irk could have stopped it then, ended the murders, taken Rodya into custody. He'd failed.

Svetlana and Galina were back at the apartment. They didn't know where Rodya was. Rodya, Irk thought. My friend, my enigma – my quarry. Irk had seen the ease with which Rodion moved among children. Young people see clearly; they know with one look, and those poor boys and girls who'd gone with Rodion had done so because they'd seen who he was: a victim.

What option did he have, given the circumstances, but to surrender to the dark side, and to his addictions: vodka, death, life, blood . . . The innocent and pure blood of the children, which he knew would be untainted by vodka. That was why Rodya had chosen children, Irk realised. None of the victims had drunk vodka; they'd been scared that it would stunt their growth, or they hadn't yet got used to the taste. Rodion got drunk to commit the crimes, and the drunker he got, the more he feared his blood was turning to vodka, and so the more he needed to go out and kill.

The children were dead and he was alive. Indeed, they'd died so that he might live. But what kind of life was this? Rodion was already halfway to the other side. He'd lost his soul in Afghanistan, and what was a man without a soul? Rodion was neither dead nor alive, but living in death. How fearful a destiny is that of the vampire who has no rest in the grave, but whose doom it is to come forth and prey upon the living. Can a man be victim and fiend at the same time? All too easily. Rodion was driven and constrained to endless, fruitless repetition. With no way out, he could have ended it all – but what a waste that would have been, when he'd survived everything else. He was afraid of dying. Rodion wanted to live.

Rodya was due home at seven. At half past eight, he rang: there was trouble down at the orphanage, he'd spend the night there. It was Galina who spoke to him; Irk gestured that he wanted a word, but Rodya had hung up before Irk reached the phone.

"I have to go," Irk said.

"Where to?" Sveta asked.

"Back to Petrovka." It was halfway true: Petrovka would be his first stop.

He rounded up a dozen policemen and went down to the orphanage. "We've come to see Rodion Khruminsch," he explained to the 21st Century man on the door.

"Rodya? Went home hours ago."

"He's just phoned from here."

"He left at six. Haven't seen him since."

Irk's stomach began to twist like a moray eel. "He said there was some trouble here."

The gatekeeper gestured towards the building. "Go ahead and look, if you want. You won't find him."

He was right. They didn't.

# 86

*Tuesday, 17 March 1992*

There was a whole list of things Rodion couldn't do before he went on a mission. He couldn't use the word "last", or shave, or shake hands, or be photographed. That was how it had been in Afghanistan; that was how it was now.

He'd been in the sewers all night looking for a target, without joy. Now he was above ground, hidden in the flat morning shadows, and he was still. He could wait as long as he needed. The blood lust never really started until he was committed to the attack, though when it did he couldn't hold it. Even knowing the price of exposure – the Chechens were no longer going to be the fall guys – he hadn't been able to hold it.

A crocodile line of children passed on their way to school, singing jauntily:

*"Marushka met her lover; she asked him where he lived;*
*His dark eyes merely laughed at her; no answer would*
  *he give.*
*So on his shining button she looped a piece of thread,*
*Unwound it and then followed where it led.*
*It led her out the village through a grove of silver birch,*
*It led her to a bolted doorway at a silent church,*
*Up upon a ladder through a window she did peer,*
*And watched a scene which chilled her heart with fear.*
*Upon the church's altar, a rustic coffin lay.*
*Within it was a dead man, his skin as cold as clay;*
*Leaning o'er the body, the man whom she would wed*
*With hungry gulps was eating up the dead."*

There was a boy off the back, five or six paces behind the rest. People hurried this way and that on their way to work, but none of them would suspect him. No one ever did, not when he was half a man and so good with children. "Hey!" he hissed.

The boy turned, and Rodion winked. "Give us a hand, would you?"

The boy glanced at the retreating backs of his classmates.

"You can spare a moment for a man with no legs, my friend," Rodion said.

The boy took a step closer, and then paused again. His eyes were large under his school cap.

One on one, Rodya and the boy; that was how it always was, that was how it had been in Afghanistan.

When you found a mine, everything suddenly became very still, as if someone had turned the volume right down. Like when a violinist has just taken his bow from the strings, and the final note hangs dying in the auditorium, only the note faded inside you rather than outside.

A minesweeper had to work alone – even if the mine you were working on exploded, the others still had to check the road ahead. You worked in sixty-degree fields with a fifty-metre arc; no one else was allowed in that zone. It was just you and the mine, one on one, each trying to second-guess the other. Sometimes you'd be concentrating so hard that you didn't notice how much your hands were bleeding from where you'd scraped them. And if the mine went off – well, there'd be nothing left but your head, still intact inside your helmet. If it did go off, you hoped it was a big one and it killed you and killed you quick, because all the tension came not from the thought of being killed, but of being maimed and surviving.

Do you wonder that we took all the help we could get? Sheep, cows, horses, dogs – we'd throw food for them into any area we suspected of being a minefield, then wait to see if they set anything off when they went to get it. And yes, we used children too. A handful of sweets, thrown high in the air, and they'd be off and running before your hand was back by your side. You're shocked. *Even* children? *Especially* children. For every child that stepped on a mine, that was one less to grow up and hunt us down in years to come. Because everyone was the enemy there. They'd smile at you before putting a bullet in your back or a mine under your car. That's the way it was; there were no borders between civilian and military, hard and soft, legitimate and illegitimate. They were all guerrilla fighters and it was us or them.

"I've got to go," said the boy, and he was running after his friends even as Rodion's hands closed into claws of impotent frustration.

Gorky Park was full of people – the place was free, after all. Traffic fumes faded into the burnt sugar smell of candyfloss; despite the temperature, a man clad only in a loincloth marked 'Tarzan' was performing bungee jumps from the top of a crane, yodelling and beating his chest on the way down. Alice dodged sad rows of hawkers posing morosely chained animals for snapshots with giggling adolescents, and she was still beating off the hucksters when she came face to face with a colossal German beer hall, every one of its two thousand seats empty. Whatever else the Soviet Union had lacked, Alice thought, there'd always been hope, but here even that seemed to have gone.

Snow was piled car-high on the verges, and the paths were littered with malevolent grey chunks of ice. Beyond tracts of whitened grass and shrubs wrapped in sacking against winter, skaters glided serenely on the ice rink. Recognising Lewis and the others waiting in line to hire skates, Alice went to join them.

Alice had always been a good skater – figure skating, of course, not speed skating, because to be a good speed skater you need thighs which can kickstart Concorde. For Alice, skating was virtually the only method of human propulsion that wasn't in some way ungainly, and when she got it right she felt as if she were soaring.

They took to the ice with varying degrees of grace and success: Harry was surprisingly good, Christina unsurprisingly bad, and there was nearly an international incident when Lewis managed to stop by the simple but antisocial method of ploughing straight into the nearest babushka. One by one they retired to sit beside the rink and eat their picnic, leaving Alice to skate alone, her thoughts turning in circles with her blades.

Lev was gone, her job was gone. Should she leave Lewis or stay with him, leave Moscow or stay here, stay in finance or try journalism – or just keep on skating, drinking, spiralling, until she'd eliminated every course but one?

Alice skated on. Her nose and lips were cold and doubtless turning purple, but the rest of her felt warmed by all the vodka she'd drunk. She imagined her insides pulsing like the core of a reactor. Hadn't one of the early privatisation proposals she'd received been from a company wanting to make 'Thermonuclear' vodka?

Her eye was suddenly caught by a man pushing himself along on a trolley. He had no legs, she saw, but he was amazingly sure-footed – well, sure-wheeled – riding over the iced ruts rather than through them. It was Rodion, she realised, pumping away with his massive arms.

"Rodya!" She skated over to the side of the rink. "Rodya!"

He slowed and smiled at her. "You skate well. I saw you."

She smiled. "Thank you."

"You're certainly well equipped." He pointed at her clothes – skates, fur coat, gloves, fur hat – and then looked past her to Josh. "Yours?"

Alice indicated Bob and Christina. "Theirs."

Josh, perpetually inquisitive, was already on his way over, chewing extravagantly on a toffee. "All those sweets." Alice tutted in mock disapproval. "Won't your ass get stuck shut?"

Christina was talking loudly about how Moscow was no place for children, not really, not American children at any rate; she made Josh sit under a sun lamp every other day, she said, to counteract the lack of sunlight and Vitamin D.

Whenever Alice worried that she was a bad person, she was re-assured to discover that Josh loved her as much as ever. Children were clear-sighted judges of good and evil, weren't they? Malice can deceive the wisest and shrewdest man, but, however cunningly it may be hidden, a child will sense it and be repelled by it. Alice might have been wrong-headed, muddled, out of control, confused, all that – but malicious and deliberately hurtful, definitely not. Quite the opposite, in fact. What had all her lying to Lewis been about, if not to keep him from being hurt?

Josh was chatting to Rodion as if he were a favourite uncle. Rodion grinned at him and began to sing in a deliberately absurd falsetto and Josh clapped his hands and laughed. Rodion asked if he could have a sweet, and when Josh gave him one, he pretended to swallow it and then magicked it out of Josh's ear.

"What's going on, Alice?" Christina shouted.

"We're fine," Alice replied, resisting the urge to flip Christina the finger.

"You've got another one in your ear," Rodion told Josh.

Josh felt inside both ears. "Have not."

"Have too." Rodion leant forward and plucked the sweet from his ear again.

"More!" Josh cried. 'More!"

Rodion ducked out of the sling he used to carry his belongings, hopped off his trolley and, placing his hands flat on the ground, slowly turned his head and trunk through a full circle, like a gymnast on the rings. Then he began somersaulting down the path, Josh tumbling end over end to keep up with him, all the way to the nearest corner, and all the way back.

"Auntie Alice," Josh said, "will you give me a piggyback? On the ice?"

"Sure."

There was a pile of vodka bottles – all empty, of course – heaped against the edge of the rink. Alice took eight bottles, four in each hand, their necks between her fingers, and set them out in a line on the rink, each one a couple of paces from the next. Then she squatted down, let Josh climb on to her shoulders, and gripped his legs under her armpits as she straightened up.

"Alice, what are you doing?" Christina said.

"Aw, Mom, we're fine," Josh replied.

"You tell her, Josh," Alice giggled. She skated once round the perimeter of the rink, minutely but constantly adjusting her balance as Josh shifted on her shoulders, before approaching the row of vodka bottles at speed and passing through them in an expert slalom.

"Yeah!" Josh shouted. "Way to go, Auntie Alice! Again!"

She turned and made a second approach run, except this time she span round at the last moment and took the line backwards, crossing and uncrossing her legs for each alternate bottle.

"Do be careful," Christina said. "That looks awful dangerous."

The vodka hummed in Alice's brain; she felt invincible. She squeezed her upper arms tighter against Josh's legs. "Ready for a jump and spin?"

"Yeah!"

"OK, here goes. Katya Witt, eat your heart out."

Alice hadn't done a jump in years, but she could remember the basics: speed and confidence, speed and confidence. She took long strides to get herself moving, feeling her quadriceps stretching as her legs extended, and then shorter steps to maintain the velocity. One deep breath as she gathered herself, and up they went.

It was all wrong, Alice knew that the moment her skates left the ice. Her balance was hopelessly off, and Josh's weight above her shoulderline was making it even worse. She was falling backwards, and if she landed on her back then Josh would hit the ice hard – and she couldn't have that. But if she managed to twist herself so she was falling forwards instead, his knees would take both her weight and his, and she couldn't have that either. All these thoughts came pinging through her head in fractions of a second, as did the solution. And so Alice ducked her head and flipped Josh over the top of it, still holding him, so that she would hit the ice first and he would land on top of her.

The impact didn't hurt as much as she'd thought it would. She was drunk enough to be reasonably limp, and the padding of her jacket and hat helped cushion the blow. A moment after she'd landed, she caught a mouthful of downy parka as Josh landed on her face. But he was all right, and so was she. He bounced off her with high-pitched squeals.

"Brilliant! Let's do it again, Auntie Alice! Let's do it again!"

Alice lay still for a moment, her eyes filled with the unrelenting grey of the Moscow sky, and then she began to laugh hysterically.

"Josh! Josh!" It was Christina. "Are you OK?"

"Mom, I'm *fine*. That was *great*."

Lewis appeared in Alice's vision, on his knees beside her. "I was over by the shoot-da-chute, I didn't see anything. What happened?"

"I fell. I'm fine."

"Let me check. Where did you hit your head?" He removed her hat and ran a hand over her head, probing through her hair for any damage. She reached up and guided his hand to a place on the back of her skull. "There."

His fingers moved like a pianist's. "Just a bobo. You'll have a bump and a headache."

"That's called a hangover, Lewis."

"Don't joke, Alice." He felt again, to be sure. "You're lucky. A hickey, nothing more."

"A hickey?" Harry said. "You'd better be worried if your wife's got a hickey . . . I mean . . ." He trailed off into communal silence; memories of Alice and Lev were still too raw.

"A hickey in New Orleans is a bump on the head," Lewis said neutrally. "We call the other thing a passion mark." He hopped to his feet, and Christina took his place in Alice's face. "What the hell were you playing at, Alice? How could you be so irresponsible?"

"Probably," Alice giggled, "because I'm drunk."

"You're damn right. It's disgraceful."

"Christina –" Alice propped herself up on one elbow – "it was an accident. Josh isn't hurt, and neither am I."

"You think I could care less about you? He's not hurt by sheer chance; you're not hurt because you're so pickled. I don't want you touching my son ever again, you hear me?"

"I love your son as though he were mine."

"Then maybe you should *have* your own."

"Maybe you should shut the fuck up."

"Come on, Alice," said Lewis. "I'll take you home."

"Home? Why home?"

"Don't start this."

"Home, because that's where a woman should be? Not me. I have a brain and I have balls and I use them both, and fuck you all."

"I think we should *all* go home," said Bob. He was making damping motions with his hands, to calm things down. "Come on, Christina. Josh! Home!"

Alice was looking at Lewis, and she saw the panic flash in his eyes as he realised.

"Josh!" Bob shouted again, swivelling on the spot as he looked for his son.

Josh was nowhere to be seen. Nor, for that matter, was Rodion.

"He'll be all right," said Alice weakly.

"Well, he's clearly not, is he, you stupid bitch?" Christina snapped.

"We can play the blame game afterwards," said Bob. "Wherever they've got to, they can't have gone far. Let's split up. Christina and I will go over yonder –" he pointed north, up towards the Kremlin. "Harry, you go there –" West, in the direction of the river. "And Alice and Lewis, that way –" South, to the main body of the park. East was across the ice rink, and they could see that Josh and Rodion weren't there. "If you see a policeman, tell him what's happened. We'll meet back here in fifteen minutes."

It was hard enough to stay balanced on Gorky Park's ice-slippery paths when walking normally; panic and haste made it twice as difficult. Harry and Christina both fell over within a few strides of setting off, and Bob and Lewis looked in danger of following suit. Alice was the only one who seemed unaffected. As she ran, she wondered whether it was because she'd started walking like a Russian, carrying her weight above her belt.

Through the trees, she could hear Christina's keening, a mother crying for her child.

Alice ran as though the hounds of hell were at her heels. Vodka and adrenalin had made her extraordinarily alert. When she scanned opening vistas of startled passers-by and empty fairground rides, she felt as though her brain were capable of processing vast amounts of information in the blink of an eye. Lewis was finding it hard to keep up. She heard him yelp, and when she looked round he was emerging from a pile of blackened slush.

They stopped, looked and ran; stopped, looked and ran; and nothing, no sign. There were too many people – perfect for a legless man to hide himself and a small boy. "Have you seen them?" she asked passers-by breathlessly. "Have you seen them?" Shrugs, blank looks, commiserations; nothing helpful.

Round another corner and there they were, more than a hundred metres ahead, glimpsed fleetingly through a gap in the throng. It looked as though Josh was slung over Rodion's shoulder. Alice cupped her hands to her mouth and hollered. "Rodya! Josh!"

Rodion looked round and then turned away. She was about to shout again when she saw them disappear into the ground, and the sight stopped her dead. *Into the ground?*

Later, Alice wouldn't remember covering the gap between where she'd been standing and where they'd vanished. Suddenly she found herself standing by a manhole cover, sitting slightly askew, improperly replaced, and she knew.

Lewis was at her side. "What the –?"

"Quick!" she barked. "Give me a two-kopeck piece!"

Irk hadn't enough men to mount a full-scale search of the sewers, so he was left with two options. Either he could hunt Rodya by himself, and he was not sure he was mentally or physically strong enough for that; or he could finally bite the bullet, go to Lev, take a dozen mafiyosi, and be grateful for their help.

Like most things to which Russians refer as choices, it was nothing of the sort.

Alice was waiting for them at the manhole. It took them twenty minutes to get there, and each of those seemed like a lifetime. If Josh . . . if something happened to him . . .

Lewis had gone back to the rendezvous by the ice rink to collect the others. They stood and watched as Irk led his temporary allies down into the underworld. "You find him, you hear me?" Christina shouted. "You find him!" And then they were gone.

The sewers were a labyrinth. Irk had to second-guess Rodion, or they would never catch him.

Rodion had heard Alice shout, so he'd know the chase would be on. He wouldn't risk killing Josh somewhere open, where he might be found Instead he'd take him into the unknowable depths. On the other hand, he must have been desperate to snatch someone in broad daylight from a woman who knew him. Rodya had nothing left to lose now his name was known and his cover blown. Irk thought briefly of Sveta and Galya, still blissfully ignorant that they'd borne and married a monster respectively. Then he thought of the times Rodya had offered to "help" with the case, and his heart hardened once more.

Irk ran his torch down three tunnels before he found what he was looking for: tracks. They were intermittent and sometimes faint, but they were definitely there. Extended drag marks where the tips of Josh's little boots had trailed; splayed marks from Rodya's hands; knurled lines from the wheels of Rodya's trolley.

Irk led the way. In the larger pipes, the men could walk four abreast; smaller sewers forced them into a stooping single file, past electric pumps which maintained flows at least ankle-deep and thus concealed the tracks which were Josh's only lifeline. Irk lost the trail, found it again, lost and found – he needed Theseus' thread. When they came across a stream running red, Irk started; his first thought was that he was wading through blood, but the accompanying chemical smell reproached him for his silliness. The red flow was nothing more sinister than the efflux from a paintworks.

Stalactites of grease congealed round the entrance to a pipe barrel; glowing lines of worms the size of grass snakes, luminous in the darkness. The phosphorescence in turn illuminated carp with tiny horns on their heads, strange mutations caused by chemical waste.

Half an hour, an hour, perhaps two – Irk had no idea how long it had been, but suddenly there was a splashing in the tunnel up ahead. Jabbing his torch in that direction, Irk picked out a half-size man swinging from hand to hand, almost at the end of the beam's range, and with him Josh, slumped over Rodion's shoulder, held in position by the sling – it was impossible from this distance to tell whether he was unconscious or dead. Sound carried a long way in the sewers, Irk thought, and then realised that it worked both ways: Rodya must have heard them coming.

The chase was on.

Scanning the mountain ridges, looking for a dust puff on the scree, some tiny inconsistency in the shape of the upper hillside, but seeing nothing but the flowers and blue skies and mountains; then the flicker lightning above the rock walls, a thunder clap over the valley, and here came the attack: a lunar surface of sliding feet and razor-fine rock cutting shins and knees and hands and elbows, mujahidin running for firing positions, bullets whipping up little fountains of dirt all around, and you'd think how close that was, how you must write to your friends and tell them, but not your mum, of course, you didn't want to worry her, but that's the way it was when you lived next to death like that, you didn't think about it any more – never think, never think, the first to think died, keep moving if you wanted to stay alive, move and fire, move and fire, your trigger shiny with use, never look back, bullets slapping into the cliffs, you hoping that they were the ones that exploded on impact, because then they wouldn't ricochet and get you on the rebound, when a bullet hit someone it was an unmistakeable sound, you never forgot it, a wet slap and down went your mate right next to you, and the first time it happened you reacted like you were in a dream, but soon there was nothing left of you but your name, you'd become someone else, someone who wasn't frightened of a corpse, some-one who just wondered how the hell he was going to drag a hundred kilos of man and equipment down the rocks, especially in that heat.

Rodion scampered ahead of the pursuers, a fox before the hounds. It was a hideously uneven contest, of course. There were many of them and only one of him, they had legs where he didn't, they were armed where he wasn't, and they weren't being slowed down by having to carry a child. But he could move fast on those strong hands, and he used them well, keeping to the narrow tunnels wher-ever he could, doubling back on himself and leading them round in circles, second-guessing those detachments which boxed the long ways round to try and cut him off up ahead. No matter how many tunnels they covered, Rodion always had one more up his sleeve, and like a fish he was gone from the net again. He swung across gangways and abseiled down waterfalls using ladders like ropes.

Where streams joined each other in larger channels, he scooted across the current as fast as possible, ignoring the echoing shouts which bounced off the walls and the torchlights that danced with the effort of pursuit, sounds and shadows wild and distorted as light and shade churned together. When they were close, he could hear the urgency of their puffing breath.

"Give it up, Rodya!" Irk shouted, but he knew he was wasting his time.

Rodion knew he couldn't run for ever; there were simply too many people after him. Gradually his options began to narrow. Three times he almost set off down a tunnel before realising there were men coming through it towards him. They were getting better organised, that was what was happening; rather than simply following him, they had spread out in a large circle and were slowly closing in.

Nearer and nearer still, and Rodion was tiring with Josh's weight, but he couldn't let the child go. He darted into a side tunnel and realised too late it was a dead end. Then they were with him, and all he could do was push himself flat against the wall – he didn't want to be shot from behind – and put a knife to Josh's neck as Irk advanced.

"I'll slash him, I swear I will," he shouted. Slash him and then carve the hammer and sickle, as they'd done to the bodies of the mujahidin – a kind of signature, to show it was the Red Army and not the Afghan government troops who'd done the killing. It wasn't the kind of thing you bragged about back at home. Most things in war were best left on the battlefield.

The pipeline bubbled with noise, the hunters coming back to the quarry, calling each other; all they needed was trumpeting horns. Irk saw the rise and fall of Josh's chest: still alive.

"Let him go, Rodya." Irk's voice quavered.

"Let *me* go," Rodion replied, "or I'll kill him." The knife nicked at Josh's skin, blood welling like rose petals. Rodion bent his head to Josh's neck and licked the droplets off.

Irk looked at the nearest mafiyoso. He had his pistol outstretched, sighting down the barrel.

"In the shoulder," Irk whispered. "Shoot him in the shoulder."

The man looked quizzical, but all Irk did was nod slightly: *Just do it, don't ask why.*

"You'll get a fair trial," Irk told Rodion. "I'll tell the court you're insane. You'll go to hospital, not prison. That's the best you can hope for."

Rodion shook his head, and then tilted forward to lick Josh's neck again. The report from the mafiyoso's gun came so loud that it made Irk jump, flash and crack simultaneous in such a confined space.

The shot pushed Rodion up the wall, but it was not that which made him lose his grip on Josh, it was the dark stain which suddenly flowered on Rodion's shirt, the slick which had him clamping his hands to it and screaming in agony that he was losing his blood, losing his blood, they had to help him or he'd die.

It took four mafiyosi to hold him down, he was flailing around so much. Only when one of them pistol-whipped him did Rodion stop struggling.

There were crates of vodka as far as Rodion could see, and he knew where he was: the underground warehouse, a stone's throw from the orphanage. Lev was tugging at the tourniquet on Rodion's arm, testing it for tightness.

"The bullet went straight through your shoulder," he said. "No lasting damage."

"Where's Juku?" Rodion asked.

"Back in the real world."

The 21st Century men had escorted Irk and Josh to the surface, where they'd told Irk that they would handle Rodion from here. Irk had, of course, wanted to take him into custody so that due process could take its course. Due process be damned, they'd replied; the courts were useless, the mafiya was the only outfit which worked around here, and they'd dispense justice themselves. Irk had insisted that Rodya was his collar; he'd lived and breathed this case for weeks. Yes, came the reply, but if it hadn't been for their manpower, Josh would have been dead and Rodion would still be trawling the underworld for his next victim. Besides, the attacks had been against Lev. Now Lev had plans for him – that was the bottom line.

Realistically, there was nothing Irk could have done other than return Josh to his parents and then try to round up reinforcements, as if that would do any good. The 21st Century hadn't told him where they were taking Rodion, much less what they planned to do with him. By the time Irk found them again, it would be too late.

All the mafiyosi who'd helped in the hunt were there to see Rodion's fate. They watched him with bewildered curiosity, as if he were an exotic exhibit in the zoo.

Lev came in, and every man rose to his feet. He took a chair in the centre and bade them sit.

"This is a thieves' court," he said, "convened for those who've transgressed our rules. You're not a vor, Rodya, of course, but you've killed my children and betrayed my friendship, therefore you'll be tried under thieves' law. I'll be judge, jury, and if necessary executioner. We'll take the prosecution as read. You know the charges: you've killed at least six children. You can ask for a defence lawyer or defend yourself, it's your choice."

"I demand to be tried by a proper court," Rodion said. The words seemed to have come from somewhere other than inside him; the courage of a desperate man, perhaps.

"You're in no position to demand anything. This *is* a proper court, a damn sight more so than the shambles that passes for official justice."

"This is *not* a proper court, it's a show trial. Stalin himself would have been proud of this. You've only brought me here by force, and it's force alone that gives you the right to sit in judgement and find me guilty. Why bother with a trial at all? It's obvious what the outcome will be."

"Is that all you have to say?" Lev asked.

Rodion thought for a moment and shook his head. He cleared his throat and began hesitantly, speaking for his life.

Afghanistan was a strange place, a clear place. Everything was understandable there, I knew my purpose. In a war, you have to learn to live by the rules, and the quicker you learn them, the longer you'll have to live by them. I didn't think about whether I was defending the revolution or the motherland. I just shot at those who were shooting at me. In the mountains, it was always obvious who was who. The war peeled people's shells off. It taught me not to believe words, only actions.

I hated being in Afghanistan; now I hate not being there. The moment I got home, I wanted to go back. The place which had made me half a man was the only place which could make me whole again. Here, I'm fighting against myself all the time, pursuing myself. My only release is in the actual act of killing, just like the alcoholic's only release is in the act of drinking. For me, vodka's become blood, and blood's become murder – I need my fix, it's that simple. When I gain my release, nothing else matters, place and time seem to telescope. The attacks feel as though they're over in seconds, but when I come round, I find that I've been there for hours. Once the adrenalin's gone, I get so tired I can hardly keep my eyes open.

My crimes aren't the kind which can be punished, either by the courts or by your underworld, so why do you have me here? I'm a monster, a psychopath. I live outside the law – outside the government's law, outside your law, outside anybody's law but my own.

As a vor, Lev, you chose to be an outsider. I don't have that choice. I'm possessed by evil, so I'm no longer responsible for my actions. The war did this to me. The war in Afghanistan, the war against communism, the war against capitalism, the war we're always waging, the war against ourselves – they all did it to me.

I know that I won't leave here alive. I accept that. In fact, I welcome it, because it'll put me out of this endless torment; it'll save another child, another two, several, many. I want you to know that I never tortured them – it was bad enough that I had to kill others to survive, so I did it as quickly and humanely as I could. They trusted me, you see. People like me, the crippled and invalids, we're used to the adults who shrink from touching us, who at best ignore us and at worst abuse us. But children, they're curious about us, not threatened. How else did I get so close to them, how else could I have subdued them?

I couldn't have done it to adults, they'd have shrunk away from me, the men would have been too strong for me. Besides, they're all awash with vodka, not like the kids. I'd offer them a hundred grams first, just to check, and if they didn't drink it then that was it, fate sealed. Those children were victims of the Afghan war, through no fault of their own, just like we who fought there were victims. Those children died because of that war, as surely as if they'd stood on a landmine or been gunned down by a sniper.

I'm sorry for one more thing: that I did it so close to home. You've always been good to me, Lev, and it was never aimed at you. The first ones were those who were nearest and easiest, and that meant Prospekt Mira. After that, when you suspected the Chechens and Karkadann used that against you, well, it was perfect for me, I could keep on knowing that your suspicions were elsewhere. I put Modestas' body in the warehouse – in *here* – after the Chechens attacked, knowing the two would be linked. That wasn't the Chechens who broke into our apartment and killed the Archangel blues – it was me. I was desperate, I thought if I could drink their blood I wouldn't have to kill another child, but it was no good, my body rejected it. Only human blood would do.

432

I ask only one thing: when you kill me, make sure it's final. Sever my head from my body and place it between my legs. Perhaps I'll still be able to hear, at least for a moment, the sound of my own blood gushing from my neck. Or put a stake through my heart, bury me near a crossroads to confuse me, stake my corpse into its grave, bind my feet and legs to prevent my body from escaping, dismember my corpse and bury the pieces separately, burn my corpse to ashes, tear out my heart, throw boiling oil on my grave, bury me face down, or with a willow cross under each armpit and one on my chest, put garlic in my mouth, break my neck, string wild roses round the outside of my coffin. Just make sure you release me from all this.

In the warehouse, not a trace of movement.

After long beats, Lev stood up and went over to Rodion. He was three or four times his size; a man was this much bigger than his pet dog.

"You've made your own law, Rodya, and lived by it. But it's not for you to decide how you die. I won't indulge your wish to be beheaded, but nor will I make you suffer unnecessarily. You've suffered enough. I sentence you to ten years without the right of correspondence."

*Ten years without the right of correspondence* was the Soviet euphemism for a death sentence.

Lev stepped round behind the amputee, held Rodion's head still with one massive hand, raised his own revolver with the other, and dispatched a single bullet through Rodion's brain.

Rodion's body was dumped outside Petrovka at dusk.

Sveta and Galya hadn't wanted to see Irk. He'd led the chase for Rodya, and so they blamed him for Rodya's capture and death. He'd abandoned Rodya to the mafiya, they'd said, and now no one would ever be brought to justice for his murder.

No, Irk had said, he hadn't abandoned anybody. He'd simply been given no choice.

They hadn't listened. "Out, out," they'd screamed, "Fuck off, leave us to our grief!" It wasn't rational, it wasn't how he'd have reacted, but what else could he do but obey? Even if they *had* known, what would they have done? A wife might have turned her husband in, but a mother her son? Never.

Irk remembered the relief and joy on the faces of the Americans when he'd brought Josh home, but it was scant consolation. The Khruminsches had been Irk's only friends in Moscow. He was on his own again.

# 87

*Wednesday, 18 March 1992*

The phone was ringing when she returned to the apartment, and she ignored it. Alice didn't feel like answering, whoever it was. She put the food into the fridge and freezer, and still the phone rang; she ran her hands under the tap and dried them on a dishcloth, and still the phone rang. They'd surely hang up the moment she went to pick it up, but no, it was still going.

"Hello?"

"I need to see you."

It was Lev, his voice rolling like thunder as it jagged lightning in her heart. It seemed aeons before Alice managed to speak.

"No."

"I need to see you," he repeated.

"I've a good life here. I'm calm. I don't need to stir everything up again."

"Alice, *please.*"

He'd never begged her before, not that she could remember.

You can tell yourself you're not in love with someone, you can erect thousands of barriers in your mind against them, and if you try hard enough you can convince yourself that you've stepped over the very thin line into hatred. You can do all this, as Alice had done, and sometimes it's simply not enough.

"Where are you?" she asked.

Lev took her in his arms and held her for long minutes of silence. She froze against him at first, but gradually his warmth seeped into her and began to thaw her. When he started to apologise, she turned her face to his and kissed him to shut him up.

A sort of homecoming. They'd been apart two weeks; for them both, it felt like two lifetimes.

Alice drank her first and second glasses to get over the shock of seeing Lev, her third and fourth to celebrate their reunion. She was halfway through her fifth when he put a hand over the rim.

She looked at him first in sharp rebuke, and then with uncertain wariness. Finally, his silence made her understand what he meant.

"Do you think I need help?" she asked.

There, she'd said it. It hung like a pendulum, swishing back and forth in the air between them.

"Yes."

"Why?" It sounded too defensive; he hadn't given her the answer she wanted.

"In all the time I've known you, sweetheart, I've never once seen you do this –" Lev moved his hand across his throat as though he were cutting it, the gesture Russians make when they're full. "You drink and drink. You've never said, 'That's enough.'"

"If I need help, are you going to make me seek it?"

"No."

"Why not?" Surprised.

"How could I make you do something, Alice? You'd just dig your heels in and do exactly the opposite. You know what you're like. If I *asked* you to do something, you'd cross an ocean; if I *told* you to do something, you wouldn't cross the room. You'll seek help when you want it, not before, and only you can decide when that'll be. But yes, I think you do need help. And, yes, when you go and find it, I'll be there for you."

She knew all the cold medical facts; as a teenager she'd tried to lecture her mother with them. Alcohol abuse can affect the brain, the liver, the kidneys, the stomach, the intestines, the pancreas, the heart, the arteries and veins. It can lead to memory loss, blackouts, premature ageing, chronic coughing, malnutrition, the shakes, tingling sensations in toes and fingers, skin problems and ulcers. Social considerations aside, women are more at risk than men; because they're lighter, they can absorb and metabolise alcohol quicker, and can therefore end up sustaining greater damage even if they drink less.

"I drink in the evenings, sometimes in the afternoons too – at parties, or when work demands it, or when I'm with you, nice and relaxed and happy like we are were now," she said. "I know what alcoholism is – my mother was one, remember? Real alcoholics drink all the time, morning, noon and night. I've never missed a day off work because of alcohol; I've never called in sick, I've never had to go home because my hangover was too bad to concentrate. Real alcoholics can't keep jobs, they can't get out of bed in the morning because they're so paralysingly hungover.

Sometimes they even sleep in the gutter. I've certainly never done *that*."

"I never said 'alcoholic', Alice." Lev's voice was soft. "You did."

Alice slugged a capful of vodka when Lewis was getting his coat and followed him out to the car. She had the keys; he slid reluctantly into the passenger seat. They'd have walked, but it was hardly a night for promenaders: the wind circled and searched, trying to suck their hearts from their chests and the flesh off their bones.

They went to the Aragvi, a Georgian restaurant on Tverskaya next to a statue of Yuri Dolgoruky, Moscow's founder. Georgians like to say, only half in jest, that Dolgoruky had at least had the sense to create his city near a good place to eat.

A car alarm was blaring by the restaurant entrance, its tune shifting every few seconds – now simple two-tone, now a police siren, space invaders, something that sounded like a Tarzan imitation. It stopped just as Alice and Lewis passed it.

"That's a shame," she said. "I was hoping it would launch into the '1812 Overture'."

The moment they were inside the Aragvi's front door, they began to shed layers. The restaurant, like almost every other building in Moscow, was overheated. Some buildings needed their air-conditioning on constantly, even during winter, to stop their rooms turning into saunas. Exterior and interior temperatures were rarely, if ever, in synch.

The cloakroom attendant gave Lewis and Alice ticket numbers 40 and 42 for their coats; there was no 41, as that was when Hitler had invaded Russia, and no 45 either, because victory over the hated Nazis was sacred, to be enjoyed by everybody rather than any specific individual.

A waiter led them to their table and asked them what they wanted to drink.

"I'll take me a glass of red wine," Lewis said.

"I'll have a Smirnoff Black," Alice said.

The waiter nodded approvingly. "Large or small glass?"

"A bottle."

"I don't think so, Alice," Lewis said. He turned to the waiter. "A glass will be fine."

"A bottle," Alice repeated.

"A real man would help you drink it, rather than argue about it," the waiter muttered to himself, and Alice laughed as he departed.

They sat in uncomfortable silence. Alice picked a couple of

wrapped sugar lumps from the bowl and turned them over in her hands. The wrappers were patterned in an unfortunate brown, white and black motif which made them look at first glance like cigarette butts. Lewis inspected the artificial flowers.

When the waiter returned, Alice virtually snatched the Smirnoff from him. She drained her first glass in one gulp and was halfway through her second when she saw Lewis' expression.

"Are you going to be like this all evening?" he said.

His tone made her childishly defensive. "Probably."

"Well, if you won't have a good time, I will."

The waiter was still there, ready to take their order and pretending not to hear their argument. Alice asked for mushrooms baked in sour cream and trout with nuts and plum sauce. Lewis chose a selection of cold fish delicacies and spicy red bean stew.

Alice was still just about sober enough for Lewis' determined jolliness to soften rather than irritate her. To forestall another argument, she tacked away on to neutral topics – films, books, plans for the summer – anything, in fact, other than the invisible elephants around which they skated with studied nonchalance.

The level in the bottle of Smirnoff Black went steadily south. She was getting very drunk.

"I think it's time we left," Lewis said.

"Why? We've still got dessert and coffee to come."

"Not the restaurant – Moscow. I think it's time we left Moscow."

"Why?"

"Because I hate it here. And it's not as if you've got any reason to stay, is it?"

Lewis could make the most throwaway comments sound hurtful. Alice bit her lip. The vodka afterburn hummed under her tongue.

"Is it?" he persisted.

It was bubbling inside her now, a rising tide: *Tell him, tell him and get it over with*. Alice lifted the candle from the centre of the table and began to play with it, twisting it through two planes to make the wax drip in different patterns down the side.

"For God's sake, Alice, it's a simple enough question."

Nerves jangling, she started suddenly, involuntarily tipping the dangling columns of molten wax on to her fingers, right on her wedding ring. She yelped in pain and scrabbled to pull the ring off, metal on both sides hot against her skin. It came off in a rush, spinning across the table while Alice shook her hands to ease the pain. A livid crimson weal marked the place where the ring had been. She'd been branded.

"I saw him today," she blurted. "I saw him, I saw Lev, and I'm going to do it to you again, I'm sorry, I'm so, so sorry, but it's him I love, him I can't live without, and I want to be here with him, here in Moscow."

Alice was up and out of the door before Lewis could speak. She couldn't bear to look at his face or hear his reply, she couldn't bear to watch his heart being broken again. She didn't pause to get her coat from the cloakroom; she didn't even take what was left of the vodka.

There were grim flashes which may or may not have been the green snake of drunken hallucination; fleeing from herself like a dog with rabies, Alice could no longer tell. The shaggy, ragged smoke of street fires, the crunch of footsteps and the whine of passing cars all helped give her the impression that she'd been travelling for ages and was on her way to some terrifyingly remote place.

She passed a conga line of babushki standing shoulder to shoulder, stamping their feet while their blank eyes gazed into the distance. The women's grey heads and black ankle-length coats made them look like crows, and their rough hands held out merchandise varied enough to have filled several bazaars: loaves, Ukrainian sausages, Chinese handkerchiefs, T-shirts, used boots, old cameras, taps, shower heads, milk, laundry detergent, lamps, washbasins, doorknobs, frying pans, toothpaste, glue, string, old shoes, and ersatz designer clothing.

Next to the babushki, two men were slumped underneath a statue of Lenin with his right arm flung out before him as if he was directing traffic. There was nothing else for him to direct any more, after all. The men were brandishing a bottle of vodka. As Alice staggered past, they called out to her. "Hey, you! Yes, you, will you be the third one?"

Aha, she thought – a vodka troika. When it comes to drinking, three is the lucky number. She changed course, listing like a galleon, and headed for her new-found companions.

A well-dressed woman hissed at Alice. "It's bad enough for the men, let alone you."

Alice put her right thumb between her first and second fingers and jabbed the ensemble in the woman's direction. "Get stuffed," she snarled.

She knelt down by the river of vodka and drank deeply, trying to drown herself.

* * *

She must have fallen asleep, because the next thing she knew, she was alone in the cold and the dark. There was a weight on her chest, which she felt was a rough, heavy coat; someone must have left it for her, seeing how she was so unsuitably dressed. Beside her was a bottle of vodka. *Drink me*, it whispered to her, sweetly seductive, and she knew that if she did, she'd die, either of alcohol poisoning or exposure. Her job was gone, and now her husband too. Would it be so wrong to open up the hemlock? All she'd have to do was stay here and let death come; it wouldn't be long before he found her.

Alice was in that non-material world on the borderline between sleep and wakefulness, where her surroundings consisted of visions and thoughts that momentarily arose and dissolved in consciousness; a transitional woman in a transitional nation.

There was a man in uniform standing over her, and then all was black.

# 88

*Thursday, 19 March 1992*

When Alice woke again, the acrid smell and the drying dampness around her groin let her know even before she'd opened her eyes that she'd soiled herself, and badly. For one horrifying moment, she thought she was back in captivity again, but the voices she could hear were female and Russian, not Chechen. When she forced her eyelids apart, she found herself looking on to a vision of hell: a room full of harridans, their faces drunken, torpid and unwomanly, their clothes thick with dirt, all of them expectorating staccato bursts of foul language in between hysterical giggles. Alice didn't know where she was, or what time it was; she'd lost all those senses, and if she wasn't careful she'd lose herself too.

With the special tenderness and patience that a Russian feels for a drunkard, someone had placed a pillow under Alice's head and some sheets of newspaper under her legs.

A young woman in jeans and a jumper came over. Her black hair was streaked with grey and cropped close to the skull; her front teeth were askew, and her nose was so wide that her small oval glasses could hardly make it over the bridge. It was not a pretty face, but it was a kind one.

"Where am I?" Alice asked.

"You're in the aquarium," the woman said, then, seeing Alice's baffled expression: "one of the sobering-up centres. I'm a volunteer here. My name's Nadhezda."

'Nadhezda' meant hope. Alice looked around the room again. Hopeless would have been a more appropriate name. "Who are all these people?" she asked.

Nadhezda pointed to five women in quick succession, going right to left. "That's Ivana Babushkina. She's twenty-seven, a technical assistant; she was found in the middle of the road, unable to walk unaided. The one next to her was lying in the doorway of an apart-ment block; the one next to *her* was sleeping in a market gateway; that one –" she indicated a woman of pensionable age, still clutch-ing a dog in her arms – "was brought in from the outskirts; and the worst of all, that one in the corner, well, she was drinking away her own son. Cute kid, four years old, and she was offering him to anyone who'd give her a bottle of vodka."

Alice screwed her eyes shut, as though when she next opened them she'd be in her own bed, safe and clean and warm. "I don't belong here, you know," she heard herself say.

"Oh, but you do," Nadhezda replied simply. "Everyone's equal when they come here."

Alice opened her eyes again. The harridans were still lined up in front of her.

"I'm going to be sick," she said.

Stomach empty and throat raw, she asked Nadhezda how she'd got there.

"A policeman brought you in. Not before time, either. A few more minutes out there and you'd have been gone." A policeman; Alice vaguely remembered a man in uniform standing over her. "Oh!" Nadhezda's mouth formed a perfect circle. "He said to give you his name. I told him it didn't matter, but he was insistent." She inserted two fingers into the pocket of her jeans – they were too tight for her to get a whole hand in – and pulled out a slip of paper.

"Uvarov, Grigori Eduardovich," she read. "Said you'd saved his ass, and now you're quits."

It was the first time Alice had seen the underbelly of Russia, warts and all. On the wall above her was a poster of a woman face down in a puddle, her untied shoelaces spelling out the message *Know Your Limit*. Next to the poster, a noticeboard was speckled with the recipes of some of the concoctions drunk by the inmates here. Alice read them with horror. There was Canaan Balsam – 100 grams of meths, 200 grams of milk stout, and 100 grams of clear varnish; Spirit of Geneva – 50 grams of White Lilac toilet water, 50 grams of sock deodoriser, 200 grams of Zhiguli beer, and 150 grams of spirit varnish; The Tear – 15 grams of lavender water, 15 grams of Verbena, 30 grams of Forest Water eau de cologne, 150 grams of mouthwash, and 150 grams of lemonade; and finally, spectacularly, Dog's Giblets – 100 grams of Zhiguli beer, 30 grams of Sadko the Wealthy Guest shampoo, 70 grams of anti-dandruff solution, 12 grams of superglue, 35 grams of brake fluid, and 20 grams of insecticide.

Moscow has scores of these 'aquariums' – overnight holding stations into which the police toss drunkards – but only one of them is for women only. This rarity, Alice realised, reflects the Russian belief that it's worse for a woman to be an alcoholic. A man can get away with heavy drinking, but a woman can't. A female alcoholic has failed as a woman, though a male alcoholic hasn't necessarily failed as a man; men prove their virility through vodka, just like the man who sleeps around is a stud where his female counterpart is a whore.

A female alcoholic is polluted, and as such is seen to reject her identity as a woman, the symbol of moral purity. In Russia, women are not only emotional carers, carriers and copers; they're also custodians, champions, caretakers and guardians of society's morals. If a woman falls from social grace, she falls harder and further than a man.

Nadhezda took a Polaroid of Alice and gave it to her. Had Alice not watched the picture being taken, she'd scarcely have believed the image was her own. Her face was lumpy and swollen; bruises rose from her skin like foothills stained mauve by the setting sun.

"Fight or fall?" Nadhezda asked.

"Pavement sickness." Fell over.

Nadhezda's eyes betrayed her thoughts: they all said that, even the ones battered by their husbands. "How much did you drink?"

"A horse's dose." A large amount.

"Here –" Nadhezda handed Alice a clipboard with a questionnaire pinned to it and a biro hanging from a string. "There are eight questions here. Answer them honestly – your instinctive reaction, mind, not what you think you should write. OK?"

Alice nodded. She gripped the biro, watching it shake between her fingers, and began.

Are you always thinking about the next opportunity to
    have a drink?
Do you drink alone?
Do you drink for effect rather than taste?
Do you use alcohol to calm your nerves or help you sleep?
Do you protect your alcohol supply?
Do you use more alcohol than planned?
Do you have a higher tolerance than other people of the
    same age and gender as you?
Do you have blackouts?

It was only when she'd got to the bottom that Alice realised she'd ticked 'yes' to every one.

It was the first time Alice had ever been left without her props. All the things she'd quoted to differentiate herself from alcoholics – that she had a fantastic job, she always looked good, she was always organised, she never slept in the gutter – no longer applied. She was no better than what she'd despised. She was just like her mother, no matter how much she'd pretended otherwise.

It was the first time she'd been totally honest with herself when it came to drinking. Simple questions, simple answers. It wasn't that hard, if you didn't fight it.

It was the first time she'd ever cleared her throat and said the words which had hitherto stuck in her craw.

"I'm an alcoholic," she told the room.

Alice felt lighter the moment she'd said it. She'd broken through the looking-glass of her final deception. The realisation that she no longer loved Lewis had come some time ago, but her mind had allowed her to handle only one massive revelation at a time.

It was as though her perspective, which had been so warped, had suddenly been flipped back to normal. She saw in a rush that all her problems stemmed from vodka rather than the other way round. She'd started drinking heavily because she was unhappy, a physical solution to an emotional problem; but, as her drinking had become ever heavier, the cure had become the disease, and the equation had been reversed. Now, she was unhappy because she was drinking.

Alcoholism is a parasite that destroys everything in its path – hope, trust, honesty, love and relationships – and which is utterly arrogant in its demand for total control, determined to have the answers in any discussion, determined to make everyone else feel helpless, angry, frustrated, and isolated. It was as though Alice had been possessed, and even as she shrunk from so melodramatic an analogy she knew it was accurate. She had to exorcise this strange beast which was living inside her and intertwining itself with her personality.

There was no longer any alternative. She couldn't cut down or drink only on certain days, she had to stop altogether. Alice knew she was on an elevator that only went down. She could get off at any time, but if she didn't, she'd end where the elevator did: six feet under. The cure would be long and painful, and there was no guarantee of success, but recognising the problem was the first step to solving it. Wasn't she the woman who relished challenges? And what was this if not just another one?

One was too many. A million wasn't enough.

There were Western AA groups meeting in the Anglican Church on Voznesensky Lane, Tuesday through Sunday – why not Monday, Alice thought, when that was the worst day for alcoholics? There were Russian AA groups all over the city. She didn't want either. They'd all be full of men, and she'd have to spend too much time and energy dealing with their shit to concentrate on herself. Nor would she feel comfortable about unburdening herself to strangers. The abduction had unnerved her to the point where she could not endure the company of friends, let alone strangers, without several drinks inside her. The memory of what it felt like to be stripped and humiliated – knowing all the while that her ordeal was being filmed – made it impossible for her to consider exposing that corner of her innermost self that had remained private to public view.

No. She'd do this herself, the hard way, cold turkey, and she'd take help from one source and one source only: the only man strong enough to deal with her. She'd been conducting twin illicit affairs, with Lev and with the vodka bottle, and she'd finally confirmed one to her husband at the same time as she'd confessed the other to herself. It seemed only logical that she should use one to defeat the other.

She saw that Lev's love for her was unconditional. That was why he'd wanted her to sort herself out, and that was why he'd been

prepared to alienate her. Lewis would go on protecting and protecting until the end of time, because he'd do anything to avoid the
confrontation. Two men, very different from each other, both of
whom loved her; but only one of them would deal with it in the
right way, for her at least.

Healing could only occur in the heart of the wound itself. Alice
had to go to the wound and examine why she drank, what she was
like when she drank, and what part of herself she was losing. If she
was to heal and truly recover, she must first take a good look at
herself, and that meant finding something she could use to get over
the hate, the contempt, the denial of the good she had in herself.
Her marriage was gone, her friends and job too. The self-love would
come from the one person she knew could give it to her.

Nadhezda showed Alice to the phone, and she called Lev.

He didn't seem at all surprised to hear from her. When she told him
what had happened, he said nothing. When she told him the clinic's
address, he laughed. "I know that place."

"You're sure?"

"Sure I'm sure. We run it."

"You do *what*?"

"The 21st Century runs the clinic."

"You're a vodka gang, and you run a drying-out clinic?"

"Sure. Having people get shitfaced doesn't make sense, socially
or economically. Most of the women in there have moved beyond
vodka to those vile cocktails listed on the boards there." Sell people
drink and then help them recover; only a Russian could read that
sentence without seeing a contradiction.

"You'll help me?"

"Of course. But only if you trust me, only if you do whatever I
say."

"Put my life in your hands?"

"If you want to see it that way, yes."

"What are you going to do – sew in a torpedo?" A torpedo was
an anti-alcohol pellet implanted beneath the skin. "I don't want any
chemical shit."

"No, no torpedoes. But you must believe in me; you must trust
me to be fair even when I'm being cruel."

"I don't want to be anybody's prisoner," she said.

"Your choice, Alice."

She was strong and independent, or at least that was how she'd
always seen herself. She'd never asked for help before. Alice had

never allowed herself to be truly naked in front of Lev before, not metaphorically. Yes, she'd told him everything about herself, but she knew that this process would expose her soul far more comprehensively than weeks of pillow talk could ever do. Would he love her less, if he saw her flayed?

"Do whatever you like, Alice, whatever you need." He'd read her mind, she was sure of it. "I love you, and my love can't be made or marred by anything that you do. Nothing you confess could make me love you less."

In the heart of every storm, there's a quiet light.

"I smelt it on you," he said, "the odour of an alcoholic. Not the actual fumes, but the emotional aroma, the way you weaved and ducked and blocked questions about alcohol. There was this deep, dreadful silence. I sensed that you didn't want to talk about it, or even that you *couldn't* talk about it, it was so forbidden to you. I just heard the silence, that mute shame, or denials that included a lot of explanations."

"Do you think I'm a bad person?" she said.

"Bad? Good? What do they mean, Alice? I know that people do things for reasons which way transcend notions of right and wrong. I believe that what I do is right, but it doesn't necessarily mean that those who oppose me are wrong. Do you understand that?"

"I think so."

"Good. Because it's a very Russian thing to think."

He could see her better than she could herself. It was one of Lev's strengths, his ability to pinpoint other people's attitudes, identities and state of mind, and equally one of his weaknesses that he was relatively incapable of doing this to himself. Consciousness was a beam of light directed outwards, it lit up the way ahead so he didn't trip up. But, like the headlamps on a railway engine, if you turned the beam inwards, there'd be a catastrophe.

It might be worse for a woman to be an alcoholic than for a man, Lev said, but it's also easier for them to recover. Women don't have the same problem with humility that men do. To recover, Alice would need to surrender. She would need to accept the way she was and what she'd done to herself. A man – especially a Russian man – would resist this spirit of humility, but even the strongest woman hasn't been taught how to rescue herself. The image of Prince Charming rescuing the damsel from the forest where she's strayed is too deeply embedded in the female psyche. And that is woman's salvation.

Alice laughed when he told her this. It reminded her that all Russian men are chauvinists.

They lifted Lewis at lunchtime. It was very simple: a posse of 21st Century heavies walked into the Sklifosovsky and told him that Alice was safe and that Lev would like to speak to him. Lewis was so relieved at the first that he hardly gave the second a thought. He hadn't bothered to chase after Alice when she'd left the Aragvi, assuming that she was simply being melodramatic and would return in her own time. When he'd still been sitting alone after ten minutes, he had, belatedly and with a rising sense of panic, gone out into the street. Of course by that time she'd been long gone. He'd called every police station and hospital in central Moscow, but no one had seen Alice.

Husband and lover, alone in a penthouse drawing-room. Lev offered him a seat; Lewis said he'd rather stand. "Where's Alice?" he asked.

"She's safe, and she's going to be all right, that's the most important thing."

"I'm her husband."

"Alice is an alcoholic."

"She's not."

"Alice is an alcoholic."

"She has a drinking problem, sure, and I'd rather she drank less, but that doesn't make her an alcoholic."

"You're a doctor, you must know better than anyone that she fits every medical definition. Alice is an alcoholic. She knows exactly the time of her last drink. She has no control over alcohol. She can't predict what'll happen after the first vodka. Every day she says she'll have just two drinks and go home, and every day there's an excuse to have more – a work event, or she's had a hard day, or she's depressed, or angry, or celebrating, whatever. 'Just this one time' – I've heard her say it, and you must have too: the most dangerous words in your language or mine, because that's how you start not to notice. When have you ever heard her say 'enough'?"

"Plenty of times."

"No. *Never*. Alcoholism is a disease of more; enough is when you pass out."

"I've tried to help her."

"No, you haven't."

"How *dare* you?"

"You've done anything but help her. You've just mirrored her problem. Her addiction is alcohol; yours is her. You've cleared up after her, you've apologised for her, you've let her think this can go on indefinitely. Instead of making her see how much she's been messing up her life, you've let her keep thinking that what she's doing is normal. Your love for her is soft, when it needs to be tough."

"You think I can't see what you're trying to do here?"

"I'm trying to help Alice."

"No. You're trying to prise her away from me. What do you think I'll do? Throw up my hands and say, 'OK, she's all yours.' I married her for better or for worse, and I'm going to stick through both – that's what marriage is about. It's this shithole you call a city that's done this to her. She made her vows to me, not to you. You're in no position to tell me what to do."

The gunpowder sparked in Lev. "I could have you killed in an instant if that's what I wanted, and no one would be any the wiser. I brought you here because you're Alice's husband and it's only fair that you know she's all right. We both love the same woman, sure, but this isn't a competition to see which one of us she prefers. She needs help from herself before she needs either of us, can't you see that? Don't get me wrong, I can understand why you don't want to listen to me. But for Alice's sake, consider the merits of my suggestion, not its provenance."

"That's nothing to do with –"

"I'm taking charge of Alice's recovery," Lev said with finality. "I'm going to help put her back on her feet. After that, as ever, she's free to choose."

"No."

"You've had years of marriage to make it better, and you haven't done so. I'm sorry, but that's the truth. If you really love Alice, you owe it to her to let someone else have a go."

Alice had braced herself for hell, and hell was what she got. The symptoms began to start in the evening, less than twenty-four hours since her last drink and before the alcohol had completely cleared her system – a sign of reasonably severe dependence. She felt uncomfortable, even trapped, in her own body. If she could have, she'd have climbed out of her skin if like the rhinoceros in Kipling's *Just So Stories*. Her hands were shaking, she was anxious and so nervy that even the slightest sound, a door opening or a window creaking, made her start.

Lev took her temperature and frowned. It was up to thirty-nine degrees, and slimes of sweat seemed to sizzle on her forehead. Her pulse felt giddily high, and her veins thrummed with hammering blood. When he left again, she tried to sleep, and gave up after half an hour wriggling irritably from one side of the bed to the other. She tried to eat, and managed half a piece of toast before feeling as nauseously satiated as after an eight-course meal.

Each symptom came in on top of the one before, a symphony introducing each instrument of the orchestra in turn. Above them all was the haunting voice of the soloist: "Get out of here, have a drink, get away from this place."

A drink, that was all she wanted, a measly hundred grams of vodka. It was the one thing that would help. It was the one thing she couldn't have. Lev had cleared the place of every drop of alcohol, down to the toiletries in the bathroom. There was nothing which contained even trace amounts of alcohol – no mouthwash and no toothpaste, no aftershave and no eau de cologne. Bad breath and rich armpits were a small price to pay, he said.

"I want a drink," Alice said.

"No."

"One drink, just to take the edge off it."

"No."

"Lev, give me a drink, please."

"No."

"I hate you! Give me a fucking drink!"

"No."

She clung to his hand like a little girl afraid of being lost in a crowd. He wiped the sweat from her with dry lips and whispered into her ear. "Take me in into your darkest hour," he said, "and I'll never desert you."

# 89

*Friday, 20 March 1992*

Sabirzhan had taken over Lev's office at Red October, though he looked small and shrunken in the vor's outsize chair, like a small boy playing at his father's desk. There was much to do before Sabirzhan would feel secure in his position, even though – on the surface, at least – things seemed to be progressing as normal. He was confident, however, that everything would work out his way in the end. Yes, the workers had loved Lev, but he'd taken them for the mother of all rides. They would take time to get used to a new boss, but they'd love him in the end.

There was a knock on the door, which he liked to keep closed. "Come!" he shouted, settling back in the chair and steepling his fingers under his chin as though pondering questions of infinite import. The door opened, and Galina walked in. It was the first time Sabirzhan had seen her in days – she'd not been in to work since Rodya's death – and the change in her was shocking. Her eyes were ringed with dark circles of fatigue, and she walked as though the very act of movement demanded all her effort.

Sabirzhan was on his feet instantly. "Galya. Are you all right?"

She blinked at him. Perhaps she was offended by the speed with which he'd usurped Lev.

"I need your help," she said.

Alice had hoped that things would start to get better, that the first part had been the hardest, and that the pain would begin to slide away. In fact, it was becoming worse. One sleepless night on, all the existing symptoms had been augmented and intensified. Her sweats now came in torrents rather than beads, smelling vile as the poisons crawled from her; it was not normal body odour, but the kind of smell associated with corpses or chemical dumps. The shaking was no longer confined to her hands; her arms trembled all the way from fingertips to shoulders so that she couldn't hold a glass of water or a cup of weak tea without spilling half of it on the bed. When she started to suffer miniature seizures, the panic clawed at her through momentary paralysis.

Let me see you through, Lev said, let me see you through. I've seen the dark side too.

The hallucinations came next, though at least she understood them as such. They felt benign, amusing even, as a dream does when you know you're dreaming. The vegetarian Tolstoy with his padded coat and fake silver beard was standing there. "Look," Alice heard herself say, "you're sweating as much as I am." Tolstoy was holding Surikov's *The Morning of the Execution of the Streltsy*, and as she watched he morphed into the Lenin impersonator she'd seen sometimes on Red Square.

Alice had always thought she dreamt of things which had made

449

a particularly strong impression on her, but now she felt it could just as easily be the opposite. Her hallucinations were, often as not, things to which she'd paid relatively little attention at the time: vague thoughts she hadn't bothered to think out to the end, words spoken without feeling and which had passed more or less unnoticed, and which now returned to her clothed in flesh and blood, as if to force her to make up for having neglected them in her sentient hours.

She watched as a fuchsia-pink banknote wafted across the ceiling: five hundred roubles, once so enormous, now so risibly worthless. Voices bounced off the walls: Borzov adamant that "we're not going to lose hope – hope we do have"; Borzov again, quieter but even more insistent, "there are always eighteen drops of vodka left in a bottle. *Always*." Mirages bloomed in the room. There was a plank laid across a bench, to signify that the roof above was being cleaned, and when she looked up it was snowing, or at least that was what she thought, until she looked closer and saw that the snow was in fact fluffy white flakes of poplar pollen which came down in June, she'd always wanted to see the summer snow, and when these flakes settled on the floor they formed rows of business cards with which people were playing poker, and the people were Lev and Bob and Harry, and here came the tax police brandishing thick wads of demands for umpteen tariffs, and the wads had dollars on the outside and cut-up newspapers inside, and Alice was saying, "You've fallen for the oldest trick in the book" – that was her voice, those her feet banging on metallic gangways as she ran, and Borzov again, chortling as he said, "Anatoly Nikolayevich fears you've been sleeping with your head in the west."

Things were becoming ever worse. The shaking in her arms and legs had turned to twitching, great jerking jack-knifes which sent her sheets scurrying halfway down the bed. When she staggered to the bathroom, the floor seemed to slide beneath her feet, first one way and then the other. Her heart was palpitating, bouncing around in her chest; chairs, sofas, television sets all seemed to zoom in and out.

Worst of all, the hallucinations were no longer quixotic reverie; they'd become fused, and she believed that they were real, not benign or amusing but terrifying and armed with chains and clubs and knives and baseball bats and knuckledusters. Lev's suite was now the Terem Palace in the Kremlin, covered with angels and demons, knights and maidens, all soaring across the ceiling and swooping down the walls. Electric tramlines exploded in small blazes above her, and the floor was carpeted with candle stands glowing like softly burning trees. Arkin was by her bed, jabbing at her with his stiletto blade, and she flung up her hands to protect herself as a mushroom-coloured Borzov, clad only in a tiny pair of swimming trunks obscured at the front by the pendulous overhang of his belly, clambered dripping over her prostrate body, she felt his weight on her stomach, and he was followed by a Japanese family moving in splashes of mauve and lime and throwing books at her as they passed; Alice batted away Agatha Christie and James Bond, computer manuals and analyses of the USSR's collapse, translations of Smith, Keynes, Hayek and Galbraith, Bibles, books on yoga and meditation, Sakharov's autobiography.

Lenin's bust was on the bedside table, spinning round as though it had seen *The Exorcist* one too many times. Then it stopped, abruptly, as Sabirzhan disconnected it from the wall, clicking his tongue as he bemoaned the shoddy wiring and then laughing as Galina rubbed her hands over his ass. Galina cooing mockingly at Alice, "You're so *glamorous*, Alice, I'd be you if I could be anyone else," as she took groceries from Lewis' arms and smeared them over Alice – Marmite, Ribena, Cadbury's crème eggs, corned beef – and Alice dived under the covers as Lewis came back into the room with a hunting rifle and started blazing away round the room, she heard glass tinkling and it was Uvarov smashing his baton into her headlight, the high-pitched shattering segueing into a falsetto human voice, Rodya singing "Along Peterskaya Street" before he lunged at Alice to snatch a sweet from her ear, and as she turned her head away he went for her fur hat instead and sprang no-legged from the room.

Lev smoothed her hair from her forehead; it stuck to his fingers in damp tendrils. "Alice?" It was like looking at a waxwork. "Alice?"

She started shaking again, all over, as though wired up to the city grid.

Delirium tremens can be fatal if left untreated. Lev knew that Alice needed immediate hospitalisation; he knew equally that the best place in Moscow was the Sklifosovsky, where Lewis worked. He didn't even hesitate. He called his bodyguards and they drove in convoy, mafiya-style. They couldn't have got there quicker if they'd taken police outriders with them.

Lewis wasn't on duty, and even if he had been he wouldn't have been allowed to look after a patient in whom he had an emotional

451

investment. A Russian doctor took charge of Alice, and he was quick and efficient. He linked her to a drip, rehydrating her with intravenous physiological fluids, including Vitamin B; and he gave her a loading dose of diazepam, a long acting sedative-hypnotic drug. She passed out. She was nothing but a repository expelling bad chemicals and ingesting good ones.

Lev rang Lewis at home and told him what had happened.

# 90

*Saturday, 21 March 1992*
Morning came and went with Alice still unconscious. Her condition had stabilised, however, and the doctor was not worried. Her vital signs – temperature, blood pressure and respiratory rate – were all fine. She was still relatively young, and her constitution was sturdy, she'd get through this, no problem.

That was where the doctor's expertise stopped. He made no comment on the unusual sight of two men in the corridor outside her room, one of them his colleague and the other instantly recognisable throughout Russia; both clearly ill at ease with each other, both desperate to know what news he could give them.

When the doctor had gone, they sat together in silence, lover and husband. What could they say? Perhaps in other circumstances there might have been some kind of accommodation, an understanding that what had happened was not the other's fault and that the blame lay mainly with the slender figure in the bed beyond the door. But how could that be, when their love for her was so raw?

Lev turned his head away from Lewis before smiling, less for fear that Lewis would see than that he would misunderstand. It would have been very Russian, Lev was thinking, to have come this far and then die from renouncing something because you knew that in the end it would kill you.

There was a television in the corridor, and they watched the news together. A former army colonel had robbed a bank and held the cashiers hostage after his life savings had been wiped out. Seduced by the siren songs of Russia's new capitalists, the colonel had taken his hidden stash of cash, what the Russians called his 'independence fund', and invested in the Eynabejan Bank, a newly established outfit which had promised phenomenal rates of investment return. When it had collected millions of dollars, mainly from its clients' life savings, the Eynabejan Bank had simply disappeared. Only then did a TV reporter covering the story realise that Eynabejan, spelt backwards, read *najebanye* – 'fuck you'.

The colonel had needed the money to pay for an operation to save his wife's sight. The policemen who'd talked him into ending the siege gave him vodka and looked after him. The officers from the Ministry of Finance shrugged their shoulders and said they'd added the names of the Fuck-You Bank's board members to a wanted list already several thousand strong. Eynabejan was hardly the first bank to swipe easy cash and do a runner, nor would it be the last.

"Look at that shit," Lewis said. "What kind of place is it where people are reduced to that? Damn country – it's going to the dogs, whoever's in charge."

Alice regained consciousness later in the day, and when she did, it was Lev for whom she asked. He went in to see her with no sense of triumph, outward or inward. He held her and told her what had happened, where she was, and that Lewis wanted to see her; then he left the room so that Alice could have time alone with her husband, for Lewis' sake if not for hers.

Alice was discharged that afternoon. Lewis came to the main entrance to see her off. She climbed into the back of Lev's Mercedes 600, and didn't look back once as the convoy eased out into the traffic and headed towards the Kotelniki.

Lev's love was a bubble that kept Alice safe. He understood that she was missing the structure of addiction, the way drinking rituals had marked her time. To keep this framework filled, he made sure that she always had something to do, no matter how minor. They drank tea, they watched videos, they read to each other – the usual bottle-necks through which sands trickled.

There was still a void at the heart of her, of course. Her physical cravings were slowly dwindling, but the mental ones remained as strong as ever. Her existence felt stale and colourless, and she panicked that she'd cut herself off not only from people, but from life itself. Only now she was eschewing alcohol did Alice realise how much her existence had revolved around it. She was scared that everything she prized – fun, intimate conversations, hammering out grandiose plans for social transformation – would be denied her for ever, because they were all soaked with vodka.

She remembered why she used to drink: to turn herself into

someone she liked. Alice Mark II seemed boring and unattractive in contrast; emotionally naked, walking on eggshells and worrying about panic attacks. Without her liquid protector, everything seemed different and scary. Alice kept finding herself twitching for the warm and comforting option of vodka rather than the cold and threatening one of abstinence. The one thing which could give her courage was the very thing she was forbidden.

With anxiety and insecurity came anger, forking and sparking at diffuse targets: at being singled out by the disease, at being unable to achieve the control which she'd fought so hard to obtain, at being forced to accept defeat and go into recovery, at having to face up to issues she wanted to forget and make amends. She shouted and beat her fist into the pillows; she cried, sobbing so much that she almost felt herself shrinking. At dinner, when one of her tears fell to the table, Lev tenderly drew a heart with it. There wasn't quite enough liquid for him to finish the down slope; she laughed through her tears, and the shaking of her head released another drop, perfectly completing the shape.

Lev was infinitely patient. She was having to remaster life itself, he pointed out. She'd only rejoin the human race if she reversed all the beliefs which alcoholism had fostered. Her disordered sense of self had made it hard for Alice to see that anyone could love her for her own merits. She'd been concentrating on her own demerits to such an extent that she'd been living a lie. It was what the Russians had been told when the old system had collapsed, he said; they'd all been living a lie, they simply had to accept that and change their lives accordingly.

Yes, she replied; and look how well they were managing *that*.

He made her keep the Polaroid which Nadhezda had taken in the clinic, to remind her of what alcohol had done to her and would do again if she gave it half a chance. Like the soldiers in Afghanistan or the men in the gulag, Alice had to take life twelve hours at a time, her next goal never further away than the next sunrise or sunset. The moment she projected too far into the future, the daunting scale of the task would become all too clear, and she would almost certainly relapse. Recovery would take a lifetime. The quicker she tried to go, the quicker she'd ruin it.

Lev brought in Oligarchy – a local version of Monopoly. "'The object of the game'," Lev said, reading from the instruction manual, "'is to acquire as much money as possible through legal and illegal means, to control commerce and the press, to bankrupt your opponents, and finally to seize the entire board.'"

In concept, Monopoly perfectly suits the Russian mentality; its problem is that it has too many rules and too many scruples. Oligarchy changed all that. Players' progress around the board was still marked with little silver emblems, but they were no longer hats, irons, boots and dogs; instead, they were Mercedes 600s, TT pistols, cell phones and Armani suits. The 'GO' square had been renamed 'US Aid'; 'Free Parking' was now a Swiss bank account; property holders demanded bribes rather than rent from those who landed on their squares; railroads and utilities had been replaced by ministers, who were just as easily bought, of course; and chance cards and community chest had been replaced by *kompromat* and presidential decrees respectively.

Lev chose the Mercedes 600, Alice the Armani suit. Even in this prosaic, workaday aspect of her being, dishevelled and with her sleeves rolled up as she kissed the dice for luck and shook them extravagantly between her hands, she almost frightened him with her beauty. They played long into the night, and no amount of laughter and joking could disguise the vigour of their competitiveness. There was a vast, churning intensity to everything they did; they'd never just simply been together, doing not very much, the way she'd managed with Lewis, even when things were going wrong.

To sit in companionable silence is one of the joys of being a couple, but with Alice and Lev such downtime felt like a dereliction of duty, a waste of the energy which crackled between them. She'd once likened him to vodka, and she saw now that the comparison hadn't been idle. Just as she'd always remembered when and where and what her last drink had been, so Alice could always recall when she'd last seen Lev, what he'd been wearing, what they'd talked about or what they'd done, how they'd made love . . .

. . . except they hadn't, not since she'd come back to him. It wasn't just her physical cravings for vodka that had gone; those for sex had vanished too. Alice began to count back through all the times she and Lev had screwed, but even before she was halfway through, she knew that there'd be no exceptions to the rule. They'd never made love when she hadn't had at least one drink beforehand. Entirely sober, the prospect of physical intimacy terrified her.

When, hours into Oligarchy and with the game more or less level, they'd argued playfully about which square Lev had landed on, and she'd plucked the Mercedes from the board and refused to give it back until he agreed with her, and he'd gone to wrestle her for it, she'd suddenly frozen, squealing laughter dying in her throat. It was the way his arms were moving over her, too sexual for her sober comfort, even though all he was doing was trying to get his token back, and she'd rolled away from him and burst into tears, apologising over and over, he'd been so good with her and she couldn't explain why she was reacting this way, but she *was*, and she needed time and she hoped to God he'd give it to her because she couldn't imagine being without him . . .

"Alice, stop beating yourself up. You expect more of yourself than I do. Let things come naturally, there's no hurry, not for anything. We have all the time in the world."

# 91

*Sunday, 22 March 1992*

Alice woke to find Lev staring at her so adoringly that it unsettled her.

"How long have you been looking at me?" she asked.

"Hours."

She looked so peaceful in sleep, he told her, all her worries temporarily smoothed away. There's something about the serenity of slumber which is intensely personal; he was invading every part of her now, the boundaries between them were dissolving. How could she worry about her privacy being violated, when there was none left? They were two halves of a whole, moving around and always coming back to each other.

He had to go out for a couple of hours. She tried not to worry or be resentful – she understood that he had things to do, even now – but without him she didn't have enough to take her mind off things. She was half-asleep when he left; when she woke and tried to leave the bedroom, she found that he'd locked the door from the outside. She was a prisoner. Couldn't he trust her to behave as an adult? No, she thought, as she stalked the room looking for even the tiniest smidgeon of vodka he might have forgotten to remove; he couldn't. Why did she want a drink? To assuage her baser desires and show him the defiance of her resentment, and both reactions were childish.

\* \* \*

The shade of yellow in which the presidential residence is painted appears to change colour according to the time. In the faint light of the morning, it's a thick egg yolk; the sharply angled rays of the setting sun deepen it to mustard. Now, at midday, it had the rich lustre of lemon.

Sabirzhan had come with Galina, and he was succinct: there were four people round the table and Lev had betrayed them all. He'd tried to remove first Arkin and then Borzov from office; he'd more or less accused Sabirzhan of the child murders; and he'd taken the real culprit, Rodion Khruminsch, Galya's husband, and dispensed mafiya justice without a thought for due process. Lev had given each of them a reason to want him out of the picture, permanently.

The president had struck a deal with Lev, Borzov said. He wouldn't renege on it.

Yes, Sabirzhan understood that, but what he was suggesting had nothing to do with that deal. Since the deal had been struck, Rodion had been killed, almost certainly by Lev himself, though no one present at the kangaroo court would admit it. So Galina would go and see Lev. Lev still trusted her; he was unaware of her part in helping Alice uncover his scams – though of course Sabirzhan didn't mention this to Arkin and Borzov. In fact, Lev would probably feel that he owed her an explanation at the very least, and perhaps more. Galina would wear a wire, and she'd get Lev to tell her what had happened. Their conversation could then be used in evidence against him.

Galina nodded in agreement; she wanted to do it.

"Absolutely not." Borzov was adamant. "You're untrained; it's too dangerous. You're sprinkling salt under her tail, Tengiz – you'll get her into trouble. If she's rumbled before she's got him to confess, the whole thing will be lost. There'll be no more element of surprise."

"I have to disagree, Anatoly Nikolayevich," Arkin said. "Galya's the only one that can do it. Tengiz is trained, but Lev wouldn't tell him what day it is. If Lev trusts Galya, why should he suspect that she's wearing a wire?" He turned to Galina. "You *will* get him to confess, you *will* record it; there's no two ways about it." It was Arkin at his most Marxist: the ends justified the means, and the pursuit of the desired outcome brooked no obstacles.

The question of whether or not to wear a wire settled, they now debated what type of device it should be. There were two possibilities: the Nagra tape recorder or the T-4 transmitter, both of them the most up-to-date equipment available to the Russian authorities, both long since abandoned as obsolete by the FBI. Whichever one Galina used, she was bound to pick up all kinds of surround sounds – clothes rustling, feet and chairs shuffling, radios, televisions. She wouldn't be able to test on scene for sound levels; she wouldn't be able to arrange Lev as she liked for optimum recording; she would-n't be able to ask him to raise his voice or repeat things more slowly.

The Nagra was relatively hefty, fifteen by ten by two centimetres. Manually activated, it used a three-hour tape and was able only to record, so the tape had to be transferred to another machine for playback. The Nagra's microphone was about the size of the eraser on the end of a pencil tip, and a long wire meant it could be hidden anywhere on Galya's body. With a Nagra, Galya wouldn't need to rely on back-up. As long as she got Lev to admit killing her husband within the tape's recording span, and then found a way to get the tape to the authorities, they could arrest Lev at any time afterwards.

The T-4 was half the size of the Nagra – nine centimetres by six by one – and, though it had no intrinsic recording capacity, it could transmit to monitoring agents nearby who'd listen and record. Its maximum range was perhaps two blocks, though steel structures, adverse weather conditions and passing vehicles could all reduce this. The antenna was small and flexible, with a tiny microphone bulb on the end, and it would last four hours on fresh batteries. The T-4 was less likely to be seen than the Nagra. Transmission meant that a snatch squad could move in the moment they heard Lev admit to Rodion's murder.

Galina wanted to wear the Nagra because there was less to go wrong. Sabirzhan wanted her to wear the T-4. "The Nagra's record-ing quality is rubbish," he said. "If you haven't got it clearly, there's no way you'll know until afterwards, by which time it'll be too late. With the T-4, the technicians can fiddle with the sound quality with-out you needing to worry about it."

"There's more chance of a screw-up with the T-4."

"And then we can come and get you out. With the Nagra, you're on your own."

She was untrained, she needed all the help she could get; that was what all three men were thinking. Galina sighed as she was voted down. This was Russia, she reminded herself, where you hoped for the best and prepared for the worst.

Against Arkin's will – for him, it was confession or nothing – they worked on a code phrase as a signal for the Spetsnazy to swing into action, no questions asked. It would be left to Galina's discretion as

to whether or when to use the phrase: it could be when she considered that Lev had said enough, or if she was in dire trouble and
needed to be extracted without delay. The phrase had to be something that wouldn't crop up in the normal course of conversation,
but not too eclectic to be jarring if Galya had to incorporate it into
the dialogue. They tossed ideas around – jokes, famous quotes, refer-
ences to things within Red October – before settling on something
short, sharp and to the point: *"in vodka veritas"*.

# 92

*Monday, 23 March 1992*
Above Alice's head, electric tramlines exploded in small blazes. The
authorities had laid even more snow-melting chemicals than usual
as the thaw set in, the quicker to have the streets cleared, and the
fumes were eating away at the lines' external insulation. The ther-
mometer was hovering at seven or eight degrees above zero, but
Muscovites gloomily warned that it was almost certainly a false
dawn. Spring in Russia usually hammered at the door two or three
times before winter finally decided to let it through.

Water droplets drummed on the metal of the drainpipes and the
cornices, roof tapping message to roof. As Moscow cars habitually
sported tidemarks of grime up to their door handles, so the pedestrians were now splattered from ankle to knee with water and mud.
Men in thick black jackets were hacking up blocks of ice with iron
bars and spades; planks laid across benches or trestles signified that
roof-cleaning was taking place above. Still, plenty of people were
killed by falling icicles every year, straight through the head, sharp
as a knife, usually in places where the warnings had been stolen –
planks, benches and trestles were all valuable commodities.

The need for reparations to Lewis had been playing on Alice's
mind, and the longer she left it, especially without the dampening
effect of vodka, the greater importance it seemed to assume. It was
something she had to face, not just for Lewis' sake but also for her
own peace of mind.

She'd made an inventory of the wrongs she'd done him, and it
went on for pages. Set down in black and white, she realised perhaps
for the first time exactly how much damage she'd done, and that
there was no way she could ever go back, even if she'd wanted to
and even if he'd take her. The best they could hope for was a wary

and regretful accommodation; it was the very least he deserved.

She went round early in the evening, unannounced and alone, walking fast up to the familiar block in Patriarch's Ponds and plunging the key like a dagger into the lock, fast and sharp, before she lost her – well, her bottle, for lack of a better word. The thought would have made her laugh if she hadn't so desperately wanted a drink to settle her nerves.

The apartment seemed at once familiar and distant, and it was a moment before she realised why. This was where she'd drunk herself stupid, this was where she'd thrown up on the sheets, this was where she'd yelled at Lewis in blind intoxicated fury. This place would forever be associated in her mind with drinking.

All the gang were there: Bob, Christina, Harry, and of course Lewis himself. They turned to look at Alice in horrified silence as she walked in.

"What are *you* doing here?" Christina, spiky. "Haven't you caused enough trouble?"

"Christina, please." Lewis was already on his feet. "It's my apartment, I'll deal with this. Excuse me a moment, everyone." He took Alice by the elbow and steered her into the bedroom. She glanced quickly round; looking, she realised, for the traces of another woman, though less from jealousy than curiosity as to whether his life had changed as drastically as hers.

"What *are* you doing here?" he asked.

"I'm sorry, Lewis, I didn't mean to spoil your party. I'll go, I'll come back another time. Christina was right."

"What Christina thinks is no worry of yours. Tell me why you've come."

"To say sorry." It sounded so simple, put that way.

"Sorry?" He pushed some air through his nose. "OK. You're sorry. Thank you."

"That's it? You don't want to hear any more?"

"What's there to hear, Alice? I love you and you don't love me. I keep trying to understand the meaning of this judgement on me, to see the reason for it. I look into myself, I go over our whole life together, everything I know about you, and me, and us together, and I can't find the beginning. I can't remember what it is I did and how I brought this misfortune on myself. I love you – if only you knew how much. There's no one better than you in the whole world, even after all you've done. But you love another man. What can I do?"

"You could fight it."

"Why?"

"Lewis, what's brought this on?"

Lewis almost smiled. "He did."

"*He?*"

"Lev. When he brought me to see him the day after you'd stormed out of the Aragvi, to tell me where you were and that you were OK. I didn't want to listen at the time, but when I'd calmed down and thought about what he'd said, it made sense. He made me realise something I'd been blind to before: you were my addiction just as much as vodka was yours. And by refusing to recognise that, I hadn't helped you, or me, or us."

"Lewis, you can't blame yourself for this. It was my drinking that fucked everything up."

"Yes, but there are ways and means to get round it, and I didn't choose any of them."

"This is . . ."

"Addictive behaviour's the same, it doesn't matter what it focuses on. The only way to get over it is to break it. To start with, I denied you had a problem. When I accepted there was something wrong, first I played it down, then I blamed other things for it, then I ratio-nalised it, then I intellectualised it; then I became hostile to it."

Alice could hear Christina's voice from next door, hectoring. The world would end before Christina ran out of things to moan about. Alice gestured with her head back towards the dining-room. "I'm surprised Christina and Bob are still here, after what happened to Josh. How is he?"

"A touch of concussion, but otherwise fine. He has no idea what happened to him – Bob told him he took a tumble on the ice and bumped his head. It was pretty easy to convince him that the stuff about a goblin dragging him into his cave was all just a bad dream."

"What about the others? I guess they think I'm the devil incar-nate after all this."

"You really want to know?"

They were his friends, really, not hers. Alice shook her head. "No."

"Good. You can probably guess, anyways."

"The only one whose reaction matters is you."

It sounded trite, but he knew she wouldn't have come here unless it was true. "Well, as you can see, there's one more stage after hostil-ity."

"Which is?"

"Acceptance. You're an alcoholic and I'm not; I love you and you don't love me. That's the way it is, and I don't have the energy to keep hiding from it or to hate you for it. I lost you a long time ago. If you want a divorce, I won't stand in your way."

The sobs gushed from Alice till she feared being drowned in her own tears.

# 93

*Tuesday, 24 March 1992*

The T-4 prickled against Galina's skin. It was taped to the small of her back, hidden under both a shirt and a sweater, but as far as she was concerned, it could hardly have been more obvious if she'd taken it out, painted it pink and waved it around the room. She was sure Lev would notice that something was awry. Was she walking funny, did her voice sound strained? All she had to do was leave, say she was sorry, it didn't matter; walk out and leave him none the wiser.

None the wiser, and still free. She thought of Rodya, dead because of the madness which had consumed him. She thought of Sveta, back at the school on Prospekt Mira because life must go on, she must endure, even when her only son was dead and she'd never now be a grandmother. Galina hadn't told Sveta anything of her plan, because Sveta would have tried to talk her out of it. Galina thought of what Alice had said when she'd convinced her to pass over the Nicosia phone number, about doing things properly; doing things properly meant not letting people getting away with killing other people. She collected herself and resolved that she would do this: get Lev to admit, mention, agree, confess, whatever, that he'd killed Rodya. This was the moment she'd been waiting for ever since Irk had come to tell her that Rodya was dead, and now it was on her it seemed too soon by half.

The Spetsnazy were here, vanloads and vanloads of them. Some were disguised as maintenance men and window cleaners. Others were dressed all in black and had come up the Kotelniki's fire escapes and elevator shafts, ready to shoot their way in at a moment's notice. Lev's bodyguards were the best in the business, and they'd see off most attacks that rival mafiya bosses could consider, let alone anything run by the police, but a full-scale assault by army special forces was a different calico altogether.

Galina was desperately thirsty. She wanted a drink – not vodka, of course, she needed to keep a clear head – but there was no mineral water in sight, and Moscow tap water isn't safe to drink without being boiled first, especially in spring, when the melting snow cover slides a goodly proportion of the city's pollutants into the river.

Lev was looking straight at Galina. He knows, Galina thought, he knows. Don't be so stupid, her reason said, of course he's going to be looking at you, you're the only person here.

"Has that Georgian weasel wrecked my distillery yet?" he asked.

Galina shrugged. "You know how things are."

"You're working for *him* now? What's going on there?"

Galina didn't want to discuss Red October with Lev, and she didn't know how a professional would react – wait him out, or try and steer the conversation round – but she was conscious that the transmitter's batteries were finite, so she did what came naturally: she blurted out what was on her mind. "What happened to Rodya?"

Lev was perfectly still for a moment, then he sat back in his chair, nodding to himself. "*That's* what you've come about. Of course." He looked at the ceiling, as though pondering what to tell her. Was he embarrassed? That would be a first, Galina thought.

"He was my husband," she said. "Any woman would want to know."

"Rodya was sick," Lev said. "No, he was more than sick. He was wounded, in torment."

"We could have got him help. Not here – abroad, where they've got the right pills."

"He was too sick for pills, Galya. This . . . it's hard for you to understand. Don't take this the wrong way, but to me Rodya seemed like a wounded animal. He was in agony. There's only one way to deal with a wounded animal, Galya. If you see a dog on the road, hit by a car but still alive, what do you do? Do you drive round it? Not if you have a heart. You line it up under your wheels and put it out of its misery."

"No!" The wounded animal was in Galina's cry.

"It was the best thing to do, Galya. It was the *merciful* thing to do."

She was crying now, and Lev was on his feet, enveloping her in his vast arms. Her husband's executioner, she thought, trying to comfort her for what he'd done. She pushed back against him, and when he didn't yield she surrendered to it, burying her face in a chest so massive that she could suffocate herself there, and he pulled her closer, pressing the wire harder against her skin.

The sensation jerked Galina through her tears. Would he feel the transmitter under her clothes? Why weren't the Spetsnazy here? Lev had told her what had happened, more or less . . . That was it, she thought: more or less. He'd implied much, but what had he actually said? They wouldn't come in until they had a proper confession, and they wouldn't get a confession if he found the wire. She wriggled free of him.

"Let me get you some vodka," Lev said.

"Did you kill Rodya?" she said. Too bold?

He was walking across the room, towards the sideboard, and answered her without turning round. "What I did was for the best, Galya. Please don't ask any more."

"I need to know."

He poured two glasses and came back with them. "Why?"

"Because . . . of course I do."

He handed her a glass and sat down. "Don't do this to yourself, Galya."

"Just tell me. Please."

Alice walked into the room.

"Galya! I didn't know you were here." Alice started across the carpet towards her, and then stopped. Her instinctive reaction at seeing Galya had been happiness; it was only afterwards that she'd remembered they weren't friends, and why. They'd liked each other once. To Alice, it seemed as though their quarrels – like everything else – had taken place in another lifetime.

Lev saw Alice's confusion, and misinterpreted it. "It's for medicinal purposes, darling," he said, gesturing at the vodka. "I'm about to give Galya a nasty shock. Perhaps you'd prefer to leave the room."

"I want to see what's happening in the world," Alice said, and turned on the television.

Lev, ignorant of the schism between Alice and Galina; Galina, ignorant of Alice's long fall to the bottom of the bottle and slow rise back; Alice, ignorant of the magnitude of what Galina had come for. Lev opened his mouth to order Alice out, but that would spark an argument, and he was aware, too aware, of her fragility. Perhaps, he thought, this would be easier if she were here. She could give Galya some support, woman to woman. It was a feeble excuse, and Lev was disgusted at himself for making it, but he turned to Galina anyway.

"It was quick. He felt no pain."

"What was quick?"

"Rodya's death."

Noise from the corner; a reporter talking excitedly. Would the

464

Spetsnazy still be able to hear over the noise from the television? Galina moved closer to Lev, no longer caring if it seemed strange. "How did he die?"

"He was shot."

"Who shot him?"

Lev was a vor, and vory killed people, even when those people had worked for them, even when the vor had befriended their families. Vory killed people, and until now Lev had never found it hard to admit. Until a young woman's relentless, naïve probing had weakened him in a way that decades in a jail cell could never have.

"I shot him."

"You shot him?" You, *you*: that was where she'd laid the emphasis.

"Yes, I shot him – who else?"

Where time had raced before, eating up the transmitter's precious batteries, it suddenly juddered to a halt. For Galina, every second that the Spetsnazy didn't come kicking down the door and smashing through the windows stretched as long as a Brezhnev speech; and every moment that passed unchanged brought with it imagined scenarios of doom. The transmission had broken down; they were fighting with Lev's men outside; 21st Century thugs were raping and killing Sveta in revenge for Galina's treason.

Galina couldn't believe what Lev had said; she could believe it all too easily. She raised her glass unsteadily at him, mockery of a toast. "*In vodka veritas,*" she said.

"There was no alternative," Lev said. Why did he feel the need to explain himself? "Years in one of those stinking jails waiting for . . ." he stumbled over his words, as his voice had seemed momentarily to be coming back at him from the television set: ". . . waiting for some judge to get off his ass" – there it was again, definitely coming in stereo, and he knew what it meant even as Galina and Alice shot puzzled looks at each other, finally reunited, albeit only in bewilderment. The frequency on which the T-4 was transmitting was too near that of the television channel Alice was watching, and so it was broadcasting Lev's voice back through the set. Lev knew what the sound meant, every gangster did, they were paranoid about wires.

Galina, confused, stepped away from Lev's chair towards Alice, near enough the television set to send a piercing shriek of feedback round the room, and Lev fixed her with the certainty of his glare, deepest hurt and murderous hatred. She knew it must be something to do with the wire. This wouldn't have happened with the Nagra, Galina thought helplessly. She should have been firmer back at the Kremlin – *her*, against the two most powerful men in the land, how could she have been?

"*In vodka veritas*," Galina said, and then again, more frantically, "*in vodka veritas, in vodka veritas –*" the last one little more than a yelp.

Galina was backing towards the door, Lev hissing and spitting as he rose from his chair like an erupting volcano, Alice asking: "What the hell's going on?" and it was all Galina could do to keep her legs moving through mists of white panic, and suddenly the world exploded, light and smoke everywhere, and Galina thought for a moment, really believed, that Lev had somehow spontaneously combusted with rage, and as her eyes streamed and she lost all notion of which way was up, she realised that it was of course the Spetsnazy with their thunderflashes coming to the rescue, and not a moment too soon.

Two Spetsnazy trussed Galya's hands behind her back and pressed her head against the floor. When she tried to shout her innocence, she took a smack in the mouth. This was how they worked: secure everyone first, then sort it out later. Bodies writhed through the smoke, disorientated, choking and eyes streaming, Lev was struggling against six men, and it was all they could do to keep him in check.

There were people everywhere, barking shouts and gunfire in staccato flicks. Alice's throat hurt, that was the only way she knew she was screaming, because she sure as hell couldn't hear it above the shots and the yelling and the wet slaps as bodies hit the floor or were flung against walls. She was on her feet now, out into the fresh air of the fire escape and down, down, down, Lev and Galya with her, shins and ankles cracked hard against the metal rungs and the leathered lumps of dead mafiyosi, and this was where the endless circles of deceit had got them all, into the back of Spetsnaz trucks and howling through the streets of Moscow.

Galina was taken home; Lev and Alice were brought to the Kremlin. They were confined to one of the guest apartments, a gilded prison where they were provided with all the comforts and told absolutely nothing. There were guards at their door and outside their window, all silent as Trappist monks; there were no telephones in the apartment, and the nearest they had to contact with the outside world was a television set and the view over the battlements out across the river. In the square below, staff bustled with tables and chairs. Saturday would be Borzov's seventieth birthday, and a ball was being held in his honour.

Lev kept constant watch over Alice, reassuring and protecting her in equal measures. They talked until the small hours before curling round each other, their clothes firmly on. Alice muttered about being embarrassed with all the guards there, and not knowing what was happening to them, but they both knew that excuses did not equal reasons.

# 94

*Wednesday, 25 March 1992*

Borzov had summoned Lev; just Lev, not Alice. Before he left her, Lev kissed her hard and told her everything would be all right, and he said it with such sincerity that he almost believed it himself. As they walked to Borzov's office, he dwarfed the guards who surrounded him. Watching from the window, Alice thought of tugboats escorting a super tanker from harbour.

Borzov and Arkin were waiting. Vodka was poured and pleasantries exchanged. Arkin handed Lev a copy of *Pravda*. "A country abandoned by its government," the headline screamed. Underneath, the text continued in more sober fashion. "Under communism, there was a social contract, guaranteeing a safety net in return for political acquiescence. Now the government continue to run things, but for their own benefit only. They have abandoned the social contract."

The figures made depressing reading. Three per cent thought the government guaranteed timely payment of wages, pensions and salaries. Another three per cent – or perhaps the same three per cent – thought that social protection of the unemployed, homeless and needy was all it could be. Six per cent thought Russia was moving in the right direction; double that number thought it was stationary. They were clearly misguided, Lev thought; Russia was never stationary. Four per cent thought the government was doing a good job fighting organised crime, and eight per cent approved of the way in which law and order was maintained.

"What do you think?" Arkin said.

"The eight per cent who approve of law and order is promising."

467

"Anatoly Nikolayevich wants you to come to the Chief's birthday on Saturday," Borzov said happily, "and he wants you to try and kill him there."

The assassination attempt would not be for real, of course. Lev's gun would be loaded with blanks. The important thing was that it would *look* real, and therefore engender public sympathy for Borzov and swing back in his favour the public opinion which had been ebbing ever since the August coup and was now, after the shelling of the White House, approaching dangerously low levels. Borzov had no qualms about being authoritarian – a state of emergency was still in effect – but he didn't want to be unpopular with it. All good dictators are popular at least for a time; one in six Russians still think of Stalin as their greatest leader. But things were changing, and he couldn't rule as they had in the old days, not indefinitely.

"Anatoly Nikolayevich believes absolutely in what he's trying to do," Borzov said, "and in time the Russian people will too; but he needs that time."

So this was the plan, as audacious, radical and hare-brained as most Russian programmes tend to be. Lev would fire the gun; the bodyguards would overpower him and bundle Borzov out of the room; the press would be told that Lev had gone berserk, even after Borzov had been decent enough to extend him an olive branch by inviting him to the ball; and Lev would be ostensibly jailed. In reality, he and Alice would be free to start a new life wherever they pleased, and Borzov would afford them every resource necessary to do this.

"It's absurd," Lev said.

"It's perfect," Arkin said. "Motive, means, opportunity. It'll take Anatoly Nikolayevich back to the people, which is where he belongs."

It was an article of faith among many Russians that Gorbachev had organised the August coup, Lev thought. Why couldn't Borzov set up an assassination attempt against himself?

"You're asking me to give up everything I have here. Everything I've worked for; everything I've believed in." Neither Borzov nor Arkin demurred. "And if I don't?"

"You've confessed to the murder of Rodion Khruminsch," Arkin said. "We have it on tape. You'll spend the rest of your life in Butyurka."

Butyurka is one of Moscow's most notorious jails. It had been the starting-point for czarist convoys of prisoners bound for Siberia, a wasteland they'd reached not in cattle trucks or on horseback, but on foot, and in fetters. After the revolution, Butyurka had become an overcrowded transit prison, cramming cells to six times their supposed limit and squeezing two thousand men, including Solzhenitsyn, into the church, where they'd been obliged to drink soup from their coat-tails. Borzov wasn't going to dignify Lev as an enemy of the state by sending him back to the Lefortovo, where he'd still have an active network of accomplices.

He laughed. "Butyurka? I've spent half my life in the gulag. You think I could care less about going to Butyurka?"

"Before, no. Now . . ." Arkin let the word hang in the air. "You'd never see your lover again."

Borzov was silent, Lev noted. It was Arkin playing the hard man, stabbing home the president's wishes, his master's voice.

"I need time to think," Lev said.

"No. No time. Decide *now*. If you say no, you'll never see her again. You'll go straight from here to Butyurka. We'll take her out of the Saviour Gate and dump her in Red Square. You're all she has left. You can do that to her, abandon her, and then spend the next twenty years climbing the walls of your cell because you chose wrong."

"Your methods stink."

"My methods are for the greater good."

"*My?*"

"Our."

Lev turned to Borzov. "You have mixed eyes, Anatoly Nikolayevich."

"How so?"

"I see a dreamer in one eye and a fool in the other."

Arkin stiffened at the insult, but Borzov laughed; he recognised the truth of it. "Perfect to lead a nation of dreamers and fools, then," he said.

# 95

*Thursday, 26 March 1992*
The *Izvestiya* front page carried the story of the cosmonaut Sergei Krikalev, who'd returned to earth yesterday after ten months in space only to discover that, on a salary of fifteen hundred roubles a month, he was more or less broke. Krikalev, Russia's own Major

Tom, had blasted off last May as a resident of Leningrad in the Soviet Union; he'd returned as one of St Petersburg in Russia. This was the third time he'd tried to land; the coup attempt had kept him aloft last August, and a dispute between Russia and Kazakstan over who owned the Baikonur cosmodrome had repeated the process two months later. Judging by the shock and consternation on his face, Alice thought, Krikalev would rather have stayed up in space until the end of time, far from the madding crowd and all the bullshit. She wondered whether he'd had enough vodka to last him.

Lev and Alice would go and live in the middle of nowhere. A couple could lose themselves in Russia's vastness till the end of time, safe from any pursuers. There were places where the locals still didn't realise communism was no more, and where they'd have cared even less if they had known; places that took days to reach, accessible not by train and car but boat and horseback; places where they didn't even know who Borzov was.

In the lamp-washed glow of their Kremlin apartment, they planned their new life together: they'd have a small cottage, outbuildings, a garden with tomato plants down one end, some livestock too, a well, they'd be entirely self-sufficient, at one with the earth like true peasants.

They'd go to villages where the women would wait for the bread truck, and where they'd gather round and take their loaves, simply and without fuss, when it arrived. There'd be no pushing or jostling, let alone raised voices; everyone would know that they'd get their allocation, so they'd stand in line and gossip quietly. One of the babushki would begin to sing "By the Long Road", and the rest of them would take up the chant, slowly coming in when it felt right to them. An old Russian folk song is like a weir; it may look as though it's no longer flowing, but in its depths it's ceaselessly rushing through the sluice-gates, and its stillness is an illusion.

Lake Baikal, Lev said; that was where they should start, because Baikal is the perfect metaphor for Russia. It's unimaginably vast in both dimensions. It holds more water than all five of America's Great Lakes combined, and it's steeped in its own ecosystem, teeming with plant and animal species, many of them unique.

Alice had changed. Before, she couldn't even have considered living such a timeless existence. Now, she was ready to give everything up for Lev. She'd die for him, she said, and insisted on this when

470

he demurred. It's something that people always say, but she really meant it: she really would.

It was mutual, he said.

For Lev and Alice, everything they'd ever believed and lived for had been swept away. That was how they saw each other now, stripped to the bone and beyond.

# 96

*Friday, 27 March 1992*

The waiting was almost over. This was the last night they'd spend in Moscow, the city Alice loved so much.

The schedule for tomorrow had been fully worked out. In the evening, just before the ball, Lev would be given a gun filled with blanks. There'd be dinner, and then Borzov would make a speech. It was then, when everyone was watching, that Lev would make the apparent assassination attempt. Afterwards he would be taken to Lefortovo prison, just for show. Any would-be presidential assassin would automatically be taken to Lefortovo, the traditional place of incarceration for enemies of the state. Lev's presence there, no matter how brief, was therefore imperative to the charade. With appearances satisfied, he'd be secretly removed from Lefortovo later that evening and driven to Domodevo Airport, where Alice would be waiting. They'd board a military plane bound for Baikal, and they'd disappear.

"He refused to negotiate for your life," Lev told Alice. "He tried to kill me in the White House. And now he puts us through this senseless farce. The fucker's lucky they're only giving me blanks."

Another day drowned in the river beyond the battlements of the old fortress.

They went to a banya in the Kremlin. Lev lifted Alice over the threshold. When she looked quizzical, he explained: "It's an old superstition. Stillborn children are often buried underneath the banya; a man carries a woman inside so that their own kids don't suffer the same fate."

The steam and heat swarmed at them, tangible entities. They undressed in silence. Lev checked the fire under the rocks; the smoke smelt like Siberian cedar, one of the commonest banya woods, along with birch and pine – but never aspen, regarded as a sorrowful tree.

471

Satisfied the logs were burning strongly, he tossed some water on the rocks, and Alice giggled as the steam hissed.

The attendants had left them some switches made of birch branches. Lev picked a couple up and soaked them in the hot-water bucket for a few moments, to make sure that the leaves were soft. When he took them out, he flicked through the branches carefully, checking for stray shrubs. "I've heard unhappy stories from people who've unwittingly added a sprig or two of poison ivy," he said, and smacked one of the switches across Alice's back.

"Ow!" she said. "That hurt!"

"It's supposed to." He handed her the other one. "Here, do it to me."

She whipped the switch across his back, at first reluctantly; then, as she saw it was part of the ritual, with more confidence, driving the scalding steam deeper into Lev's skin, seeing the crimson weals through his tattoos and the way sweat sprang from the marks.

"Here," he said eventually, and guided her to one of the wooden benches. He reached into the small bag he'd brought with him and brought out a small container of milk, which he opened and poured over her, watching the creamy streams part on the ridges of her shoulders and flow down both sides of her, front and back. She shivered, and not from cold.

"It collects the sweat," he said. And it did, too: little oily globules tumbled over each other towards her navel.

"It feels lovely."

"You want some honey? It's good for your skin."

She looked at him with widening eyes. "Yes, please."

Lev found the honey jar, dipped his fingers inside, and pulled them out trailing sticky golden tendrils which he smeared over her stomach, moving slowly upwards in circles at first small and tight, becoming gradually wider, larger, right up to the underside of her breasts and, when she gave a little nod that came with a gasp, over them as well.

"Golden one," he said.

"Use your tongue," she breathed.

He knelt to her and began to lick, collecting stripes of honey on his tongue and tracing them back elsewhere on her body, and at last she found herself rising to him, catching the relief that her desire had not deserted her as she'd feared, and that she could still respond without needing the drip-feed of vodka. Alice's hair hung in a matted curtain around her face. Her tears sluiced down her neck and between her breasts to Lev, salt and sweet. He began to touch her

472

with the very ends of his fingertips, light stroking which made her skin feel effervescent.

Now he was holding something against her; a nettle, she felt. He was pressing the plant's hairs very gently on to her, brushing lightly to sensitise her skin and then pushing a little harder, sharp hot stings to excite her. Lev's fingers ran lines over and inside Alice, spelling out words of love incomprehensible and illegible. When he paused, it was all she could do to choke: "Don't stop!", and she could tell by the shape of his mouth against her skin that he was grinning. It was at once familiar and new, letting him seduce her all over again, and she knew why she was at last allowing herself to give in.

She had armoured herself in layers against him. She had wanted to hide. She'd felt shame and inadequacy, anxiety and anger, both inside and out. Now she yielded and gave herself up to him, gave herself *back* to him, soft and welcoming. Her eyes closed as though he were rising inside along her spine up to her throat. She carried him deeper, as if they could shed their bodies, shed the pain, save each other, two persons in one skin. The present was the only reality, there was no world beyond the banya.

They were flushed pink in their nakedness, emerging reborn from the dark womb of the banya, free from impurities, refreshed and cleansed into their true selves after so much lying and deception.

They would build their own banya, he told her; and they'd make love there, and what they did when they'd finished would depend on the time of year. In the summer, they'd retire to a cooling room with wall-to-wall mirrors and a servant waving stork-feather fans. In the winter – well, in the winter, they'd jump into a frozen lake or tumble in the snow, there was nothing better. "You get so hot that you can't stand it and all you want to do is get cold," he said. "So you run outside and jump through the hole in the ice until you're so cold you can't stand it and all you want to do is get warm." He thought for a moment. "It's the kind of pleasure you experience when someone stops hitting you."

It was time to leave. Alice pushed herself sharply upright, and immediately felt woozy. "Take it easy," Lev said. "Your vessels are all relaxed; the blood's rushed down from your head."

She clung to him until the sensation abated, and then moved to pick up all the stuff they'd brought in with them: the soap and the lye, nettles and milk and honey.

"Leave them," Lev said.

"We should clear our mess up."

"No. Leave them for the *bannik*."

"The *bannik*?"

"The spirit of the banya. He's an old man with hairy paws and long nails, and he lives behind the stove or under the benches."

"Fuck the stupid old *bannik*."

"Ssssh!" He seemed truly concerned. "We've annoyed him enough by making love here."

"We have?" She still wanted to treat it as a joke, but it was clear that Lev was serious.

"Sure. Bathers have lost their skin and had their bodies wrapped round the stove for less. Loud singing, talking, swearing, lying, boasting; the *bannik* can get you for all of those."

"But we haven't done any of those."

"All the more reason to leave our stuff for him, just to make sure. An angry *bannik* can throw red-hot rocks and boiling water; he can even transform harmless steam into deadly coal gas. So –" He ushered her out of the door. *"Da svidanya!"* Lev called to the *bannik*.

Back in their room, overlooking the zoo, Lev pressed a small box into Alice's hands.

"It's not a marriage proposal," he said, reading her face. "It's more than that."

She opened the box on to a gold ring in the shape of the infinity symbol, forever curling round on itself. The two holes fitted perfectly over her third and fourth fingers, pinning them together.

"As you and I will always be with each other," he said. "We can never escape; we whirl round in an endless dance, independent and interdependent. Our love binds us together as this ring binds your fingers together, and like this ring our love goes on for ever."

# 97

*Saturday, 28 March 1992*

Stripped to the waist, Borzov was unconscious on his bed. His stomach, as large and slack as a sack of sand, had spread across itself and down his flanks, as a basset hound's ears flop to the sides of its head. A drip ran from the inside of his right elbow to a transparent bag bulging thick red; the president was being sobered up by the simple method of changing half his blood.

There was a single prerequisite for those soldiers wishing to serve in the presidential guard, the Kremlin's private army: they all had to have blood type AB, the same as the president's. Borzov received a blood transfusion before virtually every major occasion; it was the only way to be sure of having him halfway sober when it mattered. The medical staff had initially tried keeping a quantity of frozen plasma on the premises, but it had soon become apparent that they'd need a walk-in freezer to cope with demand, and it had been deemed easier to have a large supply of donors permanently on site.

The presidential suite at the Kremlin is magnificent, of course. Around Borzov were walls hung with silk of vermilion and pearl, beneath him a sheened floor of marble, above him a ceiling fresco which twirled and whirled to infinity. An ante-room overflowed with gifts; it seemed as though half the country had given Borzov a present. Huge floral arrangements covered a conference table; a mountain bike with a yellow bow tied round the handlebars rested against a wall. The floor was littered with rose petals. There were skis, boots, poles, suits, stereo systems and video recorders, Moroccan carvings and Mexican sculptures. In pride of place was the famous picture of Lenin conferring with his advisers, though here Lenin had been repainted in Borzov's own image.

Russia's elite spend a million dollars on a birthday present for a helpful politician – and none come more helpful (at least potentially) than the president – as casually as they send him a card. Those further down the scale are less expansive but no less heartfelt; they give to demonstrate their loyalty and keep themselves in the frame for future favours. So many petitioners had wanted to prove their devotion today that the staff had been obliged to organise visits in waves: twenty minutes for the vodka distillers, twenty minutes for the political correspondents, twenty minutes for the precious metals faction.

And the most absurd thing about this grotesque feeding frenzy was that the recipient couldn't have given two shits. This grotto of bounty and largesse, right next to his bedchamber, was entirely lost on him. He wouldn't use a single one of these items. Rapacious underlings would remove half of them; the remainder would be given or simply left to rot.

Borzov had put the Kremlin wardrobe at the disposal of Lev and Alice, and she at least had made full use of it. Her outfit was relatively simple – an unfussy black dress, a pearl choker, gold and silver bracelets, and a bronze butterfly in her hair – but somehow the effect far outweighed the constituent parts. She'd seen it in the re-action of those through whose presence her beauty had rippled: Lev, as he'd stood behind her and watched them both in the mirror; the sentries whom they'd passed on their way to the ball; and the other guests who made minute and perhaps even unconscious changes in their positions so they could see her better. Tonight she was a traffic-stopper, and even the most beautiful can't manage that at will.

The ball was being held in the three imperial palaces which clus-ter around a courtyard in the south-west corner of the Kremlin, and the guests were to be taken from palace to palace as the evening progressed: drinks in one, dinner in another, dancing in the third, each more beautiful than the last. They began in the Terem Palace, the oldest building in the Kremlin. Waiters hovered against the gilded stucco with trays outstretched: some offered lanky champagne flutes and stubby tumblers of vodka, others caviar blini and devils on horseback, each of them urging Alice with a smile to indulge, indulge, whenever would this happen to her again? She smiled through gritted teeth, shaking her head at the waiters with their poisonous flutes and tumblers, and she stuck to mineral water and orange juice.

All of Moscow's great and beautiful were here, pulsing beneath the painted vaultings and between the elaborately gilded stoves. Every time Alice turned she saw someone she recognised: a cabi-net minister adjusting the collar beneath his chins, a ballerina drop-ping kisses like confetti, a tycoon moving like a lizard through the crowd. She laughed at the reactions of those who saw her and Lev there, after everything that had happened. When she realised that all these people had absolutely no idea what would happen later, she laughed harder.

Lev and Alice stood in the lower of the Terem's two medieval churches and lost themselves in the iconography. The pillars spread up to the roof like spring flowers in bloom, and not a square inch was left uncovered: angels and demons, knights and maidens, all soared across the ceiling and swooped down the walls. It was like being inside the head of a tattooist.

At eight o'clock sharp, the guests were politely but firmly taken out past the Church of the Deposition of the Robe and into Sobornaya Square, from where they'd ascend the Red Staircase to the diamond-patterned Hall of Facets. Borzov and his wife were standing at the top of the staircase like a modern-day czar and czarina, the comparison underscored by the imperial double-headed eagles which perched on the arches above their heads. The guests clapped and cheered, and Russia's first couple – for tonight, its royal couple – clapped back and beckoned for the guests to come up and join them. As Alice climbed between stone lions, the light from the arc lamps brushed the steps beneath her feet, and she remembered that this staircase had once run with blood; it was down these treads that Peter the Great had tossed his mutinous relatives in 1682.

Above the Kremlin, Borzov's face had been projected demigod-like on to the clouds.

Dinner was served in the banqueting hall where Ivan the Terrible had treated foreign ambassadors to roast swan and elks' brains, and where more recently Gorbachev had entertained Ronald Reagan and Margaret Thatcher. A single massive pillar in the centre of the room supported the vaults, as though Atlas himself had stopped by and had the place built around him.

Courses came and went: sorbet, soup, ham sliced laser-thin, fish, lamb, pancakes filled with curd cheese, potato and nut dumplings with cinnamon and soured cream, more sorbet. Each course was served with its appropriate vodka: the ham came with bison zubrowka (a Russian version, of course) to accentuate the mustard; the pancakes were offset beautifully by Starka; and the lingering aftertaste of pure cherry vodka made it seem as though the dumplings had drawn the alcohol clean away.

Alice had the Kyrgyz prime minister to her right and a telecommunications chairman on her left, and they tried to impress her with tales of yurts and bandwidths respectively. The Kyrgyz was funnier and more charming, and she spent most of her time talking to him. On the wall behind her, Prince Vladimir of Kiev stood immortalised in icon, forever showing his twelve sons how to live righteously and wisely.

Lev had the pistol in the inside pocket of a tuxedo cut generously enough to leave no bulge. He chatted amiably with his neighbours. If there was turmoil within, he gave no sign; but when Arkin stood and called for silence, Alice noticed Lev make the slightest, quickest of inhalations. Arkin was to introduce Borzov, Borzov was to speak, and Lev was to make his move then.

There were two official videographers here tonight, and they swung their cameras towards the prime minister. Borzov had wanted the event recorded for posterity; Arkin wanted taped proof of the attempt on Borzov's life, to show the nation how close they'd come to losing their leader.

The crowd quietened, and Arkin began to speak. The evening was yet young, he said, and there was much more to come. They'd go from here through the Holy Vestibule, a multiplicity of doorways gilded with ornate golden latticework, and into the Great Kremlin Palace itself for dancing. Before that, however, the president wanted to say a few words.

Borzov rose unsteadily to his feet. The effects of the half-completed blood transfusion had worn off, sped on their way by furious quantities of vodka. He thanked everyone for coming, and had just launched into a story about his time as head of the Sverdlovsk party committee when he stopped suddenly and peered across the room.

"The chief's grandson is here!" he exclaimed. "So long past his bedtime, but what a lovely surprise! Come, Edik. Come and give your grandpa a birthday kiss."

The room was held in a terrible hiatus.

"Anatoly Nikolayevich," Arkin said, "that's not your grandson. That's a camera tripod."

There was a smattering of laughter from those who thought that the joke was deliberate.

Lev looked across at Arkin, and the prime minister silently willed him forward. *The time is now*, Arkin's handsome face urged, *do it, do it.* Arkin would trust Lev when it was all over and he'd done his bit, but not a moment before. It would of course be insane for Lev to do anything other than what he'd agreed, knowing what the consequences would be both for him and for Alice; but illogicality has never been a bar to any course of action in Russia.

It was not a conscious decision on Lev's part. He felt like an actor who'd just heard his cue, and his feet were taking him to his destination whether he wanted to go there or not, because there was no alternative; any course of action other than the ordained one was unthinkable. He jabbed his hand into his pocket and closed his fingers around the pistol butt. The touch seemed to impart tremendous clarity to his vision. He saw everything as though it were momentarily frozen, with him walking through a tableau: Borzov's mouth as he talked, drunk enough to have forgotten or not to care that in a few seconds he'd have to pretend to have been shot; Arkin, tense as he waited for events to unfold; the turning faces of the guests as they wondered what Lev was doing interrupting the presidential toast.

Lev was a stride and a half from Borzov now. Out came the gun from his pocket, smooth as he could have hoped, no problems with the barrel catching on the lining, safety off with his left hand, and even though it made no difference he was still careful to aim properly, nine inches below Borzov's shoulders and dead centre, to take out as many vital organs as possible, the reports cracking loudly in the vast hall as he squeezed the trigger, once, twice, again, and the Kremlin guards were already on him and slamming him to the ground, there was nothing fake about their tackles, six of them hitting him at once to ensure that he was taken down, and as the wind whistled from Lev's lungs he saw Borzov's bodyguards bundle their president from the room, Arkin following fast behind them.

The Kremlin has a hospital, but it's not capable of dealing with gunshot wounds, so the charade had been extended to encompass the Sklifosovsky. Russian leaders are usually treated at the Kremlinovka, far out to the west, but in a crisis such as this they'd go closer to home, and the Sklifosovsky has the best emergency department in the country.

The presidential limousine and its motorcycle outriders shot from the Saviour Gate and across Red Square. Shimmering in upturned lights behind them, the Kremlin was midway between reality and dream, an immense, oppressive vision. In the floodlamps, the walls hovered and the swallowtail battlements shivered.

Four frantic minutes through the streets, and then they were pulling up outside the main entrance of the Sklifosovsky, where paramedics were on hand to lay Borzov on a stretcher and wheel him inside. "It's an emergency!" they shouted, and indeed it was. There was blood gurgling from sucking wounds in Borzov's torso; he was unconscious, his breath came in shallow pants, and his pulse was fading. The surgeons preparing their instruments under Lewis' direction would have been amazed to know that the shooting was supposed to have been a set-up, as this was definitely not for show. The president was dying.

The ball had broken up in panic and confusion. Alice had been taken back to her apartment in the Kremlin, where she was watching television. Normal programmes had been suspended; every channel carried live footage from Red Square, and the feeds from the video cameras at the ball were already being broadcast. There was Borzov, standing up; there was Lev, walking towards him – they'd removed any footage of Borzov actually speaking, Alice noticed – there was Lev, taking aim; the shots; Borzov staggering, Lev being wrestled to the ground.

Reporters gabbled urgently to anchormen, and then a switch to the Sklifosovsky. Arkin was standing on the front steps. He was covered in blood, and his face was streaked in tears. Alice saw Lewis in the background, still in his surgeon's scrubs. His clothes were splattered red, his face bathed blue in the revolving lights of the police cars parked nearby. It was the expression on his face which kicked deep into Alice's senses: Lewis, who usually showed as much emotion as a man doing the weekly shopping, looked as if he was about to be sick, burst into tears, or both.

"Following the shooting incident at the Kremlin this evening," Arkin said, "Anatoly Nikolayevich Borzov was brought to the Sklifosovsky Hospital with severe external injuries and internal haemorrhaging. The hospital's finest surgeons have fought to save him, but to no avail. Life extinct was declared ten minutes ago. The president is dead."

The warders at the Lefortovo came to get Lev a good few hours earlier than he'd expected. He knew better than to ask them why he was being released so soon; they wouldn't tell him if they knew, and if they didn't know then they couldn't tell him. A gaggle of reporters was waiting at the main entrance, so they took him out through a back door which led into a courtyard where a limousine was waiting. The rear seat was all his, but two Spetsnazy sat opposite with their submachine guns trained on him. When they pulled out of the courtyard, two more cars joined them.

The roads were deserted. Virtually the only vehicles on the streets were police cars slewed across intersections with the policemen leaning against them and slapping luminous traffic-control batons against their thighs as they tried to keep warm. The car Lev was in had special presidential markings; not a single policeman moved to challenge them.

They more or less followed the course of the Yauza River as it headed back into the city. Lev looked around him with the wide eyes of a yokel arrived from the provinces for the first time. After today, he'd never see Moscow again.

The car glided across the Garden Ring and on to Nikoloyamskaya.

"Hey! We should have turned left there –" Lev pointed out of the window. "Domodevo's that way." The Spetsnazy remained silent. "What's going on? Where are we going? What the fuck's going on?"

Something was very wrong. There was no reason for them to be heading back towards the city centre, let alone for no one to be telling him what was happening. Lev thought of flinging open the door and jumping for it, but the car was going too fast, he'd be dead the moment he hit the pavement; and besides, there were no interior handles on the rear doors. He was trapped here until they chose to let him out.

Lev may not have been told where they were going, but he knew the moment they got there. His destination was a vast concrete labyrinth, one of Moscow's most recognisable buildings – and certainly its most feared. They were at the Lubyanka.

He was numb beyond reaction. He'd done everything he'd been asked to. The charade in the Kremlin was supposed to have been the end of it all. There was nothing left in him any more; he didn't have the energy to respond.

The tunnel which led down to the Lubyanka's underground car park swallowed the car. Lev tried not to gag. He hated the smell of car parks, too many exhaust fumes in too small an area.

They were waiting for him in a corner; a dozen or so Spetsnazy, and in the middle Sabirzhan, trembling with the suppressed thrill of a teenage boy about to lose his virginity.

When they opened the door, Lev stepped from the car with as much dignity as he could muster. He wasn't going to let Sabirzhan's thugs drag him out like terriers down a rabbit warren.

The Lubyanka's corridors were cream and green, the colours of institutions. On the first basement floor, the paint was scratched and chipped, and the further down one went below the ground, the more the walls were stained with patches of rusty brown, the colour of dried blood.

No one was telling Alice anything; her guards were as silent as ever. Lev's words span in her head. "The fucker's lucky they're only giving me blanks, let's put it that way."

The bullets must have been real. She'd no idea how he had got hold of them, but then again Lev had contacts everywhere. He'd spent decades running criminal empires from behind the wire – a couple of bullets in the centre of Moscow would surely be child's play.

What Alice couldn't see was *why* he'd done it. Even if Lev had really wanted to kill Borzov – and she was sure what he'd said was hyperbole rather than serious intent – he must have known it'd solve nothing. Quite the opposite, in fact, as it had instantly destroyed their escape and all their plans for the future. What about

481

Baikal, and jumping in the snow after making love in the banya? What about their own vegetable garden and long, lazy days in the summer heat? What about *her*? How could he have done this to her?

Alice had questions for everything and answers for nothing.

It was too much for her to take in at once. If the guards had been talking to her, she'd have asked them for a vodka, no question. Just one glass, to take the edge off it all. Just to be normal again.

# 98

*Sunday, 29 March 1992*

Sabirzhan's face filled the darkness round Lev. Dripping Poison, they called him, and it suited him well. There were no inherent contradictions in Sabirzhan's character, Lev thought, and he had only one side to him – evil – which was rather un-Russian. Well, Sabirzhan was a Georgian really, so perhaps it was unfair to apply Russian criteria.

When Lev thought more, he realised he was wrong. Sabirzhan was no more or less unilateral than the next man. He was boorish, disgusting and without kindness, but he was also intelligent and astute. Who would have guessed his darker undercurrents on first acquaintance? It was a good thing when a man differed from his image; it showed he wasn't a type. When a man can't be placed in a category, it means that at least part of him is what a human being ought to be: he has a grain of immortality.

Sabirzhan's breath was coming in short, tongue-lolling pants, anticipation at the pleasure to come. He wasn't racing a deadline, as he'd been with Sharmukhamedov. He would have as long as he needed, and this time the end would come when *he* chose. He thought of the way Lev had thrown him to the wolves at Petrovka; it felt good to win now.

He pressed a ring of cold metal against Lev's right ankle, moving it as a dog would sniff as he sought the best spot: on the ankle bone itself, or against the webbing of skin which wrapped round the Achilles tendon? The gun barrel slipped, adjusted, settled.

Lev heard the shot and smelt the gunpowder burn. It seemed a long, long time before he felt his joint explode.

\* \* \*

Alice gave up the search for sleep at dawn, and turned on the television, more for comfort than anything else. The assassination – though she was forcing herself still to think of it as a pantomime, as it had been intended – was being aired continuously. If she missed it on one channel, she didn't have to wait long until another channel ran it. She watched the footage over and again. On the fourth or fifth showing, by which time she could have closed her eyes and replayed the scene stride for stride in her head, she saw something which jagged at her.

There was a video recorder in the apartment, and piles of recorded films – pirate copies of Western movies, mostly. Alice inserted a tape in the machine, found the playback channel, and began searching through the stations using the video's controls. The next time the shooting was shown, she recorded it; then she replayed it, watching carefully.

The speech, the walk, and then the gun bucking and cracking and blooming fire in Lev's hand. And there was Borzov . . .

. . . And there was Borzov doing nothing. *That* was what had caught Alice's eye. Lev was no more than a man's height away from Borzov when he fired, and he was aiming dead centre, yet the shots didn't push Borzov backwards. Borzov kept standing for a full second, perhaps even more, before finally staggering back, as though he'd only just remembered what he was supposed to do. He'd been blind drunk; he should have gone down like a ninepin.

Alice backed the tape up and watched again. This time, she saw that none of Lev's shots even tore the material of Borzov's tuxedo.

Rewind. Play.

The carpet was a deep cream; any blood would surely have shown up on it. There was none visible. Alice watched all the way though. Not a drop.

Lev had clearly used blanks as instructed. Borzov was clearly dead. One of those statements couldn't be true; not even in Russia.

Lev's right ankle was in pieces, but Sabirzhan had yet to give him a matching pair. He was not going to do one immediately after the other. He wanted to prolong Lev's agony, and make the gap between bullets linger as long and excruciating as the shots themselves, give the pain time not merely to kick but to gurgle and flow round Lev's body, oozing into the smallest parts and carving agony in the crevices.

"I'm going to pull your eye over your ass," Sabirzhan said. "I'm going to punish you more severely than you could ever have imagined. I'm going to tear off your balls."

Alice called the Kremlin guards into the television room. They came reluctantly, acceding only when she told them that the whole episode had been a lie. Every Russian is used to having the wool pulled over their eyes; many secretly revel in it. She played the video back to them, explaining what she'd seen, and asking them to tell her if she'd misunderstood anything.

None of them said a word. Alice was right; Lev *had* been using blanks.

"Then take me to the Sklifosovsky," she said. "My husband" – they looked surprised – "*ex*-husband" – even though he wasn't, not officially – "whatever, he's a surgeon there; he'll tell us what's going on."

They argued with each other. They hadn't been given any orders to move, they should try and find out what was going on first.

"Your president is dead," she shouted. "Your president is dead. You're the Kremlin guards, the elite, so show some fucking initiative."

They argued some more. Why didn't some of them stay and some go? That last suggestion met with general agreement.

"Come," they said to her. "To the Sklifosovsky."

Time loses all meaning in a room without windows. Lev couldn't tell whether minutes, hours or days had passed when Sabirzhan next entered. This time, Sabirzhan didn't show Lev the gun, nor did he need to look for the best place to rest the barrel. He simply placed it against Lev's left ankle and fired.

It seemed that half of Moscow's police were at the Sklifosovsky, and they weren't letting anyone in. Alice sat in the car while the Kremlin guards shouted, argued, gesticulated and waved guns around. This was debate Russian-style, and she sunk lower in her seat, hoping that making herself as invisible as possible would help if shooting started. The police wanted to see authorisation papers; the presidential guard said they had a perfect right to be here. The situation was sufficiently heated to be beyond resolution through bribery, which was saying something.

One of the presidential guard eventually ended the stand-off in a typically Russian way, by upping the ante. He grabbed the nearest policeman and held a gun to his head. Before any of the other policemen could react, every one found himself covered by a gun. If it was going to come down to shooting, they all knew which side would end up on top. The Kremlin guard were among the cream of the Russian army, such as it was; the police would hardly have counted as the cream in a collective dairy. The two policemen nearest the hospital gates could hardly open them fast enough. The presidential guards jumped back inside the car and drove through with a few well-considered oaths by way of farewell.

"I want to see Lewis Liddell," Alice said, when they reached the main desk.

"Everyone's very busy right now," the receptionist said.

"Nurse!" someone cried from down a corridor.

"Lewis is my husband," Alice said, "and I need to see him, *now*."

The receptionist looked beyond Alice to her escort, thought better of whatever she'd been about to say next, and swung in her chair to point down the corridor behind her. "Follow the signs first to pathology and then to neurosurgery," she said. "When you get to the large picture of Khrushchev – you can't miss it, it's hideous, makes him look like a boiled egg – turn left, then first right. His office is the second door on your right."

Alice had never been here before. She'd never once visited Lewis at work, and the realisation pricked her with guilt. They hurried down long corridors and found his office at the second time of asking. He was deep in conversation with two of his colleagues, and looked up sharply when they entered. He hadn't been home all night, that was clear; hadn't shaved or slept either, by the look of him.

"Alice! What are you doing here? Who are these people with you?"

"I need to talk to you," she said. "Urgently."

He turned to his colleagues. "Could you excuse us for a moment, please?"

They got up and left, casting anxious glances at the presidential guard as they went. Alice turned to her escort. "You guys can wait outside too."

"We'll stay," one of them replied.

"This man is my husband, and I'd like to talk to him in private." That did the trick; whatever they wanted to know about Borzov, they wouldn't impinge if they thought there was something personal to discuss. "But stay right outside the door, OK?" she added. "Don't let anyone in."

She was gabbling at Lewis almost before the escort had closed the door behind them. "I don't know what's happened, Lewis, but Lev didn't kill Borzov, you have to know that –"

"Alice –"

"– whatever you think of him, it was all a set-up, that was the whole point, and . . ." And what? That after tonight, if all had gone well, Lewis would never have seen her again?

"Alice! Will you let me speak?"

She was breathing hard enough to be swallowing air. "OK," she gulped. "Sorry."

"I know Lev didn't kill Borzov."

"How do you know?"

Lewis picked up a manila folder from his desk and opened it on to a series of photographs. Alice caught glimpses as he flicked through them: Borzov's body on the slab, even less dignified in death than he'd been in drunken life. Lewis found the photograph he'd been looking for and handed it over. It was Borzov's dress shirt, drenched in blood.

Alice shrugged. "I don't understand."

Lewis pointed to a tear in the shirt, presumably where a bullet had entered; more specifically, to the area around it, almost imperceptible against the lake of red until she looked closer and saw what he was indicating. There, there, and there: darker areas, black against the crimson.

"Lewis, stop fucking around. What are they?"

"Scorch marks," he replied.

"Scorch marks?"

"From the barrel of a gun. But to leave scorch marks on someone's clothes, you have to be firing very close. *Very* close. A few inches kind of close." He swallowed. "I saw the TV footage, Alice, a few hours ago. When he fired, Lev was too far away to have left scorch marks."

Sabirzhan wanted Lev to beg him for mercy. Both ankles gone, Lev spat at him through the pain.

"You're a coward, Tengiz, you know that?"

"I'm not listening."

"You know why you've got a patronymic? So your mother could remember who your father was, that's why."

Cold metal on skin, and the hot blast of a bullet through Lev's right kneecap.

Lewis told Alice everything: how they'd done all they could to save Borzov, but he'd already lost too much blood, and the faster they'd pumped new plasma into him, the faster it had leaked out. Even though the limousine had got there as quickly as it could, the outriders clearing traffic all along the route – the motorcyclists had been adamant about that, just in case anyone had tried to blame them, they'd insisted they couldn't have got Borzov there a second earlier – it was a minor miracle that he hadn't been dead on arrival.

After life extinct had been declared, Arkin himself had come into the operating theatre and demanded they hand over Borzov's body to him. He was president now, under the constitution, and would be for at least the next three months until elections were held. He would arrange for an autopsy and a state funeral. He had thanked them all for their efforts, and reminded them that they weren't to breathe a word of what had happened in the hospital to anyone. The president's assassination was the most heinous of crimes, and the mood in the country wouldn't be helped by sensationalist tattle from surgeons who should have known better. Anyone who breached these conditions would find themselves detained long enough for their wives to have fucked every man inside the Boulevard Ring before they were out again.

Lev's kneecaps were bullet-shattered porridges of cartilage and tissue. From the wounds, blood and fluid oozed through the holes which the slugs had ripped in the table. His pain leached into the silence.

Alice traced back what she knew. Borzov had been unharmed when he'd got into the limousine, and more or less dead when he'd arrived at the Sklifosovsky. Therefore he must have been shot en route. The limousine had barely slowed, let alone stopped, in its headlong rush for the hospital, so Borzov must have been shot by someone already in the car with him. It couldn't have been the driver, clearly, since he was driving; nor anyone in the front seat, since front and back compartments were sealed off from each other. It could only, therefore, have been someone who'd been in the back with Borzov.

"Have you got security cameras here?" she asked. "At the main entrance, in particular?"

"Of course." Soviet paranoia had dictated as much.

"Can you get a look at last night's tape; for the time when the limousine arrived?"

Sabirzhan came in with plates laden with food. "Look at all this," he said. "You haven't eaten since you arrived, you must be hungry,

487

no? Ravenous, that's what I'd be, if I were in your shoes. Well, all this could be yours. Look at it, Georgian cooking. There's beef soup, delicious and hearty, just what a man in your condition needs; here we've got some vegetable paste with spinach, walnuts and cabbage. It looks awful, it sounds awful, it tastes great. All this could be yours. You know what you have to do."

Lev gasped through the rolling waves of agony. "You were conceived on a train, weren't you, Tengiz? All a guy had to do was to barge into your mother's compartment with a bottle of vodka, and within seconds her panties were hanging from the curtain rod."

Lewis was reluctant; he'd already proved to her that Lev couldn't have killed Borzov, what more did she want? He was a surgeon, not an activist. Why couldn't Alice just leave things alone?

This was the murder of a head of state, she said. It wasn't theirs to leave alone. If he was that scared, they'd go straight from here to the embassy and demand protection.

She didn't need to add the rider: if she found out who'd killed Borzov, she might have an idea of what had happened to Lev.

Lewis rang down to the security department and asked to see the tapes for last night.

"Why do you want them?" the supervisor asked.

"To ensure that all proper procedures were followed when the president was brought here. There'll be an inquiry – it's in all our interests that we can say we did everything by the book."

The supervisor promised to bring the tapes straight up. When Lewis rang off, Alice was smiling at him. "Who'd have guessed it?" she said. "Three months here, and at last a bit of Soviet ass-covering rubs off on you."

Lev knew that his strength of mind would destroy his body, but would could a man do, if not be true to himself? He would never break, never lie down, never bend over, not for anybody. Body and soul are two complementary vessels; after crushing and destroying a man's physical defences, an invading party nearly always succeeds in sending its mobile detachments into the breach in time to triumph over a man's soul, and to force him into unconditional capitulation.

Not with Lev. Perhaps he'd have been more inclined towards surrender, or at least less firmly set against it, had it been someone other than Sabirzhan inflicting the pain. But however much it hurts to lose, it always hurts twice as much when that loss is against a best friend or a worst enemy. So, just as Sabirzhan was determined that Lev would crumble and plead with him for a mercy which would never come, so Lev was one precious iota more resolved that he would not.

The black-and-white footage unspooled before the Liddells. Here were the motorcycles, flashing lights diffusing like halos in the low-resolution pictures; here came the limousine, men spilling from its doors even before it had stopped. All four doors were flung open, the driver was out, the front passenger was out, both of them anonymous protection officers. Borzov was being carried on to the stretcher. And there, emerging from the far door, was Arkin.

There had been no one else inside. The leather bench seat was clearly visible, and clearly empty. There was only one person who'd ridden all the way with the president, and that was Arkin.

The pain came in swells, and when it got really bad Lev simply went away. He thought of Alice and their love together, and he was sure he could endure anything in the knowledge that she'd always remember and cherish him. What man craves most in life is the sense that someone somewhere treasures him; if that idea holds fast, anything can be borne. He'd sacrificed everything he had for her, and it didn't occur to him for a moment that he'd been wrong to do so. Beside Alice, nothing had any value.

Sabirzhan had told Lev enough for him to know that Borzov was dead, but Alice wouldn't believe he'd done it. She would work out the truth, and she would also be beside herself with worry, because she still wouldn't have found him, and the fear and anxiety would be overwhelming.

The American Embassy is one of the vilest buildings in Moscow, an eyesore in custard and bile on the edge of the six-line Novinsky Highway near the White House. It's so revolting that the rooftop Old Glory had this day curled itself round its flagpole in apparent protest at being associated with this architectural monstrosity. The embassy staff joke that if the garish colour scheme isn't enough to make then feel nauseous, then the microwaves from all the nearby listening posts are. The smart new building down by the river which had been intended as the new embassy has stood empty since the Americans had found the Russian builders planting enough bugs during its construction to keep a small town powered for around a year. So the Americans are still in the carbuncle on Novinsky, and it was here that Lewis came.

Just as he'd rescued Alice from the pit of alcoholism, so Lev now hallucinated that Alice had come to liberate him. She battled in the doorway with the *bannik*, and the *bannik* had Sabirzhan's face. He was a crazed devil, vengeance itself, Lev's punishment for that exquisite time outside time in the banya.

Alice didn't sit in the chair Arkin indicated, she didn't take the vodka he offered, and she didn't listen to his platitudes about what a shock this whole thing had been. She told him quickly and clearly what she'd done and what she knew. The confidence drained from Arkin as Alice watched. Then she watched as it refilled as if from a cistern. She knew what had happened, but he still held the key to what she wanted.

"You see those books there?" He gestured to a couple of volumes on his desk. "I keep them to hand because they're the most invaluable guides to Russian politics."

Alice read the spines. *Alice in the Land of Miracles. Alice in the World Behind the Mirror.*

"Where's Lev?" she asked.

"It wasn't the reforms that were the problem," Arkin said. "The problem was Borzov's readiness to water them down whenever he felt his power threatened. The first night of the parliamentary plenum, when the deputies voted to remove me, he would happily have cast me out – until every capital from Washington to Warsaw reminded him of his obligation to reform. Would you have let that pass, if you were me?"

"Where's Lev?"

"That's why he clung on to power so doggedly, of course; for what does a man have left after he's been the most powerful figure in the nation? Russia's merciless to those on the down slope. Gorbachev and Khrushchev were the only two Soviet leaders to have left office alive, you know. Gorbachev's now the most hated man in the country; Khrushchev was banished to internal exile and had his death reported in a single paragraph in *Pravda.*"

"Where's Lev?"

"Lord Acton said that power corrupts. I've always thought that slightly inaccurate. Power *addicts*. Borzov had surrounded himself with yes-men – myself apart – and excluded all potential threats. If left unchecked, he'd have ended up turning us into a giant North

Korea: no outside investment, no prospects, nothing working, none of the things a modern country needs."

"Where's Lev?"

"As a young, idealistic reformer, I dreamt for years of marching into Gosplan and tearing it apart. When he told me to do just that a few months ago, I was terrified, absolutely terrified. Now I realise I wasn't scared enough. I underestimated the determination of many to keep Russia bound in permanent tutelage. If we're not careful, we'll be dragged back to the bloody Bolshevik swamp, where so many seem to think that everything was fine. There was sausage, and someone was thrown in jail. Everyone worked so hard, and people were shot for being late for work. Everyone lived so well, and millions were in the gulag. I won't allow Russia to be turned back into an enormous concentration camp. I will not."

"Where's Lev?"

"What did Lenin say? A revolution is only worth something when it knows how to defend itself. Revolutions are made by fanatical men of action with one-track minds, men who are narrow-minded to the point of genius. The Russian people are a great race. A great race deserves a great leader, and I tell you this, without either bombast or false modesty, I have no doubt whatsoever that I'm up to the job. A great man can be cruel or harsh, even wrong sometimes; but he's strong enough to do what's necessary. I am that man. I am the future for Russia. I believe that as sincerely as I believe that the sun rises in the east."

"Where's Lev?"

Finally, Arkin seemed to hear her. "Lev? I needed to eliminate him, of course."

"*Eliminate?*"

"He was the only one who could have known the truth. I didn't think you would work it out."

"What do you mean, *eliminate*?"

"I gave him to Sabirzhan." He saw her face. "Oh, don't worry. Sabirzhan will be taking his time with him; he won't have killed him yet. You know how much he hates him."

"Get him out of there."

"Or what?"

"Or I'll tell the world what you've done."

"That would be hard, if I make sure you never leave."

"You're being serious?"

"Perfectly."

His dark eyes showed her nothing, and she knew he was telling the truth. He'd killed Borzov, he'd abandoned Lev to his fate, he'd been prepared to let Alice die with the Chechens, he'd . . . "Those men who attacked me down by the river last month," she said. "They didn't want my money. They weren't muggers. You sent them to kill me, didn't you?"

"Everything's deniable, Alice."

"Not this. If not me, then my husband will tell. He's in the American Embassy."

"Your government thinks I'm the best thing in this country."

"Not to the point of murder they don't."

Arkin was very still as he thought. Alice looked at him, as handsome as he was cruel.

"Three of you know that Lev didn't kill Borzov: you, your lover and your husband." Arkin had spelled out the triangle with deliberate cruelty. "You and your husband also know who did. I need your silence, both of you; or I'll have you locked up and let Lev die."

"Lewis will tell the world what's happened if I don't come back safely."

"But he wouldn't abandon you like that – though God knows you deserve it. And you won't let it happen, because you want Lev back alive." Arkin had played on Alice's ambition to keep her in the privatisation programme; he played on her love now. He always knew her weak spots.

Arkin picked up a phone and dialled the American Embassy. "I remember phone numbers," he explained as he waited for the connection. "Don't know how; just do. American Embassy? This is President Arkin. I believe you have a Lewis Liddell on your premises? I'd like to speak to him, please." He and Alice waited in silence while Lewis was paged and brought to the phone. "Lewis Liddell? Nikolai Arkin. I sincerely hope you've yet to tell anyone what you know. You're still waiting for the ambassador? Excellent, because your wife's here with me. Give me your word that what you know stays with you to the grave, or she won't see the end of today."

Eight bullets fired now, through ankles and kneecaps and wrists and elbows; eight joints reduced to bloody pulp. There was only one more shot: through the temple. Sabirzhan was going to kill Lev, of course he was, and Lev was stoic. He'd faced death so many times already that it no longer seemed such a big deal. It wasn't that he didn't care, of course he did, but he knew there was nothing he could do about it. Death had come for him many times already, and many times it had turned away at the last moment in search of someone else. If it came this time and didn't turn away, he would accept it. Fate can be benign or malign, but it can't be changed or evaded.

Like all Russians, Lev knew his literature. He thought of the passage in *Crime and Punishment* – and remembered that Dostoyevsky had in turn taken this part from Victor Hugo's *Notre Dame de Paris* – about a man who'd said, or perhaps just thought, in the hour before his death, that even if he had to live somewhere high up on a rock, on a summit so small that he could only just stand on it, with nothing around but sheer unclimbable precipices and an ocean which stretched as far as he could see in every direction, the weather always either thick fog or raging storms, never bright sunshine and warm breezes, and of course without ever seeing or hearing another human being, even if that was all that life had to offer for fifty years, or a hundred, a thousand, even for eternity, then it'd be better to live like that than to die so very soon! If only he could live, live and live some more, no matter what life was like.

"What was that?" Sabirzhan said, seeing Lev's lips move.

"I don't hate you," said Lev, feeling curiously light-headed. The sands of his life were almost done. He'd do what Russian men did before death: put a white shirt on his soul. They may have lived sinfully, but they died like saints.

The Spetsnazy came for them, on Arkin's orders. Sabirzhan heard the commotion outside and assumed it was about something else entirely. He wasn't at all prepared when they came barrelling through the door, one with the battering ram and the others throwing the stun-grenades and spraying bullets. They saw a body motionless on a table, and that was Lev; a flash as Sabirzhan fired into Lev's head before the broadside from the Spetsnazy picked him from where he was standing and flung him clean against the wall, dead even before he'd slid to the floor.

Where else would they take Lev but the Sklifosovsky, keeping him alive en route with cardiac massage and injections of adrenalin? It was like Borzov, Lev's supposed victim, all over again, and once more Lewis, back from the embassy with the ambassador left unseen and wondering what the visit had been all about, was the surgeon in charge.

This time, however, it was his wife's lover whom he was trying to save.

Lev had lost a lot of blood, and that in itself was a problem, but the only reason he wasn't dead already was because Sabirzhan, startled by the Spetsnazy, hadn't got the final head shot quite right. It had entered Lev's skull through the mastoid bone, an inch behind his ear, and had travelled onwards to sever the branches of the superior cerebral artery and pass into the brain, scattering fragments of lead and bone. Successfully removing them all would be a feat in itself. Keeping Lev alive would be a whole new level of achievement.

Lewis was honest about Lev's chances, and equally honest about his willingness to do everything he could to save him. Lewis was the best surgeon here; there was no question of him standing down.

Arkin walked round the Kremlin.

He went to the museum and stared for long minutes at a crown of eight gold-filigree triangles joined to form a cone, studded with rough-cut gems and trimmed with sable. It was the crown of Monomakh, the symbol of the Russian leader.

He went inside the Assumption Cathedral, where, in the first winter of the Great Patriotic War, with the Nazis in Moscow's suburbs, Stalin had flouted his regime's atheism and secretly ordered a service to pray for the city's deliverance.

He paused by the giant cannon which couldn't be fired and the giant bell which had fallen down before it could be rung, and thought that it was an amazing town in which the objects of interest were distinguished by their absurdity, or perhaps that the great bell without a tongue was a hieroglyph symbolic of this huge dumb land.

Across the square, a row of black Zils backed on to the presidium, squatting low to the ground under the weight of their armour-plating. Beyond them, and all around him, was the Kremlin, this curious conglomeration of palaces, towers, churches, monasteries, chapels, barracks, arsenals and bastions; this complex which had in its time functioned as fortress, sanctuary, seraglio, harem, necropolis and prison; this violent contrast of the crudest materialism and the most lofty spirituality. Was there not bound up in here the whole history of Russia, the whole epic of the Russian nation, the whole inward drama of the Russian soul?

The pistol Arkin used to shoot Borzov had been identical to the one he'd given Lev. He had fitted a silencer to suppress the noise and then shot Borzov point-blank, in the chest, with hollow-nosed bullets that would spread out inside Borzov and leave no bullet marks in the car. Borzov had looked at him in surprise, suddenly very sober, and through the pain he'd smiled. Arkin had got his aim slightly wrong; Borzov wouldn't die instantaneously, but he wouldn't last long either.

"If you think you can do it better, Kolya, just try," Borzov had gurgled, the haemorrhaging drowning him from within. "Take care of Russia," he said, the lights of the Sklifosovsky reflected in his dying eyes.

# 99

*Monday, 30 March 1992*
Alice had been given a private waiting-room. She'd clenched her hands so tight, dug her nails so deep into her palms, that she'd drawn blood, dripping reddened globules on to the white leather sofas like rose petals on snow.

Lewis came to see her at breakfast. "We've got rid of most of the bullet and bone fragments," he said, "and those still left there aren't doing any particular harm. But his vital signs are seriously impaired."

He walked with her into the intensive-care unit, where Lev had been taken after the operation. The even rise and fall of Lev's chest offered Alice the only reassurance that he was still alive. His head was bandaged, and his blackened eyes and white cheeks were frightening in their absence of colour. Alice bent to Lev and whispered in his ear. There was no response.

"There's very little brainwave activity," Lewis said. "That mechanical ventilator is the only thing keeping him alive."

"What are his chances of recovery?"

"None."

"None?"

"Not to any life outside this bed. We can keep him going on the ventilator indefinitely, but the brain damage is too deep."

The television was showing old footage of Arkin performing martial arts; *sombo*, to be precise, a mixture of judo and wrestling which places a premium on quick moves, a calm demeanour, and the ability to keep oneself from showing emotions or uttering a sound, no matter how intense the struggle or the pain. As Arkin fought, hard but fair, his judo teacher was being interviewed. "Nikolai Valentinovich is not a wrestler of physicality," the teacher was saying, "but more of intellect – a smart wrestler. He always does the unexpected, because he's versatile, very strong, so the speed of the fight is intense."

As if on cue, Arkin ended the fight with his favourite move, a swift attack which knocked his opponent off his feet. The beaten man picked himself up off the mat. He and Arkin bowed to each other, then clasped hands and shared an unheard joke.

Arkin would need more than judo to save Russia, Alice thought; he'd need voodoo.

She sat in the waiting-room all day, refusing food or company. Lev was in a coma, and he'd almost certainly never come out of it. She'd nurse him, of course, if that was what he needed, she'd nurse him day and night, feed him and empty his catheter and watch over him with all the love in the world; but whatever that existence would represent for her, it would be no life for him.

Night fell, and with it came the darkness in her soul.

# 100

*Tuesday, 31 March 1992*
Alice left the waiting-room and went back to the intensive care unit. Lewis was there, looking silently at Lev. Alice came up beside Lewis and rested her head against his shoulder. They stood like that for a moment, husband and wife, both looking at Lev as the ventilator opened and closed his lungs; both facing the enormity of what they'd lost.

"Turn the ventilator off," Alice whispered.

In the depths of his soul, way deeper than anything that man's machines could detect, Lev felt the world slipping from him. There was to be no miraculous recovery, and that was only fitting; the reason why none of Russia's great novels have happy endings is because Russians wouldn't know what to make of them if they did.

Lev thought once more how grateful he was that he'd lived long enough to love Alice. "Goodbye, goodbye," he said to himself; "goodbye my only love, my love forever lost, until we meet again in the next world." He was Lev, and he was dying, and yet he wasn't Lev, because Lev was the name he'd been given as a vor, and how could he still be a vor when he'd broken so many of their rules? How could he still be a vor when he'd have given every-thing up to be with a woman? He'd lived his life in the brother-hood, and right at the last he'd chosen to forsake it; his love for Alice was too great.

Lev saw images which seemed strange and unfamiliar: him in a church, holding hands with a woman in white; him splashing in a brown ocean under a blazing sun, somewhere hot; him in a large hospital, and he couldn't work out why until he heard a baby fill its lungs and yell out a life-affirming squawk, and he knew. Lev had always thought his life would flash before him when he died, but he didn't remember any of these things. Then he realised that what he was seeing was not his life past but his life future, all the things he was meant to have done with Alice and now would never have time to.

How appalling it is, how terrifying, to stand up and face death, to run towards death rather than away from it. How terrible it is to die before your time. Lev wanted to stay alive. He'd already resigned himself to fate, but this desire was stronger than any thought. This desire was so vast that nothing could be compared to it; it could not be measured.

It was not enough.

Lewis showed Alice which button on the ventilator to press, and she did so without fuss or ceremony. The machine's humming wound down to silence, Lev's chest ceased its endless rise and fall, and on the monitor at the head of his bed, the spiky line of his heartbeat smoothed to the flatness of a spirit level.

"What's life, if you live it on a flat line?" Lev had told her once. "No great downs, true, but no great ups either. You might as well be dead. Ups and downs are proof that you're alive. Flatlines are what happen to patients in hospital when their bodies give out on them."

The body in the bed was so unlike Lev that Alice concluded he simply wasn't there. His sufferings were over; he was free. But the extinction of the last, faintest hope that he might recover had inten-sified her agony even further. She felt the world becoming darker and darker; it must have been the unbearable pain in her soul that was dissolving the boundary between her inner existence and the real world.

The lights in the room flickered briefly, fading before burning strongly again. "Fluctuation in the power supply," Lewis muttered, "it happens all the time," but Alice shook her head; she knew better.

It was Lev's soul on its way out, and the motes of the air stirred and rearranged themselves as it went.

Lev's soul came to visit Alice, as she'd known it would. It was not a sensory manifestation – she didn't see or hear him, let alone smell or taste or touch him – but rather an indefinable sense of his presence. She walked the streets for hours in the watery sunshine, visiting all the places they'd been together; she stood outside the gates of the distillery and sat down on the steps of the Kotelniki, she walked round the Kremlin and sat at the bar of the Vek restaurant, letting the tears fall into her mineral water. Lev was in all these places as surely as if he'd been standing next to her.

The prospect of the soul's journey – for death is the beginning of a voyage, undertaken either by boat or in a sledge drawn by a troika of wild horses – is a dreadful one, a reckoning and a test. The soul isn't alone, for its guardian angel accompanies it, but the companionship is not necessarily consoling. The angel isn't simply benign, a good fairy by another name; its task is to reveal to the astonished soul the true meaning of its lifetime's deeds and choices, however terrible they might appear. The prayers that mourners offer for the soul's peace at this time are in deadly earnest, for few can contemplate this kind of truth, unmediated, without fear.

The journey is in three stages. Firstly, the soul remains on earth for three days and three nights, visiting the places where it spent most of its mortal hours. Next, it ascends to heaven to meet its god, where it stays for six days. On the ninth day after death, it is taken down to hell for a month. After a total of forty days traversing the regions inhabited by various demons who tear asunder a consciousness infected by sin comes the moment of individual judgement, when everything the soul has learned on its journey becomes real, when it begins to face the consequence of actions it might have chosen to forget, and when it faces the genuine prospect of torment stretching onwards to the end of time.

This was what the future seemed to hold for Alice. Eternity retreated before the agony of her lost love.

# EPILOGUE

*Saturday, 9 May 1992*
Victory Day is the biggest holiday in the Russian calendar. Deliverance from the Nazis is a celebration which will always endure, no matter what political system is in place. Bemedalled old women and bowlegged ex-cavalrymen in archaic uniforms reminisced, wept, sung and danced to accordion music. Almost everywhere, it seemed, people recalled the autumn of 1941.

Off the Stalinist squares and avenues, the back streets were deserted, a mellower Moscow of courtyards and lanes in every hue of crumbling brick and stucco; a city of hidden charms. The sun was warm, and pedestrians strode purposefully in shirtsleeves; the mud and slush had finally receded, and the first dandelion leaves were pushing through the concrete pavements. Moscow is seen as a city of endless winter, but this is a myth. Yes, it has to endure six months of snow, but no sooner has the thaw begun than the race for summer is on. Days lengthen and begin to simmer, nights are fire and smoke. The heat obliterates all memory of the cold that has been and is yet to come.

It was the fortieth day since Lev's death, the day on which his soul would return from its wanderings and face the final judgement. Alice wanted to get to Lev's grave as quickly as possible, but he stilled her: *Hush, my love, hush, we have all the time in the world.* So she slowed her pace and looked around. She was a Russian now, and as such she should appreciate the way in which her people deal with death.

Feeling as though the legions of dead were watching her, Alice walked through thickets of tombstones, staggered by their variety and artistry. In a country where everyone was dying, cemetery space was so tight that husbands and wives were sometimes buried on

499

top of each other. Perhaps that was where Alice would end up too, on top of Lev; she thought briefly of the times they'd made love, her above him, him above her.

Headstones were engraved not simply with names but with pictures and sculptures too. She saw gold eagles, outsize boxing gloves and maple leaves; a winding road commemorated a woman killed in a car crash. Husbands and wives bumped each other in little oval portraits, the men dignified and the women strict, hairstyles as flattened as their expressions. Olympic champions with medals hooked around their necks, dancers stopped forever in stone; explorers holding compasses, pilots peering from behind aviator goggles. They shared a sombre, communal gaze, restless and restful at the same time. Pine needles were gathered in wreathes, bright flowers bunched in bouquets.

When Alice had first arrived in Moscow, she'd have found these decorations tacky and twee; because she'd have looked at them with Western eyes trained to abhor gaudy sentimentality. Now, she found them moving; she understood them.

A freight train tooted a mournful refrain as it chugged slowly past the cemetery's north wall. Alice found Lev's grave and sat down. It was just the two of them now.

She rummaged in her bag and brought out a bottle – mineral water, of course. Vodka had been her lover before she'd found her real lover, and her real lover had saved her from the traitorous vodka; he'd pledged to stand by her, and he'd not let her down. He'd have been proud of her today, standing there with her bottle of water. He'd have been proud that she'd not drunk yesterday, that she was not drinking today, and that she'd not drink tomorrow. That was how she was getting through it, a day at a time, and she'd keep her eyes on the road in front and never dare lift them to the summit for fear it would seem too daunting. It was hard by the yard, they said, but it was a cinch by the inch.

Now, finally, when she'd renounced vodka, she understood why the Russians love it so deeply. No other spirit is half as compatible with their soul. The subtle lithesomeness of wine, best taken in the open air with fine cheese and warm bread, is a bad fit with Russia's long winters and short growing seasons. But vodka, so pure and purposeful, so ideal for warming the despondent soul in February or for cooling passions in August, is a feast or famine sort of drink, and Russia is a feast or famine sort of place.

* * *

500

Alice wondered how everyone else was spending their Victory Day. Arkin was still interim president, and stood a good chance of making the job his permanently in the elections next month. She'd stuck to their agreement, regardless of what had happened to Lev. Arkin had told her he was the best man for Russia, and Alice agreed, he was. She'd seen Irk in the street the other day, and chatted to him briefly; Canute-like, he was still trying to stem the tide of lawlessness. When she'd asked about Sveta and Galya, he'd wiped his hand across his face and shaken his head. Lewis had gone back to the States, as had Bob and Christina. Harry was still here, and still pestering her to set up a business with him. Perhaps she would, in time. She didn't need to work for a while, she still had plenty of money from her days on Wall Street. She hoped they were all happy, but she was no longer for them, nor they for her.

She'd chosen the design of Lev's memorial herself. The tombstone was black and white, as Khrushchev's was, reflection of the light and dark which had existed side by side in Lev. He'd been dangerous, emotional and irresponsible, and yet haunted by conscience; he'd been cruel, yet fundamentally childlike. He'd been broad yet narrow, reckless yet cautious, tolerant yet censorious, independent, docile, tough, malleable, kind, hateful, naïve, cynical . . . Most of all, he'd been Russian, and what are Russians if not human beings writ large? There's duality in everyone, it's the most universal of human characteristics, and though this isn't unique to the Russians, they take it to greater extremes than other peoples.

Most people experience love without noticing that there's anything remarkable about it. To Alice and Lev – and this was what had made them unusual – the moments when passion visited their doomed human existence were moments of revelation, greater understanding of life and themselves.

Maybe she'd known all along that he was doomed, maybe that was why she'd fallen so deeply for him. A famous Russian fairytale tells of a princess made of ice who knows how she'll die; one day she'll meet a mortal man, their passion will last a day and a night, and then she'll melt and expire. What was the story of Lev and Alice, if not that very fairytale in reverse? "A man considers himself frozen, stagnant, halfway lifeless," he'd told her; "then the right flame draws him as though he were a moth, and when he gets close, it melts him."

But does life stop with death? No, she thought, of course it

501

doesn't. A man is not dead until he's forgotten, and Alice would never forget Lev. When someone you love dies, Alice thought, they take a piece of you with them; but equally they leave a piece of themselves with you. She felt a stirring deep inside her. It was nothing so prosaic as a biological changing; it was a feeling, a hunch, rooted in nothing more than the absence of a monthly occurrence and the sure knowledge of herself and him, and therefore as irrefutable as a mathematical proof. She was already at the disposal of the future which she carried within her; she was no longer only herself, she was Lev too, and another, a fusion of them both, and one day she'd sit her son down and tell him everything about his father; that this, truly, had been a man.

She'd been at his grave for some time. The sun was burning down the west, and the skies were darkening. The twilight above Lev's gravestone seemed to rearrange itself momentarily in the shape of his grin, hanging in the air as it had always seemed to – and then the apparition was gone, his soul spiralling upwards towards its judgement, and she was alone.

Alice walked back through the cemetery, past a shed where green-stained copper tongues lolled from the mouths of drainpipes and where two old gravediggers were playing chess with vodka bottles as pieces. Whenever one player took a piece, he had to drink the contents; judging by the state these particular combatants were in, this game had been going on for some time. Each man was left with a king, a queen and a rook – a gangster, his moll and their body-guard, perhaps – and these figurines chased each other endlessly round the board, white on black, black on white, radiating lines of force and magnetism, attraction and repulsion, permission and inter-diction, from and to and across every square. The chessboard is a haven of precision and clarity, Alice thought, and as such it's an inaccurate reflection of the world. There's no black and white in real life; there's only grey.

   The gravediggers saw Alice watching them, and greeted her cheer-ily. She pointed to the bottles and laughed. "You'd better watch it. They'll be the death of you."

   "Well, vodka's a poison which kills slowly," said the man playing white.

   "And as it happens," Black added, "I'm in no hurry."

   She laughed again. "Who's winning?"

   "He is," said Black.

"No, he is," White said. "We both want to play with black, that's the problem."

"Surely that's a disadvantage? Doesn't white have the first move?"

They shrugged. Maybe so, but that was how it was; black was white, white was black, a disadvantage was an advantage. It all made sense, if you stepped through the looking-glass and surrendered yourself to the peculiar principles of logic that held sway in Wonderland. Alice had never felt more Russian than now, when she'd gone teetotal and forsworn the very soul of Russia itself, and if *that* wasn't a Russian thing to think, then she didn't know what was.

"You'd stay without me," Lev had said; and he'd been right, she would.

Alice paused a moment at the gate, orienting herself by the embers of the setting sun, and then began to retrace her way through the streets of Moscow at dusk, the great city hanging suspended in all its contradictions: halfway between day and night, past and future, east and west, sanity and madness, picturesque and squalid, good and evil.